Pokémon™ Adventures

COLLECTOR'S EDITION

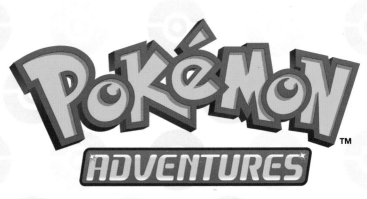

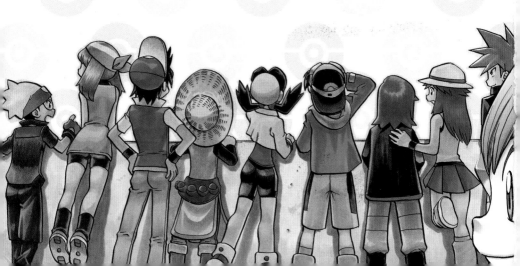

CONTENTS

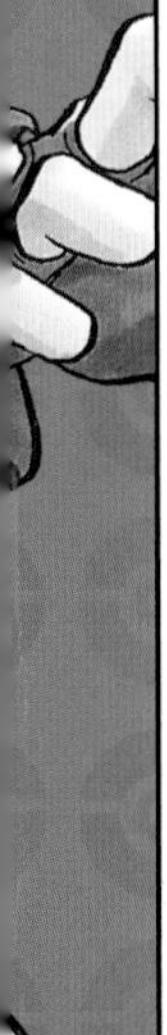

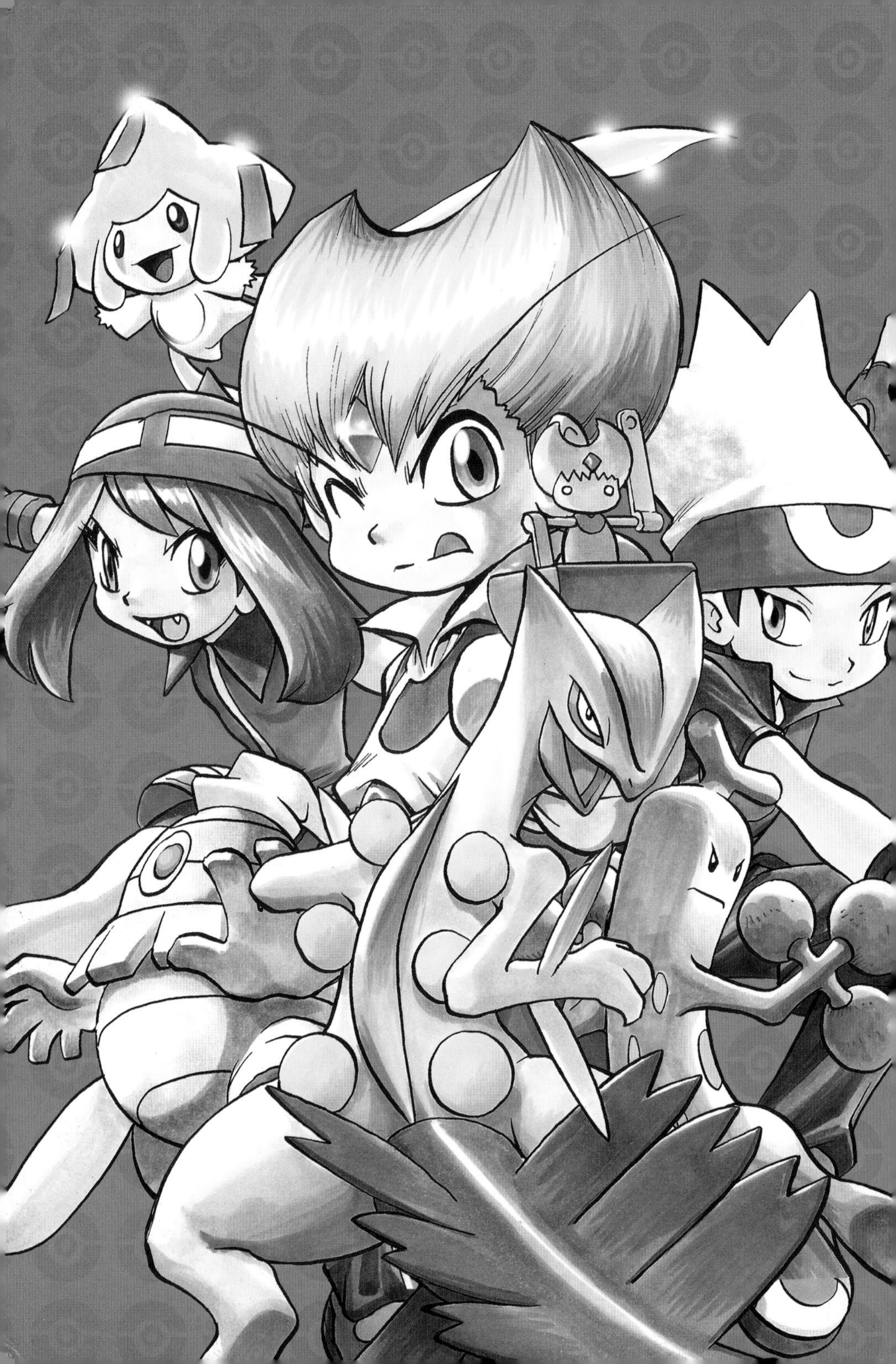

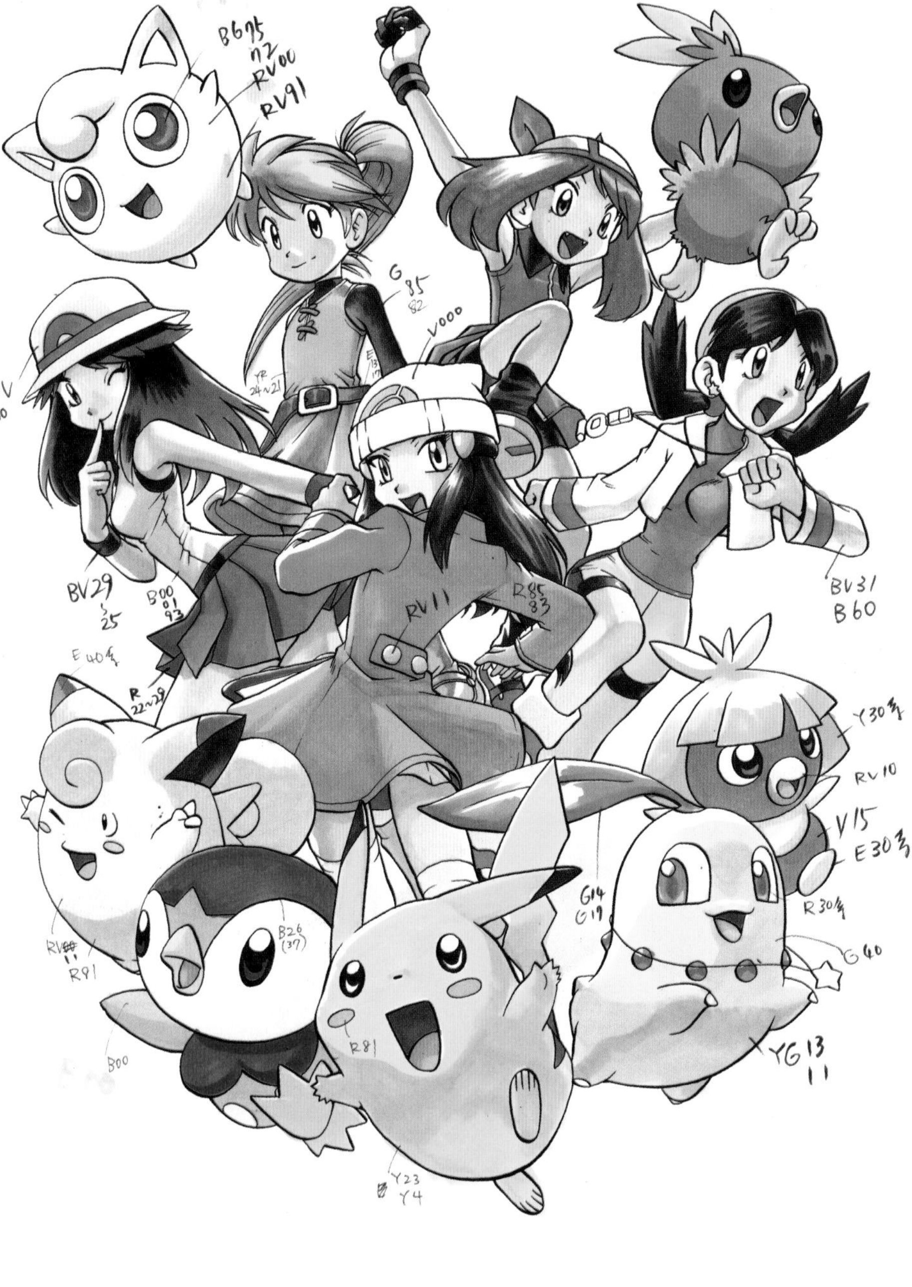

RV91
RV00
G
85
82
V000
BV
00
BV29
25
B00
01
93
RV11
R85
83
BV31
B60
E40
R
Y30
RV10
V15
E30
G14
G19
R30
G40
B26
(37)
R81
R81
B00
YG13
11
Y23
Y4

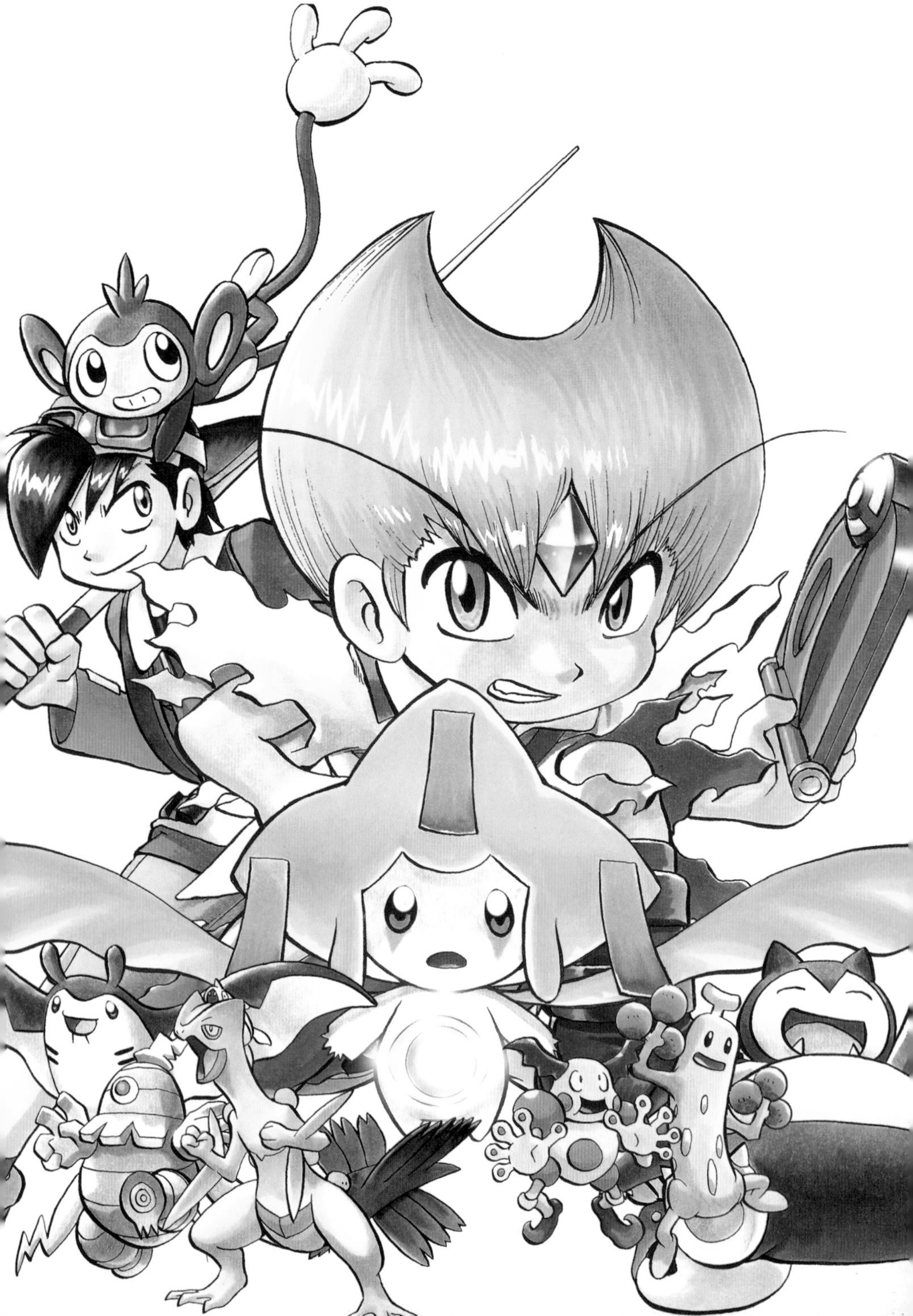

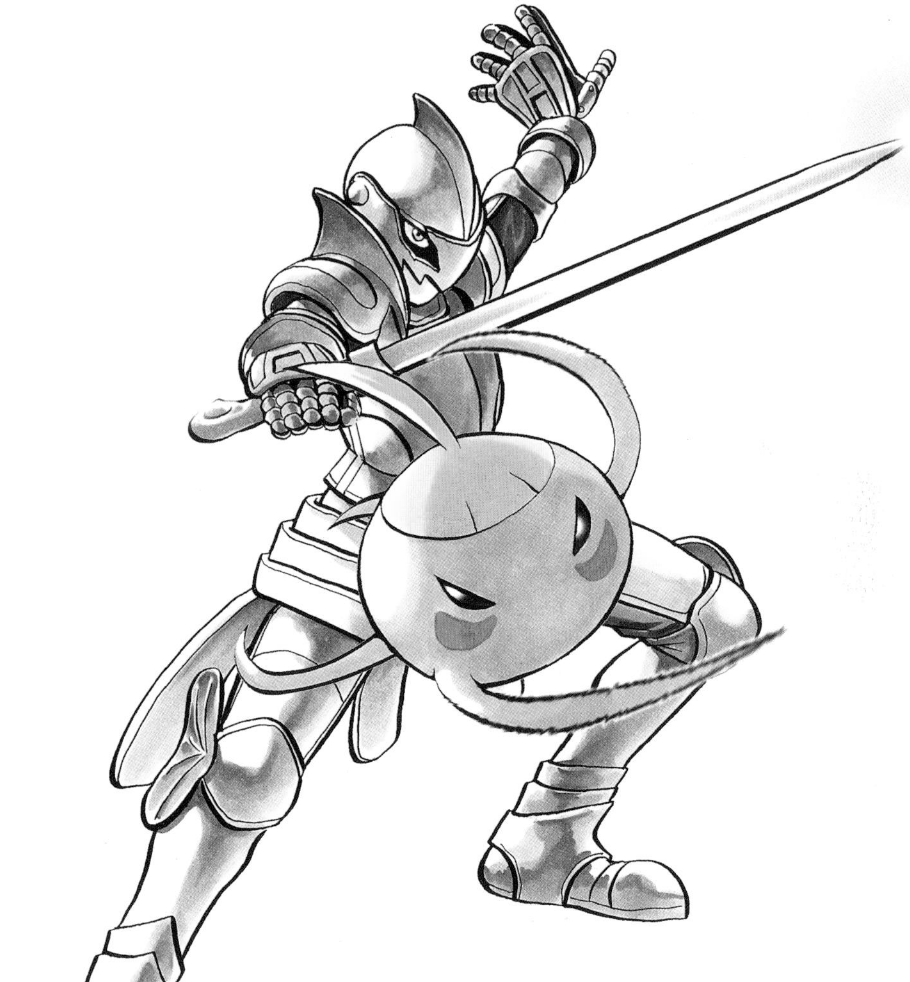

Message from
Hidenori Kusaka

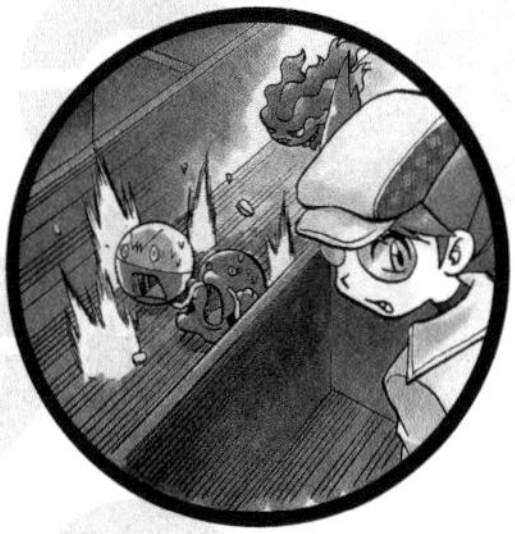

The year 2007 has almost come to an end. I can hear the footsteps of 2008 coming around the corner. I've also been hearing about new Pokémon projects, and I'm looking forward to them. Some of those projects might be connected to the Diamond and Pearl Adventure story arc that I'm currently working on... I often receive questions like "Isn't it hard to have to suddenly change the entire direction of the story because of the new games and plots?" Don't worry about me! I believe manga is like a living creature–I'm just weird that way–and so I enjoy how it morphs into new things! (*laugh*)

–2007

Message from
Satoshi Yamamoto

Ruby and Sapphire have finally joined Emerald! Emerald has been pushing the Frontier Brains around so much that it's fun to see someone boss him around for a change. Meanwhile, Emerald's battle against Guile and the race to capture Jirachi intensifies! Who is Guile anyway...?! Brace yourself for the heart-pounding excitement of this part of the Emerald story arc!

–2007

SPECIAL OBJECT

The Pokédex holders and their stories

Kanto region

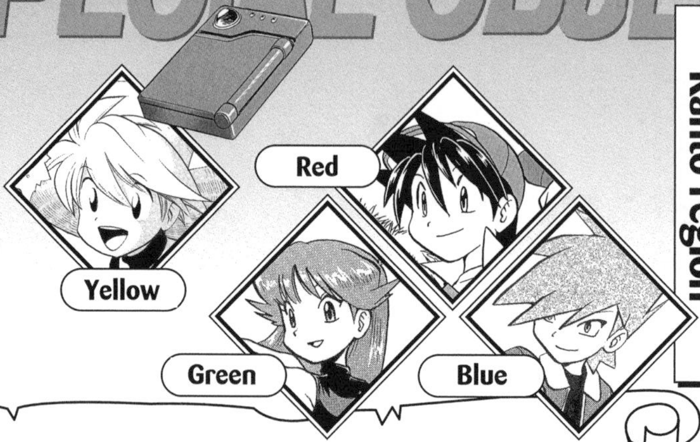

Red
Yellow
Green
Blue

1st Chapter

Red, a young boy from Pallet Town, receives a Pokédex from Professor Oak and heads out on a Pokémon training journey. Along the way, he meets two other Trainers–Blue, who becomes his rival, and Green. Red fights evil Team Rocket with his new friends and then becomes Champion of the Pokémon League.

2nd Chapter

Two years later, Red suddenly disappears, and Yellow, a mysterious new Trainer, appears at Professor Oak's laboratory in search of him.

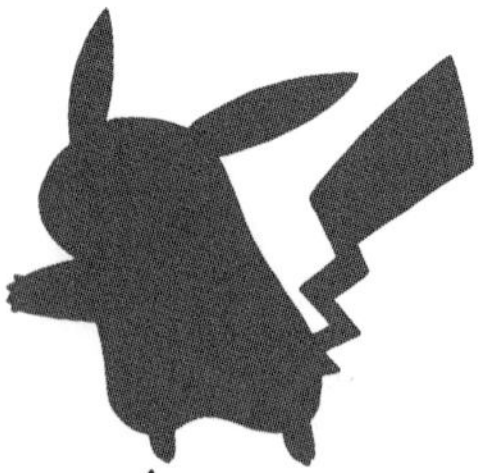

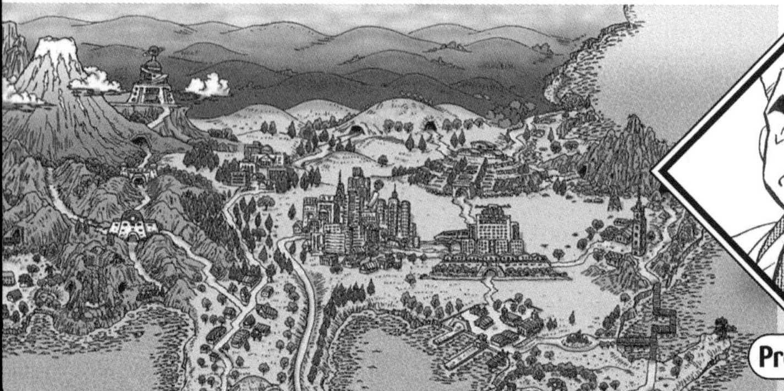

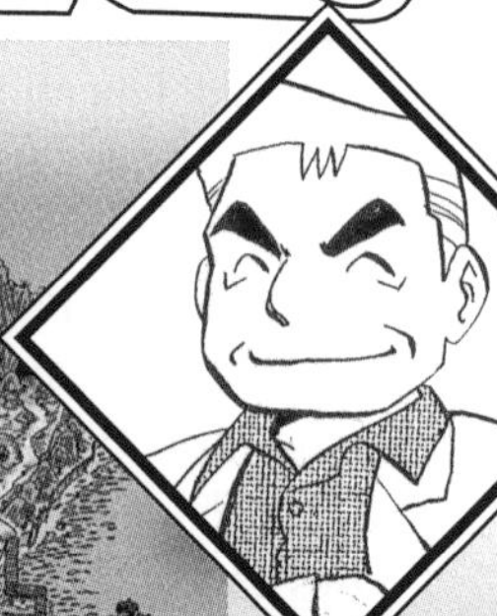

Professor Oak

POKÉMON

Johto region

Gold
Silver
Crystal

Standing in Yellow's way is the Kanto Elite Four, led by Lance. In a major battle at Cerise Island, Yellow manages to stymie the group's evil ambitions.

3rd Chapter

A year later, Gold, a boy living in New Bark Town in a house full of Pokémon, sets out on a journey in pursuit of Silver, a Trainer who stole a Totodile from Professor Elm's laboratory. The two don't get along at first, but eventually they become partners fighting side by side. During their journey, they meet Crystal, the Trainer whom Professor Elm entrusts with the completion of his Pokédex. Together, the trio succeed in shattering the evil scheme of the Mask of Ice, a villain who leads what remains of Team Rocket.

Hoenn region

4th Chapter

Pokémon Trainer Ruby has a passion for Pokémon Contests. He runs away from home right after his family moves to Littleroot Town. He meets a wild girl named Sapphire, and they pledge to compete with each other in an 80-day challenge to...

Professor Elm

Professor Birch

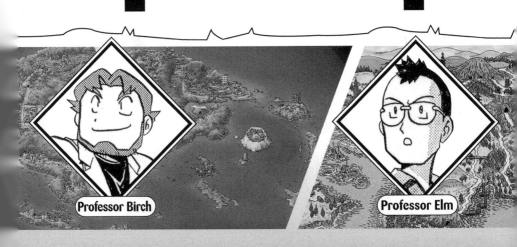

SPECIAL OBJECT

Kanto region

Red

Green

Blue

Sapphire

Ruby

5th Chapter

Six months later, a new adventure unfolds for Red and his friends on the Sevii Islands. After a deadly battle, Red manages to defeat Deoxys, who has fallen into the hands of Giovanni. Silver, in search of his true identity, is faced with the shocking truth that Giovanni is his father. Red and his friends manage to safely land the Team Rocket airship, which was flying out of control thanks to Carr, one of the Three Beasts, who betrayed Team Rocket. But then another of the Three Beasts, Sird, appears, and in a mysterious flash of light the five Pokédex holders—Red, Blue, Green, Yellow and Silver—are petrified. Literally!

...win every Pokémon Contest and every Pokémon Gym Battle, respectively. Meanwhile, in the Hoenn region, Team Aqua and Team Magma set their evil plot in motion. As a result, Legendary Pokémon Groudon and Kyogre are awakened and inflict catastrophic climate changes on Hoenn. In the end, thanks to Ruby and Sapphire's heroic efforts, the two legendary Pokémon go back into hibernation.

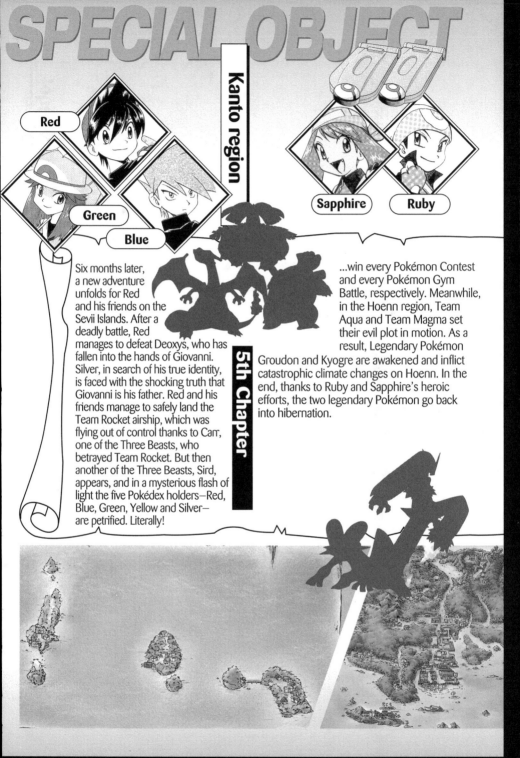

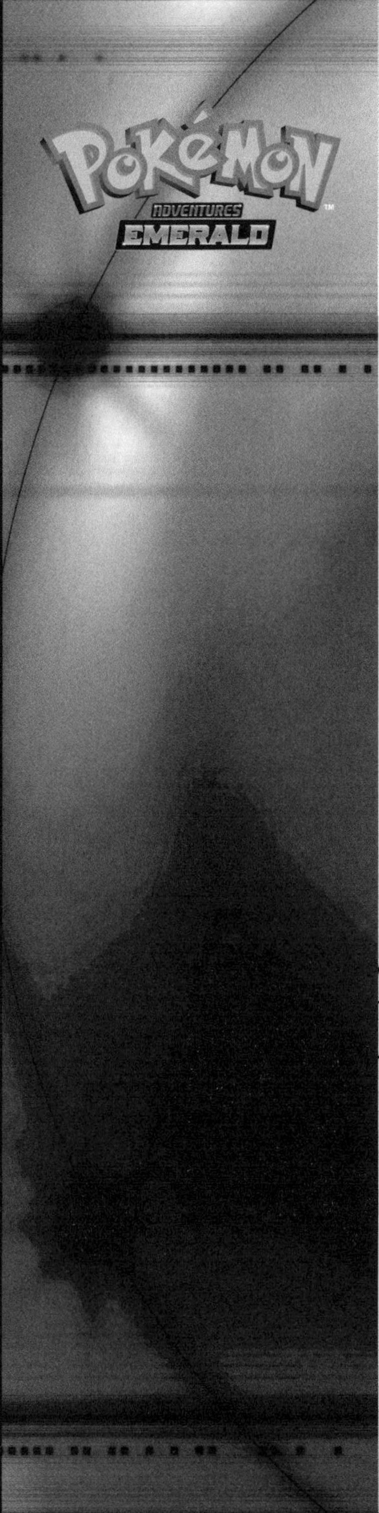
POKéMON
ADVENTURES
EMERALD

POKÉMON

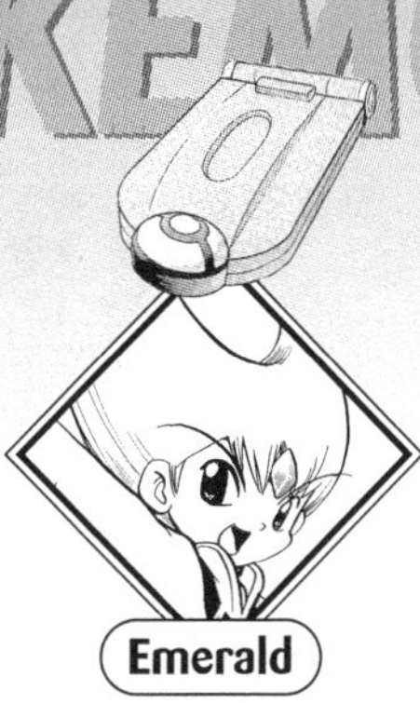
Emerald

Hoenn region

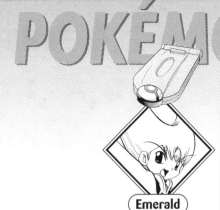

6th Chapter

A few months later, construction is completed on a thrilling new Pokémon Battle facility, the Battle Frontier, located in the Hoenn region. A young Trainer named Emerald crashes the press opening for the media to challenge the facility's Frontier Brains. Now he has just seven days to defeat them all!

Thus far, Emerald has won his battles against Factory Head Noland, Lucy and Brandon. His other mission is to capture and protect Jirachi, the Wish Pokémon, who awakens every thousand years for seven days and can grant any wish. Now the battle to prevent mysterious armor-clad Guile from getting his hands on Jirachi first continues...!

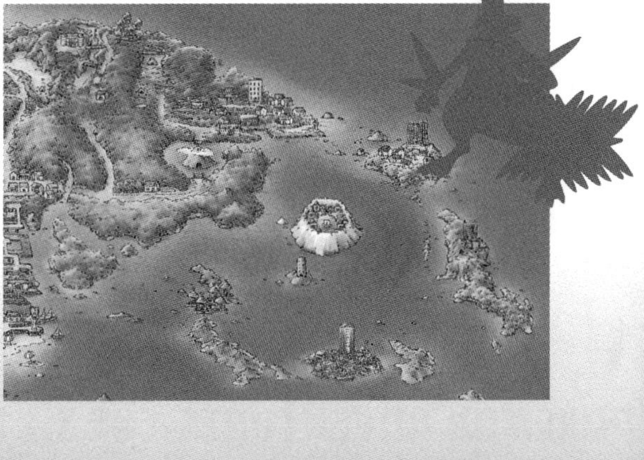

Sneaky like Shedinja, Part 2

POKÉMON ADVENTURES·THE SIXTH CHAPTER·EMERALD

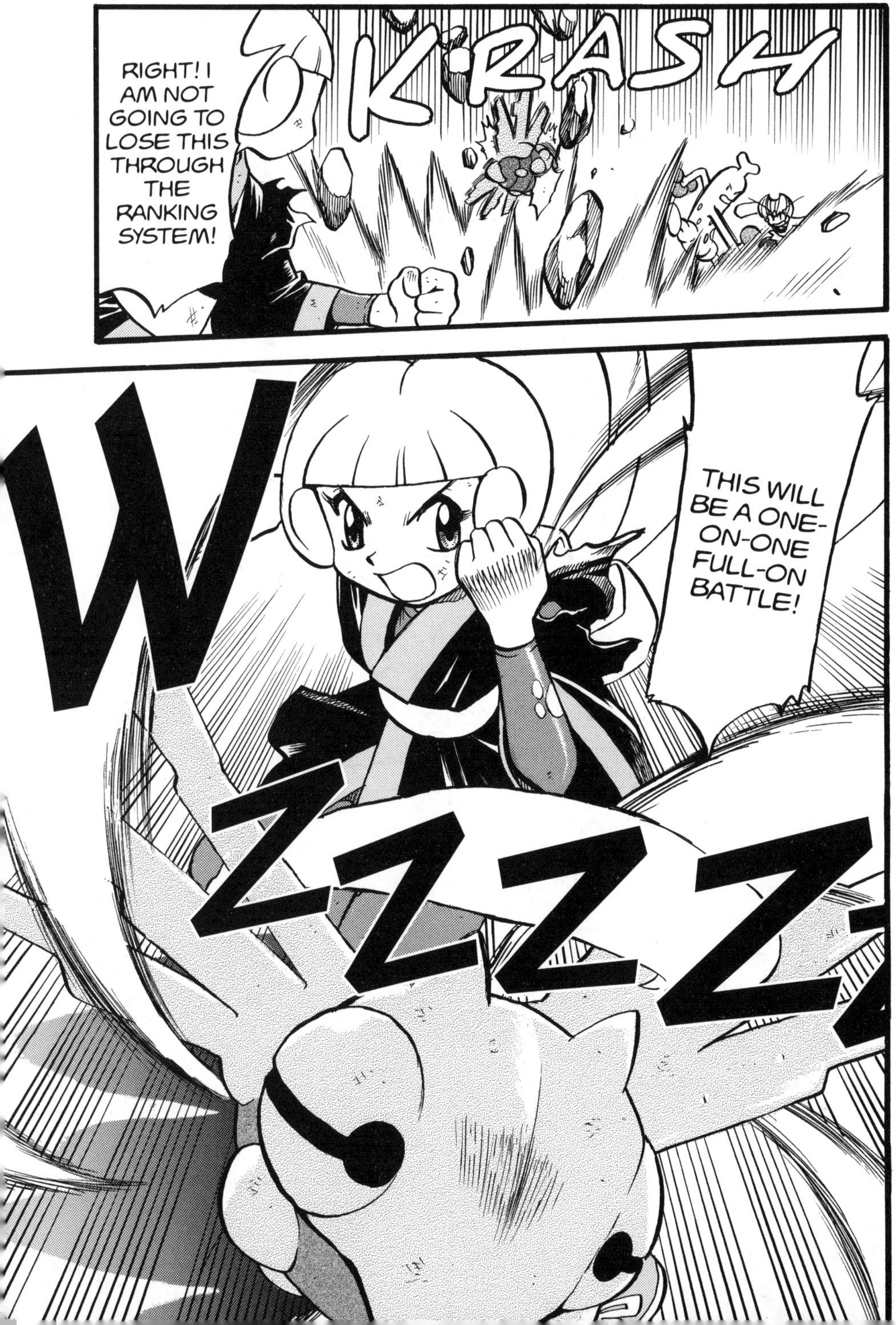
KRASH
RIGHT! I AM NOT GOING TO LOSE THIS THROUGH THE RANKING SYSTEM!
THIS WILL BE A ONE-ON-ONE FULL-ON BATTLE!
WZZZZ

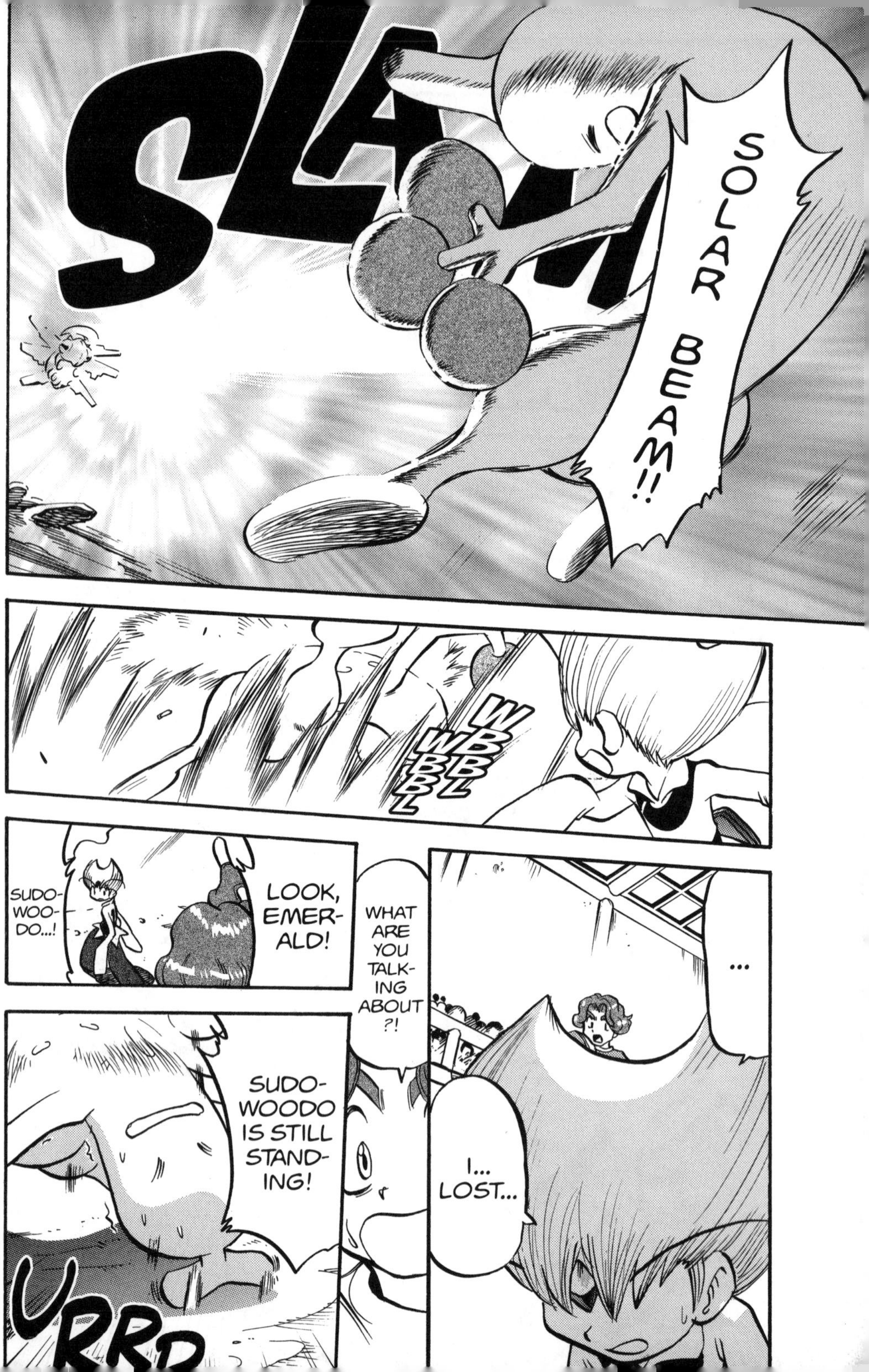
SOLAR BEAM!!
SLAM
WBBBL WBBBL
...
I... LOST...
LOOK, EMERALD!
SUDOWOODO...!
WHAT ARE YOU TALKING ABOUT?!
SUDOWOODO IS STILL STANDING!
URRD

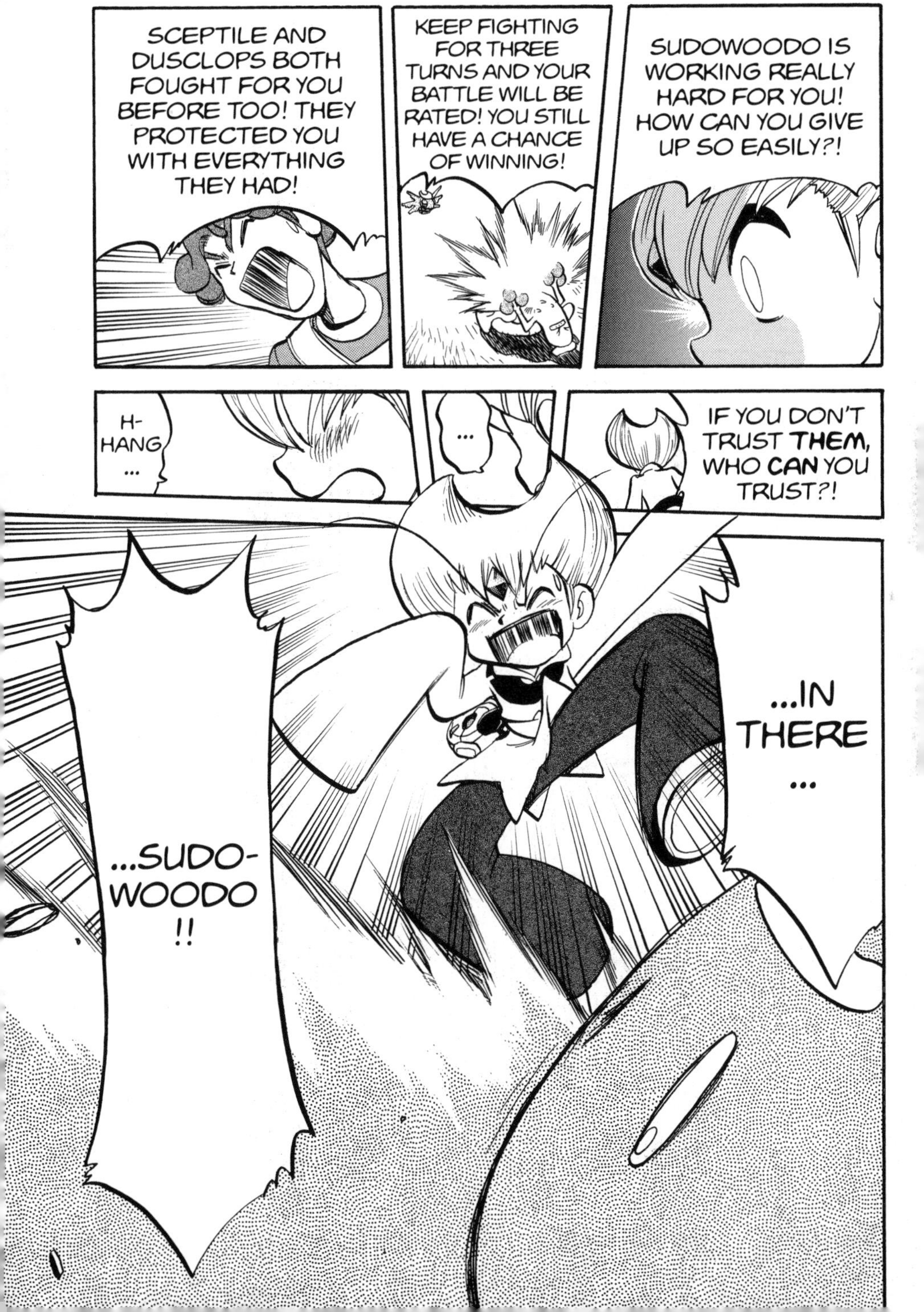
SUDOWOODO IS WORKING REALLY HARD FOR YOU! HOW CAN YOU GIVE UP SO EASILY?!
KEEP FIGHTING FOR THREE TURNS AND YOUR BATTLE WILL BE RATED! YOU STILL HAVE A CHANCE OF WINNING!
SCEPTILE AND DUSCLOPS BOTH FOUGHT FOR YOU BEFORE TOO! THEY PROTECTED YOU WITH EVERYTHING THEY HAD!
IF YOU DON'T TRUST **THEM**, WHO **CAN** YOU TRUST?!
...
H-HANG ...
...IN THERE ...
...SUDO-WOODO !!

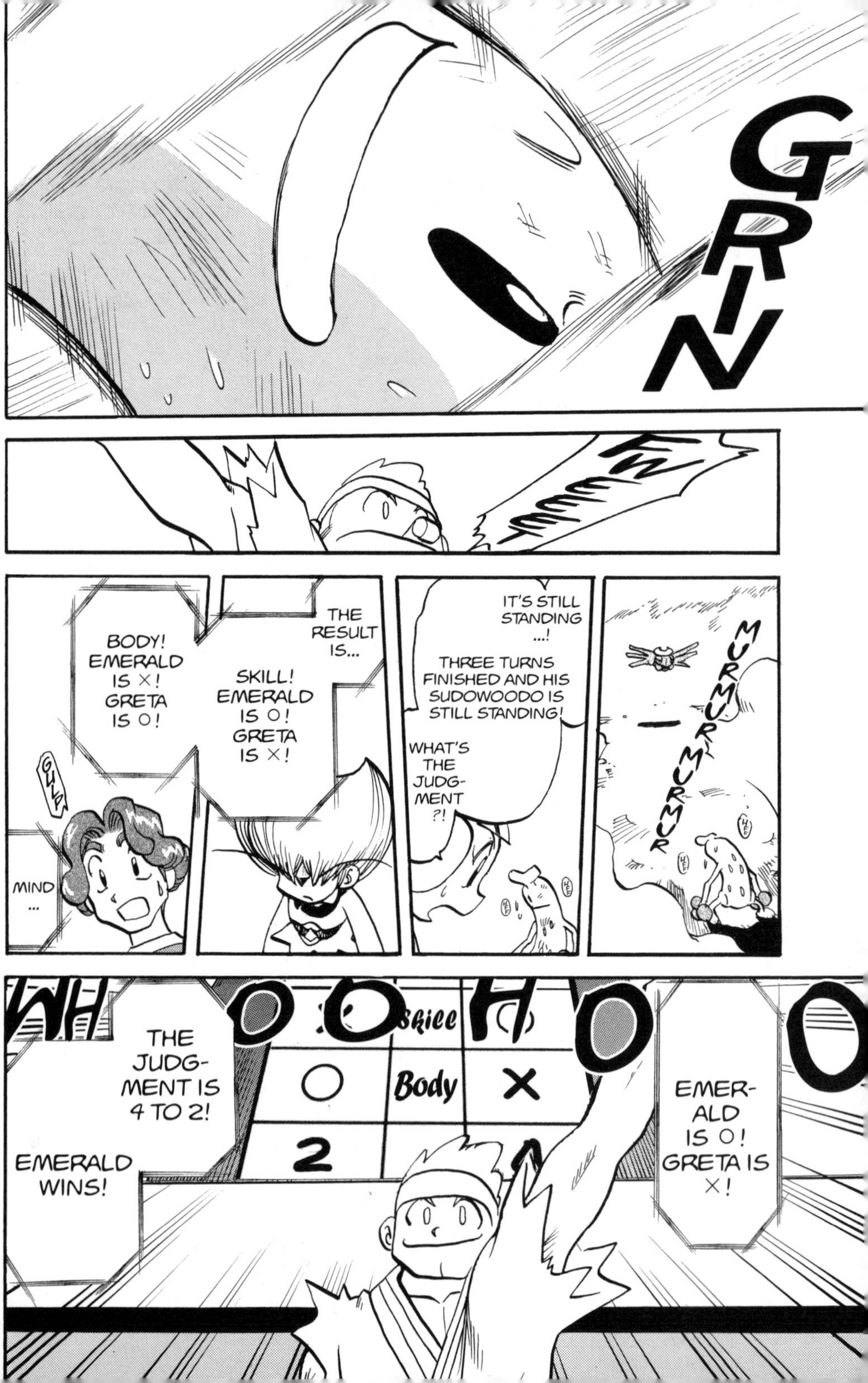
GRIN
FWUUUP
MURMUR MURMUR MURMUR
IT'S STILL STANDING ...!
THREE TURNS FINISHED AND HIS SUDOWOODO IS STILL STANDING!
WHAT'S THE JUDG-MENT ?!
THE RESULT IS...
SKILL! EMERALD IS ○! GRETA IS ×!
BODY! EMERALD IS ×! GRETA IS ○!
GULP
MIND ...
WHOOHOOO
Skill
Body
2
EMER-ALD IS ○! GRETA IS ×!
THE JUDG-MENT IS 4 TO 2!
EMERALD WINS!

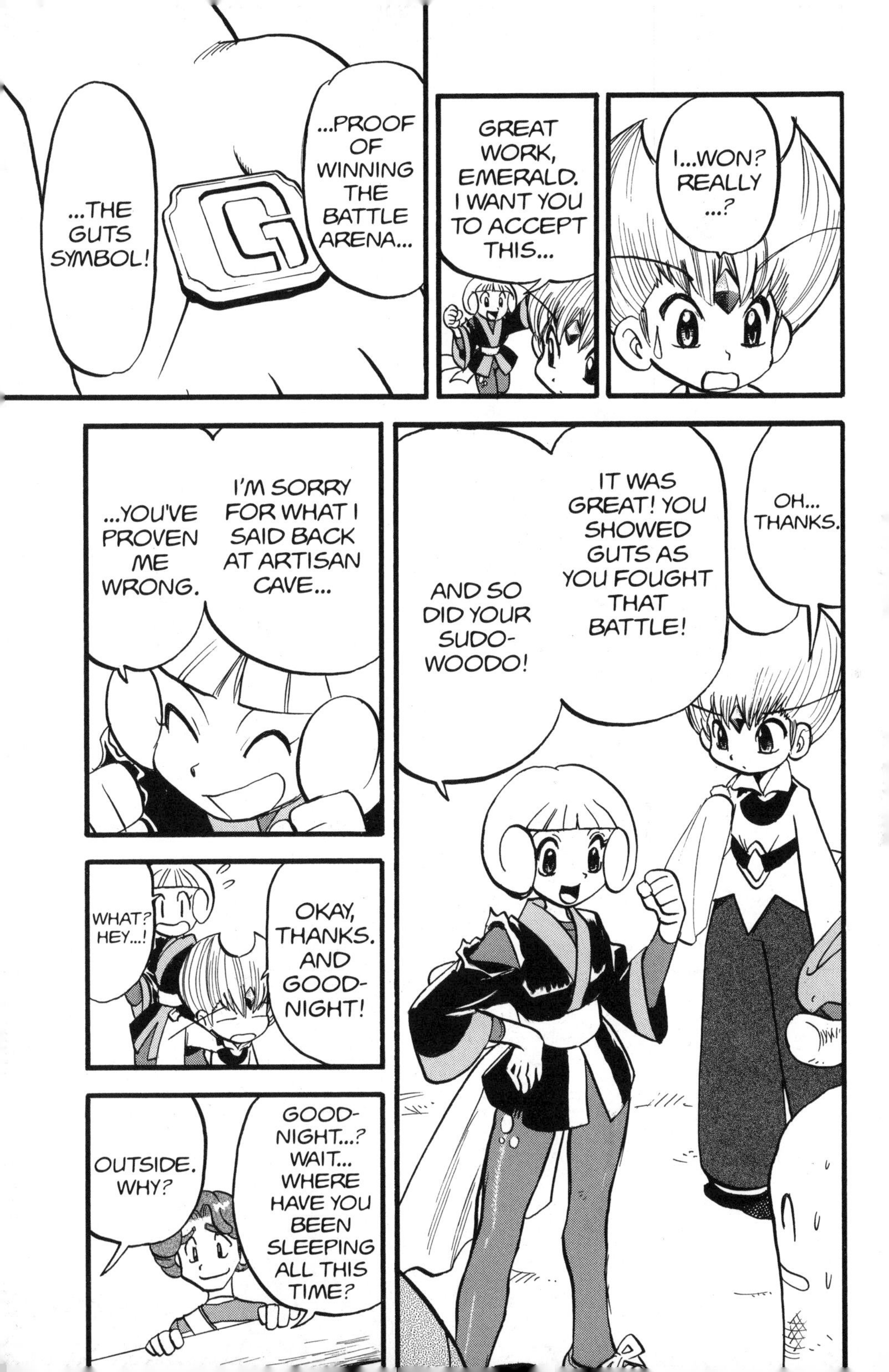
I...WON? REALLY ...?
GREAT WORK, EMERALD. I WANT YOU TO ACCEPT THIS...
...PROOF OF WINNING THE BATTLE ARENA...
...THE GUTS SYMBOL!
OH... THANKS.
IT WAS GREAT! YOU SHOWED GUTS AS YOU FOUGHT THAT BATTLE!
AND SO DID YOUR SUDO-WOODO!
I'M SORRY FOR WHAT I SAID BACK AT ARTISAN CAVE...
...YOU'VE PROVEN ME WRONG.
OKAY, THANKS. AND GOOD-NIGHT!
WHAT? HEY...!
GOOD-NIGHT...? WAIT... WHERE HAVE YOU BEEN SLEEPING ALL THIS TIME?
OUTSIDE. WHY?

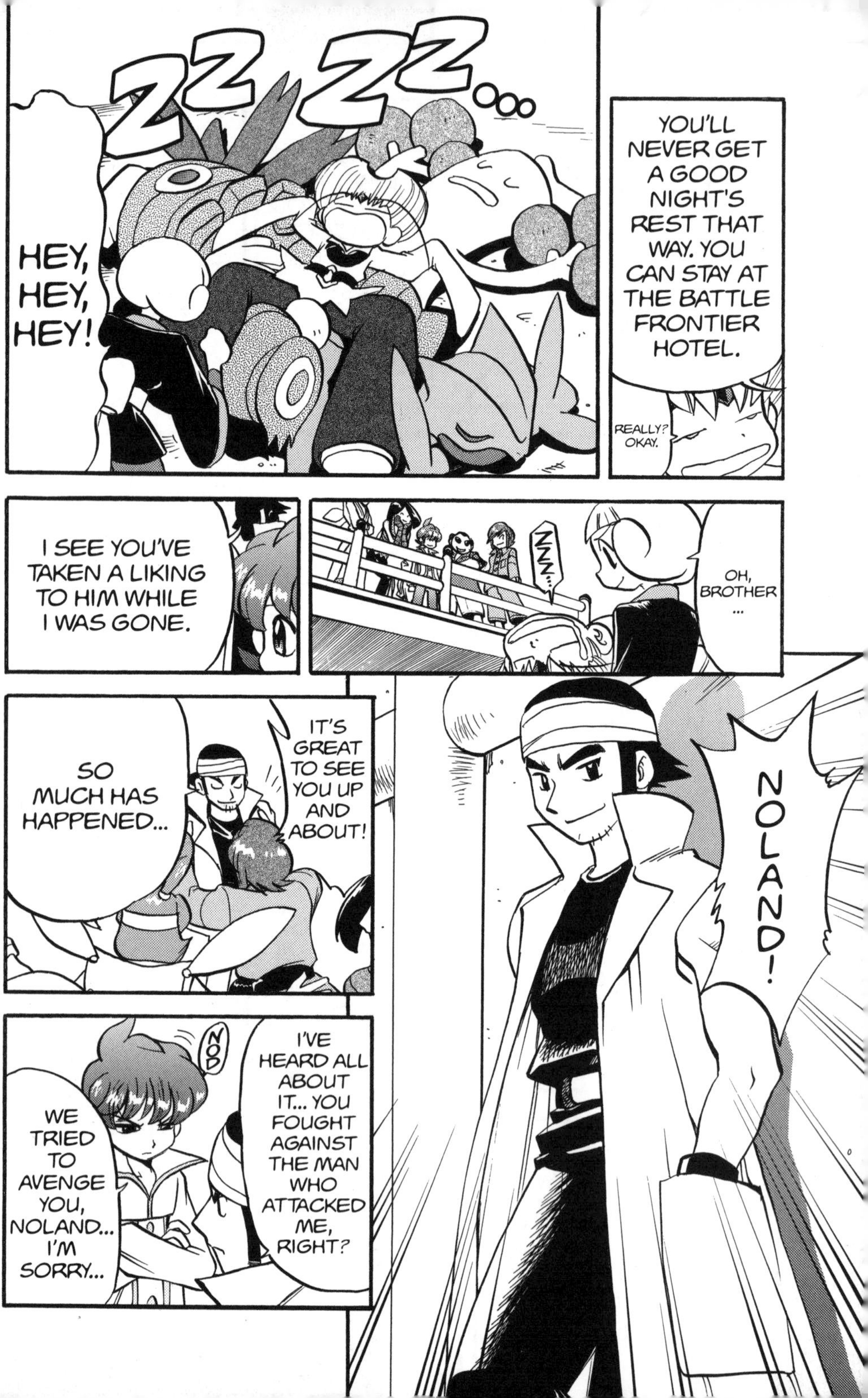
YOU'LL NEVER GET A GOOD NIGHT'S REST THAT WAY. YOU CAN STAY AT THE BATTLE FRONTIER HOTEL.
REALLY? OKAY.
ZZ ZZ...
HEY, HEY, HEY!
ZZZ...
OH, BROTHER ...
I SEE YOU'VE TAKEN A LIKING TO HIM WHILE I WAS GONE.
NOLAND!
IT'S GREAT TO SEE YOU UP AND ABOUT!
SO MUCH HAS HAPPENED...
I'VE HEARD ALL ABOUT IT... YOU FOUGHT AGAINST THE MAN WHO ATTACKED ME, RIGHT?
NOD
WE TRIED TO AVENGE YOU, NOLAND... I'M SORRY...

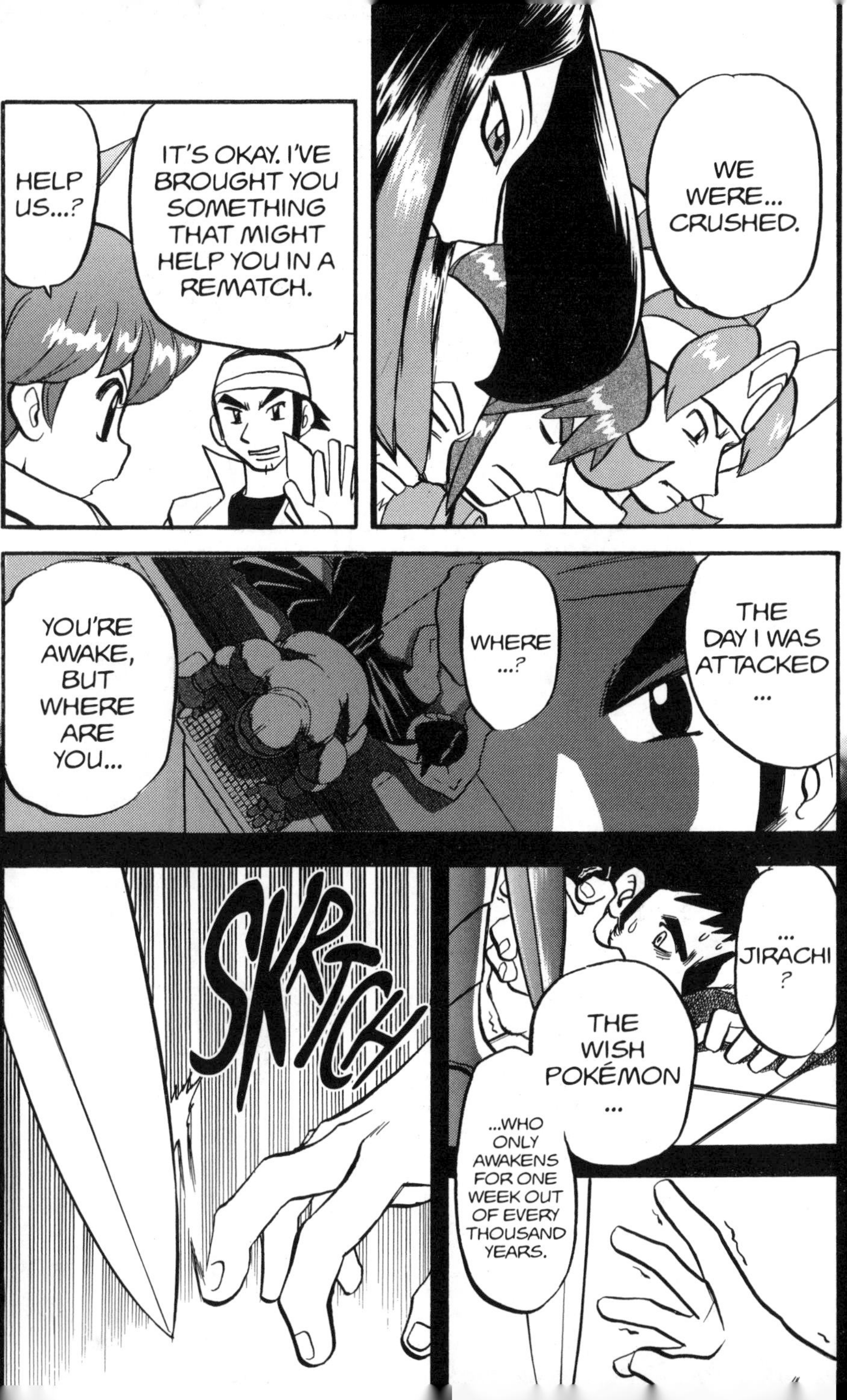
WE WERE... CRUSHED.
IT'S OKAY. I'VE BROUGHT YOU SOMETHING THAT MIGHT HELP YOU IN A REMATCH.
HELP US...?
THE DAY I WAS ATTACKED ...
WHERE ...?
YOU'RE AWAKE, BUT WHERE ARE YOU...
... JIRACHI ?
THE WISH POKÉMON ...
...WHO ONLY AWAKENS FOR ONE WEEK OUT OF EVERY THOUSAND YEARS.
SKRTCH

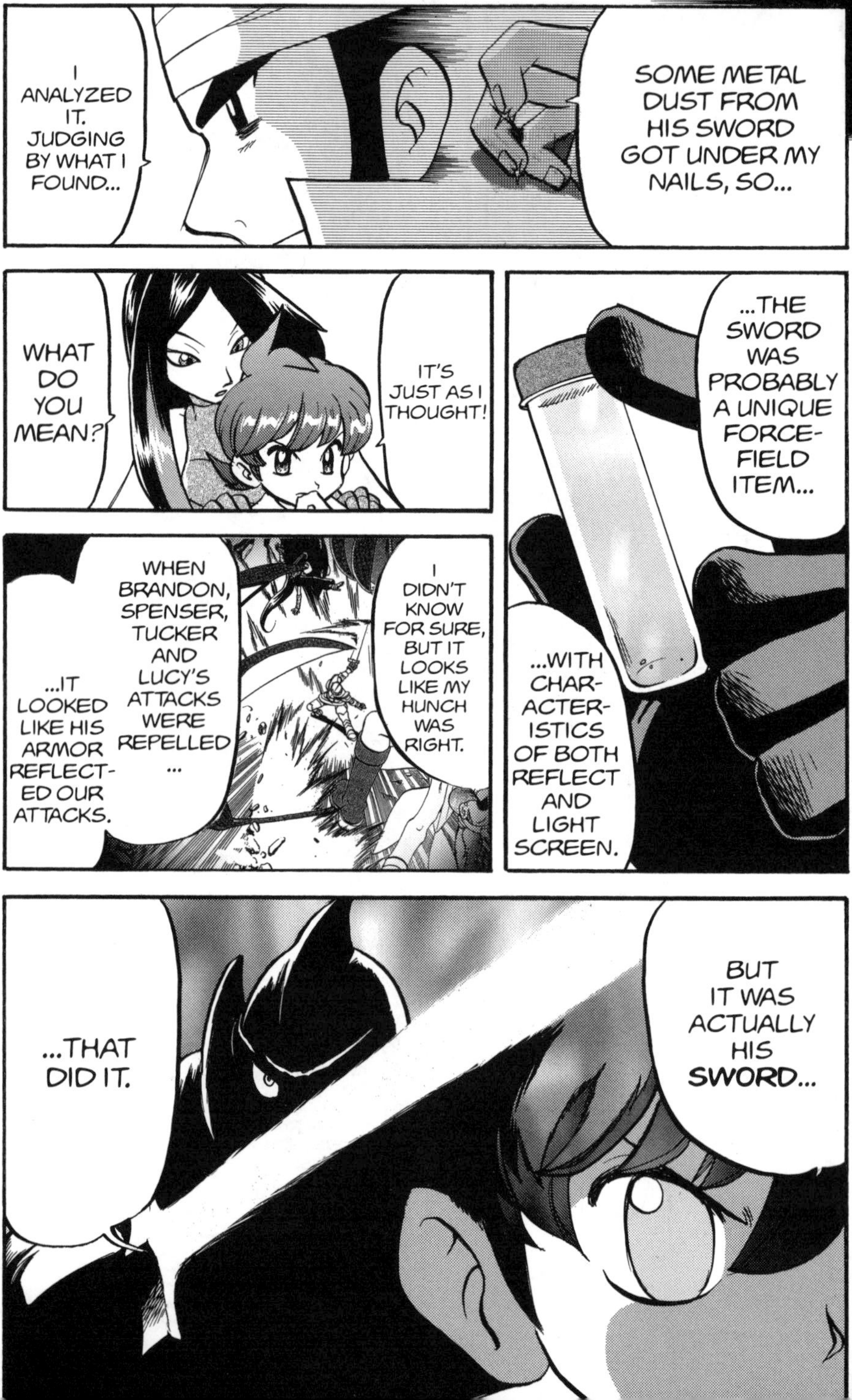
SOME METAL DUST FROM HIS SWORD GOT UNDER MY NAILS, SO...
I ANALYZED IT. JUDGING BY WHAT I FOUND...
...THE SWORD WAS PROBABLY A UNIQUE FORCE-FIELD ITEM...
...WITH CHARACTERISTICS OF BOTH REFLECT AND LIGHT SCREEN.
IT'S JUST AS I THOUGHT!
WHAT DO YOU MEAN?
I DIDN'T KNOW FOR SURE, BUT IT LOOKS LIKE MY HUNCH WAS RIGHT.
WHEN BRANDON, SPENSER, TUCKER AND LUCY'S ATTACKS WERE REPELLED...
...IT LOOKED LIKE HIS ARMOR REFLECTED OUR ATTACKS.
BUT IT WAS ACTUALLY HIS **SWORD**...
...THAT DID IT.

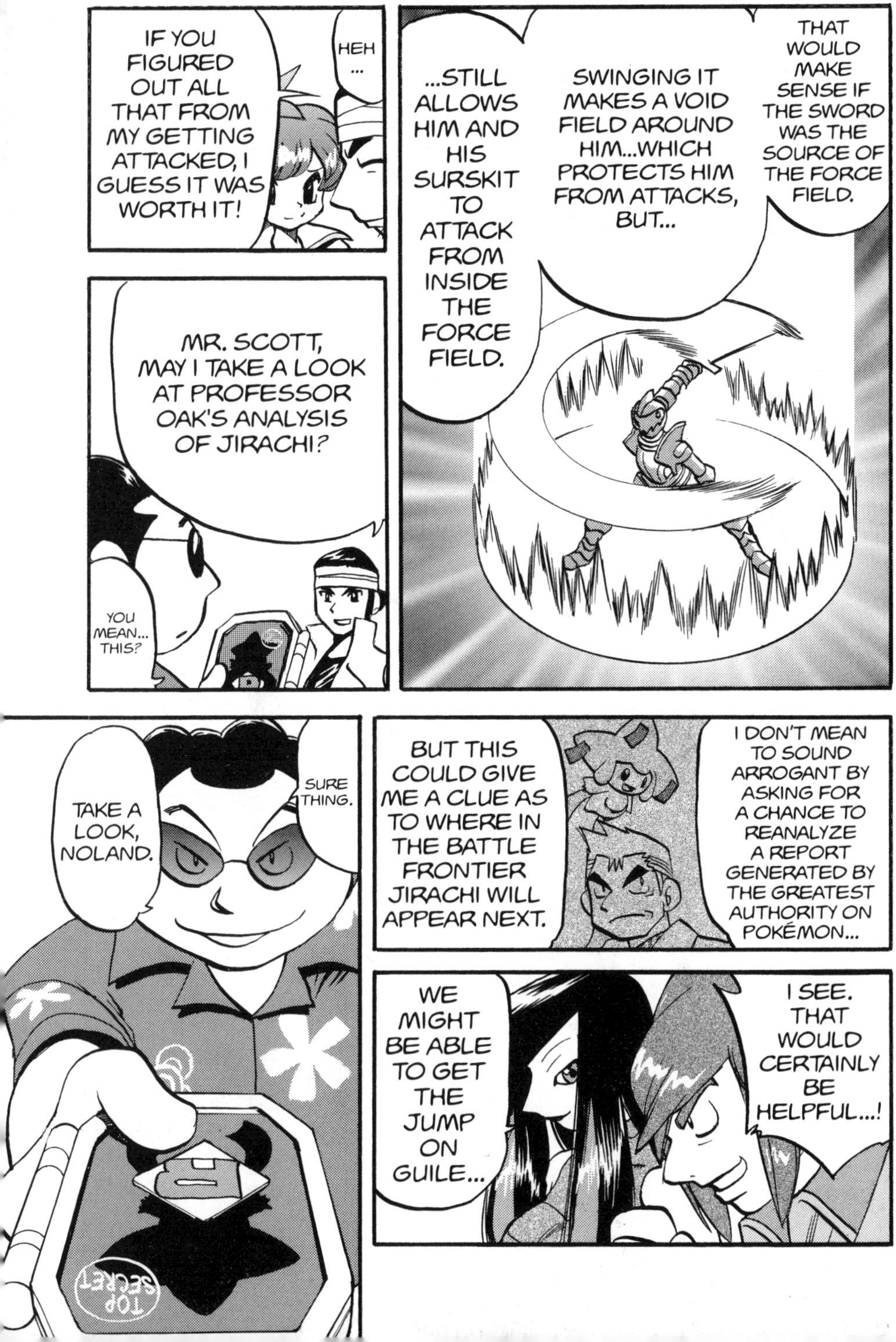
THAT WOULD MAKE SENSE IF THE SWORD WAS THE SOURCE OF THE FORCE FIELD.
SWINGING IT MAKES A VOID FIELD AROUND HIM...WHICH PROTECTS HIM FROM ATTACKS, BUT...
...STILL ALLOWS HIM AND HIS SURSKIT TO ATTACK FROM INSIDE THE FORCE FIELD.
HEH ...
IF YOU FIGURED OUT ALL THAT FROM MY GETTING ATTACKED, I GUESS IT WAS WORTH IT!
MR. SCOTT, MAY I TAKE A LOOK AT PROFESSOR OAK'S ANALYSIS OF JIRACHI?
YOU MEAN... THIS?
I DON'T MEAN TO SOUND ARROGANT BY ASKING FOR A CHANCE TO REANALYZE A REPORT GENERATED BY THE GREATEST AUTHORITY ON POKÉMON...
BUT THIS COULD GIVE ME A CLUE AS TO WHERE IN THE BATTLE FRONTIER JIRACHI WILL APPEAR NEXT.
I SEE. THAT WOULD CERTAINLY BE HELPFUL...!
WE MIGHT BE ABLE TO GET THE JUMP ON GUILE...
SURE THING.
TAKE A LOOK, NOLAND.
TOP SECRET

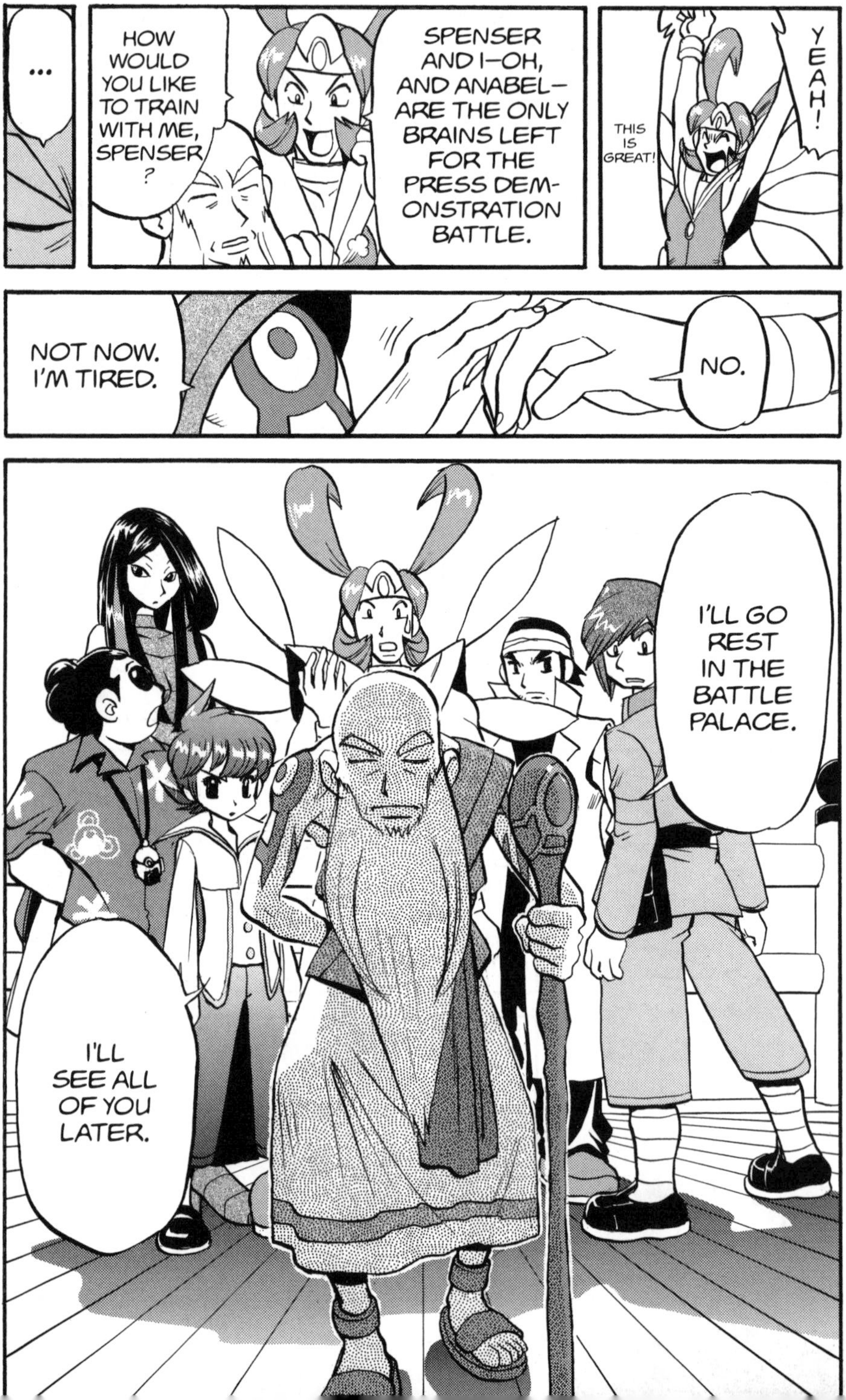
YEAH!
THIS IS GREAT!
SPENSER AND I—OH, AND ANABEL—ARE THE ONLY BRAINS LEFT FOR THE PRESS DEMONSTRATION BATTLE.
HOW WOULD YOU LIKE TO TRAIN WITH ME, SPENSER?
...
NO.
NOT NOW. I'M TIRED.
I'LL GO REST IN THE BATTLE PALACE.
I'LL SEE ALL OF YOU LATER.

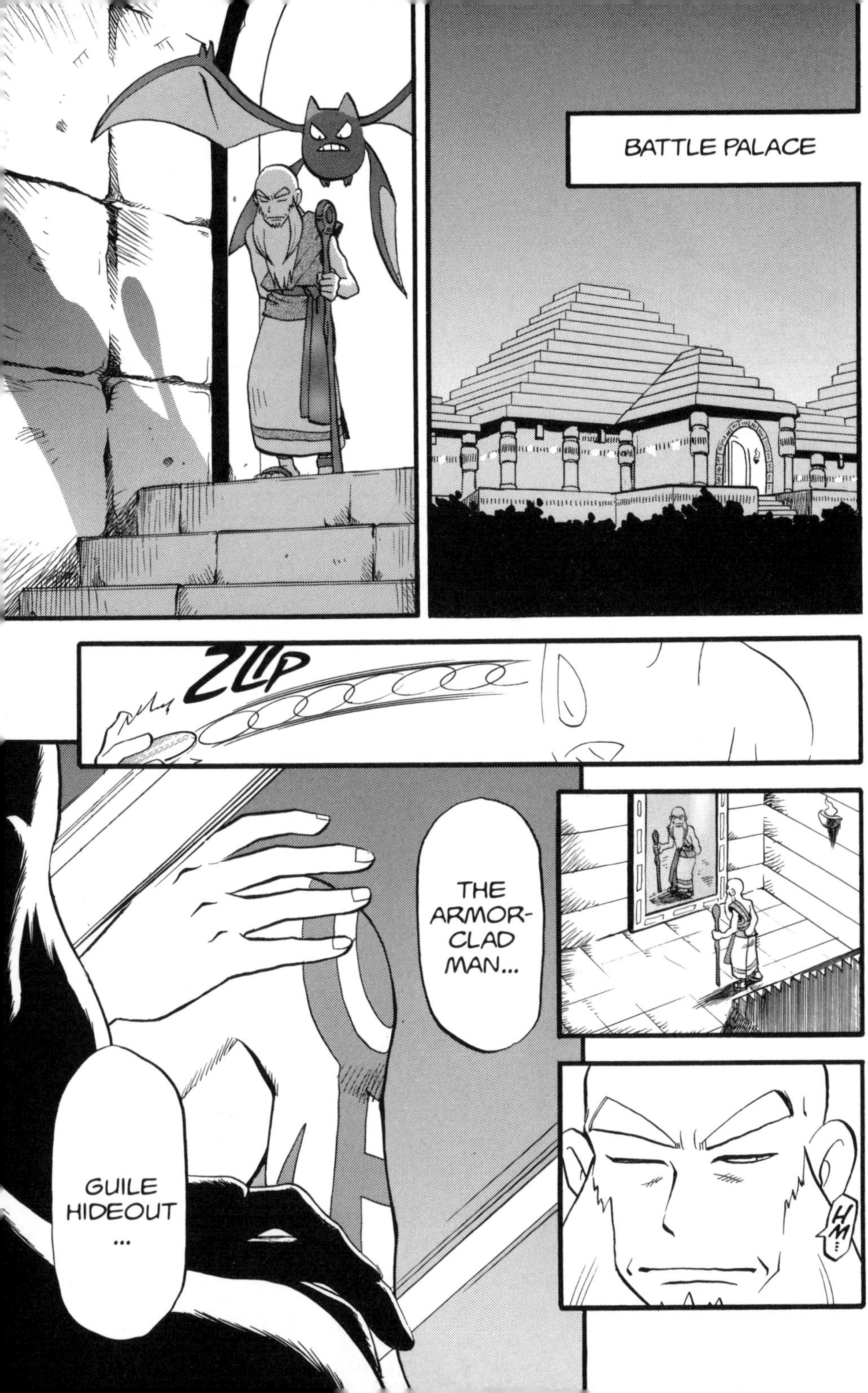
BATTLE PALACE
ZLIP
HM...
THE ARMOR-CLAD MAN...
GUILE HIDEOUT...

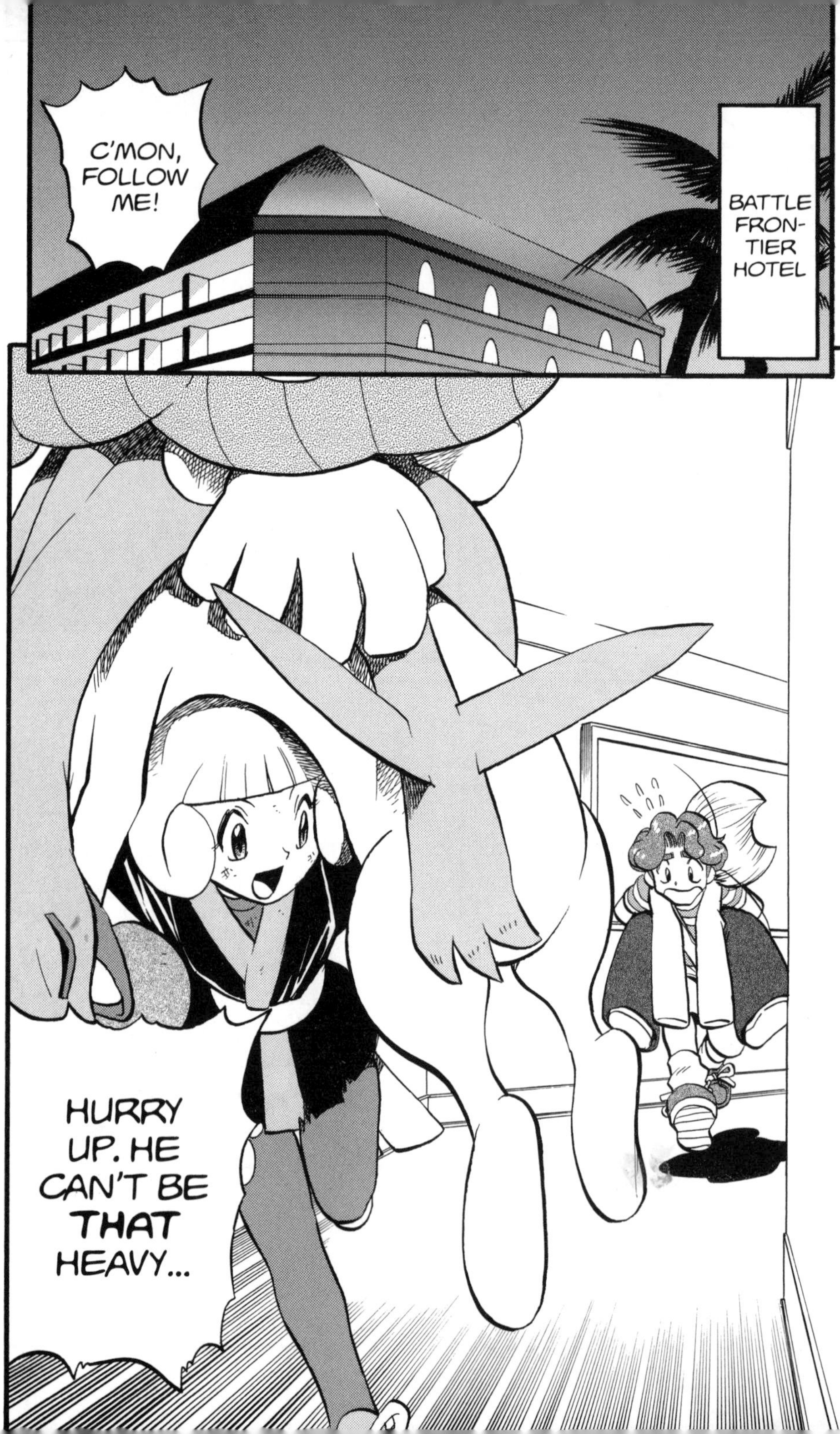
BATTLE FRONTIER HOTEL
C'MON, FOLLOW ME!
HURRY UP. HE CAN'T BE **THAT** HEAVY...

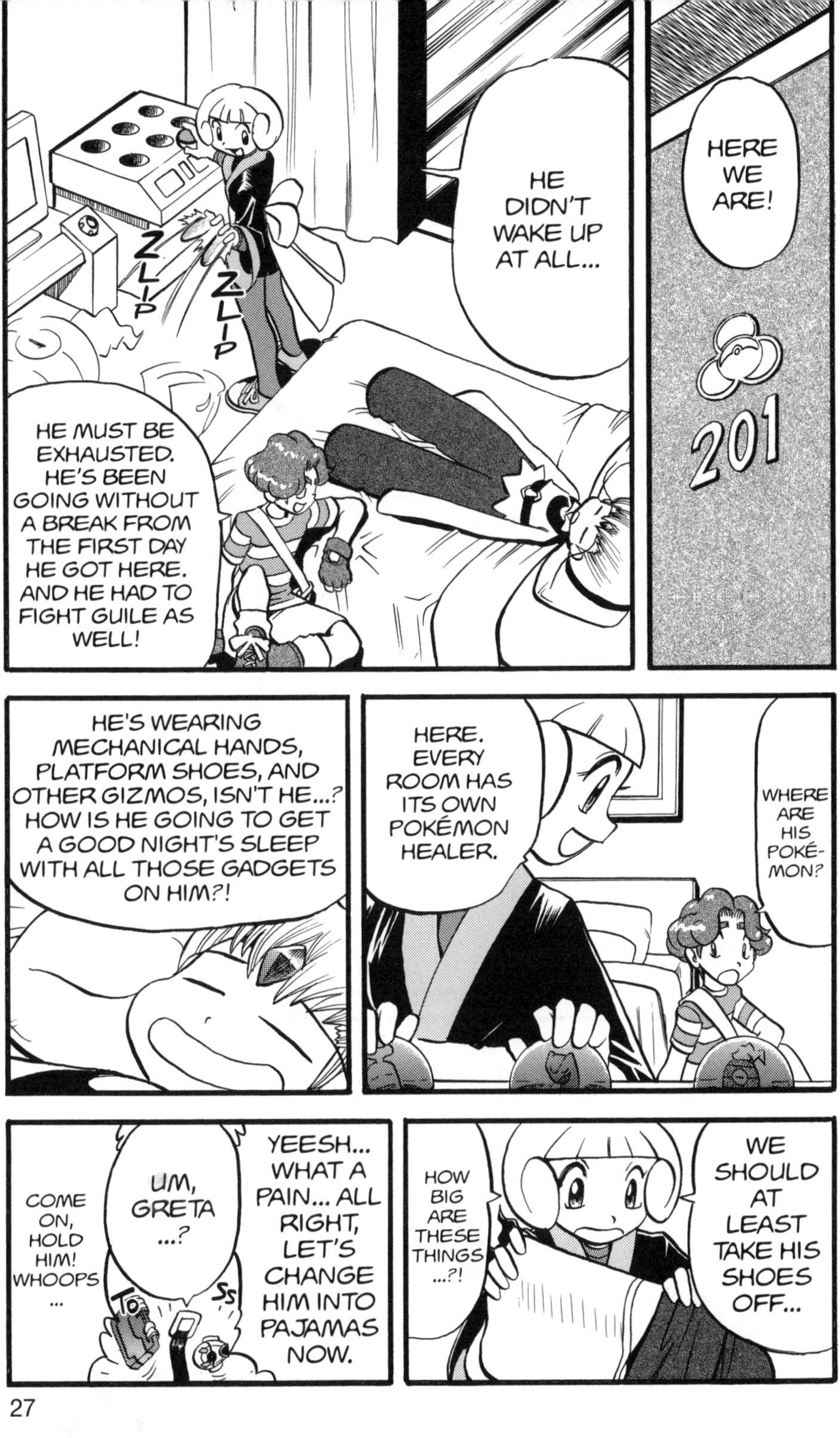
HERE WE ARE!
201
HE DIDN'T WAKE UP AT ALL...
ZLIP
ZLIP
HE MUST BE EXHAUSTED. HE'S BEEN GOING WITHOUT A BREAK FROM THE FIRST DAY HE GOT HERE. AND HE HAD TO FIGHT GUILE AS WELL!
WHERE ARE HIS POKÉ-MON?
HERE. EVERY ROOM HAS ITS OWN POKÉMON HEALER.
HE'S WEARING MECHANICAL HANDS, PLATFORM SHOES, AND OTHER GIZMOS, ISN'T HE...? HOW IS HE GOING TO GET A GOOD NIGHT'S SLEEP WITH ALL THOSE GADGETS ON HIM?!
WE SHOULD AT LEAST TAKE HIS SHOES OFF...
HOW BIG ARE THESE THINGS ...?!
YEESH... WHAT A PAIN... ALL RIGHT, LET'S CHANGE HIM INTO PAJAMAS NOW.
UM, GRETA ...?
COME ON, HOLD HIM! WHOOPS ...

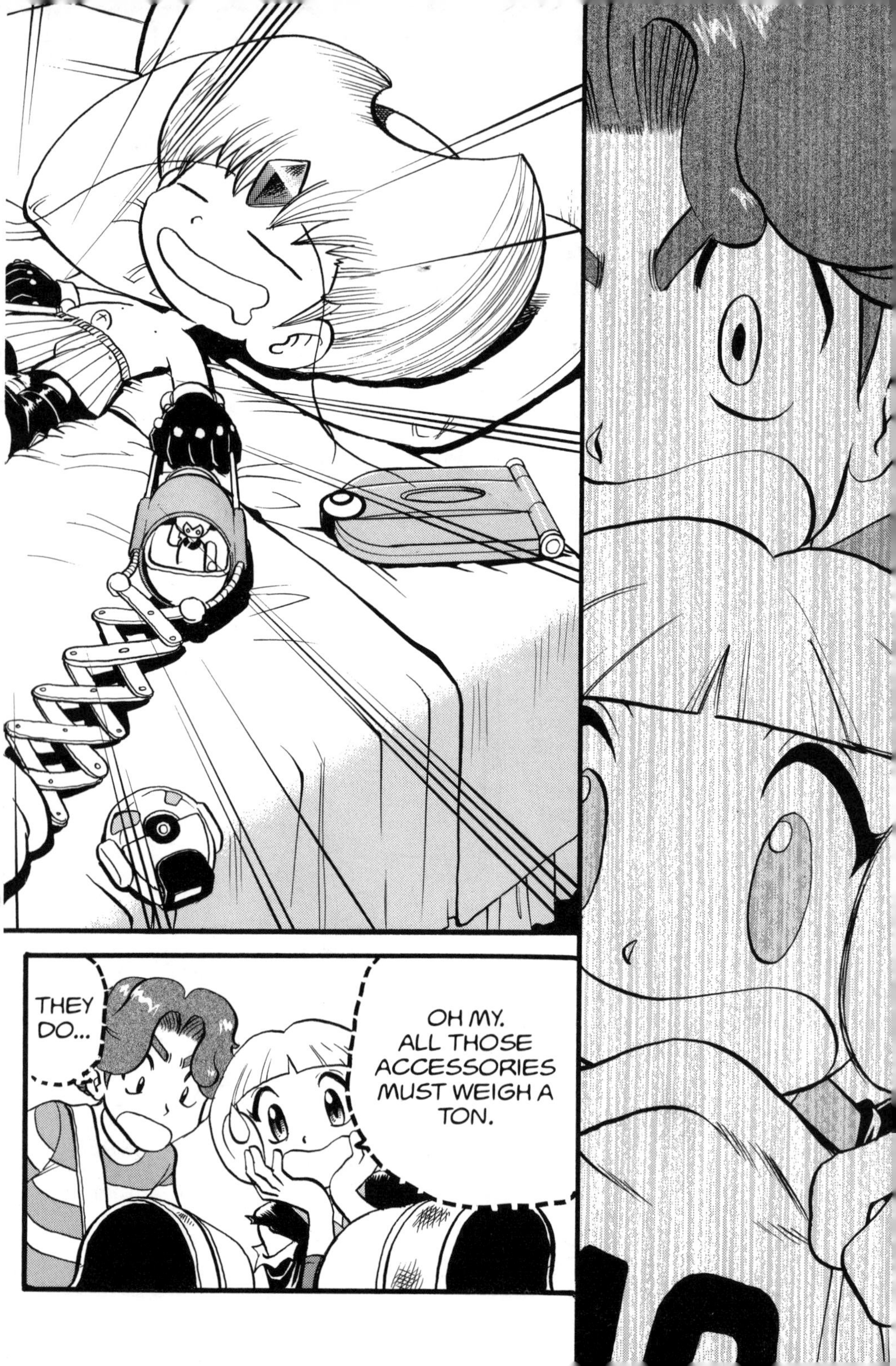
OH MY. ALL THOSE ACCESSORIES MUST WEIGH A TON.
THEY DO...

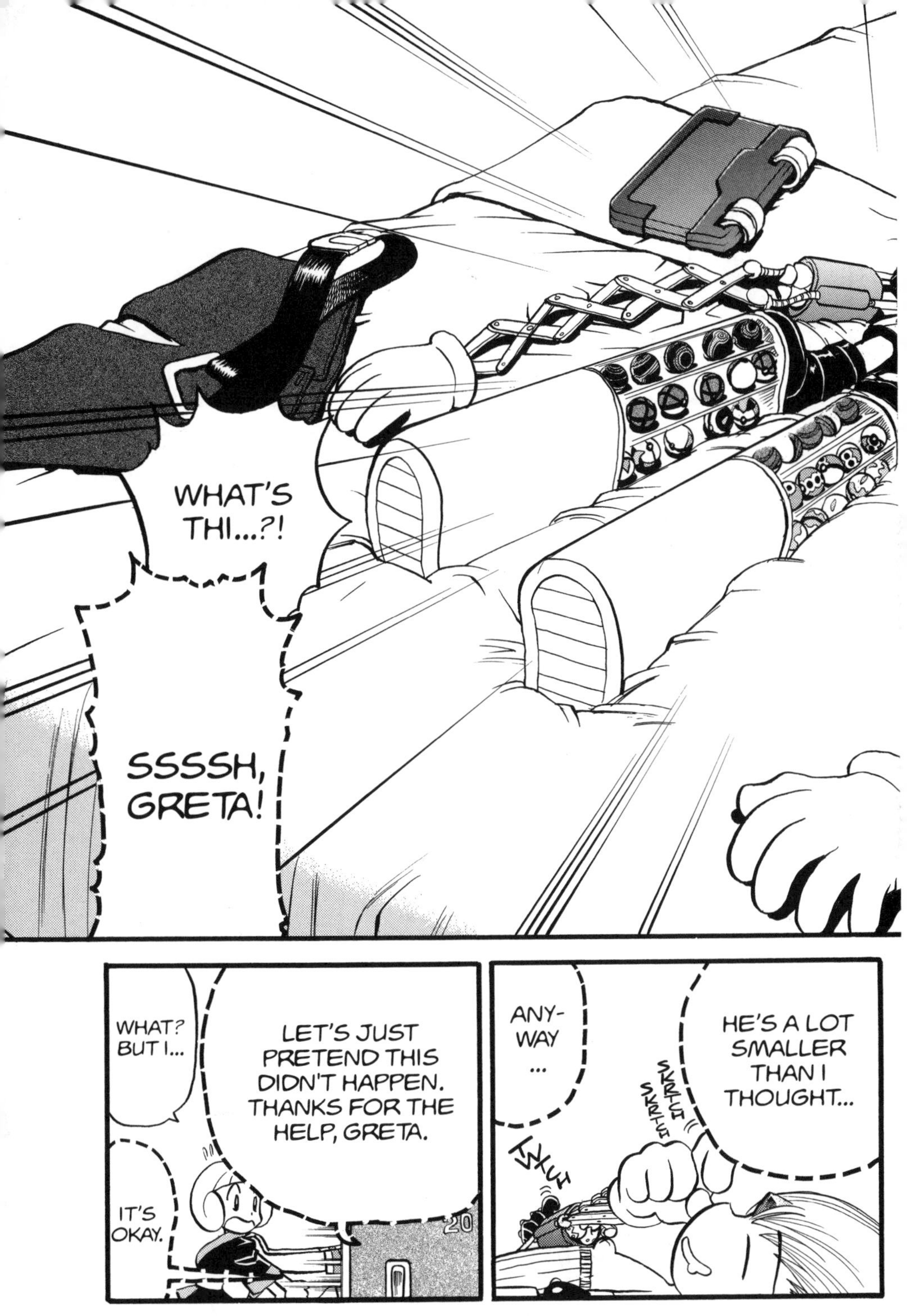
WHAT'S THI...?!
SSSSH, GRETA!
HE'S A LOT SMALLER THAN I THOUGHT...
SKRTCH SKRTCH
ANY-WAY...
LET'S JUST PRETEND THIS DIDN'T HAPPEN. THANKS FOR THE HELP, GRETA.
WHAT? BUT I...
IT'S OKAY.
20

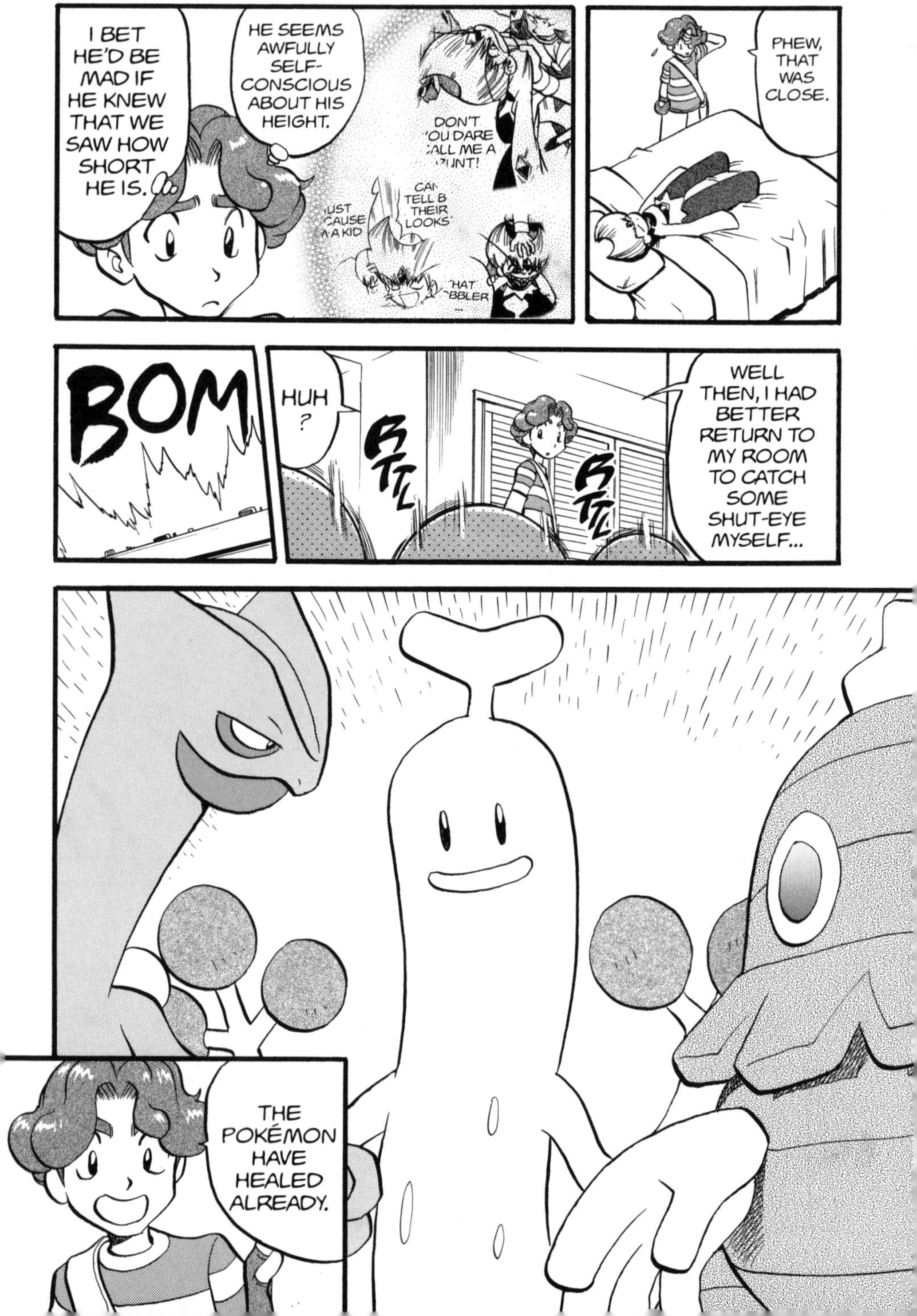
PHEW, THAT WAS CLOSE.
HE SEEMS AWFULLY SELF-CONSCIOUS ABOUT HIS HEIGHT.
I BET HE'D BE MAD IF HE KNEW THAT WE SAW HOW SHORT HE IS.
WELL THEN, I HAD BETTER RETURN TO MY ROOM TO CATCH SOME SHUT-EYE MYSELF...
RTTL
RTTL
HUH?
BOM
THE POKÉMON HAVE HEALED ALREADY.

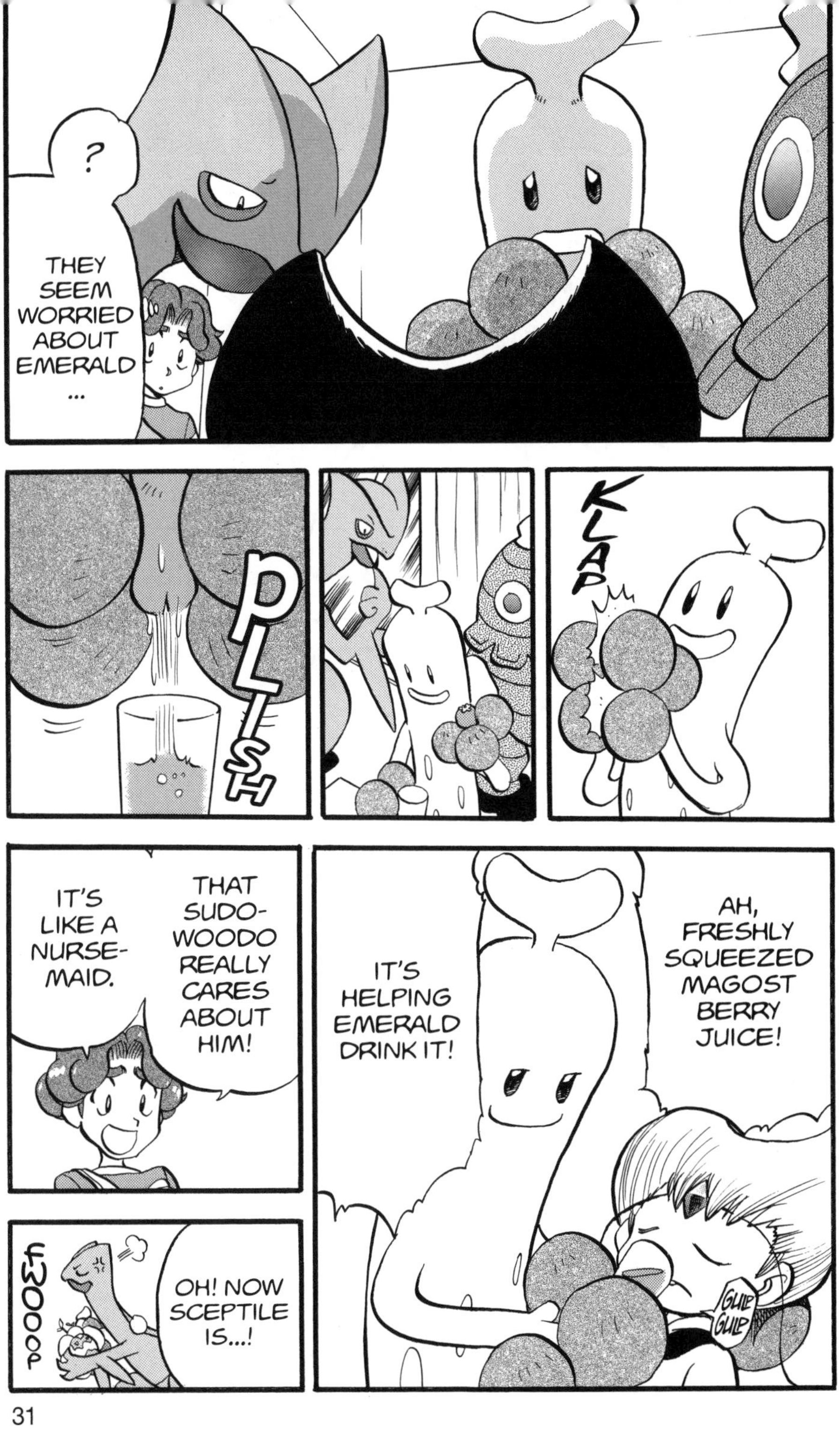
?
THEY SEEM WORRIED ABOUT EMERALD ...
KLAP
PLISH
AH, FRESHLY SQUEEZED MAGOST BERRY JUICE!
IT'S HELPING EMERALD DRINK IT!
GULP GULP
THAT SUDO-WOODO REALLY CARES ABOUT HIM!
IT'S LIKE A NURSE-MAID.
OH! NOW SCEPTILE IS...!
FWOOOP

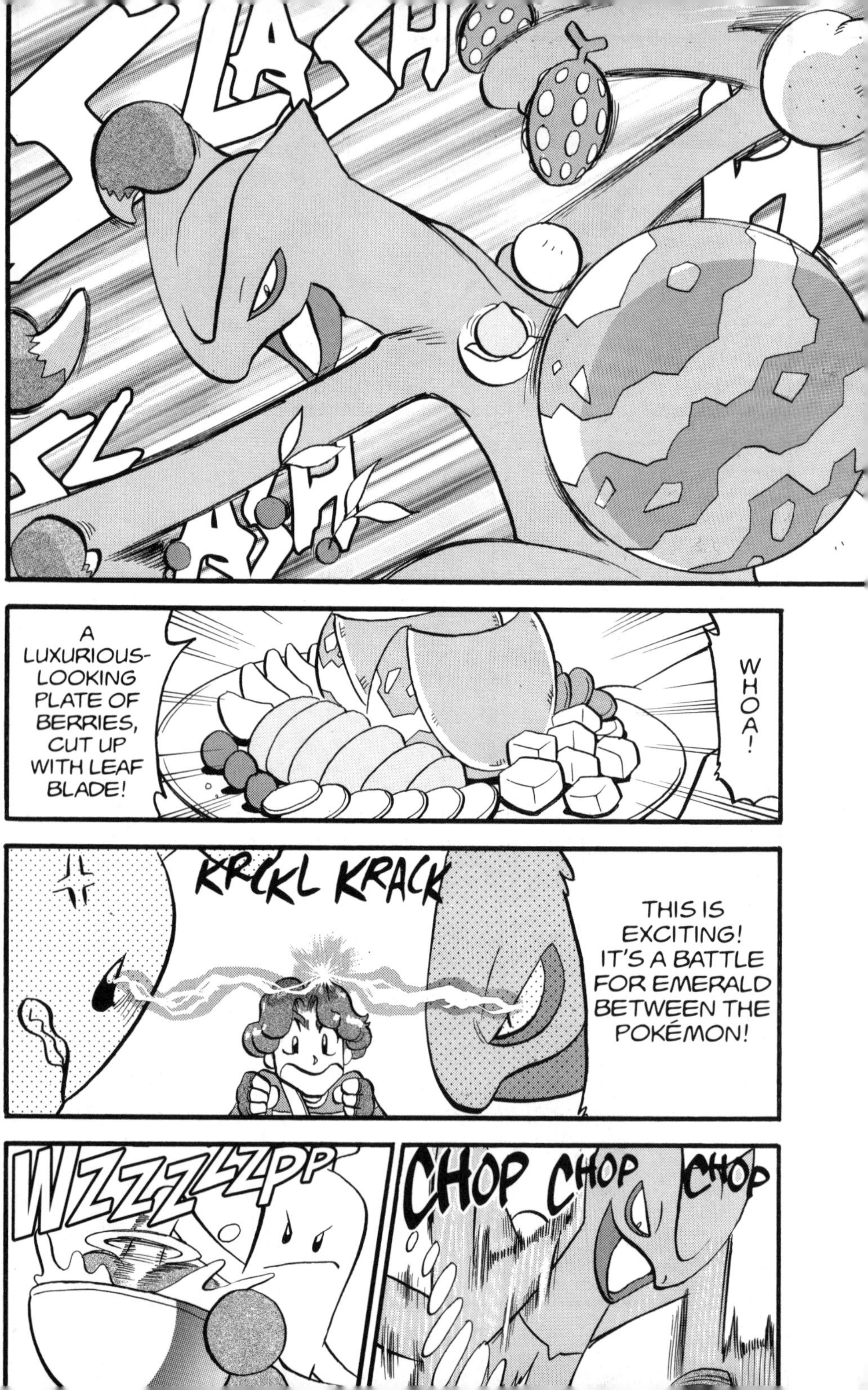

WHOA!
A LUXURIOUS-LOOKING PLATE OF BERRIES, CUT UP WITH LEAF BLADE!
THIS IS EXCITING! IT'S A BATTLE FOR EMERALD BETWEEN THE POKÉMON!
KRCKL KRACK
CHOP CHOP CHOP
WZZZZZPP

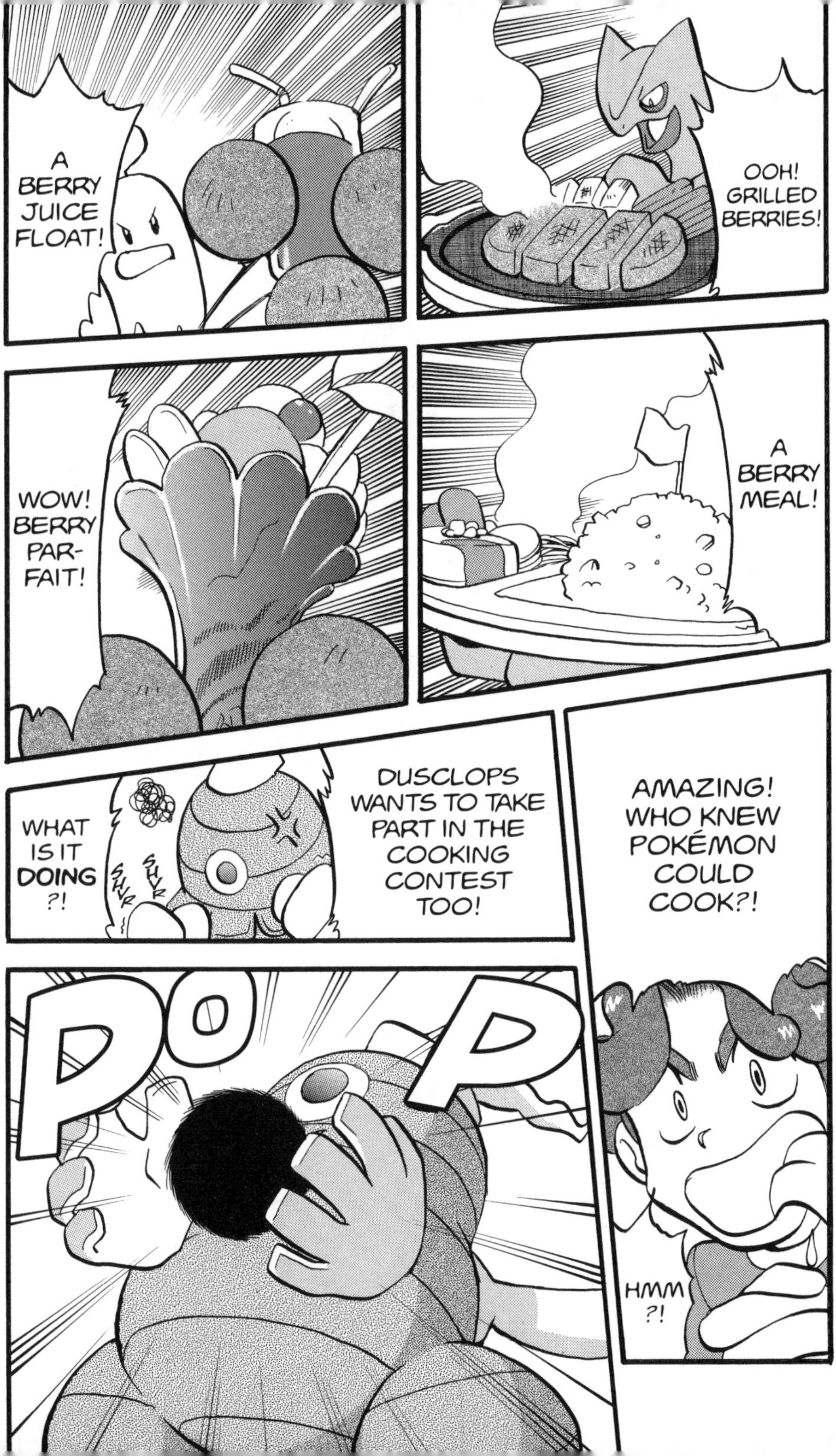
OOH! GRILLED BERRIES!
A BERRY JUICE FLOAT!
A BERRY MEAL!
WOW! BERRY PAR-FAIT!
AMAZING! WHO KNEW POKÉMON COULD COOK?!
HMM ?!
DUSCLOPS WANTS TO TAKE PART IN THE COOKING CONTEST TOO!
SHVR
SHVR
WHAT IS IT **DOING** ?!
POP

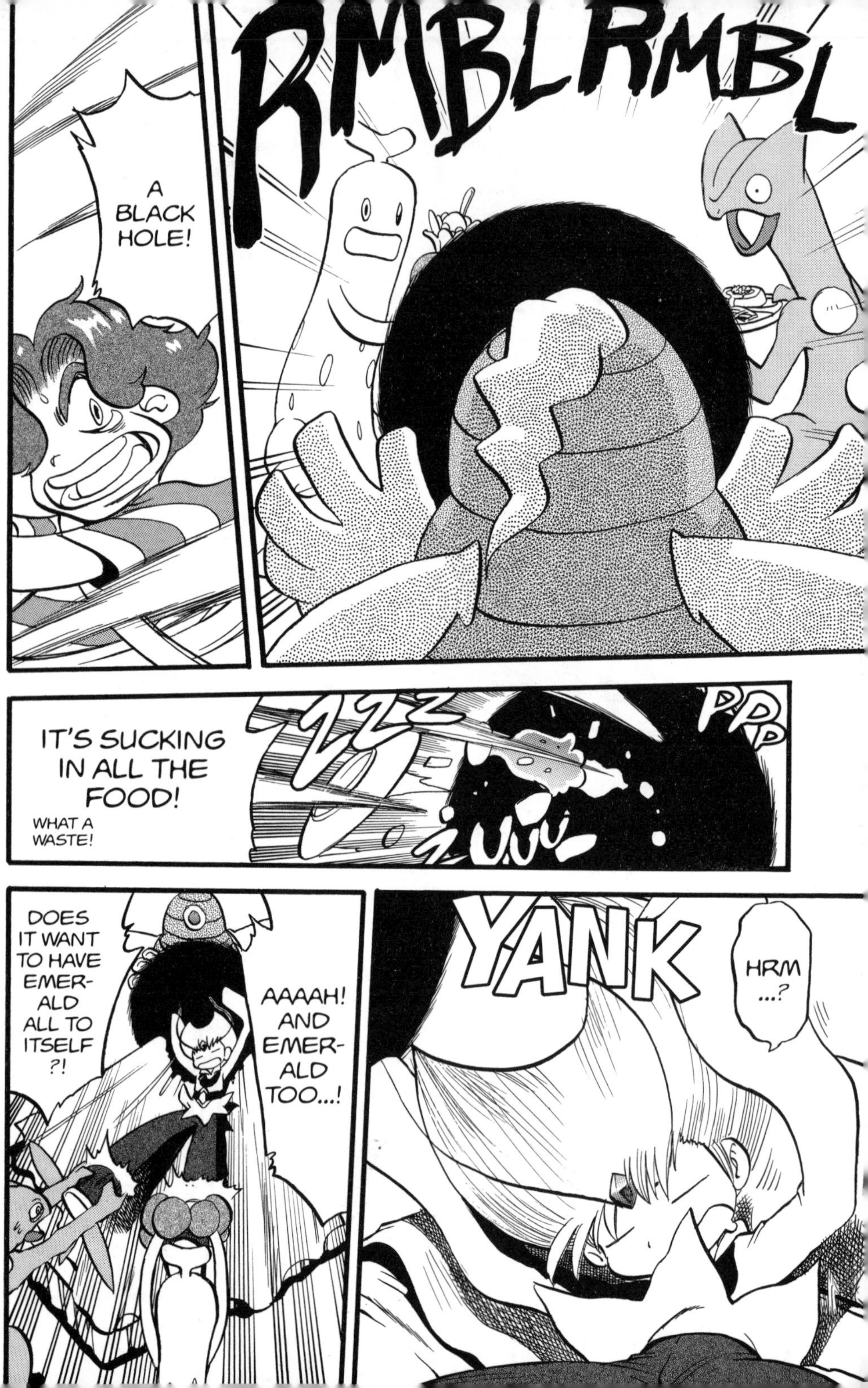
RMBLRMBL
A BLACK HOLE!
IT'S SUCKING IN ALL THE FOOD!
WHAT A WASTE!
YANK
HRM ...?
AAAAH! AND EMER-ALD TOO...!
DOES IT WANT TO HAVE EMER-ALD ALL TO ITSELF ?!

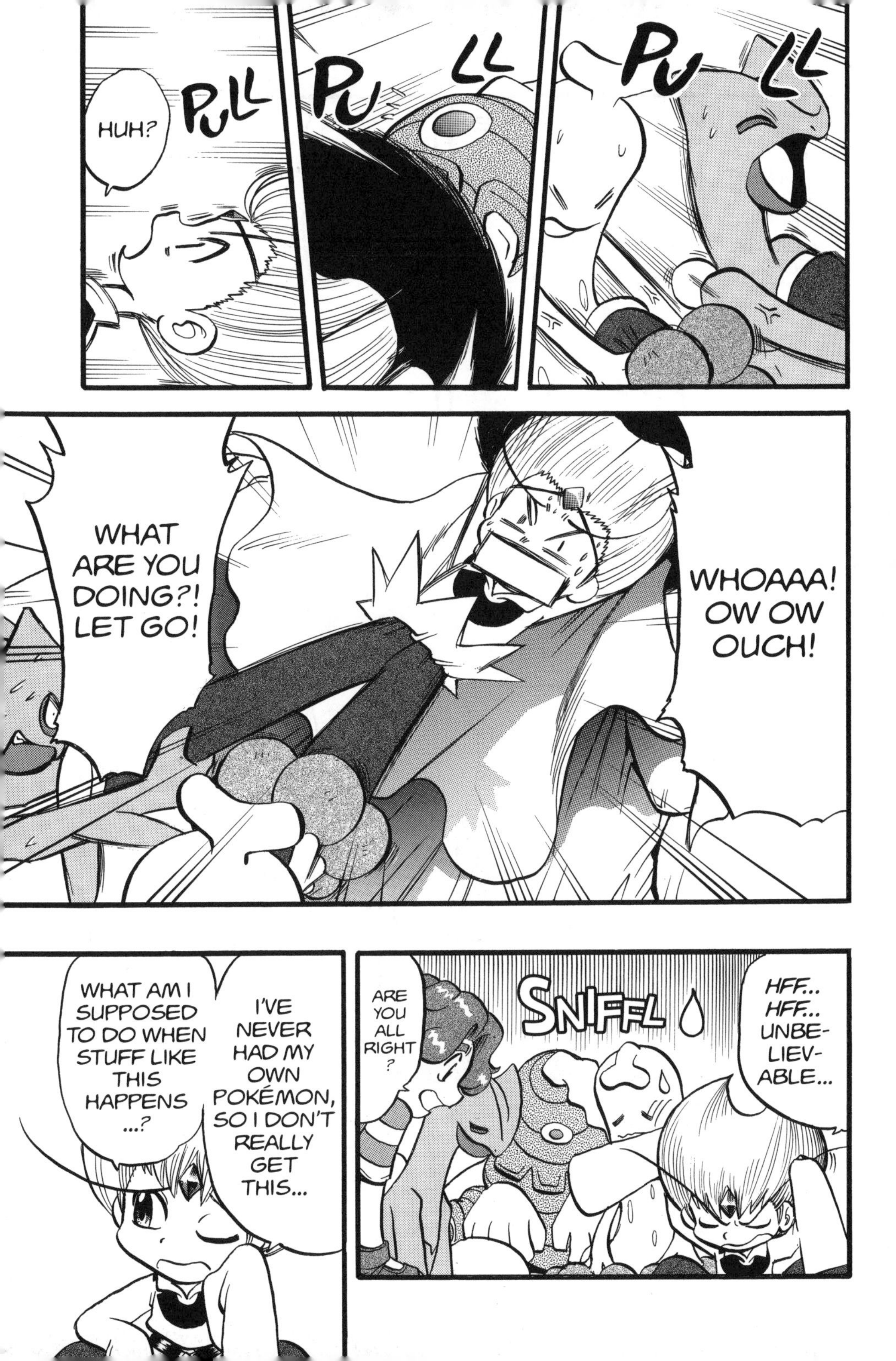
PULL
PULL
HUH?
PULL
WHOAAA! OW OW OUCH!
WHAT ARE YOU DOING?! LET GO!
HFF... HFF... UNBE-LIEV-ABLE...
SNIFFL
ARE YOU ALL RIGHT?
I'VE NEVER HAD MY OWN POKÉMON, SO I DON'T REALLY GET THIS...
WHAT AM I SUPPOSED TO DO WHEN STUFF LIKE THIS HAPPENS...?

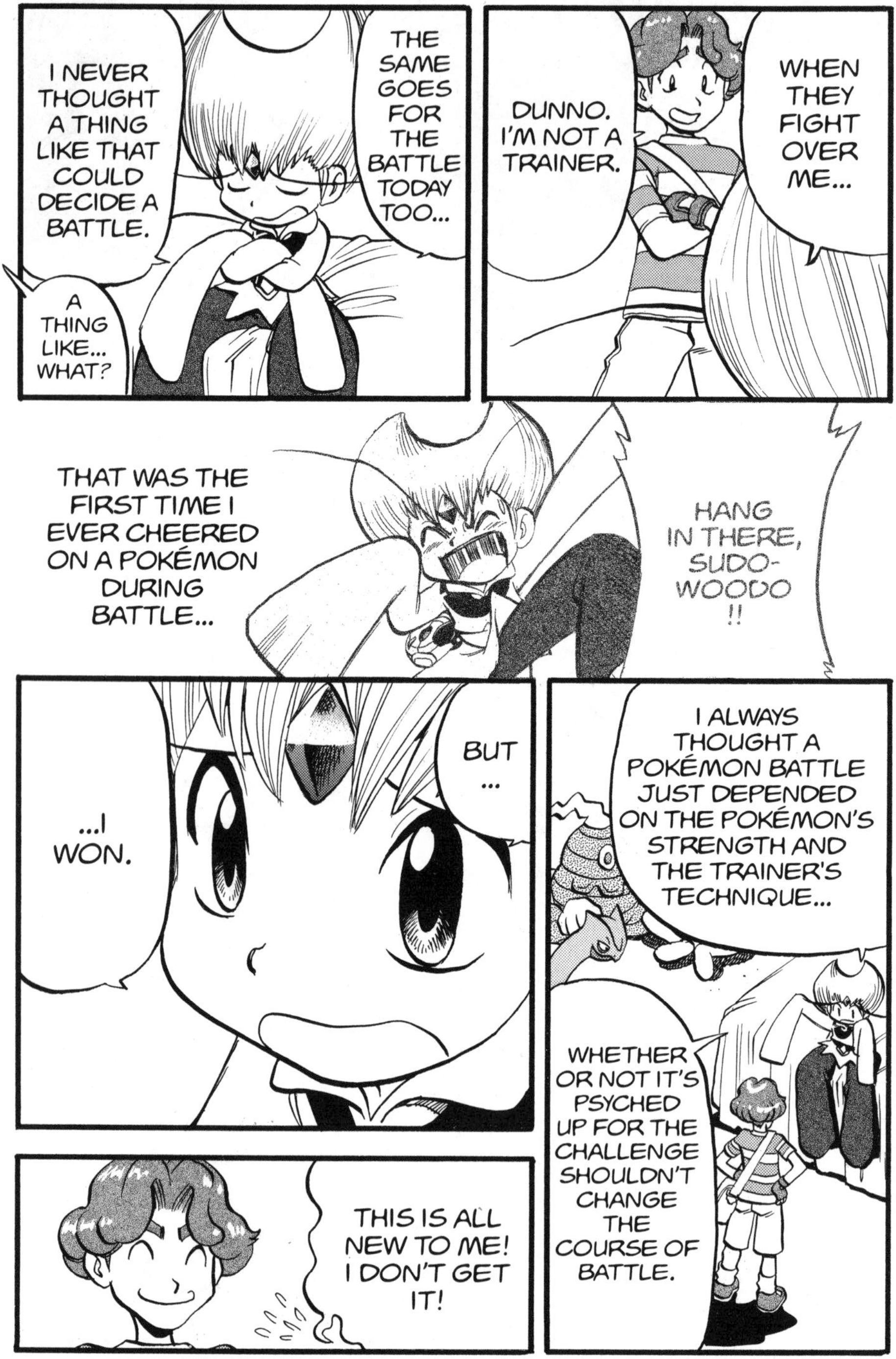
WHEN THEY FIGHT OVER ME...
DUNNO. I'M NOT A TRAINER.
THE SAME GOES FOR THE BATTLE TODAY TOO...
I NEVER THOUGHT A THING LIKE THAT COULD DECIDE A BATTLE.
A THING LIKE... WHAT?
HANG IN THERE, SUDO-WOODO !!
THAT WAS THE FIRST TIME I EVER CHEERED ON A POKÉMON DURING BATTLE...
I ALWAYS THOUGHT A POKÉMON BATTLE JUST DEPENDED ON THE POKÉMON'S STRENGTH AND THE TRAINER'S TECHNIQUE...
WHETHER OR NOT IT'S PSYCHED UP FOR THE CHALLENGE SHOULDN'T CHANGE THE COURSE OF BATTLE.
BUT ...
...I WON.
THIS IS ALL NEW TO ME! I DON'T GET IT!

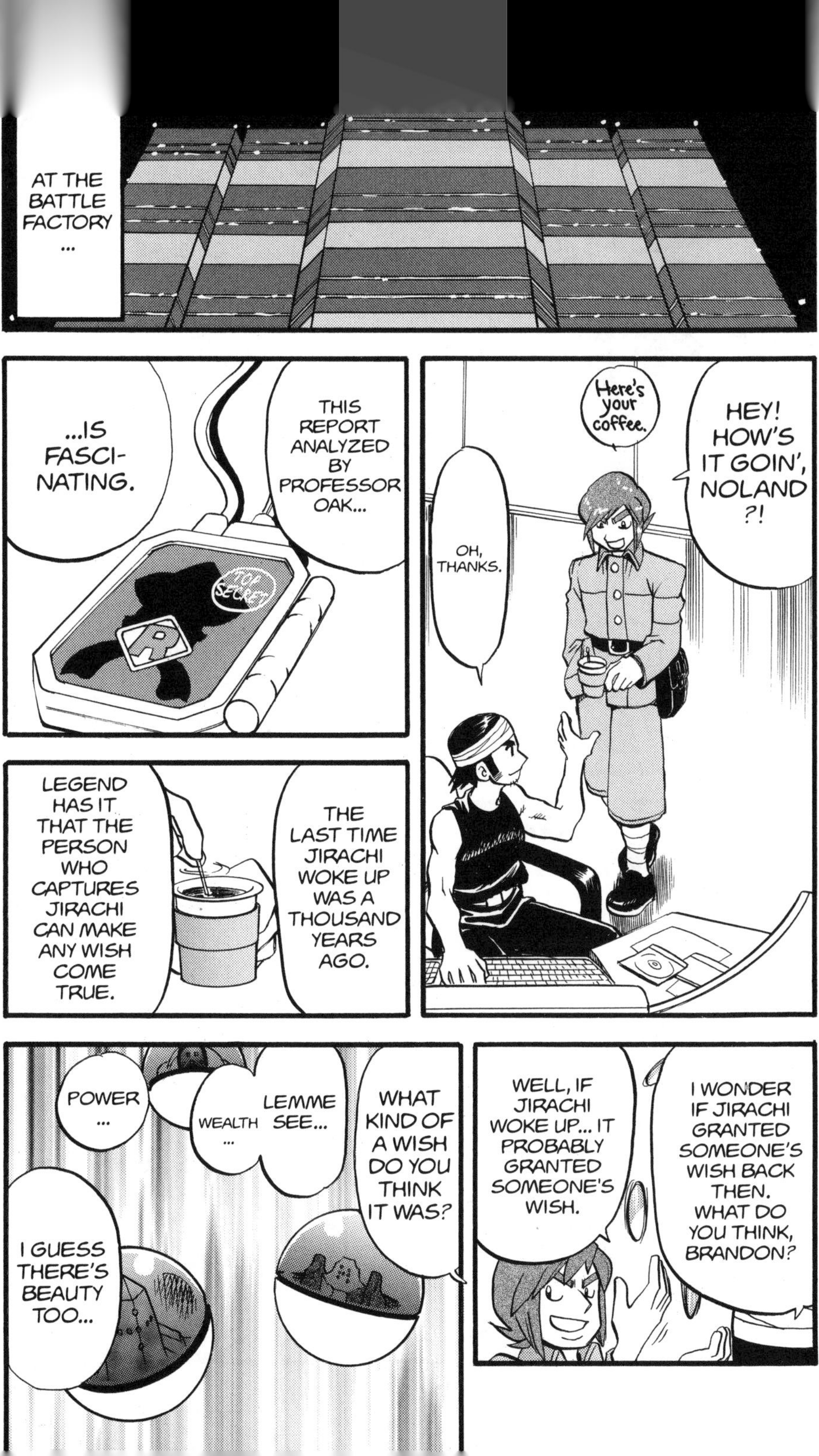
AT THE BATTLE FACTORY ...
HEY! HOW'S IT GOIN', NOLAND ?!
Here's your coffee.
OH, THANKS.
THIS REPORT ANALYZED BY PROFESSOR OAK...
...IS FASCINATING.
TOP SECRET
THE LAST TIME JIRACHI WOKE UP WAS A THOUSAND YEARS AGO.
LEGEND HAS IT THAT THE PERSON WHO CAPTURES JIRACHI CAN MAKE ANY WISH COME TRUE.
I WONDER IF JIRACHI GRANTED SOMEONE'S WISH BACK THEN. WHAT DO YOU THINK, BRANDON?
WELL, IF JIRACHI WOKE UP... IT PROBABLY GRANTED SOMEONE'S WISH.
WHAT KIND OF A WISH DO YOU THINK IT WAS?
LEMME SEE...
WEALTH ...
POWER ...
I GUESS THERE'S BEAUTY TOO...

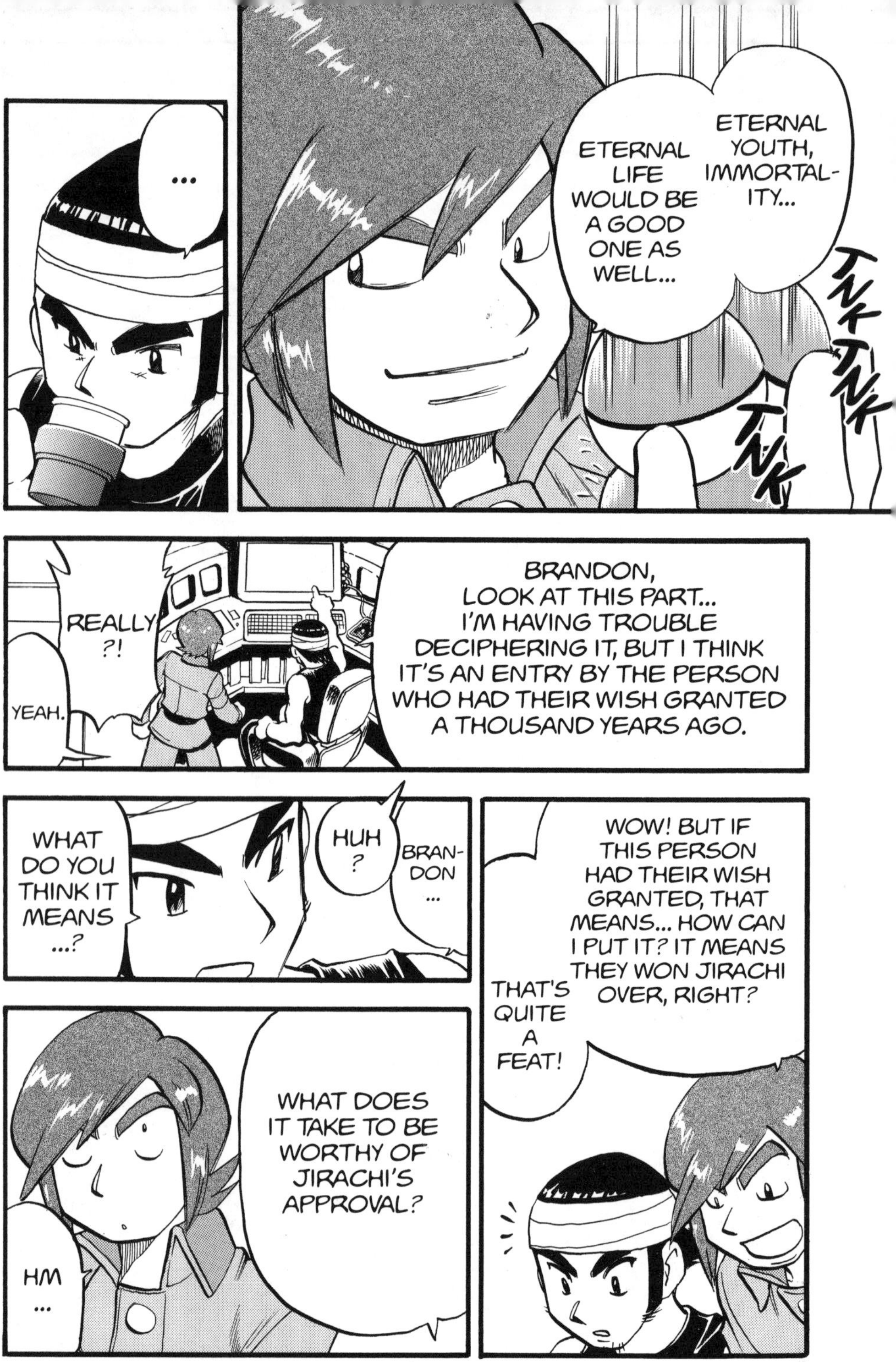
ETERNAL YOUTH, IMMORTALITY...
ETERNAL LIFE WOULD BE A GOOD ONE AS WELL...
TINK TINK TINK
...
BRANDON, LOOK AT THIS PART... I'M HAVING TROUBLE DECIPHERING IT, BUT I THINK IT'S AN ENTRY BY THE PERSON WHO HAD THEIR WISH GRANTED A THOUSAND YEARS AGO.
REALLY?!
YEAH.
WOW! BUT IF THIS PERSON HAD THEIR WISH GRANTED, THAT MEANS... HOW CAN I PUT IT? IT MEANS THEY WON JIRACHI OVER, RIGHT?
THAT'S QUITE A FEAT!
BRANDON...
HUH?
WHAT DO YOU THINK IT MEANS...?
WHAT DOES IT TAKE TO BE WORTHY OF JIRACHI'S APPROVAL?
HM...

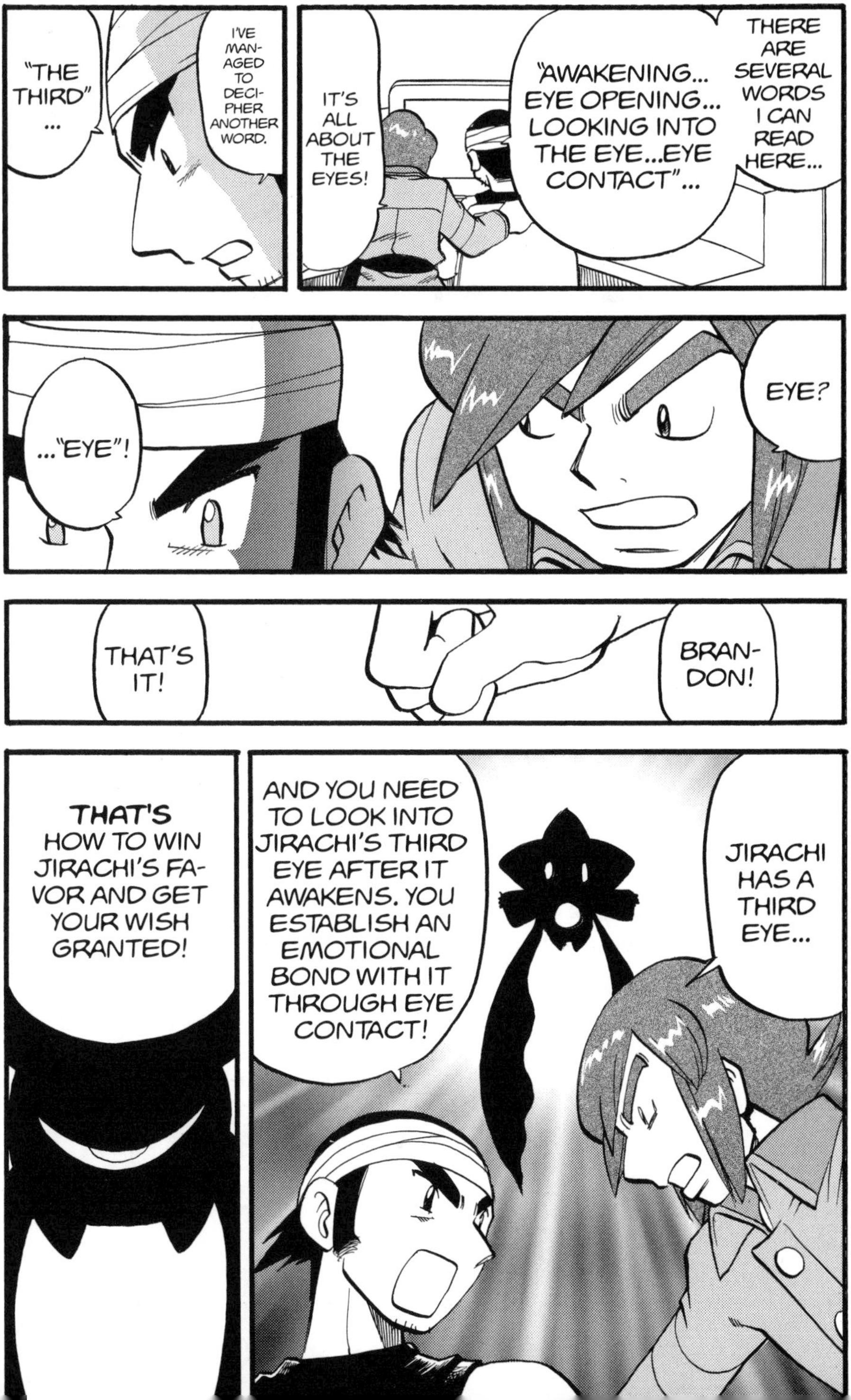
THERE ARE SEVERAL WORDS I CAN READ HERE...
"AWAKENING... EYE OPENING... LOOKING INTO THE EYE...EYE CONTACT"...
IT'S ALL ABOUT THE EYES!
I'VE MANAGED TO DECIPHER ANOTHER WORD.
"THE THIRD" ...
EYE?
..."EYE"!
BRANDON!
THAT'S IT!
JIRACHI HAS A THIRD EYE...
AND YOU NEED TO LOOK INTO JIRACHI'S THIRD EYE AFTER IT AWAKENS. YOU ESTABLISH AN EMOTIONAL BOND WITH IT THROUGH EYE CONTACT!
THAT'S HOW TO WIN JIRACHI'S FAVOR AND GET YOUR WISH GRANTED!

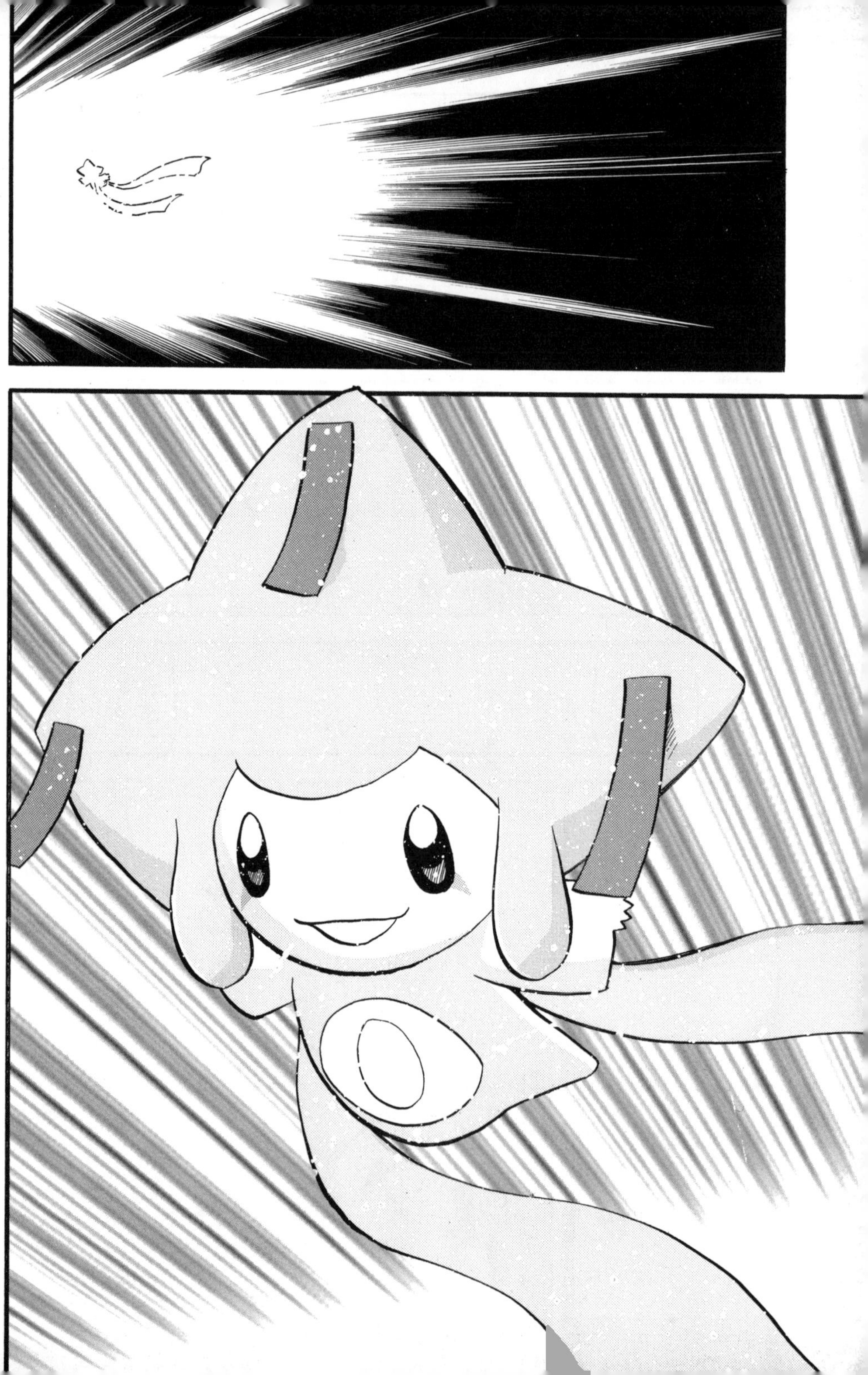

DEAR MEMBERS OF THE PRESS...

Thank you for visiting the Battle Frontier today. Permit me to continue explaining the rules of this facility...

OWNER: SCOTT

FACILITY RULES

BATTLE DOME 2

■ DETAILS OF THE BATTLE CARD ■

The challenger may learn about their opponents at the Battle Dome by reviewing their opponents' battle card.

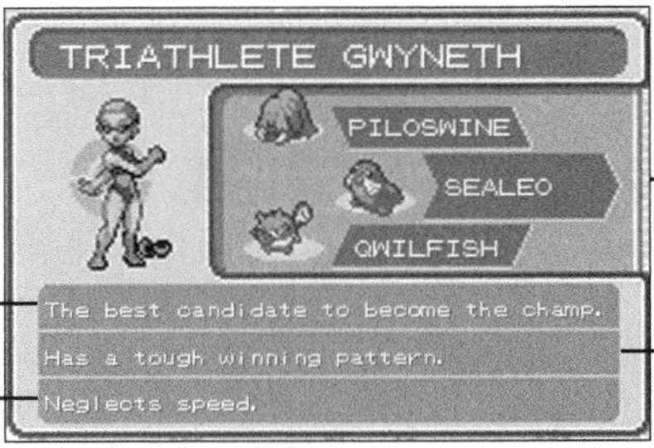

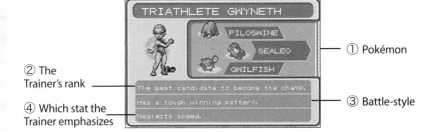

TRIATHLETE GWYNETH
PILOSWINE
SEALEO
QWILFISH
The best candidate to become the champ.
Has a tough winning pattern.
Neglects speed.

① Pokémon

② The Trainer's rank

③ Battle-style

④ Which stat the Trainer emphasizes

① Pokémon
The Trainer's three Pokémon.

② The Trainer's rank
The Trainer's rank compared to the rank of the opponent. Represents the Trainer's rank in relation to the stats of the opponent's Pokémon.

③ Battle-style
The type of battle-style this Trainer excels in. (The sentence here will differ depending on the type of Pokémon moves.)

④ Which stat the Trainer emphasizes
The stats of the Pokémon. You may also learn how the Nature of the Pokémon affects the stats.

◆ 319 ◆

Verily Vanquishing Vileplume, Part 1

■ ■ K B O G L

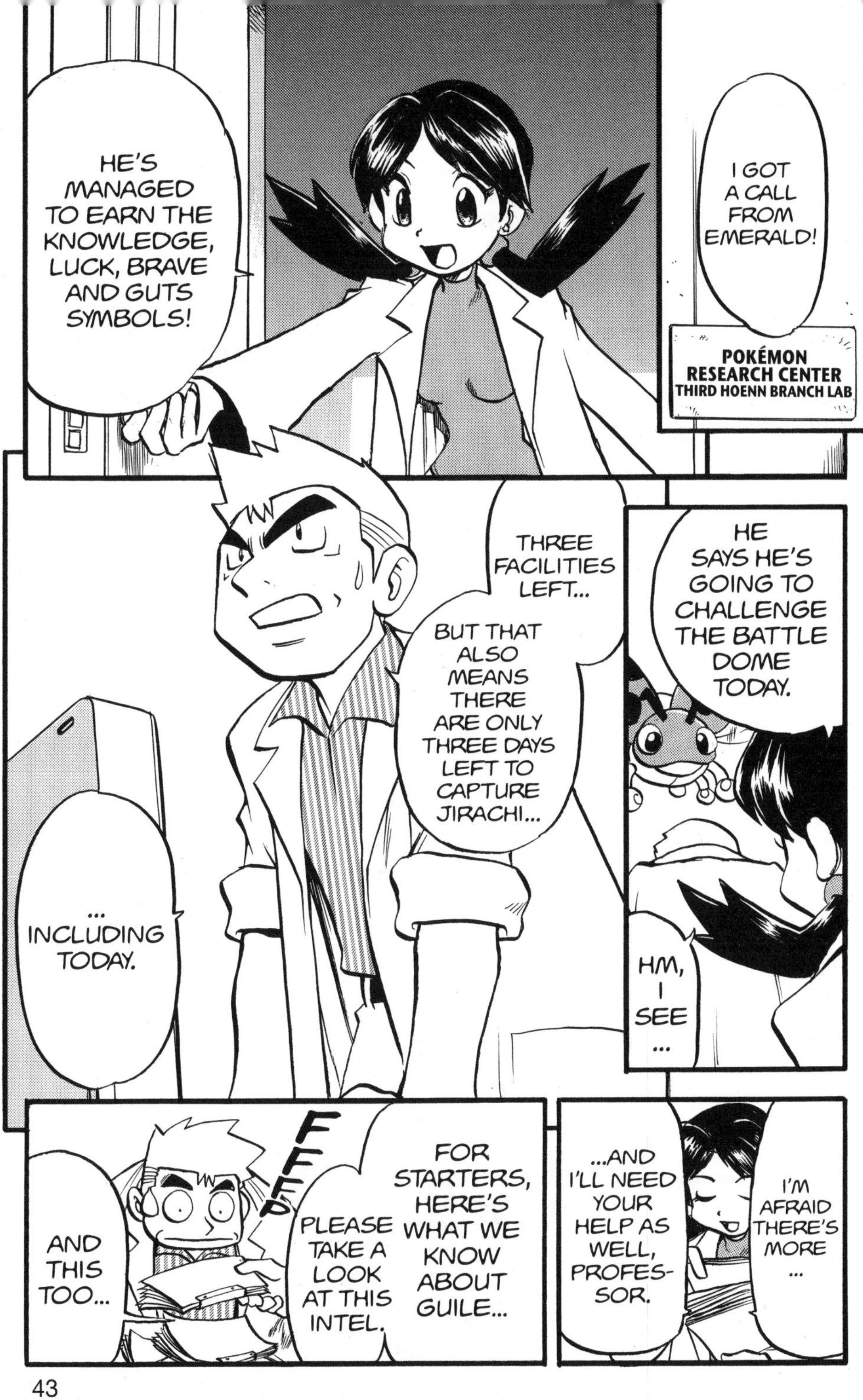
I GOT A CALL FROM EMERALD!
POKÉMON RESEARCH CENTER THIRD HOENN BRANCH LAB
HE'S MANAGED TO EARN THE KNOWLEDGE, LUCK, BRAVE AND GUTS SYMBOLS!
HE SAYS HE'S GOING TO CHALLENGE THE BATTLE DOME TODAY.
HM, I SEE ...
THREE FACILITIES LEFT...
BUT THAT ALSO MEANS THERE ARE ONLY THREE DAYS LEFT TO CAPTURE JIRACHI...
... INCLUDING TODAY.
I'M AFRAID THERE'S MORE ...
...AND I'LL NEED YOUR HELP AS WELL, PROFES-SOR.
FOR STARTERS, HERE'S WHAT WE KNOW ABOUT GUILE...
PLEASE TAKE A LOOK AT THIS INTEL.
FFFP
AND THIS TOO...

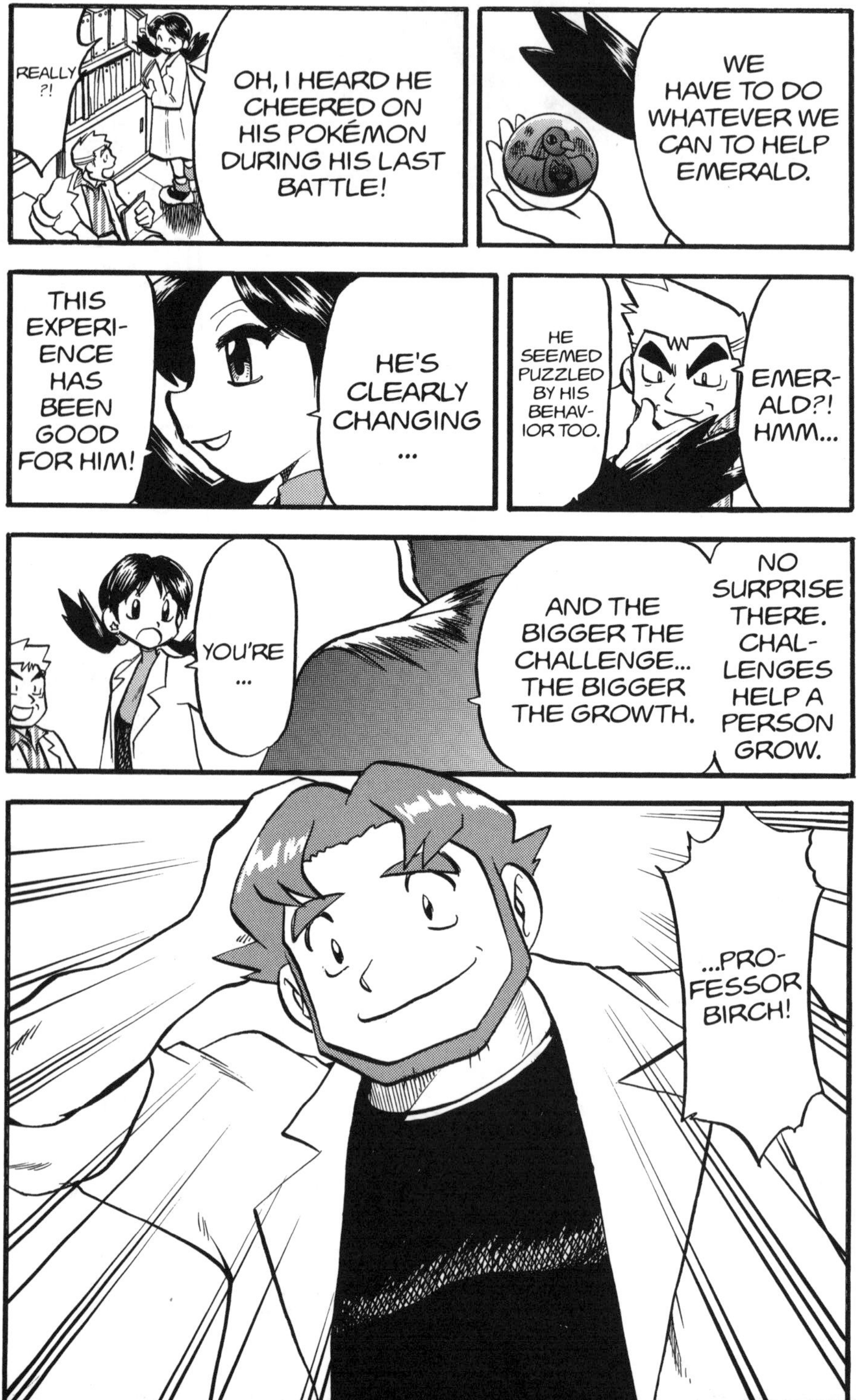
WE HAVE TO DO WHATEVER WE CAN TO HELP EMERALD.
OH, I HEARD HE CHEERED ON HIS POKÉMON DURING HIS LAST BATTLE!
REALLY?!
EMERALD?! HMM...
HE SEEMED PUZZLED BY HIS BEHAVIOR TOO.
HE'S CLEARLY CHANGING...
THIS EXPERIENCE HAS BEEN GOOD FOR HIM!
NO SURPRISE THERE. CHALLENGES HELP A PERSON GROW.
AND THE BIGGER THE CHALLENGE... THE BIGGER THE GROWTH.
YOU'RE...
...PROFESSOR BIRCH!

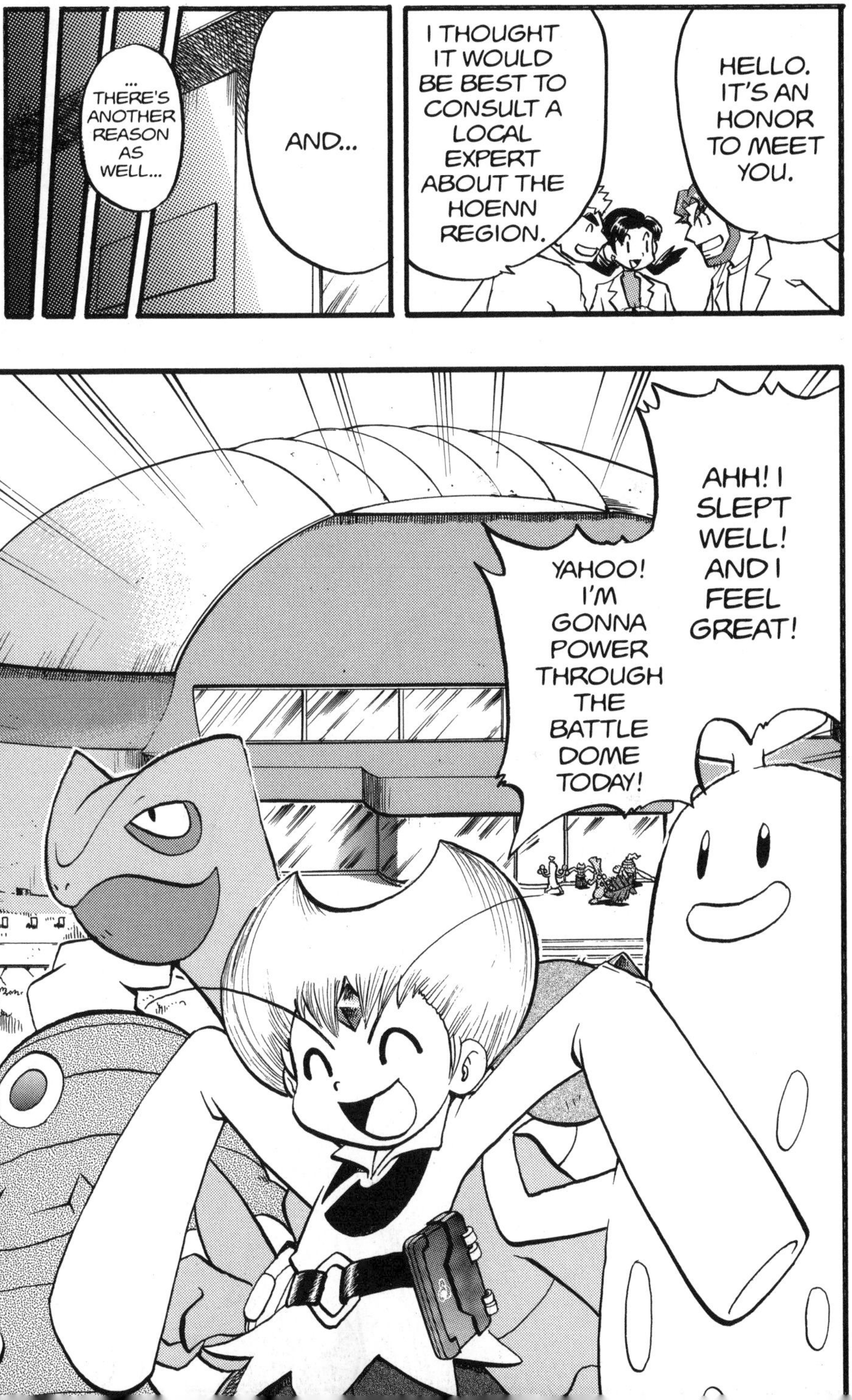
HELLO. IT'S AN HONOR TO MEET YOU.
I THOUGHT IT WOULD BE BEST TO CONSULT A LOCAL EXPERT ABOUT THE HOENN REGION.
AND...
... THERE'S ANOTHER REASON AS WELL...
AHH! I SLEPT WELL! AND I FEEL GREAT!
YAHOO! I'M GONNA POWER THROUGH THE BATTLE DOME TODAY!

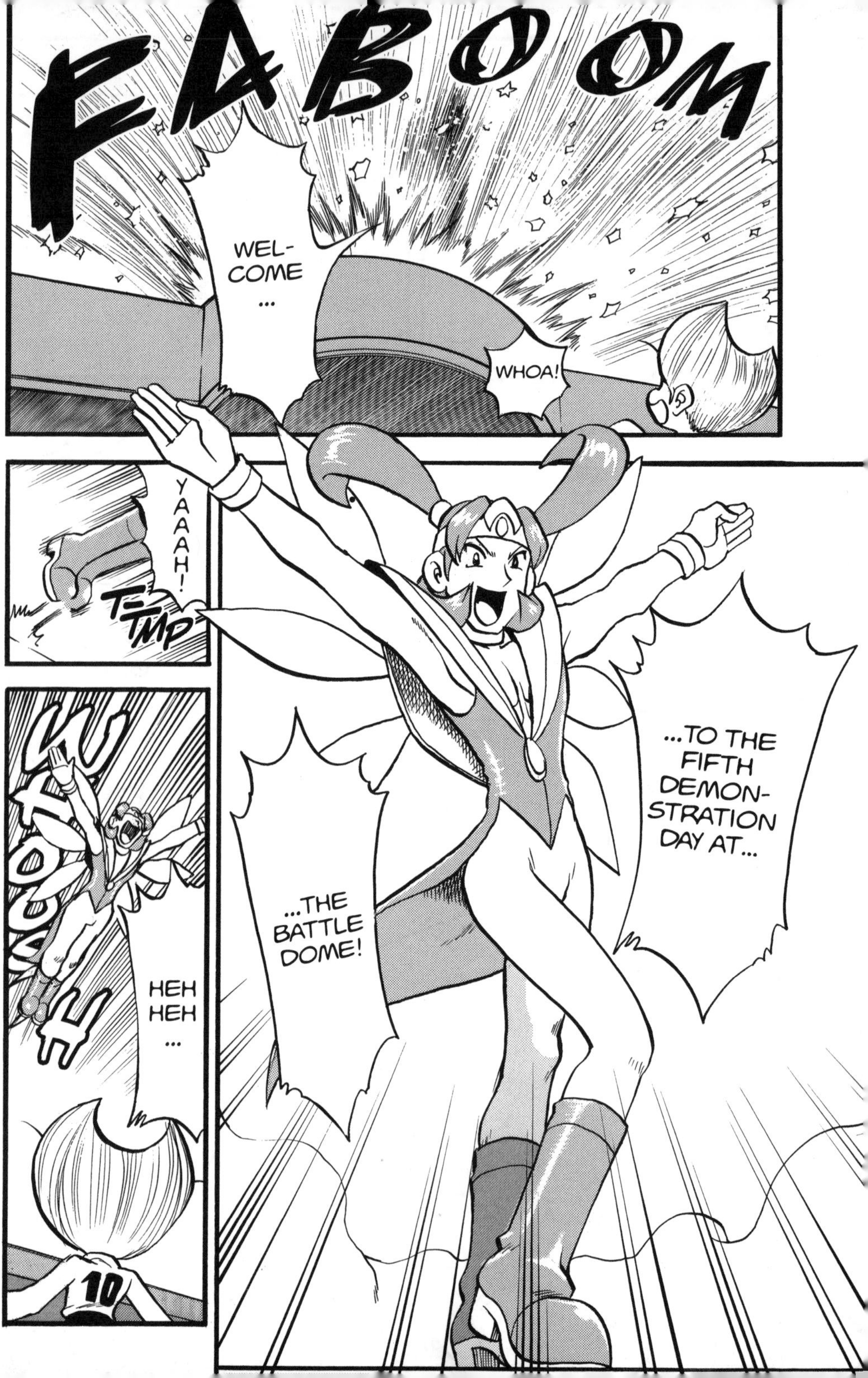
FABOOM
WEL-
COME
...
WHOA!
...TO THE
FIFTH
DEMON-
STRATION
DAY AT...
...THE
BATTLE
DOME!
YAAAAH!
T-TMP
WHOOSH
HEH
HEH
...

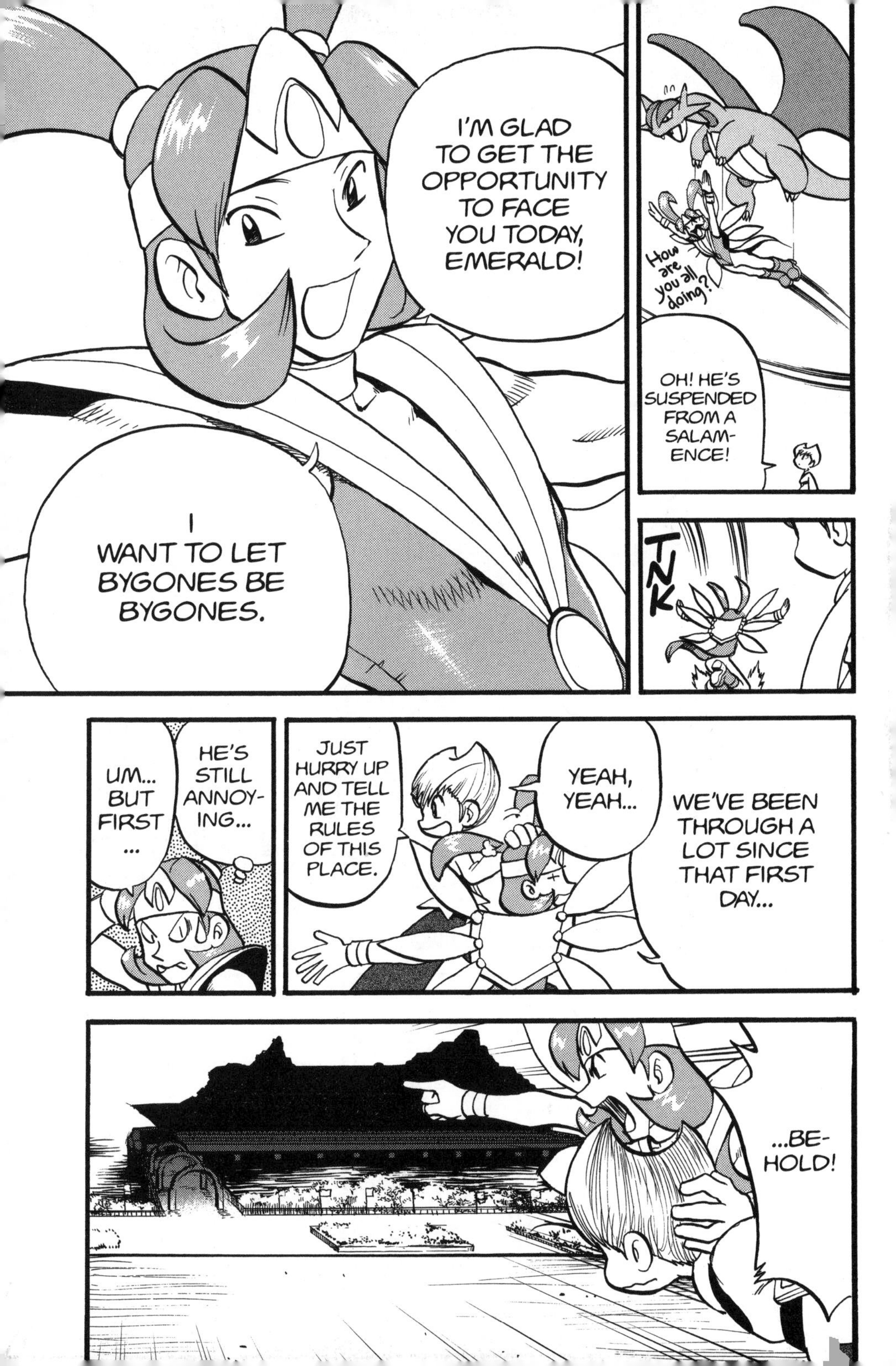
How are you all doing?
OH! HE'S SUSPENDED FROM A SALAMENCE!
TNK
I'M GLAD TO GET THE OPPORTUNITY TO FACE YOU TODAY, EMERALD!
I WANT TO LET BYGONES BE BYGONES.
WE'VE BEEN THROUGH A LOT SINCE THAT FIRST DAY...
YEAH, YEAH...
JUST HURRY UP AND TELL ME THE RULES OF THIS PLACE.
HE'S STILL ANNOYING...
UM... BUT FIRST ...
...BEHOLD!

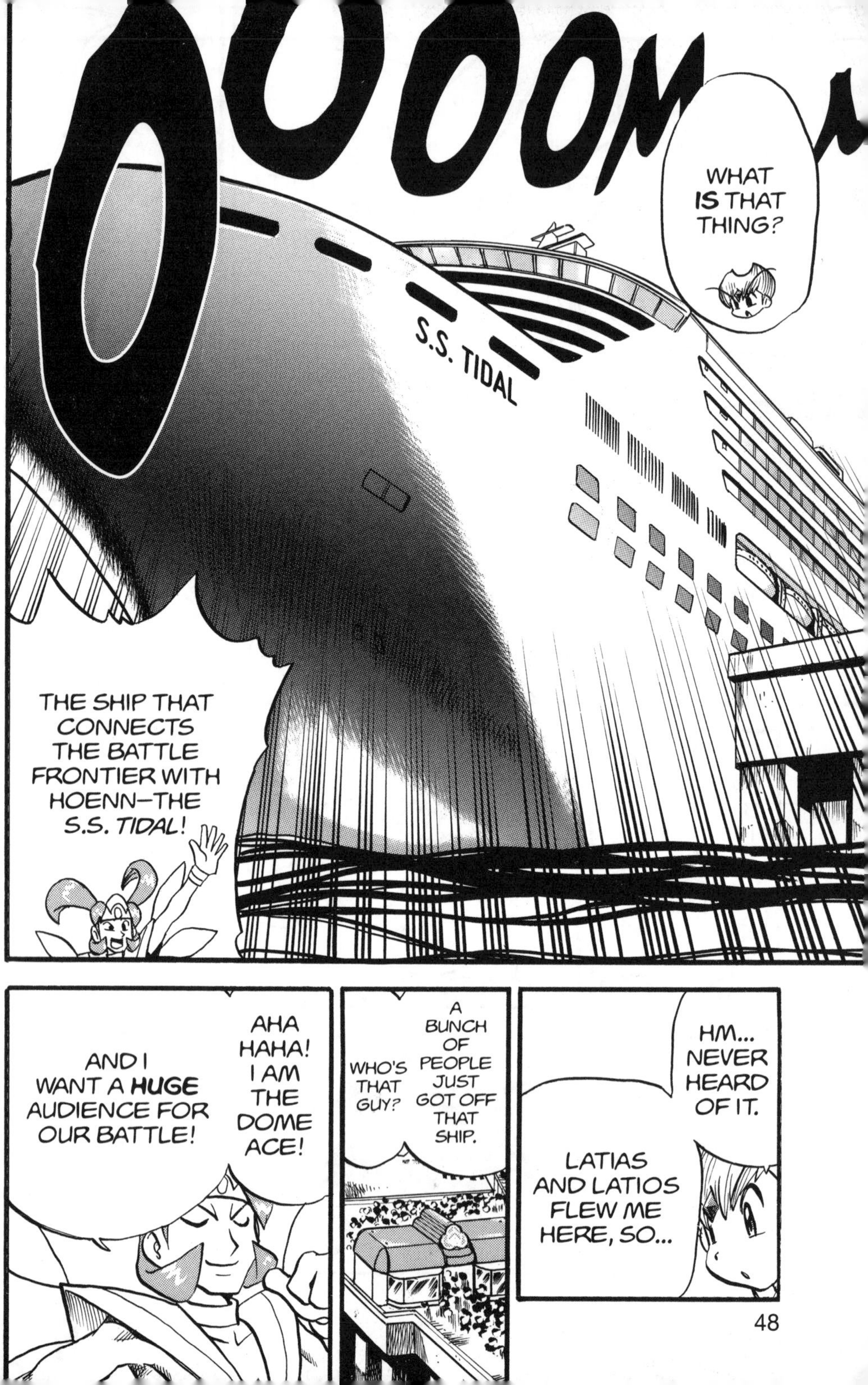
OOOOM
WHAT IS THAT THING?
S.S. TIDAL
THE SHIP THAT CONNECTS THE BATTLE FRONTIER WITH HOENN—THE S.S. TIDAL!
HM... NEVER HEARD OF IT.
LATIAS AND LATIOS FLEW ME HERE, SO...
A BUNCH OF PEOPLE JUST GOT OFF THAT SHIP.
WHO'S THAT GUY?
AHA HAHA! I AM THE DOME ACE!
AND I WANT A HUGE AUDIENCE FOR OUR BATTLE!

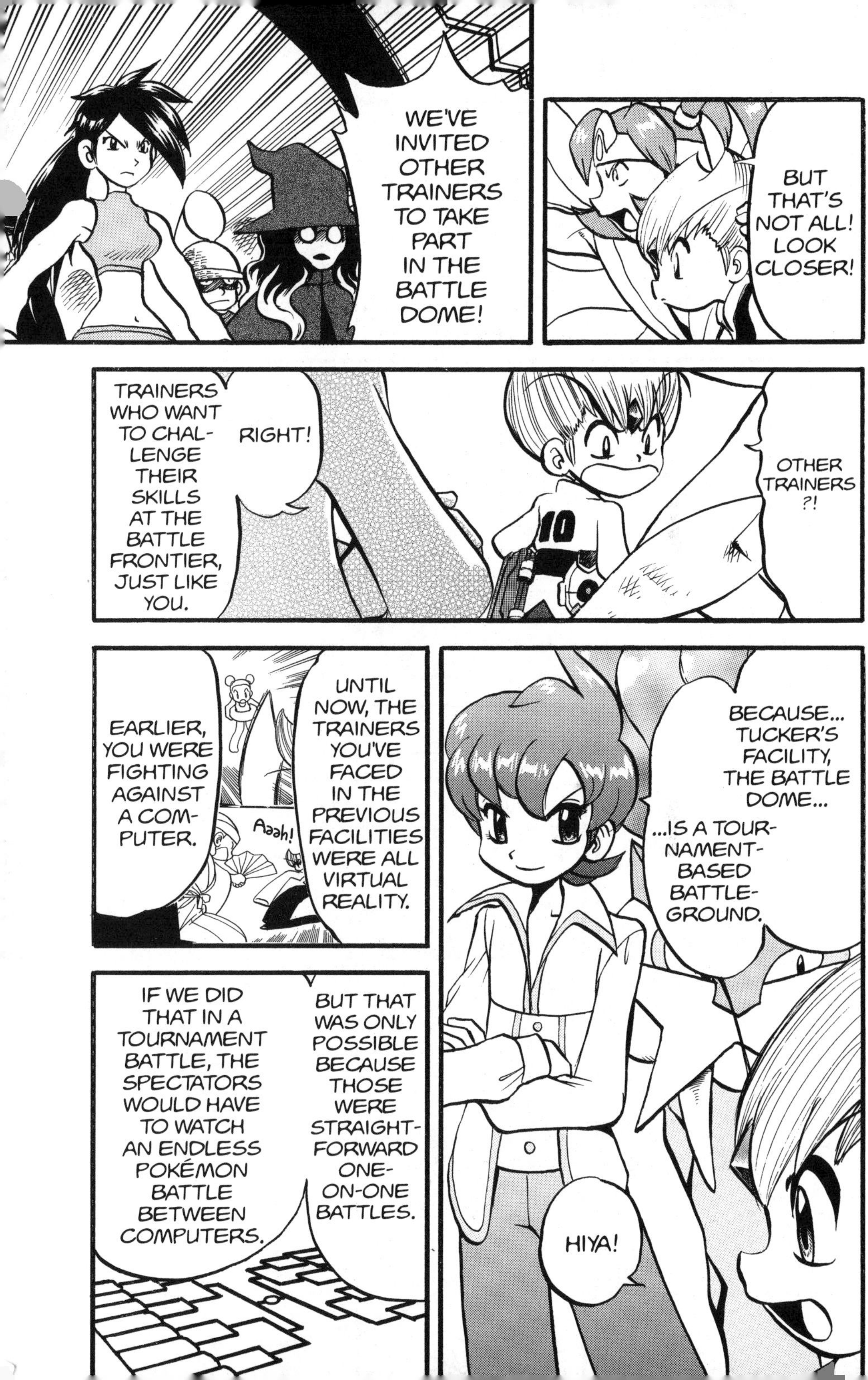
BUT THAT'S NOT ALL! LOOK CLOSER!
WE'VE INVITED OTHER TRAINERS TO TAKE PART IN THE BATTLE DOME!
OTHER TRAINERS ?!
RIGHT!
TRAINERS WHO WANT TO CHAL-LENGE THEIR SKILLS AT THE BATTLE FRONTIER, JUST LIKE YOU.
BECAUSE... TUCKER'S FACILITY, THE BATTLE DOME...
...IS A TOUR-NAMENT-BASED BATTLE-GROUND.
HIYA!
UNTIL NOW, THE TRAINERS YOU'VE FACED IN THE PREVIOUS FACILITIES WERE ALL VIRTUAL REALITY.
Aaah!
EARLIER, YOU WERE FIGHTING AGAINST A COM-PUTER.
BUT THAT WAS ONLY POSSIBLE BECAUSE THOSE WERE STRAIGHT-FORWARD ONE-ON-ONE BATTLES.
IF WE DID THAT IN A TOURNAMENT BATTLE, THE SPECTATORS WOULD HAVE TO WATCH AN ENDLESS POKÉMON BATTLE BETWEEN COMPUTERS.

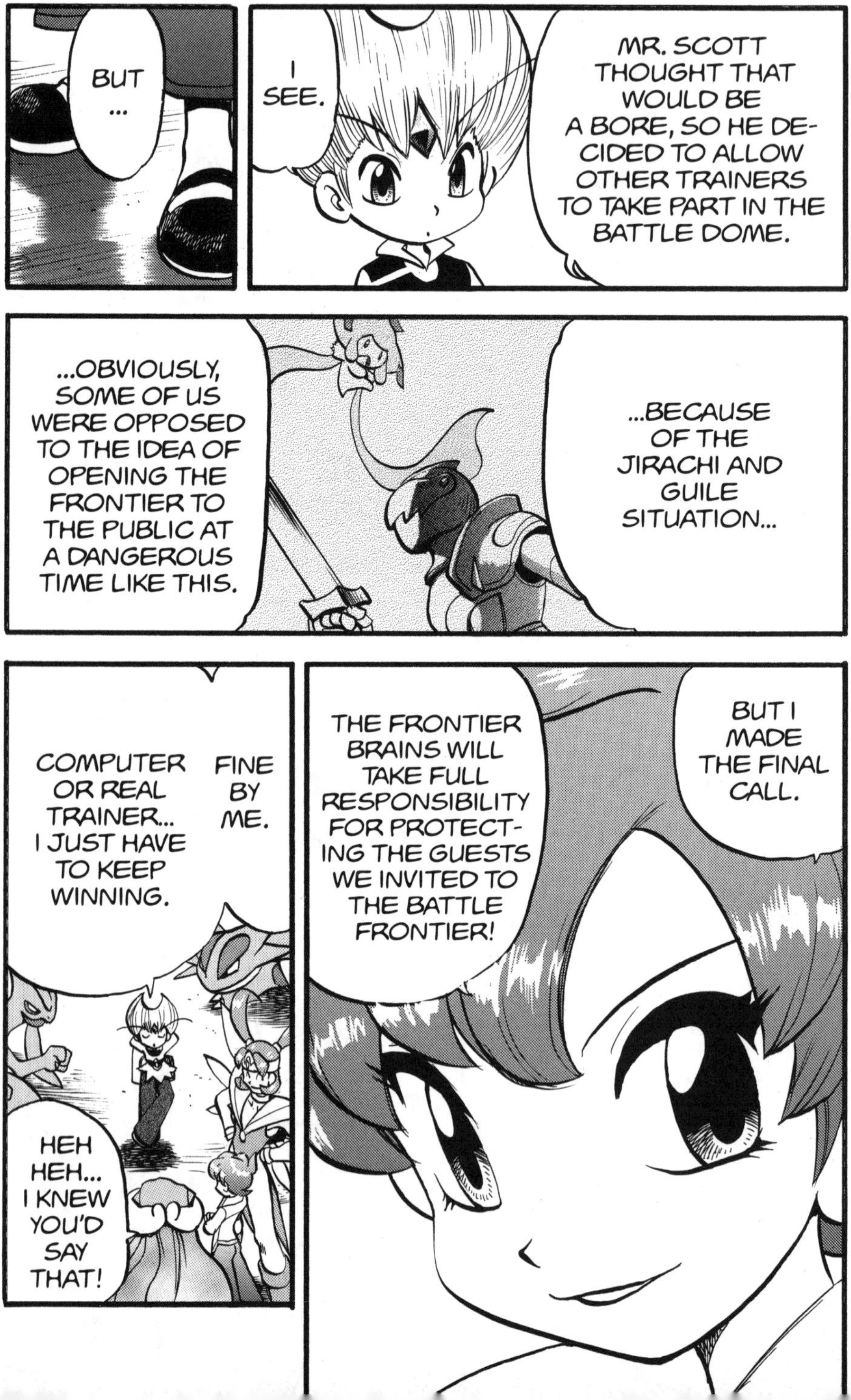
MR. SCOTT THOUGHT THAT WOULD BE A BORE, SO HE DECIDED TO ALLOW OTHER TRAINERS TO TAKE PART IN THE BATTLE DOME.
I SEE.
BUT ...
...BECAUSE OF THE JIRACHI AND GUILE SITUATION...
...OBVIOUSLY, SOME OF US WERE OPPOSED TO THE IDEA OF OPENING THE FRONTIER TO THE PUBLIC AT A DANGEROUS TIME LIKE THIS.
BUT I MADE THE FINAL CALL.
THE FRONTIER BRAINS WILL TAKE FULL RESPONSIBILITY FOR PROTECTING THE GUESTS WE INVITED TO THE BATTLE FRONTIER!
FINE BY ME.
COMPUTER OR REAL TRAINER... I JUST HAVE TO KEEP WINNING.
HEH HEH... I KNEW YOU'D SAY THAT!

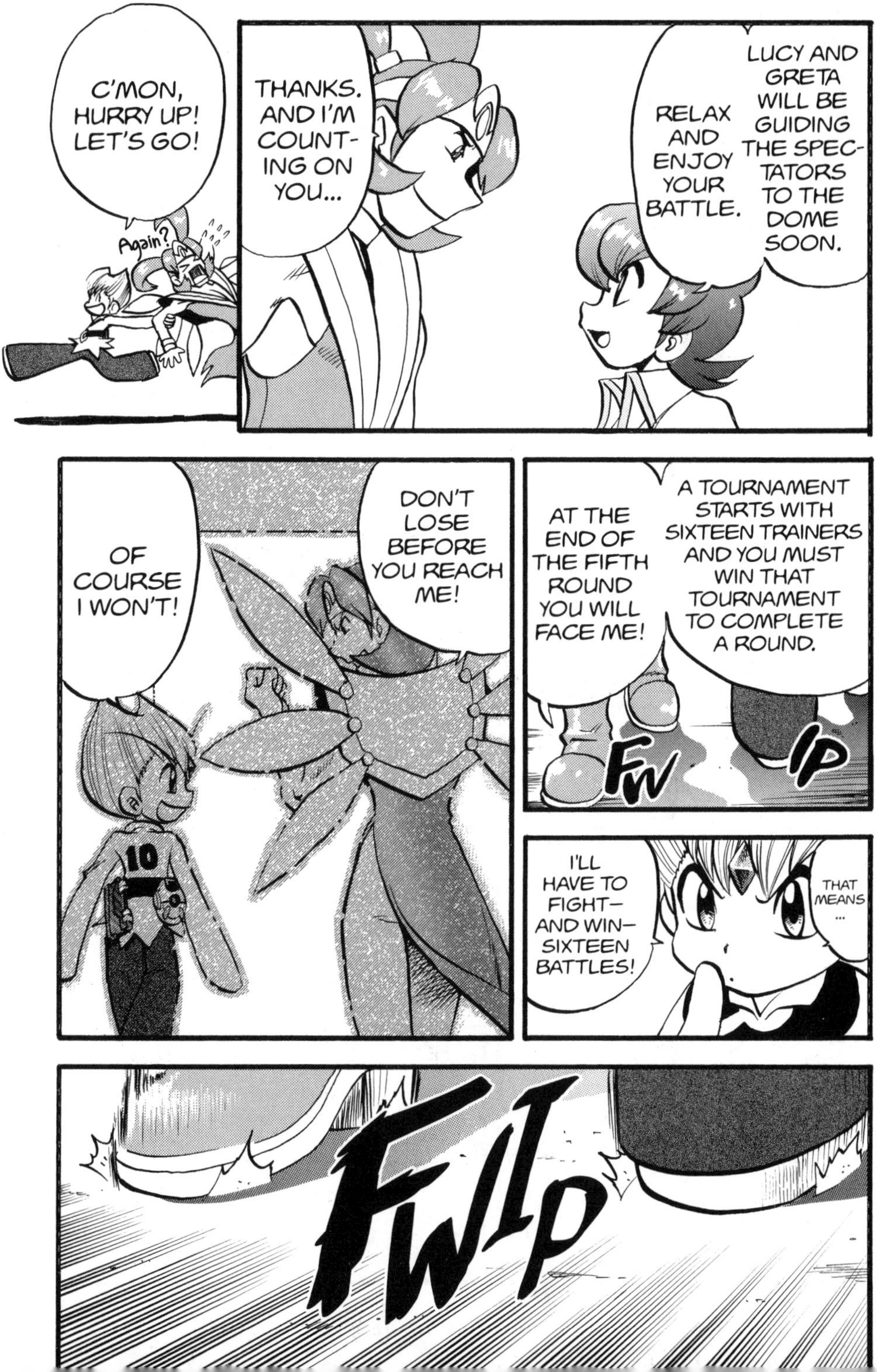
LUCY AND GRETA WILL BE GUIDING THE SPECTATORS TO THE DOME SOON.
RELAX AND ENJOY YOUR BATTLE.
THANKS. AND I'M COUNTING ON YOU...
C'MON, HURRY UP! LET'S GO!
Again?
A TOURNAMENT STARTS WITH SIXTEEN TRAINERS AND YOU MUST WIN THAT TOURNAMENT TO COMPLETE A ROUND.
AT THE END OF THE FIFTH ROUND YOU WILL FACE ME!
FW
IP
THAT MEANS...
I'LL HAVE TO FIGHT—AND WIN—SIXTEEN BATTLES!
DON'T LOSE BEFORE YOU REACH ME!
OF COURSE I WON'T!
FWIP

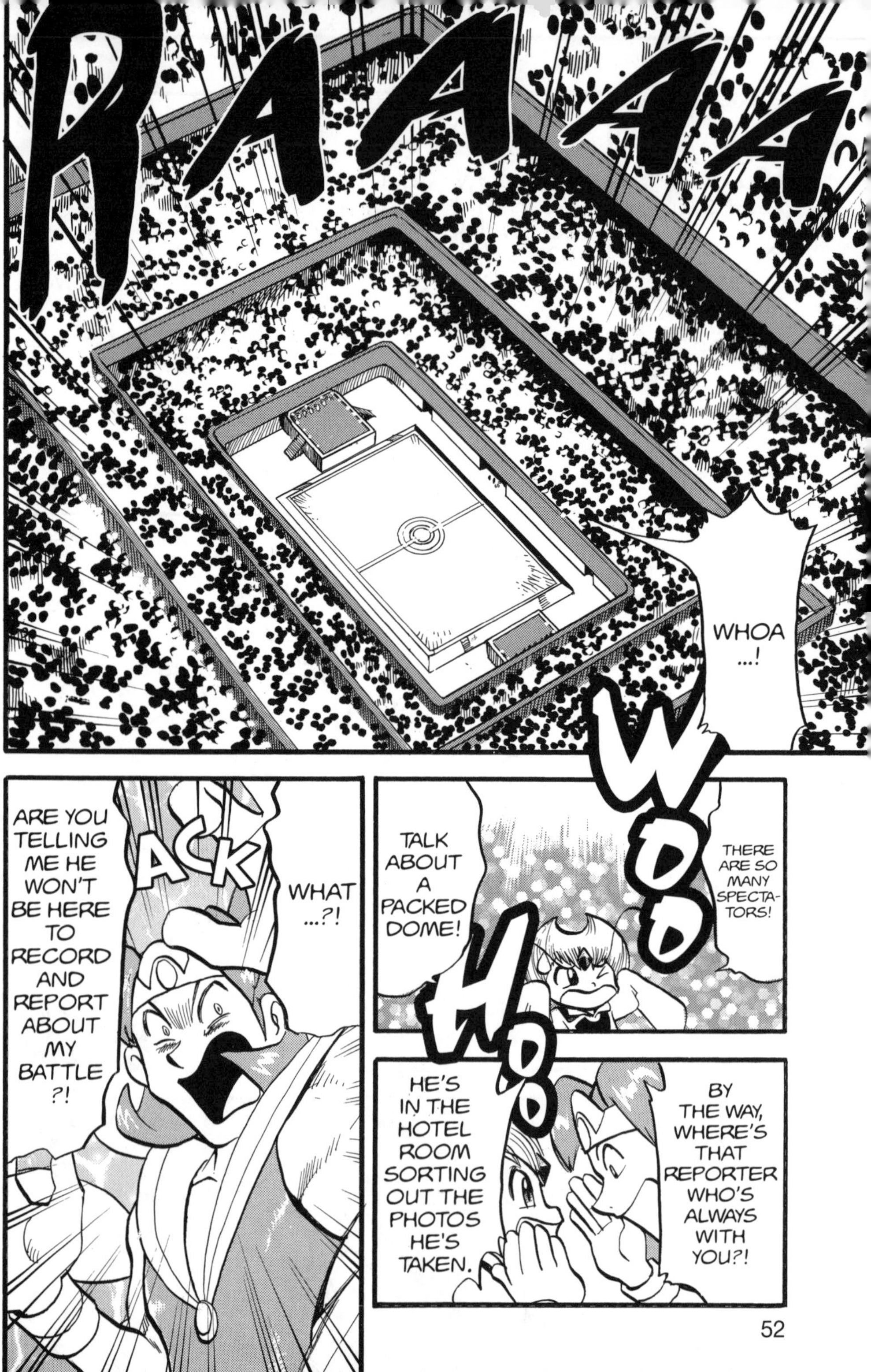
RAAAAA
WHOA...!
WOO HOO
THERE ARE SO MANY SPECTATORS!
TALK ABOUT A PACKED DOME!
BY THE WAY, WHERE'S THAT REPORTER WHO'S ALWAYS WITH YOU?!
HE'S IN THE HOTEL ROOM SORTING OUT THE PHOTOS HE'S TAKEN.
WHAT...?!
ACK
ARE YOU TELLING ME HE WON'T BE HERE TO RECORD AND REPORT ABOUT MY BATTLE?!

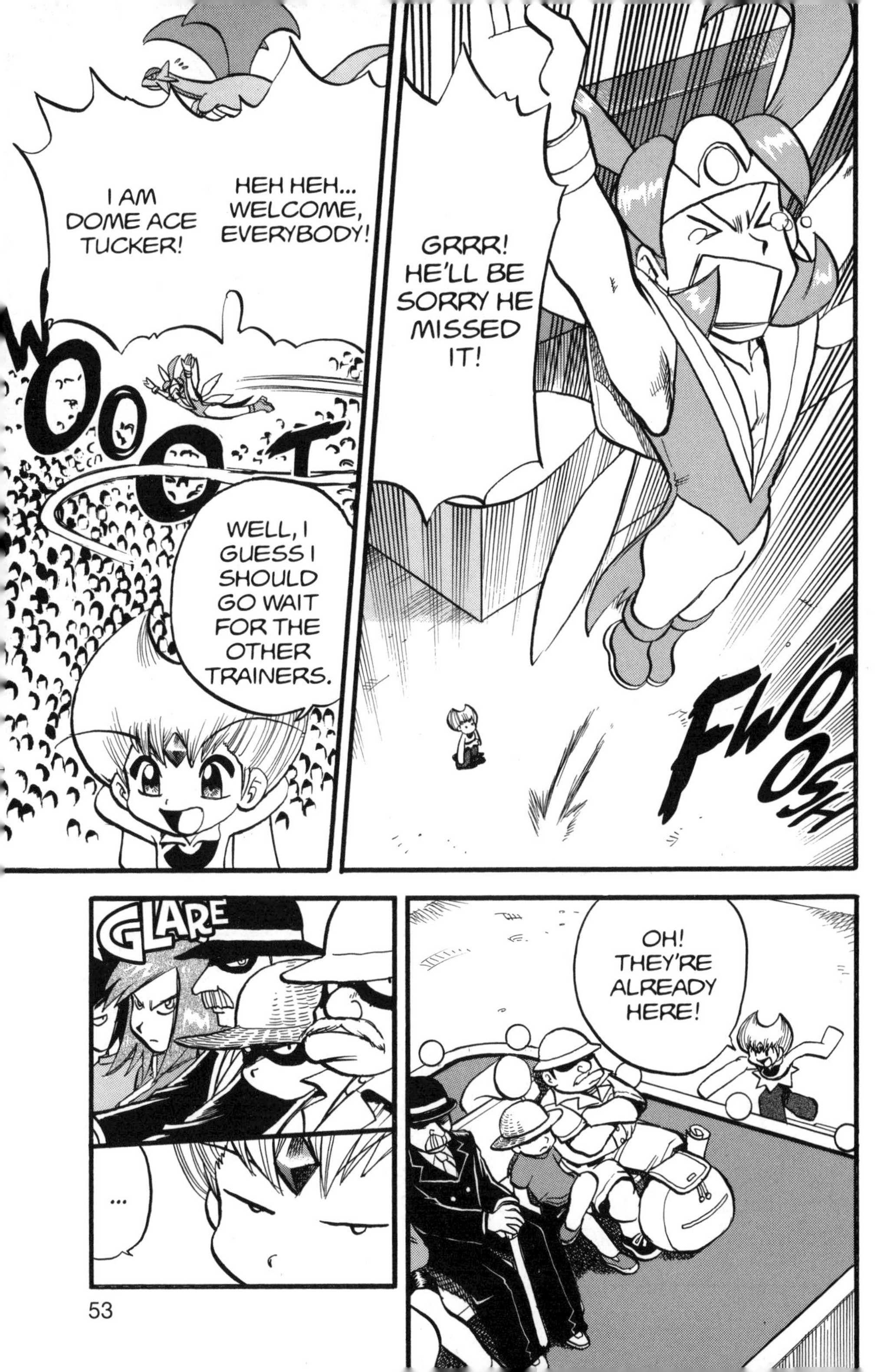
GRRR! HE'LL BE SORRY HE MISSED IT!
FWOOSH
HEH HEH... WELCOME, EVERYBODY!
I AM DOME ACE TUCKER!
WOOOOT
WELL, I GUESS I SHOULD GO WAIT FOR THE OTHER TRAINERS.
OH! THEY'RE ALREADY HERE!
GLARE
...

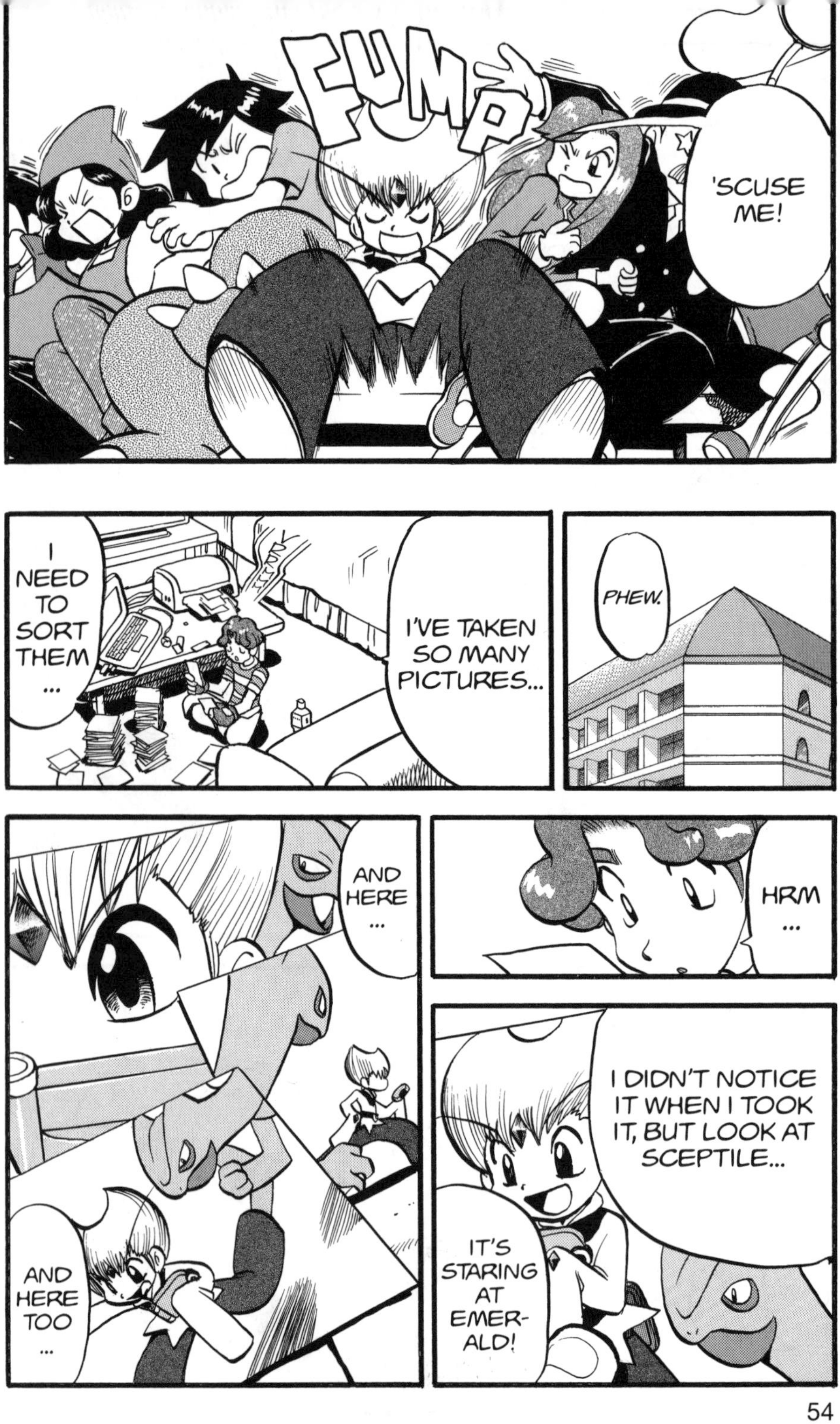
FUMP
'SCUSE ME!
PHEW.
I'VE TAKEN SO MANY PICTURES...
I NEED TO SORT THEM ...
HRM ...
I DIDN'T NOTICE IT WHEN I TOOK IT, BUT LOOK AT SCEPTILE...
IT'S STARING AT EMER-ALD!
AND HERE ...
AND HERE TOO ...

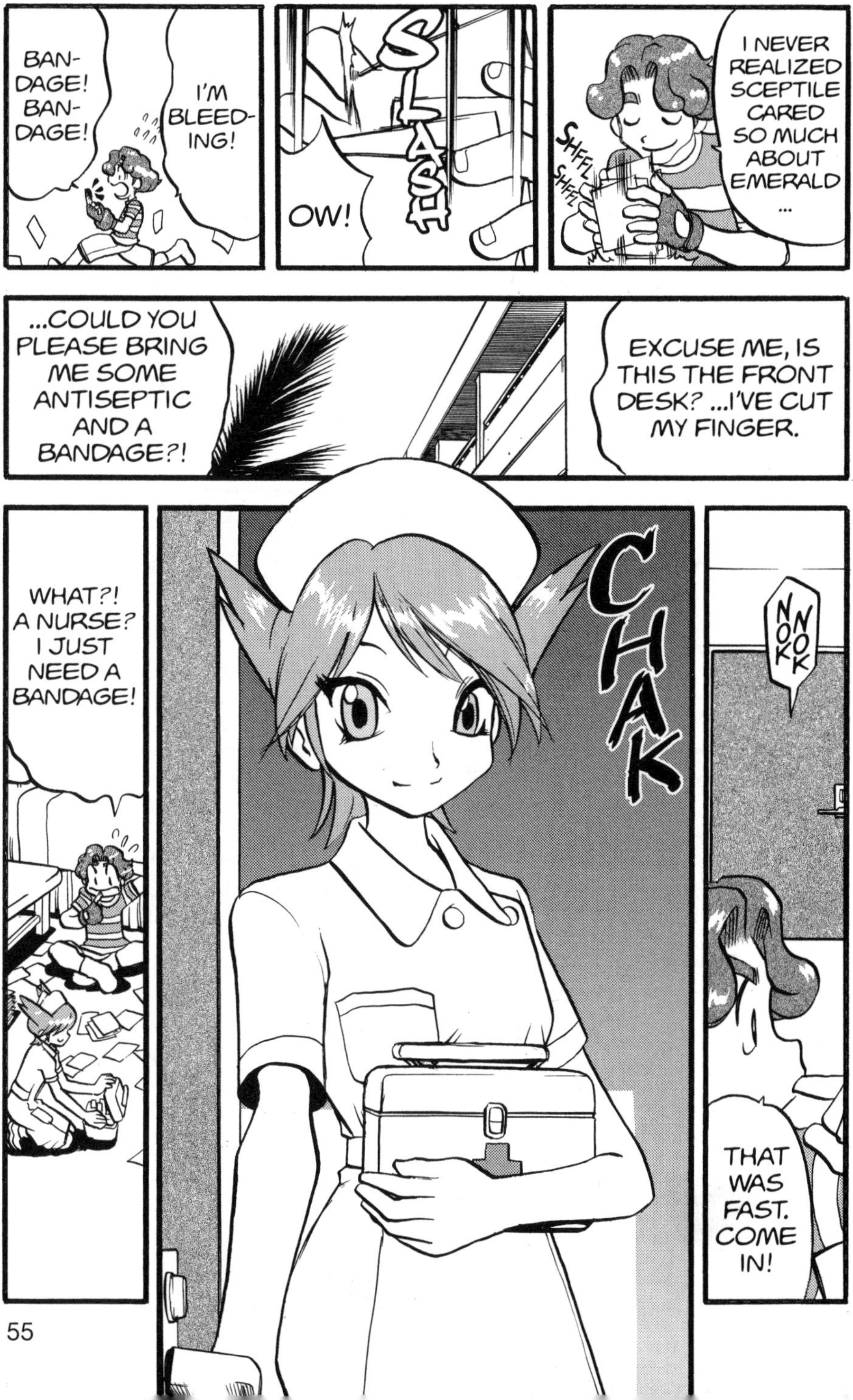

SHFFL SHFFL
I NEVER REALIZED SCEPTILE CARED SO MUCH ABOUT EMERALD ...
SLASH
OW!
I'M BLEED-ING!
BAN-DAGE! BAN-DAGE!
EXCUSE ME, IS THIS THE FRONT DESK? ...I'VE CUT MY FINGER.
...COULD YOU PLEASE BRING ME SOME ANTISEPTIC AND A BANDAGE?!
NOK NOK
THAT WAS FAST. COME IN!
CHAK
WHAT?! A NURSE? I JUST NEED A BANDAGE!

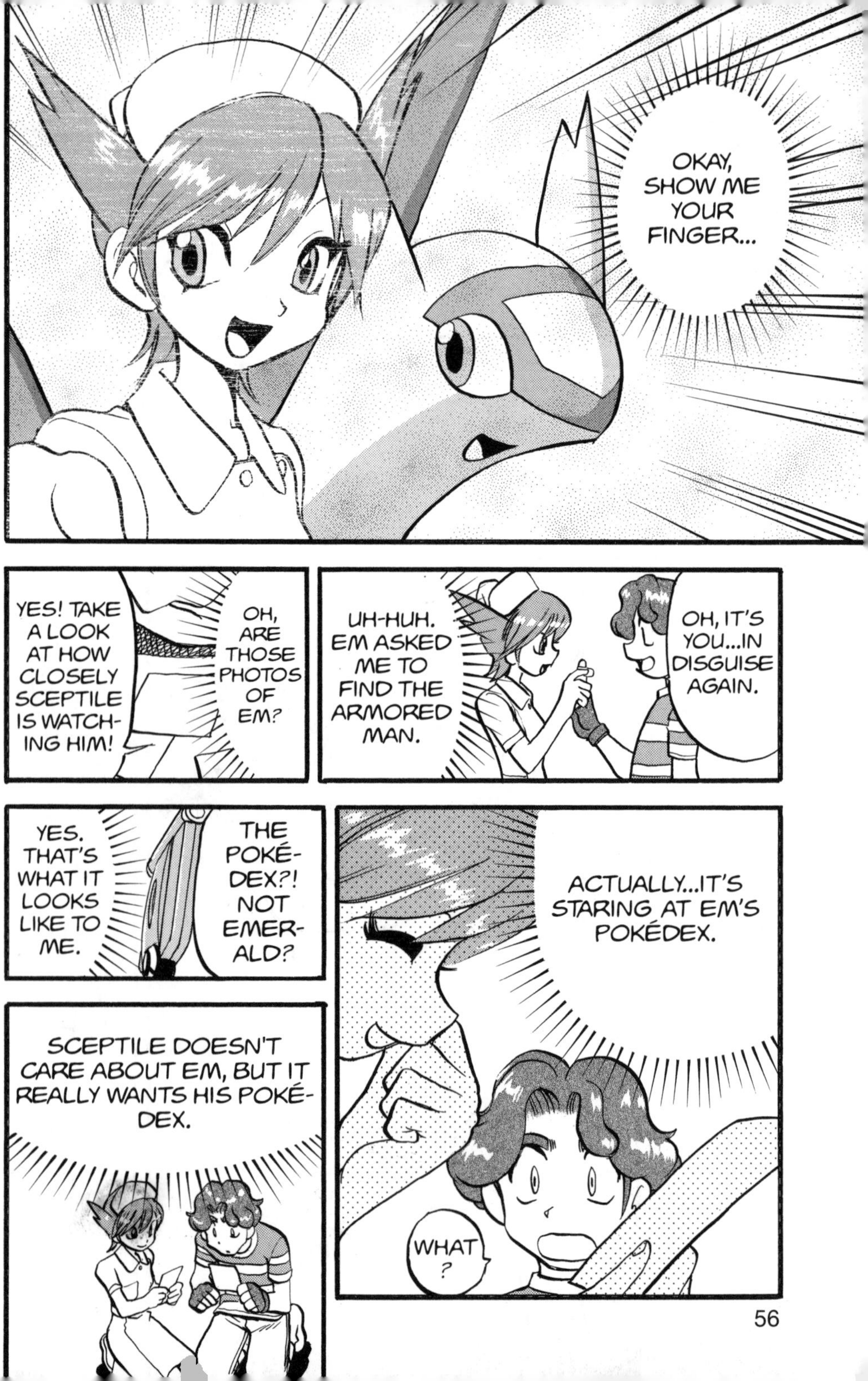
OKAY, SHOW ME YOUR FINGER...
OH, IT'S YOU...IN DISGUISE AGAIN.
UH-HUH. EM ASKED ME TO FIND THE ARMORED MAN.
OH, ARE THOSE PHOTOS OF EM?
YES! TAKE A LOOK AT HOW CLOSELY SCEPTILE IS WATCHING HIM!
ACTUALLY...IT'S STARING AT EM'S POKÉDEX.
WHAT?
THE POKÉDEX?! NOT EMERALD?
YES. THAT'S WHAT IT LOOKS LIKE TO ME.
SCEPTILE DOESN'T CARE ABOUT EM, BUT IT REALLY WANTS HIS POKÉDEX.

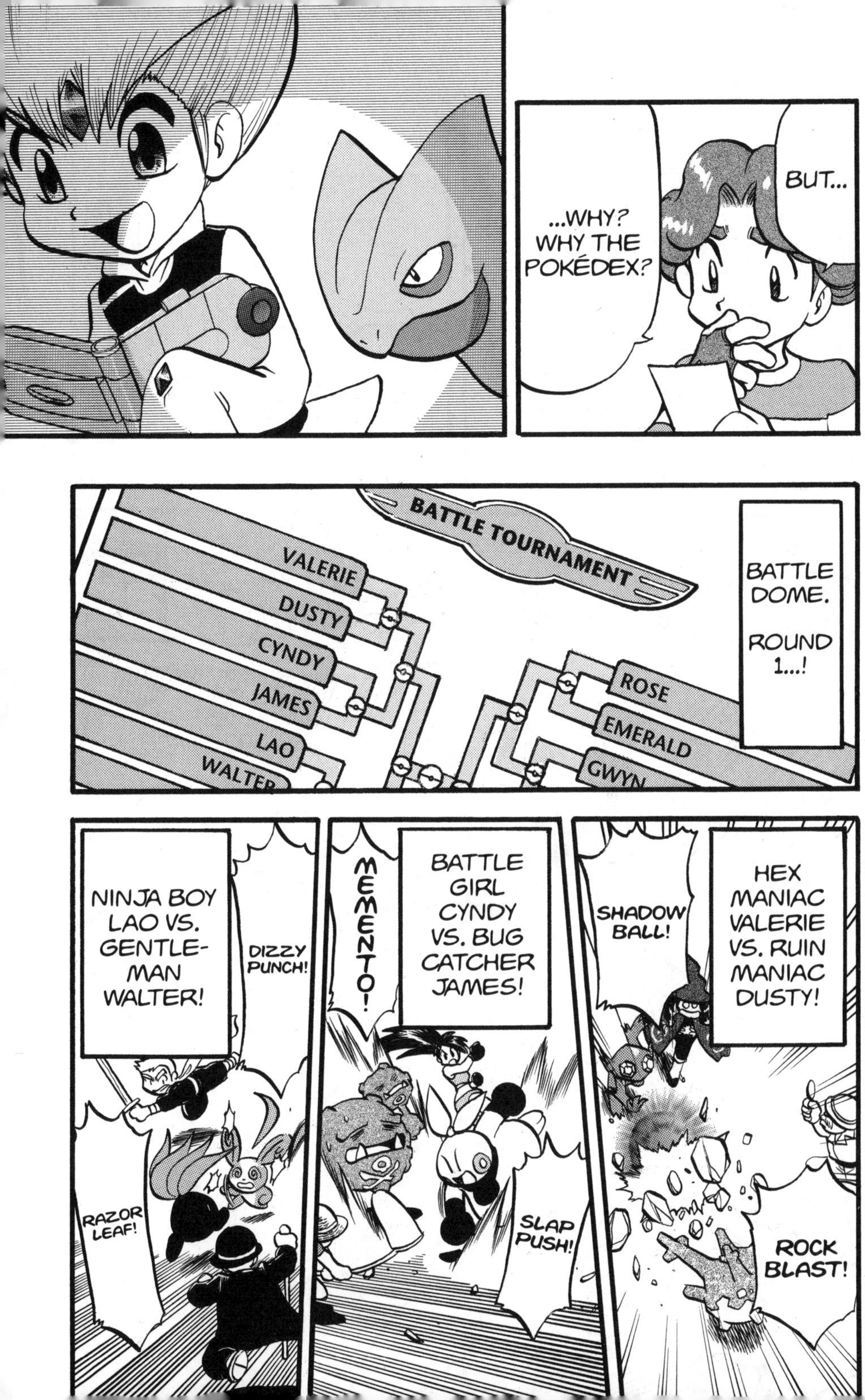
BUT...
...WHY? WHY THE POKÉDEX?
BATTLE DOME. ROUND 1...!
BATTLE TOURNAMENT
VALERIE
DUSTY
CYNDY
JAMES
LAO
WALTER
ROSE
EMERALD
GWYN
HEX MANIAC VALERIE VS. RUIN MANIAC DUSTY!
SHADOW BALL!
ROCK BLAST!
BATTLE GIRL CYNDY VS. BUG CATCHER JAMES!
MEMENTO!
SLAP PUSH!
NINJA BOY LAO VS. GENTLE-MAN WALTER!
DIZZY PUNCH!
RAZOR LEAF!

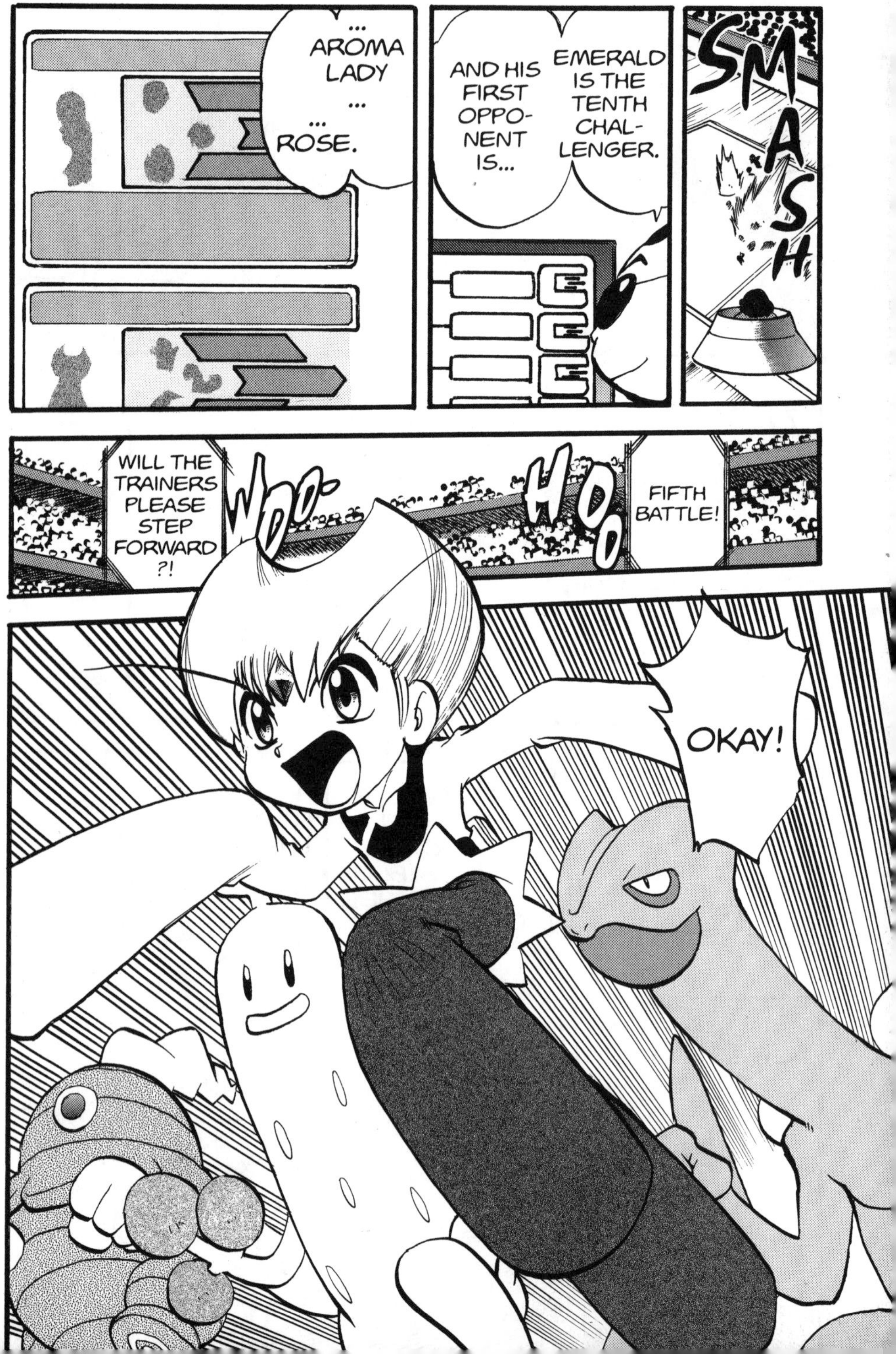
SMASH
EMERALD IS THE TENTH CHAL-LENGER.
AND HIS FIRST OPPO-NENT IS...
... AROMA LADY ... ... ROSE.
FIFTH BATTLE!
HOO
WOO
WILL THE TRAINERS PLEASE STEP FORWARD?!
OKAY!

DEAR MEMBERS OF THE PRESS...

Thank you for visiting the Battle Frontier today. Permit me to continue explaining the rules of this facility...

OWNER: SCOTT

FACILITY RULES

BATTLE DOME 3

■ ABOUT THE TRAINER RANK ■

Trainer Rank: The first line on the Trainer card describes the rank of the opposing Trainer.

➡ Please refer to the chart on the right during the tournament.

↑ High Ranking	- The best candidate to be the champ
	- A sure-finalist team
	- A likely top-three finisher
	- A team with top-class potential
	- A candidate to finish first
	- This tournament's surprise favorite
	- A better-than-average team
	- This tournament's average team
	- A team with average potential
	- A weaker-than-average team
	- A team looking for its first win
	- One win will make this team proud
	- Overall, a weak team
	- A team with very low potential
Low Ranking ↓	- A team unlikely to win the tournament
	- The team most unlikely to win

■ DOUBLE KNOCKOUT ■

In the Battle Dome, if both Trainers are knocked out, the Trainer who is ranked highest wins the battle.

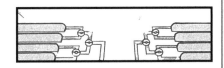

320

Verily Vanquishing Vileplume, Part 2

■ ■ ● K B ● G L

POKÉMON ADVENTURES·THE SIXTH CHAPTER·EMERALD

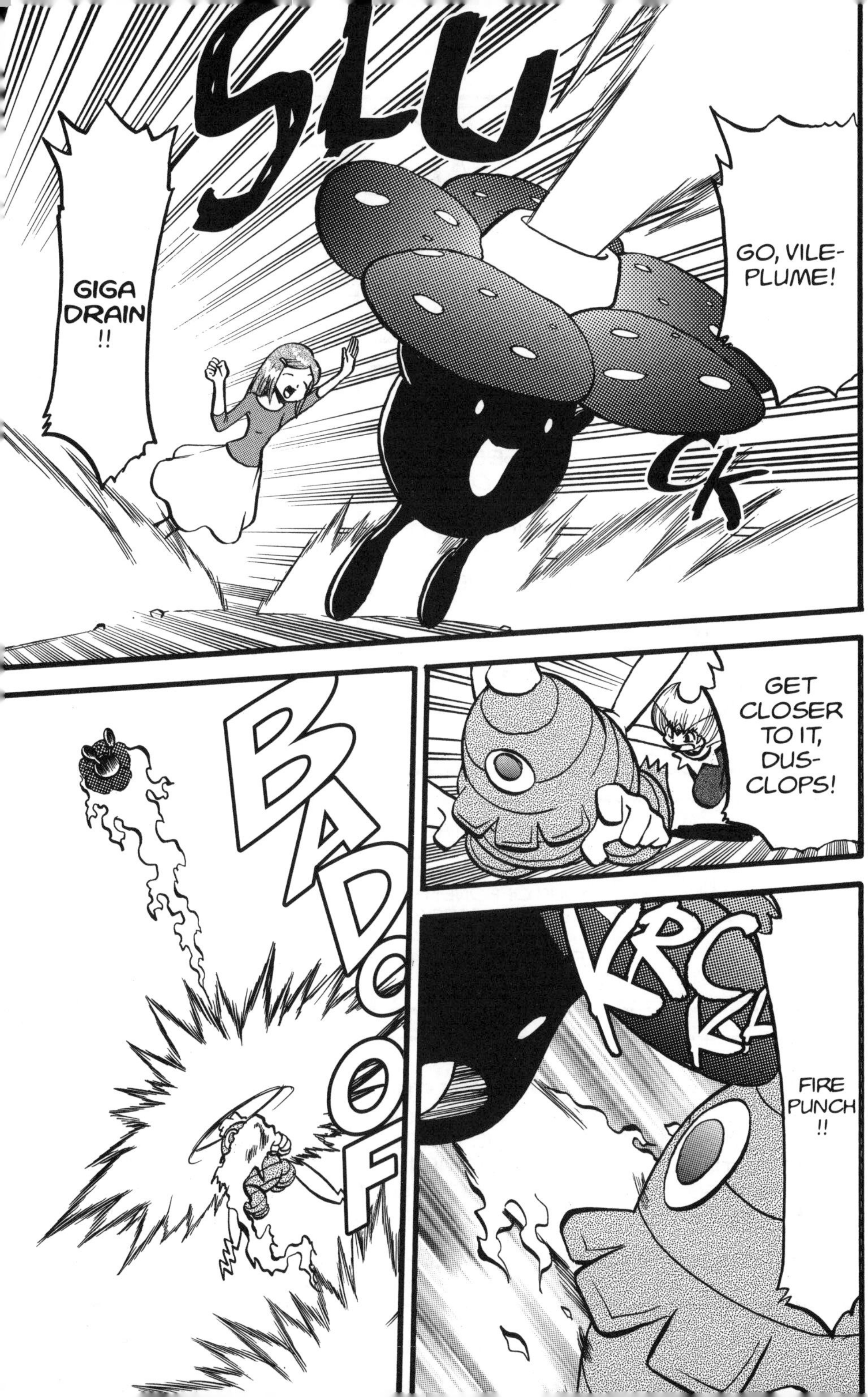
GO, VILE-PLUME!
SLU
CK
GIGA DRAIN !!
GET CLOSER TO IT, DUS-CLOPS!
KRC
KL
FIRE PUNCH !!
BADOOOF

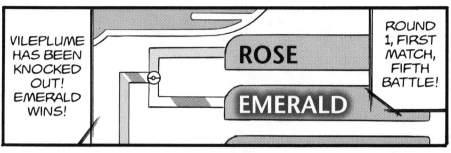

ROUND 1, FIRST MATCH, FIFTH BATTLE!
ROSE
EMERALD
VILEPLUME HAS BEEN KNOCKED OUT! EMERALD WINS!
YOU MADE IT INTO THE TOP EIGHT LIKE IT WAS NOTHING! IMPRES-SIVE!
PEACE!
I WAS REALLY SURPRISED TO SEE YOUR DUSCLOPS USE FIRE PUNCH. WHEN DID IT LEARN THAT MOVE?
THIS MORNING. I USED THE BATTLE POINTS I COLLECTED AT THE PREVIOUS FOUR FACILITIES.
THEY CAME IN HANDY QUICK-LY!
ALSO, AT THE BATTLE DOME, YOU GET TO CHECK YOUR OPPONENT'S BATTLE CARDS BEFORE YOU FACE THEM—THAT HELPED A LOT.
HEY, MY OPPONENT WAS THIS TOURNA-MENT'S SURPRISE FAVORITE!
RIGHT. THE THEME OF THE BATTLE DOME IS **TACTICS.**
THE KEY TO WINNING THE BATTLES HERE DEPENDS ON WHAT TACTICS YOU CHOOSE BASED ON THE INFORMATION YOU'RE GIVEN.

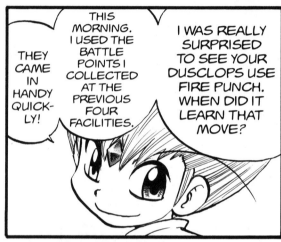

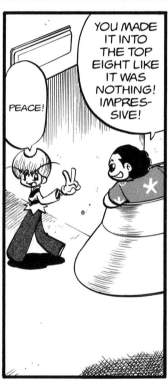

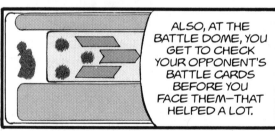

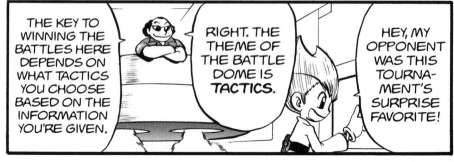

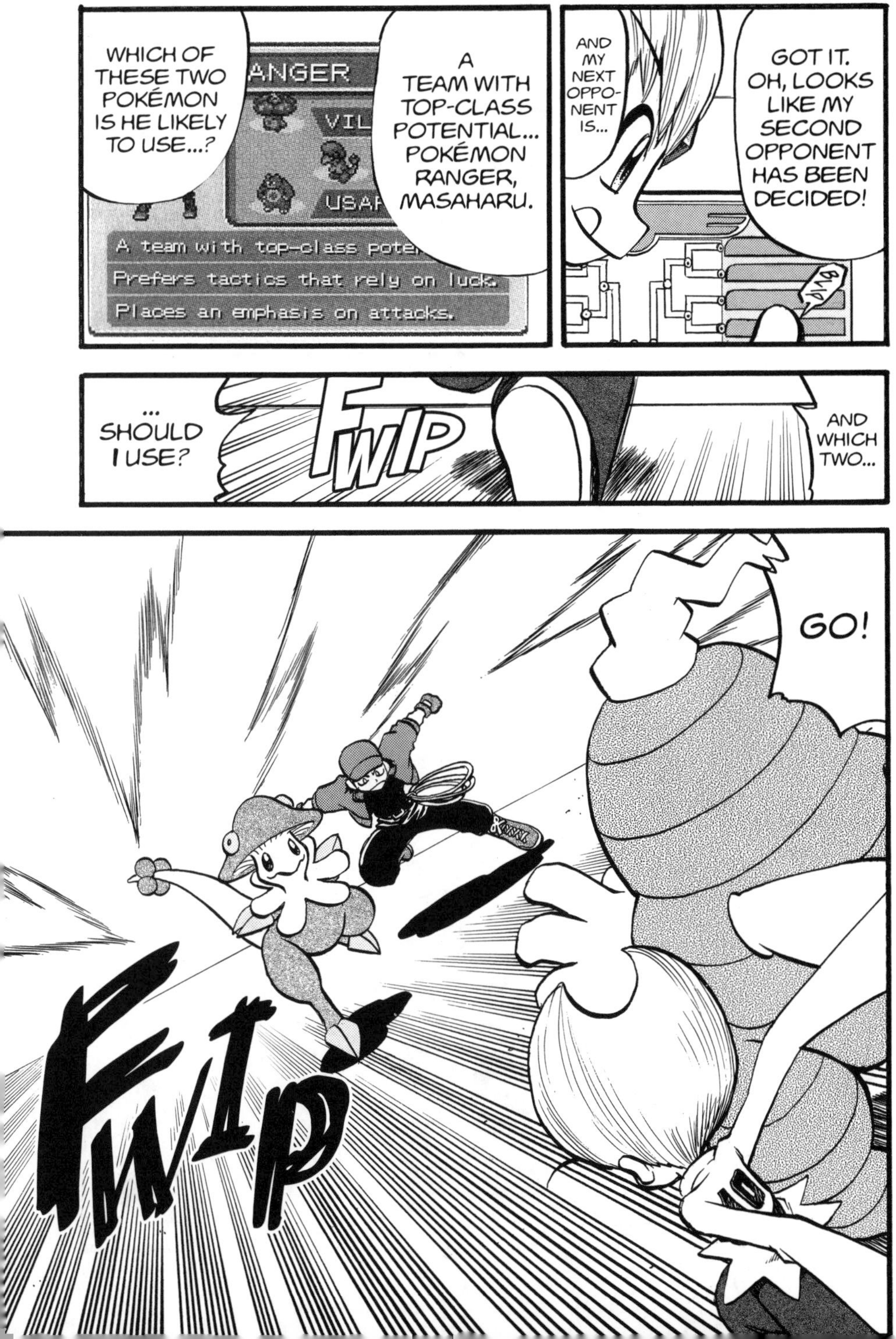
GOT IT. OH, LOOKS LIKE MY SECOND OPPONENT HAS BEEN DECIDED!
AND MY NEXT OPPO-NENT IS...
A TEAM WITH TOP-CLASS POTENTIAL... POKÉMON RANGER, MASAHARU.
WHICH OF THESE TWO POKÉMON IS HE LIKELY TO USE...?
Prefers tactics that rely on luck.
Places an emphasis on attacks.
AND WHICH TWO...
FWIP
...SHOULD I USE?
GO!
FWIP

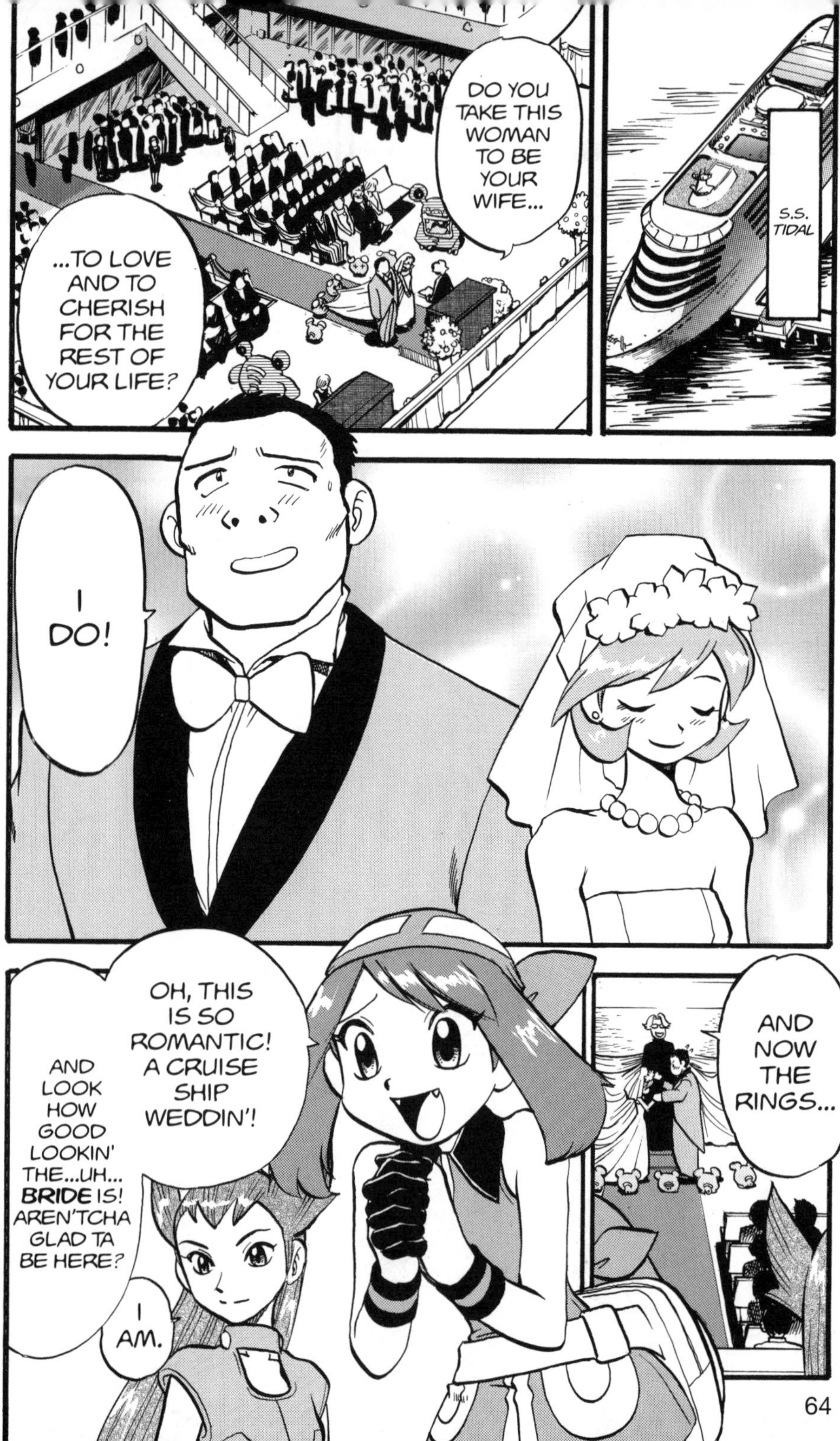
S.S. TIDAL
DO YOU TAKE THIS WOMAN TO BE YOUR WIFE...
...TO LOVE AND TO CHERISH FOR THE REST OF YOUR LIFE?
I DO!
AND NOW THE RINGS...
OH, THIS IS SO ROMANTIC! A CRUISE SHIP WEDDIN'!
AND LOOK HOW GOOD LOOKIN' THE...UH... **BRIDE** IS! AREN'TCHA GLAD TA BE HERE?
I AM.

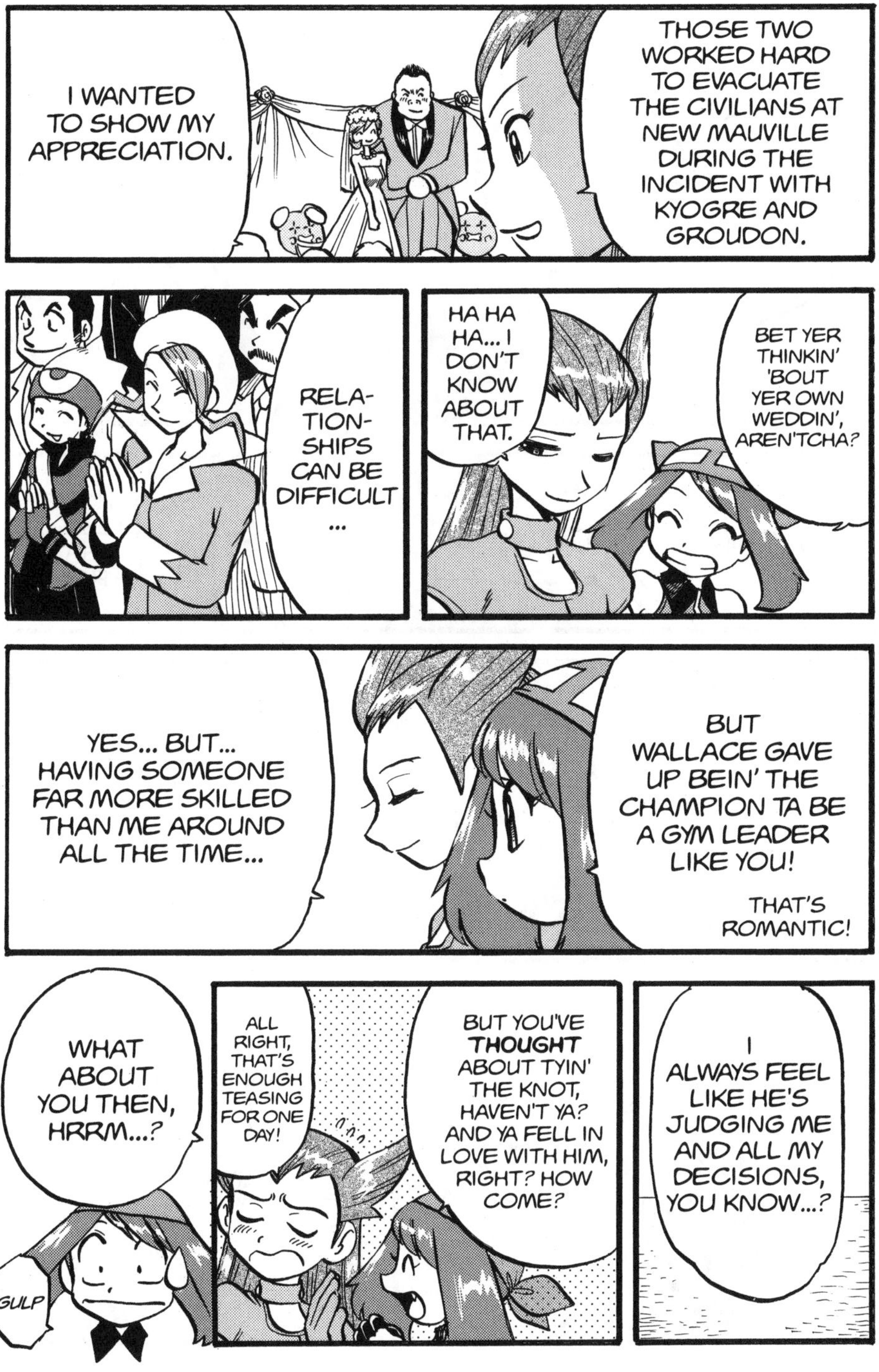
THOSE TWO WORKED HARD TO EVACUATE THE CIVILIANS AT NEW MAUVILLE DURING THE INCIDENT WITH KYOGRE AND GROUDON.
I WANTED TO SHOW MY APPRECIATION.
BET YER THINKIN' 'BOUT YER OWN WEDDIN', AREN'TCHA?
HA HA HA... I DON'T KNOW ABOUT THAT.
RELATIONSHIPS CAN BE DIFFICULT...
BUT WALLACE GAVE UP BEIN' THE CHAMPION TA BE A GYM LEADER LIKE YOU!
THAT'S ROMANTIC!
YES... BUT... HAVING SOMEONE FAR MORE SKILLED THAN ME AROUND ALL THE TIME...
I ALWAYS FEEL LIKE HE'S JUDGING ME AND ALL MY DECISIONS, YOU KNOW...?
BUT YOU'VE **THOUGHT** ABOUT TYIN' THE KNOT, HAVEN'T YA? AND YA FELL IN LOVE WITH HIM, RIGHT? HOW COME?
ALL RIGHT, THAT'S ENOUGH TEASING FOR ONE DAY!
WHAT ABOUT YOU THEN, HRRM...?
GULP

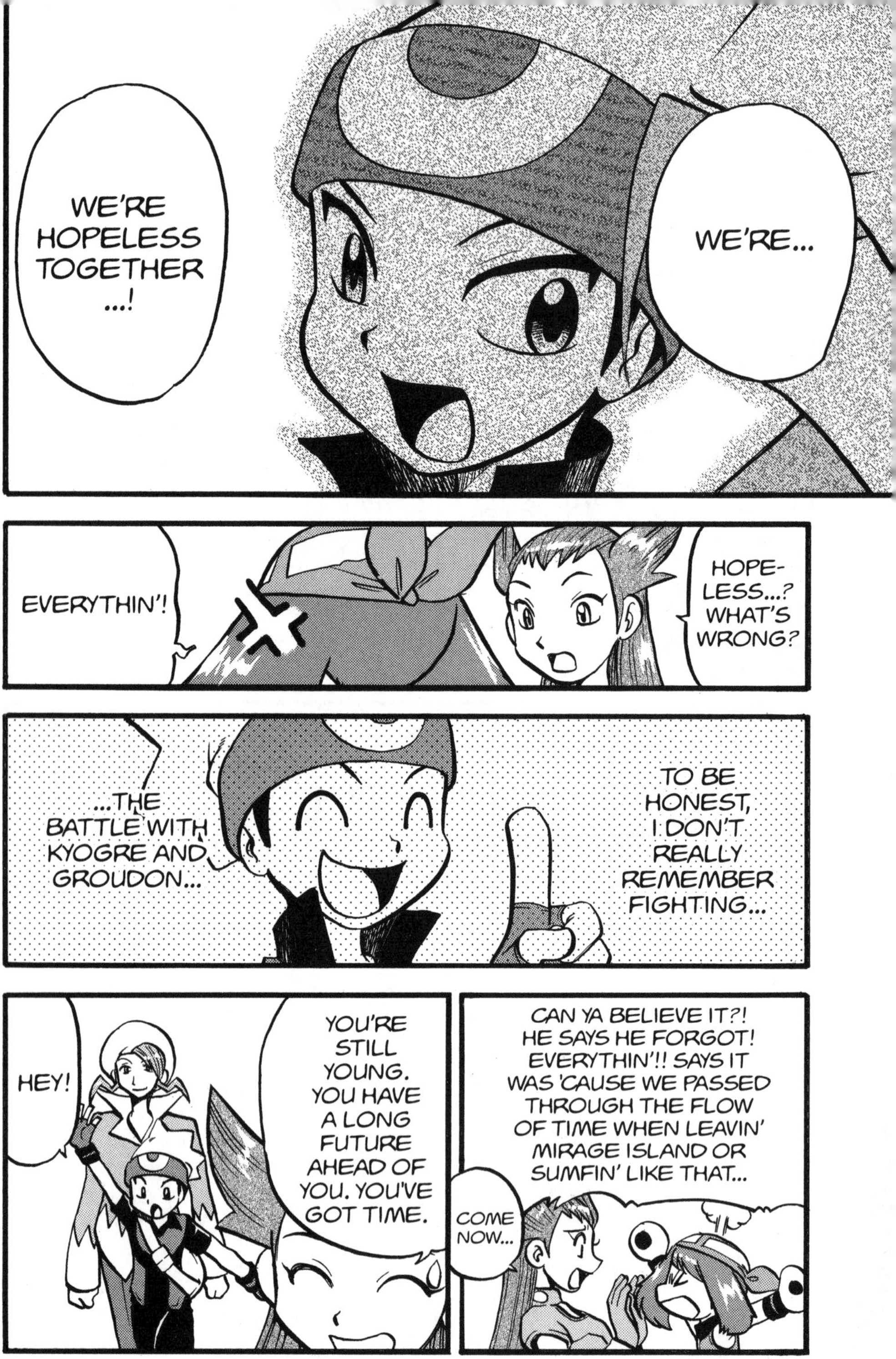
WE'RE...
WE'RE HOPELESS TOGETHER ...!
HOPE-LESS...? WHAT'S WRONG?
EVERYTHIN'!
TO BE HONEST, I DON'T REALLY REMEMBER FIGHTING...
...THE BATTLE WITH KYOGRE AND GROUDON...
CAN YA BELIEVE IT?! HE SAYS HE FORGOT! EVERYTHIN'!! SAYS IT WAS 'CAUSE WE PASSED THROUGH THE FLOW OF TIME WHEN LEAVIN' MIRAGE ISLAND OR SUMFIN' LIKE THAT...
COME NOW...
YOU'RE STILL YOUNG. YOU HAVE A LONG FUTURE AHEAD OF YOU. YOU'VE GOT TIME.
HEY!

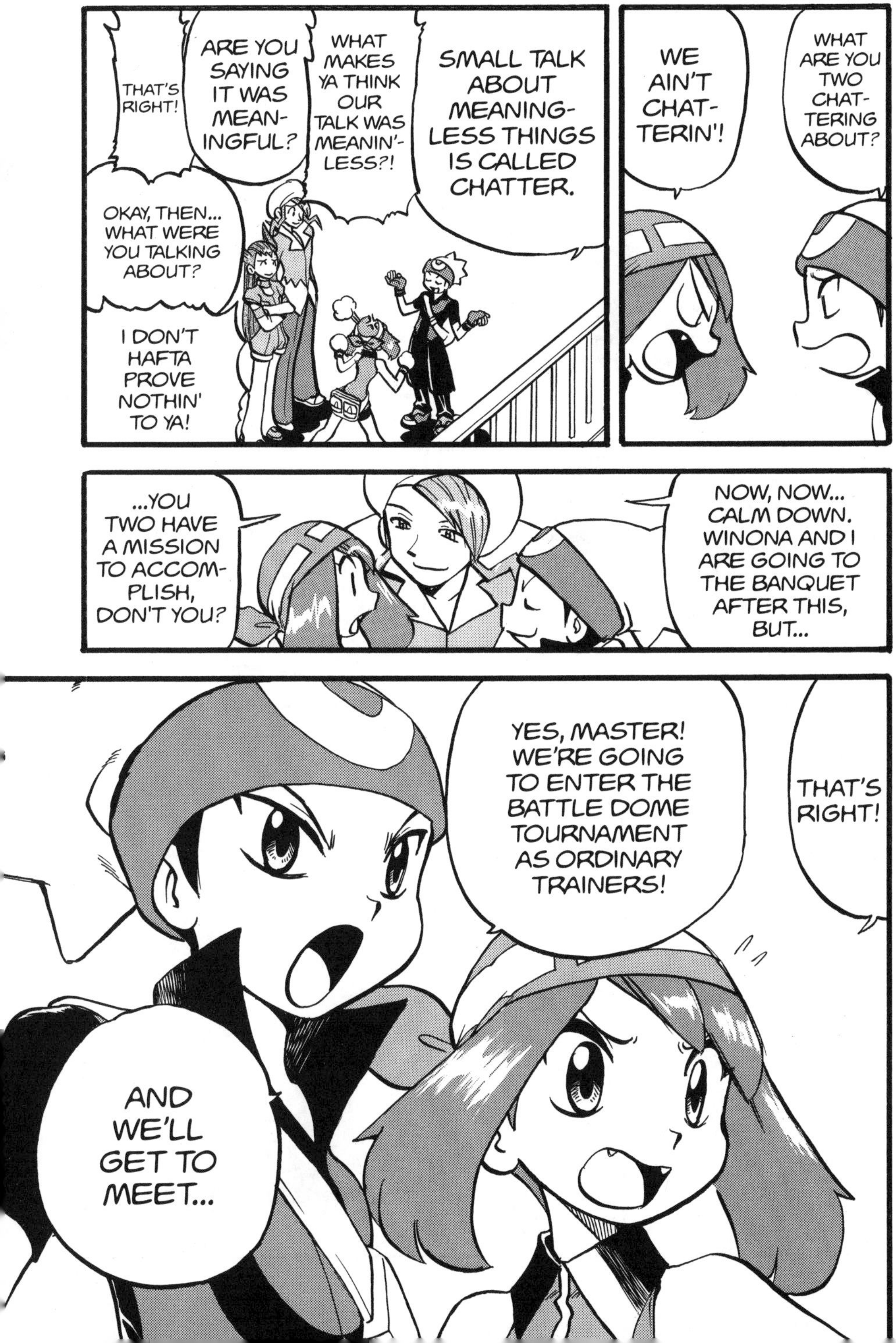
WHAT ARE YOU TWO CHATTERING ABOUT?
WE AIN'T CHATTERIN'!
SMALL TALK ABOUT MEANINGLESS THINGS IS CALLED CHATTER.
WHAT MAKES YA THINK OUR TALK WAS MEANIN'LESS?!
ARE YOU SAYING IT WAS MEANINGFUL?
THAT'S RIGHT!
OKAY, THEN... WHAT WERE YOU TALKING ABOUT?
I DON'T HAFTA PROVE NOTHIN' TO YA!
NOW, NOW... CALM DOWN. WINONA AND I ARE GOING TO THE BANQUET AFTER THIS, BUT...
...YOU TWO HAVE A MISSION TO ACCOMPLISH, DON'T YOU?
THAT'S RIGHT!
YES, MASTER! WE'RE GOING TO ENTER THE BATTLE DOME TOURNAMENT AS ORDINARY TRAINERS!
AND WE'LL GET TO MEET...

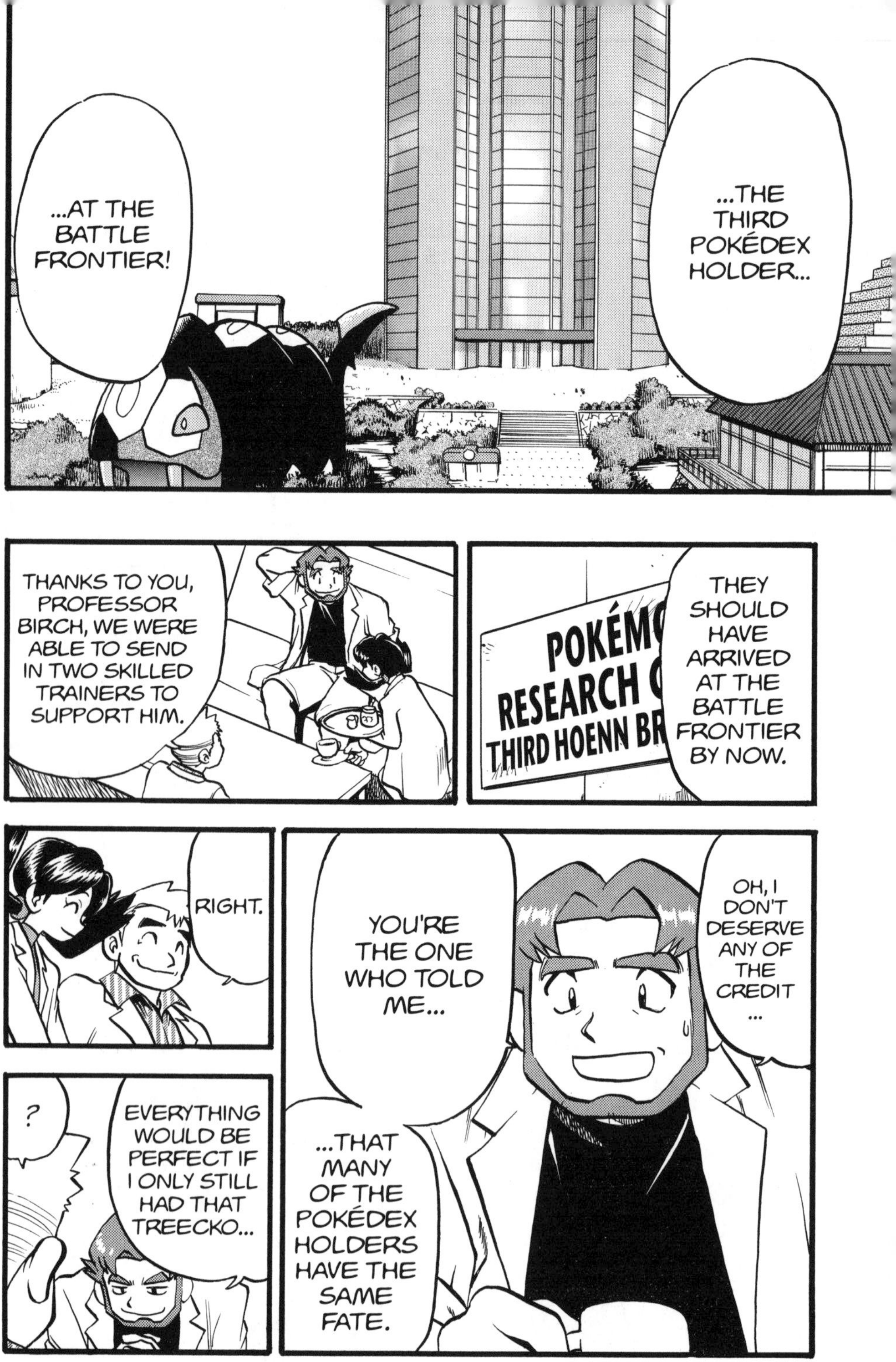
...THE THIRD POKÉDEX HOLDER...
...AT THE BATTLE FRONTIER!
POKÉMO
RESEARCH C
THIRD HOENN BR
THEY SHOULD HAVE ARRIVED AT THE BATTLE FRONTIER BY NOW.
THANKS TO YOU, PROFESSOR BIRCH, WE WERE ABLE TO SEND IN TWO SKILLED TRAINERS TO SUPPORT HIM.
OH, I DON'T DESERVE ANY OF THE CREDIT ...
YOU'RE THE ONE WHO TOLD ME...
...THAT MANY OF THE POKÉDEX HOLDERS HAVE THE SAME FATE.
RIGHT.
EVERYTHING WOULD BE PERFECT IF I ONLY STILL HAD THAT TREECKO...
?

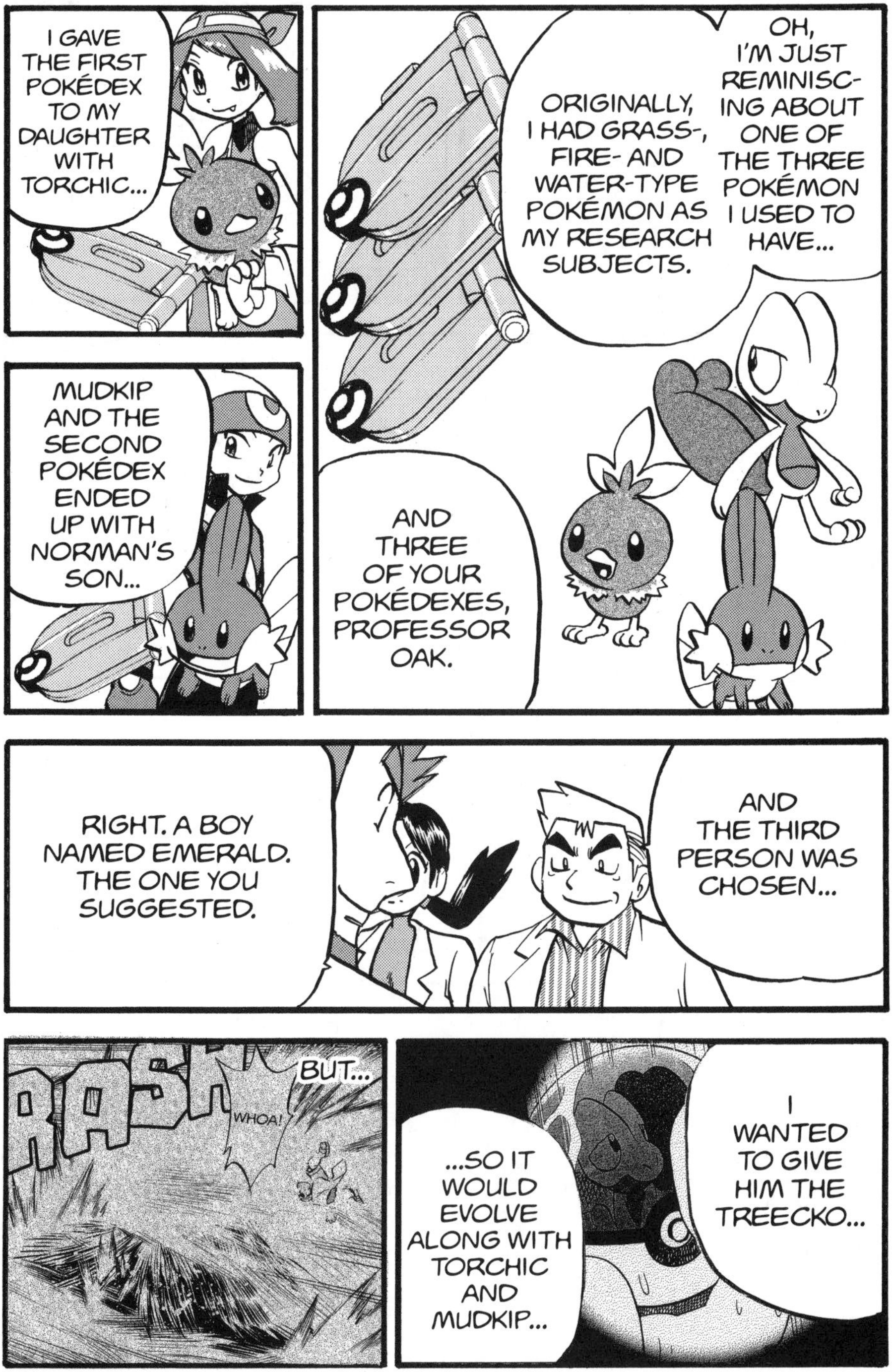
OH, I'M JUST REMINISC-ING ABOUT ONE OF THE THREE POKÉMON I USED TO HAVE...
ORIGINALLY, I HAD GRASS-, FIRE- AND WATER-TYPE POKÉMON AS MY RESEARCH SUBJECTS.
AND THREE OF YOUR POKÉDEXES, PROFESSOR OAK.
I GAVE THE FIRST POKÉDEX TO MY DAUGHTER WITH TORCHIC...
MUDKIP AND THE SECOND POKÉDEX ENDED UP WITH NORMAN'S SON...
AND THE THIRD PERSON WAS CHOSEN...
RIGHT. A BOY NAMED EMERALD. THE ONE YOU SUGGESTED.
I WANTED TO GIVE HIM THE TREECKO...
...SO IT WOULD EVOLVE ALONG WITH TORCHIC AND MUDKIP...
BUT...
WHOA!
RASH

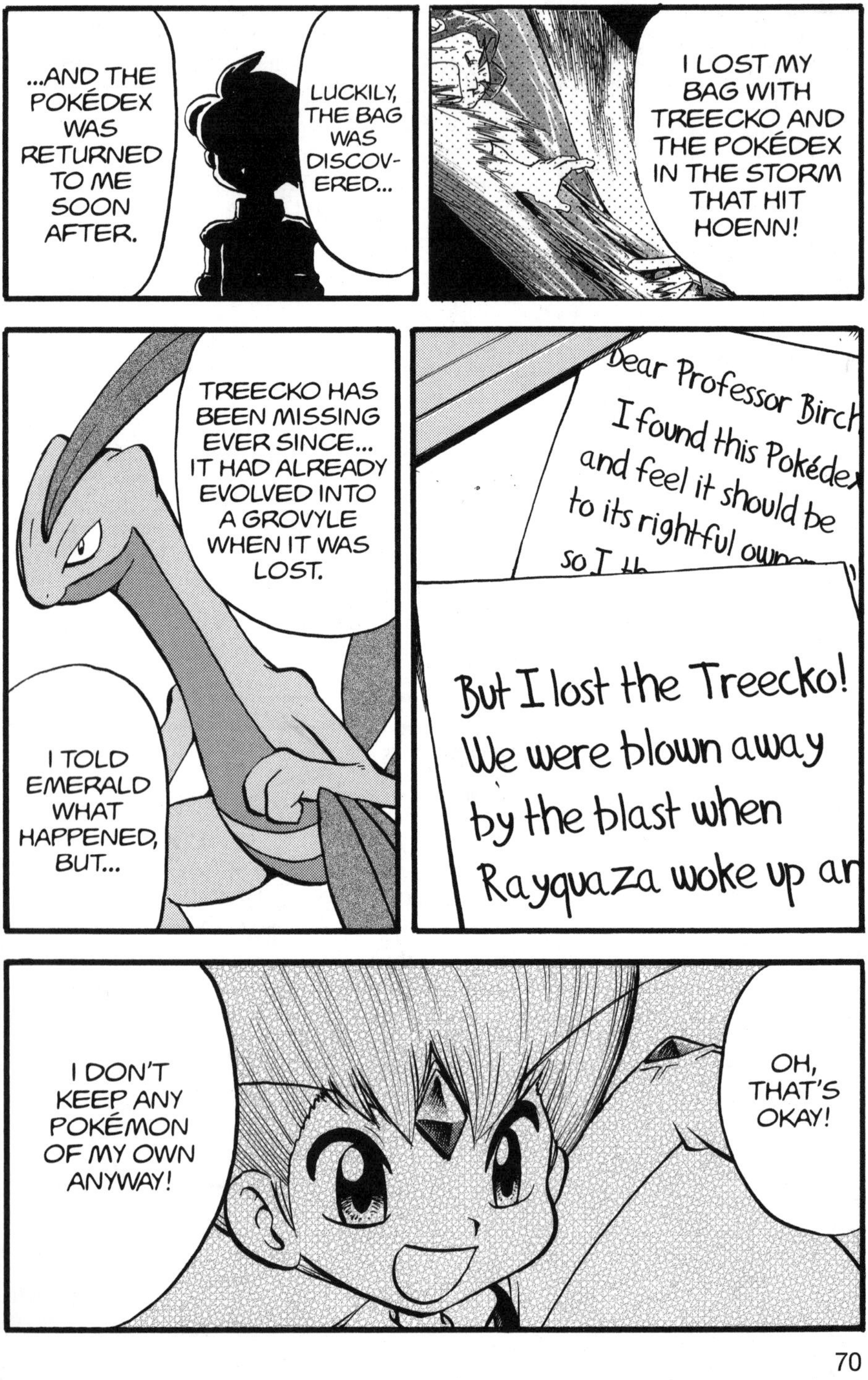
I LOST MY BAG WITH TREECKO AND THE POKÉDEX IN THE STORM THAT HIT HOENN!
LUCKILY, THE BAG WAS DISCOV-ERED...
...AND THE POKÉDEX WAS RETURNED TO ME SOON AFTER.
Dear Professor Birch
I found this Pokédex
and feel it should be
to its rightful
But I lost the Treecko!
We were blown away
by the blast when
Rayquaza woke up
TREECKO HAS BEEN MISSING EVER SINCE... IT HAD ALREADY EVOLVED INTO A GROVYLE WHEN IT WAS LOST.
I TOLD EMERALD WHAT HAPPENED, BUT...
OH, THAT'S OKAY!
I DON'T KEEP ANY POKÉMON OF MY OWN ANYWAY!

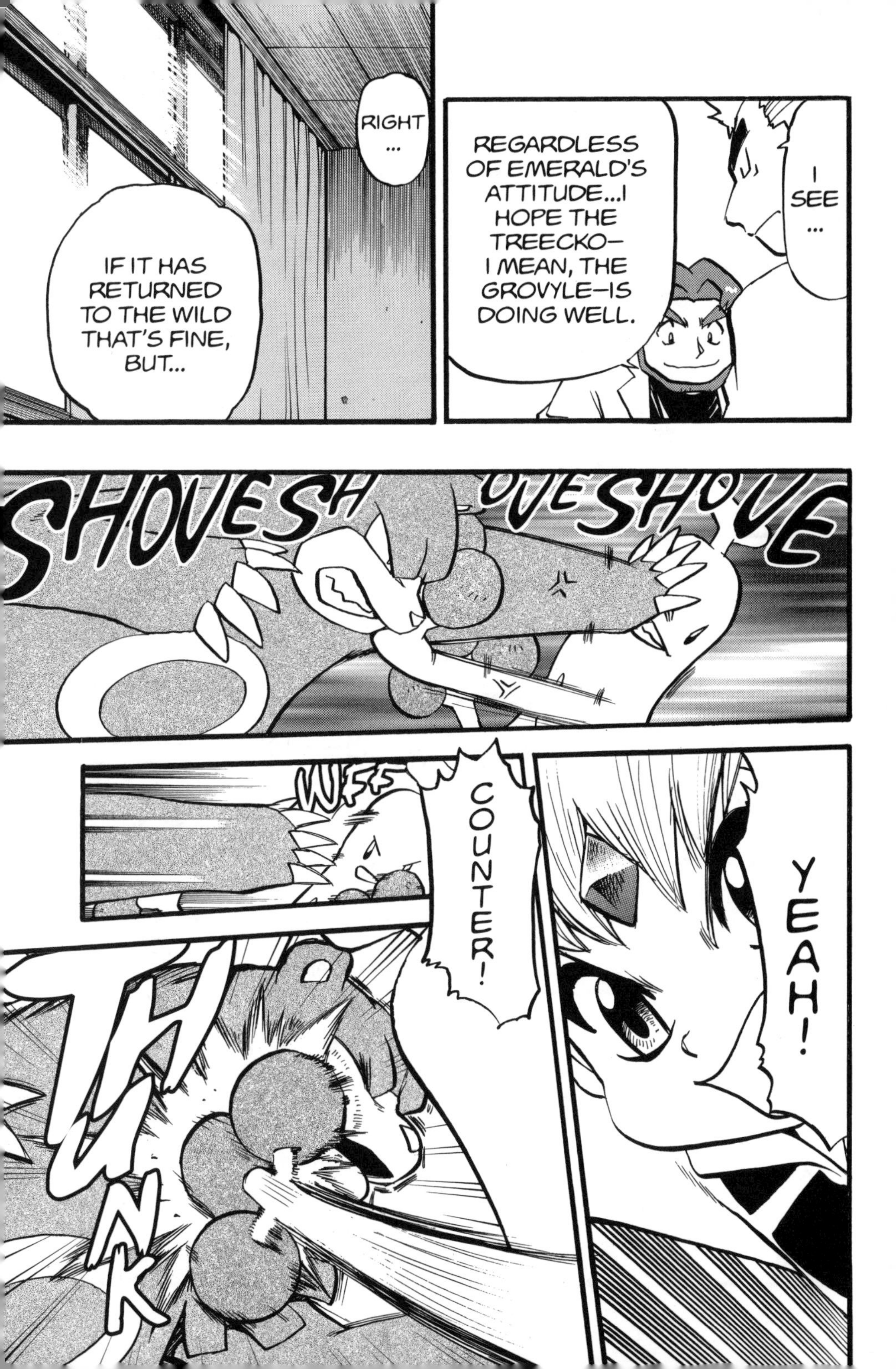
I SEE...
REGARDLESS OF EMERALD'S ATTITUDE...I HOPE THE TREECKO—I MEAN, THE GROVYLE—IS DOING WELL.
RIGHT...
IF IT HAS RETURNED TO THE WILD THAT'S FINE, BUT...
SHOVE SHOVE SHOVE
YEAH!
COUNTER!
WFF
THUNK

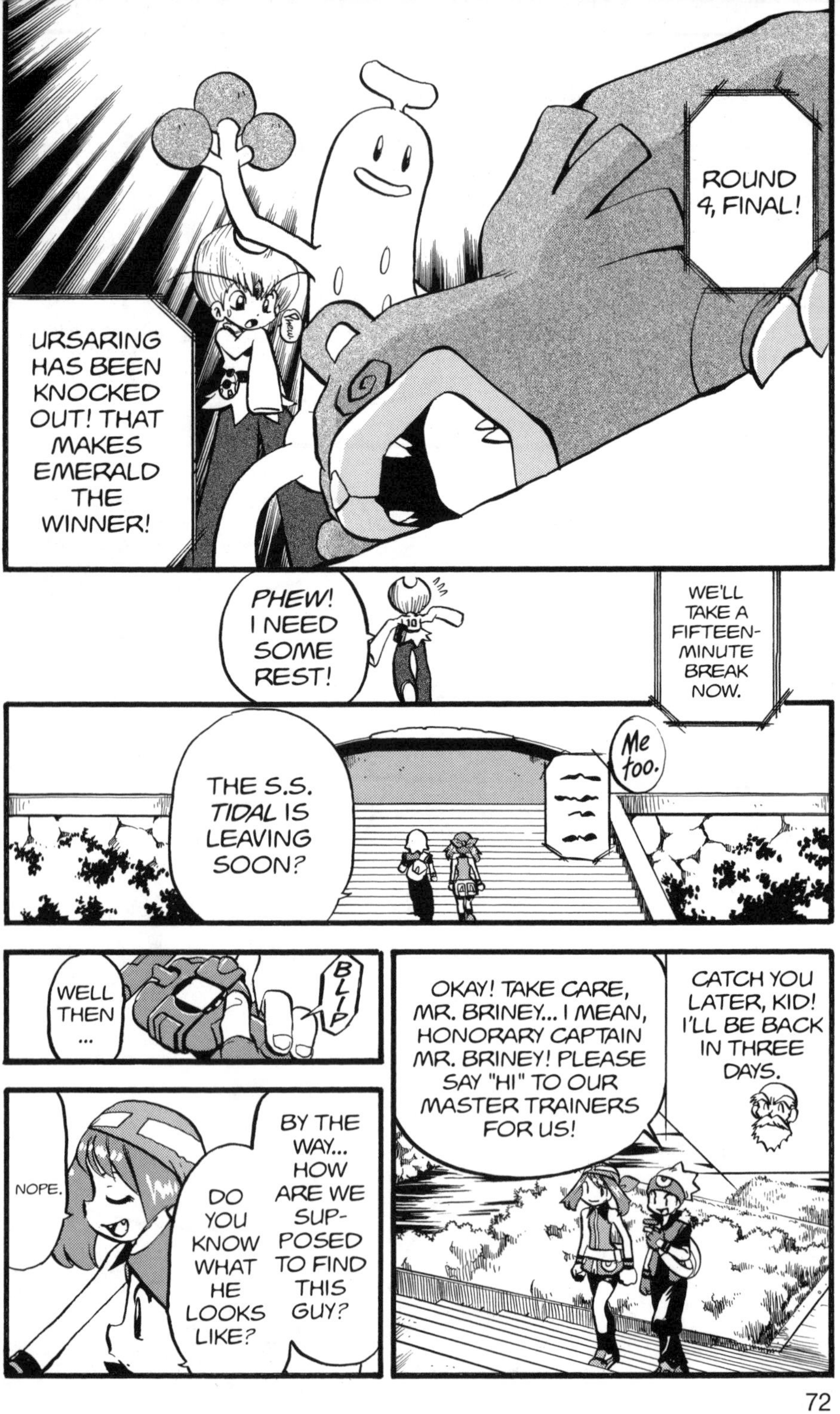
ROUND 4, FINAL!
URSARING HAS BEEN KNOCKED OUT! THAT MAKES EMERALD THE WINNER!
Phew
WE'LL TAKE A FIFTEEN-MINUTE BREAK NOW.
PHEW! I NEED SOME REST!
Me too.
THE S.S. TIDAL IS LEAVING SOON?
CATCH YOU LATER, KID! I'LL BE BACK IN THREE DAYS.
OKAY! TAKE CARE, MR. BRINEY... I MEAN, HONORARY CAPTAIN MR. BRINEY! PLEASE SAY "HI" TO OUR MASTER TRAINERS FOR US!
BLIP
WELL THEN ...
BY THE WAY... HOW ARE WE SUP-POSED TO FIND THIS GUY?
DO YOU KNOW WHAT HE LOOKS LIKE?
NOPE.

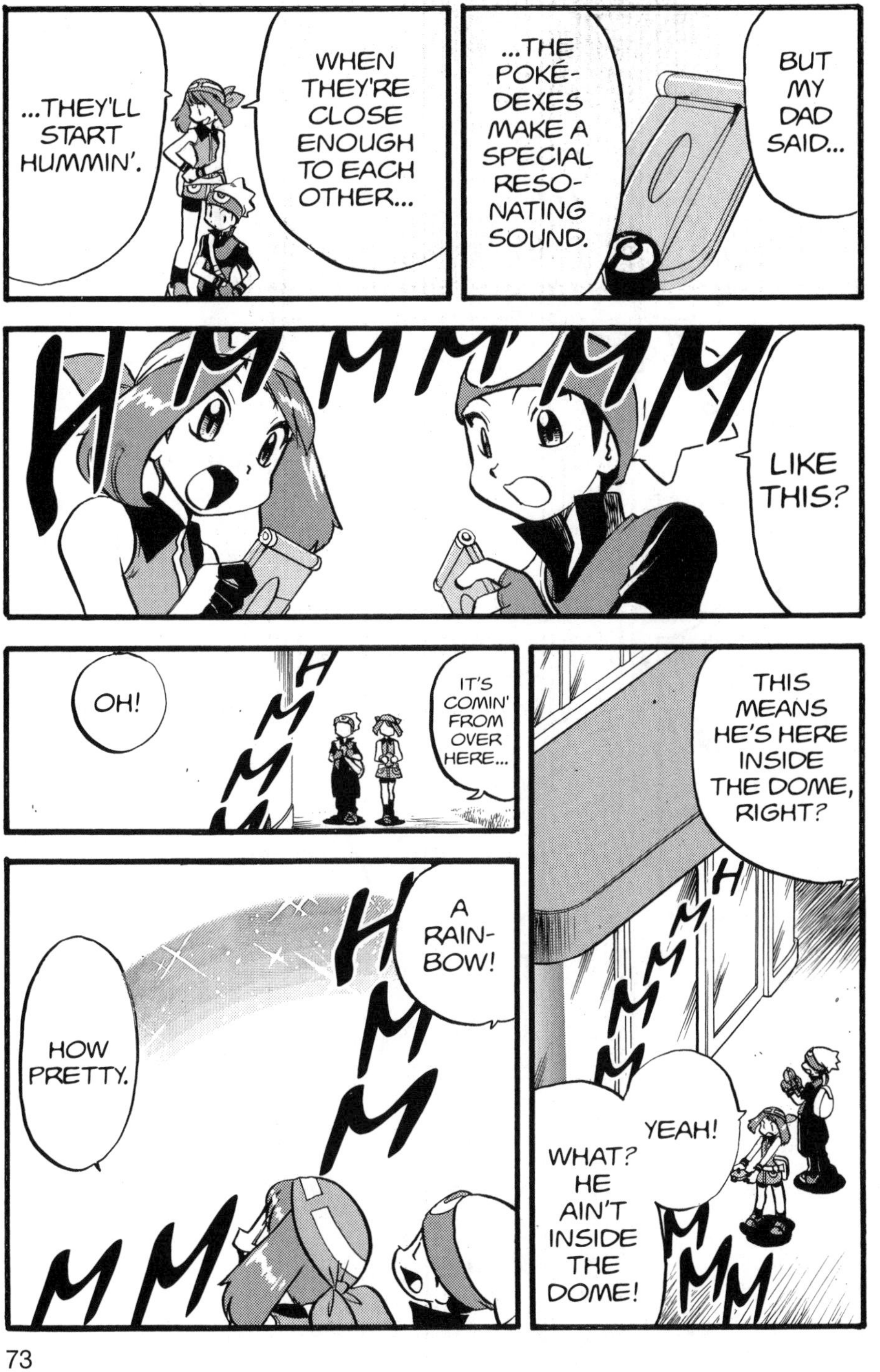
BUT MY DAD SAID...
...THE POKÉ-DEXES MAKE A SPECIAL RESO-NATING SOUND.
WHEN THEY'RE CLOSE ENOUGH TO EACH OTHER...
...THEY'LL START HUMMIN'.
HMMMMMM
LIKE THIS?
THIS MEANS HE'S HERE INSIDE THE DOME, RIGHT?
HMMMMM
YEAH!
WHAT? HE AIN'T INSIDE THE DOME!
MMM
HMMMM
IT'S COMIN' FROM OVER HERE...
OH!
HMMM
A RAIN-BOW!
HOW PRETTY.
MM

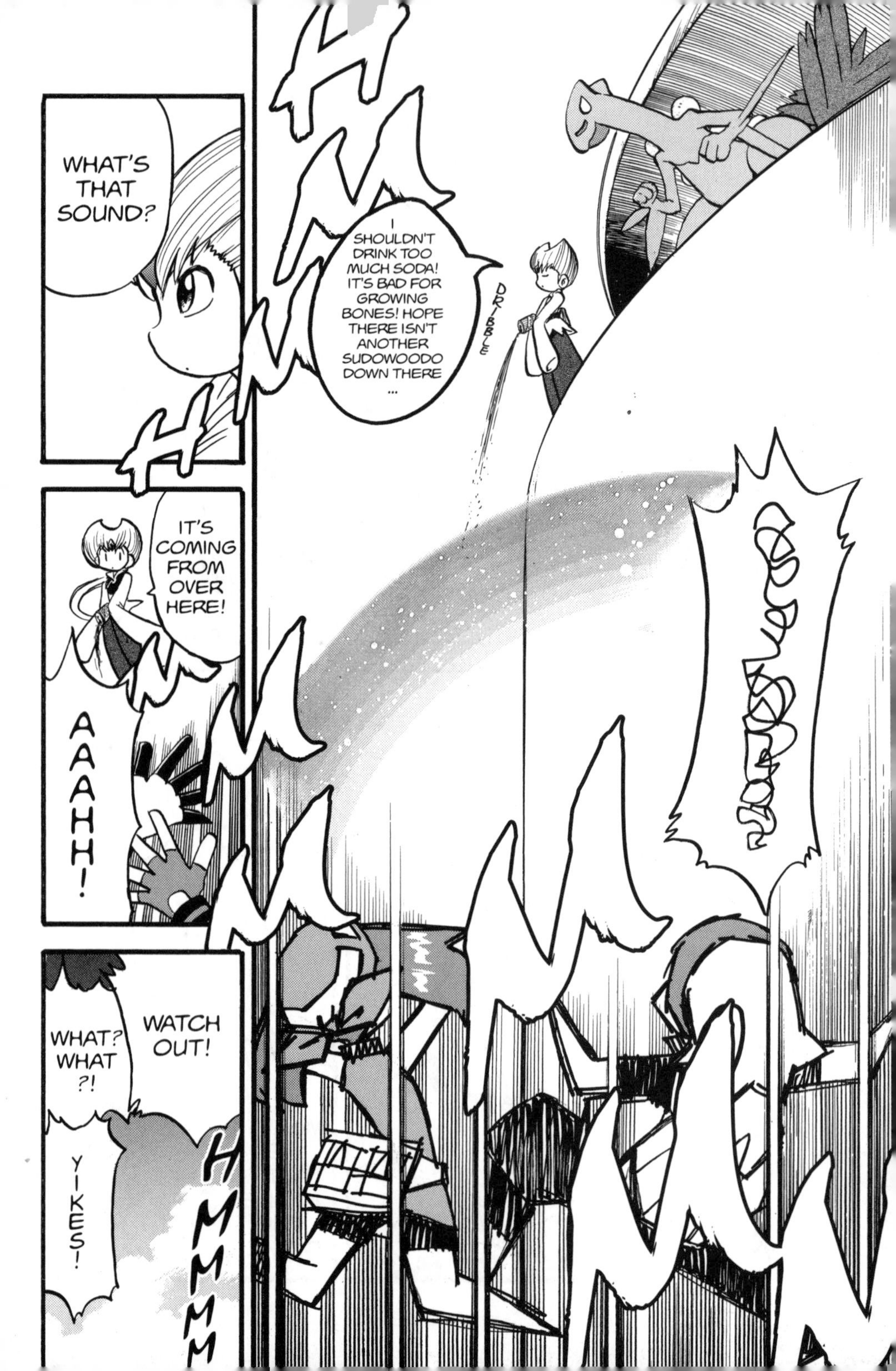

I SHOULDN'T DRINK TOO MUCH SODA! IT'S BAD FOR GROWING BONES! HOPE THERE ISN'T ANOTHER SUDOWOODO DOWN THERE ...
DRIBBLE
WHAT'S THAT SOUND?
IT'S COMING FROM OVER HERE!
AAAAHH!
WATCH OUT!
WHAT? WHAT ?!
YIKES!
HMMMM

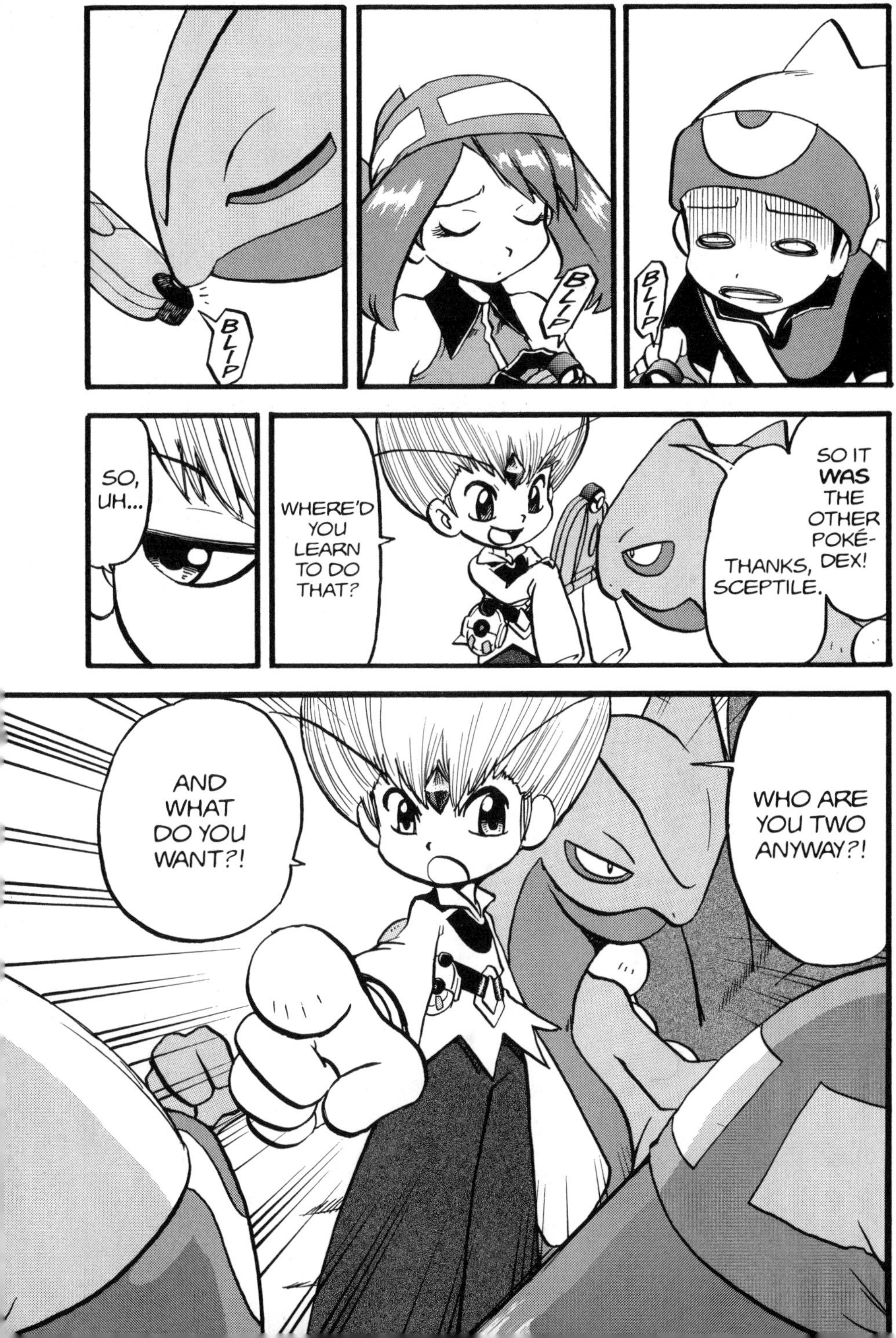
BLIP
BLIP
BLIP
SO IT WAS THE OTHER POKÉDEX!
THANKS, SCEPTILE.
WHERE'D YOU LEARN TO DO THAT?
SO, UH...
WHO ARE YOU TWO ANYWAY?!
AND WHAT DO YOU WANT?!

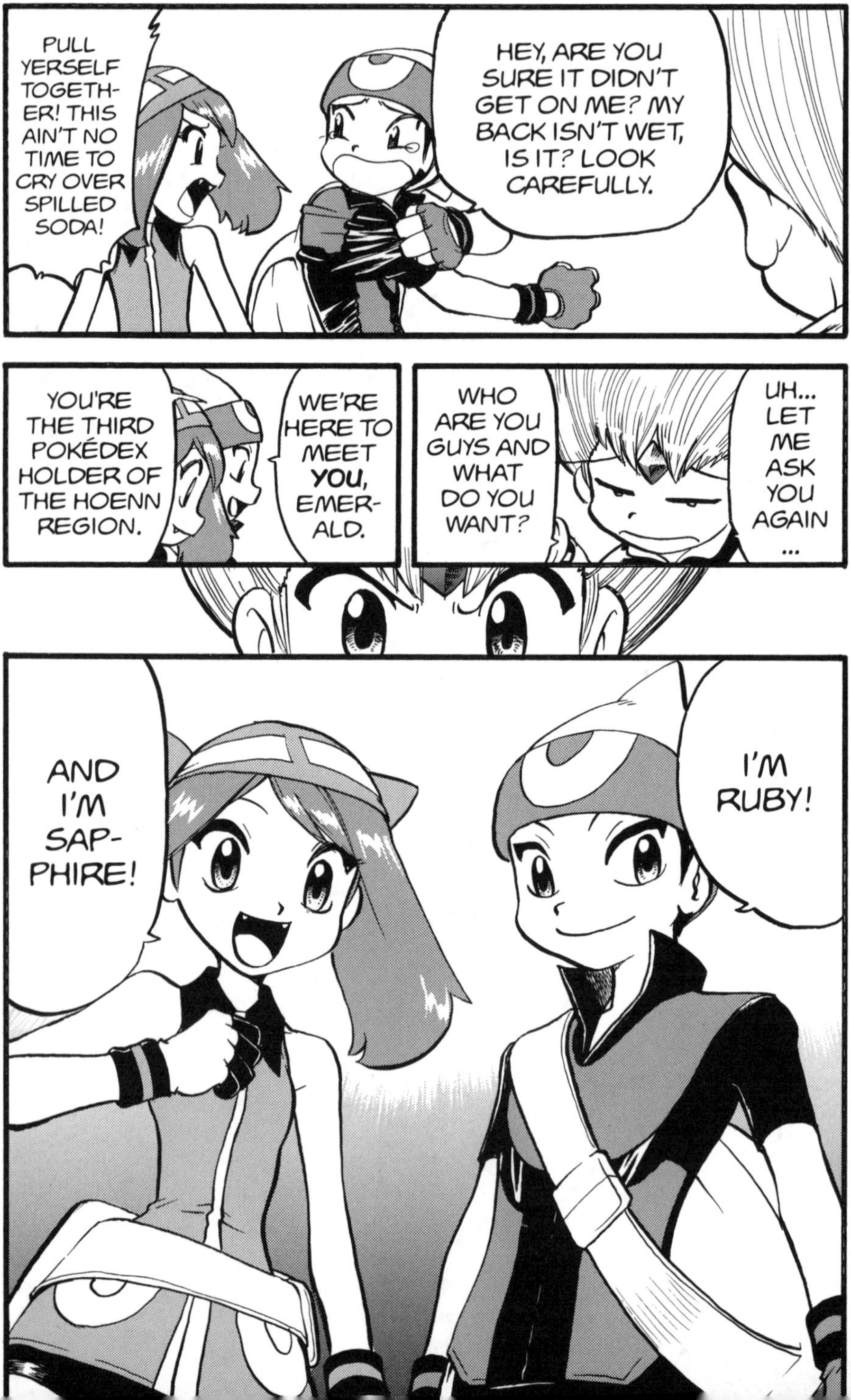
HEY, ARE YOU SURE IT DIDN'T GET ON ME? MY BACK ISN'T WET, IS IT? LOOK CAREFULLY.
PULL YERSELF TOGETHER! THIS AIN'T NO TIME TO CRY OVER SPILLED SODA!
UH... LET ME ASK YOU AGAIN ...
WHO ARE YOU GUYS AND WHAT DO YOU WANT?
WE'RE HERE TO MEET **YOU**, EMERALD.
YOU'RE THE THIRD POKÉDEX HOLDER OF THE HOENN REGION.
I'M RUBY!
AND I'M SAPPHIRE!

DEAR MEMBERS OF THE PRESS...

Thank you for visiting the Battle Frontier today. Permit me to continue explaining the rules of this facility...

OWNER: SCOTT

FACILITY RULES	Battle-type	Number of Pokémon	Type of Symbol	Wins needed to attain the Symbol
BATTLE PALACE 1	• Single • Double	3 Pokémon	Spirit Symbol	7 Wins × 6 Rounds = 42 Consecutive Wins

At the Battle Palace, battles are fought according to a unique rule: The Trainer is not allowed to give orders to their Pokémon. Pokémon must choose what move to use themselves. So, basically, the Trainer just observes the battle as it unfolds. Since Trainers cannot give orders to their Pokémon, the battles are not as complex as those at other facilities. The Battle Palace is a facility where the Trainers may enjoy a battle centered around the natural instincts of the Pokémon.

Spirit Symbol

Palace Maven Spenser

321

Cunning Kirlia

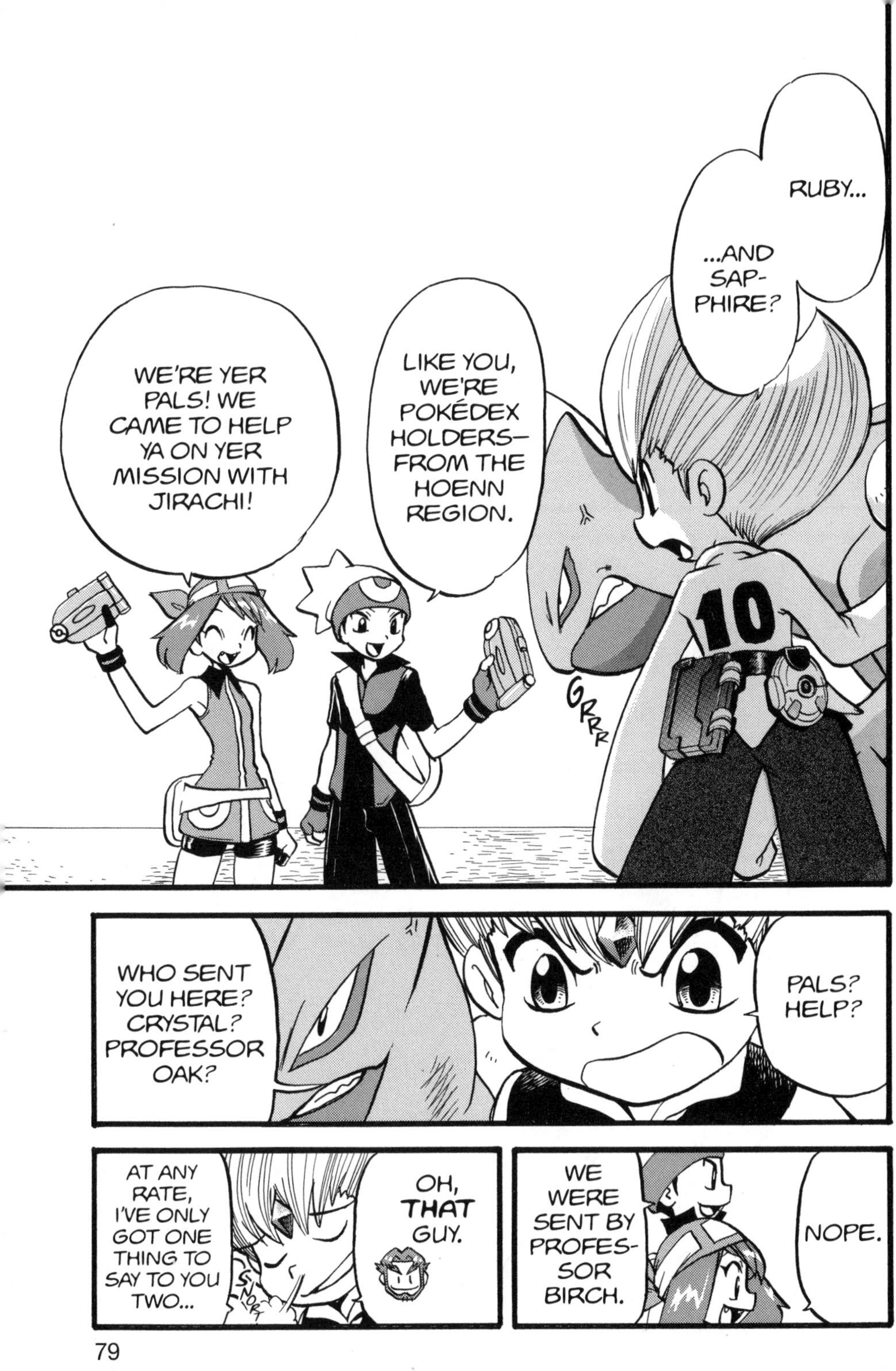
RUBY...
...AND SAP-PHIRE?
LIKE YOU, WE'RE POKÉDEX HOLDERS—FROM THE HOENN REGION.
WE'RE YER PALS! WE CAME TO HELP YA ON YER MISSION WITH JIRACHI!
GRRR
PALS? HELP?
WHO SENT YOU HERE? CRYSTAL? PROFESSOR OAK?
NOPE.
WE WERE SENT BY PROFES-SOR BIRCH.
OH, **THAT** GUY.
AT ANY RATE, I'VE ONLY GOT ONE THING TO SAY TO YOU TWO...
SNORT

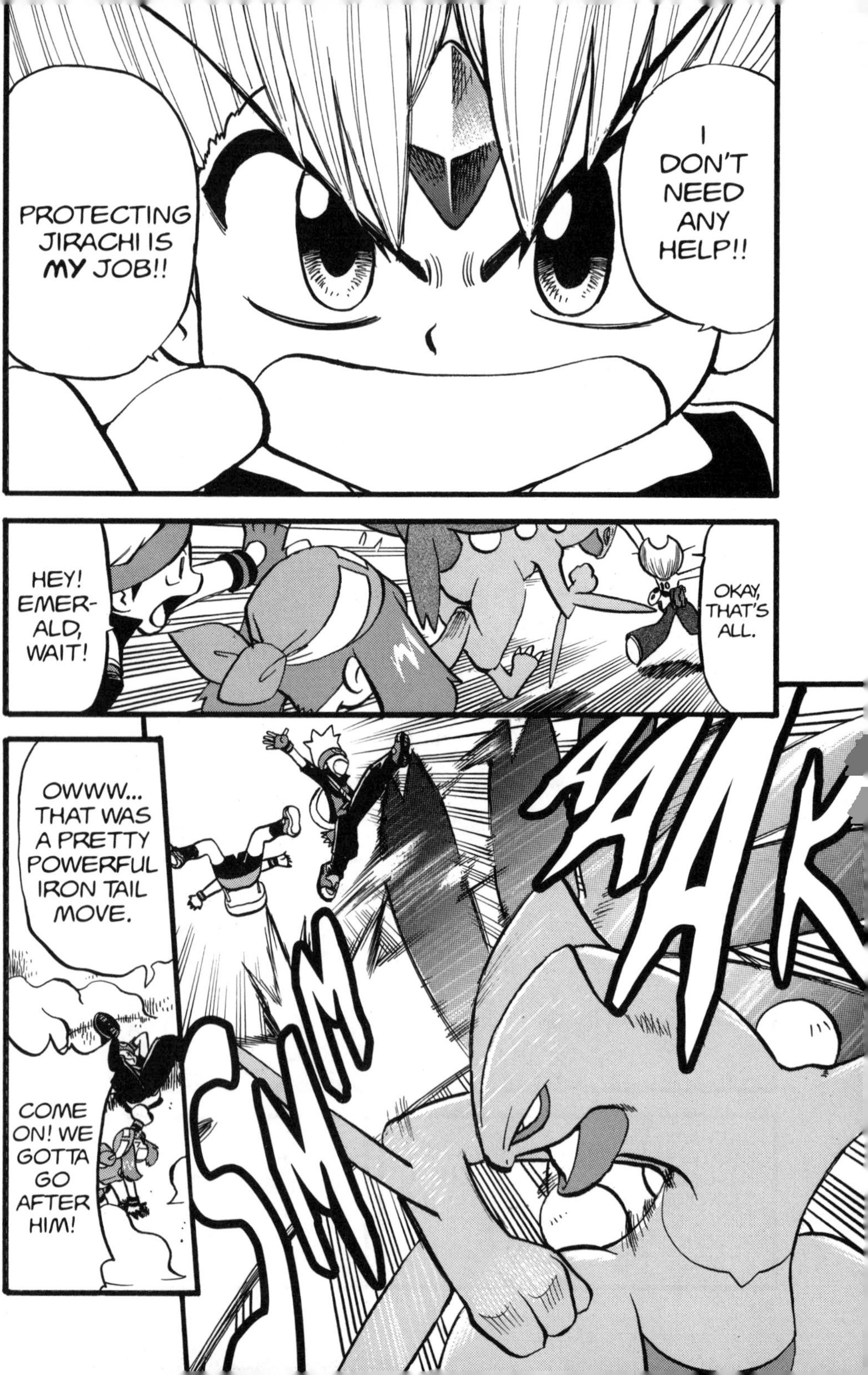
I DON'T NEED ANY HELP!!
PROTECTING JIRACHI IS MY JOB!!
OKAY, THAT'S ALL.
HEY! EMER-ALD, WAIT!
OWWW... THAT WAS A PRETTY POWERFUL IRON TAIL MOVE.
COME ON! WE GOTTA GO AFTER HIM!

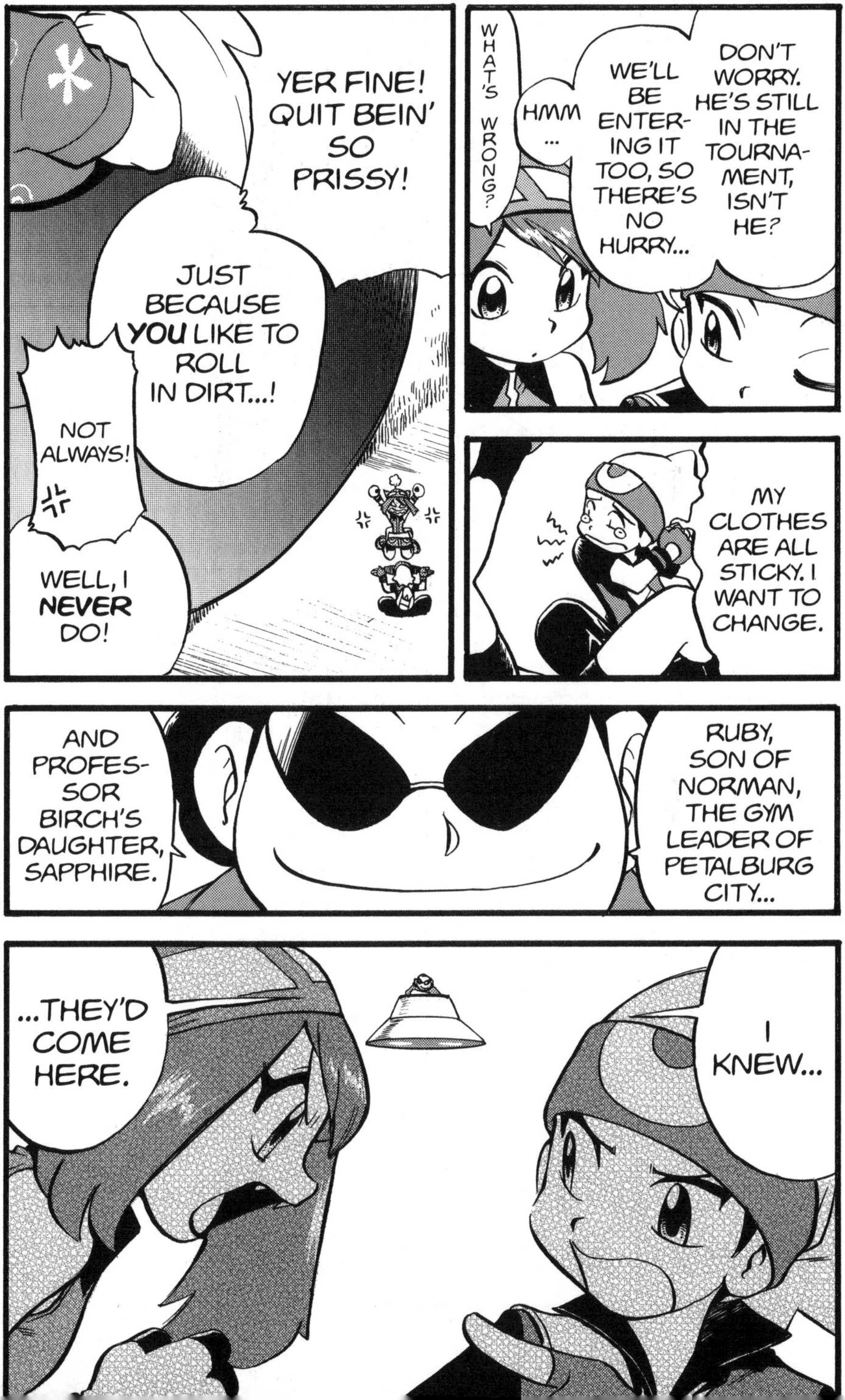
DON'T WORRY. HE'S STILL IN THE TOURNAMENT, ISN'T HE?
WE'LL BE ENTERING IT TOO, SO THERE'S NO HURRY...
HMM ...
WHAT'S WRONG?
MY CLOTHES ARE ALL STICKY. I WANT TO CHANGE.
YER FINE! QUIT BEIN' SO PRISSY!
JUST BECAUSE **YOU** LIKE TO ROLL IN DIRT...!
NOT ALWAYS!
WELL, I **NEVER** DO!
RUBY, SON OF NORMAN, THE GYM LEADER OF PETALBURG CITY...
AND PROFESSOR BIRCH'S DAUGHTER, SAPPHIRE.
I KNEW...
...THEY'D COME HERE.

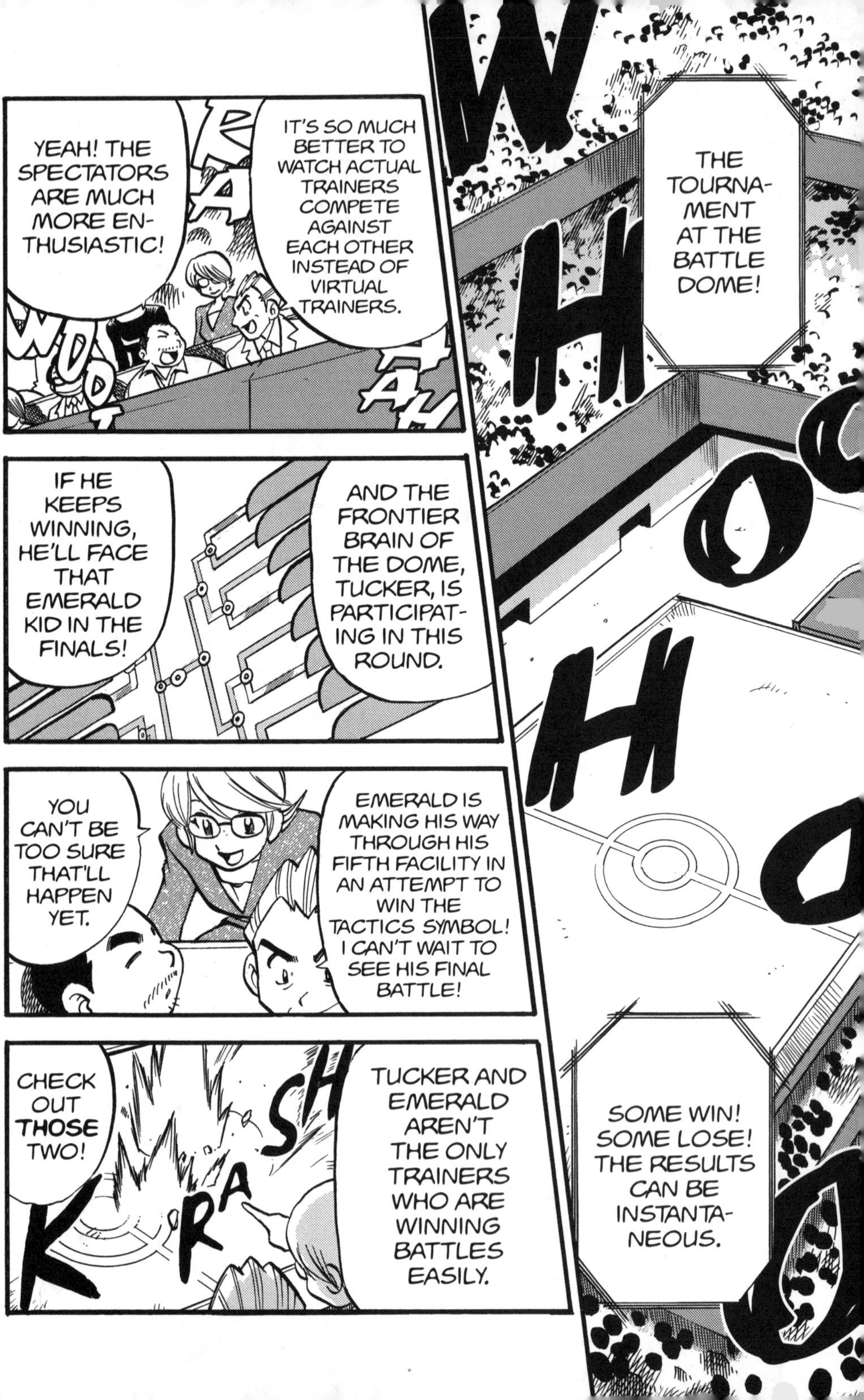
THE TOURNAMENT AT THE BATTLE DOME!
SOME WIN! SOME LOSE! THE RESULTS CAN BE INSTANTANEOUS.
IT'S SO MUCH BETTER TO WATCH ACTUAL TRAINERS COMPETE AGAINST EACH OTHER INSTEAD OF VIRTUAL TRAINERS.
YEAH! THE SPECTATORS ARE MUCH MORE ENTHUSIASTIC!
AND THE FRONTIER BRAIN OF THE DOME, TUCKER, IS PARTICIPATING IN THIS ROUND.
IF HE KEEPS WINNING, HE'LL FACE THAT EMERALD KID IN THE FINALS!
EMERALD IS MAKING HIS WAY THROUGH HIS FIFTH FACILITY IN AN ATTEMPT TO WIN THE TACTICS SYMBOL! I CAN'T WAIT TO SEE HIS FINAL BATTLE!
YOU CAN'T BE TOO SURE THAT'LL HAPPEN YET.
TUCKER AND EMERALD AREN'T THE ONLY TRAINERS WHO ARE WINNING BATTLES EASILY.
CHECK OUT **THOSE** TWO!
KRASH

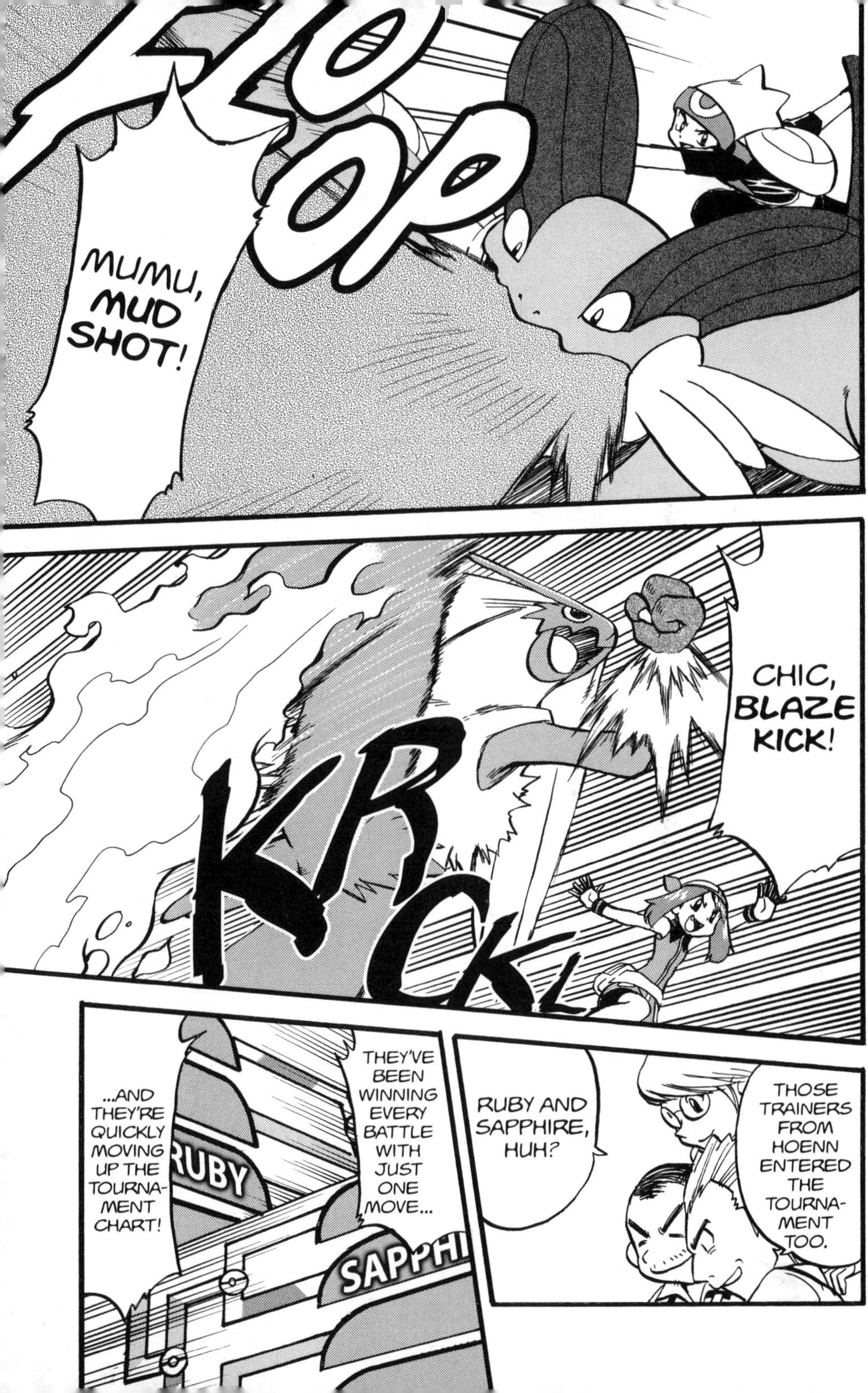
FLOOP
MUMU, MUD SHOT!
CHIC, BLAZE KICK!
KRCK
THOSE TRAINERS FROM HOENN ENTERED THE TOURNAMENT TOO.
RUBY AND SAPPHIRE, HUH?
THEY'VE BEEN WINNING EVERY BATTLE WITH JUST ONE MOVE...
...AND THEY'RE QUICKLY MOVING UP THE TOURNAMENT CHART!
RUBY
SAPPHI

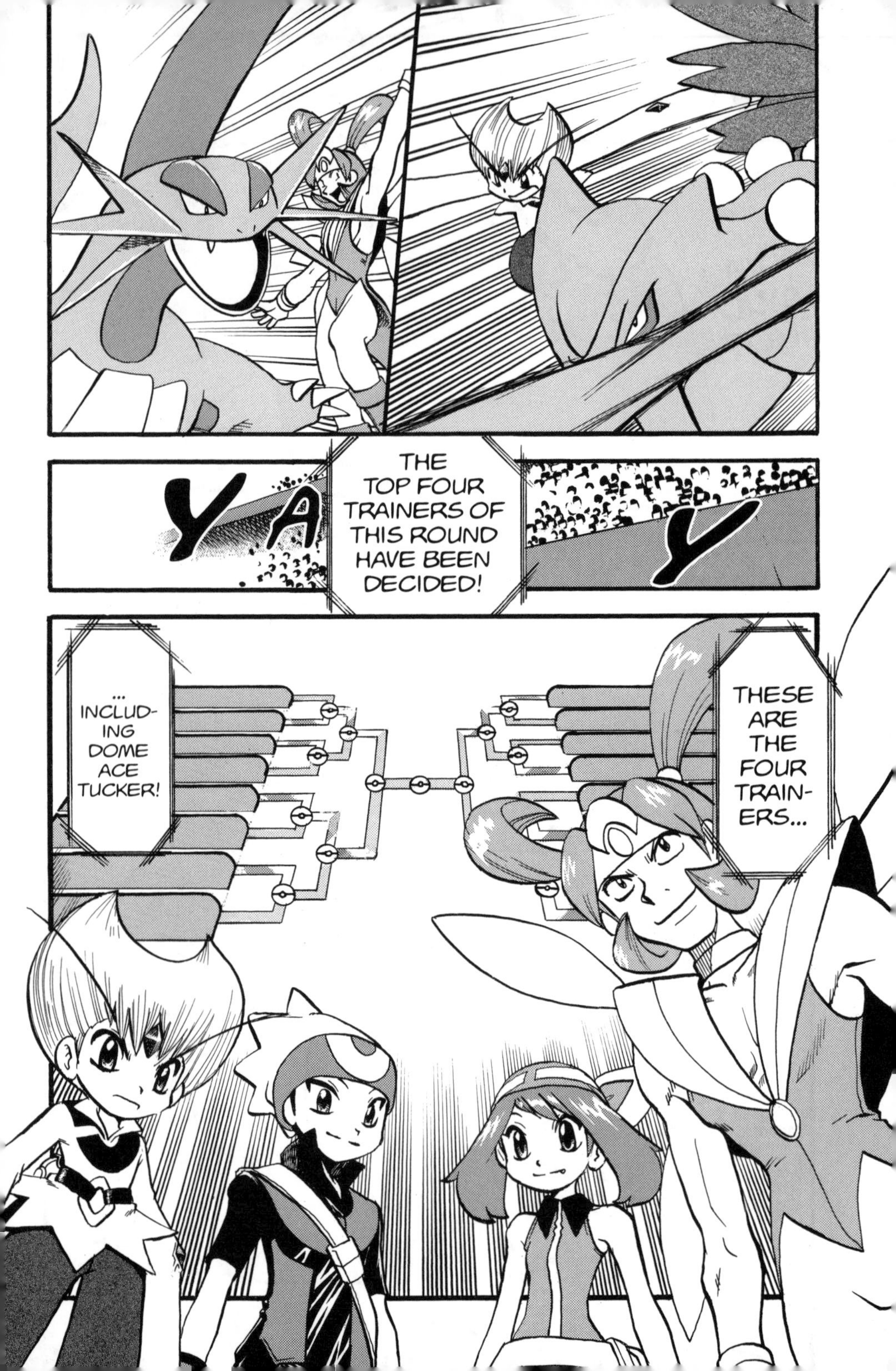
Y
THE TOP FOUR TRAINERS OF THIS ROUND HAVE BEEN DECIDED!
YA
THESE ARE THE FOUR TRAIN-ERS...
...INCLUD-ING DOME ACE TUCKER!

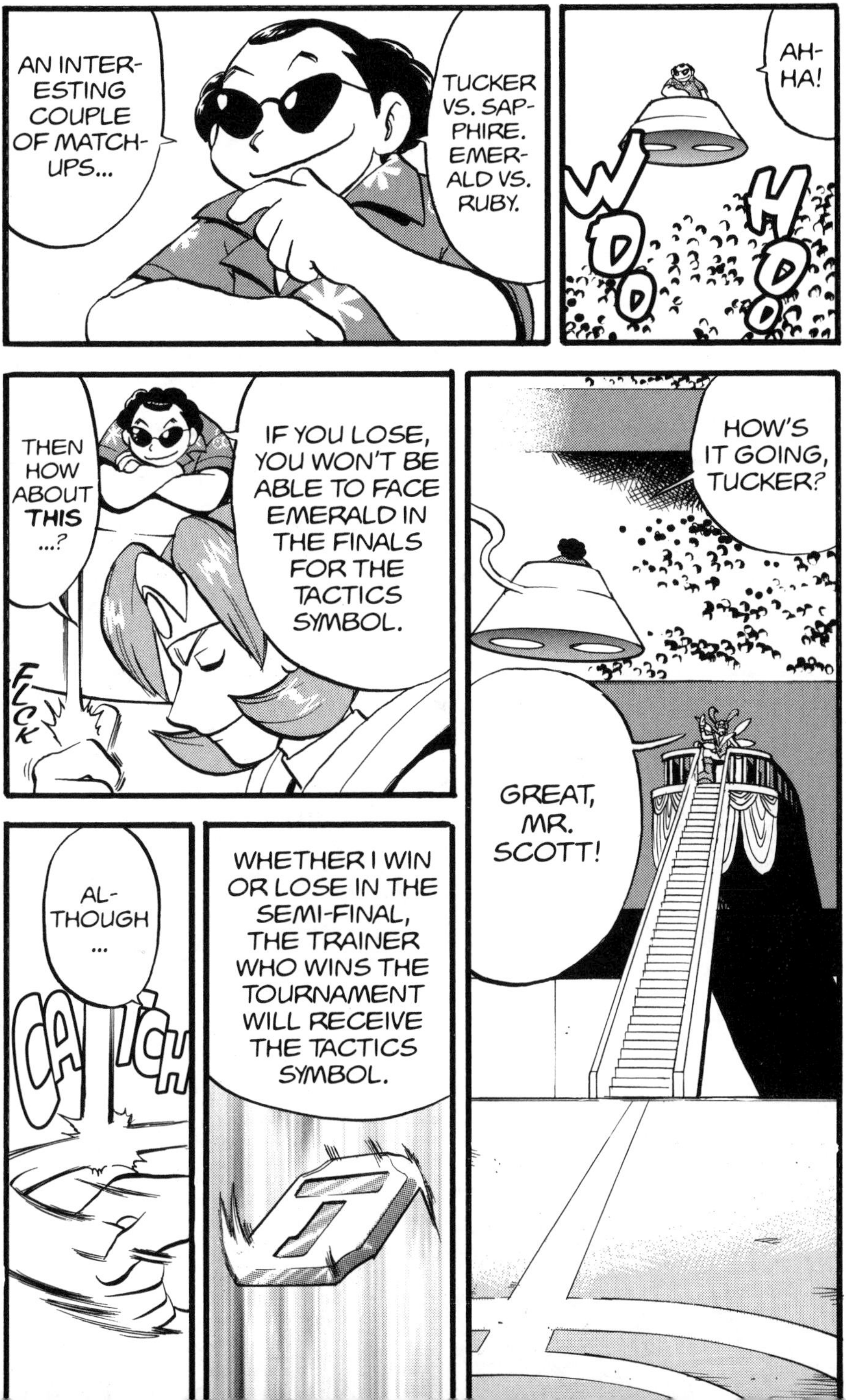
AH-HA!
WOO
HOO
TUCKER VS. SAPPHIRE. EMERALD VS. RUBY.
AN INTERESTING COUPLE OF MATCH-UPS...
HOW'S IT GOING, TUCKER?
GREAT, MR. SCOTT!
IF YOU LOSE, YOU WON'T BE ABLE TO FACE EMERALD IN THE FINALS FOR THE TACTICS SYMBOL.
THEN HOW ABOUT **THIS** ...?
FLICK
WHETHER I WIN OR LOSE IN THE SEMI-FINAL, THE TRAINER WHO WINS THE TOURNAMENT WILL RECEIVE THE TACTICS SYMBOL.
ALTHOUGH ...
CATCH

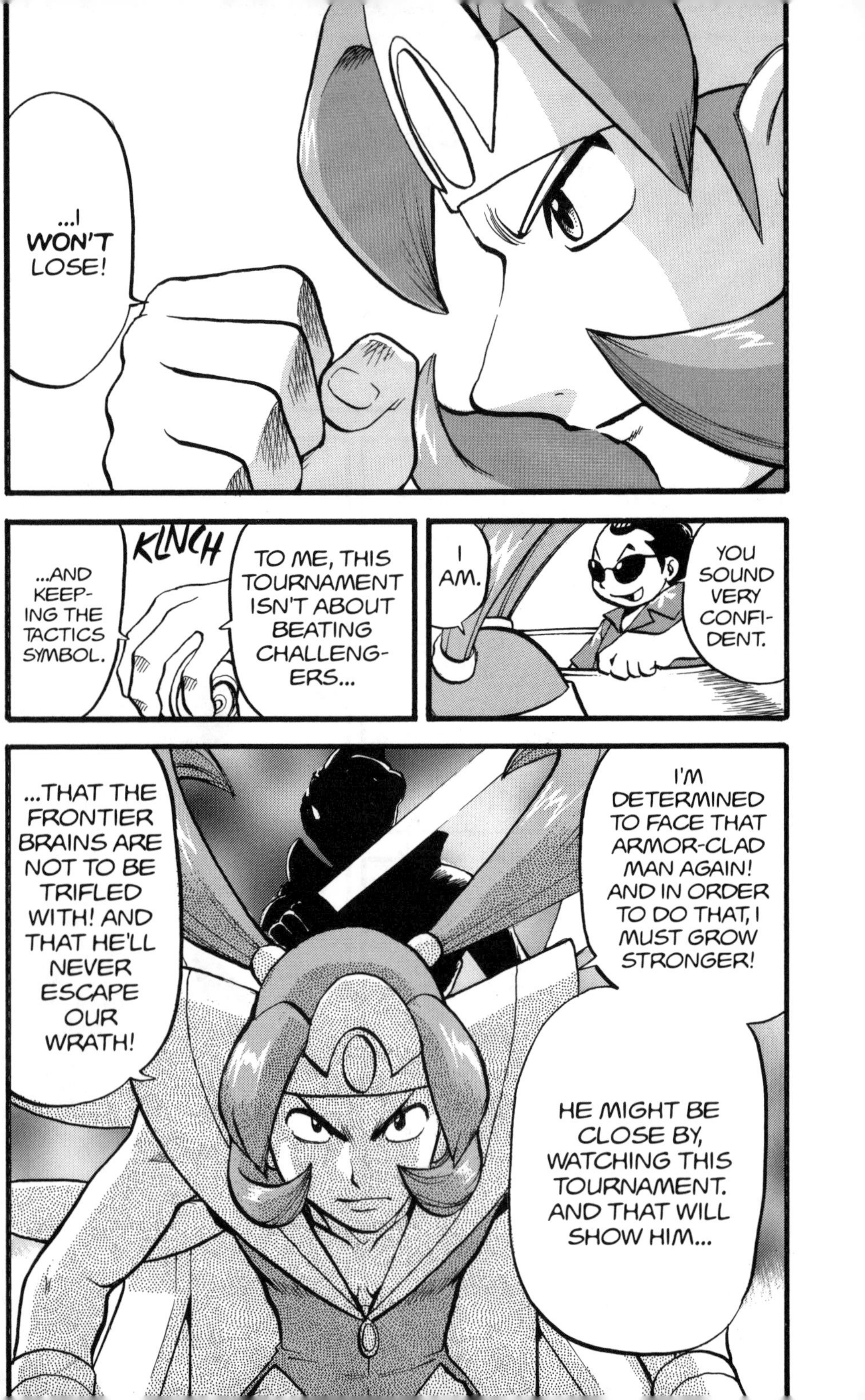

...I WON'T LOSE!
YOU SOUND VERY CONFIDENT.
I AM.
TO ME, THIS TOURNAMENT ISN'T ABOUT BEATING CHALLENGERS...
KLNCH
...AND KEEPING THE TACTICS SYMBOL.
I'M DETERMINED TO FACE THAT ARMOR-CLAD MAN AGAIN! AND IN ORDER TO DO THAT, I MUST GROW STRONGER!
HE MIGHT BE CLOSE BY, WATCHING THIS TOURNAMENT. AND THAT WILL SHOW HIM...
...THAT THE FRONTIER BRAINS ARE NOT TO BE TRIFLED WITH! AND THAT HE'LL NEVER ESCAPE OUR WRATH!

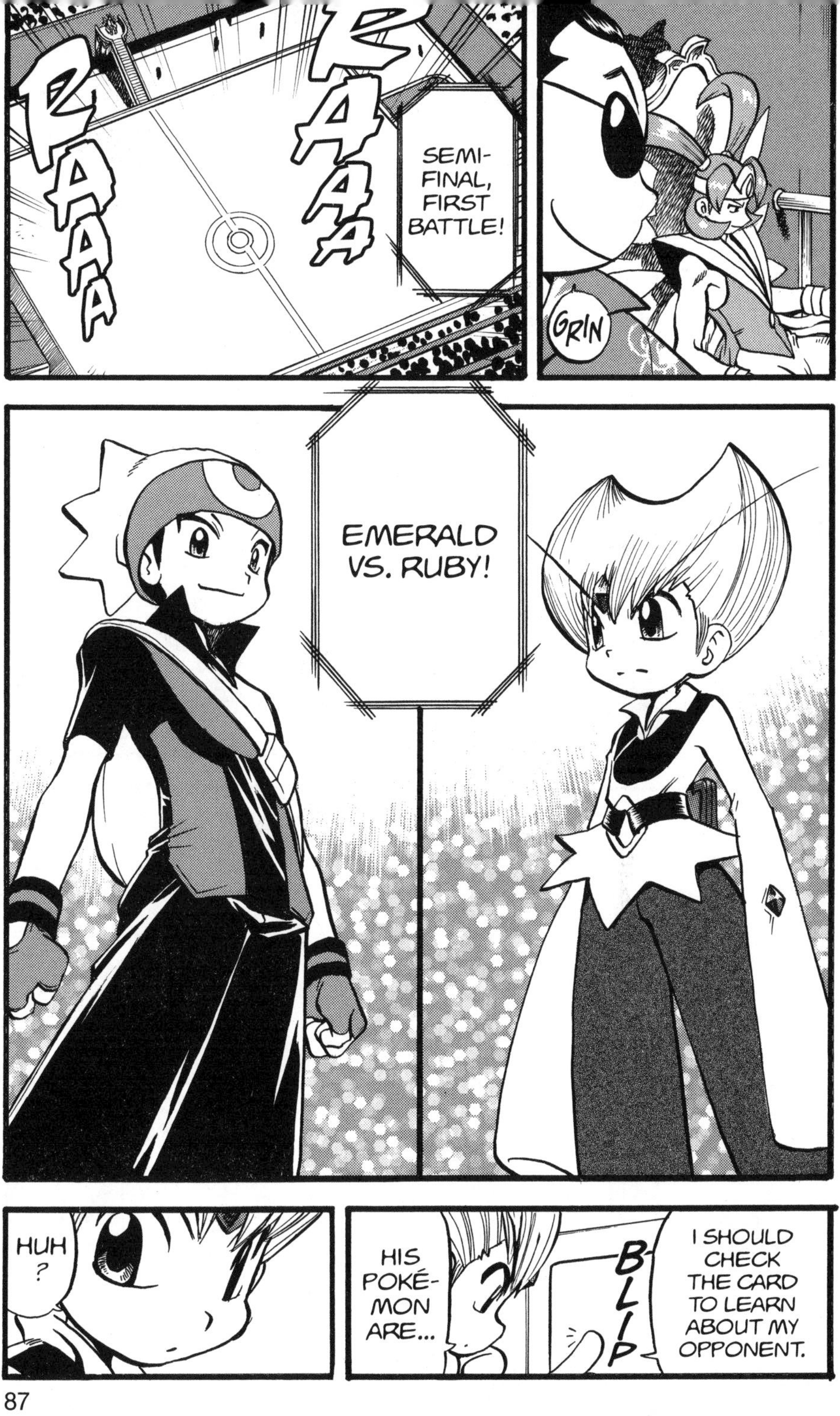
GRIN
RAAAA
SEMI-FINAL, FIRST BATTLE!
RAAAAA
EMERALD VS. RUBY!
I SHOULD CHECK THE CARD TO LEARN ABOUT MY OPPONENT.
BLIP
HIS POKÉMON ARE...
HUH?

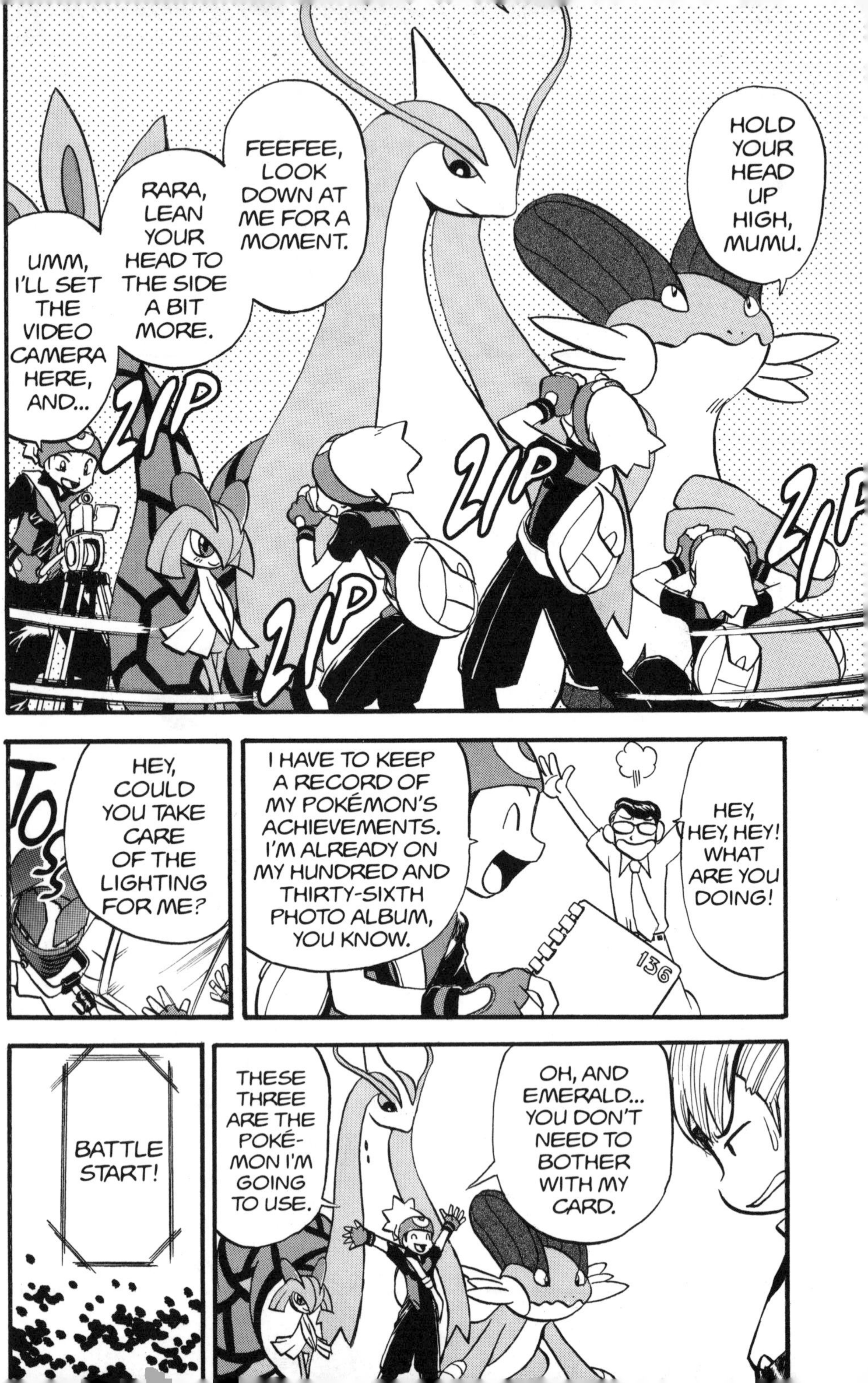
HOLD YOUR HEAD UP HIGH, MUMU.
FEEFEE, LOOK DOWN AT ME FOR A MOMENT.
RARA, LEAN YOUR HEAD TO THE SIDE A BIT MORE.
UMM, I'LL SET THE VIDEO CAMERA HERE, AND...
ZIP
ZIP
ZIP
ZIP
HEY, HEY, HEY! WHAT ARE YOU DOING!
I HAVE TO KEEP A RECORD OF MY POKÉMON'S ACHIEVEMENTS. I'M ALREADY ON MY HUNDRED AND THIRTY-SIXTH PHOTO ALBUM, YOU KNOW.
136
HEY, COULD YOU TAKE CARE OF THE LIGHTING FOR ME?
TOSS
OH, AND EMERALD... YOU DON'T NEED TO BOTHER WITH MY CARD.
THESE THREE ARE THE POKÉMON I'M GOING TO USE.
BATTLE START!

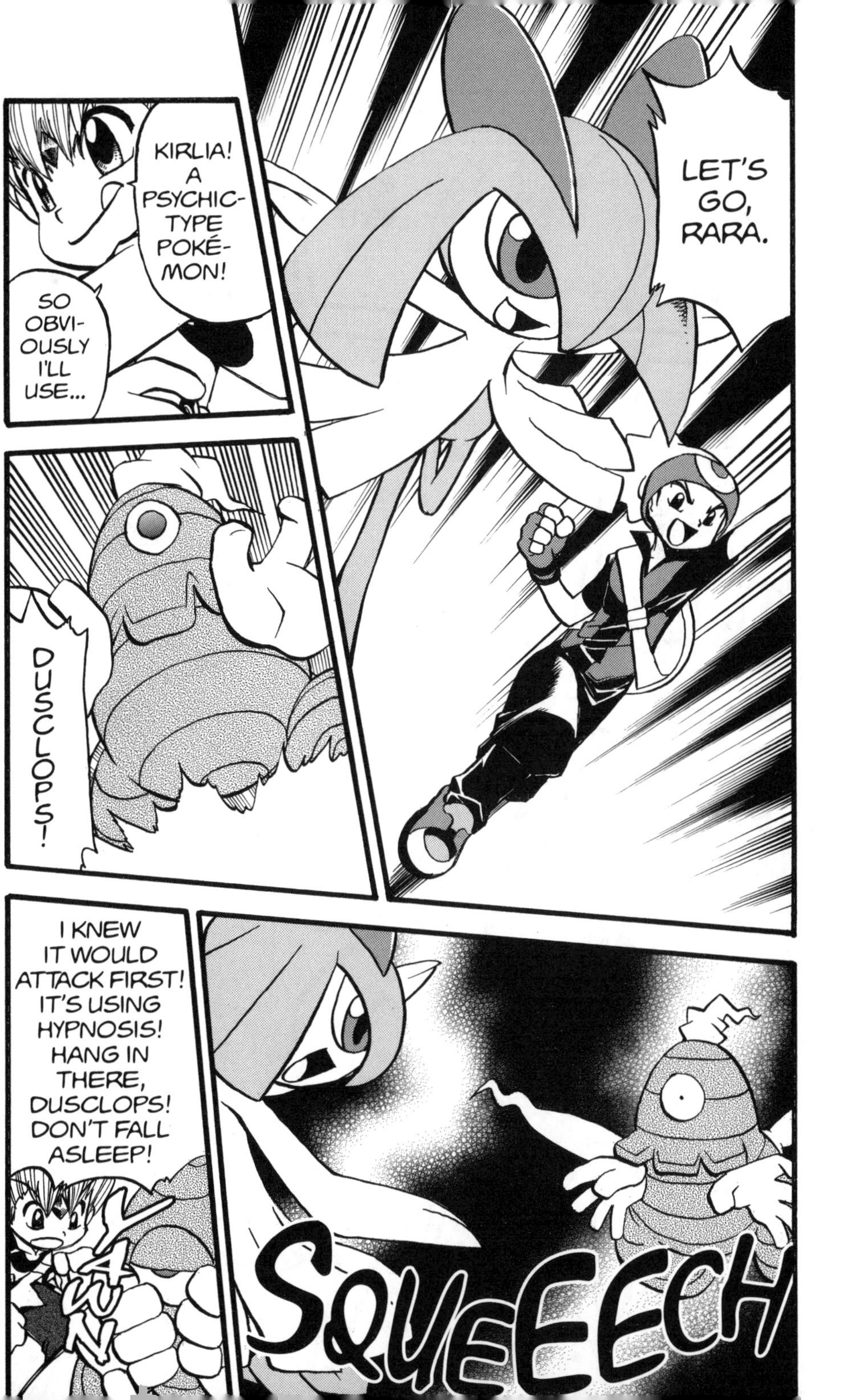
LET'S GO, RARA.
KIRLIA! A PSYCHIC-TYPE POKÉMON!
SO OBVIOUSLY I'LL USE...
DUSCLOPS!
SQUEEECH
I KNEW IT WOULD ATTACK FIRST! IT'S USING HYPNOSIS! HANG IN THERE, DUSCLOPS! DON'T FALL ASLEEP!

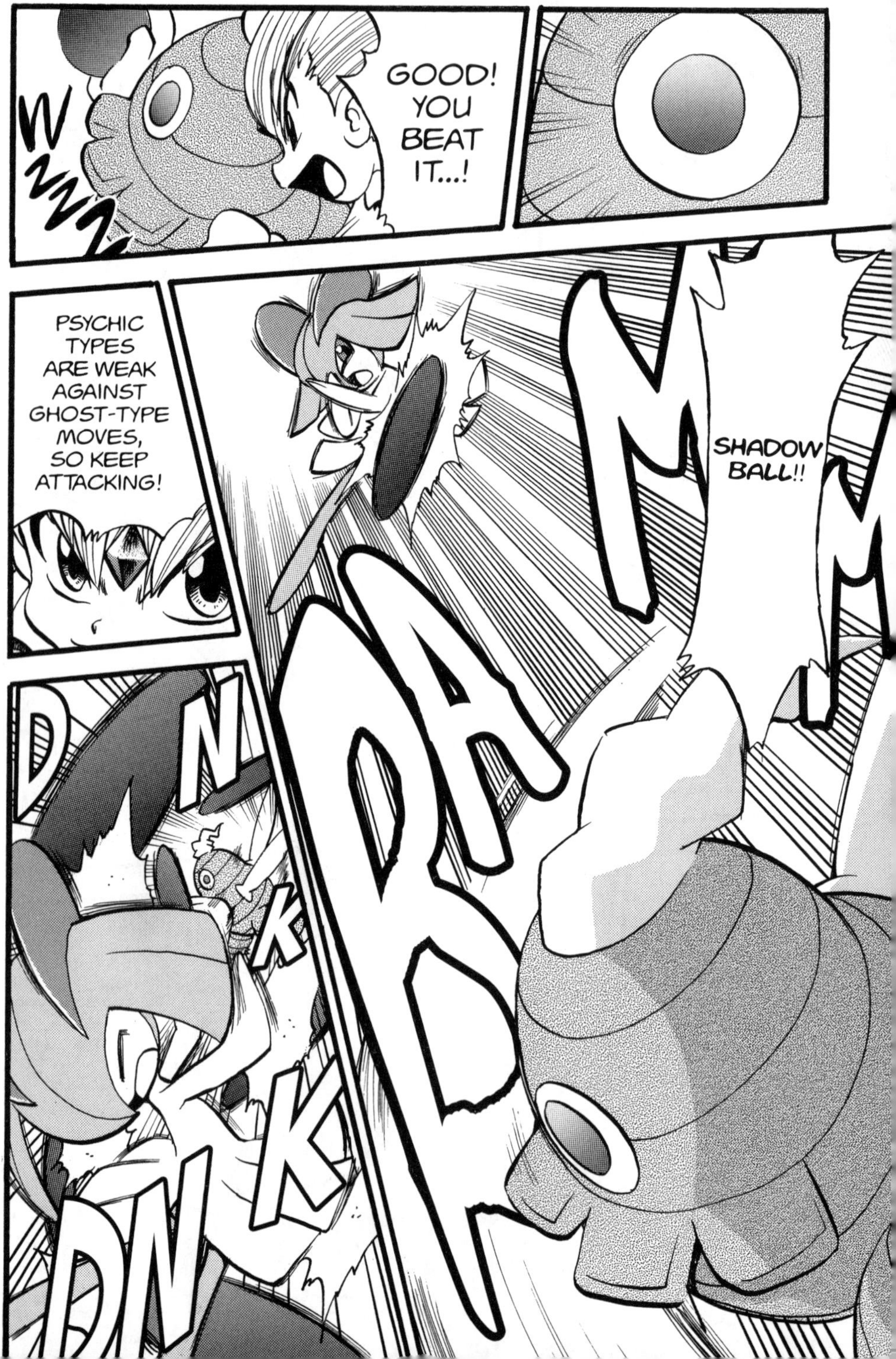
GOOD! YOU BEAT IT...!
SHADOW BALL!!
PSYCHIC TYPES ARE WEAK AGAINST GHOST-TYPE MOVES, SO KEEP ATTACKING!

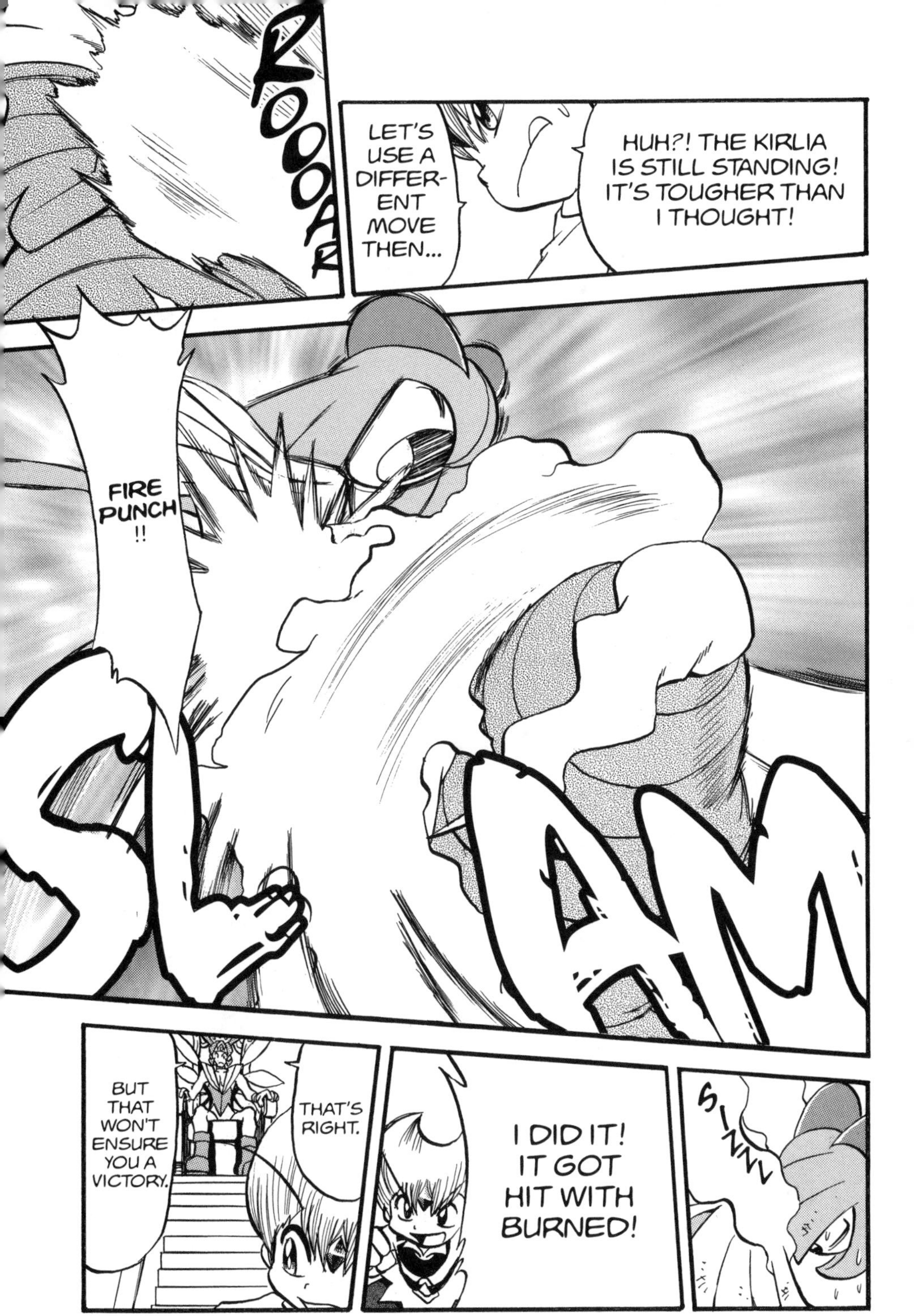
HUH?! THE KIRLIA IS STILL STANDING! IT'S TOUGHER THAN I THOUGHT!
LET'S USE A DIFFER-ENT MOVE THEN...
ROOOARR
FIRE PUNCH !!
SLAM
SIZZL
I DID IT! IT GOT HIT WITH BURNED!
THAT'S RIGHT.
BUT THAT WON'T ENSURE YOU A VICTORY.

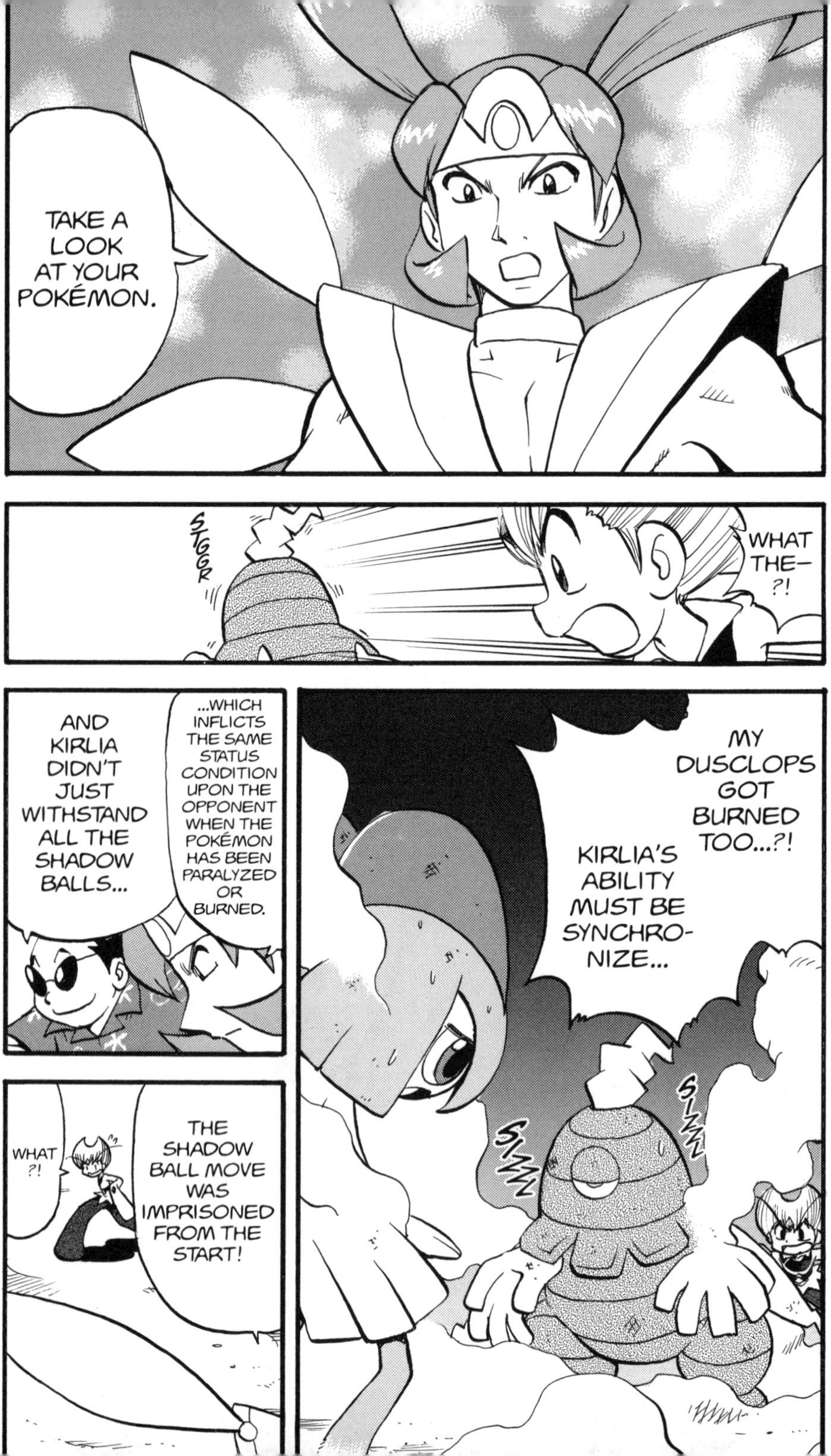
TAKE A LOOK AT YOUR POKÉMON.
WHAT THE—?!
STGGR
MY DUSCLOPS GOT BURNED TOO...?!
KIRLIA'S ABILITY MUST BE SYNCHRO-NIZE...
SIZZ
SIZZ
...WHICH INFLICTS THE SAME STATUS CONDITION UPON THE OPPONENT WHEN THE POKÉMON HAS BEEN PARALYZED OR BURNED.
AND KIRLIA DIDN'T JUST WITHSTAND ALL THE SHADOW BALLS...
THE SHADOW BALL MOVE WAS IMPRISONED FROM THE START!
WHAT ?!

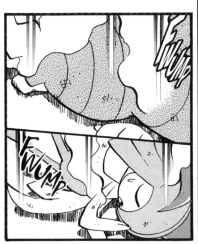

THAT MEANS ALL THOSE ATTACKS WERE MEANINGLESS!

WOOO

A DOUBLE KNOCKOUT!

RAAA

GRIN

HMM... YOU **ARE** STRONG, AREN'T YOU...?

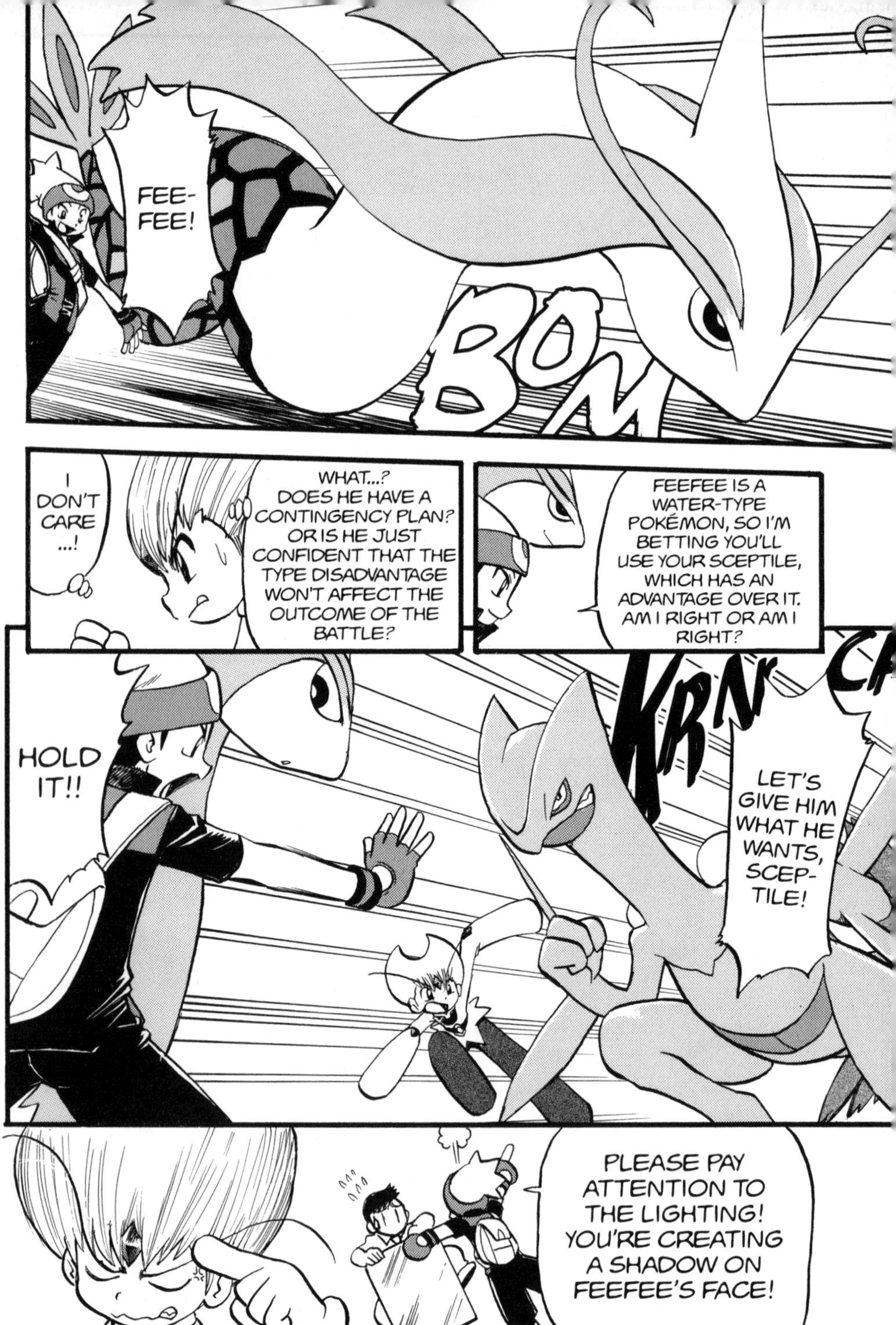
FEE-FEE!
BOM
FEEFEE IS A WATER-TYPE POKÉMON, SO I'M BETTING YOU'LL USE YOUR SCEPTILE, WHICH HAS AN ADVANTAGE OVER IT. AM I RIGHT OR AM I RIGHT?
WHAT...? DOES HE HAVE A CONTINGENCY PLAN? OR IS HE JUST CONFIDENT THAT THE TYPE DISADVANTAGE WON'T AFFECT THE OUTCOME OF THE BATTLE?
I DON'T CARE ...!
KRNK
CR
LET'S GIVE HIM WHAT HE WANTS, SCEP-TILE!
HOLD IT!!
PLEASE PAY ATTENTION TO THE LIGHTING! YOU'RE CREATING A SHADOW ON FEEFEE'S FACE!

DEAR MEMBERS OF THE PRESS...

Thank you for visiting the Battle Frontier today. Permit me to continue explaining the rules of this facility...

OWNER: SCOTT

FACILITY RULES

BATTLE PALACE 2

■ **TRAINER EXPERIENCE AT THE BATTLE PALACE** ■

At the Battle Palace, Trainers must permit their Pokémon to fight as they wish. However, the Trainers are allowed to make the following moves.

① Watch
After entering the battle area, the Trainer places their Poké Balls with their Pokémon inside in the battle area and moves over to the spectator circle. After that, the Trainers are not allowed to give any orders, but they may watch the battle all the way through.

② Switch
Trainers are not allowed to give orders to their Pokémon, but they may switch out their Pokémon during battle. If a Trainer wishes to switch their Pokémon due to a type disadvantage or status condition, they may request a change through the microphone located in their spectator's seat.

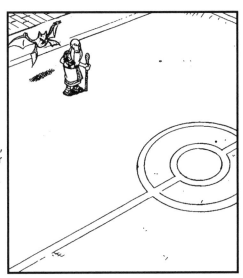

322

Susceptible to Sceptile

●● K B ● G L

POKÉMON ADVENTURES·THE SIXTH CHAPTER·EMERALD

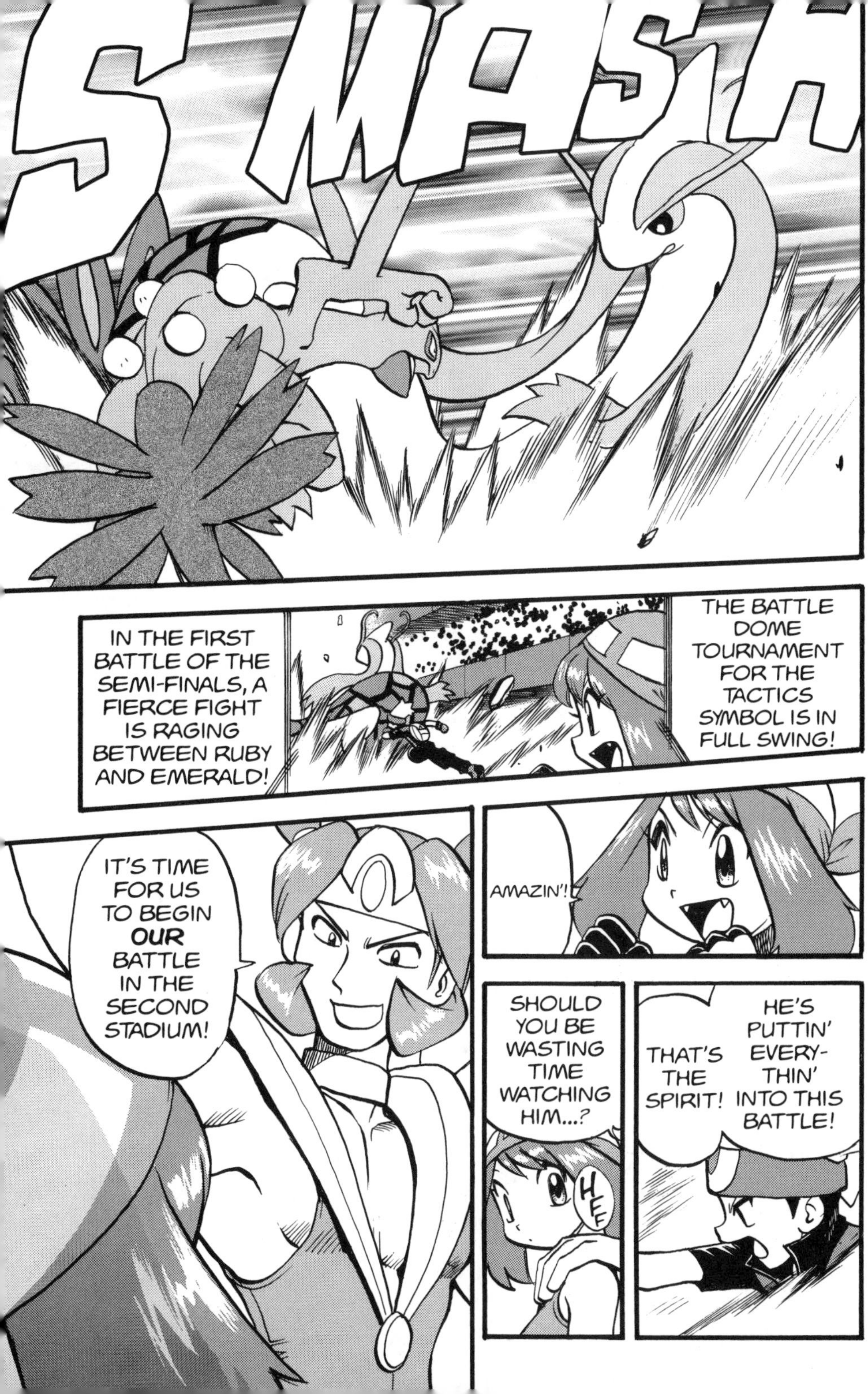
SMASH
THE BATTLE DOME TOURNAMENT FOR THE TACTICS SYMBOL IS IN FULL SWING!
IN THE FIRST BATTLE OF THE SEMI-FINALS, A FIERCE FIGHT IS RAGING BETWEEN RUBY AND EMERALD!
AMAZIN'!
HE'S PUTTIN' EVERY-THIN' INTO THIS BATTLE!
THAT'S THE SPIRIT!
SHOULD YOU BE WASTING TIME WATCHING HIM...?
HFF
IT'S TIME FOR US TO BEGIN **OUR** BATTLE IN THE SECOND STADIUM!

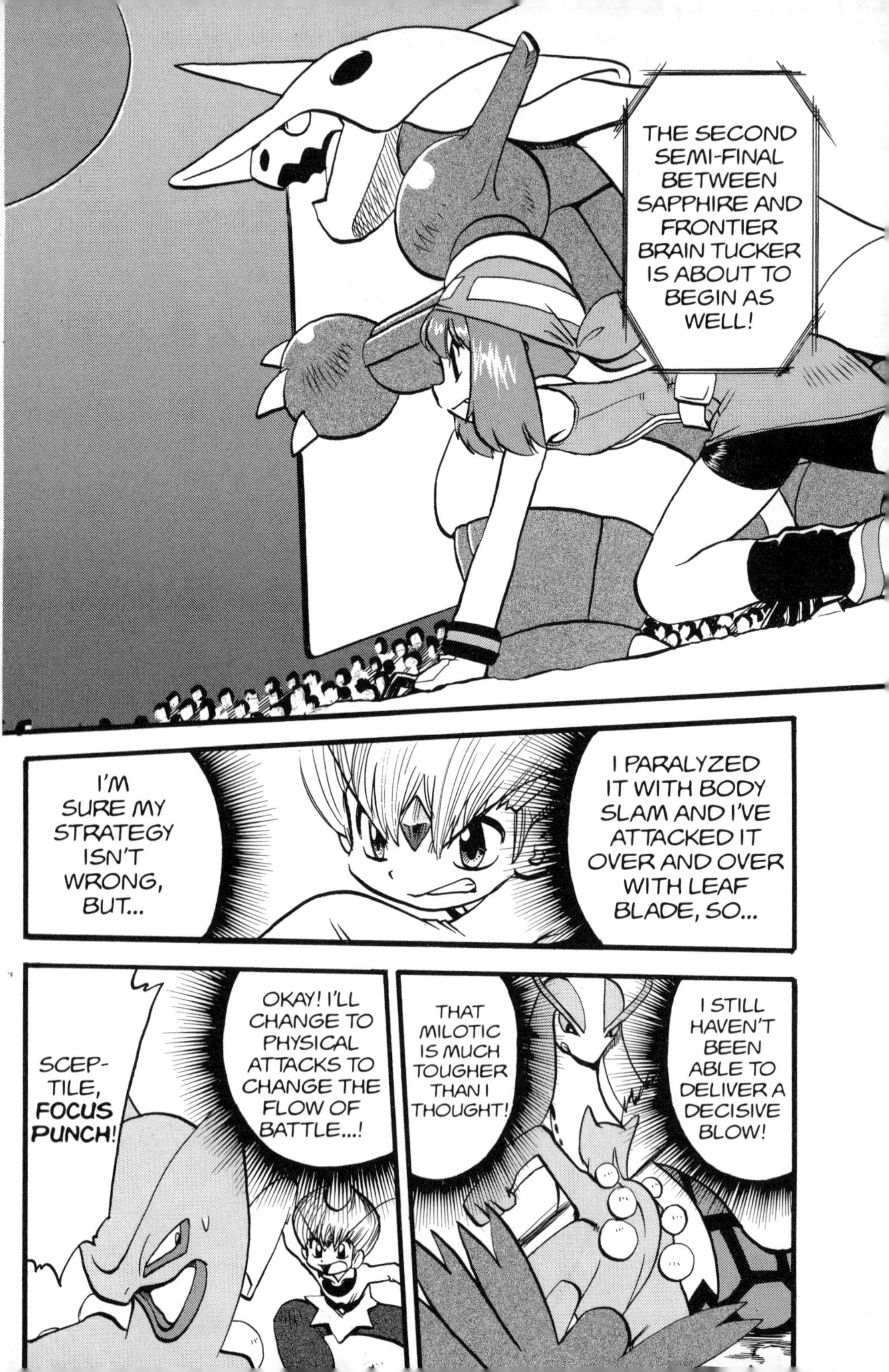
THE SECOND SEMI-FINAL BETWEEN SAPPHIRE AND FRONTIER BRAIN TUCKER IS ABOUT TO BEGIN AS WELL!
I PARALYZED IT WITH BODY SLAM AND I'VE ATTACKED IT OVER AND OVER WITH LEAF BLADE, SO...
I'M SURE MY STRATEGY ISN'T WRONG, BUT...
I STILL HAVEN'T BEEN ABLE TO DELIVER A DECISIVE BLOW!
THAT MILOTIC IS MUCH TOUGHER THAN I THOUGHT!
OKAY! I'LL CHANGE TO PHYSICAL ATTACKS TO CHANGE THE FLOW OF BATTLE...!
SCEP-TILE, **FOCUS PUNCH!**

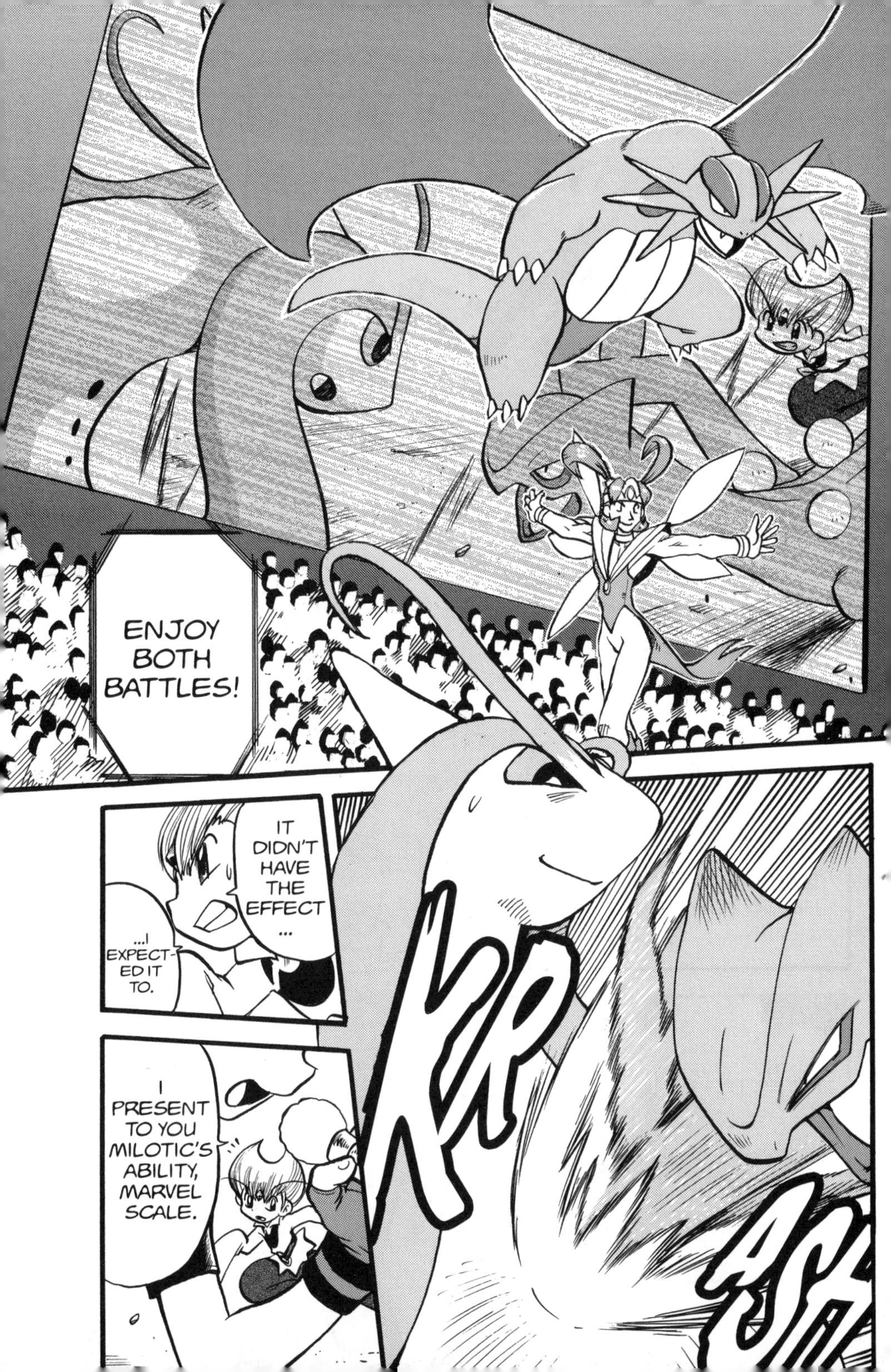
ENJOY BOTH BATTLES!
IT DIDN'T HAVE THE EFFECT...
...I EXPECTED IT TO.
I PRESENT TO YOU MILOTIC'S ABILITY, MARVEL SCALE.

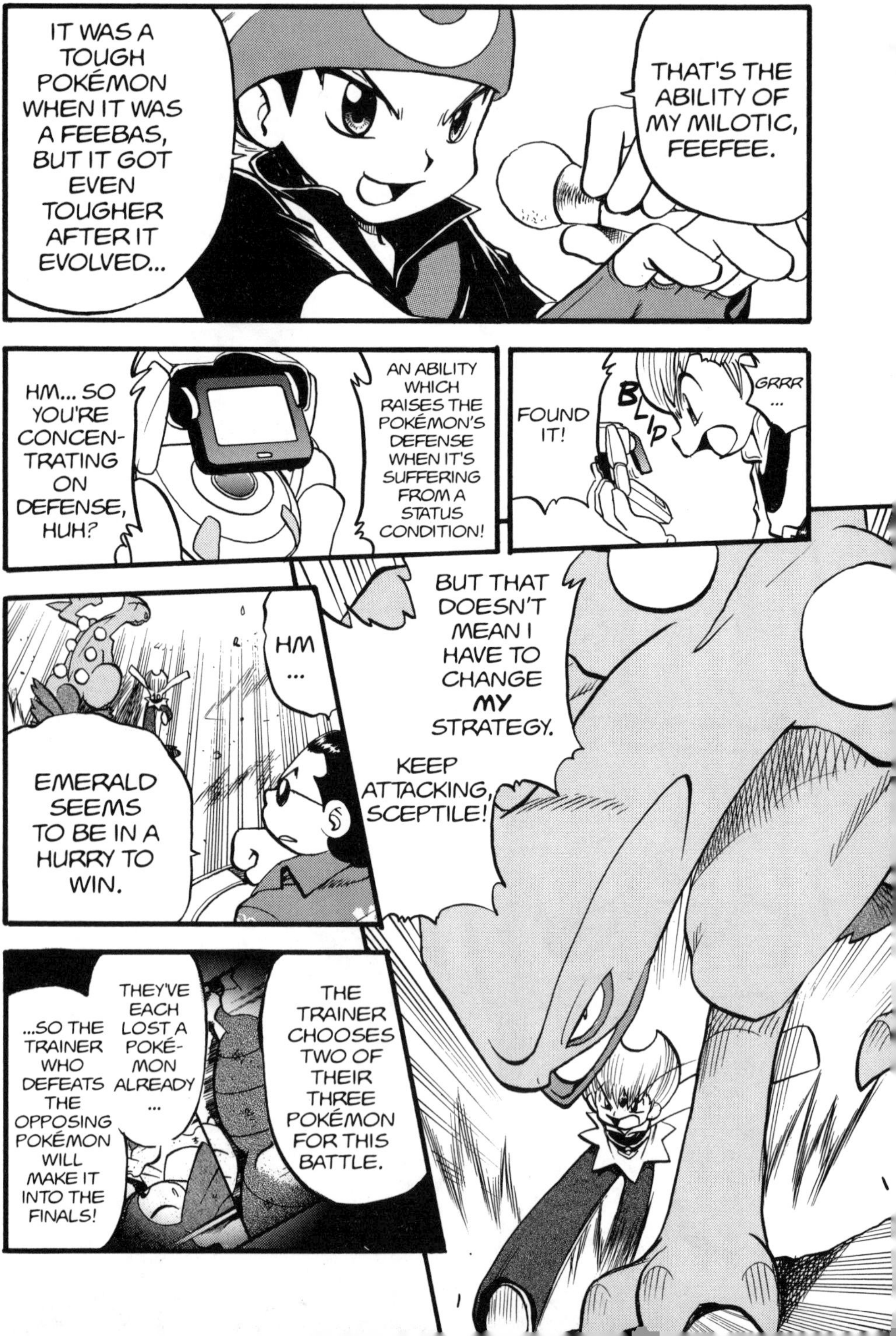
THAT'S THE ABILITY OF MY MILOTIC, FEEFEE.
IT WAS A TOUGH POKÉMON WHEN IT WAS A FEEBAS, BUT IT GOT EVEN TOUGHER AFTER IT EVOLVED...
GRRR...
BLIP
FOUND IT!
AN ABILITY WHICH RAISES THE POKÉMON'S DEFENSE WHEN IT'S SUFFERING FROM A STATUS CONDITION!
HM... SO YOU'RE CONCEN-TRATING ON DEFENSE, HUH?
BUT THAT DOESN'T MEAN I HAVE TO CHANGE **MY** STRATEGY.
KEEP ATTACKING, SCEPTILE!
HM...
EMERALD SEEMS TO BE IN A HURRY TO WIN.
THE TRAINER CHOOSES TWO OF THEIR THREE POKÉMON FOR THIS BATTLE.
THEY'VE EACH LOST A POKÉ-MON ALREADY...
...SO THE TRAINER WHO DEFEATS THE OPPOSING POKÉMON WILL MAKE IT INTO THE FINALS!

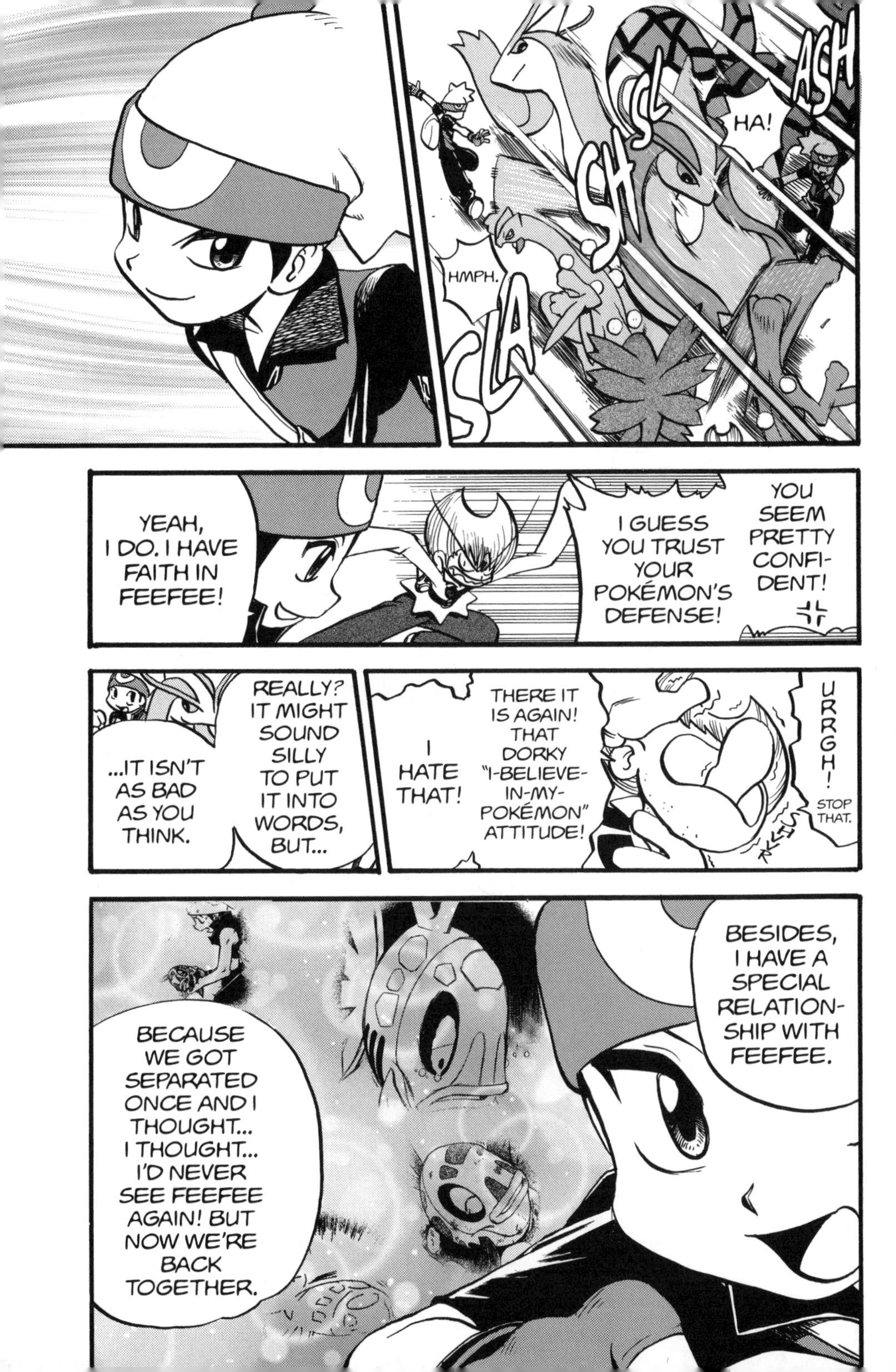
ASH
HA!
SHSL
HMPH.
SLA
YOU SEEM PRETTY CONFIDENT!
I GUESS YOU TRUST YOUR POKÉMON'S DEFENSE!
YEAH, I DO. I HAVE FAITH IN FEEFEE!
URRGH!
STOP THAT.
THERE IT IS AGAIN! THAT DORKY "I-BELIEVE-IN-MY-POKÉMON" ATTITUDE!
I HATE THAT!
REALLY? IT MIGHT SOUND SILLY TO PUT IT INTO WORDS, BUT...
...IT ISN'T AS BAD AS YOU THINK.
BESIDES, I HAVE A SPECIAL RELATIONSHIP WITH FEEFEE.
BECAUSE WE GOT SEPARATED ONCE AND I THOUGHT... I THOUGHT... I'D NEVER SEE FEEFEE AGAIN! BUT NOW WE'RE BACK TOGETHER.

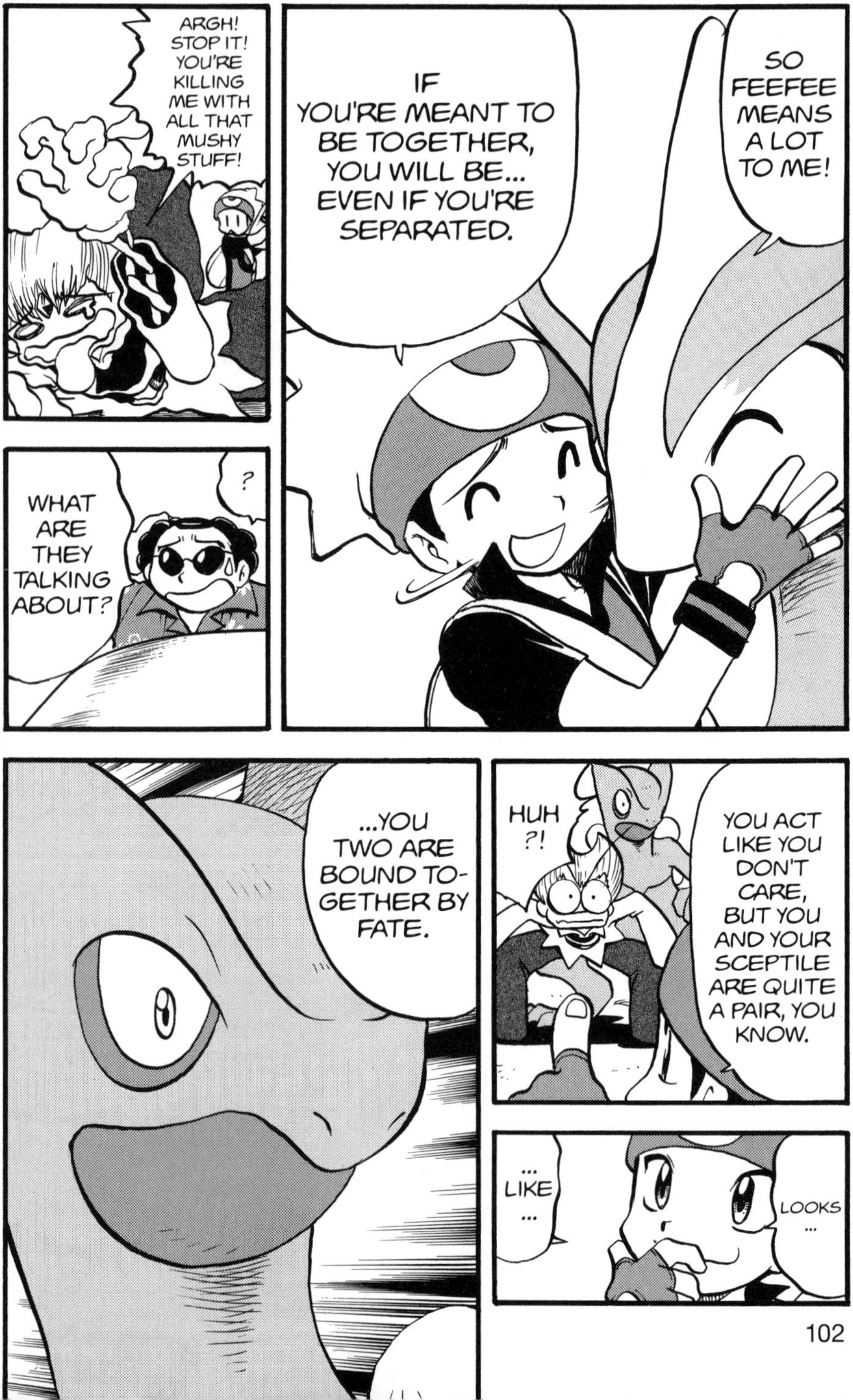
SO FEEFEE MEANS A LOT TO ME!
IF YOU'RE MEANT TO BE TOGETHER, YOU WILL BE... EVEN IF YOU'RE SEPARATED.
ARGH! STOP IT! YOU'RE KILLING ME WITH ALL THAT MUSHY STUFF!
?
WHAT ARE THEY TALKING ABOUT?
YOU ACT LIKE YOU DON'T CARE, BUT YOU AND YOUR SCEPTILE ARE QUITE A PAIR, YOU KNOW.
HUH ?!
LOOKS ...
... LIKE ...
...YOU TWO ARE BOUND TO-GETHER BY FATE.

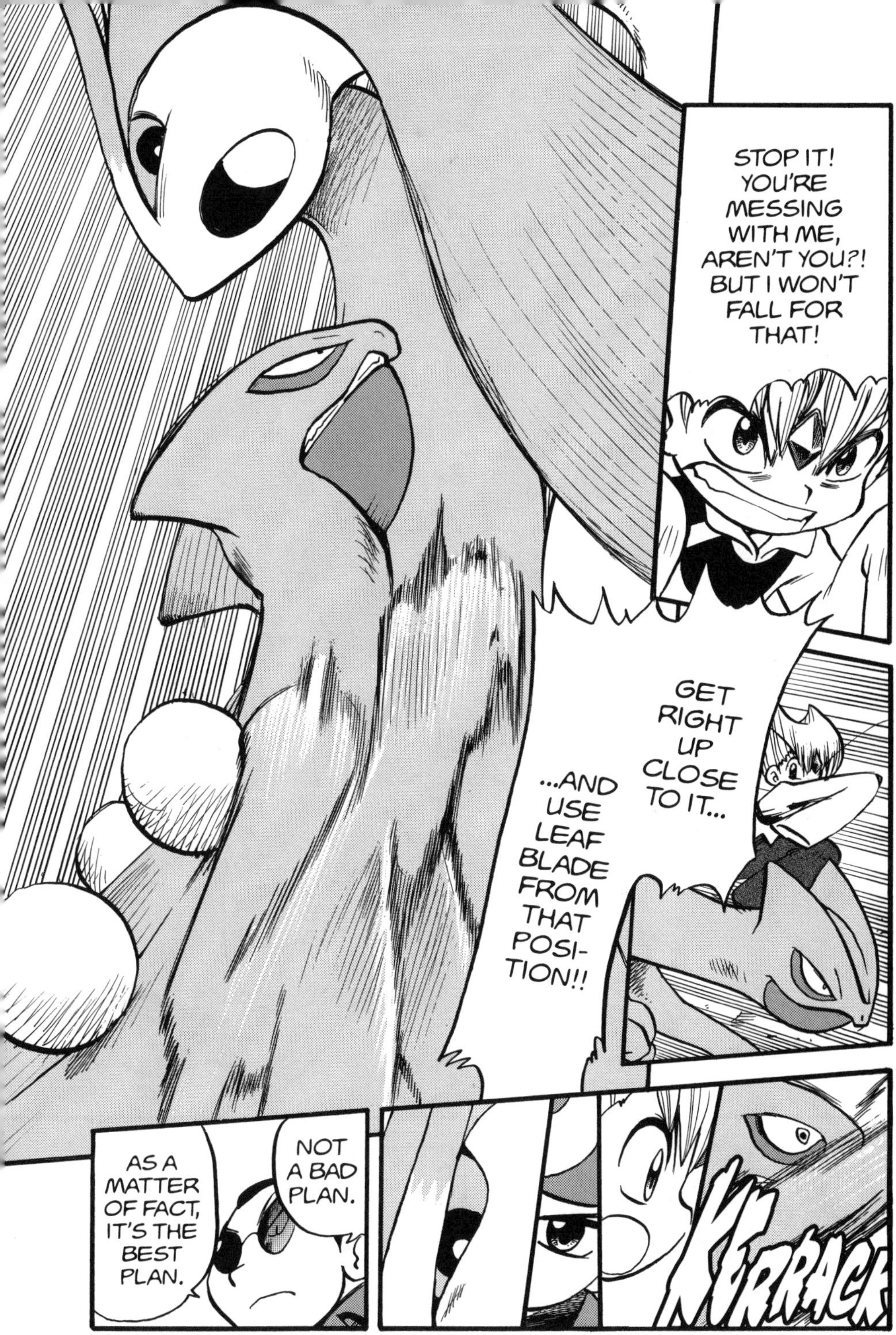
STOP IT! YOU'RE MESSING WITH ME, AREN'T YOU?! BUT I WON'T FALL FOR THAT!
GET RIGHT UP CLOSE TO IT...
...AND USE LEAF BLADE FROM THAT POSI-TION!!
KRRACK
NOT A BAD PLAN.
AS A MATTER OF FACT, IT'S THE BEST PLAN.

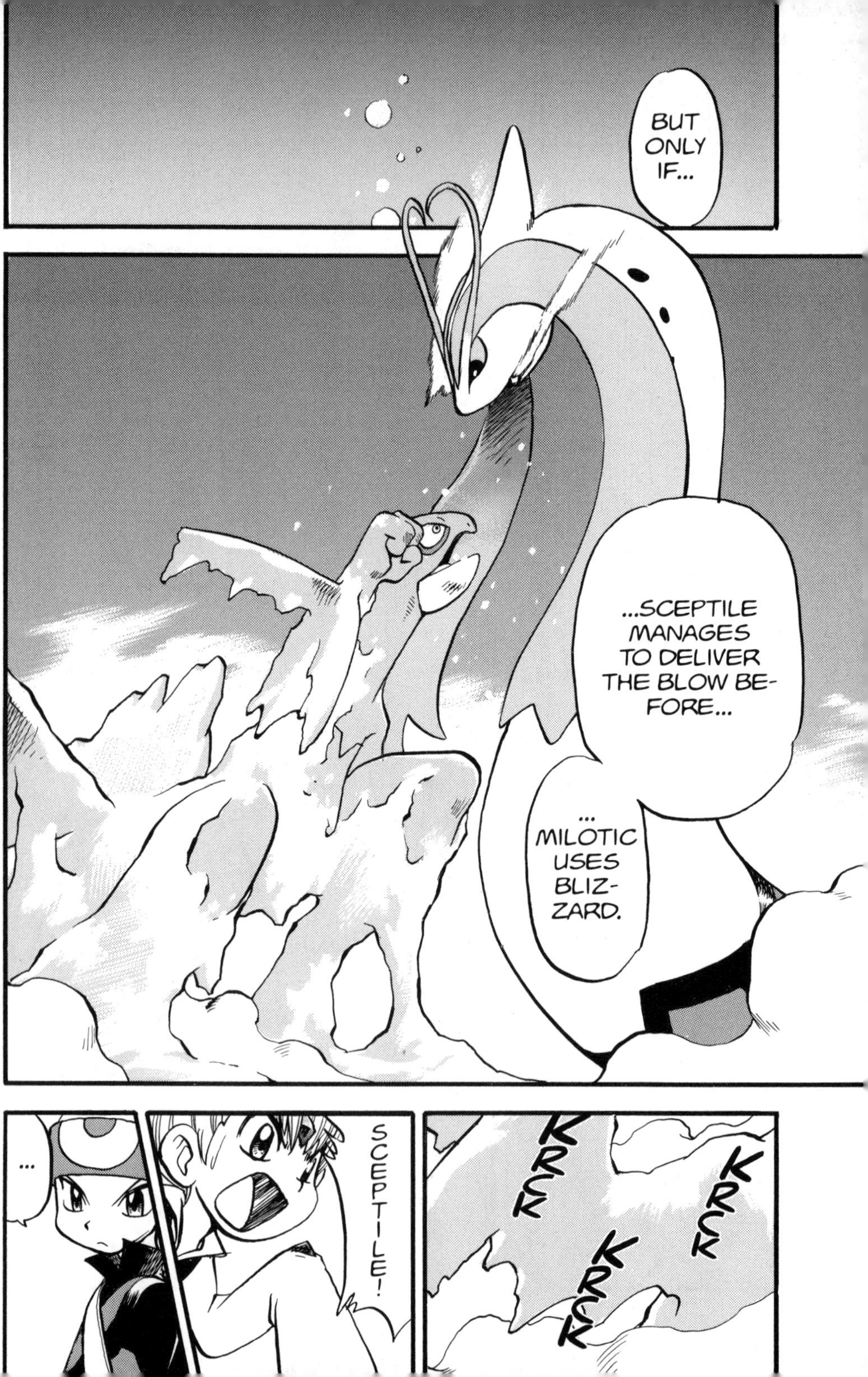
BUT ONLY IF...
...SCEPTILE MANAGES TO DELIVER THE BLOW BE-FORE...
...MILOTIC USES BLIZ-ZARD.
KRCK
KRCK
KRCK
KRCK
SCEPTILE!
...

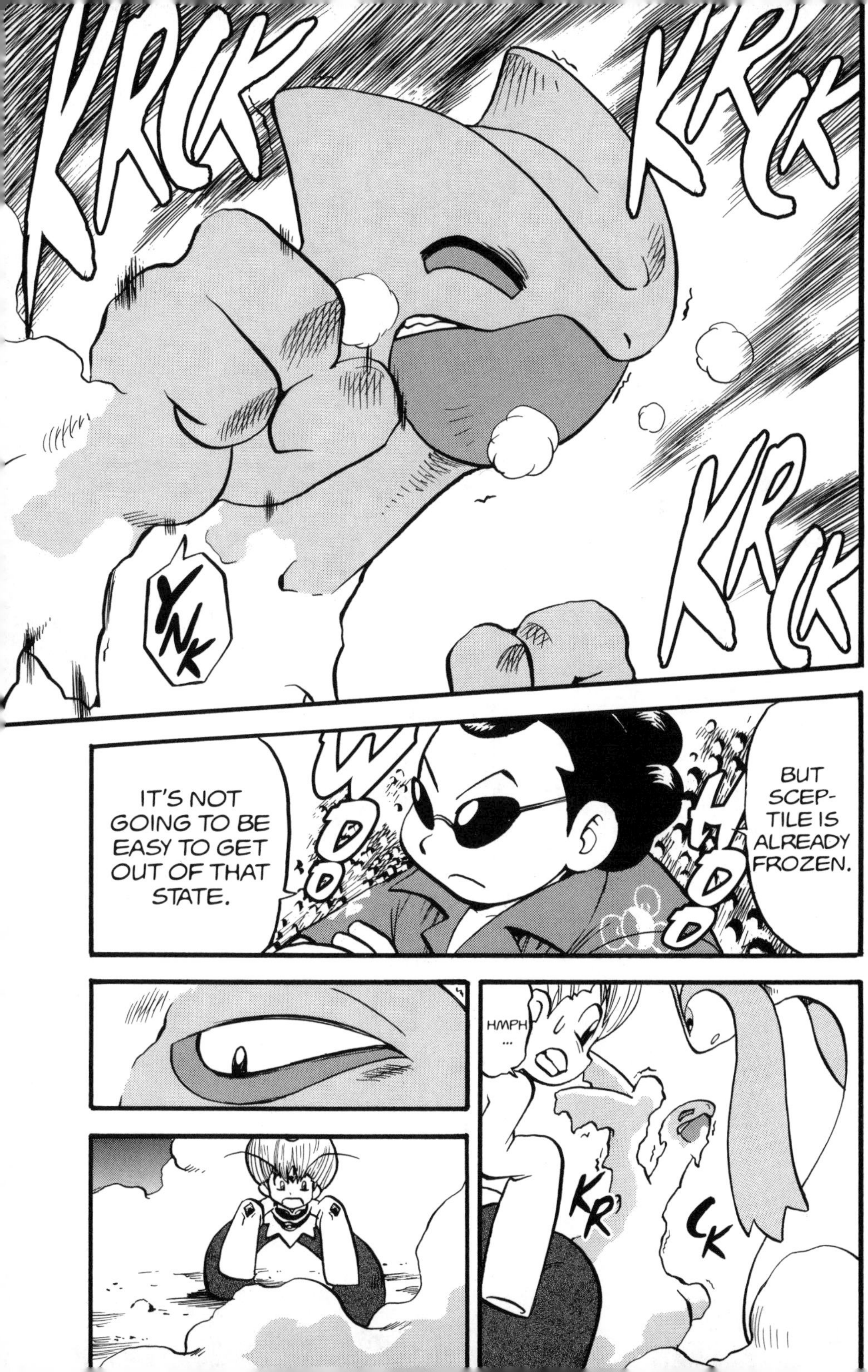

KRCK
KRCK
KRCK
YANK
BUT SCEP-
TILE IS
ALREADY
FROZEN.
IT'S NOT
GOING TO BE
EASY TO GET
OUT OF THAT
STATE.
HMPH
...
KR
CK

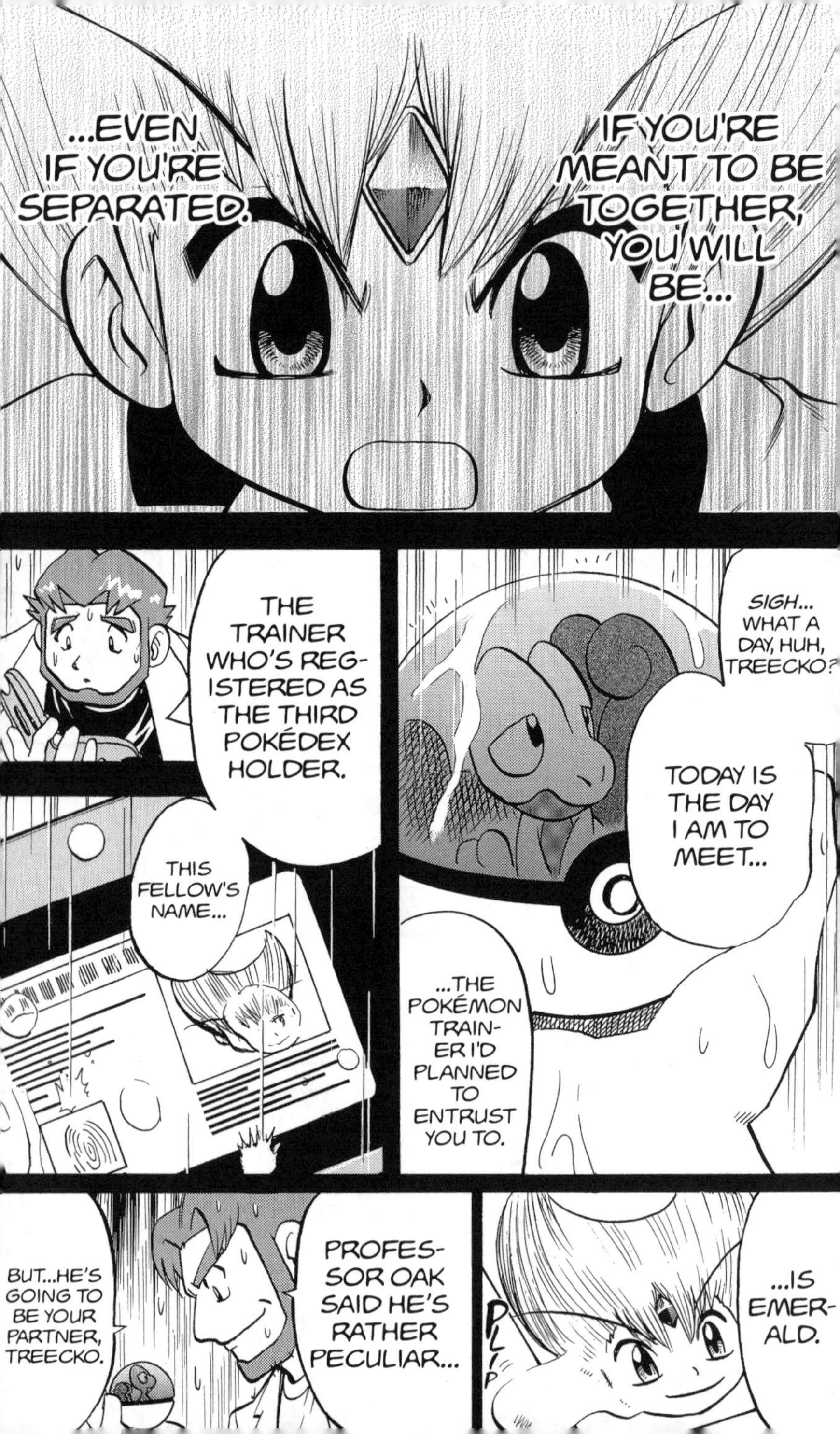
IF YOU'RE MEANT TO BE TOGETHER, YOU WILL BE...
...EVEN IF YOU'RE SEPARATED.
SIGH... WHAT A DAY, HUH, TREECKO?
TODAY IS THE DAY I AM TO MEET...
...THE POKÉMON TRAINER I'D PLANNED TO ENTRUST YOU TO.
THE TRAINER WHO'S REGISTERED AS THE THIRD POKÉDEX HOLDER.
THIS FELLOW'S NAME...
...IS EMERALD.
PLIP
PROFESSOR OAK SAID HE'S RATHER PECULIAR...
BUT...HE'S GOING TO BE YOUR PARTNER, TREECKO.

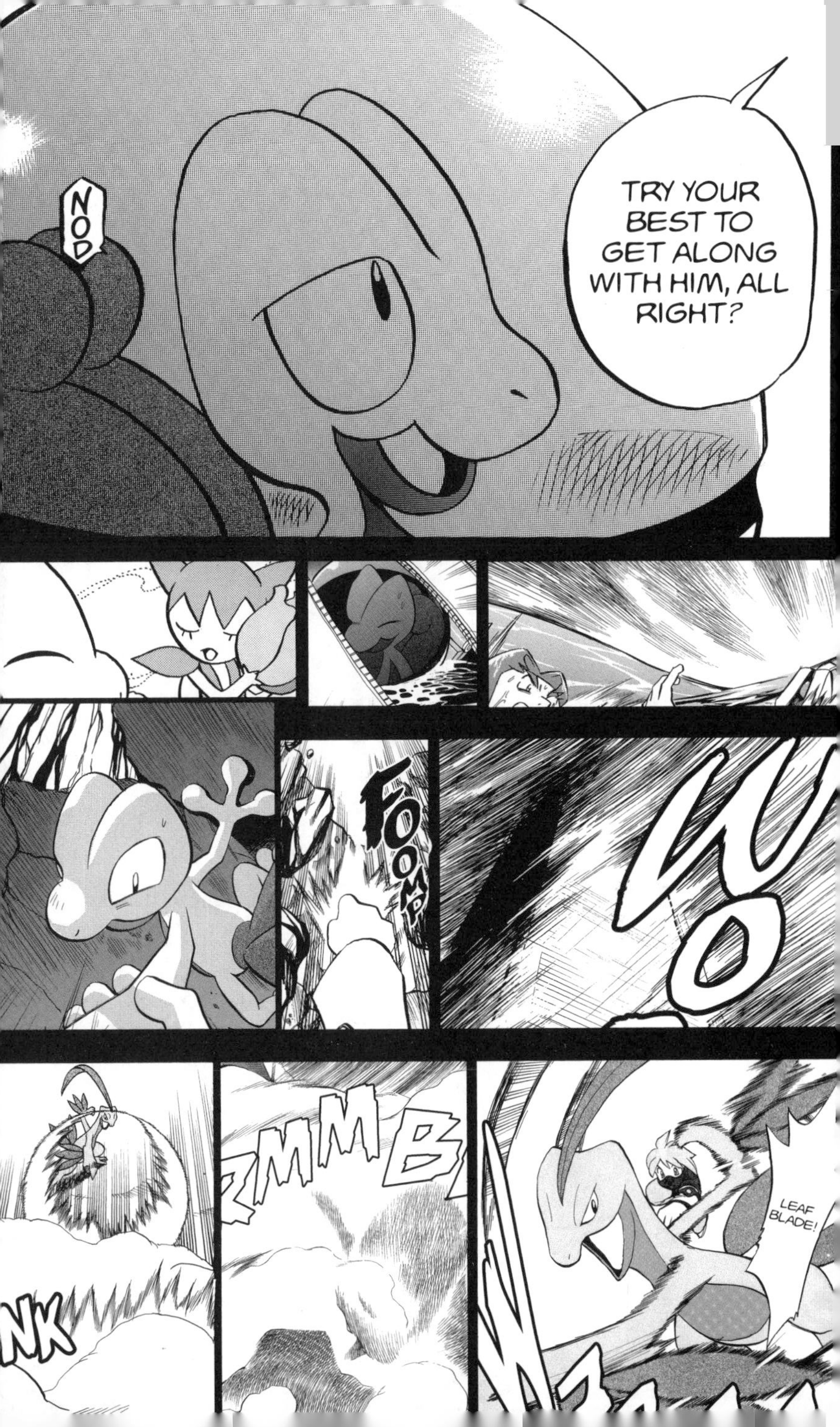
TRY YOUR BEST TO GET ALONG WITH HIM, ALL RIGHT?
NOD
FOOMP
LEAF BLADE!

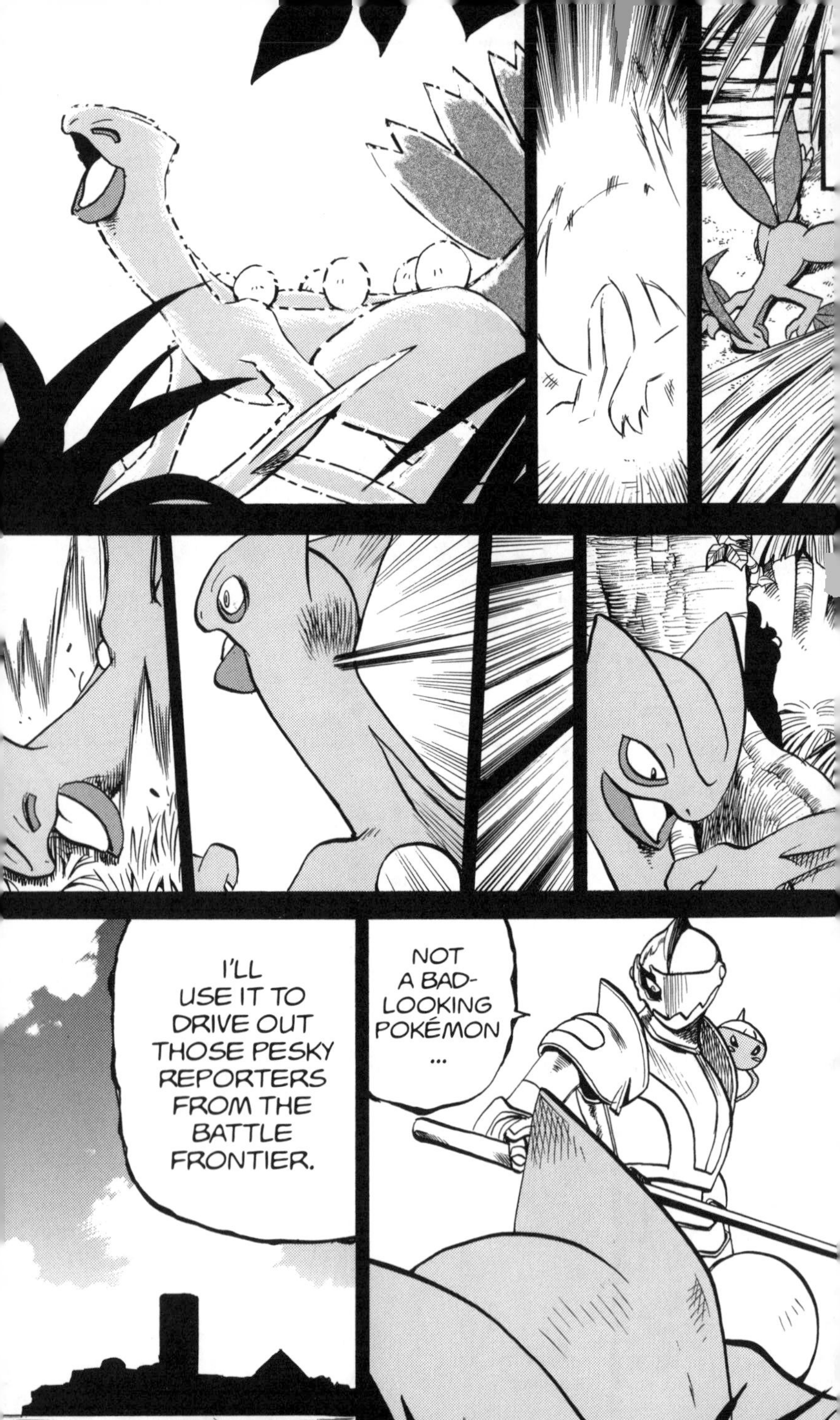
NOT A BAD-LOOKING POKÉMON ...
I'LL USE IT TO DRIVE OUT THOSE PESKY REPORTERS FROM THE BATTLE FRONTIER.

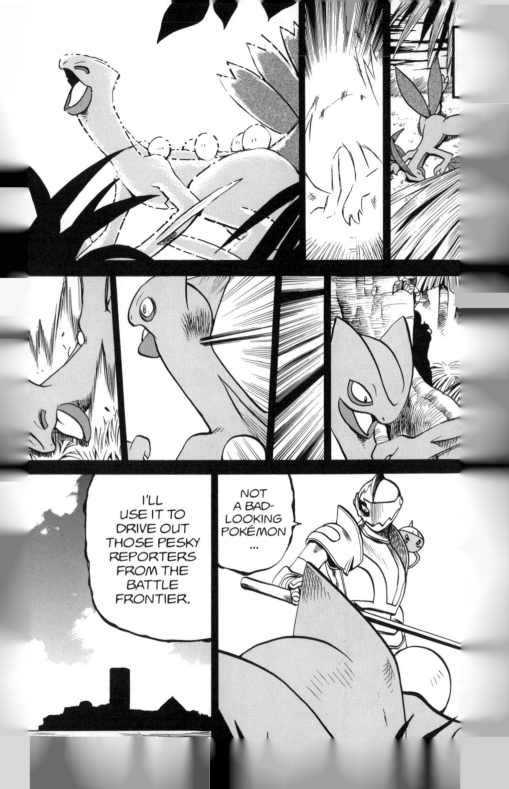

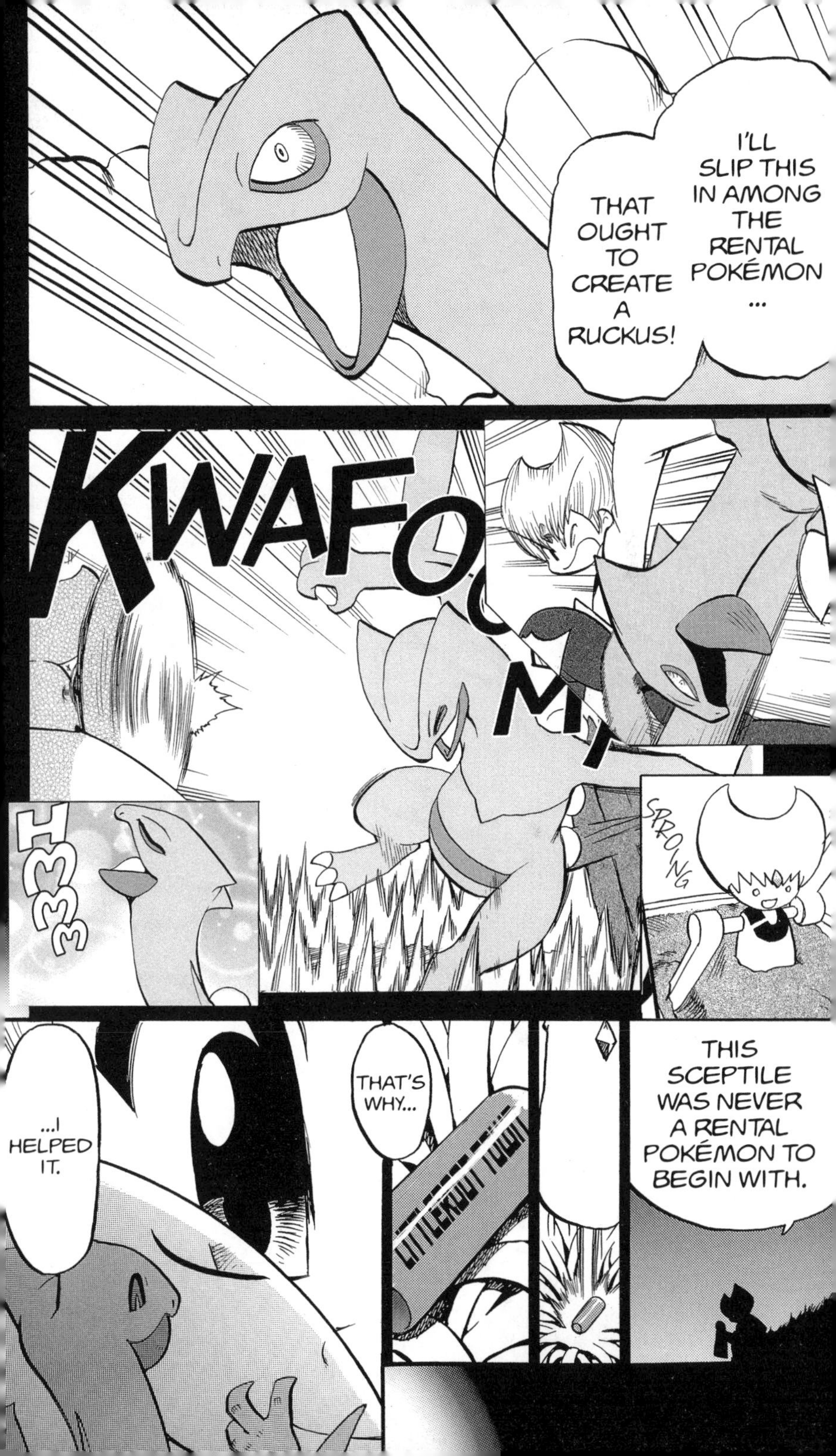
I'LL SLIP THIS IN AMONG THE RENTAL POKÉMON...
THAT OUGHT TO CREATE A RUCKUS!
KWAFOOMP
SPROING
HMMMM
THIS SCEPTILE WAS NEVER A RENTAL POKÉMON TO BEGIN WITH.
THAT'S WHY...
...I HELPED IT.

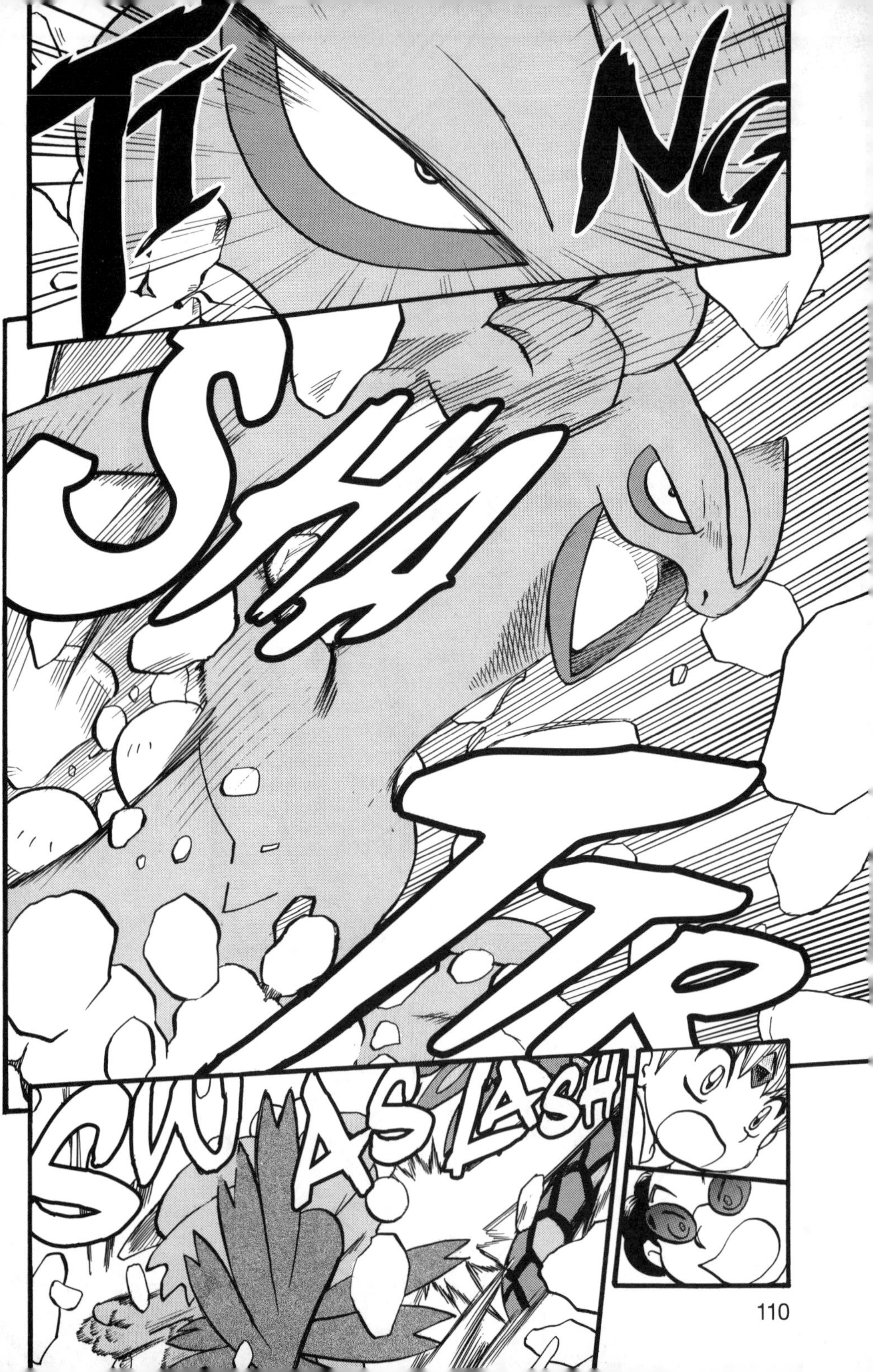
TING
SWASLASH

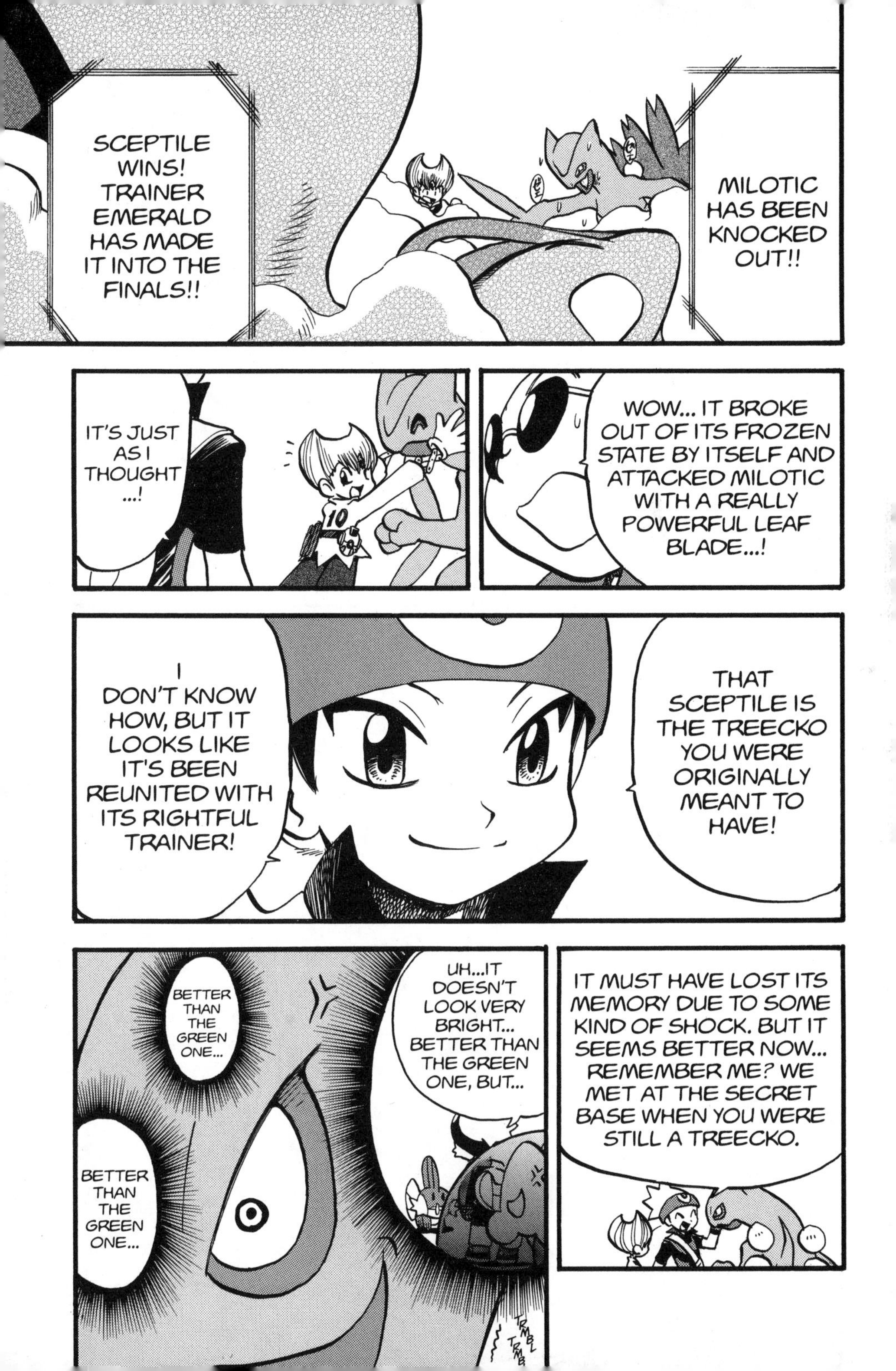
MILOTIC HAS BEEN KNOCKED OUT!!
SCEPTILE WINS! TRAINER EMERALD HAS MADE IT INTO THE FINALS!!
WOW... IT BROKE OUT OF ITS FROZEN STATE BY ITSELF AND ATTACKED MILOTIC WITH A REALLY POWERFUL LEAF BLADE...!
IT'S JUST AS I THOUGHT ...!
THAT SCEPTILE IS THE TREECKO YOU WERE ORIGINALLY MEANT TO HAVE!
I DON'T KNOW HOW, BUT IT LOOKS LIKE IT'S BEEN REUNITED WITH ITS RIGHTFUL TRAINER!
IT MUST HAVE LOST ITS MEMORY DUE TO SOME KIND OF SHOCK. BUT IT SEEMS BETTER NOW... REMEMBER ME? WE MET AT THE SECRET BASE WHEN YOU WERE STILL A TREECKO.
UH...IT DOESN'T LOOK VERY BRIGHT... BETTER THAN THE GREEN ONE, BUT...
BETTER THAN THE GREEN ONE...
BETTER THAN THE GREEN ONE...
TRMBL TRMB

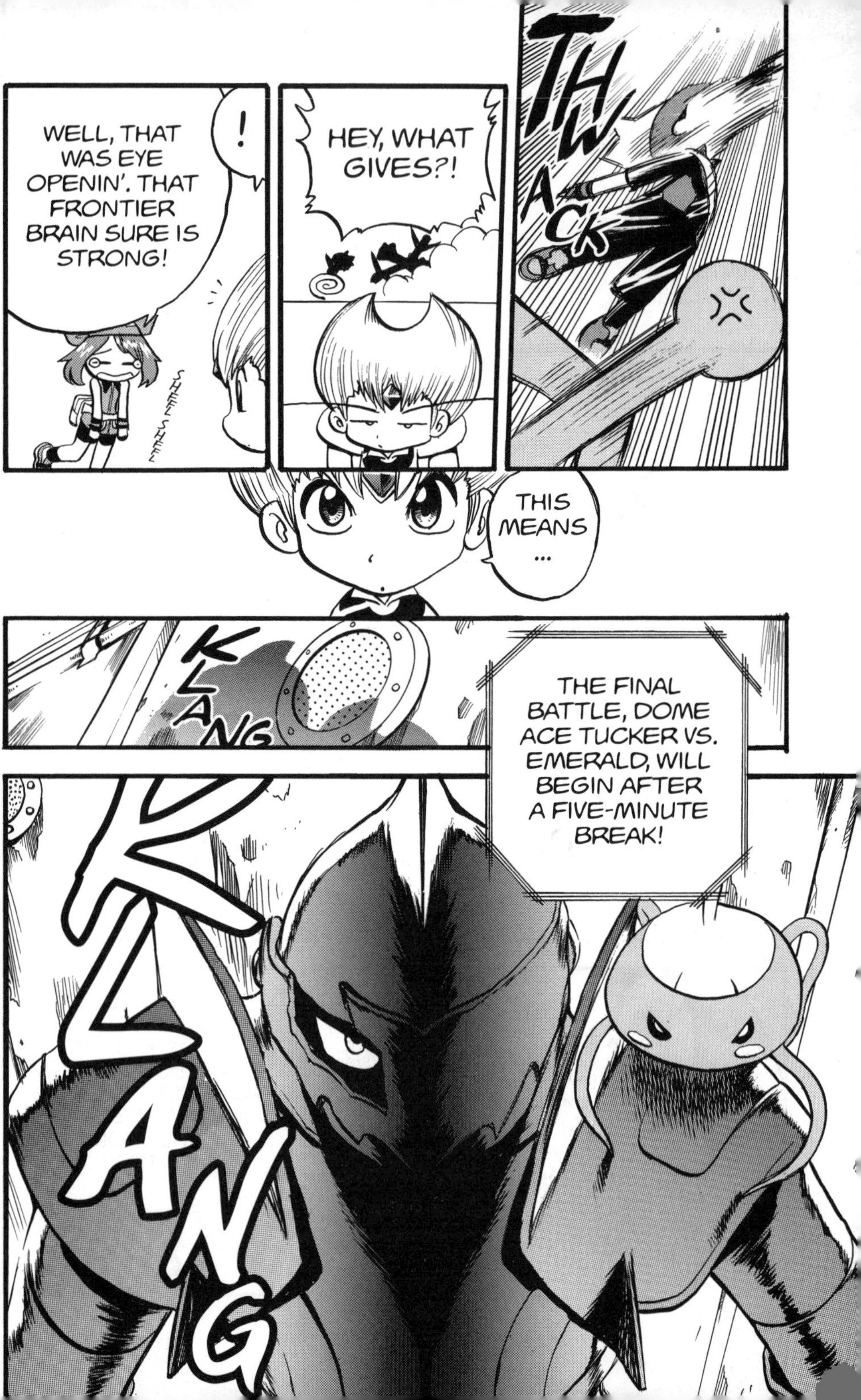
THWACK
HEY, WHAT GIVES?!
!
WELL, THAT WAS EYE OPENIN'. THAT FRONTIER BRAIN SURE IS STRONG!
SHEEL SHEEL
THIS MEANS...
KLANG
THE FINAL BATTLE, DOME ACE TUCKER VS. EMERALD, WILL BEGIN AFTER A FIVE-MINUTE BREAK!
KLANG

DEAR MEMBERS OF THE PRESS...

Thank you for visiting the Battle Frontier today. Permit me to continue explaining the rules of this facility...

OWNER: SCOTT

FACILITY RULES

BATTLE PALACE 3

■ MOVE CATEGORY ■

All the moves are uniquely categorized at the Battle Palace. These are the three categories.

ATTACK Moves like Iron Tail and Ice Beam that attack and damage an opponent.

DEFENSE Moves like Rest and Swords Dance which boost the Pokémon's stats or heal damage and status conditions.

SUPPORT Moves like Toxic and Charm which lower the opponent's stats or give them status conditions.

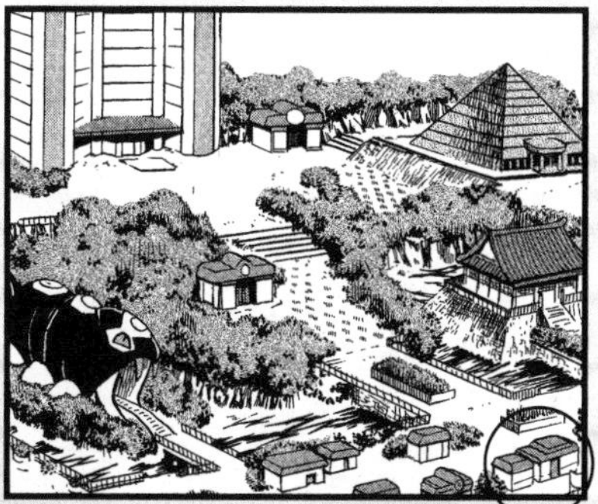

The types of moves used by the Pokémon will depend on their Nature. You can receive help from an avid fan (west of the Battle Palace) who will teach you what kind of moves your Pokémon are inclined to choose when left to their own devices.

323

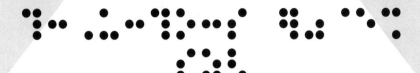

A Cheeky Charizard Change-Up, Part 1

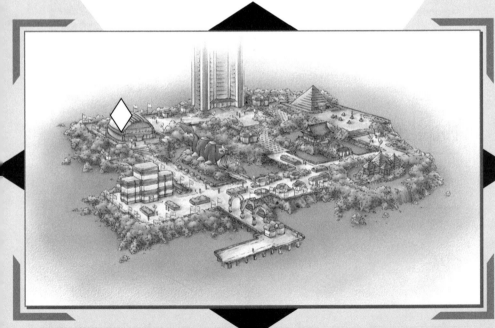

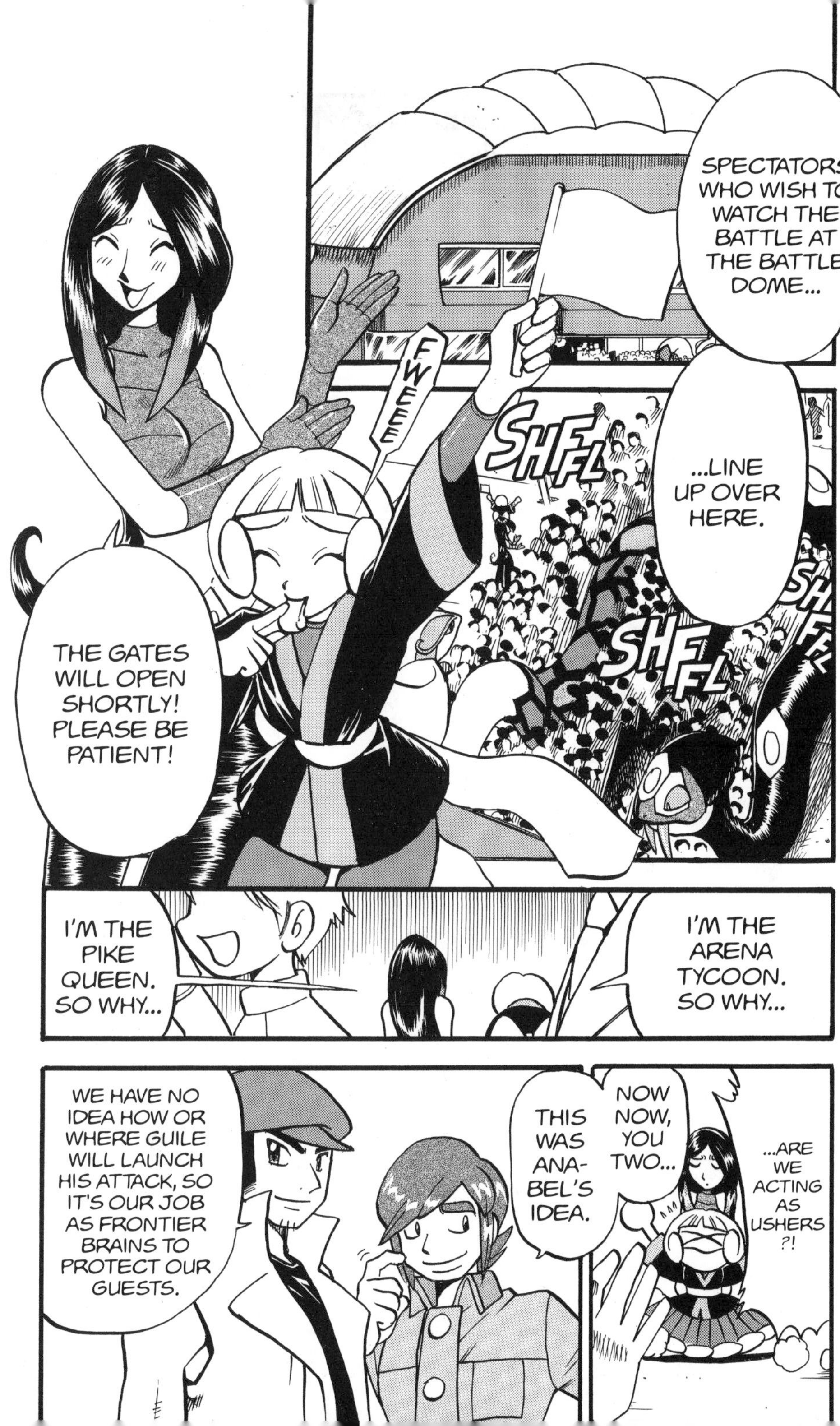
SPECTATORS WHO WISH TO WATCH THE BATTLE AT THE BATTLE DOME...
...LINE UP OVER HERE.
SHFL
SHFL
SHFL
FWEEE
SHFL
THE GATES WILL OPEN SHORTLY! PLEASE BE PATIENT!
I'M THE ARENA TYCOON. SO WHY...
I'M THE PIKE QUEEN. SO WHY...
...ARE WE ACTING AS USHERS?!
NOW NOW, YOU TWO...
THIS WAS ANA-BEL'S IDEA.
WE HAVE NO IDEA HOW OR WHERE GUILE WILL LAUNCH HIS ATTACK, SO IT'S OUR JOB AS FRONTIER BRAINS TO PROTECT OUR GUESTS.

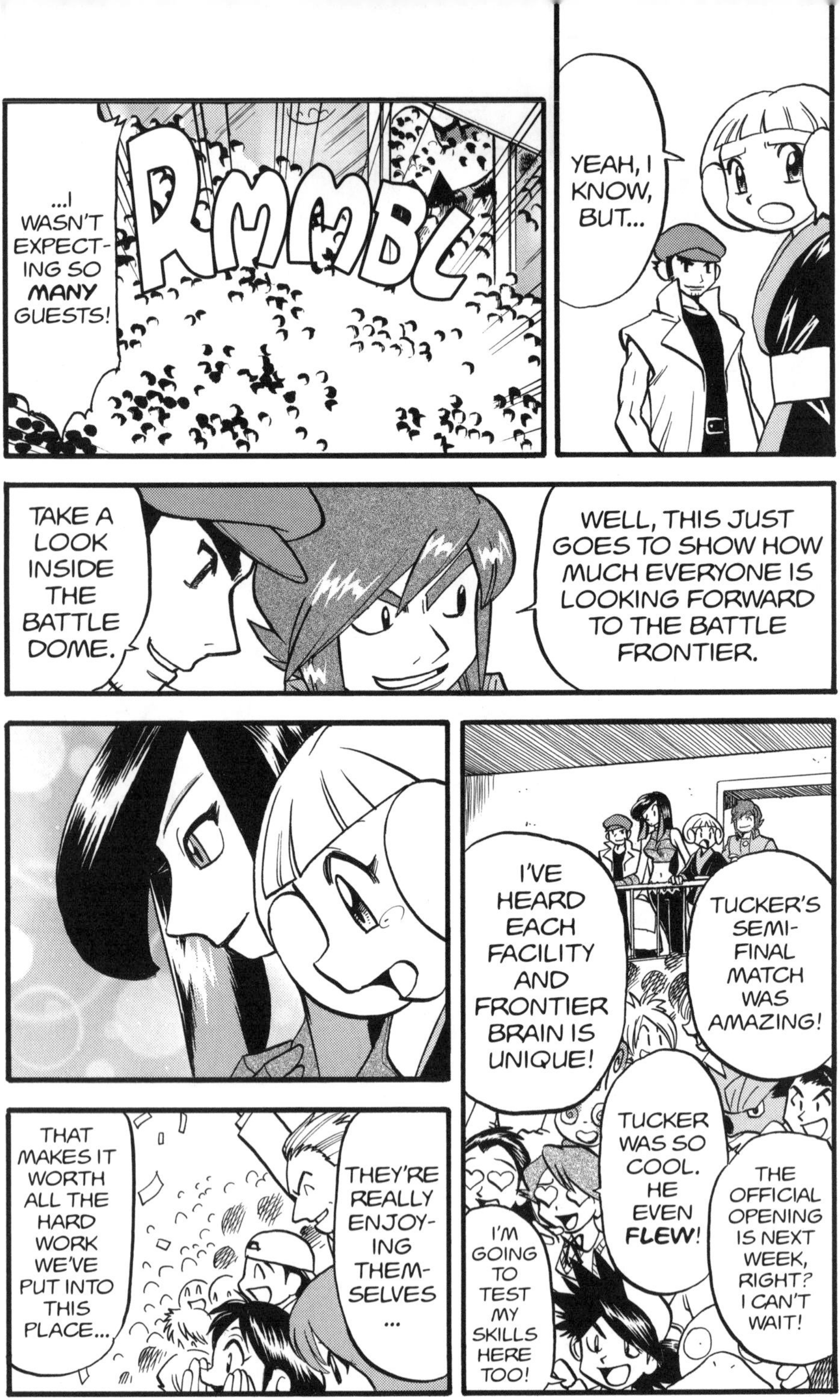
YEAH, I KNOW, BUT...
RMMBL
...I WASN'T EXPECTING SO **MANY** GUESTS!
WELL, THIS JUST GOES TO SHOW HOW MUCH EVERYONE IS LOOKING FORWARD TO THE BATTLE FRONTIER.
TAKE A LOOK INSIDE THE BATTLE DOME.
TUCKER'S SEMI-FINAL MATCH WAS AMAZING!
I'VE HEARD EACH FACILITY AND FRONTIER BRAIN IS UNIQUE!
TUCKER WAS SO COOL. HE EVEN **FLEW**!
THE OFFICIAL OPENING IS NEXT WEEK, RIGHT? I CAN'T WAIT!
I'M GOING TO TEST MY SKILLS HERE TOO!
THEY'RE REALLY ENJOYING THEMSELVES...
THAT MAKES IT WORTH ALL THE HARD WORK WE'VE PUT INTO THIS PLACE...

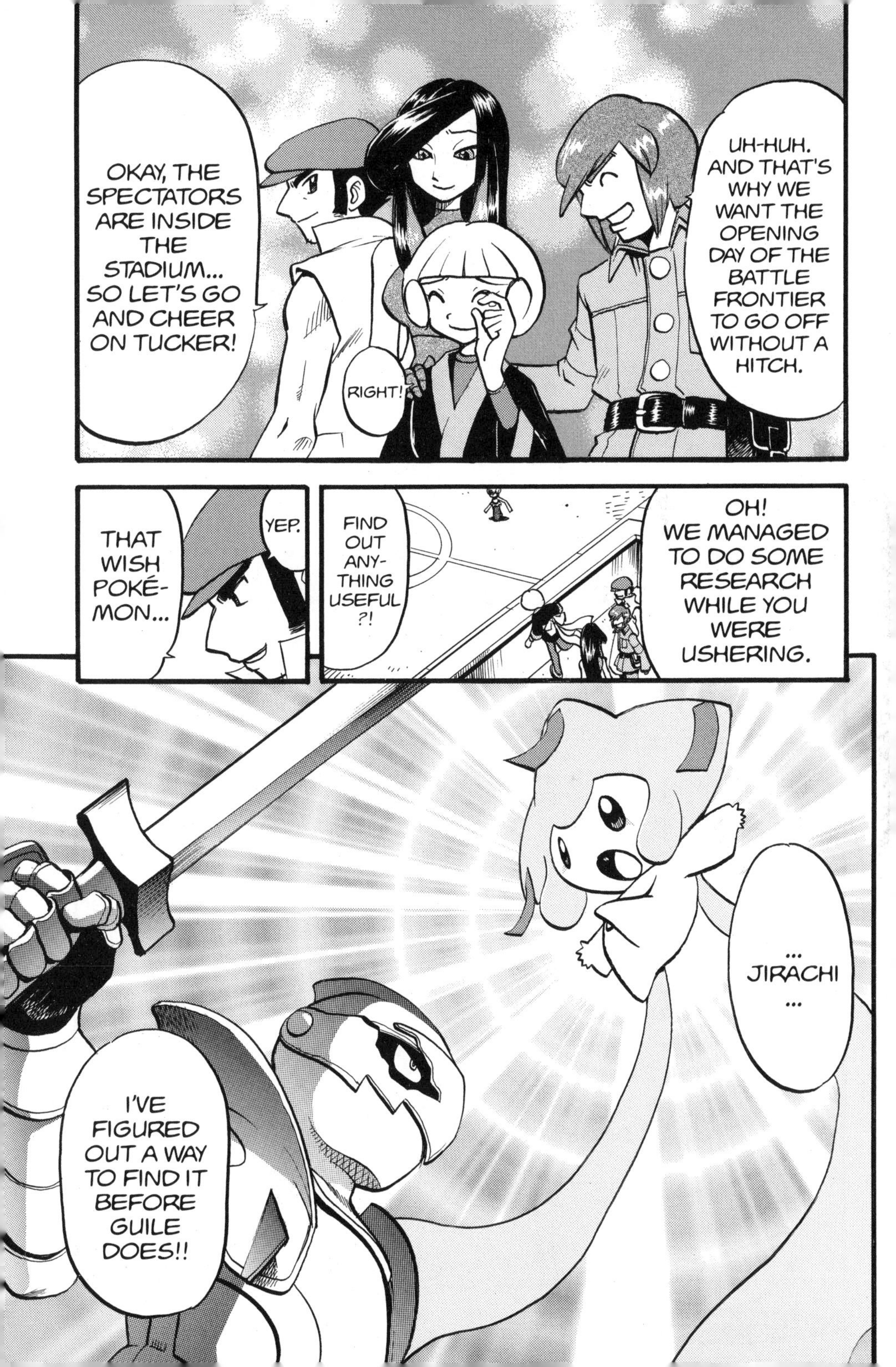
UH-HUH. AND THAT'S WHY WE WANT THE OPENING DAY OF THE BATTLE FRONTIER TO GO OFF WITHOUT A HITCH.
OKAY, THE SPECTATORS ARE INSIDE THE STADIUM... SO LET'S GO AND CHEER ON TUCKER!
RIGHT!
OH! WE MANAGED TO DO SOME RESEARCH WHILE YOU WERE USHERING.
FIND OUT ANY-THING USEFUL ?!
YEP.
THAT WISH POKÉ-MON...
... JIRACHI ...
I'VE FIGURED OUT A WAY TO FIND IT BEFORE GUILE DOES!!

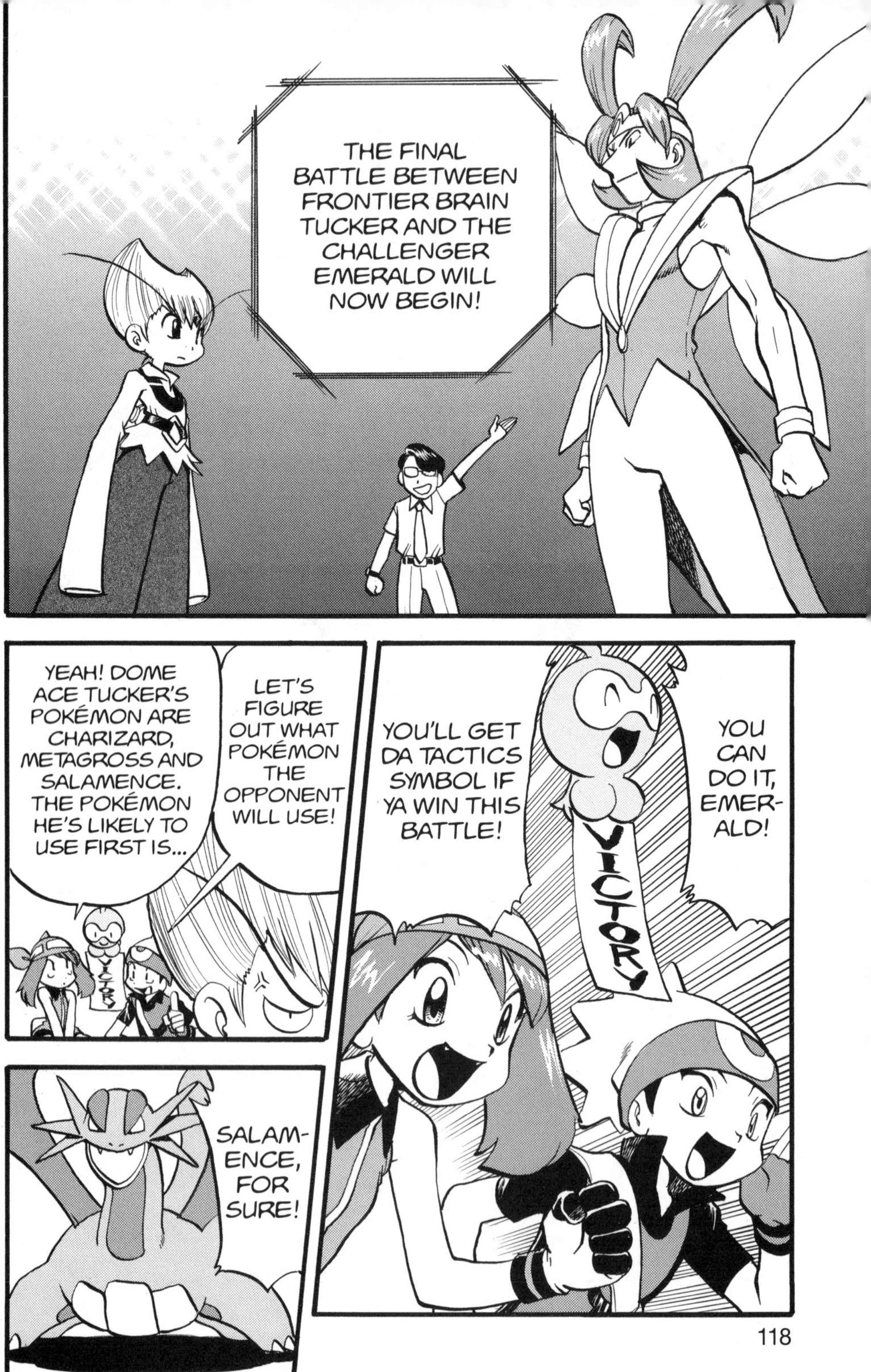

THE FINAL BATTLE BETWEEN FRONTIER BRAIN TUCKER AND THE CHALLENGER EMERALD WILL NOW BEGIN!
YOU CAN DO IT, EMER-ALD!
YOU'LL GET DA TACTICS SYMBOL IF YA WIN THIS BATTLE!
VICTORY!
LET'S FIGURE OUT WHAT POKÉMON THE OPPONENT WILL USE!
YEAH! DOME ACE TUCKER'S POKÉMON ARE CHARIZARD, METAGROSS AND SALAMENCE. THE POKÉMON HE'S LIKELY TO USE FIRST IS...
VICTORY
SALAM-ENCE, FOR SURE!

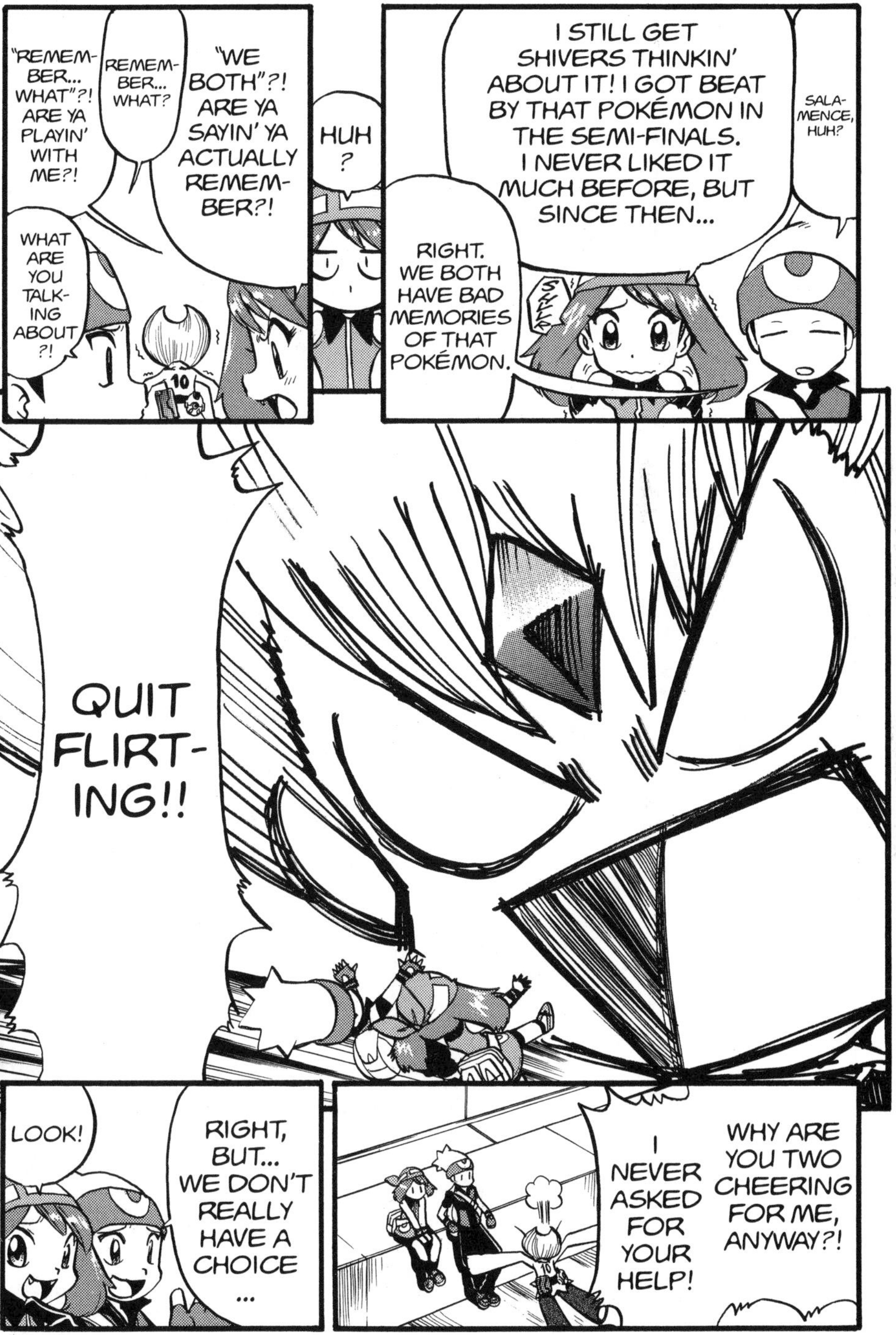
SALAMENCE, HUH?
I STILL GET SHIVERS THINKIN' ABOUT IT! I GOT BEAT BY THAT POKÉMON IN THE SEMI-FINALS. I NEVER LIKED IT MUCH BEFORE, BUT SINCE THEN...
RIGHT. WE BOTH HAVE BAD MEMORIES OF THAT POKÉMON.
HUH?
"WE BOTH"?! ARE YA SAYIN' YA ACTUALLY REMEMBER?!
REMEMBER... WHAT?
"REMEMBER... WHAT"?! ARE YA PLAYIN' WITH ME?!
WHAT ARE YOU TALKING ABOUT?!
QUIT FLIRTING!!
WHY ARE YOU TWO CHEERING FOR ME, ANYWAY?!
I NEVER ASKED FOR YOUR HELP!
RIGHT, BUT... WE DON'T REALLY HAVE A CHOICE ...
LOOK!

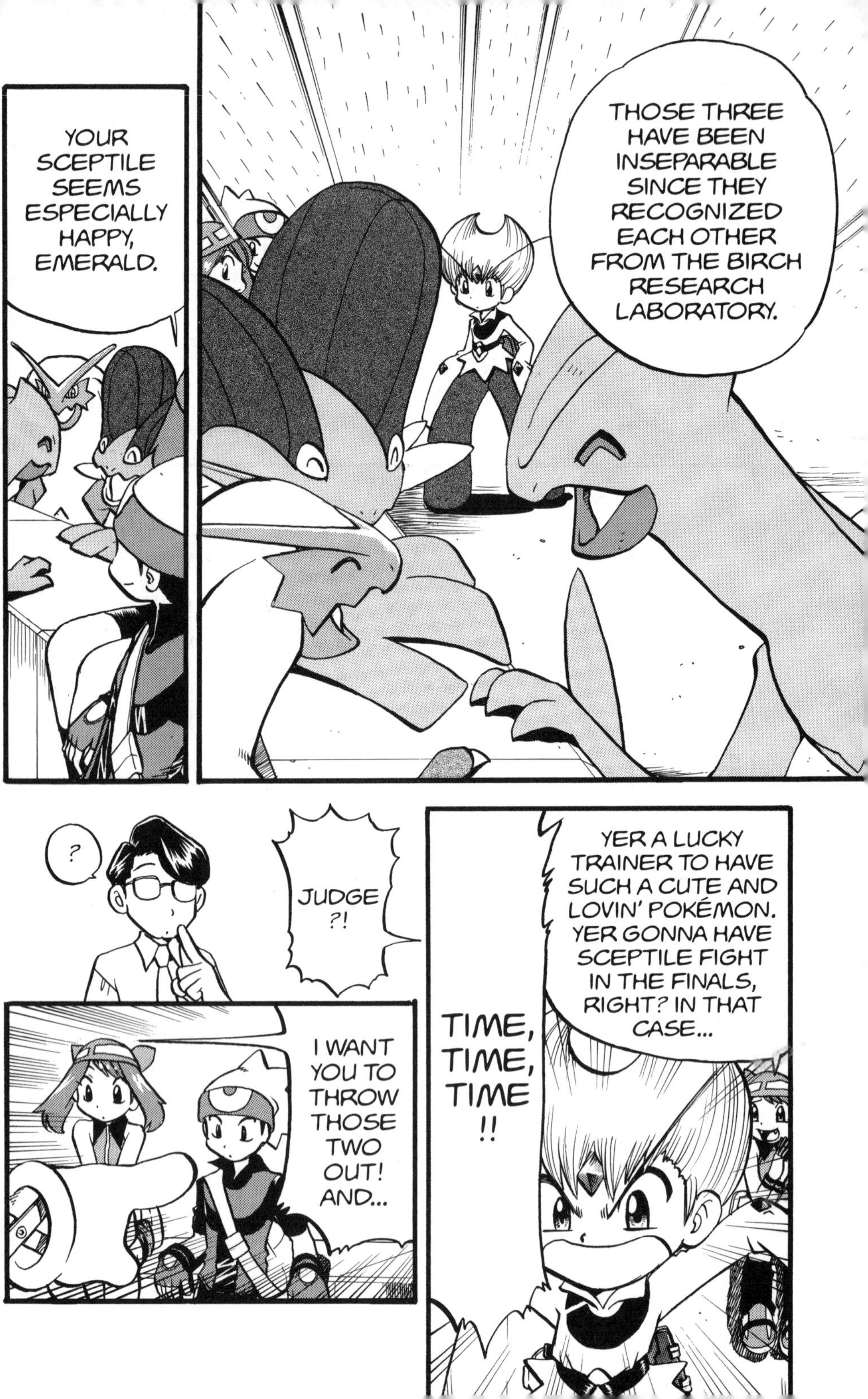
THOSE THREE HAVE BEEN INSEPARABLE SINCE THEY RECOGNIZED EACH OTHER FROM THE BIRCH RESEARCH LABORATORY.
YOUR SCEPTILE SEEMS ESPECIALLY HAPPY, EMERALD.
YER A LUCKY TRAINER TO HAVE SUCH A CUTE AND LOVIN' POKÉMON. YER GONNA HAVE SCEPTILE FIGHT IN THE FINALS, RIGHT? IN THAT CASE...
TIME, TIME, TIME!!
JUDGE?!
?
I WANT YOU TO THROW THOSE TWO OUT! AND...

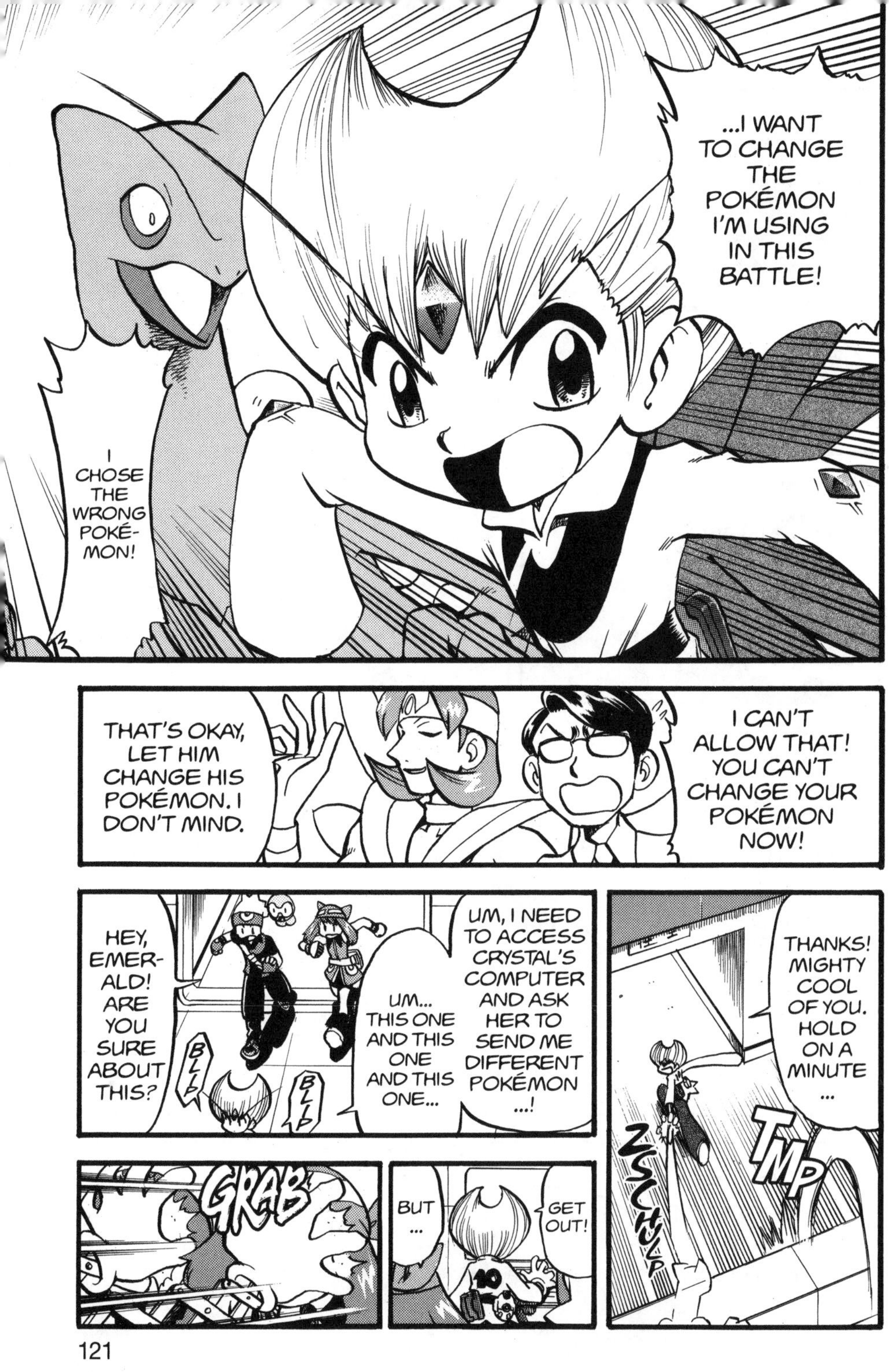
...I WANT TO CHANGE THE POKÉMON I'M USING IN THIS BATTLE!
I CHOSE THE WRONG POKÉ-MON!
I CAN'T ALLOW THAT! YOU CAN'T CHANGE YOUR POKÉMON NOW!
THAT'S OKAY, LET HIM CHANGE HIS POKÉMON. I DON'T MIND.
THANKS! MIGHTY COOL OF YOU. HOLD ON A MINUTE ...
TMP
ZSCHUP
UM, I NEED TO ACCESS CRYSTAL'S COMPUTER AND ASK HER TO SEND ME DIFFERENT POKÉMON ...!
UM... THIS ONE AND THIS ONE AND THIS ONE...
HEY, EMER-ALD! ARE YOU SURE ABOUT THIS?
BLIP
BLIP
GET OUT!
BUT ...
GRAB

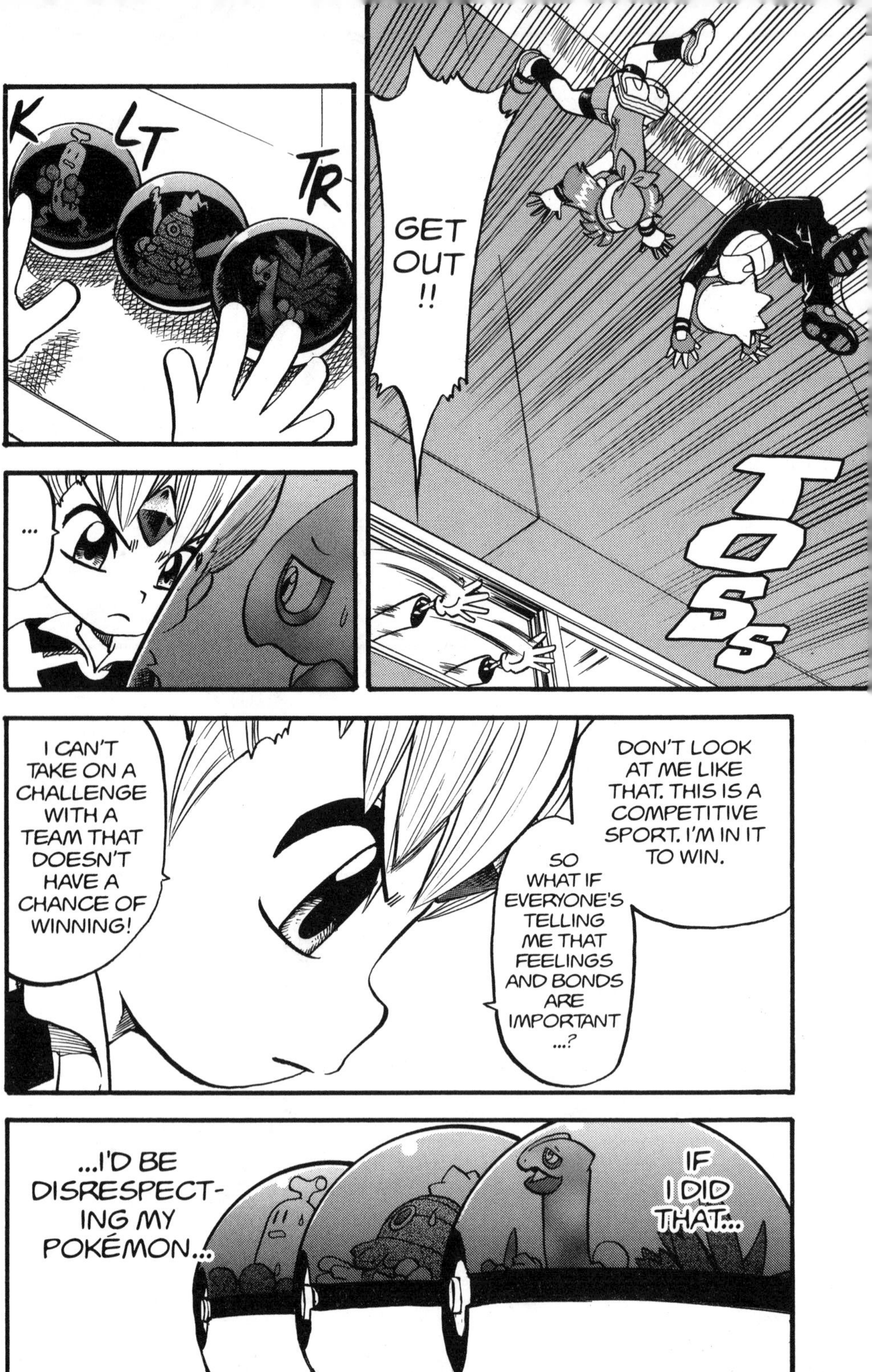
GET OUT!!
TOSS
KLTTR
...
DON'T LOOK AT ME LIKE THAT. THIS IS A COMPETITIVE SPORT. I'M IN IT TO WIN.
SO WHAT IF EVERYONE'S TELLING ME THAT FEELINGS AND BONDS ARE IMPORTANT...?
I CAN'T TAKE ON A CHALLENGE WITH A TEAM THAT DOESN'T HAVE A CHANCE OF WINNING!
IF I DID THAT...
...I'D BE DISRESPECTING MY POKÉMON...

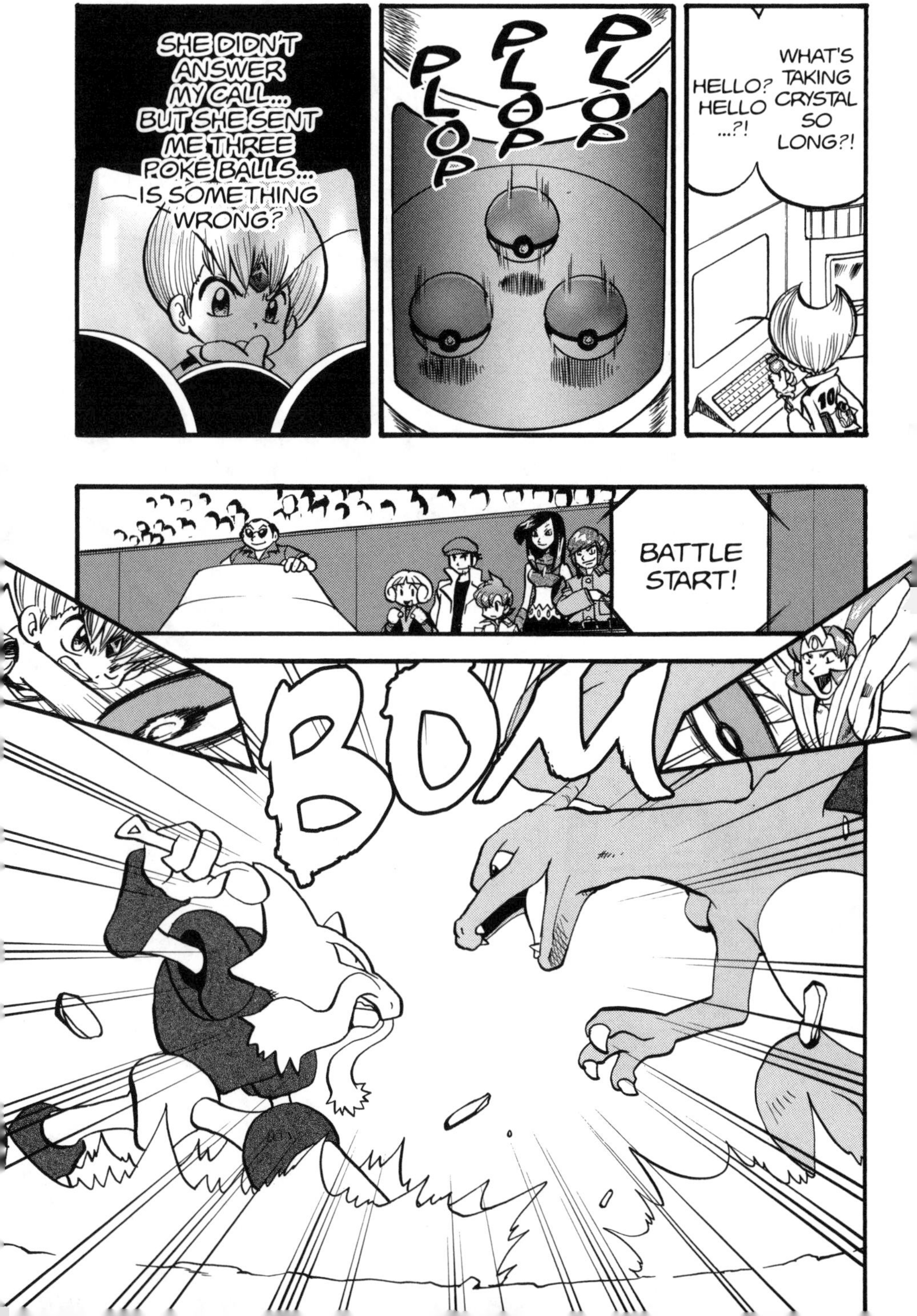
WHAT'S TAKING CRYSTAL SO LONG?!
HELLO? HELLO ...?!
PLOP
PLOP
PLOP
SHE DIDN'T ANSWER MY CALL... BUT SHE SENT ME THREE POKÉ BALLS... IS SOMETHING WRONG?
BATTLE START!
BOM

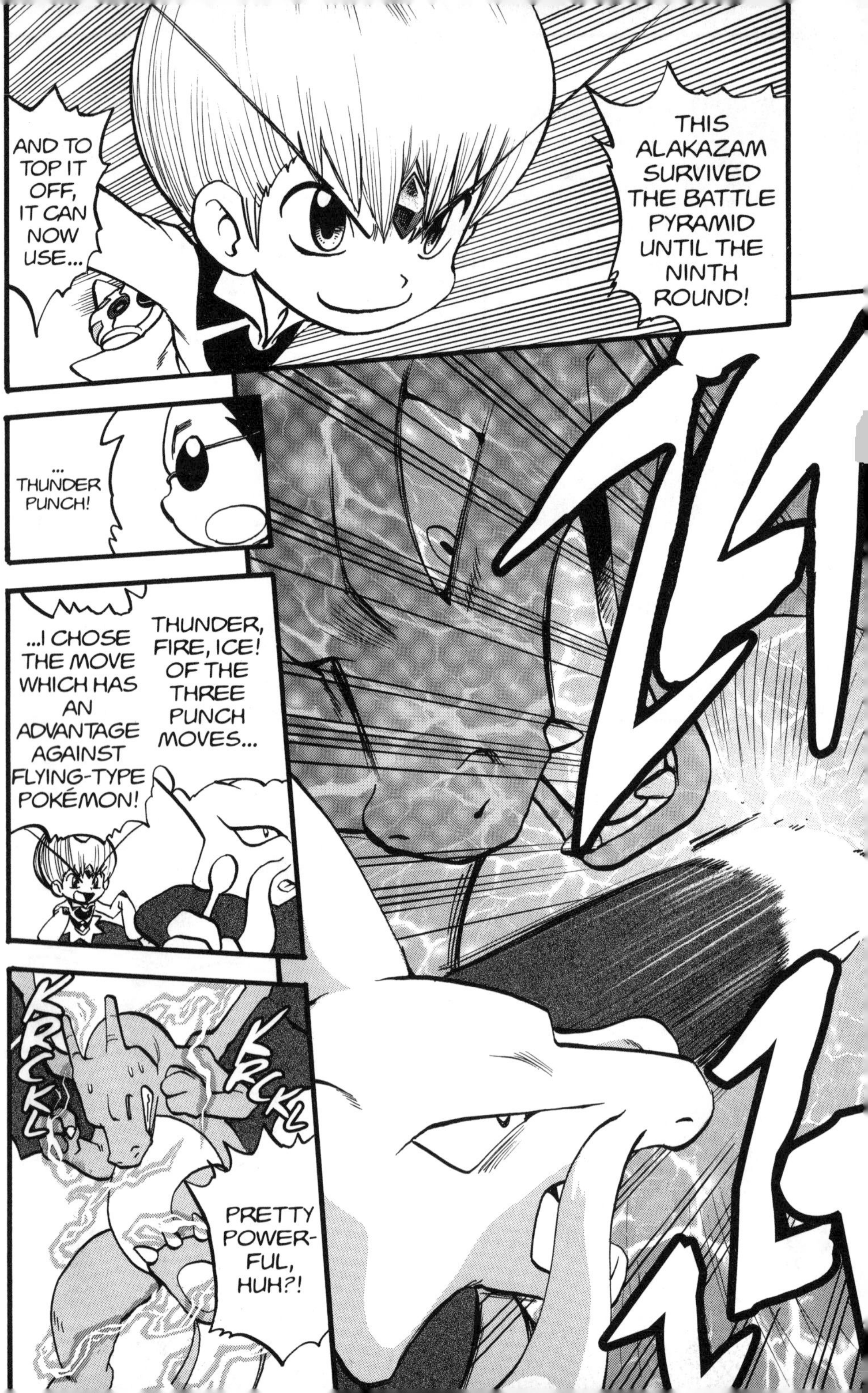
THIS ALAKAZAM SURVIVED THE BATTLE PYRAMID UNTIL THE NINTH ROUND!
AND TO TOP IT OFF, IT CAN NOW USE...
...THUNDER PUNCH!
THUNDER, FIRE, ICE! OF THE THREE PUNCH MOVES...
...I CHOSE THE MOVE WHICH HAS AN ADVANTAGE AGAINST FLYING-TYPE POKÉMON!
KRCKL
KRCKL
PRETTY POWER-FUL, HUH?!

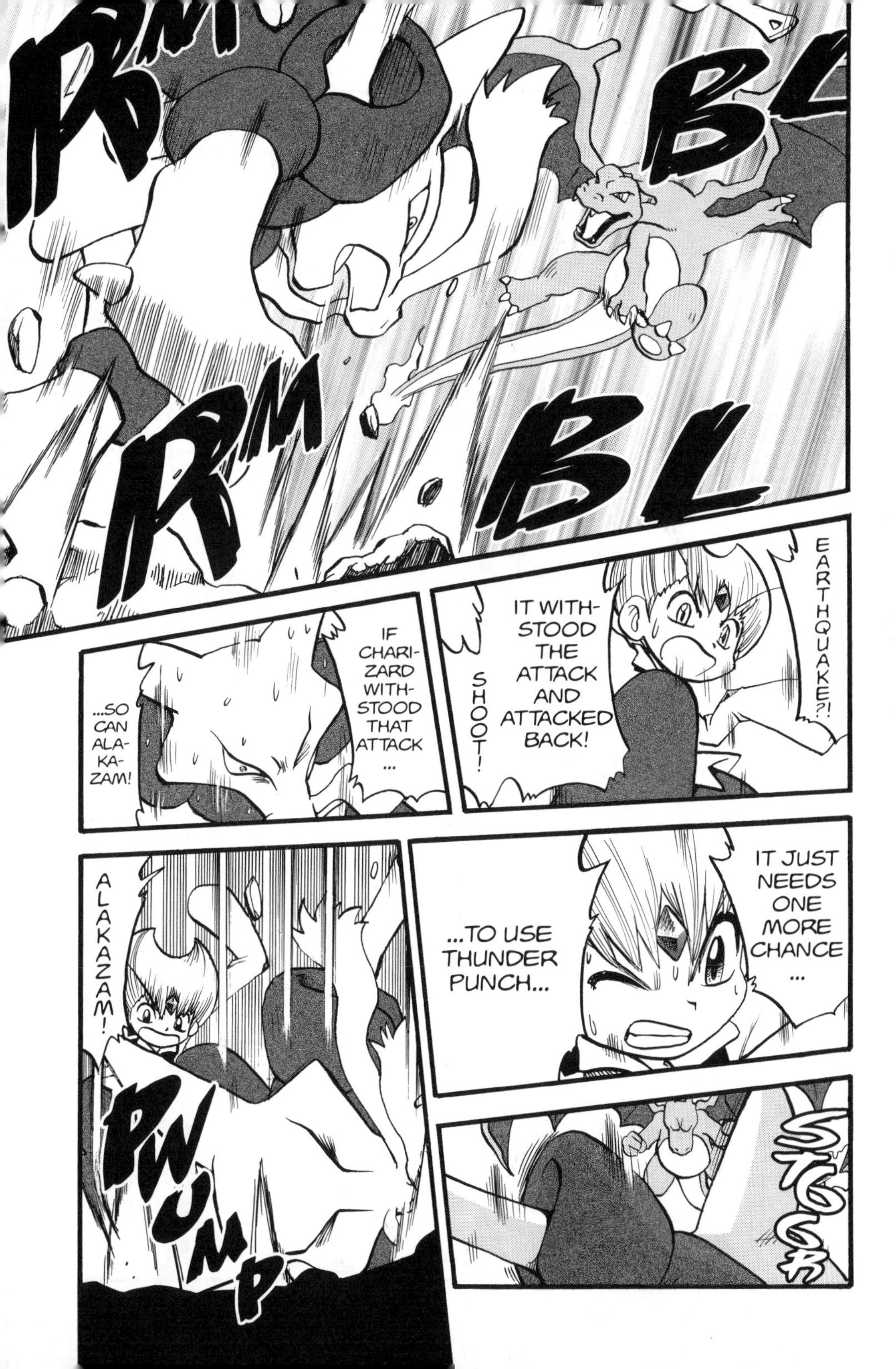

RMBL
RMBL
EARTHQUAKE?!
IT WITH-STOOD THE ATTACK AND ATTACKED BACK!
SHOOT!
IF CHARI-ZARD WITH-STOOD THAT ATTACK...
...SO CAN ALA-KA-ZAM!
IT JUST NEEDS ONE MORE CHANCE...
...TO USE THUNDER PUNCH...
STGGR
ALAKAZAM!
PWUMP

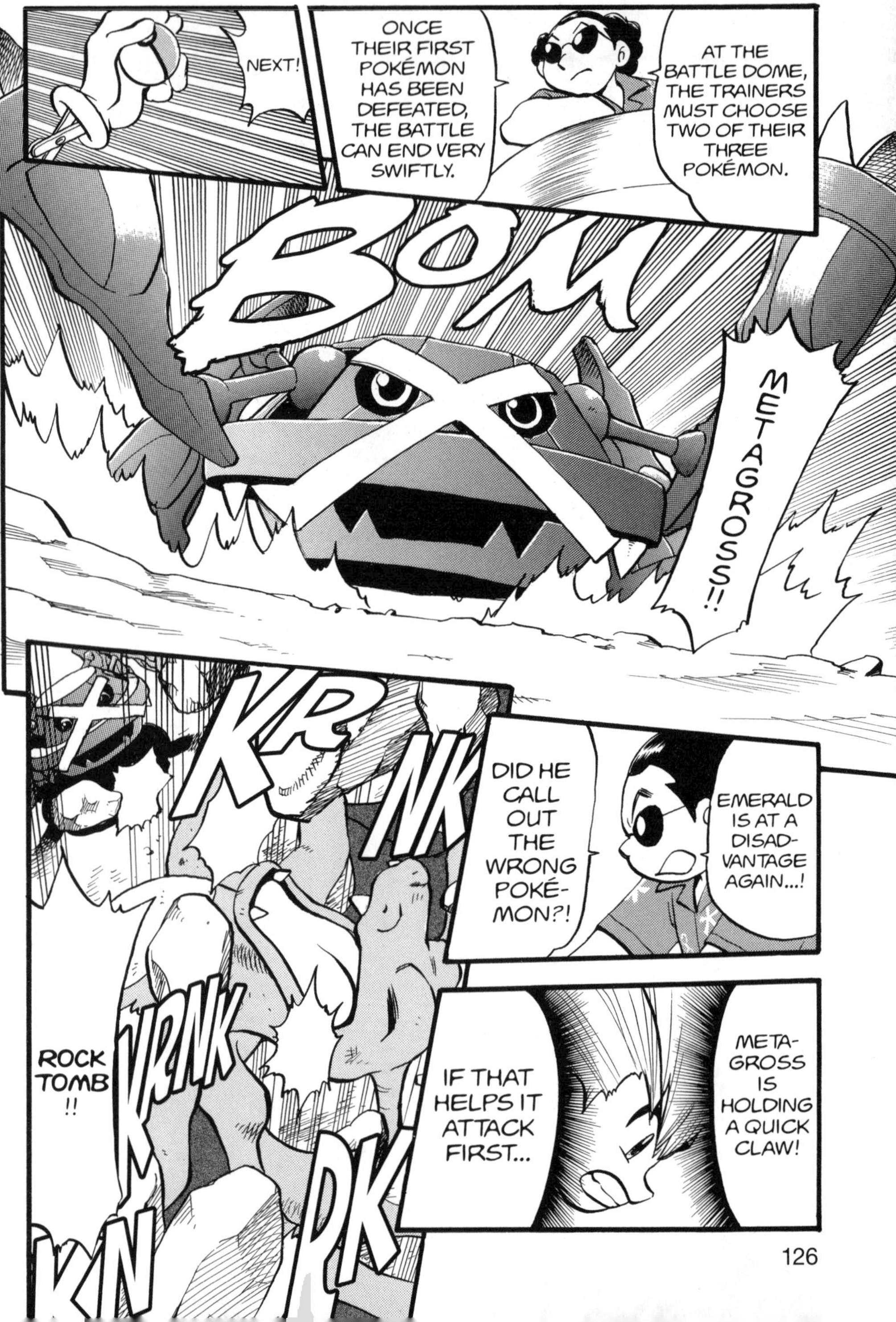
AT THE BATTLE DOME, THE TRAINERS MUST CHOOSE TWO OF THEIR THREE POKÉMON.
ONCE THEIR FIRST POKÉMON HAS BEEN DEFEATED, THE BATTLE CAN END VERY SWIFTLY.
NEXT!
BOM
METAGROSS!!
EMERALD IS AT A DISAD-VANTAGE AGAIN...!
DID HE CALL OUT THE WRONG POKÉ-MON?!
META-GROSS IS HOLDING A QUICK CLAW!
IF THAT HELPS IT ATTACK FIRST...
KRNK
ROCK TOMB!!
KRNK
KN
PK

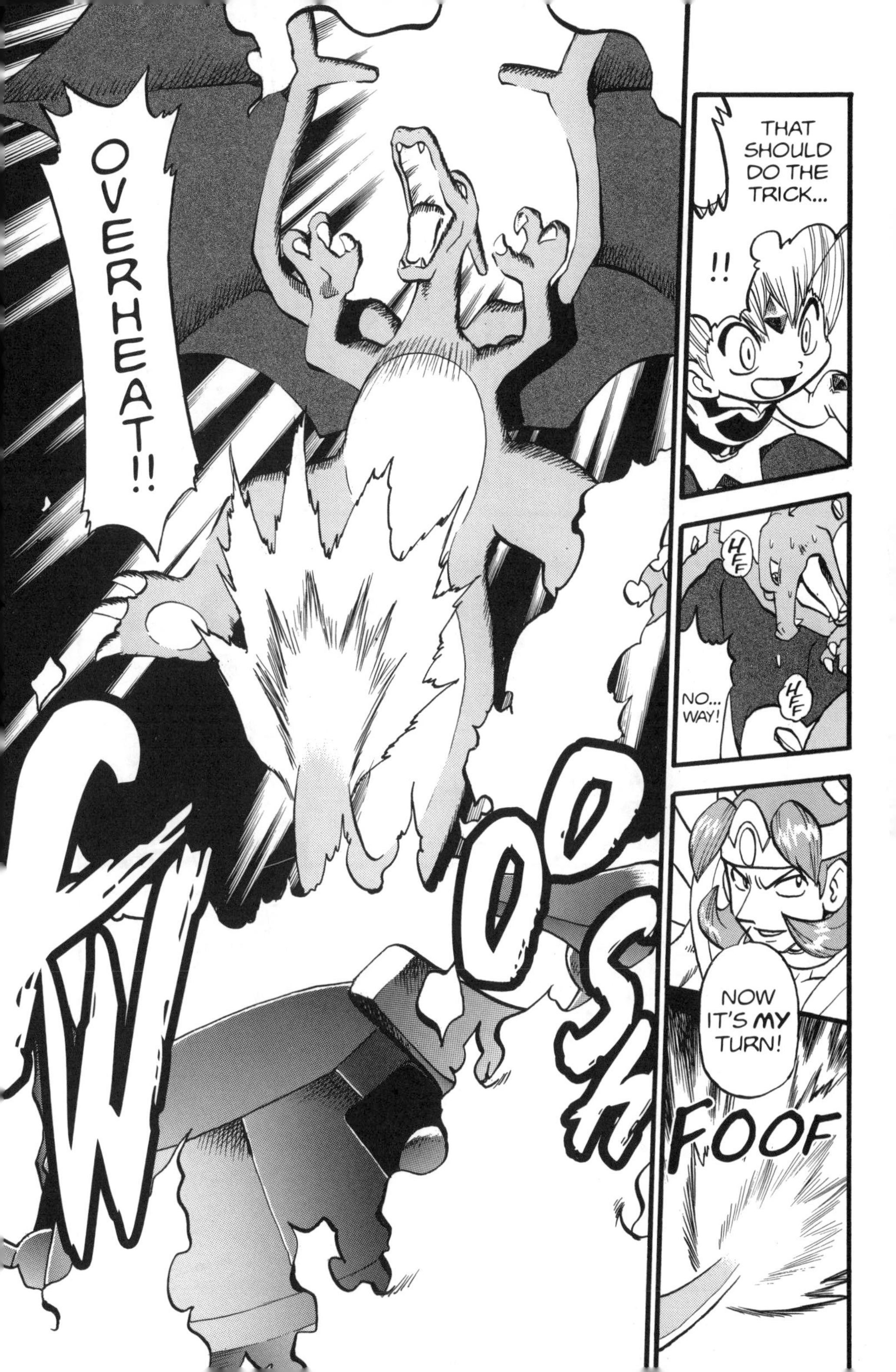
THAT SHOULD DO THE TRICK...
!!
HFF
NO... WAY!
HFF
NOW IT'S **MY** TURN!
FOOF
OVERHEAT!!

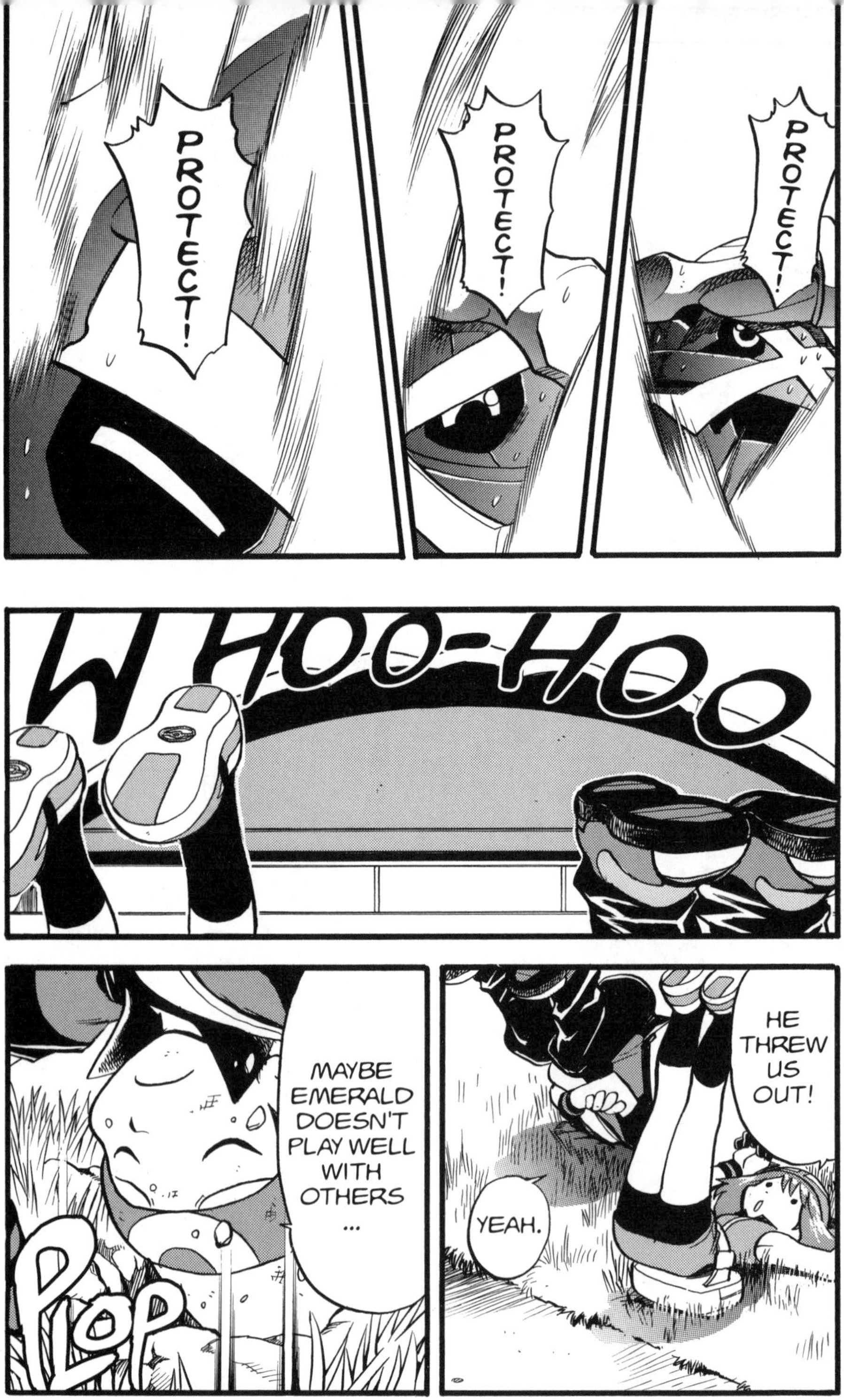
PROTECT!
PROTECT!
PROTECT!
WHOO-HOO
HE THREW US OUT!
YEAH.
MAYBE EMERALD DOESN'T PLAY WELL WITH OTHERS ...
PLOP

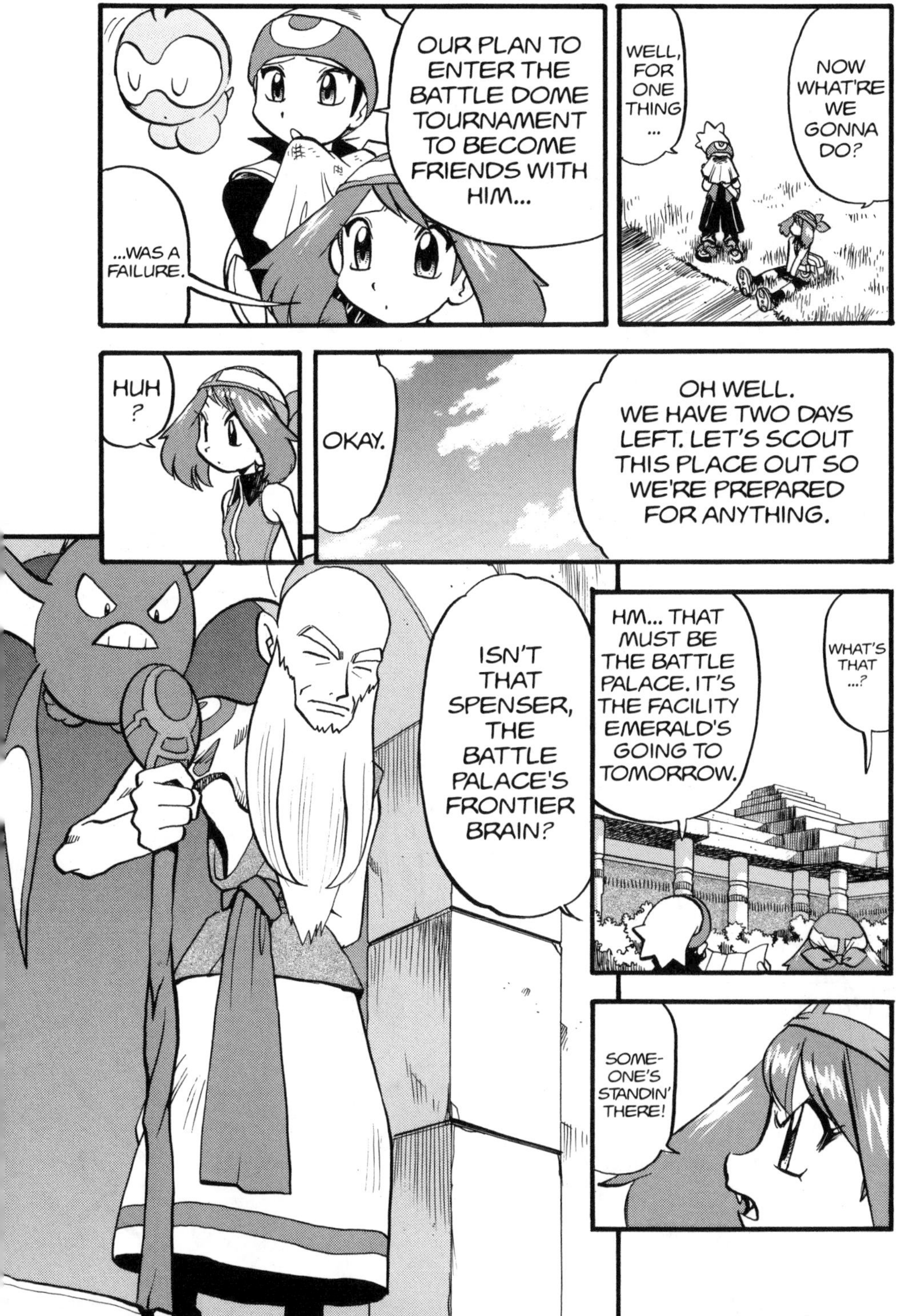
NOW WHAT'RE WE GONNA DO?
WELL, FOR ONE THING...
OUR PLAN TO ENTER THE BATTLE DOME TOURNAMENT TO BECOME FRIENDS WITH HIM...
...WAS A FAILURE.
OH WELL. WE HAVE TWO DAYS LEFT. LET'S SCOUT THIS PLACE OUT SO WE'RE PREPARED FOR ANYTHING.
OKAY.
HUH?
WHAT'S THAT...?
HM... THAT MUST BE THE BATTLE PALACE. IT'S THE FACILITY EMERALD'S GOING TO TOMORROW.
SOME-ONE'S STANDIN' THERE!
ISN'T THAT SPENSER, THE BATTLE PALACE'S FRONTIER BRAIN?

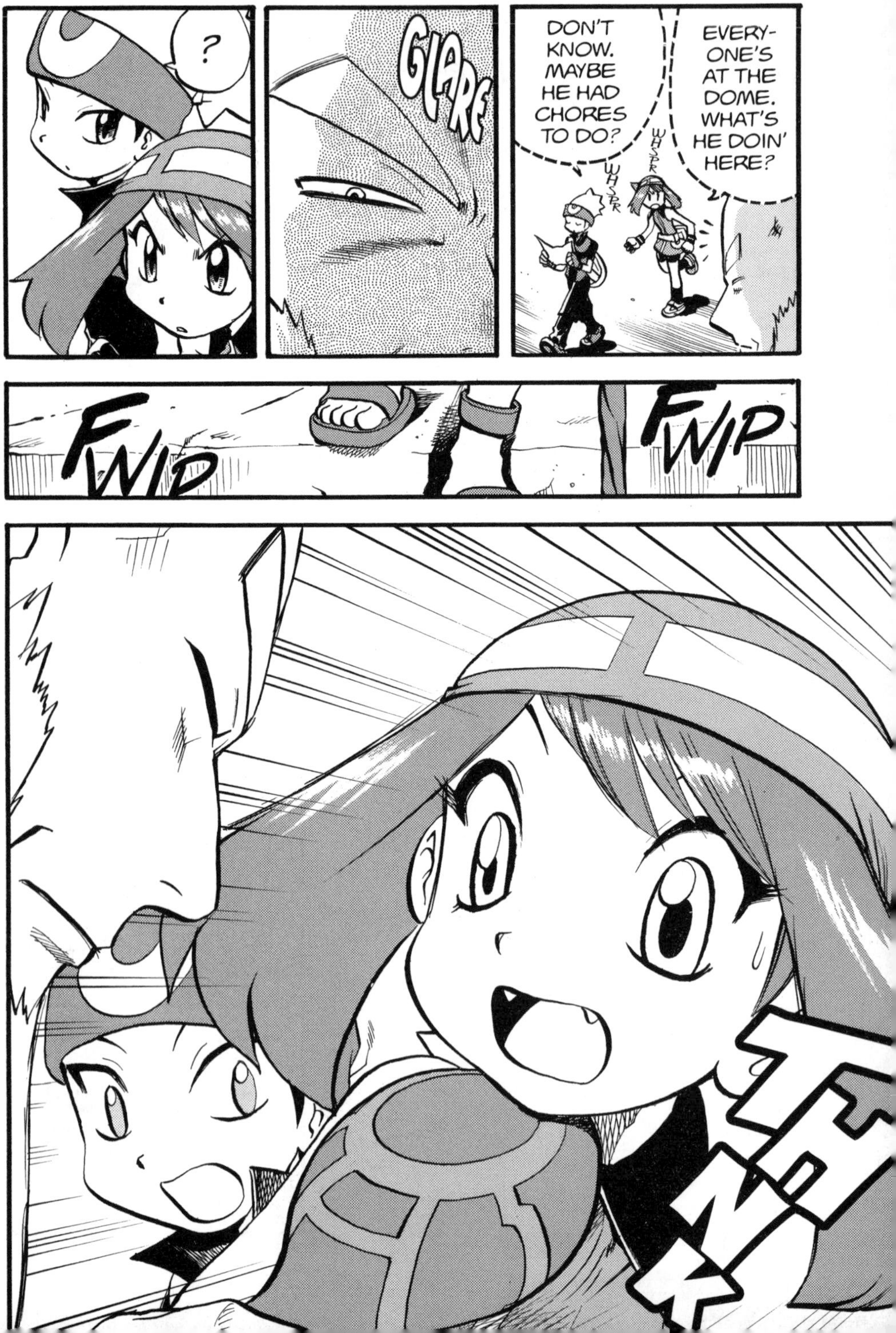
EVERY-ONE'S AT THE DOME. WHAT'S HE DOIN' HERE?
DON'T KNOW. MAYBE HE HAD CHORES TO DO?
WHSPR
WHSPR
GLARE
?
FWIP
FWIP
THNK

DEAR MEMBERS OF THE PRESS...

Thank you for visiting the Battle Frontier today. Permit me to continue explaining the rules of this facility...

OWNER: SCOTT

FACILITY RULES
BATTLE TOWER 1

Battle-type	Number of Pokémon	Type of Symbol	Wins needed to attain the Symbol
•Single •Double •Multi	3 Pokémon	Ability	7 Wins × 10 Rounds = 70 Consecutive Wins

The symbol of the Battle Frontier, the large building to the north, is the Battle Tower. This facility existed before the other six facilities were built, so I'm sure you know all about it already. It's a facility for classic Pokémon Battles, so there are no new rules or gimmicks as there are in the other six facilities. Here, the challengers may enjoy a simple battle showing off the Pokémon's and Trainer's skills.

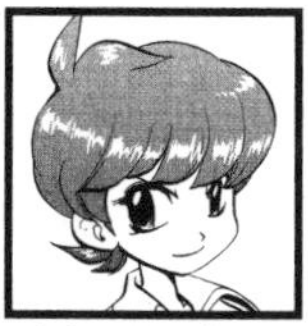
Salon Maiden Anabel

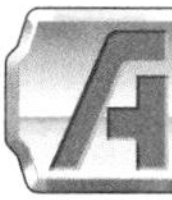
Ability Symbol

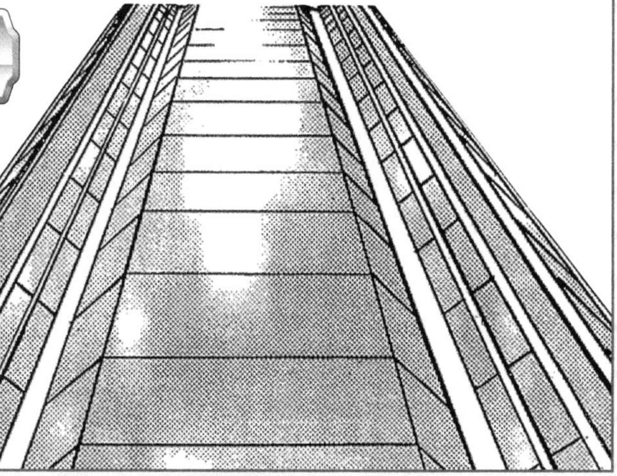

324

A Cheeky Charizard Change-Up, Part 2

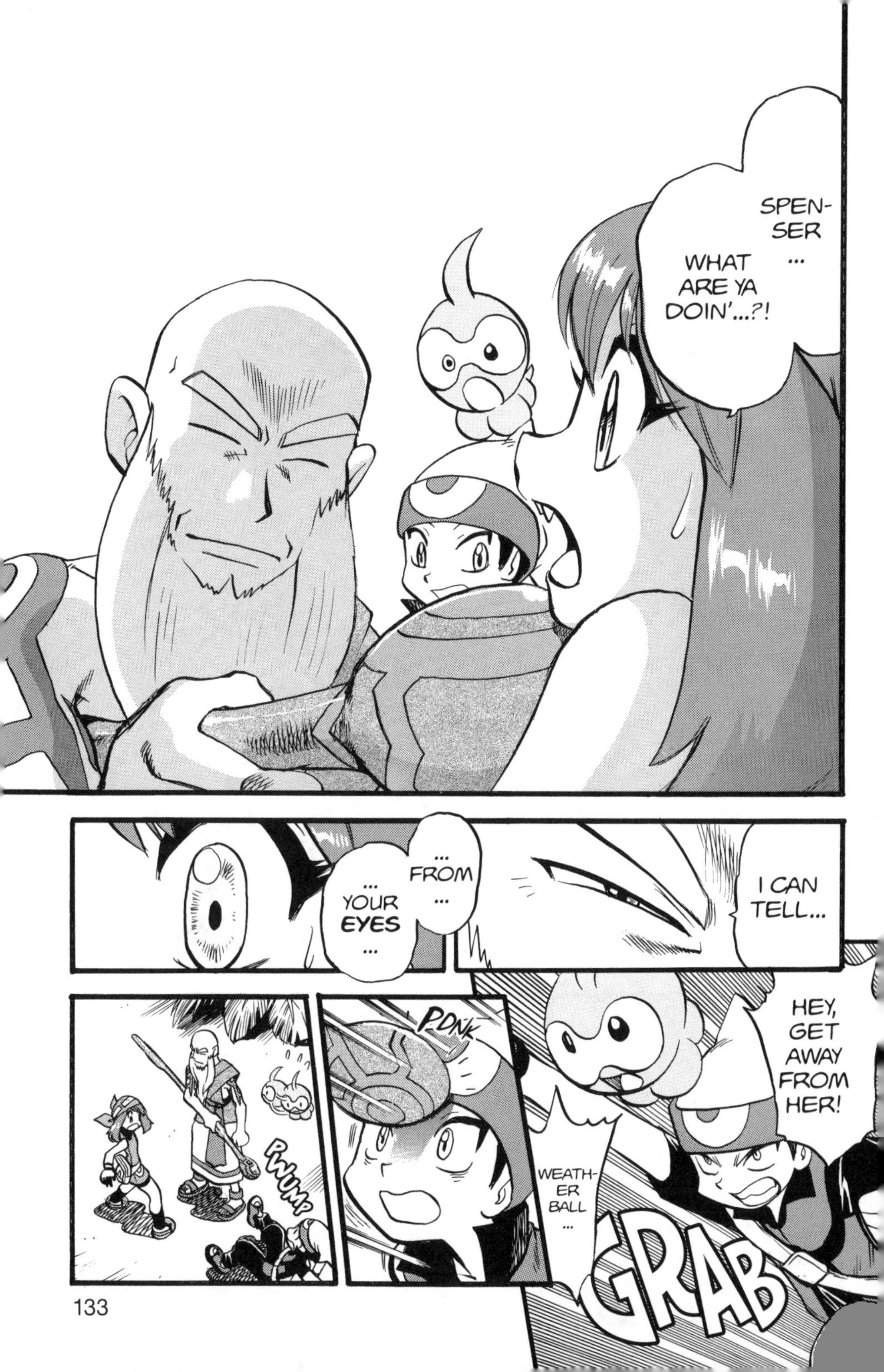
SPEN-SER ...
WHAT ARE YA DOIN'...?!
I CAN TELL...
... FROM ...
... YOUR **EYES** ...
HEY, GET AWAY FROM HER!
GRAB
PONK
WEATH-ER BALL ...
PWUMP

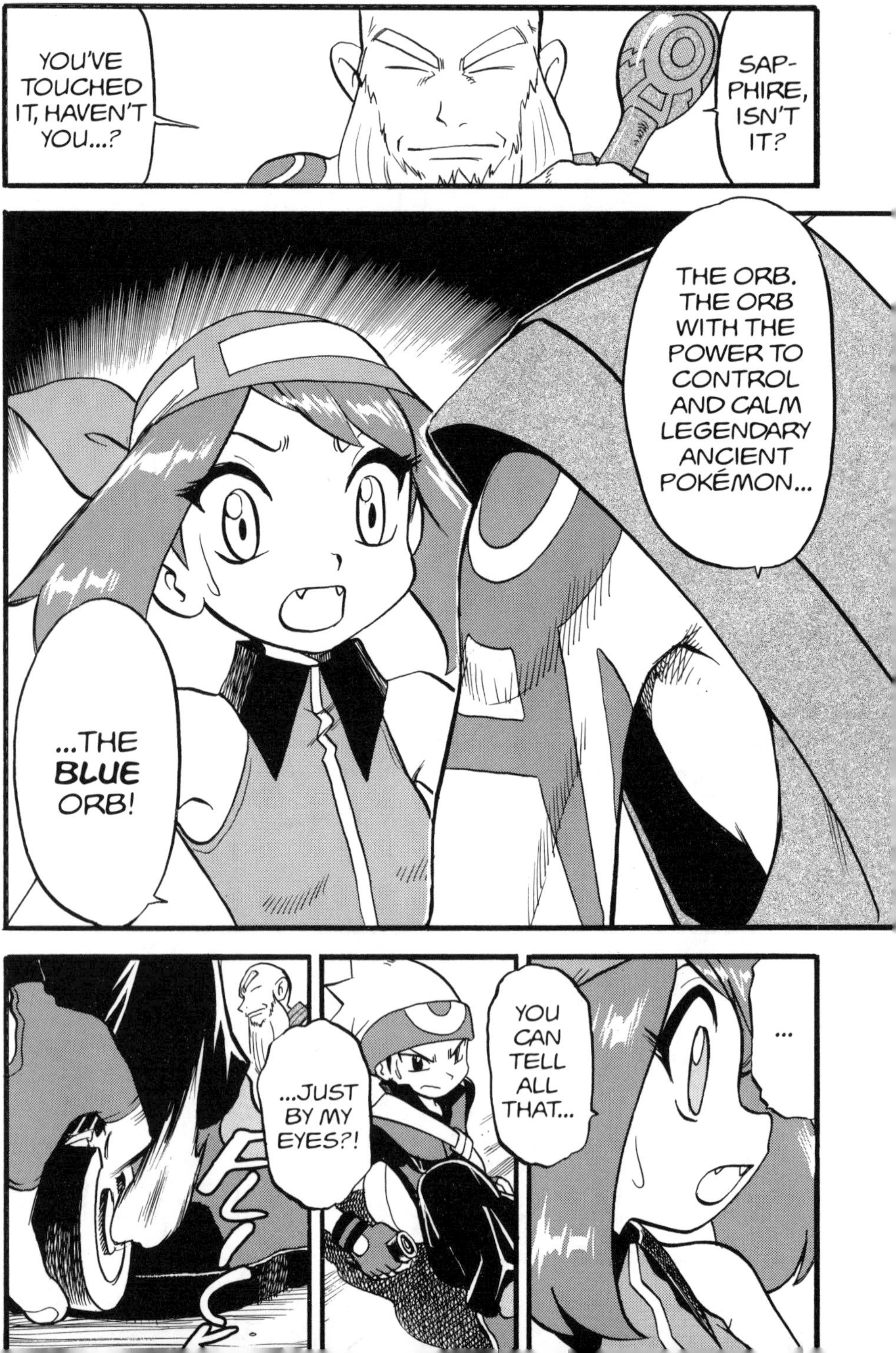
SAPPHIRE, ISN'T IT?
YOU'VE TOUCHED IT, HAVEN'T YOU...?
THE ORB. THE ORB WITH THE POWER TO CONTROL AND CALM LEGENDARY ANCIENT POKÉMON...
...THE **BLUE** ORB!
...
YOU CAN TELL ALL THAT...
...JUST BY MY EYES?!

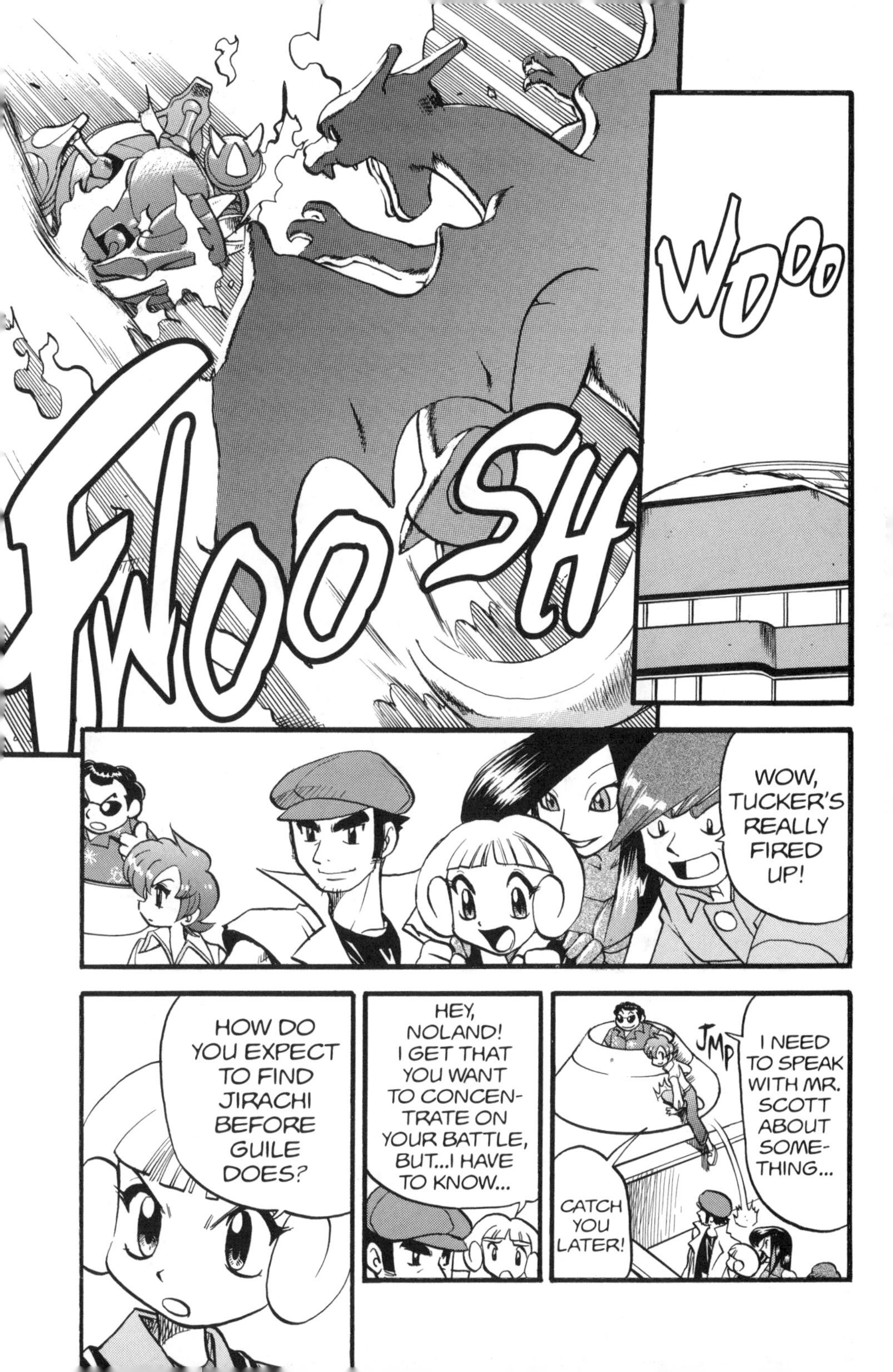
WOOO
FWOOSH
WOW, TUCKER'S REALLY FIRED UP!
JMP
I NEED TO SPEAK WITH MR. SCOTT ABOUT SOME-THING...
CATCH YOU LATER!
HEY, NOLAND! I GET THAT YOU WANT TO CONCEN-TRATE ON YOUR BATTLE, BUT...I HAVE TO KNOW...
HOW DO YOU EXPECT TO FIND JIRACHI BEFORE GUILE DOES?

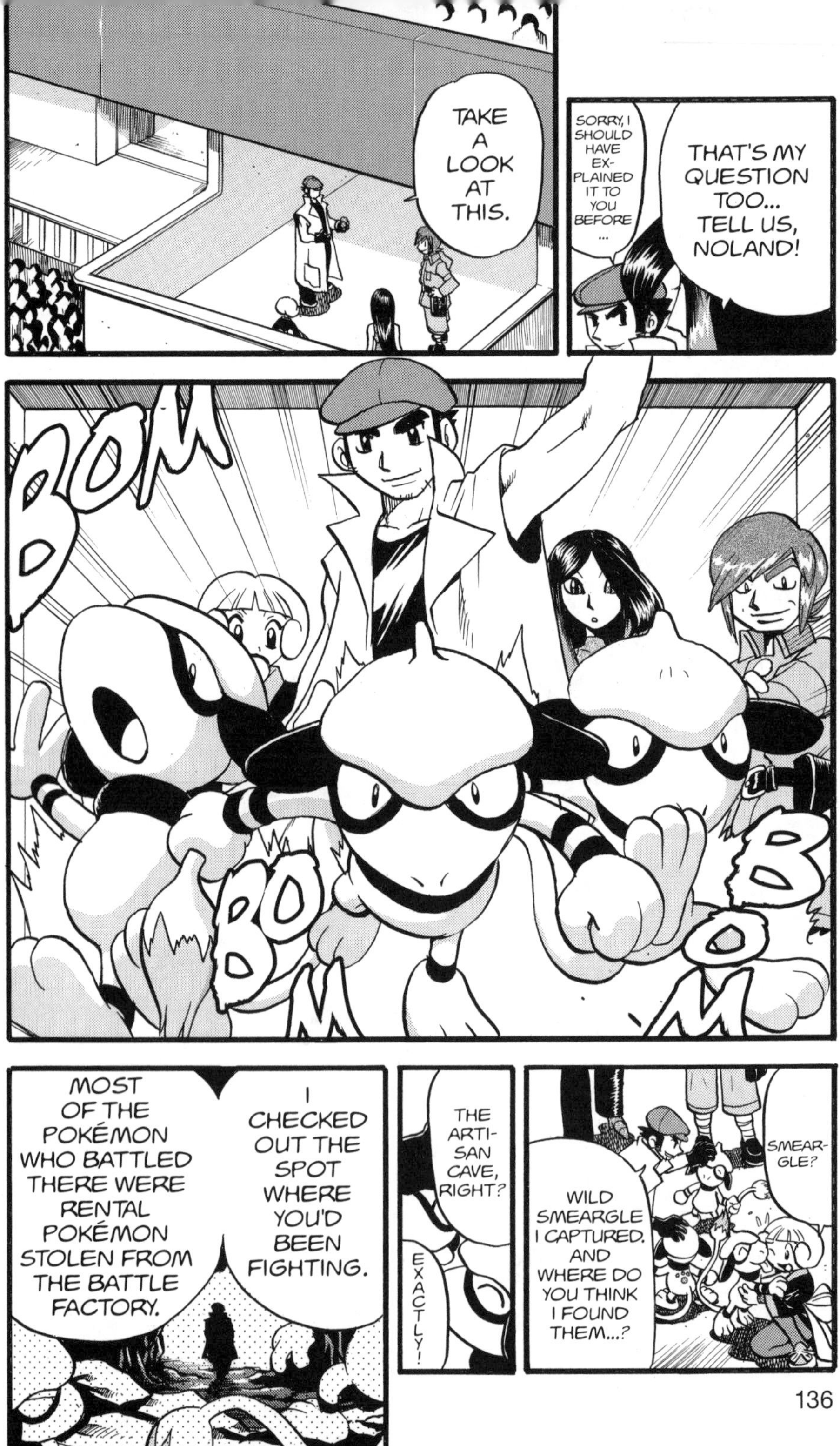
THAT'S MY QUESTION TOO... TELL US, NOLAND!
SORRY, I SHOULD HAVE EX-PLAINED IT TO YOU BEFORE ...
TAKE A LOOK AT THIS.
BOM
BOM
BOM
SMEAR-GLE?
WILD SMEARGLE I CAPTURED. AND WHERE DO YOU THINK I FOUND THEM...?
THE ARTI-SAN CAVE, RIGHT?
EXACTLY!
I CHECKED OUT THE SPOT WHERE YOU'D BEEN FIGHTING.
MOST OF THE POKÉMON WHO BATTLED THERE WERE RENTAL POKÉMON STOLEN FROM THE BATTLE FACTORY.

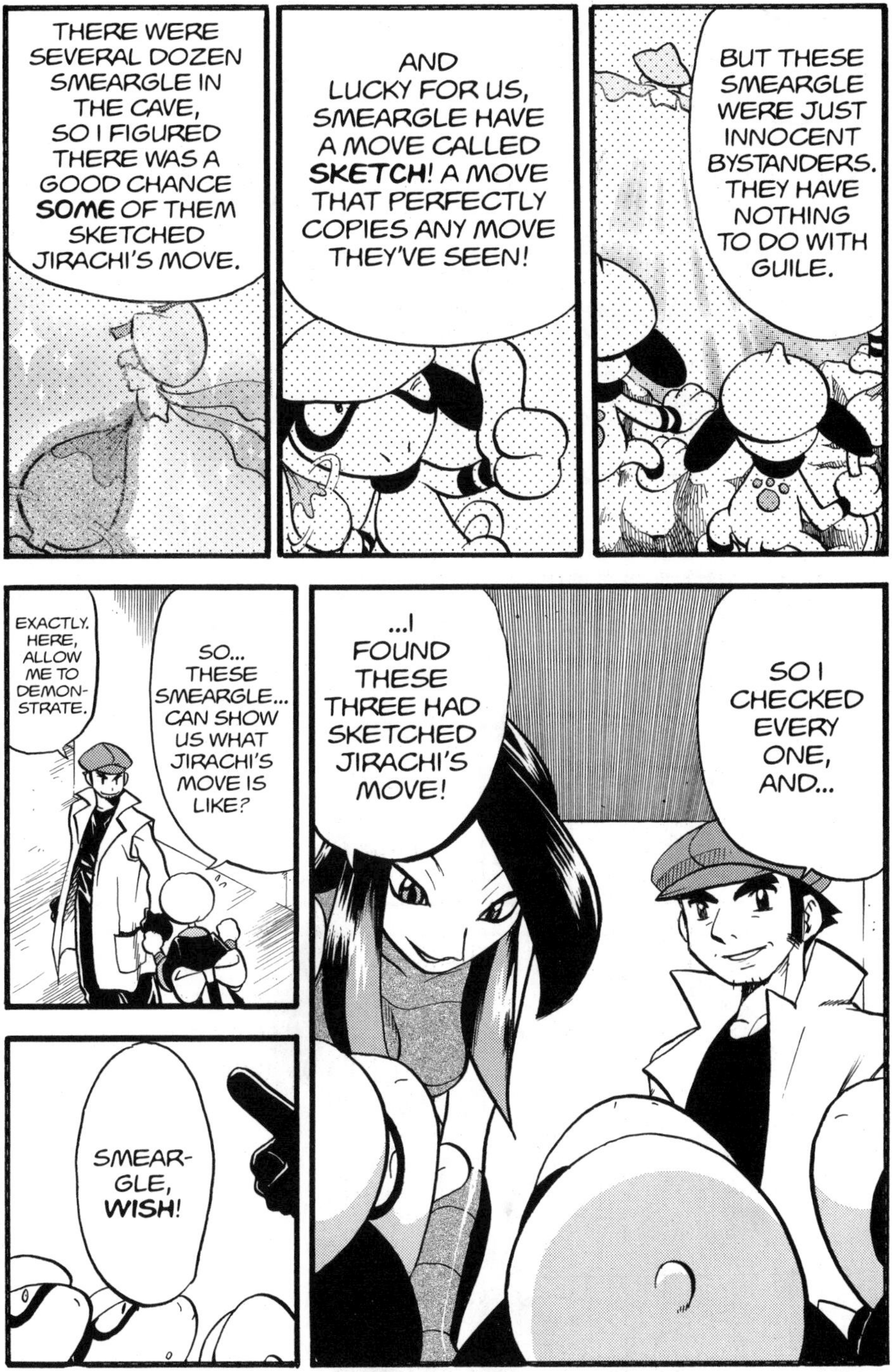

BUT THESE SMEARGLE WERE JUST INNOCENT BYSTANDERS. THEY HAVE NOTHING TO DO WITH GUILE.
AND LUCKY FOR US, SMEARGLE HAVE A MOVE CALLED **SKETCH**! A MOVE THAT PERFECTLY COPIES ANY MOVE THEY'VE SEEN!
THERE WERE SEVERAL DOZEN SMEARGLE IN THE CAVE, SO I FIGURED THERE WAS A GOOD CHANCE **SOME** OF THEM SKETCHED JIRACHI'S MOVE.
SO I CHECKED EVERY ONE, AND...
...I FOUND THESE THREE HAD SKETCHED JIRACHI'S MOVE!
SO... THESE SMEARGLE... CAN SHOW US WHAT JIRACHI'S MOVE IS LIKE?
EXACTLY. HERE, ALLOW ME TO DEMON-STRATE.
SMEAR-GLE, **WISH**!

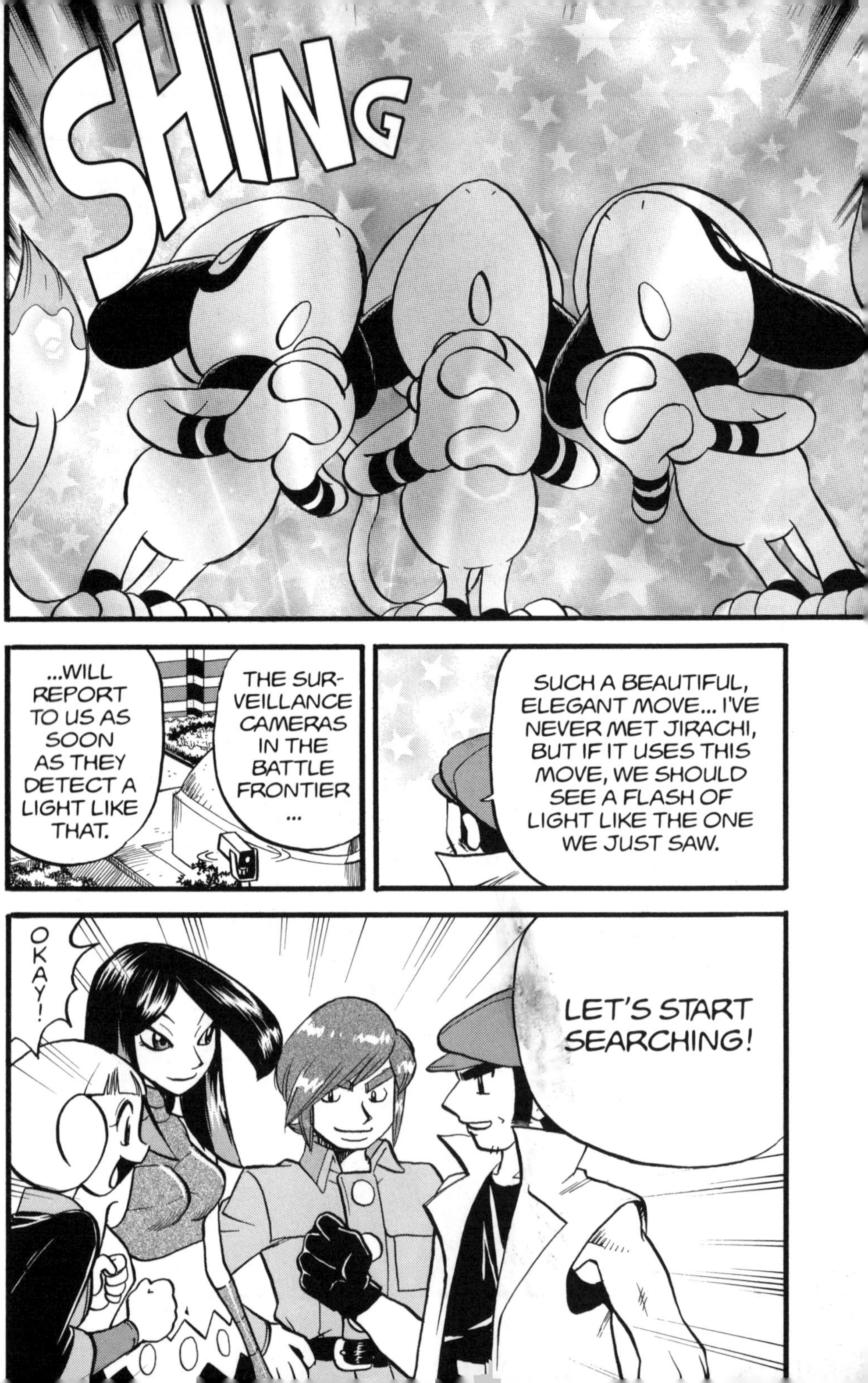
SHING
SUCH A BEAUTIFUL, ELEGANT MOVE... I'VE NEVER MET JIRACHI, BUT IF IT USES THIS MOVE, WE SHOULD SEE A FLASH OF LIGHT LIKE THE ONE WE JUST SAW.
THE SUR-VEILLANCE CAMERAS IN THE BATTLE FRONTIER ...
...WILL REPORT TO US AS SOON AS THEY DETECT A LIGHT LIKE THAT.
LET'S START SEARCHING!
OKAY!

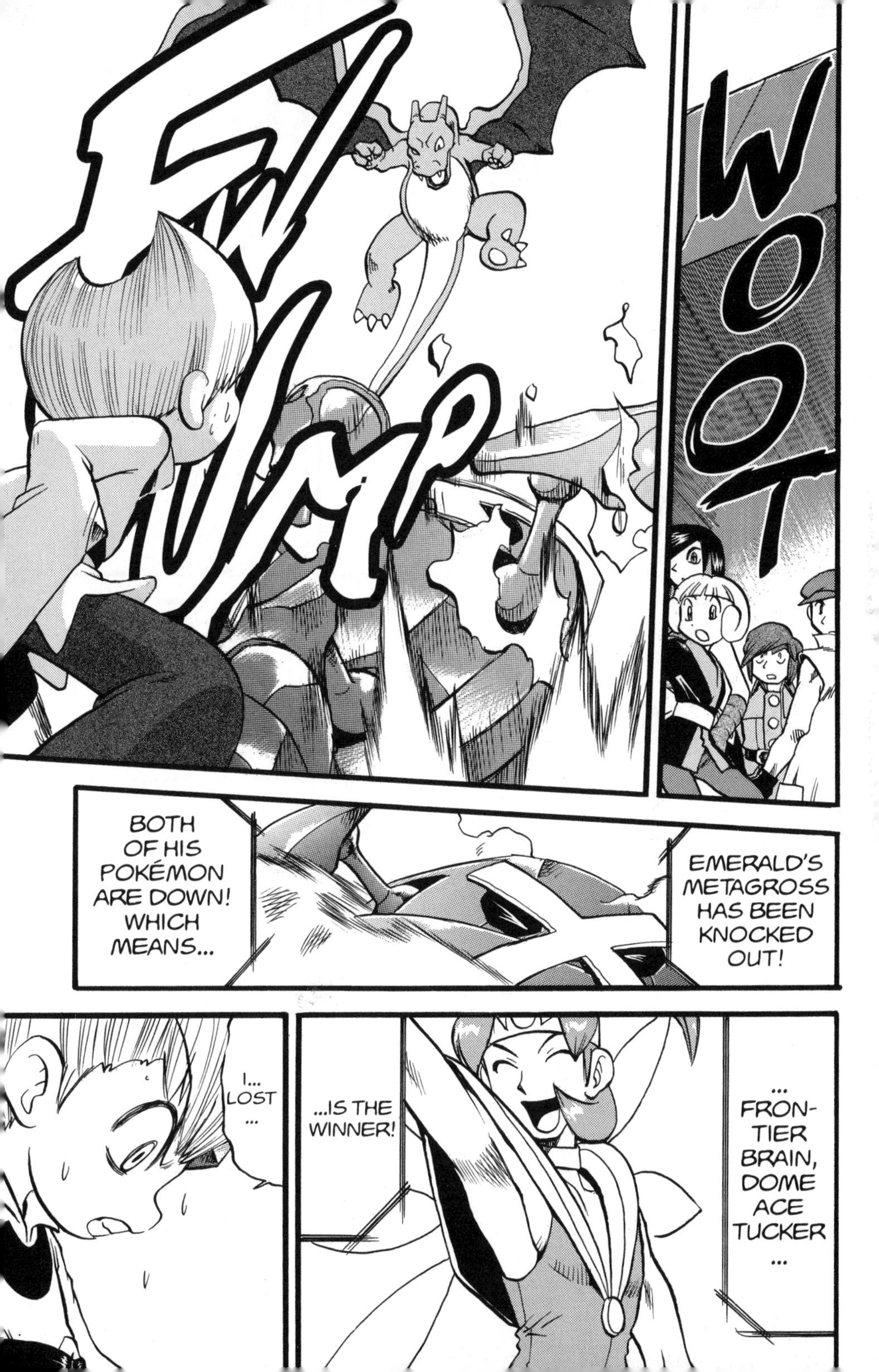
WOOT
FWUMP
EMERALD'S METAGROSS HAS BEEN KNOCKED OUT!
BOTH OF HIS POKÉMON ARE DOWN! WHICH MEANS...
... FRON-TIER BRAIN, DOME ACE TUCKER ...
...IS THE WINNER!
I... LOST ...

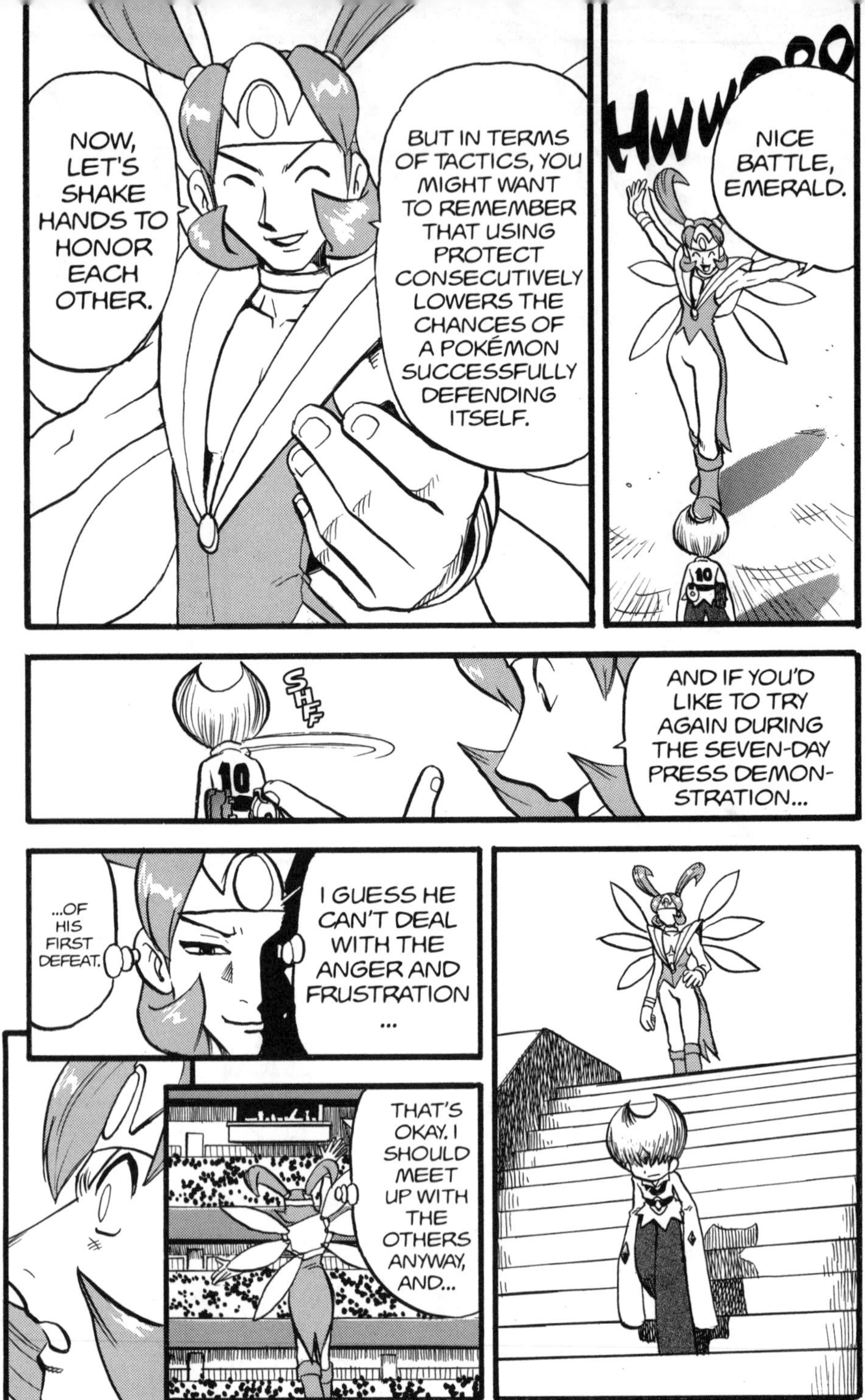
NICE BATTLE, EMERALD.
BUT IN TERMS OF TACTICS, YOU MIGHT WANT TO REMEMBER THAT USING PROTECT CONSECUTIVELY LOWERS THE CHANCES OF A POKÉMON SUCCESSFULLY DEFENDING ITSELF.
NOW, LET'S SHAKE HANDS TO HONOR EACH OTHER.
AND IF YOU'D LIKE TO TRY AGAIN DURING THE SEVEN-DAY PRESS DEMON-STRATION...
SHFF
I GUESS HE CAN'T DEAL WITH THE ANGER AND FRUSTRATION ...
...OF HIS FIRST DEFEAT.
THAT'S OKAY. I SHOULD MEET UP WITH THE OTHERS ANYWAY, AND...

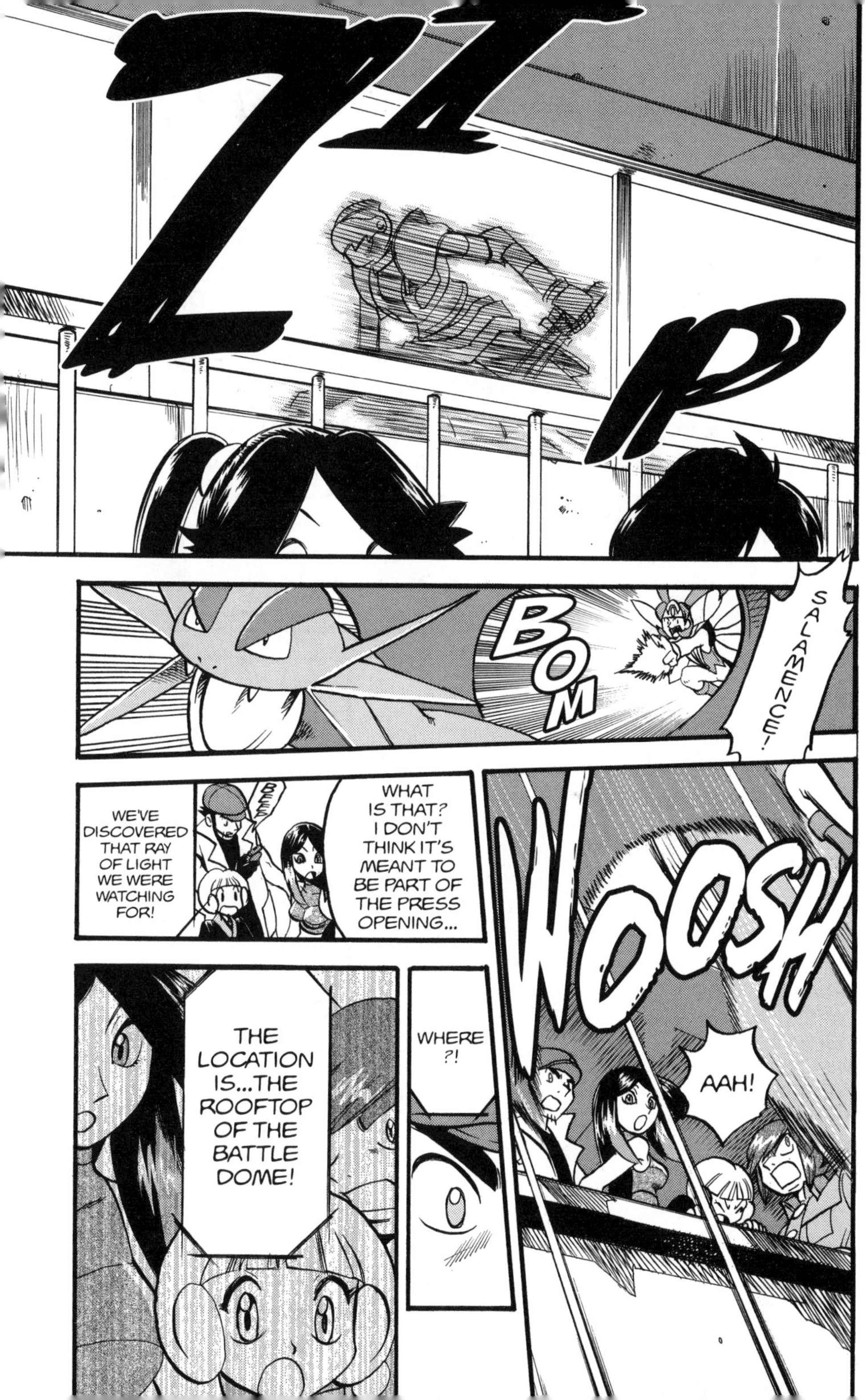
ZIP
SALAMENCE!
BOOM
WOOSH
AAH!
BEEP
WHAT IS THAT? I DON'T THINK IT'S MEANT TO BE PART OF THE PRESS OPENING...
WE'VE DISCOVERED THAT RAY OF LIGHT WE WERE WATCHING FOR!
WHERE?!
THE LOCATION IS...THE ROOFTOP OF THE BATTLE DOME!

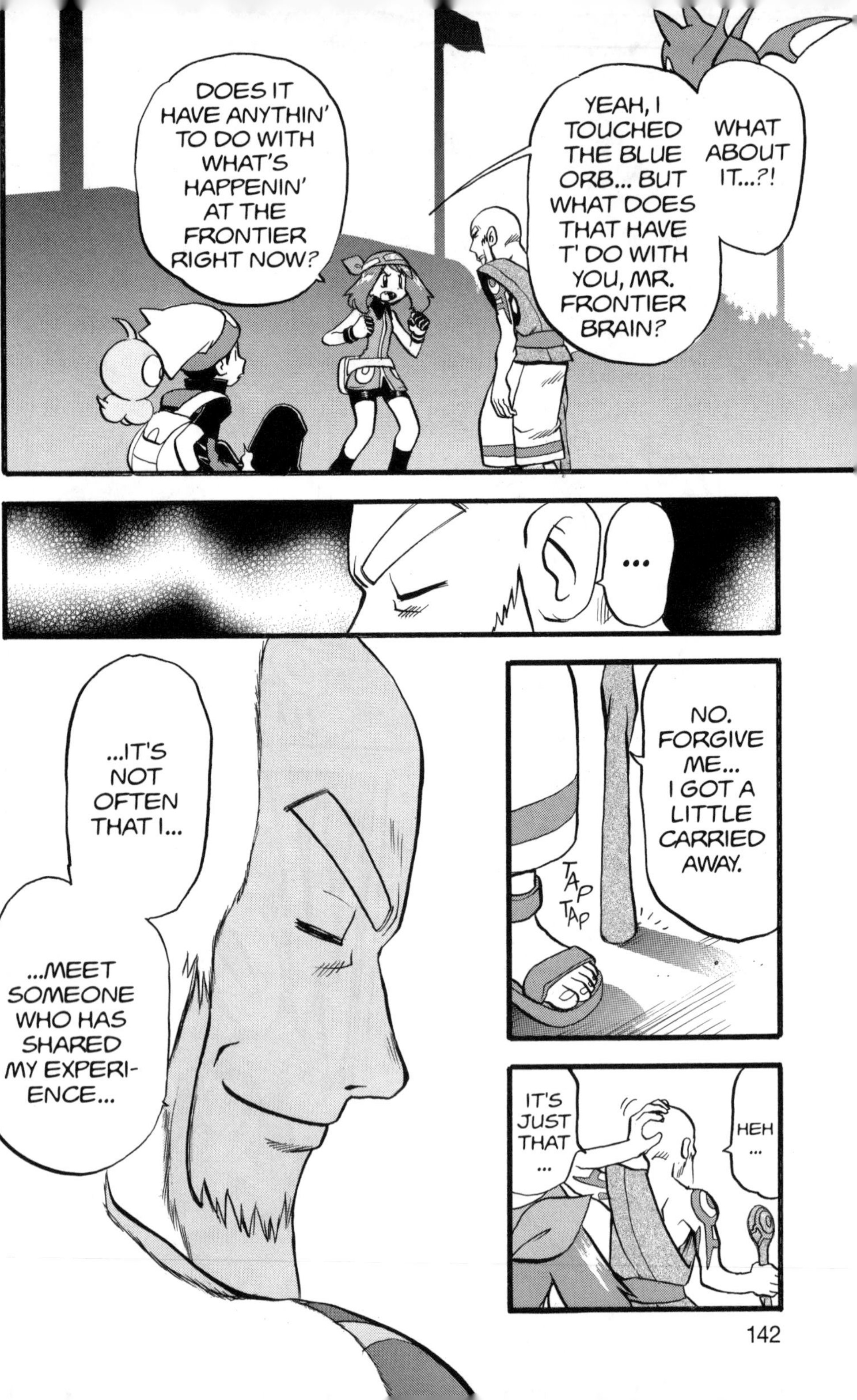
WHAT ABOUT IT...?!
YEAH, I TOUCHED THE BLUE ORB... BUT WHAT DOES THAT HAVE T' DO WITH YOU, MR. FRONTIER BRAIN?
DOES IT HAVE ANYTHIN' TO DO WITH WHAT'S HAPPENIN' AT THE FRONTIER RIGHT NOW?
...
NO. FORGIVE ME... I GOT A LITTLE CARRIED AWAY.
TAP TAP
HEH...
IT'S JUST THAT...
...IT'S NOT OFTEN THAT I...
...MEET SOMEONE WHO HAS SHARED MY EXPERIENCE...

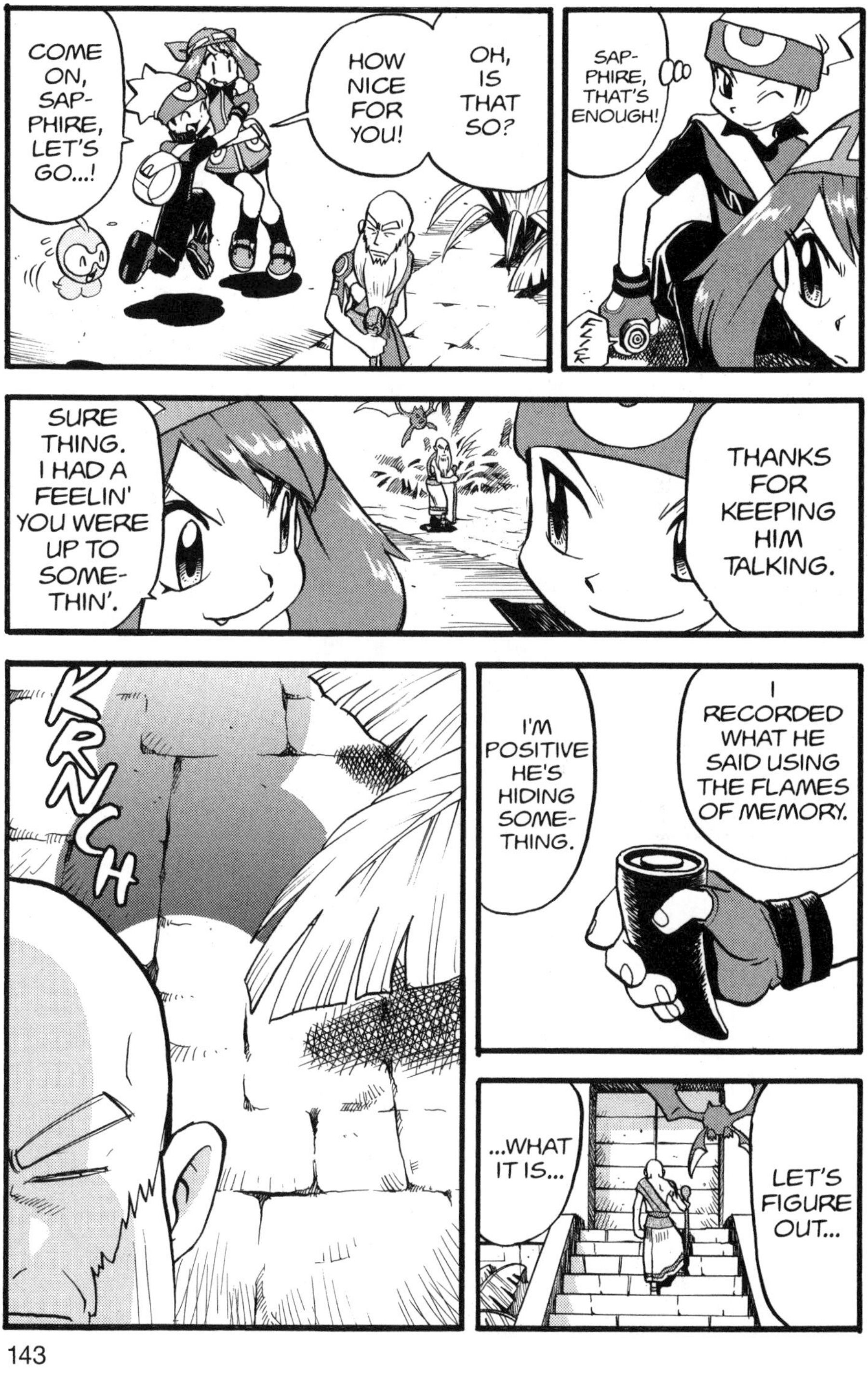
SAP-PHIRE, THAT'S ENOUGH!
FLICK
OH, IS THAT SO?
HOW NICE FOR YOU!
COME ON, SAP-PHIRE, LET'S GO...!
THANKS FOR KEEPING HIM TALKING.
SURE THING. I HAD A FEELIN' YOU WERE UP TO SOME-THIN'.
I RECORDED WHAT HE SAID USING THE FLAMES OF MEMORY.
I'M POSITIVE HE'S HIDING SOME-THING.
LET'S FIGURE OUT...
...WHAT IT IS...
KRNCH

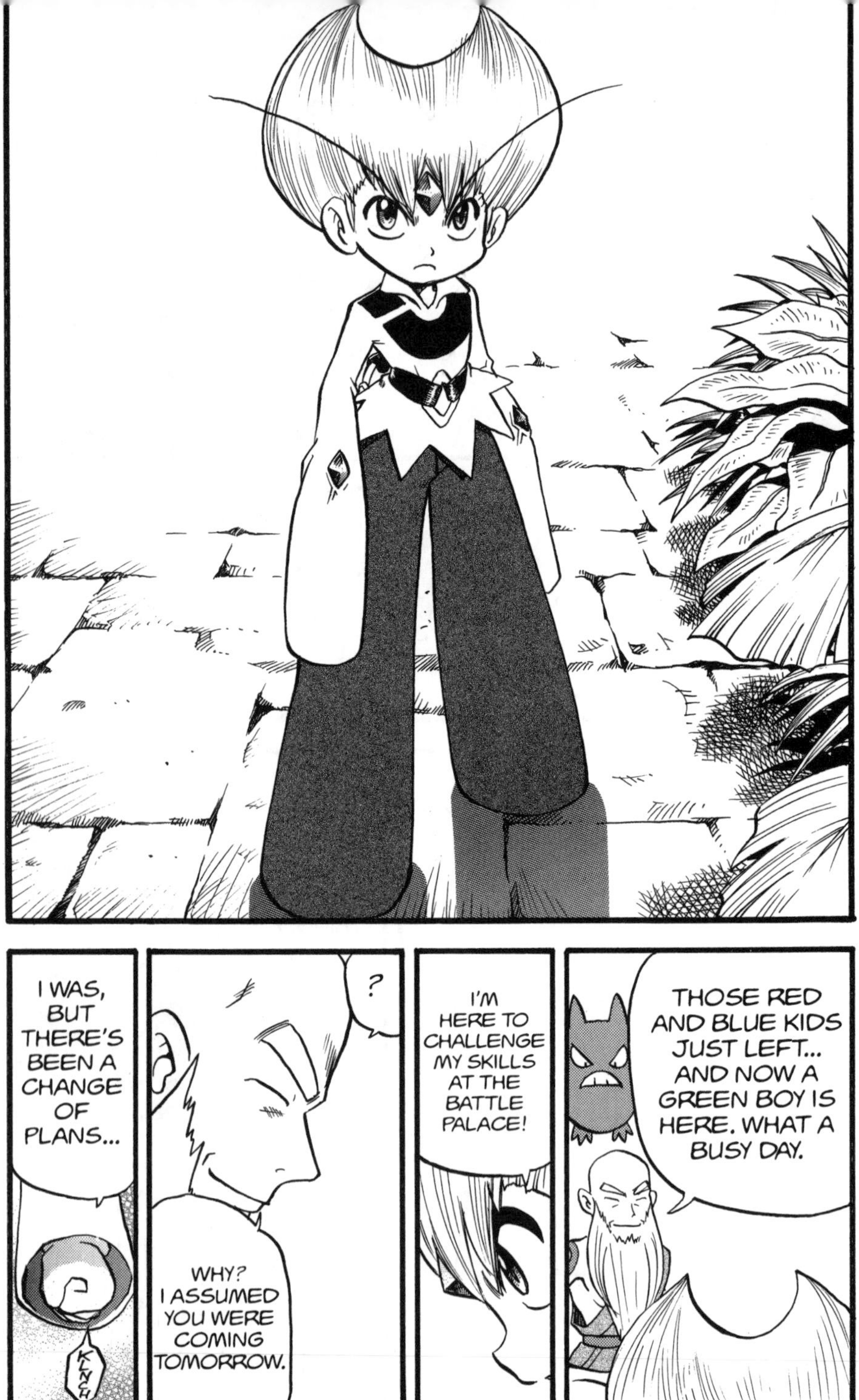
THOSE RED AND BLUE KIDS JUST LEFT... AND NOW A GREEN BOY IS HERE. WHAT A BUSY DAY.
I'M HERE TO CHALLENGE MY SKILLS AT THE BATTLE PALACE!
?
WHY? I ASSUMED YOU WERE COMING TOMORROW.
I WAS, BUT THERE'S BEEN A CHANGE OF PLANS...
KLNCH

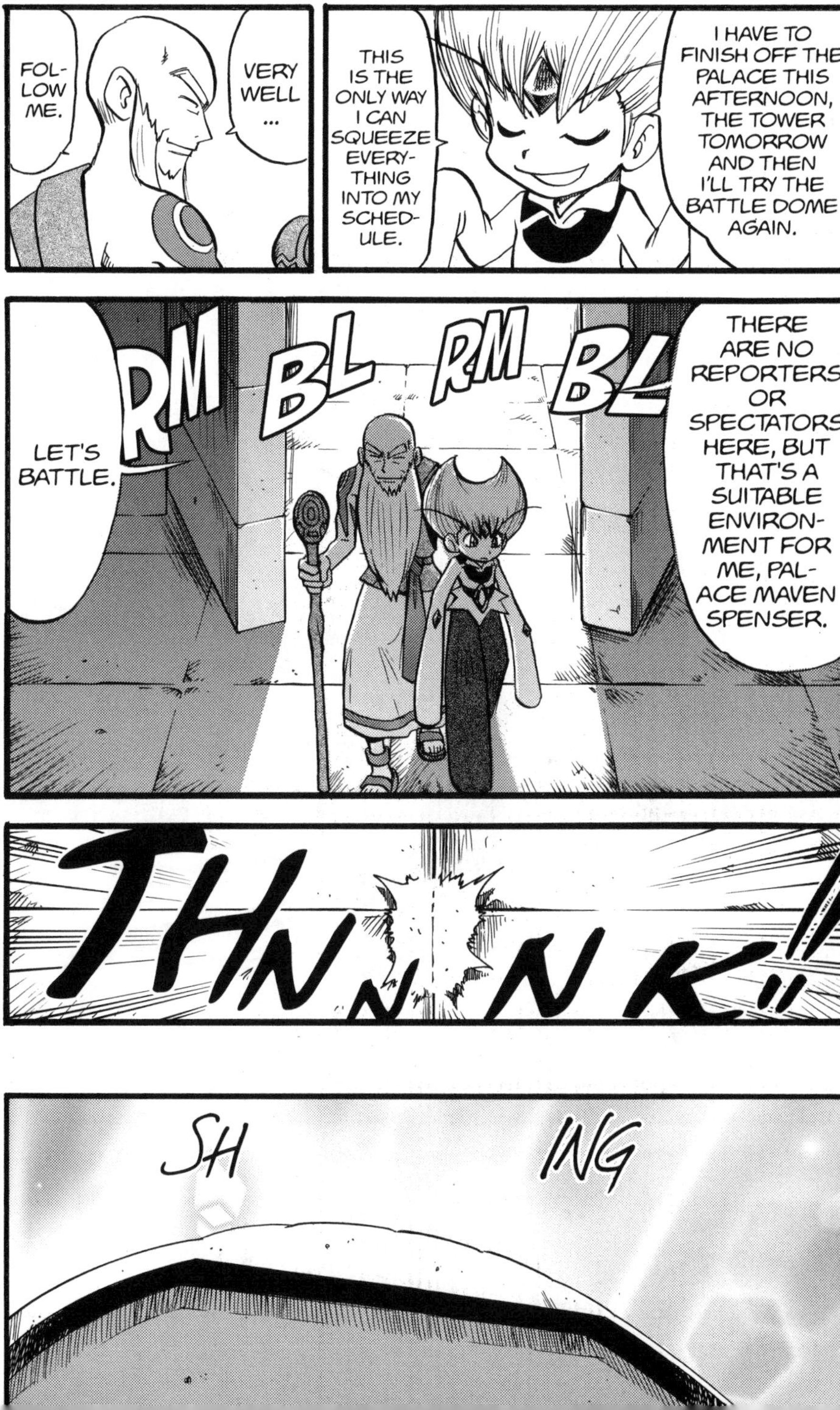
I HAVE TO FINISH OFF THE PALACE THIS AFTERNOON, THE TOWER TOMORROW AND THEN I'LL TRY THE BATTLE DOME AGAIN.
THIS IS THE ONLY WAY I CAN SQUEEZE EVERY-THING INTO MY SCHED-ULE.
VERY WELL ...
FOL-LOW ME.
THERE ARE NO REPORTERS OR SPECTATORS HERE, BUT THAT'S A SUITABLE ENVIRON-MENT FOR ME, PAL-ACE MAVEN SPENSER.
RM BL RM BL
LET'S BATTLE.
THNNNK!!
SH ING

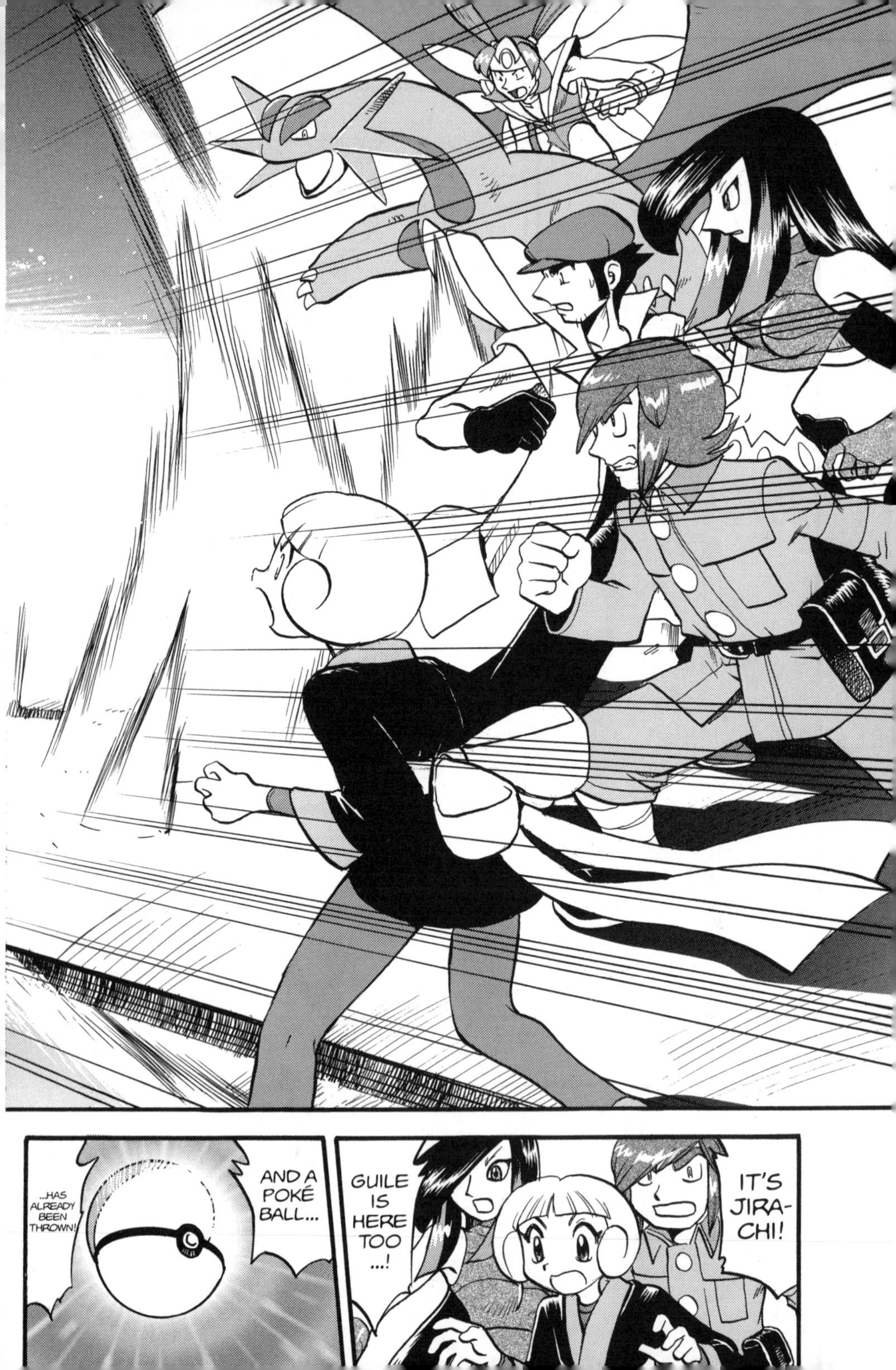
IT'S JIRACHI!
GUILE IS HERE TOO ...!
AND A POKÉ BALL...
...HAS ALREADY BEEN THROWN!

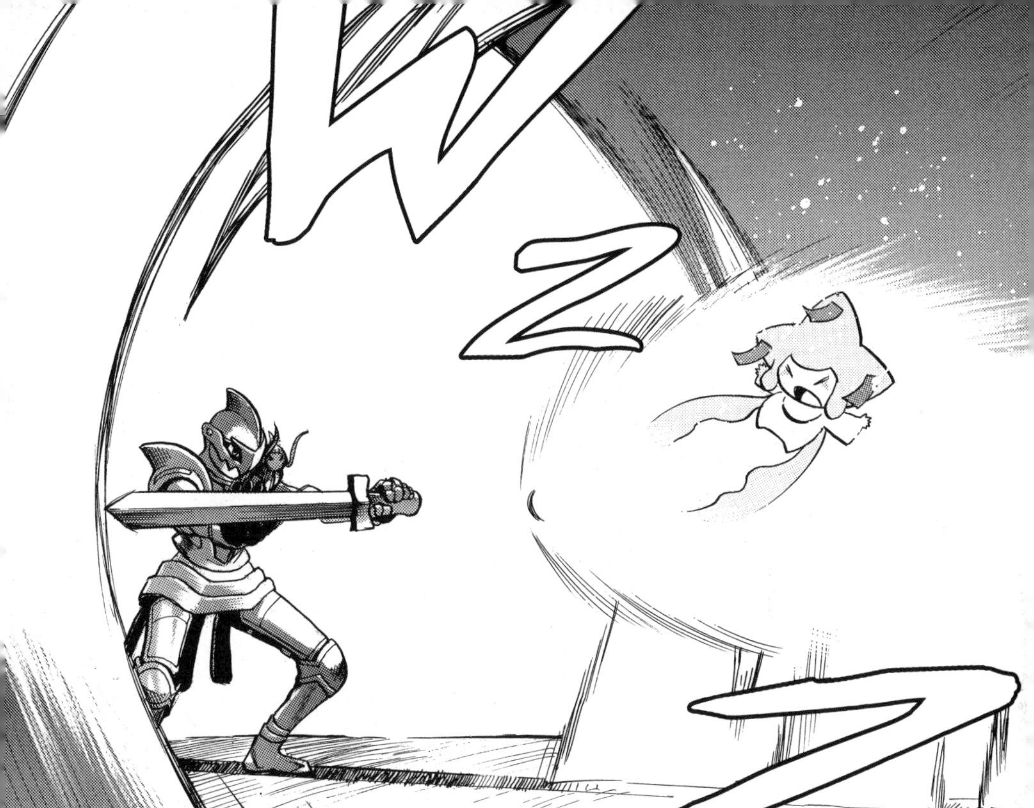
ZZZ
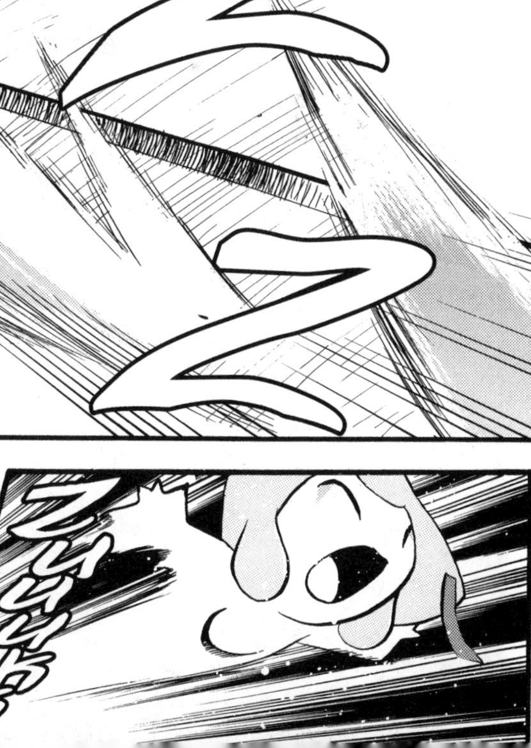
ZUUUK
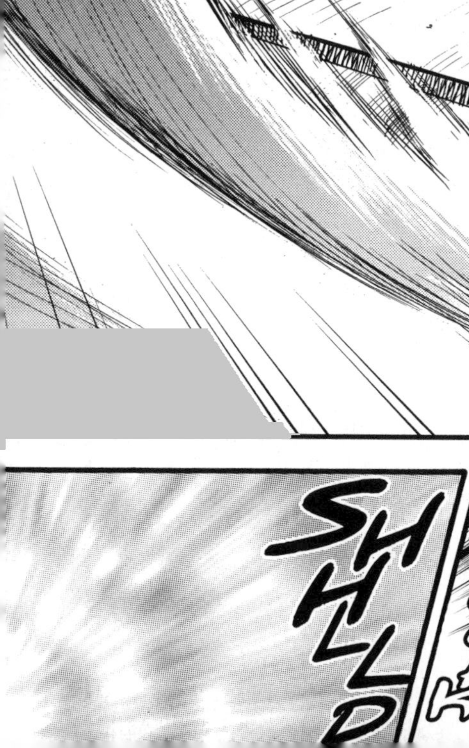
SHLLD

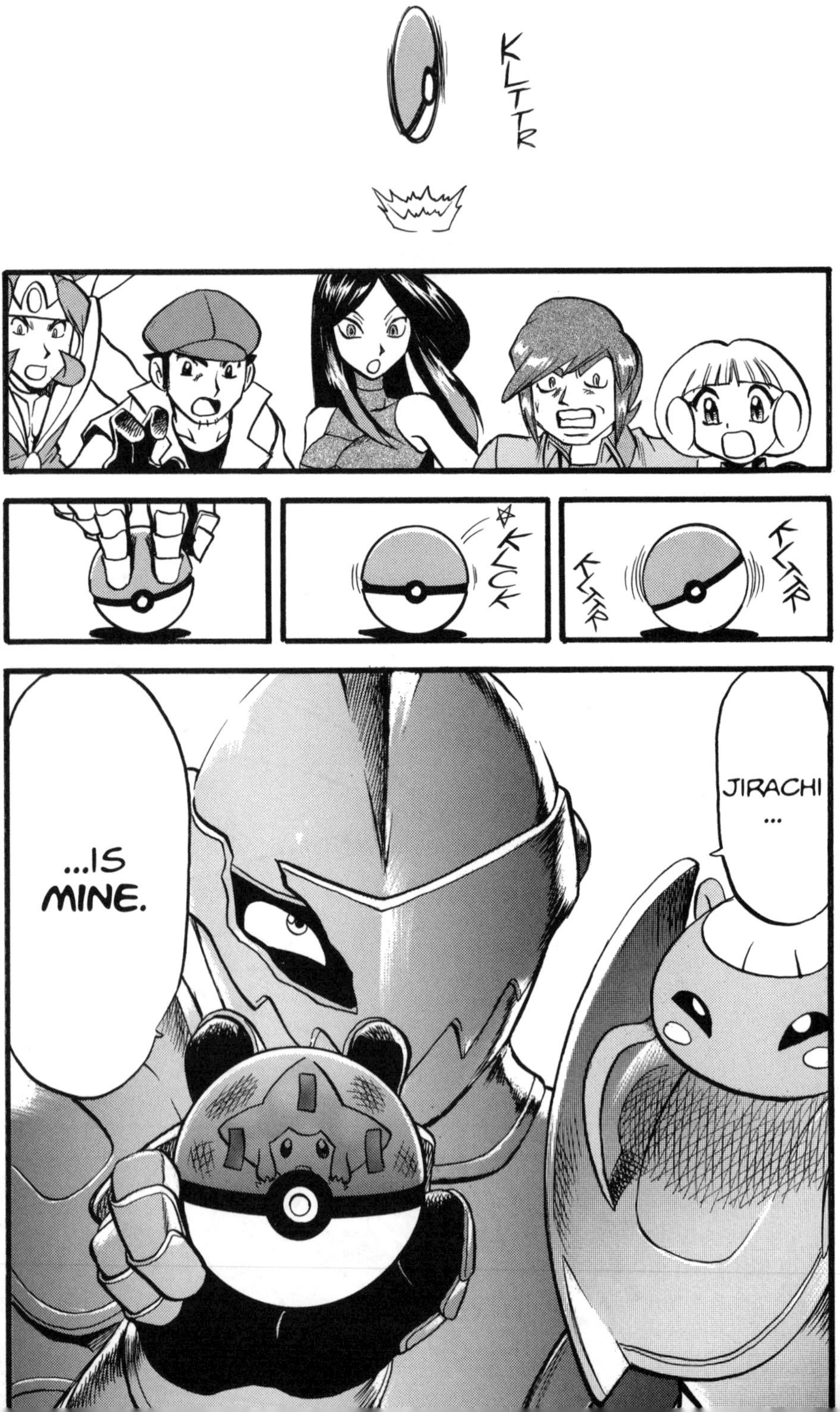
KLTTR
KLTTR
KLTTR
KLCK
JIRACHI ...
...IS MINE.

DEAR MEMBERS OF THE PRESS...

Thank you for visiting the Battle Frontier today. Permit me to continue explaining the rules of this facility...

OWNER: SCOTT

FACILITY RULES

BATTLE TOWER 2

■ **THE TYPES OF BATTLE AT THE BATTLE TOWER** ■

Apart from the three battle styles above, multiplayer battles will also be available after the official opening of the Battle Frontier. These will be Double Battles fought between Battle Towers from other regions.

① Single Battle
A one-on-one battle using three Pokémon. This is the only battle style Frontier Brain Anabel will take part in.

② Double Battle
A two-on-two battle using four Pokémon.

③ Multi Battle
A two-on-two tag battle fought by teaming up with another contestant, such as a Pokémon Breeder, Kindler, Lass and others. The battle is fought by four Pokémon, two from the challenger and two from the tag partner.

Standing in the Way
with Starmie

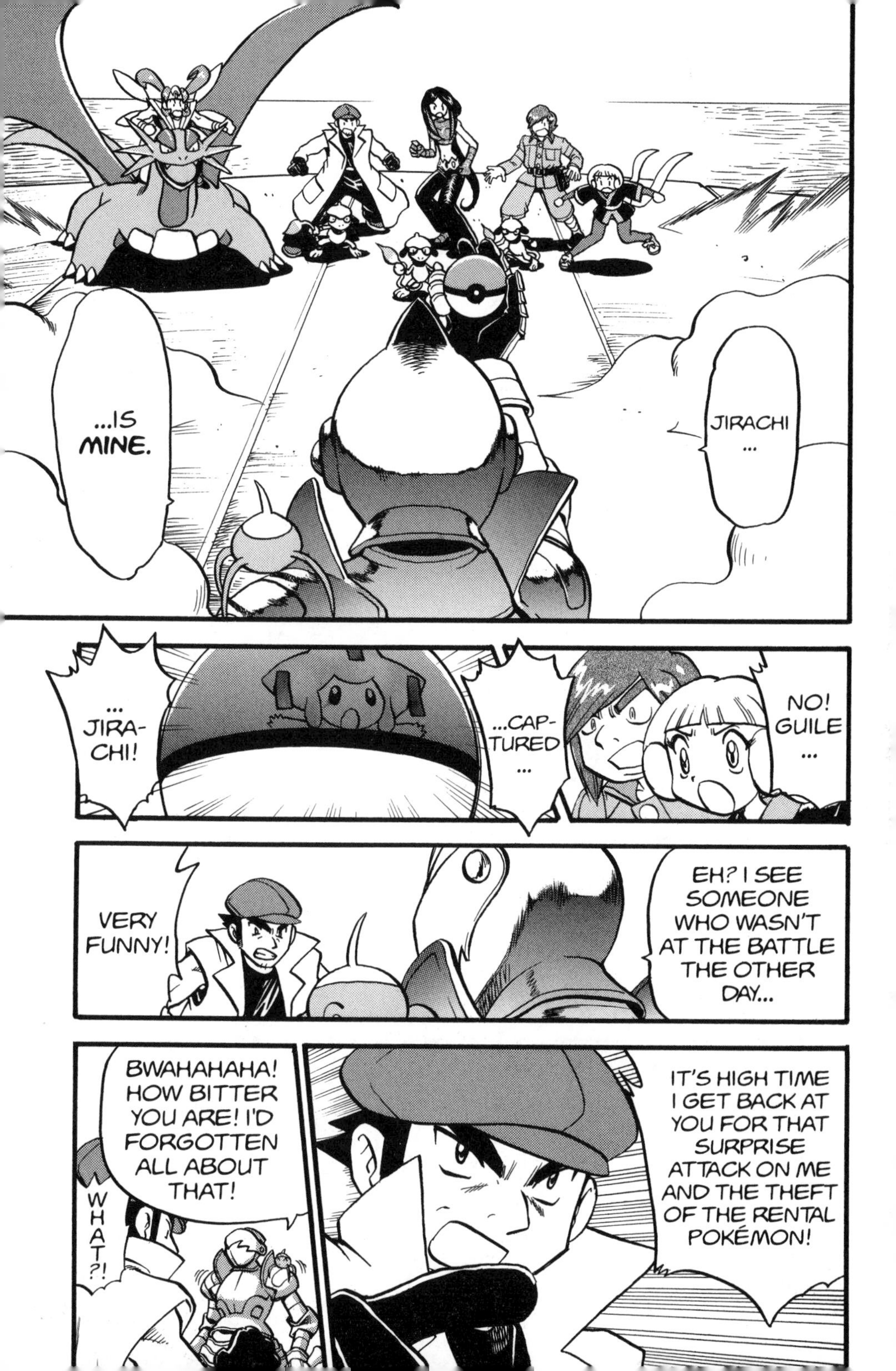
JIRACHI ...
...IS MINE.
NO! GUILE ...
...CAPTURED ...
... JIRACHI!
EH? I SEE SOMEONE WHO WASN'T AT THE BATTLE THE OTHER DAY...
VERY FUNNY!
IT'S HIGH TIME I GET BACK AT YOU FOR THAT SURPRISE ATTACK ON ME AND THE THEFT OF THE RENTAL POKÉMON!
BWAHAHAHA! HOW BITTER YOU ARE! I'D FORGOTTEN ALL ABOUT THAT!
WHAT?!

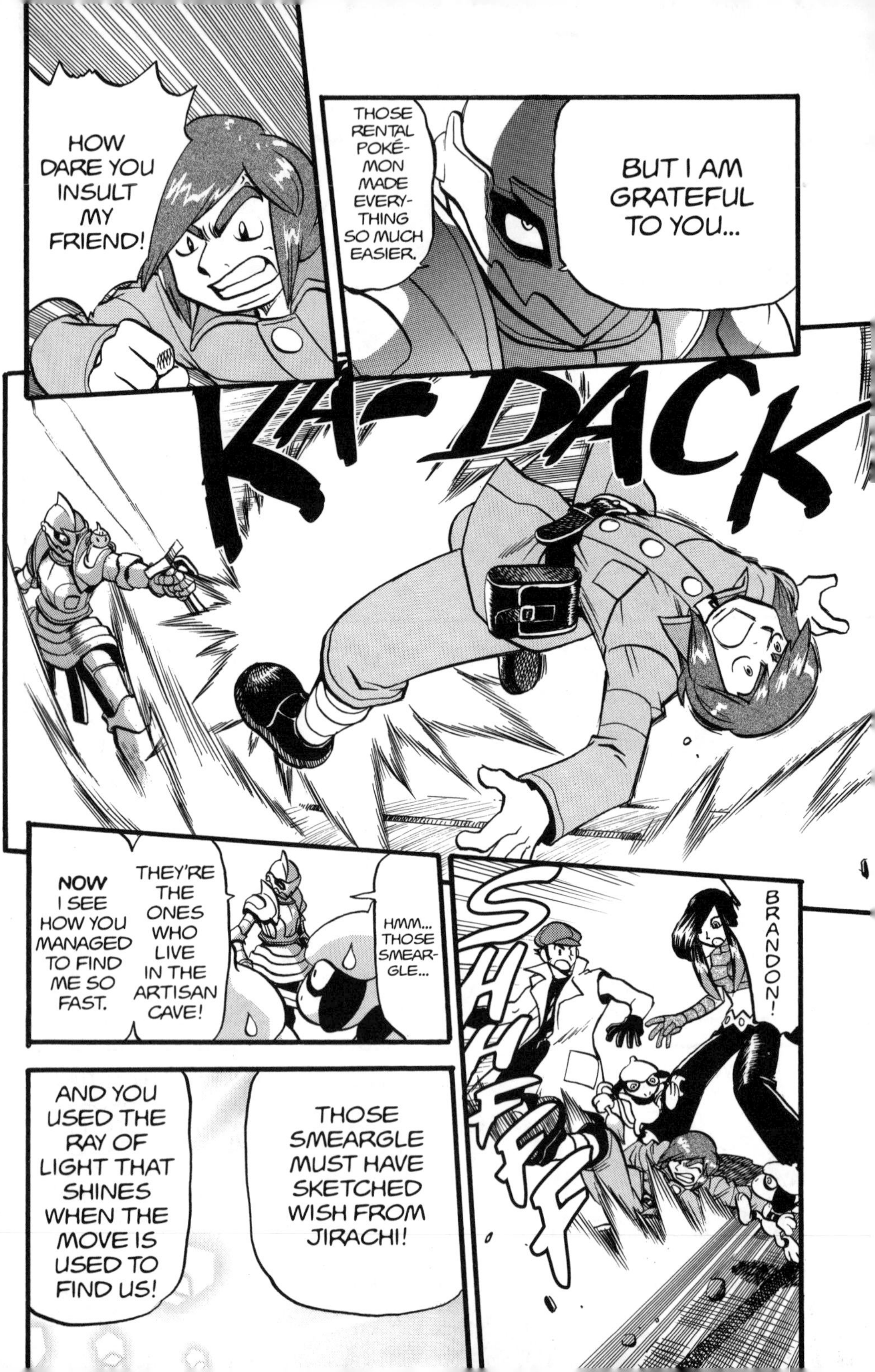

BUT I AM GRATEFUL TO YOU...
THOSE RENTAL POKÉMON MADE EVERYTHING SO MUCH EASIER.
HOW DARE YOU INSULT MY FRIEND!
KH-DACK
SHHFFF
BRANDON!
HMM... THOSE SMEARGLE...
THEY'RE THE ONES WHO LIVE IN THE ARTISAN CAVE!
NOW I SEE HOW YOU MANAGED TO FIND ME SO FAST.
THOSE SMEARGLE MUST HAVE SKETCHED WISH FROM JIRACHI!
AND YOU USED THE RAY OF LIGHT THAT SHINES WHEN THE MOVE IS USED TO FIND US!

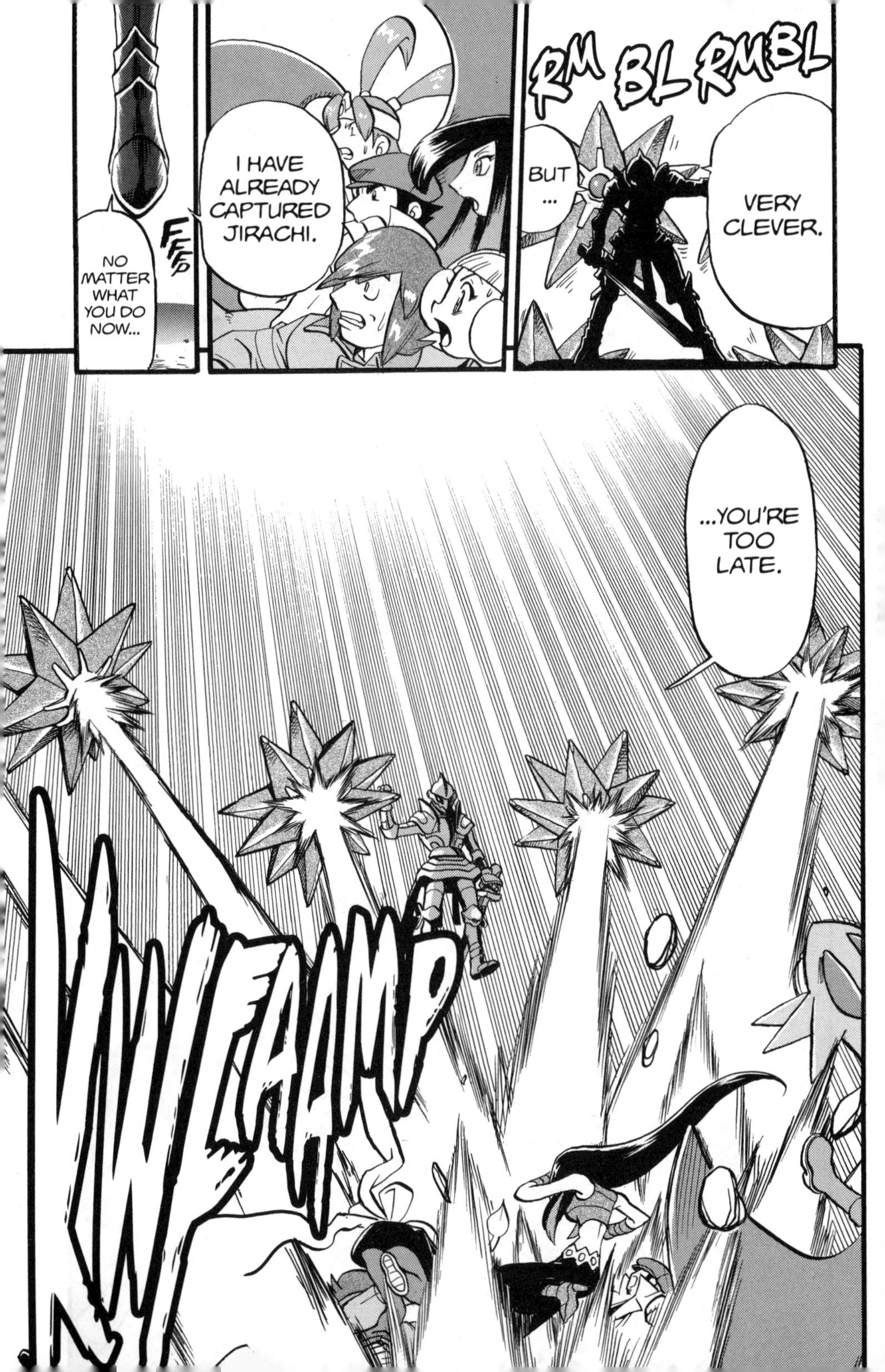
RM BL RMBL
VERY CLEVER.
BUT ...
I HAVE ALREADY CAPTURED JIRACHI.
NO MATTER WHAT YOU DO NOW...
FFFP
...YOU'RE TOO LATE.
WHAAMP

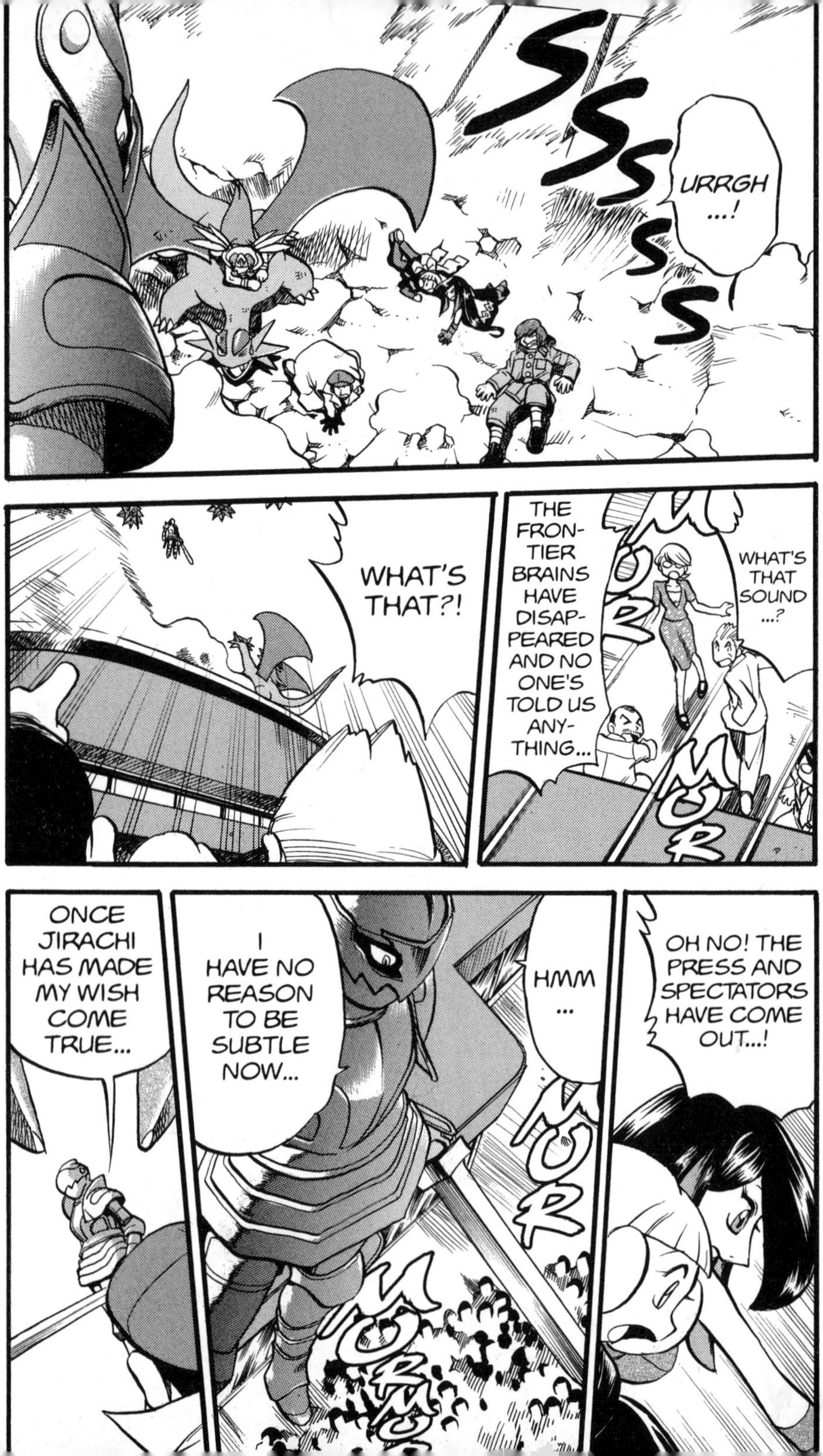
SSSSS
URRGH...!
WHAT'S THAT?!
THE FRONTIER BRAINS HAVE DISAPPEARED AND NO ONE'S TOLD US ANYTHING...
WHAT'S THAT SOUND...?
MUR
MUR
ONCE JIRACHI HAS MADE MY WISH COME TRUE...
I HAVE NO REASON TO BE SUBTLE NOW...
HMM...
MUR
MUR
OH NO! THE PRESS AND SPECTATORS HAVE COME OUT...!

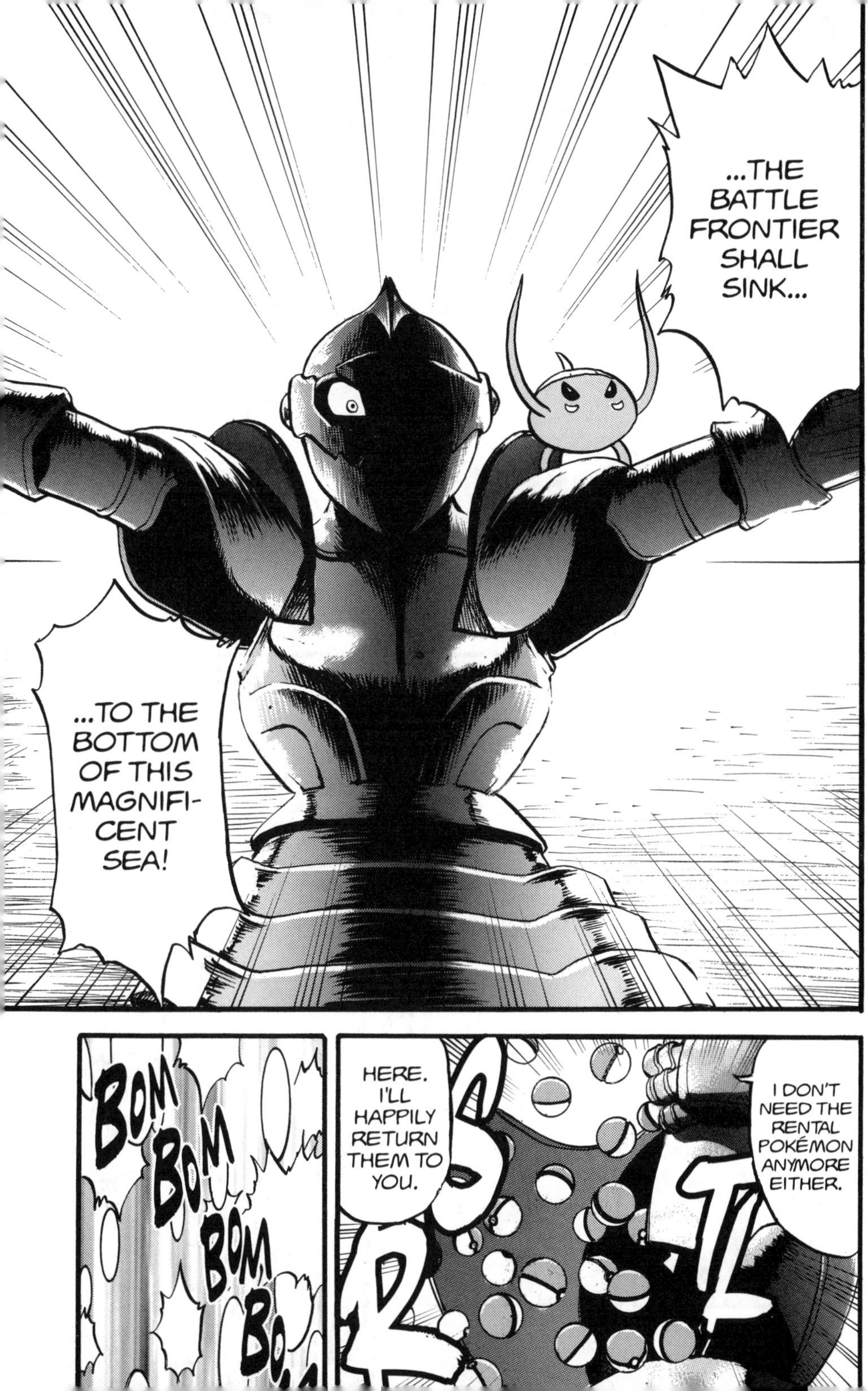
...THE BATTLE FRONTIER SHALL SINK...
...TO THE BOTTOM OF THIS MAGNIFICENT SEA!
I DON'T NEED THE RENTAL POKÉMON ANYMORE EITHER.
HERE. I'LL HAPPILY RETURN THEM TO YOU.
BOM BOM BOM

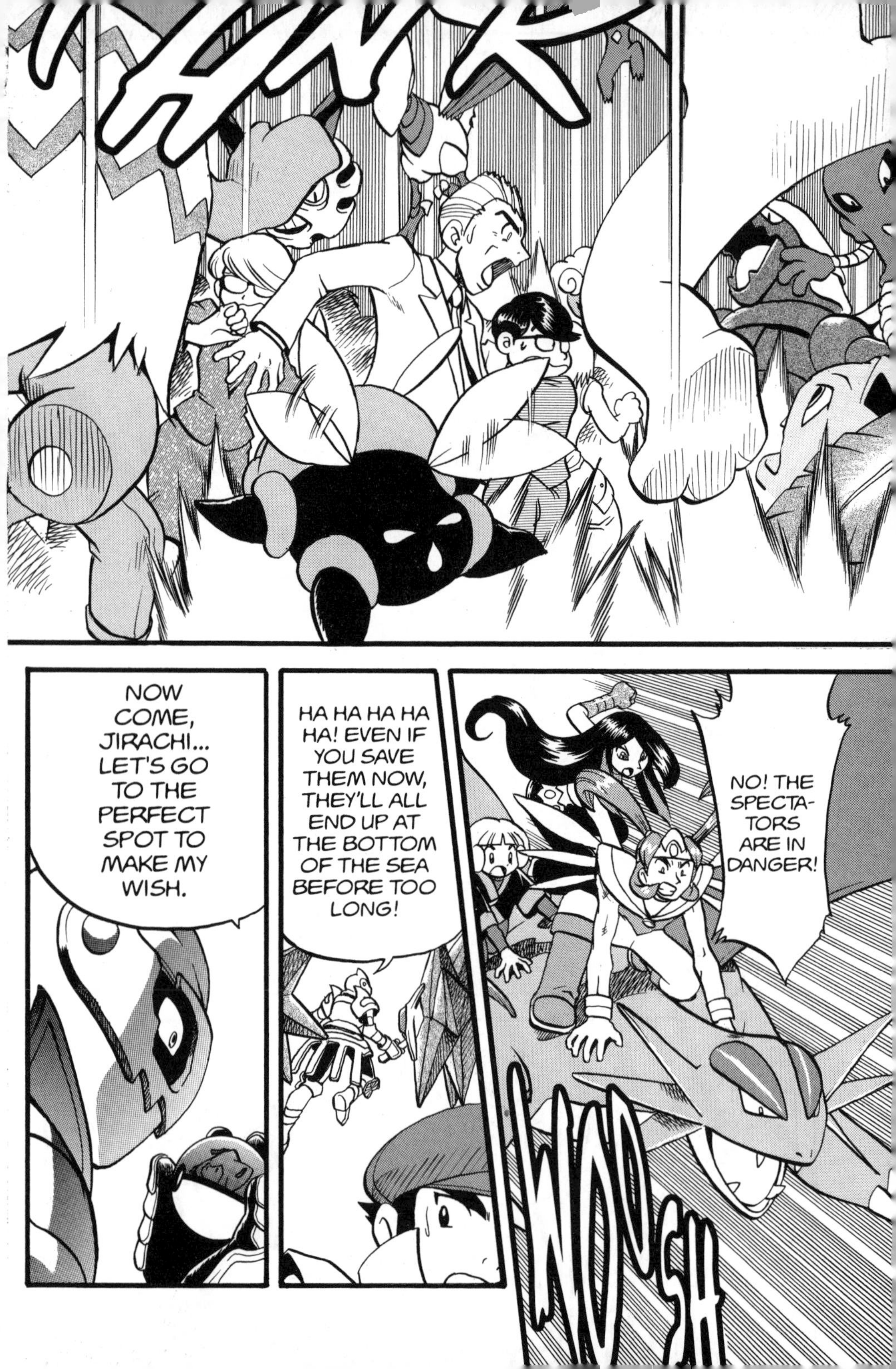
NO! THE SPECTA-TORS ARE IN DANGER!
WOOSH
HA HA HA HA HA! EVEN IF YOU SAVE THEM NOW, THEY'LL ALL END UP AT THE BOTTOM OF THE SEA BEFORE TOO LONG!
NOW COME, JIRACHI... LET'S GO TO THE PERFECT SPOT TO MAKE MY WISH.

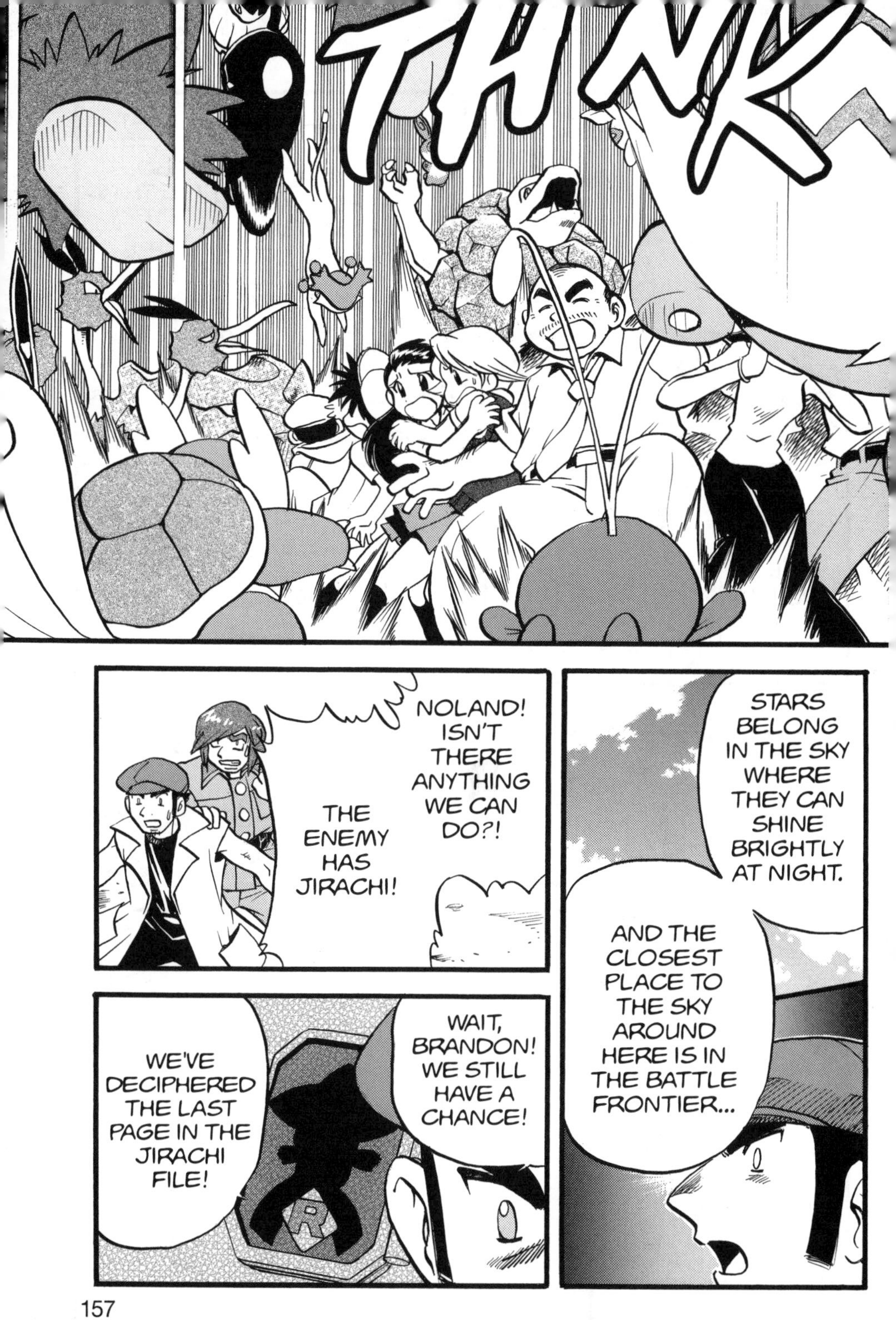
THNK
STARS BELONG IN THE SKY WHERE THEY CAN SHINE BRIGHTLY AT NIGHT.
AND THE CLOSEST PLACE TO THE SKY AROUND HERE IS IN THE BATTLE FRONTIER...
NOLAND! ISN'T THERE ANYTHING WE CAN DO?!
THE ENEMY HAS JIRACHI!
WAIT, BRANDON! WE STILL HAVE A CHANCE!
WE'VE DECIPHERED THE LAST PAGE IN THE JIRACHI FILE!

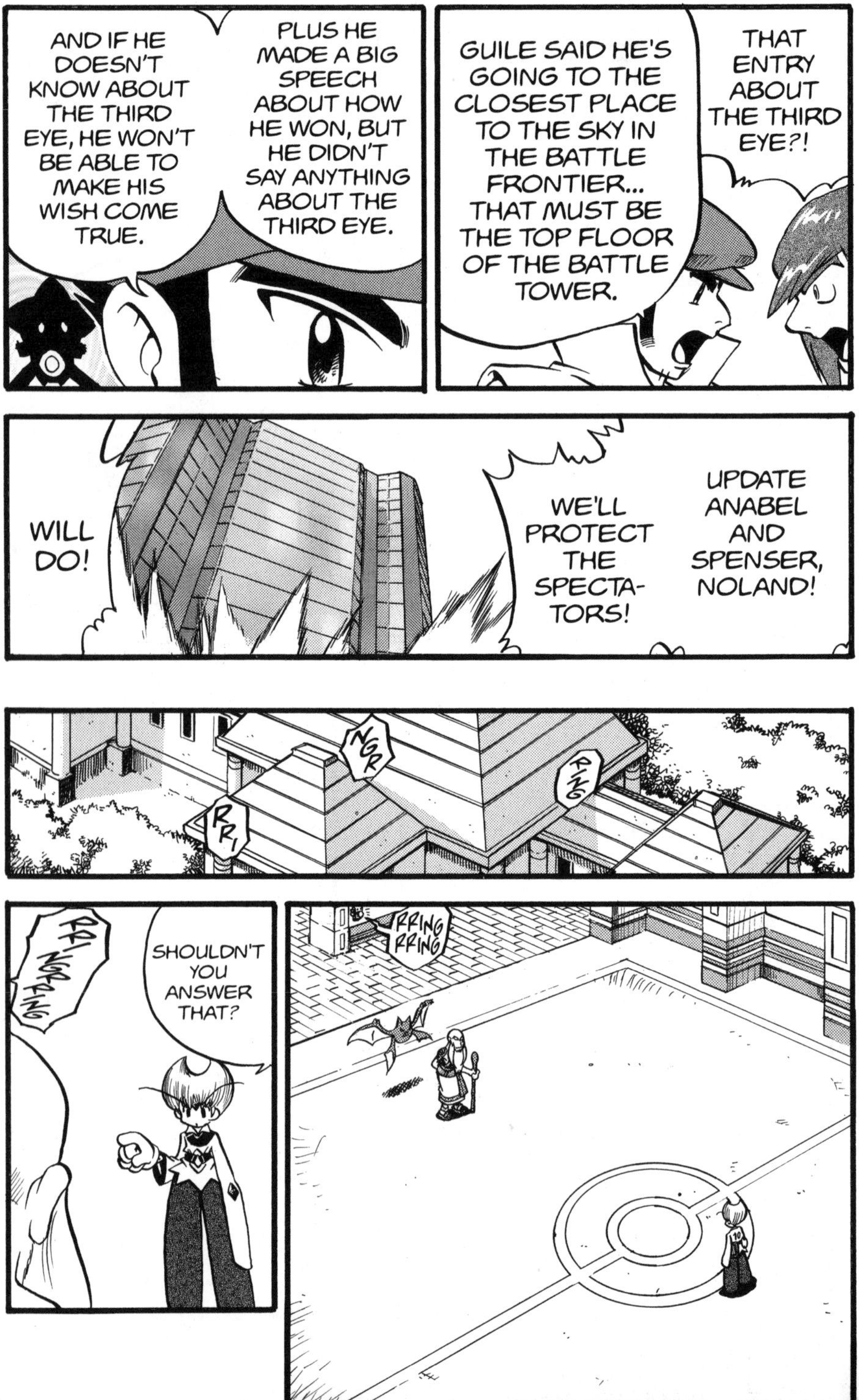
THAT ENTRY ABOUT THE THIRD EYE?!
GUILE SAID HE'S GOING TO THE CLOSEST PLACE TO THE SKY IN THE BATTLE FRONTIER... THAT MUST BE THE TOP FLOOR OF THE BATTLE TOWER.
PLUS HE MADE A BIG SPEECH ABOUT HOW HE WON, BUT HE DIDN'T SAY ANYTHING ABOUT THE THIRD EYE.
AND IF HE DOESN'T KNOW ABOUT THE THIRD EYE, HE WON'T BE ABLE TO MAKE HIS WISH COME TRUE.
UPDATE ANABEL AND SPENSER, NOLAND!
WE'LL PROTECT THE SPECTA-TORS!
WILL DO!
RING
NGR
RRI
RRING RRING
SHOULDN'T YOU ANSWER THAT?
RRI- NGRRING

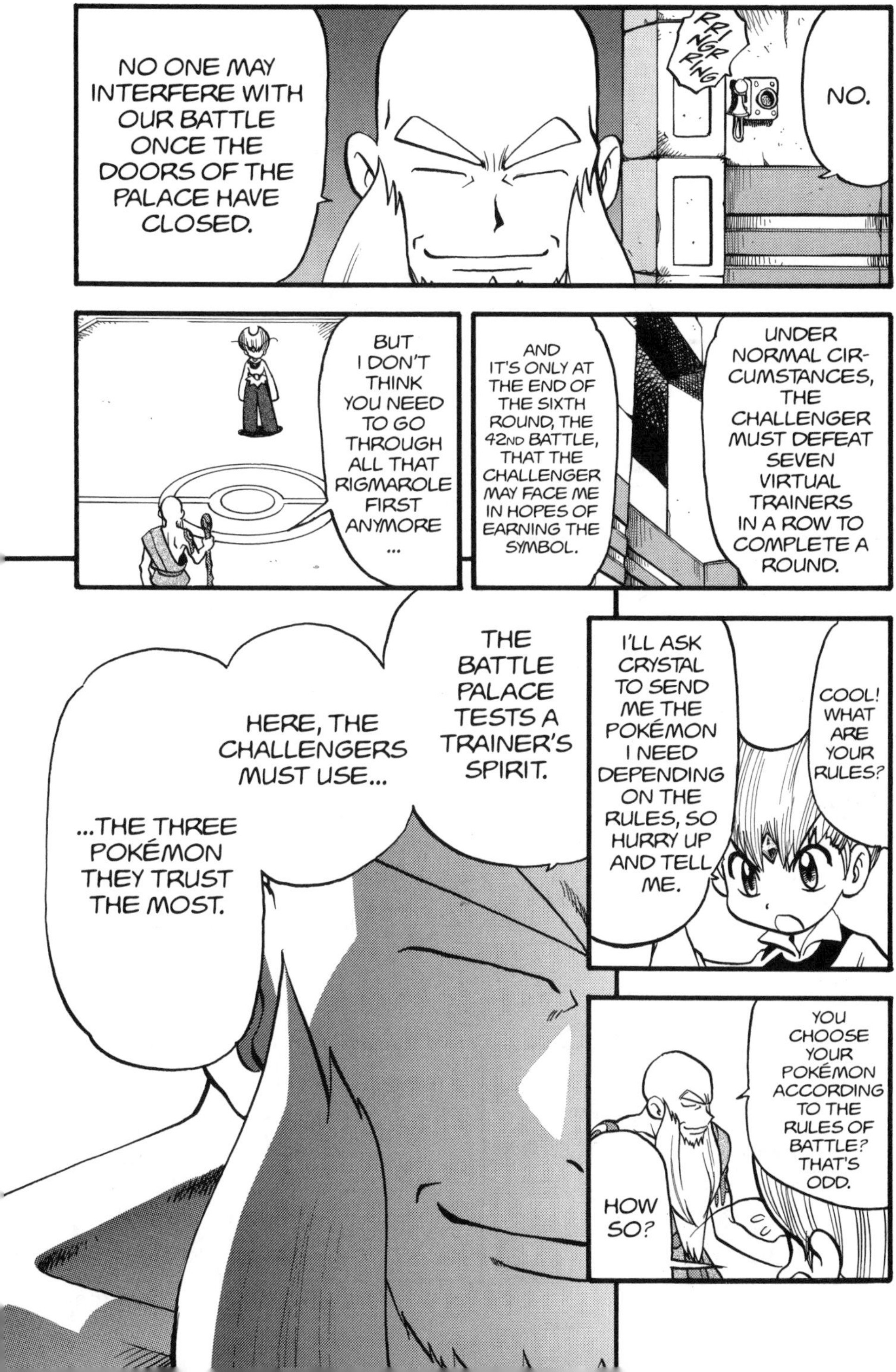
NO.
RRING RRING
NO ONE MAY INTERFERE WITH OUR BATTLE ONCE THE DOORS OF THE PALACE HAVE CLOSED.
UNDER NORMAL CIR-CUMSTANCES, THE CHALLENGER MUST DEFEAT SEVEN VIRTUAL TRAINERS IN A ROW TO COMPLETE A ROUND.
AND IT'S ONLY AT THE END OF THE SIXTH ROUND, THE 42ND BATTLE, THAT THE CHALLENGER MAY FACE ME IN HOPES OF EARNING THE SYMBOL.
BUT I DON'T THINK YOU NEED TO GO THROUGH ALL THAT RIGMAROLE FIRST ANYMORE...
COOL! WHAT ARE YOUR RULES?
I'LL ASK CRYSTAL TO SEND ME THE POKÉMON I NEED DEPENDING ON THE RULES, SO HURRY UP AND TELL ME.
YOU CHOOSE YOUR POKÉMON ACCORDING TO THE RULES OF BATTLE? THAT'S ODD.
HOW SO?
THE BATTLE PALACE TESTS A TRAINER'S SPIRIT.
HERE, THE CHALLENGERS MUST USE...
...THE THREE POKÉMON THEY TRUST THE MOST.

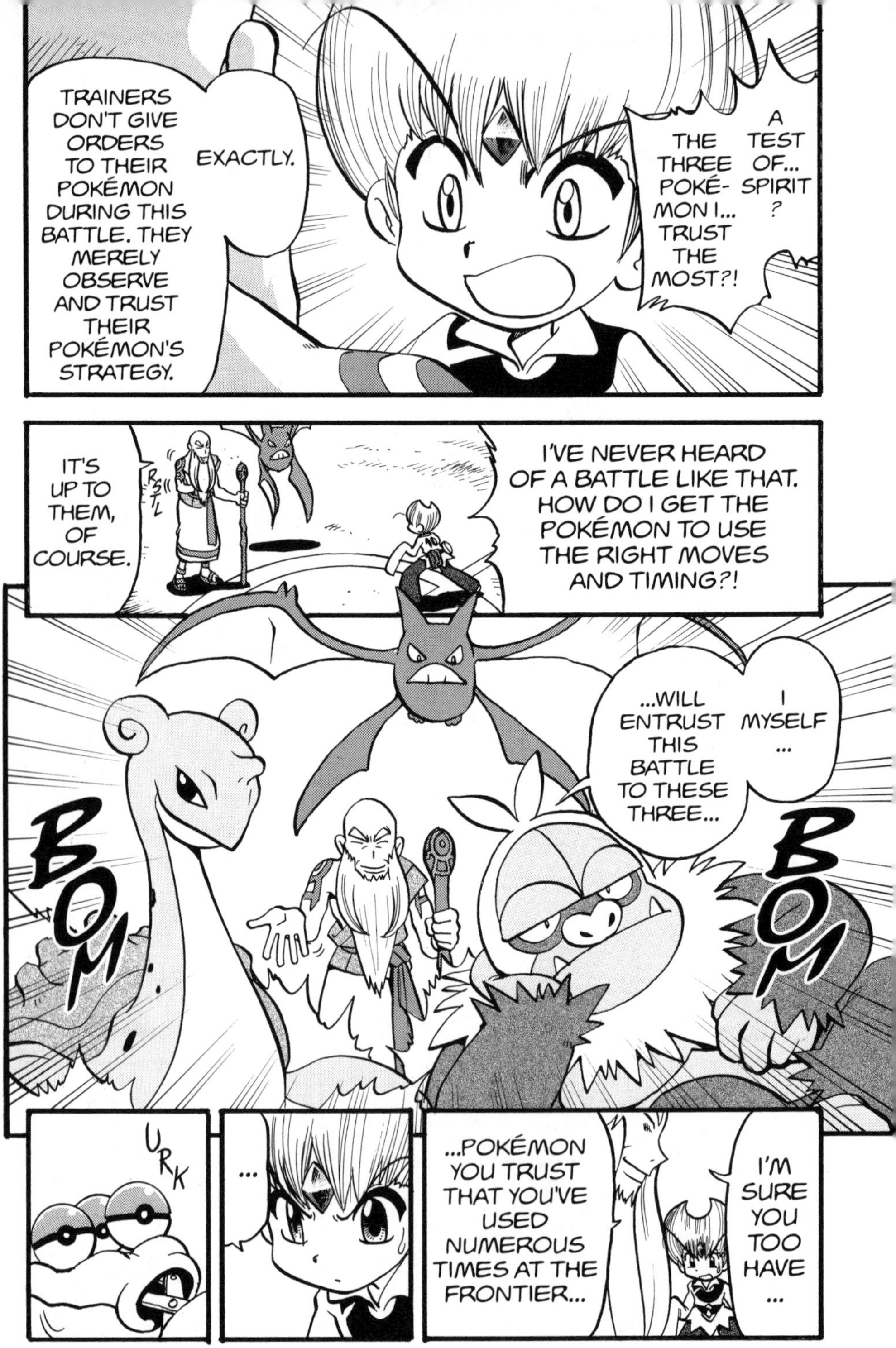
A TEST OF... SPIRIT?
THE THREE POKÉMON I... TRUST THE MOST?!
EXACTLY.
TRAINERS DON'T GIVE ORDERS TO THEIR POKÉMON DURING THIS BATTLE. THEY MERELY OBSERVE AND TRUST THEIR POKÉMON'S STRATEGY.
I'VE NEVER HEARD OF A BATTLE LIKE THAT. HOW DO I GET THE POKÉMON TO USE THE RIGHT MOVES AND TIMING?!
RSTL
IT'S UP TO THEM, OF COURSE.
I MYSELF...
...WILL ENTRUST THIS BATTLE TO THESE THREE...
BOOM
BOOM
I'M SURE YOU TOO HAVE...
...POKÉMON YOU TRUST THAT YOU'VE USED NUMEROUS TIMES AT THE FRONTIER...
...
URK

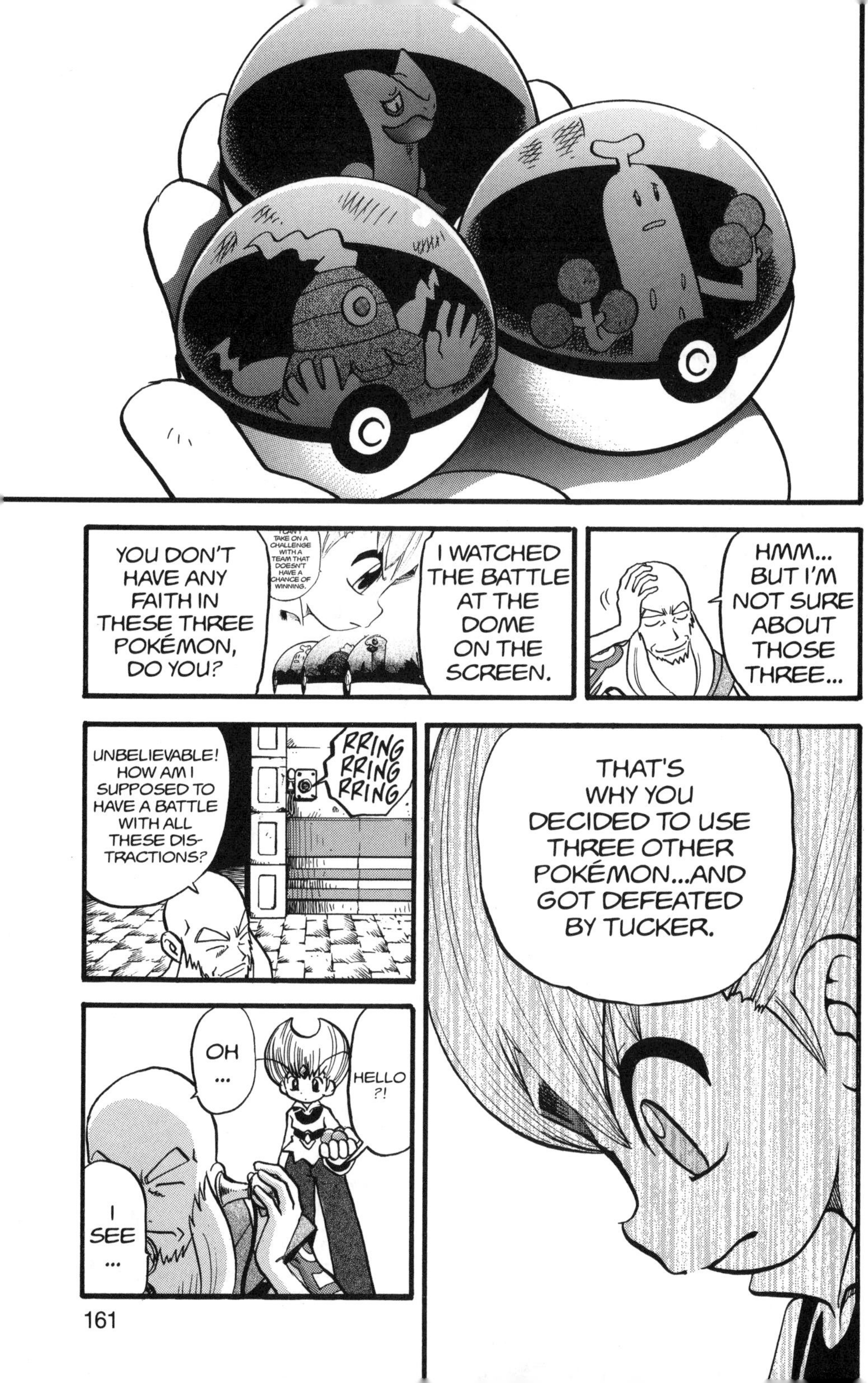
HMM... BUT I'M NOT SURE ABOUT THOSE THREE...
I WATCHED THE BATTLE AT THE DOME ON THE SCREEN.
I CAN'T TAKE ON A CHALLENGE WITH A TEAM THAT DOESN'T HAVE A CHANCE OF WINNING.
YOU DON'T HAVE ANY FAITH IN THESE THREE POKÉMON, DO YOU?
THAT'S WHY YOU DECIDED TO USE THREE OTHER POKÉMON...AND GOT DEFEATED BY TUCKER.
RRING RRING RRING
UNBELIEVABLE! HOW AM I SUPPOSED TO HAVE A BATTLE WITH ALL THESE DIS-TRACTIONS?
HELLO ?!
OH ...
I SEE ...

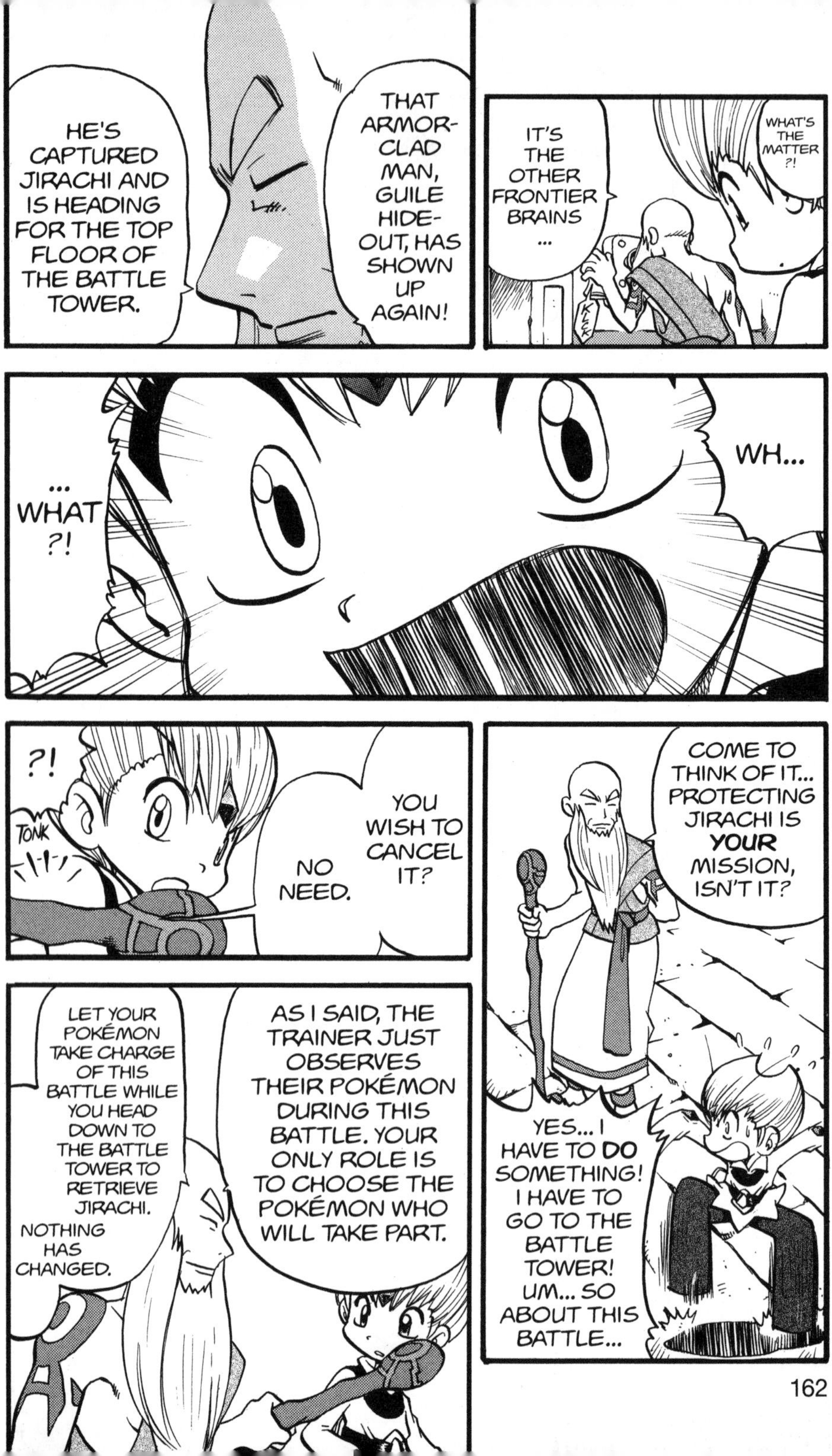
WHAT'S THE MATTER ?!
IT'S THE OTHER FRONTIER BRAINS ...
KLIK
THAT ARMOR-CLAD MAN, GUILE HIDE-OUT, HAS SHOWN UP AGAIN!
HE'S CAPTURED JIRACHI AND IS HEADING FOR THE TOP FLOOR OF THE BATTLE TOWER.
WH...
... WHAT ?!
COME TO THINK OF IT... PROTECTING JIRACHI IS **YOUR** MISSION, ISN'T IT?
YES... I HAVE TO **DO** SOMETHING! I HAVE TO GO TO THE BATTLE TOWER! UM... SO ABOUT THIS BATTLE...
YOU WISH TO CANCEL IT?
NO NEED.
?!
TONK
AS I SAID, THE TRAINER JUST OBSERVES THEIR POKÉMON DURING THIS BATTLE. YOUR ONLY ROLE IS TO CHOOSE THE POKÉMON WHO WILL TAKE PART.
LET YOUR POKÉMON TAKE CHARGE OF THIS BATTLE WHILE YOU HEAD DOWN TO THE BATTLE TOWER TO RETRIEVE JIRACHI.
NOTHING HAS CHANGED.

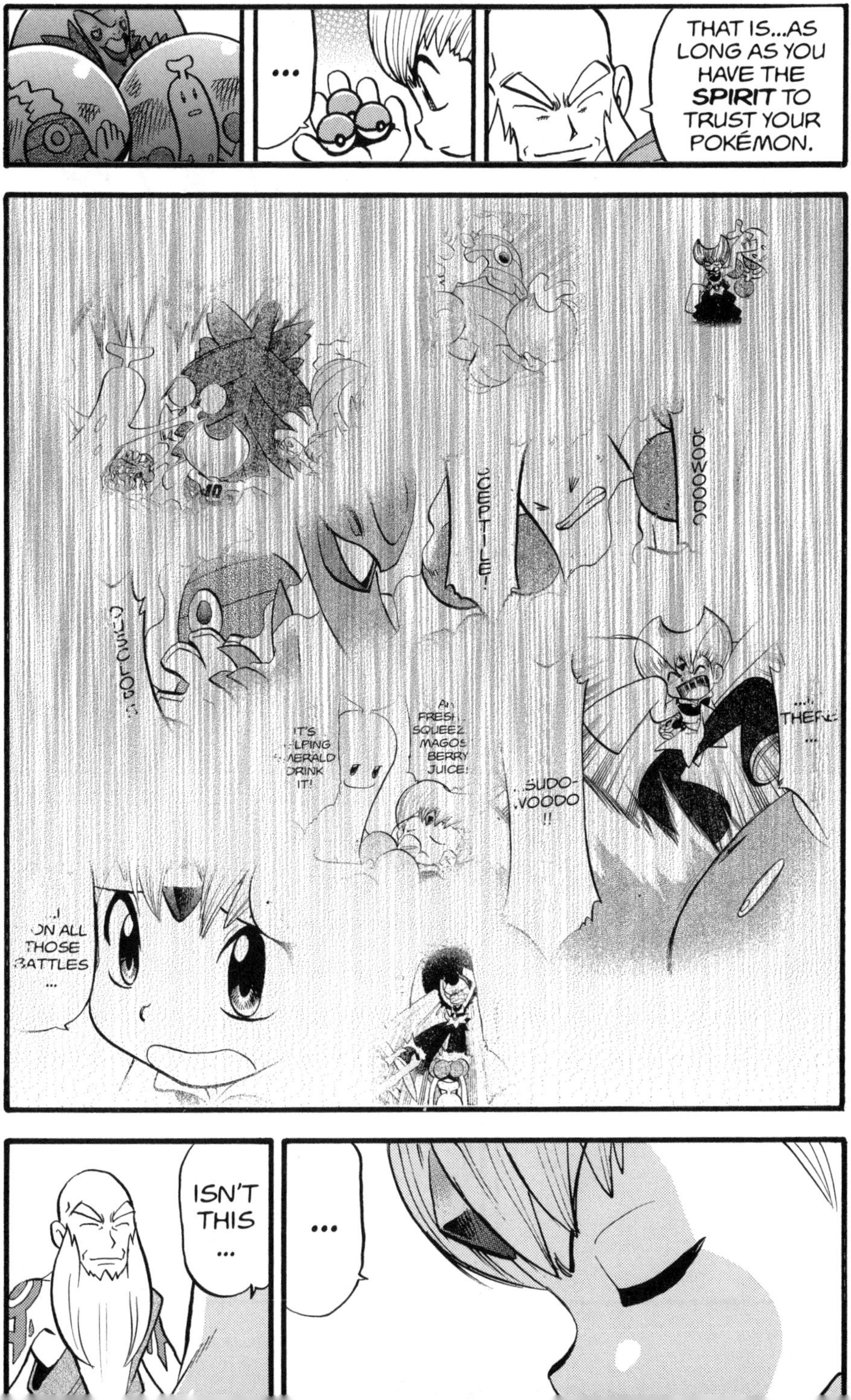
THAT IS...AS LONG AS YOU HAVE THE **SPIRIT** TO TRUST YOUR POKÉMON.
...
DOWOODO
CEPTILE!
THER
...
FRESH SQUEEZ MAGOS BERRY JUICE!
LPING MERALD DRINK IT!
SUDO-VOODO !!
ON ALL THOSE BATTLES ...
...
ISN'T THIS ...

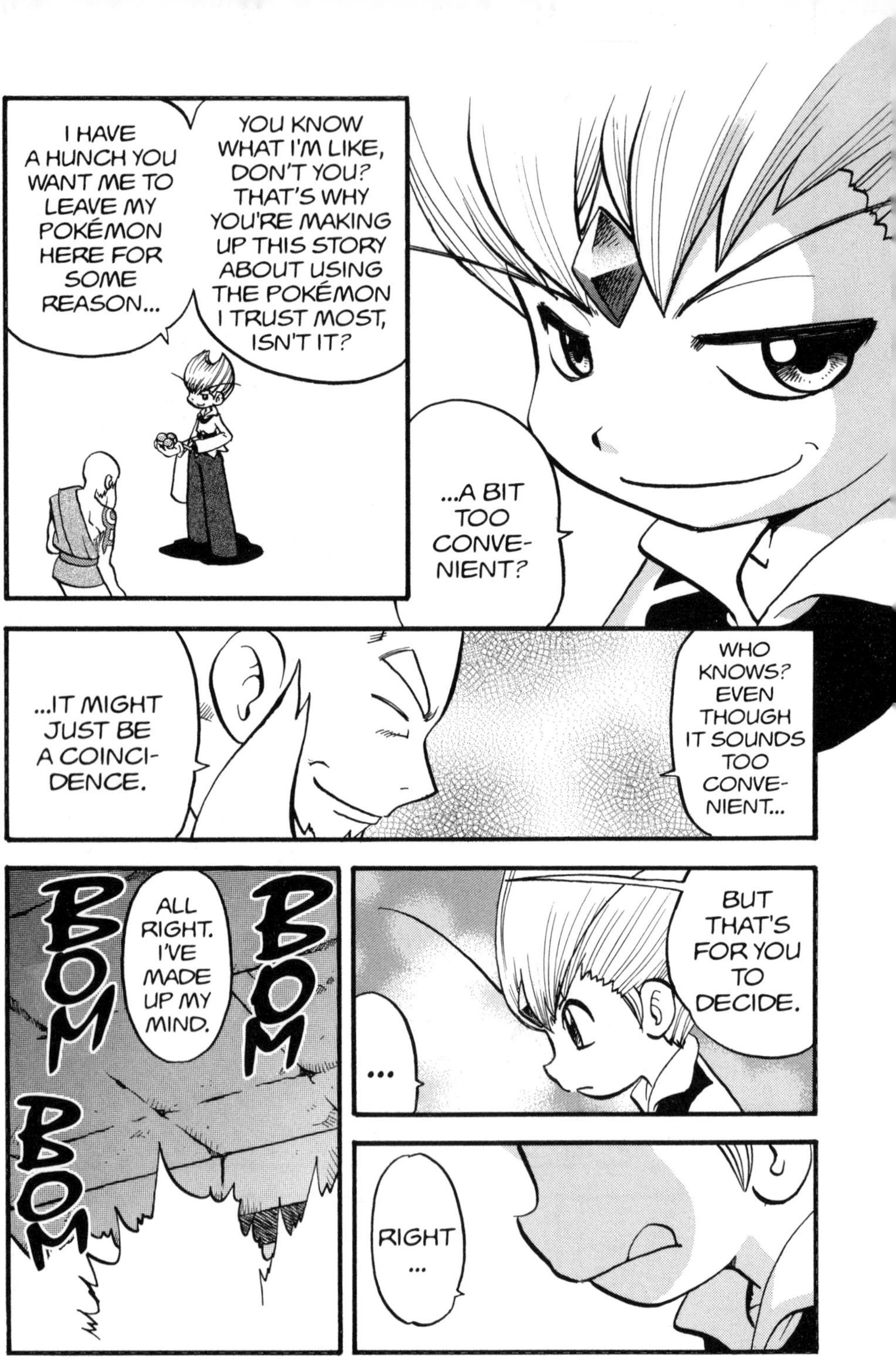
YOU KNOW WHAT I'M LIKE, DON'T YOU? THAT'S WHY YOU'RE MAKING UP THIS STORY ABOUT USING THE POKÉMON I TRUST MOST, ISN'T IT?
I HAVE A HUNCH YOU WANT ME TO LEAVE MY POKÉMON HERE FOR SOME REASON...
...A BIT TOO CONVENIENT?
WHO KNOWS? EVEN THOUGH IT SOUNDS TOO CONVENIENT...
...IT MIGHT JUST BE A COINCIDENCE.
BUT THAT'S FOR YOU TO DECIDE.
...
RIGHT...
BOM
ALL RIGHT. I'VE MADE UP MY MIND.
BOM
BOM
BOM

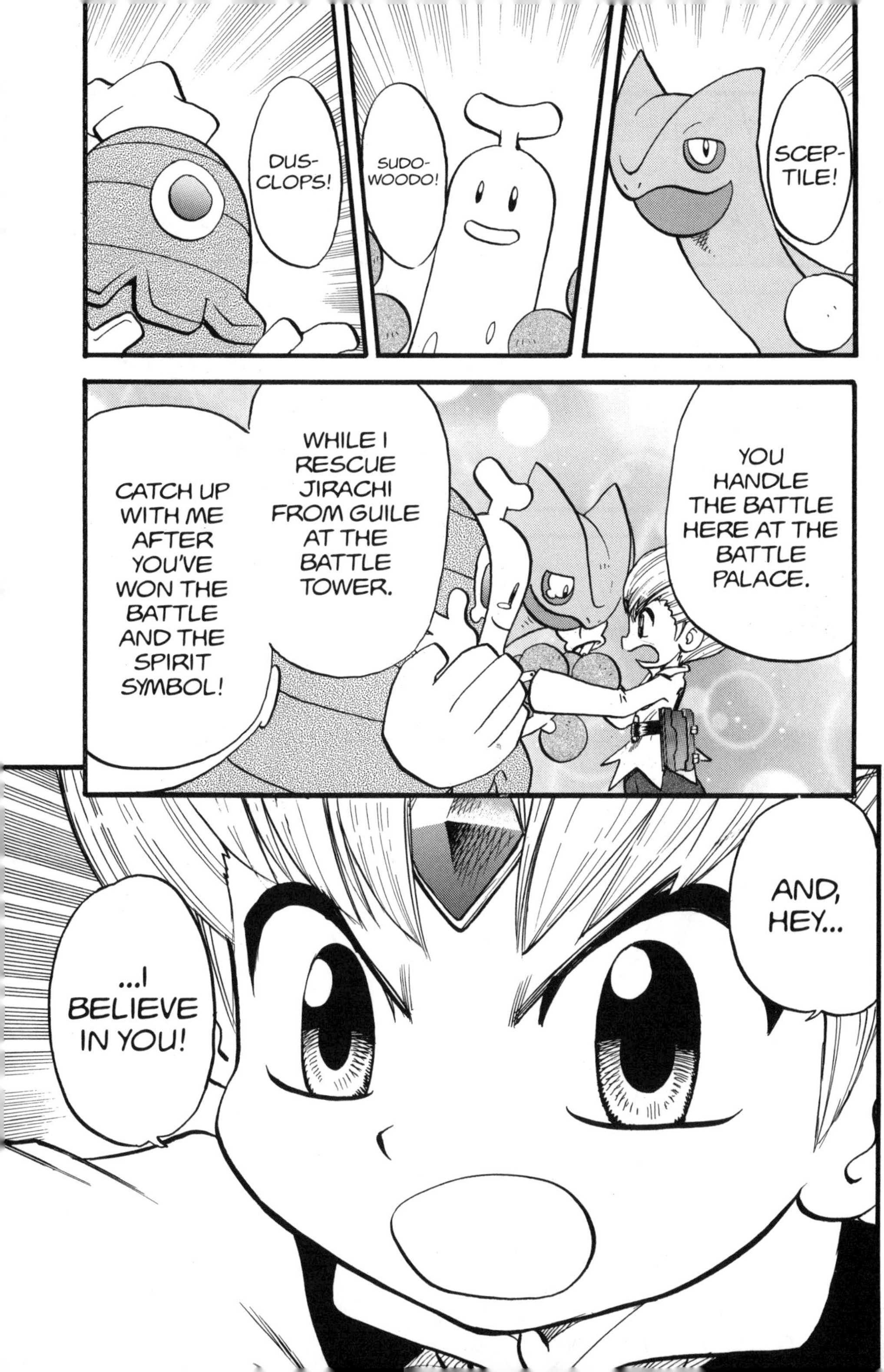
SCEP-TILE!
SUDO-WOODO!
DUS-CLOPS!
YOU HANDLE THE BATTLE HERE AT THE BATTLE PALACE.
WHILE I RESCUE JIRACHI FROM GUILE AT THE BATTLE TOWER.
CATCH UP WITH ME AFTER YOU'VE WON THE BATTLE AND THE SPIRIT SYMBOL!
AND, HEY...
...I BELIEVE IN YOU!

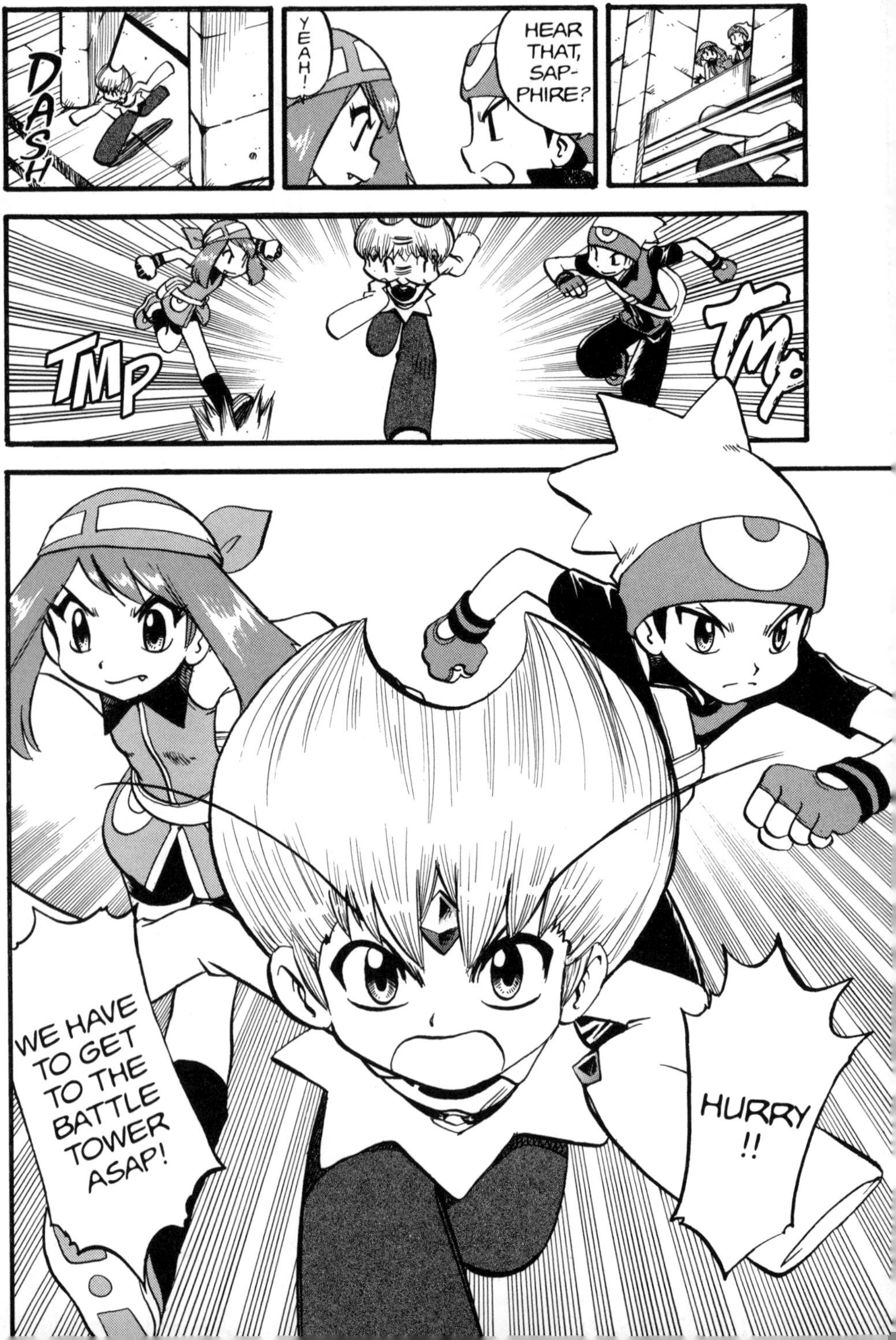
HEAR THAT, SAPPHIRE?
YEAH!
DASH
TMP
TMP
HURRY!!
WE HAVE TO GET TO THE BATTLE TOWER ASAP!

DEAR MEMBERS OF THE PRESS...

Thank you for visiting the Battle Frontier today. Permit me to continue explaining the rules of this facility...

OWNER: SCOTT

FACILITY RULES

BATTLE TOWER 3

■ THE BATTLE SALON ■

The Battle Salon is provided for Trainers who want to team up with a tag partner for Multi Battles. You can find a compatible partner here to fight on your side.

■ WINNING THE SHIELDS ■

As with the other six facilities, the challenger receives a Symbol for defeating the Battle Tower Frontier Brain. At the Battle Tower, I, Scott, will personally award Trainers with a Silver Shield after fifty consecutive wins in Single Battle and a Gold Shield after a hundred.

326

Lemme at 'Em, Lapras!

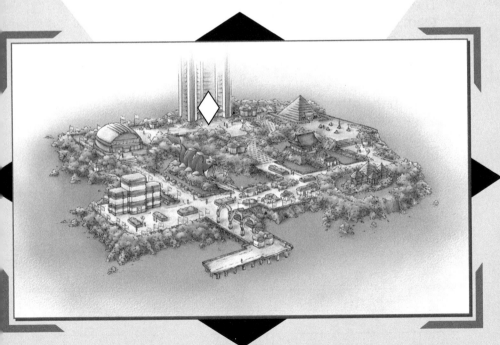

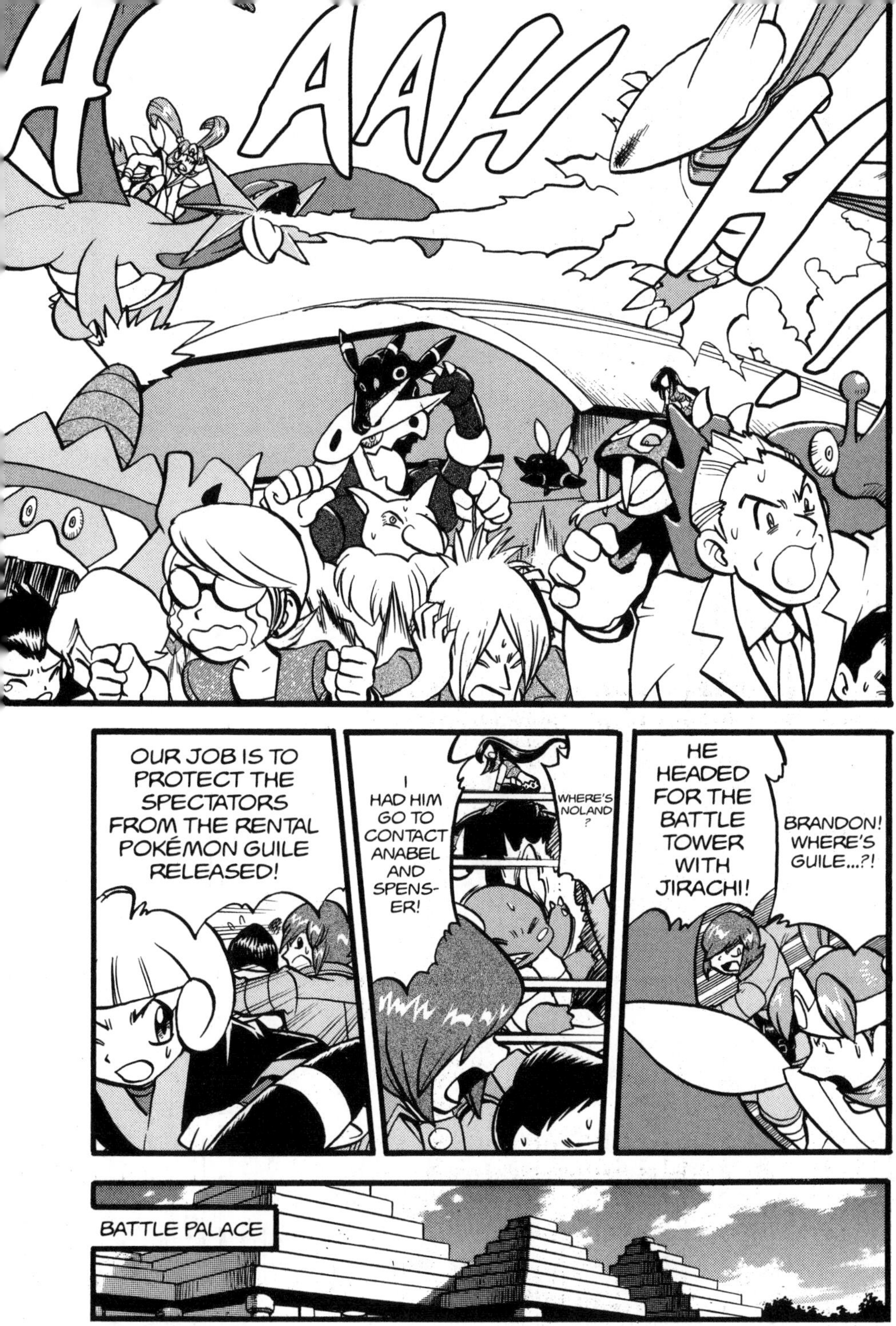

AAAHH
BRANDON! WHERE'S GUILE...?!
HE HEADED FOR THE BATTLE TOWER WITH JIRACHI!
WHERE'S NOLAND?
I HAD HIM GO TO CONTACT ANABEL AND SPENSER!
OUR JOB IS TO PROTECT THE SPECTATORS FROM THE RENTAL POKÉMON GUILE RELEASED!
BATTLE PALACE

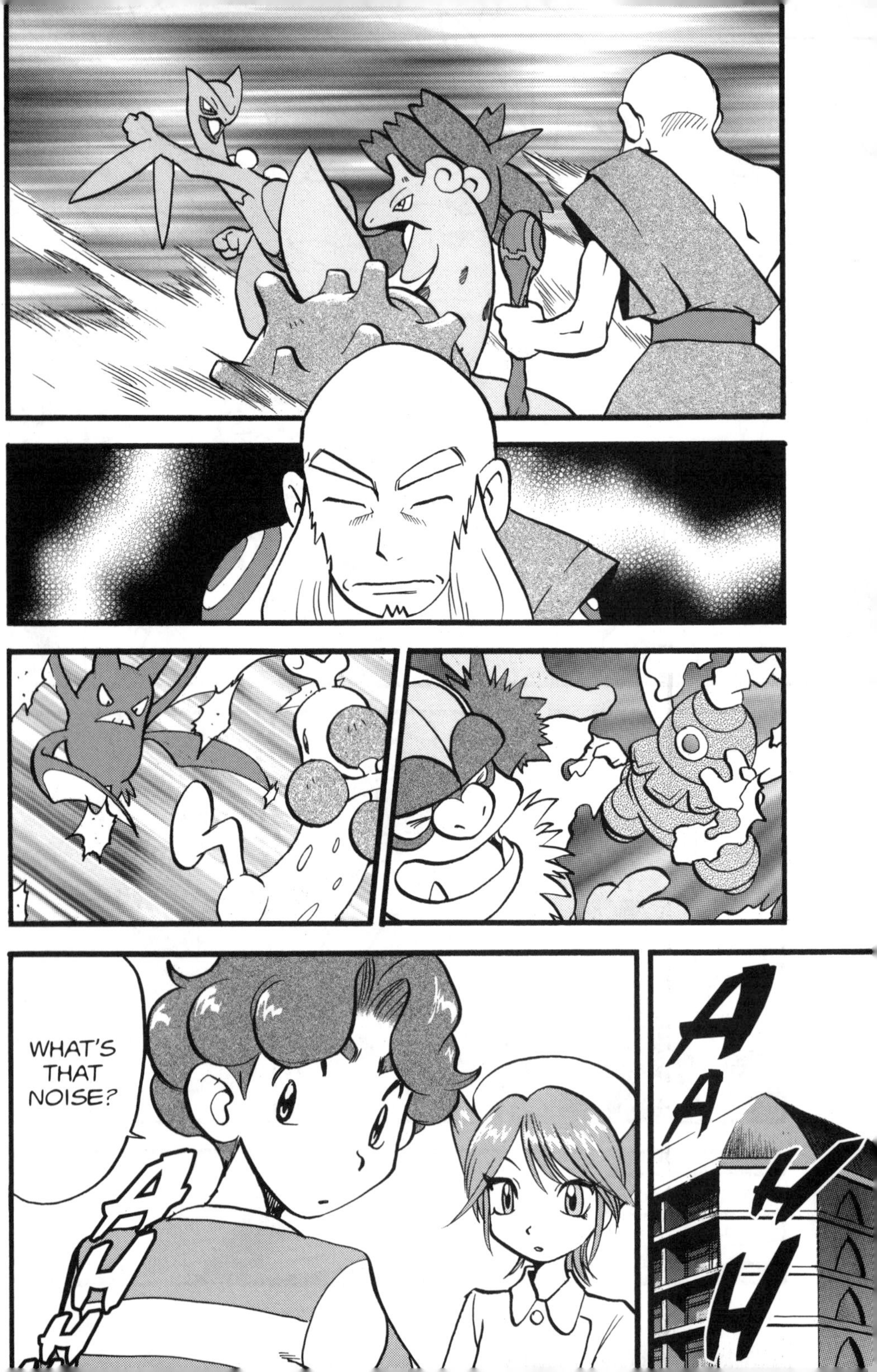
AAHHH
WHAT'S THAT NOISE?
AHH

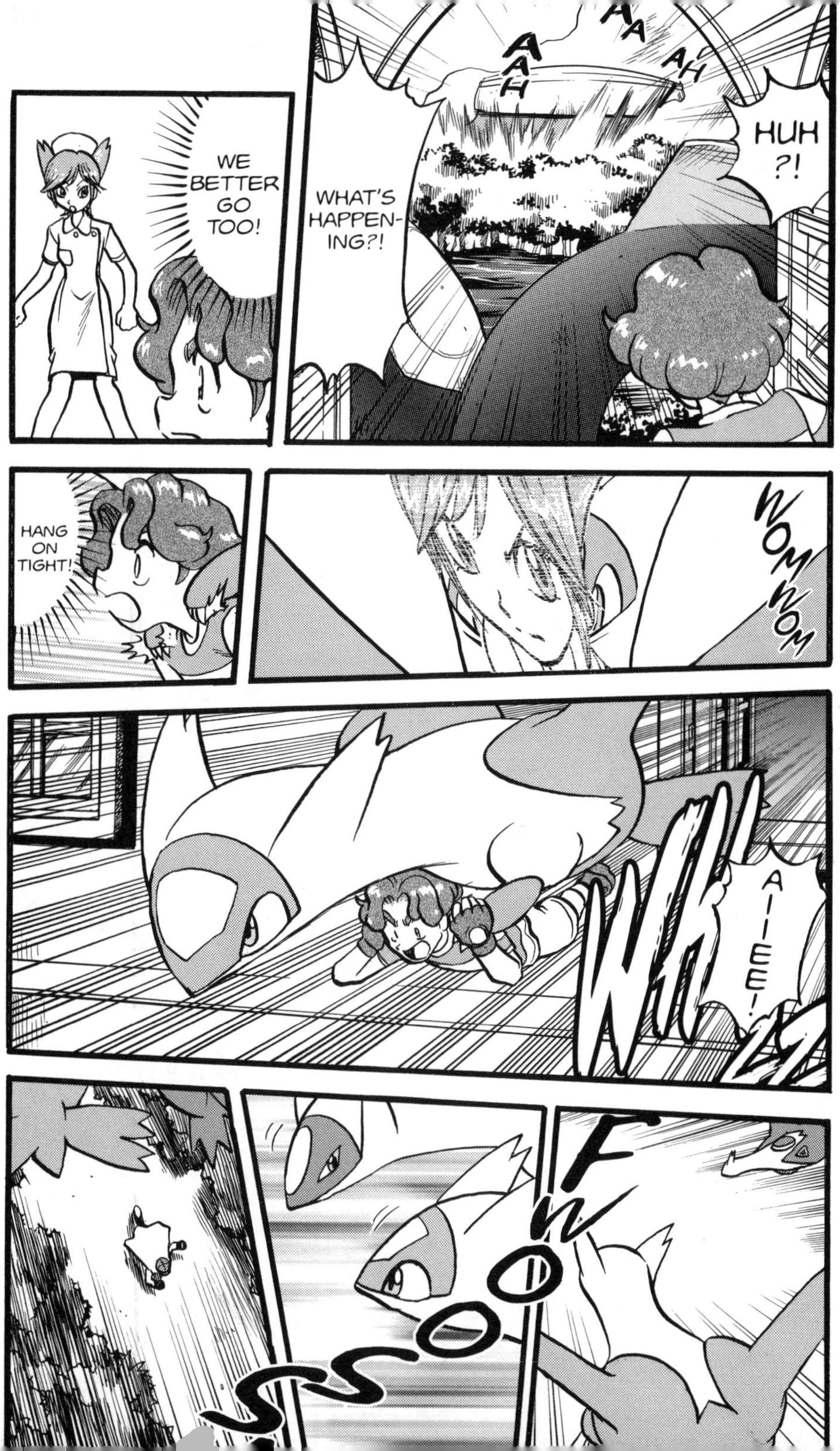
AAH AA AH
HUH ?!
WHAT'S HAPPEN-ING?!
WE BETTER GO TOO!
WOM WOM
HANG ON TIGHT!
AIIEE!

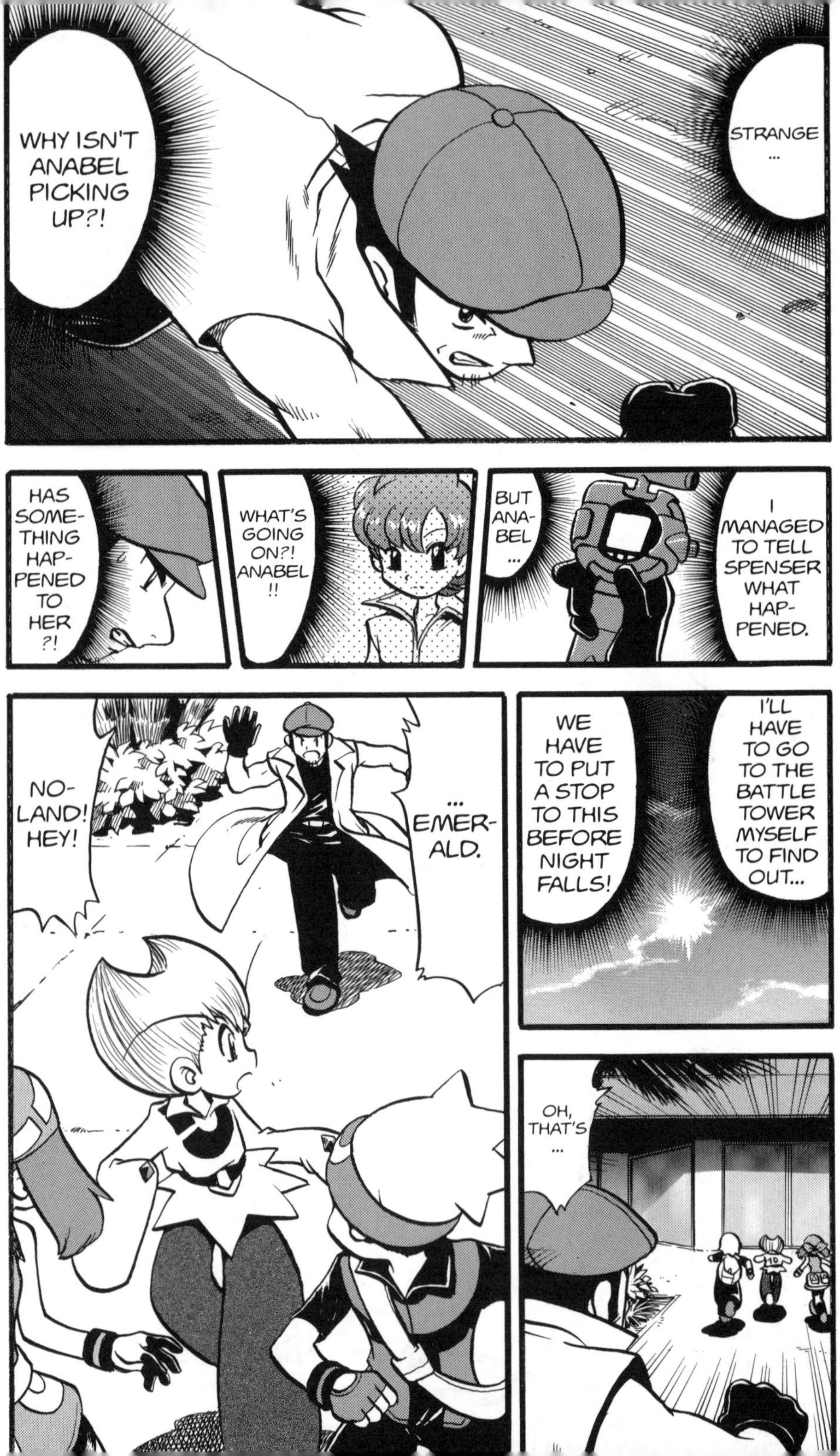
STRANGE …
WHY ISN'T ANABEL PICKING UP?!
I MANAGED TO TELL SPENSER WHAT HAP-PENED.
BUT ANA-BEL …
WHAT'S GOING ON?! ANABEL !!
HAS SOME-THING HAP-PENED TO HER ?!
I'LL HAVE TO GO TO THE BATTLE TOWER MYSELF TO FIND OUT…
WE HAVE TO PUT A STOP TO THIS BEFORE NIGHT FALLS!
OH, THAT'S …
… EMER-ALD.
NO-LAND! HEY!

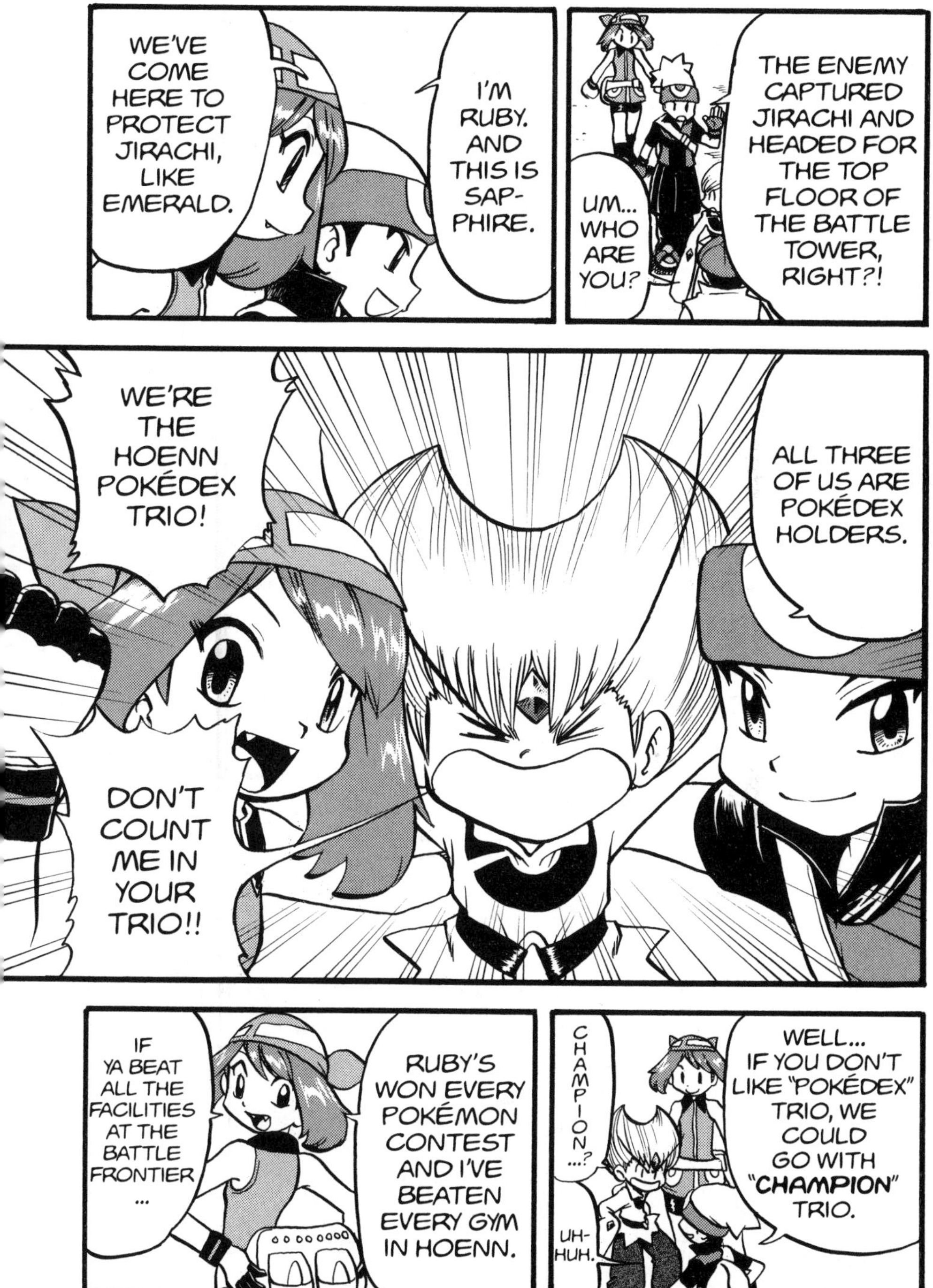
THE ENEMY CAPTURED JIRACHI AND HEADED FOR THE TOP FLOOR OF THE BATTLE TOWER, RIGHT?!
UM... WHO ARE YOU?
I'M RUBY. AND THIS IS SAP-PHIRE.
WE'VE COME HERE TO PROTECT JIRACHI, LIKE EMERALD.
ALL THREE OF US ARE POKÉDEX HOLDERS.
WE'RE THE HOENN POKÉDEX TRIO!
DON'T COUNT ME IN YOUR TRIO!!
WELL... IF YOU DON'T LIKE "POKÉDEX" TRIO, WE COULD GO WITH "**CHAMPION**" TRIO.
CHAMPION ...?
UH-HUH.
RUBY'S WON EVERY POKÉMON CONTEST AND I'VE BEATEN EVERY GYM IN HOENN.
IF YA BEAT ALL THE FACILITIES AT THE BATTLE FRONTIER ...

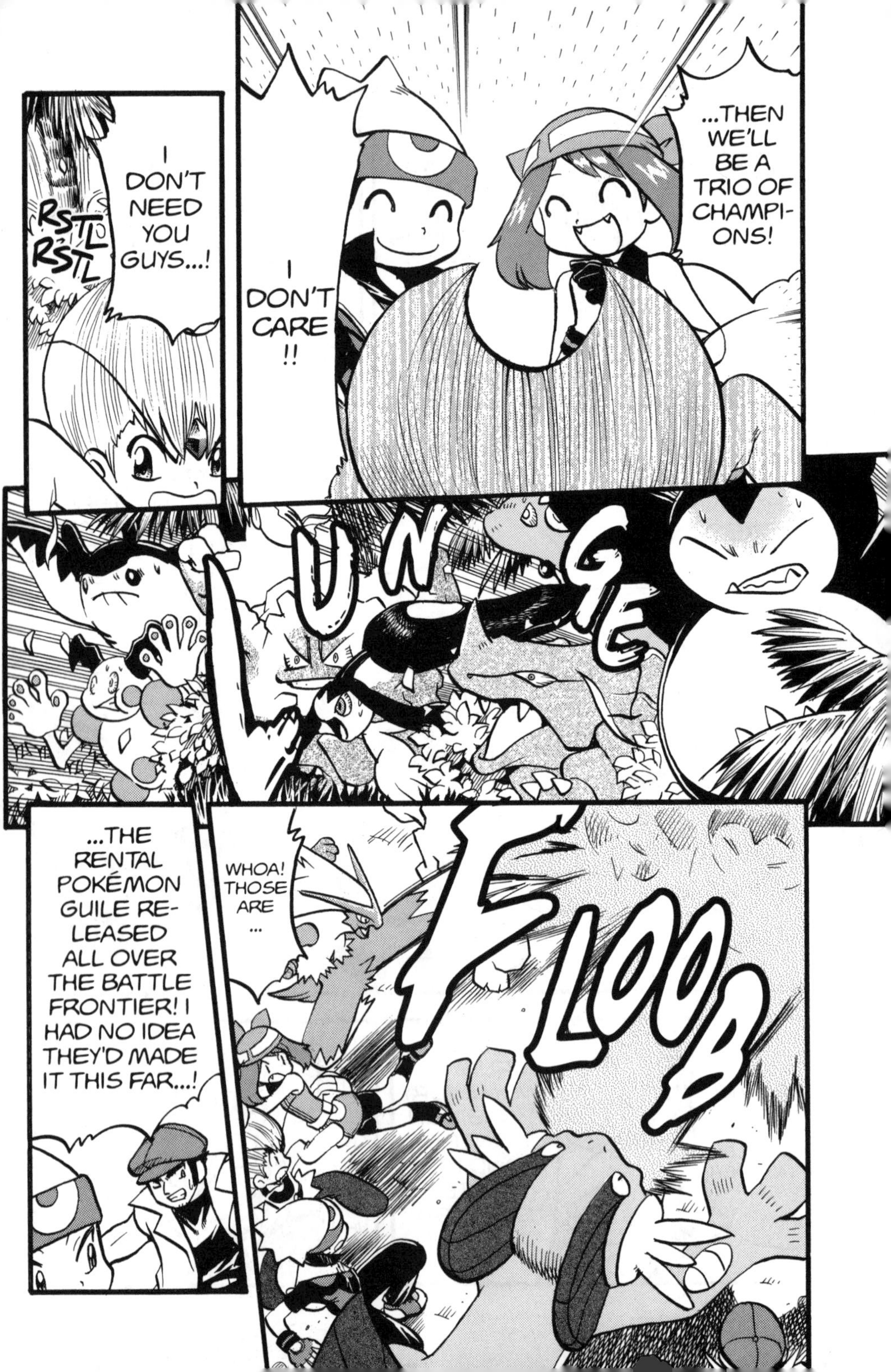
...THEN WE'LL BE A TRIO OF CHAMPI-ONS!
I DON'T CARE !!
I DON'T NEED YOU GUYS...!
RSTL RSTL
UNGE
WHOA! THOSE ARE ...
FLOOB
...THE RENTAL POKÉMON GUILE RE-LEASED ALL OVER THE BATTLE FRONTIER! I HAD NO IDEA THEY'D MADE IT THIS FAR...!

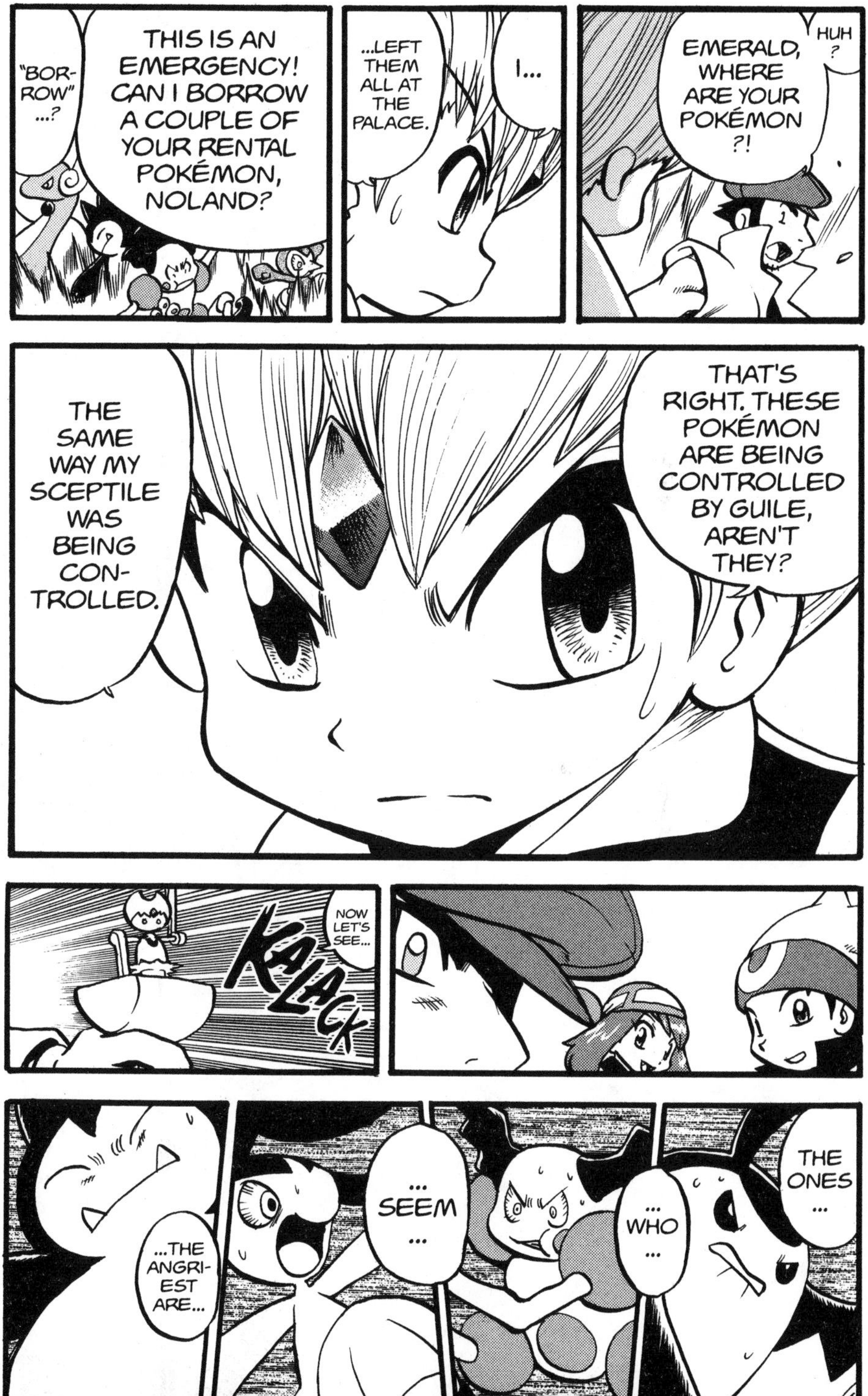
HUH?
EMERALD, WHERE ARE YOUR POKÉMON?!
I...
...LEFT THEM ALL AT THE PALACE.
THIS IS AN EMERGENCY! CAN I BORROW A COUPLE OF YOUR RENTAL POKÉMON, NOLAND?
"BORROW"...?
THAT'S RIGHT. THESE POKÉMON ARE BEING CONTROLLED BY GUILE, AREN'T THEY?
THE SAME WAY MY SCEPTILE WAS BEING CONTROLLED.
NOW LET'S SEE...
KALACK
THE ONES...
...WHO...
...SEEM...
...THE ANGRIEST ARE...

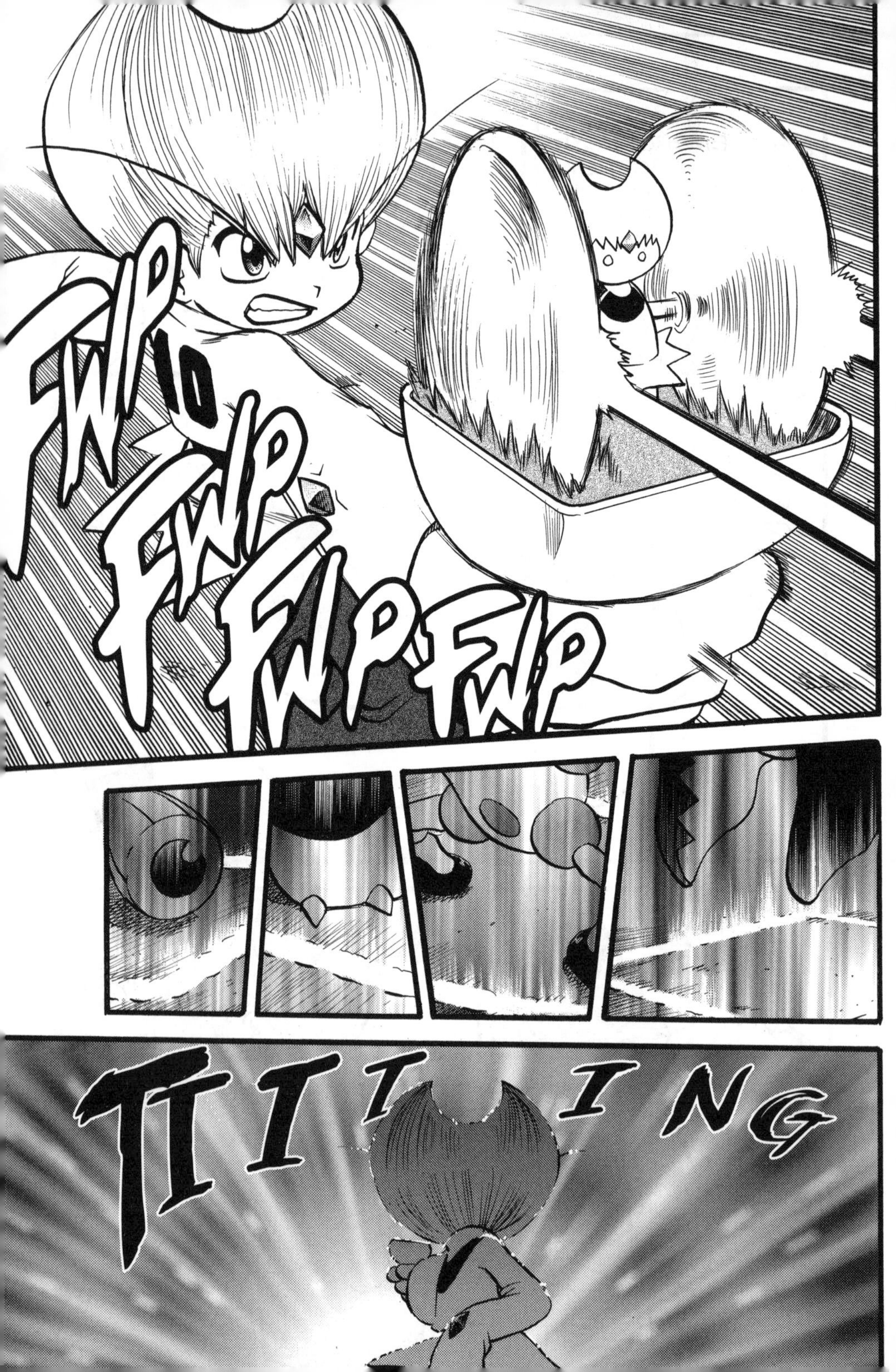
FWIP
FWIP
FWIP
FWIP
TIIIING

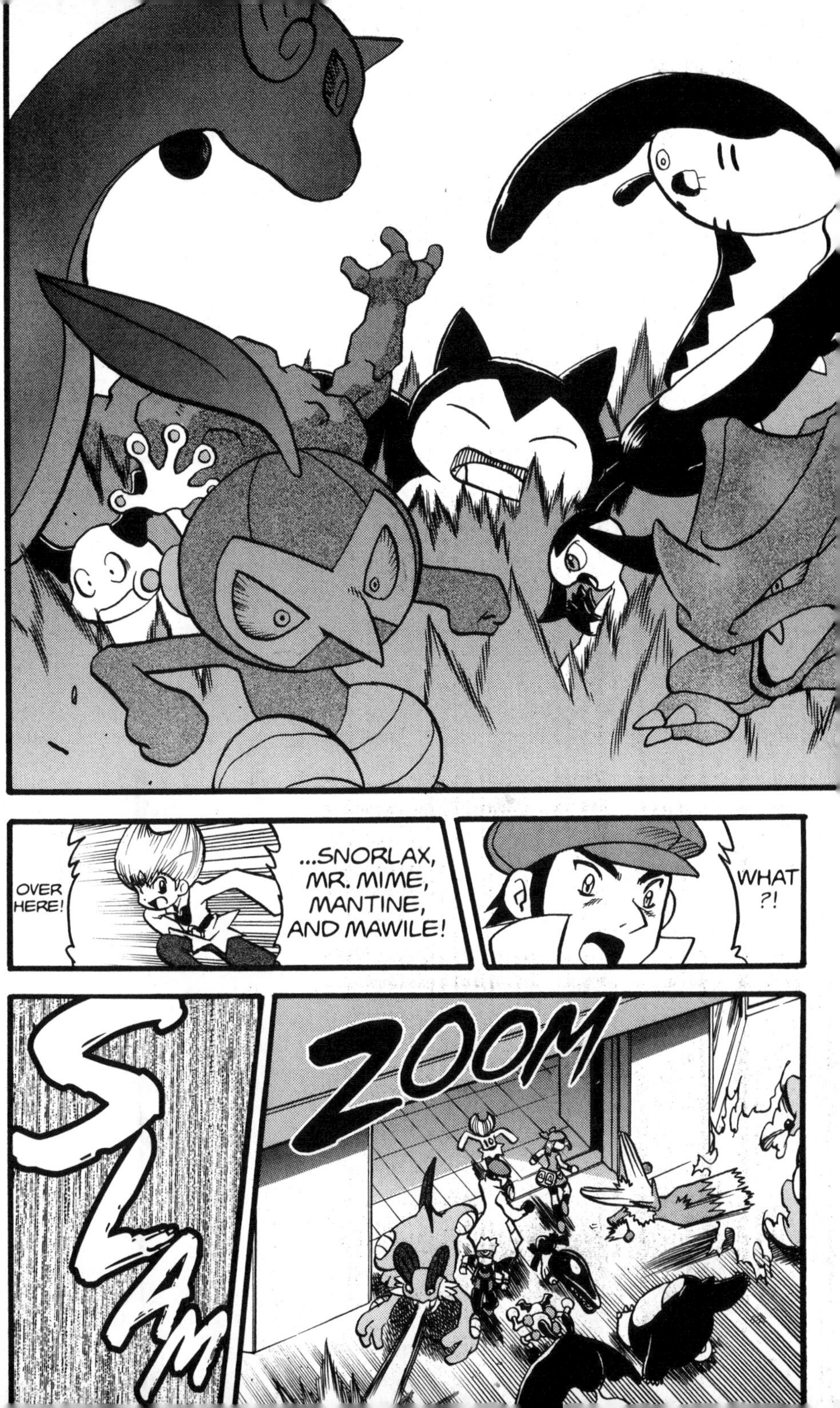
WHAT ?!
...SNORLAX, MR. MIME, MANTINE, AND MAWILE!
OVER HERE!
ZOOM
SLAM

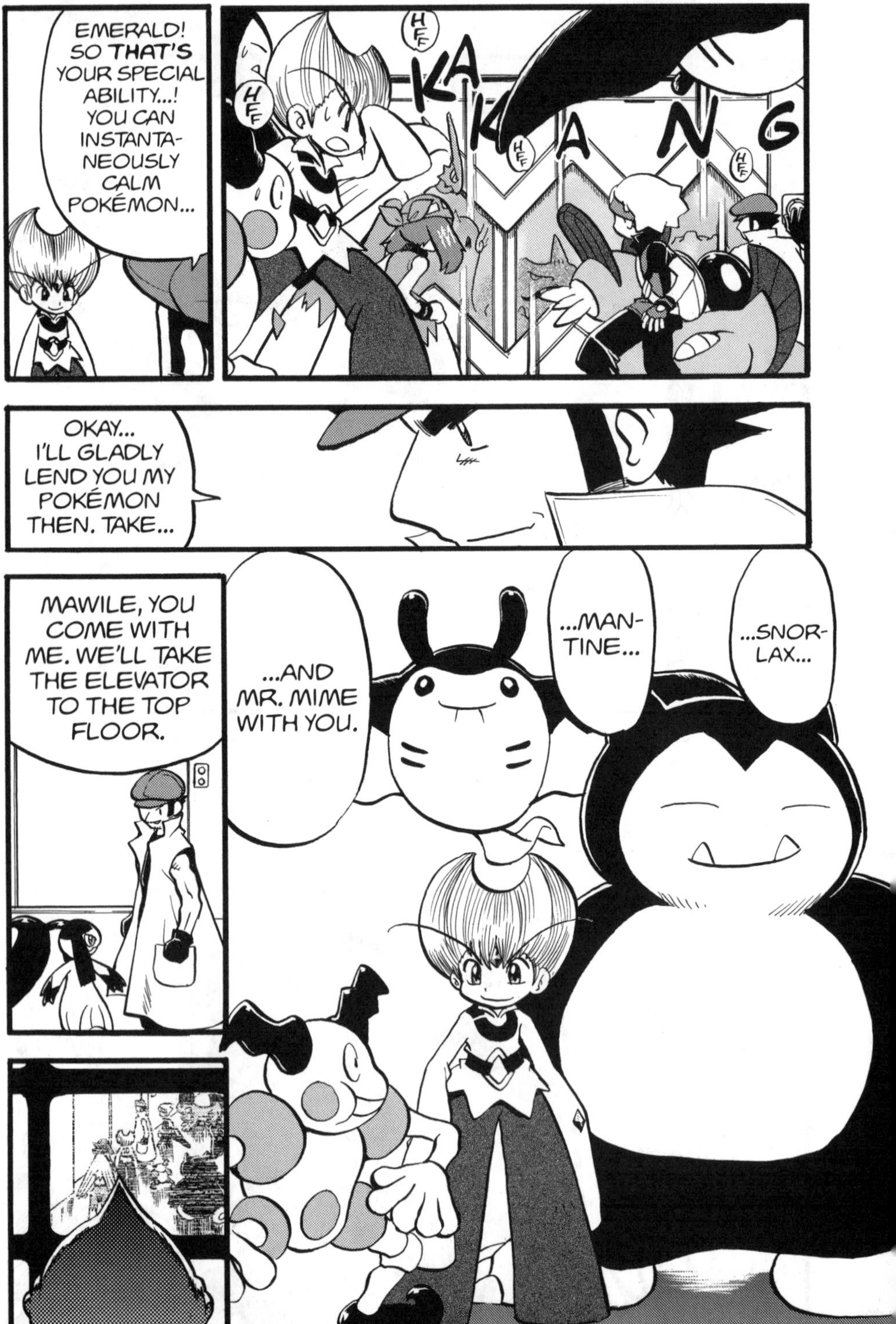
HFF
HFF
HFF
HFF
KA KANG
EMERALD! SO THAT'S YOUR SPECIAL ABILITY...! YOU CAN INSTANTANEOUSLY CALM POKÉMON...
OKAY... I'LL GLADLY LEND YOU MY POKÉMON THEN. TAKE...
...SNORLAX...
...MANTINE...
...AND MR. MIME WITH YOU.
MAWILE, YOU COME WITH ME. WE'LL TAKE THE ELEVATOR TO THE TOP FLOOR.

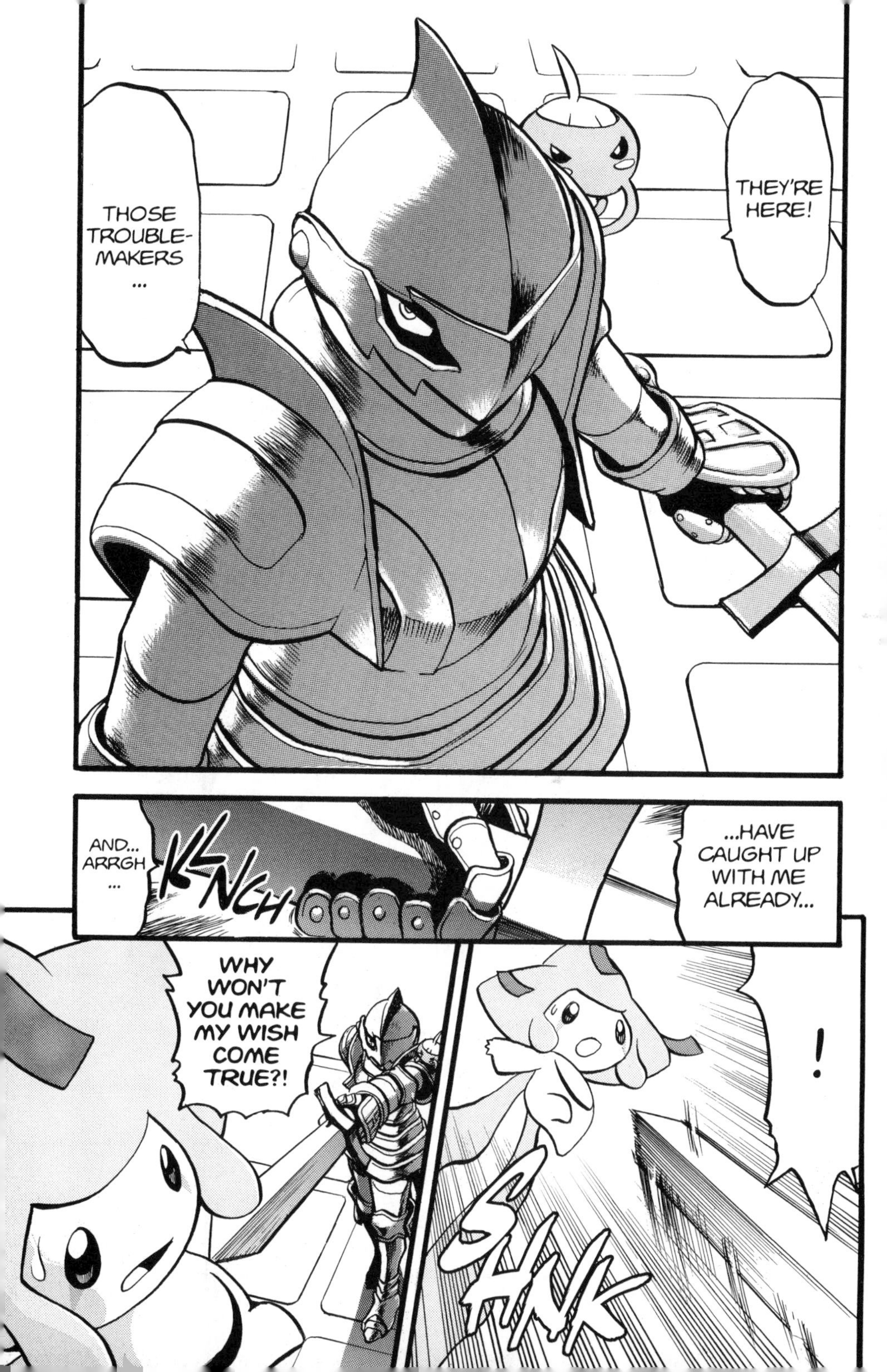
THEY'RE HERE!
THOSE TROUBLE-MAKERS ...
...HAVE CAUGHT UP WITH ME ALREADY...
KLNCH
AND... ARRGH ...
!
SHHK
WHY WON'T YOU MAKE MY WISH COME TRUE?!

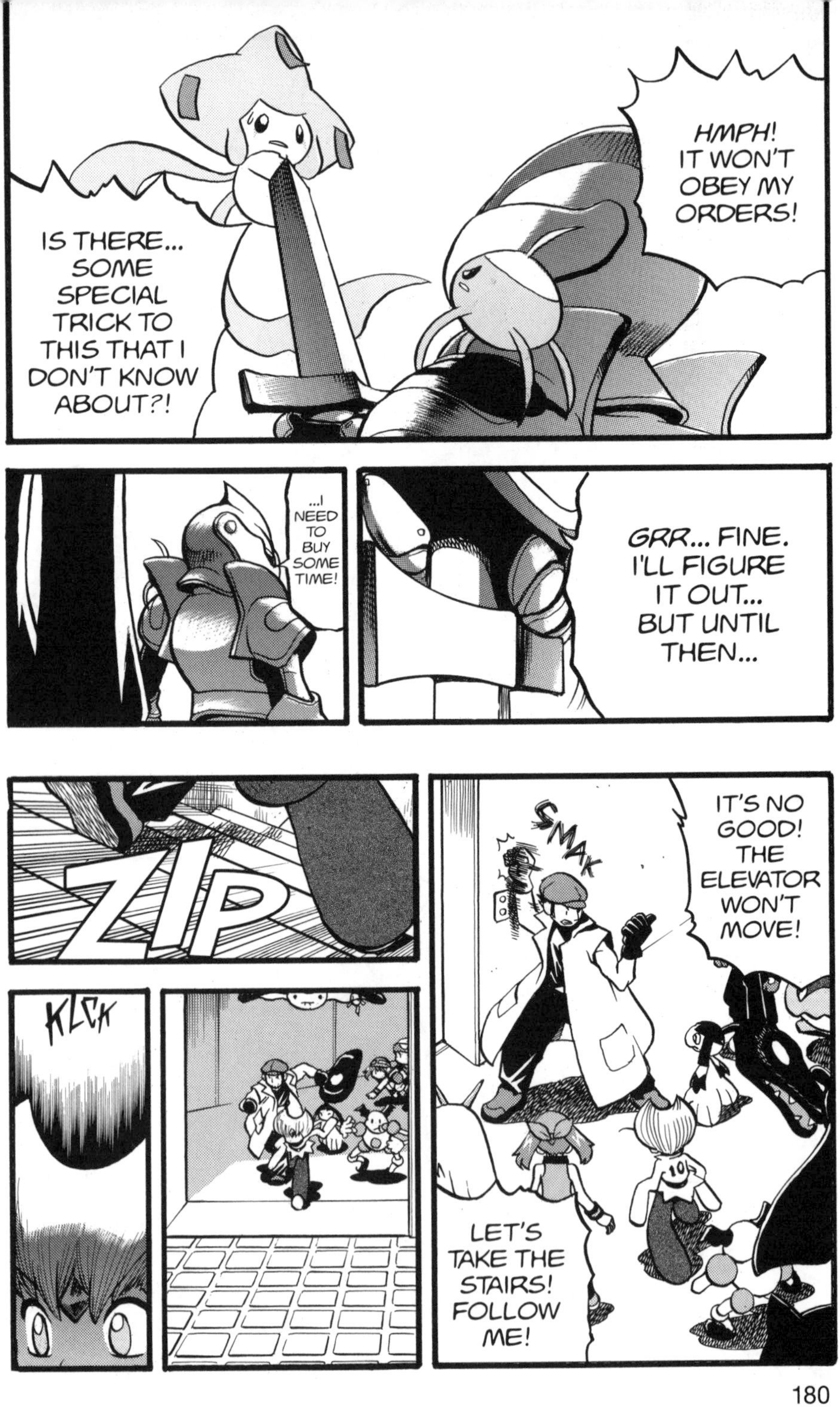
HMPH! IT WON'T OBEY MY ORDERS!
IS THERE... SOME SPECIAL TRICK TO THIS THAT I DON'T KNOW ABOUT?!
GRR... FINE. I'LL FIGURE IT OUT... BUT UNTIL THEN...
...I NEED TO BUY SOME TIME!
SMAK
IT'S NO GOOD! THE ELEVATOR WON'T MOVE!
LET'S TAKE THE STAIRS! FOLLOW ME!
ZIP
KLCK

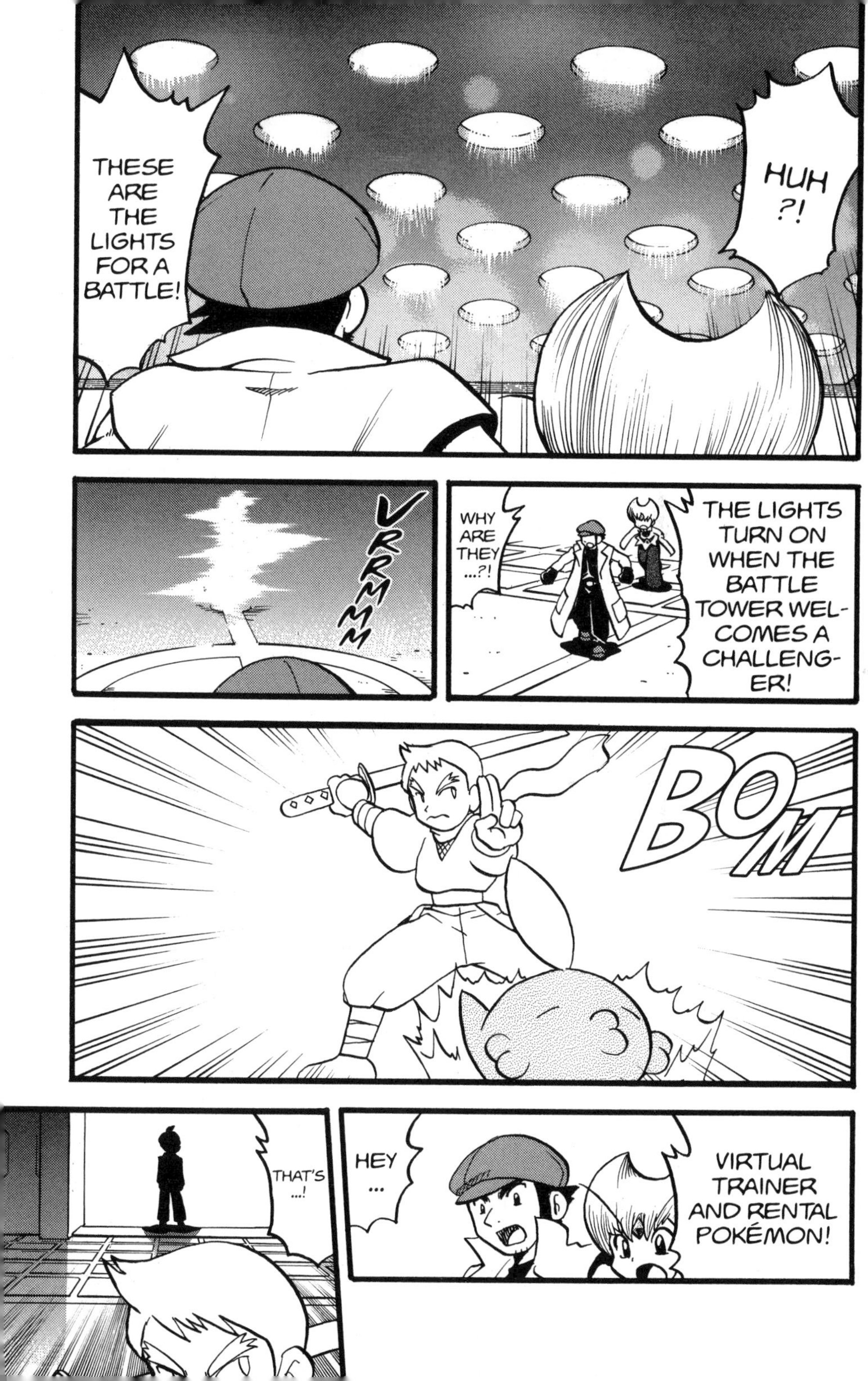

HUH ?!
THESE ARE THE LIGHTS FOR A BATTLE!
THE LIGHTS TURN ON WHEN THE BATTLE TOWER WEL-COMES A CHALLENG-ER!
WHY ARE THEY ...?!
VRRMMMM
BOOM
VIRTUAL TRAINER AND RENTAL POKÉMON!
HEY ...
THAT'S ...!

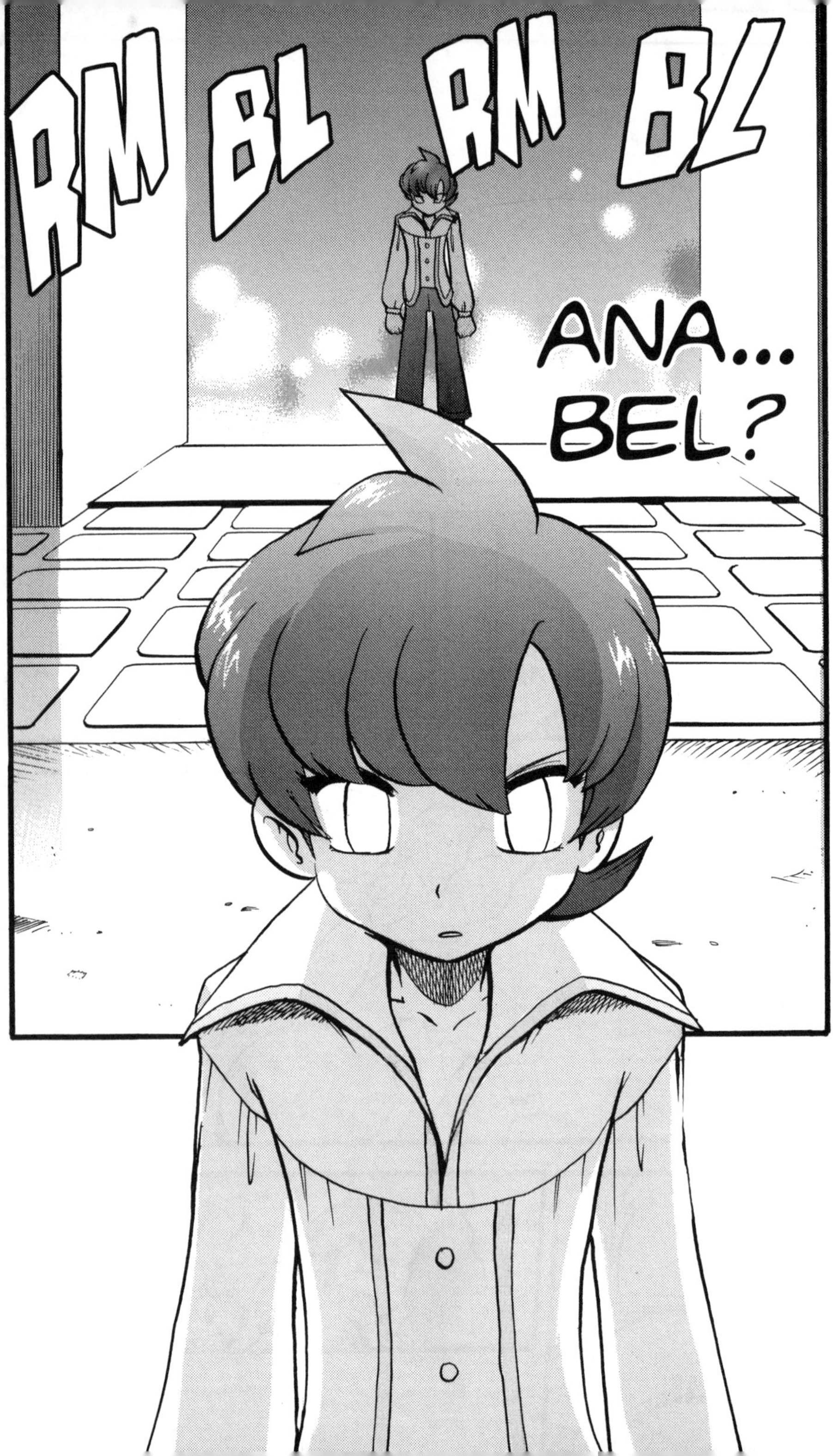
RM BL RM BL
ANA... BEL?

Facing Gulpin Is Hard to Swallow

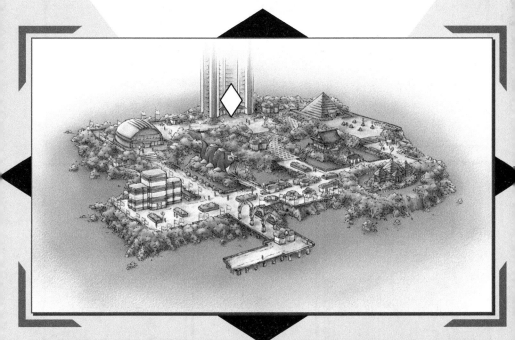

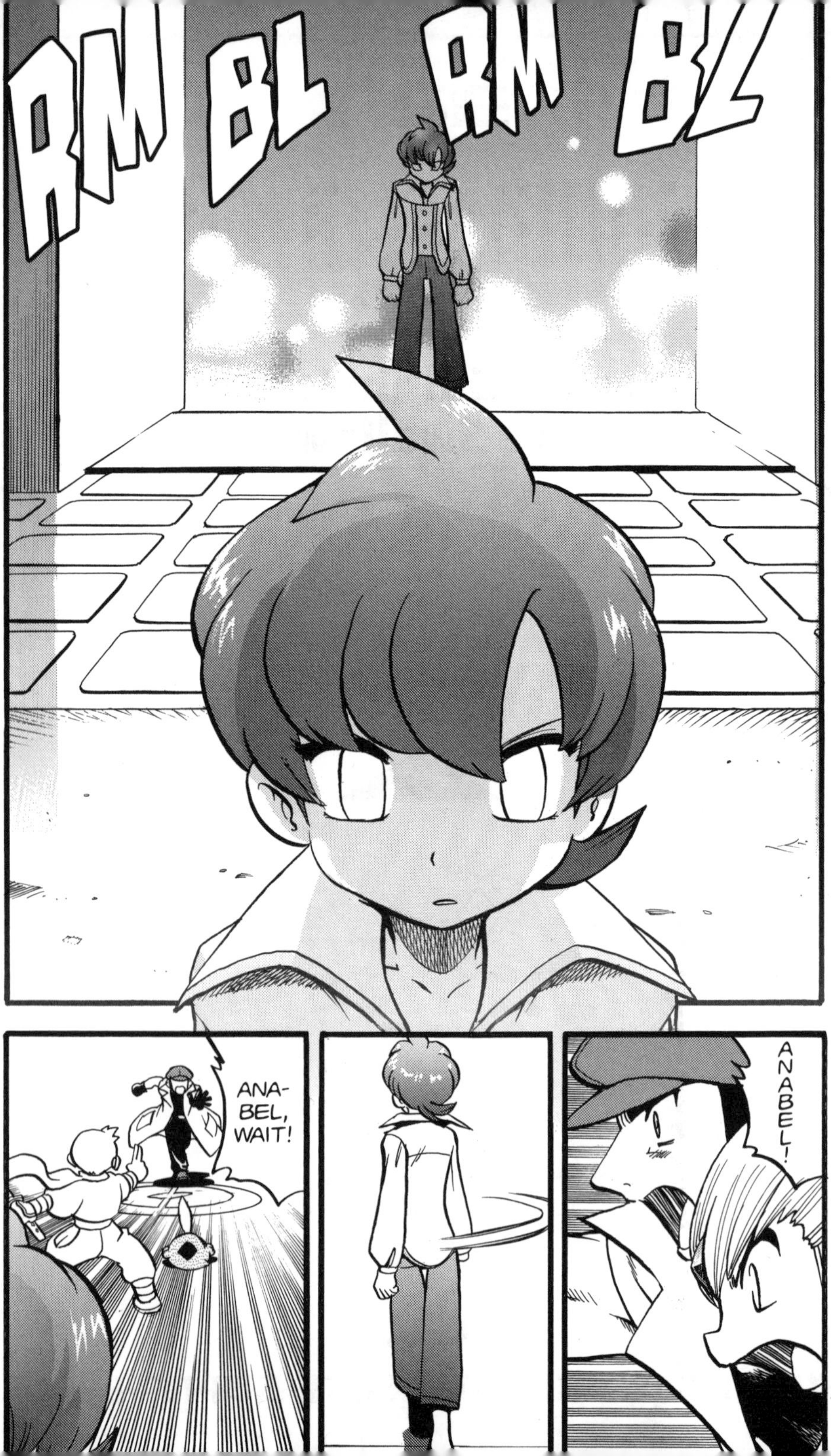
RMBL RMBL
ANABEL!
ANA-BEL, WAIT!

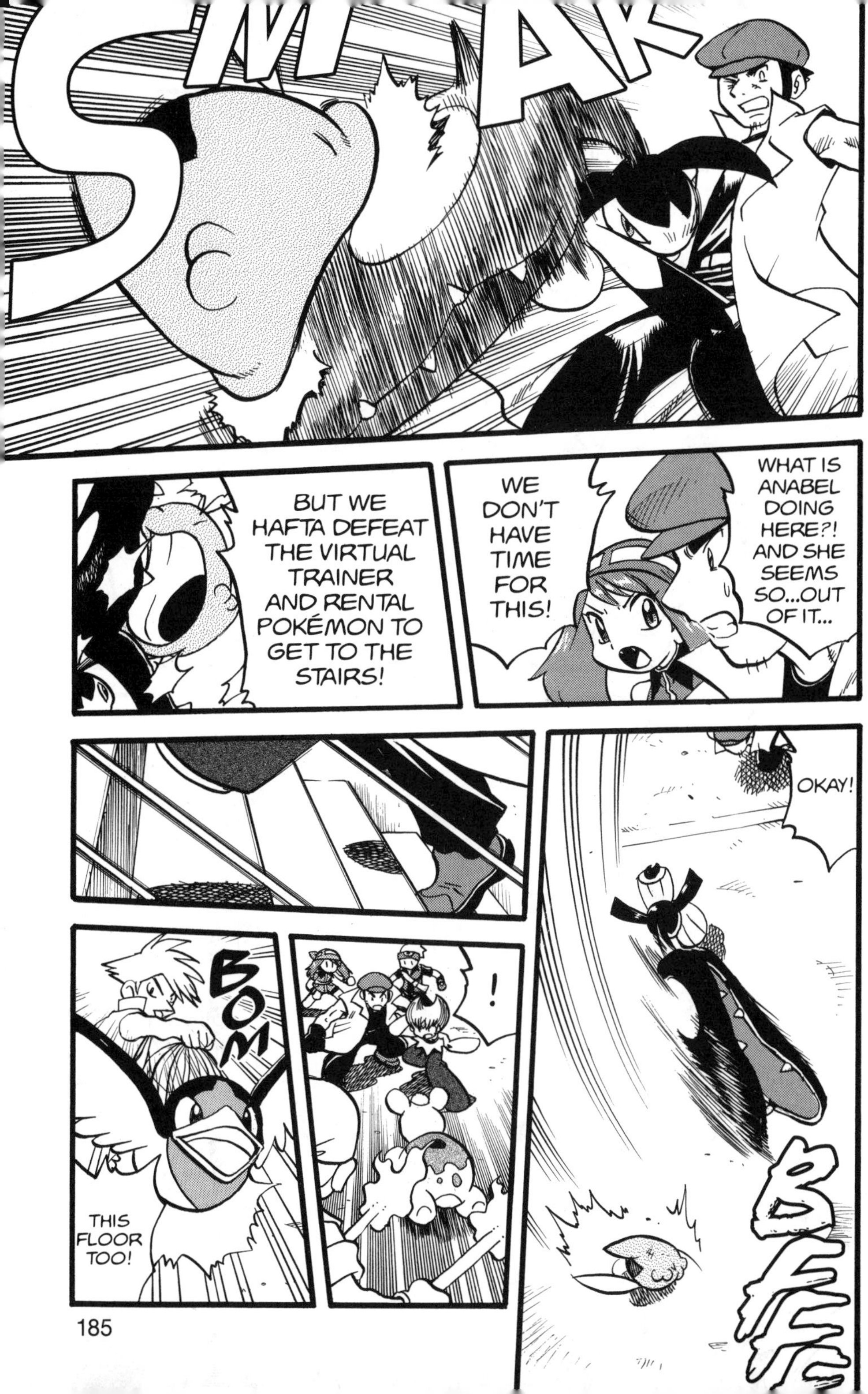
SMAK
WHAT IS ANABEL DOING HERE?! AND SHE SEEMS SO...OUT OF IT...
WE DON'T HAVE TIME FOR THIS!
BUT WE HAFTA DEFEAT THE VIRTUAL TRAINER AND RENTAL POKÉMON TO GET TO THE STAIRS!
OKAY!
!
THIS FLOOR TOO!

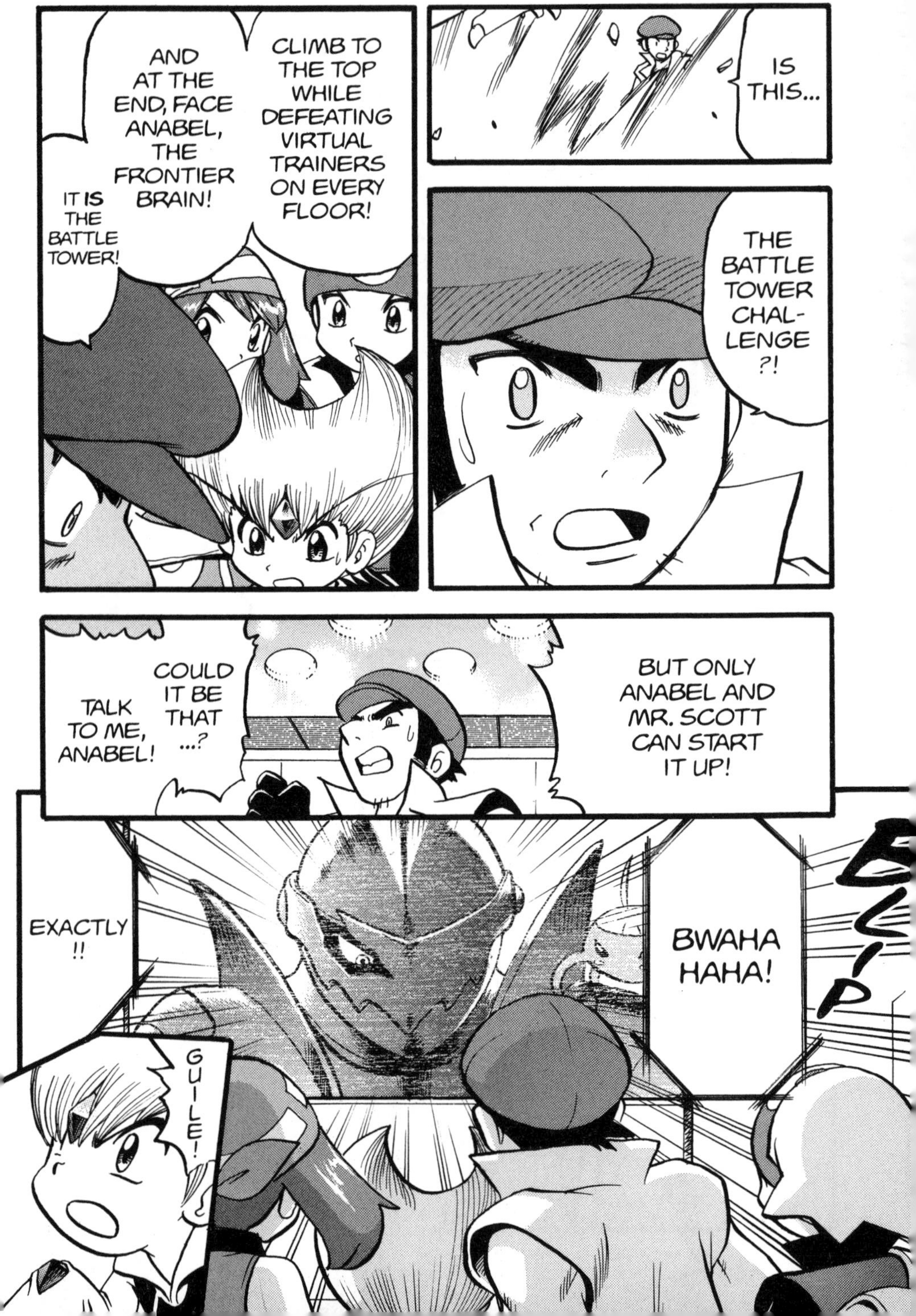
IS THIS...
THE BATTLE TOWER CHALLENGE?!
CLIMB TO THE TOP WHILE DEFEATING VIRTUAL TRAINERS ON EVERY FLOOR!
AND AT THE END, FACE ANABEL, THE FRONTIER BRAIN!
IT IS THE BATTLE TOWER!
BUT ONLY ANABEL AND MR. SCOTT CAN START IT UP!
COULD IT BE THAT ...?
TALK TO ME, ANABEL!
BLIP
BWAHA HAHA!
EXACTLY!!
GUILE!

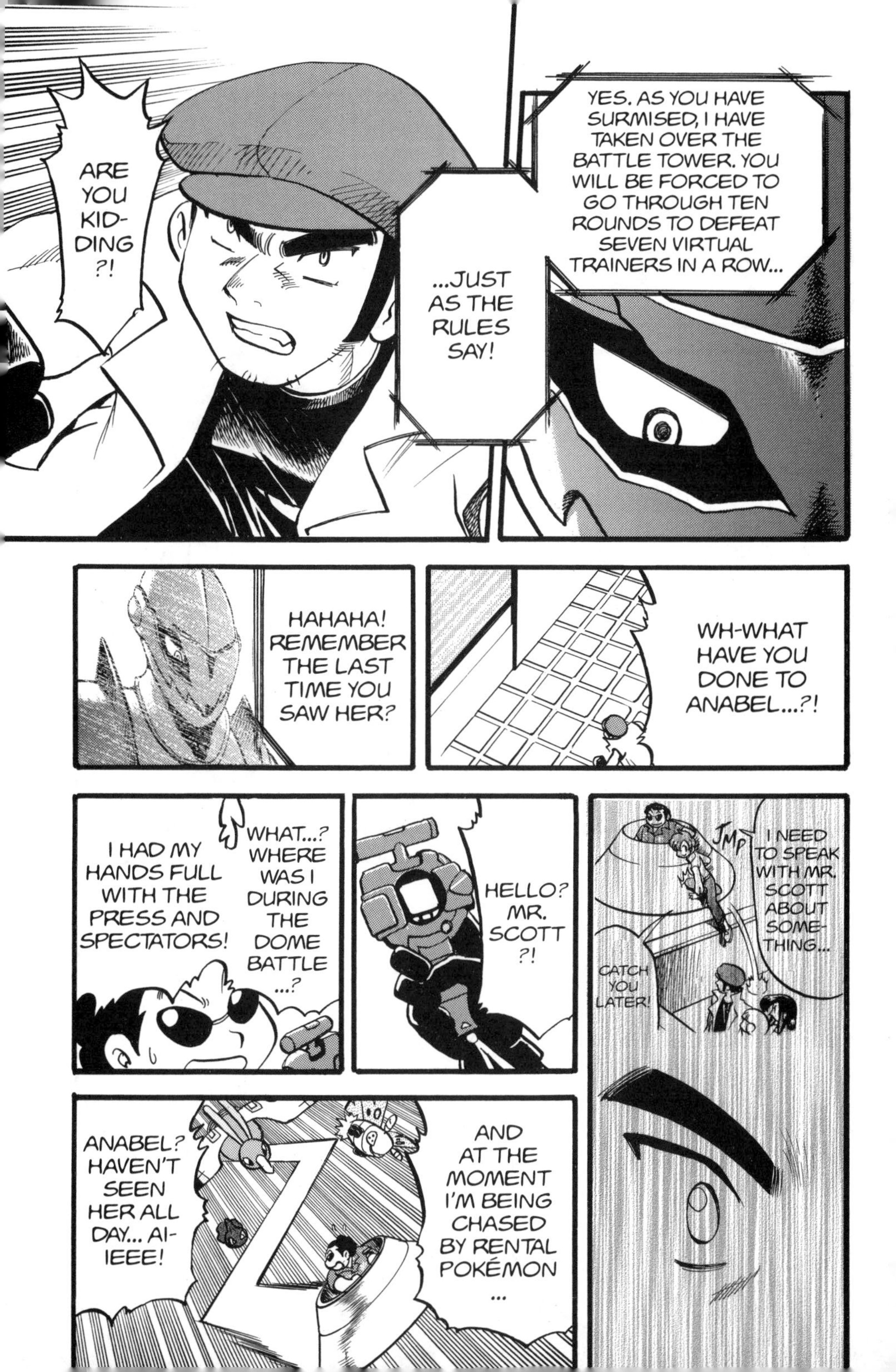

YES. AS YOU HAVE SURMISED, I HAVE TAKEN OVER THE BATTLE TOWER. YOU WILL BE FORCED TO GO THROUGH TEN ROUNDS TO DEFEAT SEVEN VIRTUAL TRAINERS IN A ROW...
...JUST AS THE RULES SAY!
ARE YOU KID-DING?!
WH-WHAT HAVE YOU DONE TO ANABEL...?!
HAHAHA! REMEMBER THE LAST TIME YOU SAW HER?
JMP
I NEED TO SPEAK WITH MR. SCOTT ABOUT SOME-THING...
CATCH YOU LATER!
HELLO? MR. SCOTT?!
WHAT...? WHERE WAS I DURING THE DOME BATTLE...?
I HAD MY HANDS FULL WITH THE PRESS AND SPECTATORS!
AND AT THE MOMENT I'M BEING CHASED BY RENTAL POKÉMON...
ANABEL? HAVEN'T SEEN HER ALL DAY... AI-IEEE!

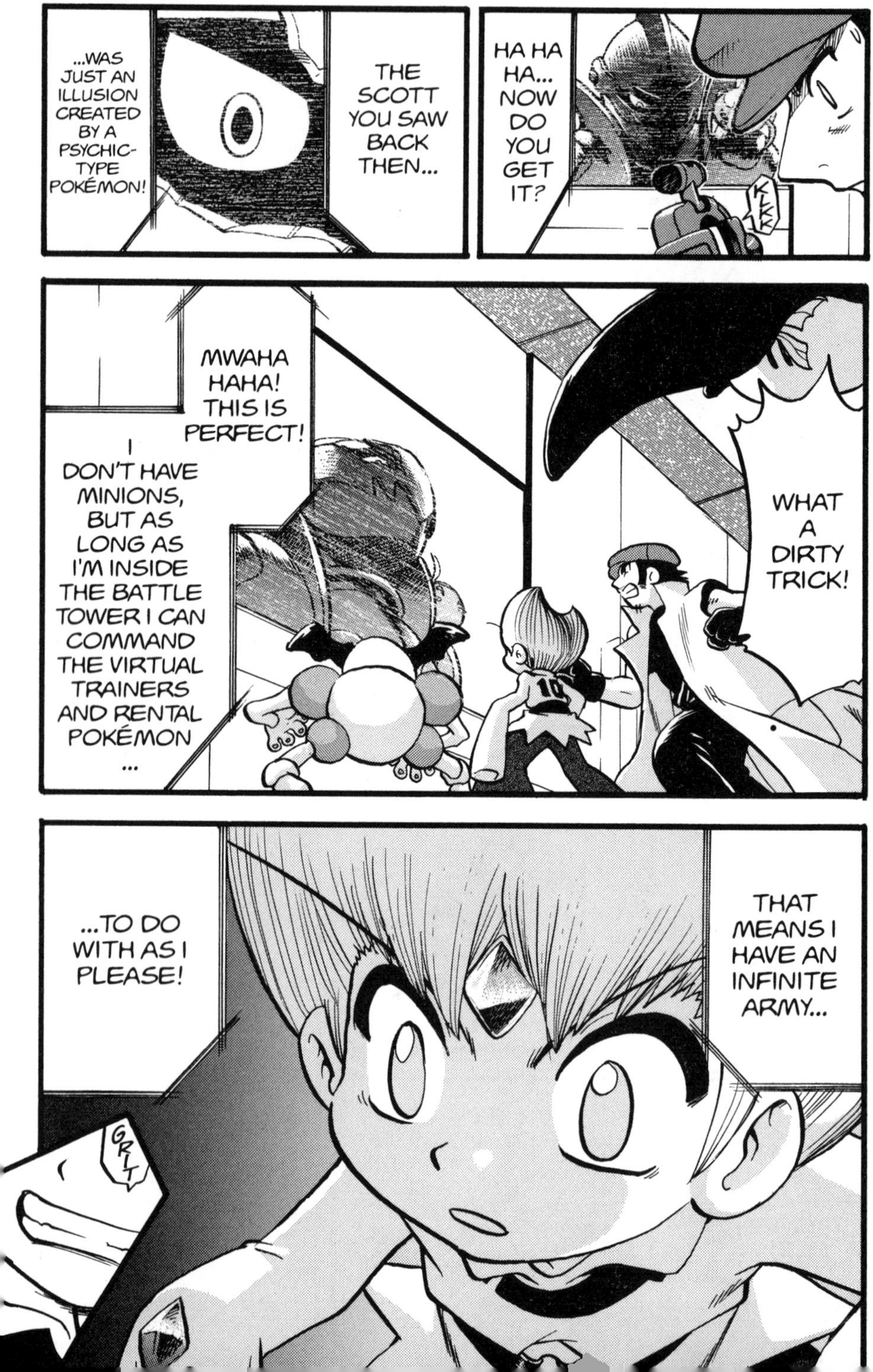
HA HA HA... NOW DO YOU GET IT?
KLIKK
THE SCOTT YOU SAW BACK THEN...
...WAS JUST AN ILLUSION CREATED BY A PSYCHIC-TYPE POKÉMON!
WHAT A DIRTY TRICK!
MWAHA HAHA! THIS IS PERFECT!
I DON'T HAVE MINIONS, BUT AS LONG AS I'M INSIDE THE BATTLE TOWER I CAN COMMAND THE VIRTUAL TRAINERS AND RENTAL POKÉMON ...
THAT MEANS I HAVE AN INFINITE ARMY...
...TO DO WITH AS I PLEASE!
GRIT

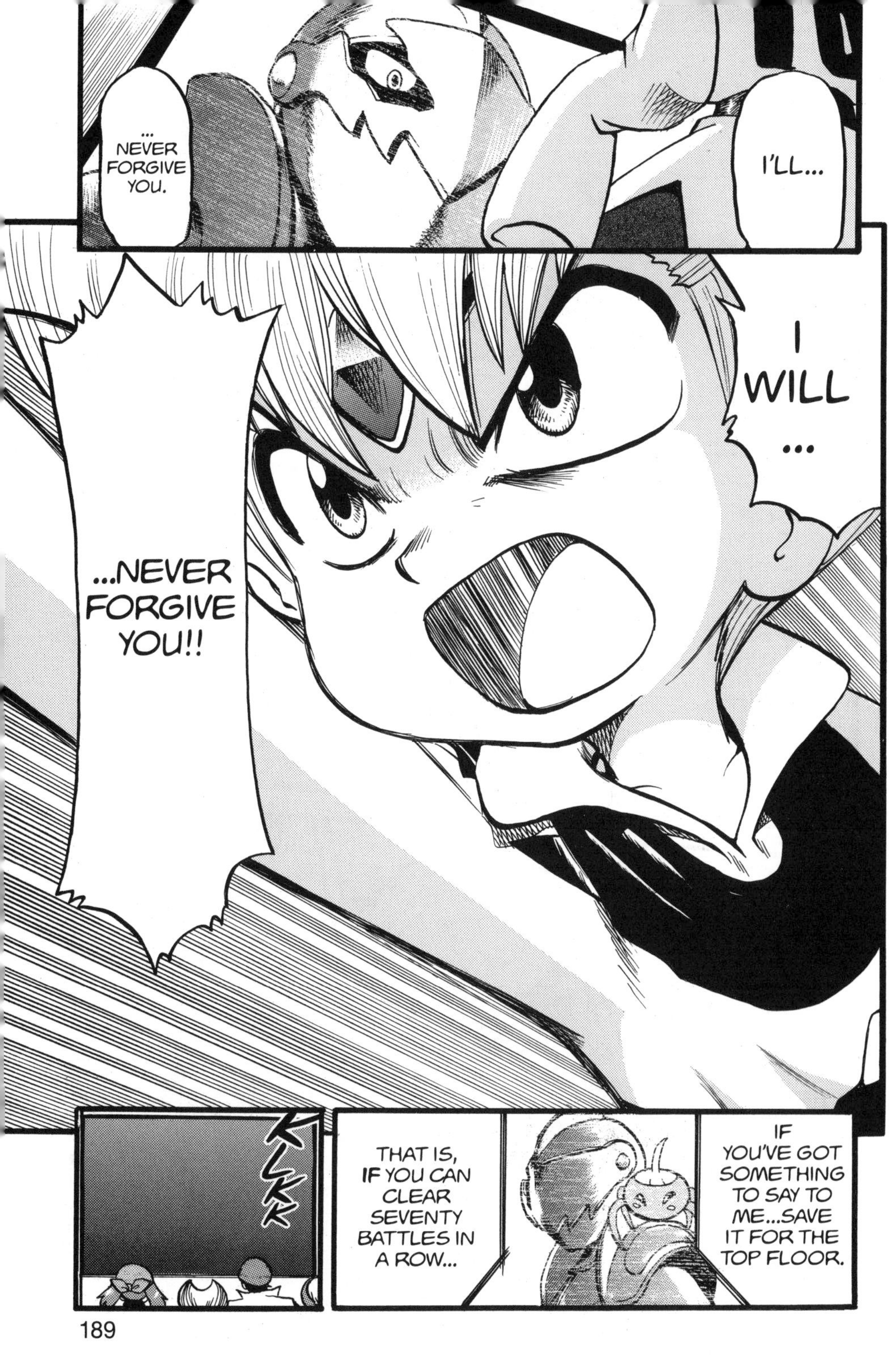
I'LL...
...NEVER FORGIVE YOU.
I WILL ...
...NEVER FORGIVE YOU!!
IF YOU'VE GOT SOMETHING TO SAY TO ME...SAVE IT FOR THE TOP FLOOR.
THAT IS, IF YOU CAN CLEAR SEVENTY BATTLES IN A ROW...
KLKK

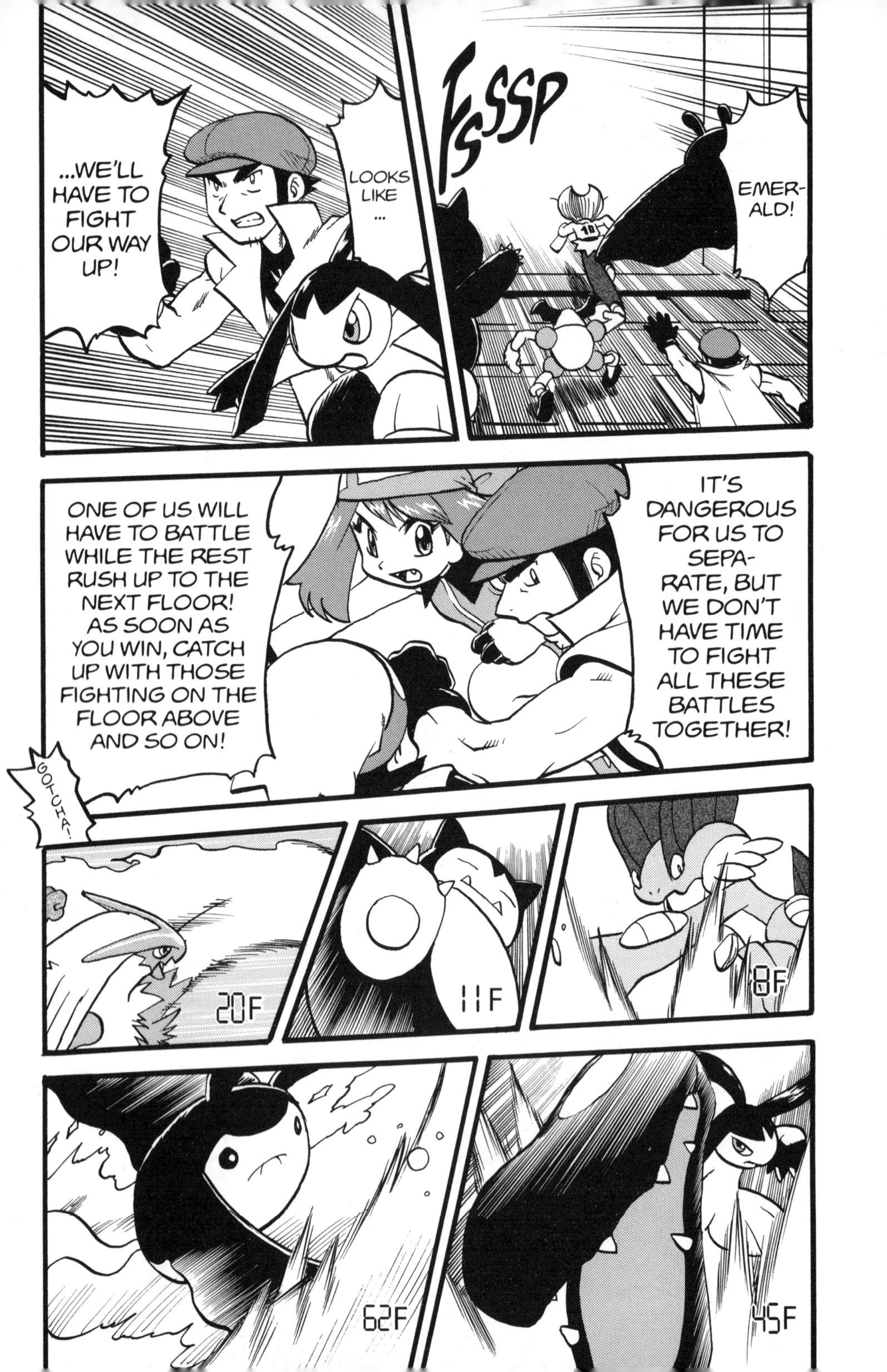
FSSSP
EMER-ALD!
LOOKS LIKE ...
...WE'LL HAVE TO FIGHT OUR WAY UP!
IT'S DANGEROUS FOR US TO SEPA-RATE, BUT WE DON'T HAVE TIME TO FIGHT ALL THESE BATTLES TOGETHER!
ONE OF US WILL HAVE TO BATTLE WHILE THE REST RUSH UP TO THE NEXT FLOOR! AS SOON AS YOU WIN, CATCH UP WITH THOSE FIGHTING ON THE FLOOR ABOVE AND SO ON!
GOTCHA!
8F
11F
20F
45F
62F

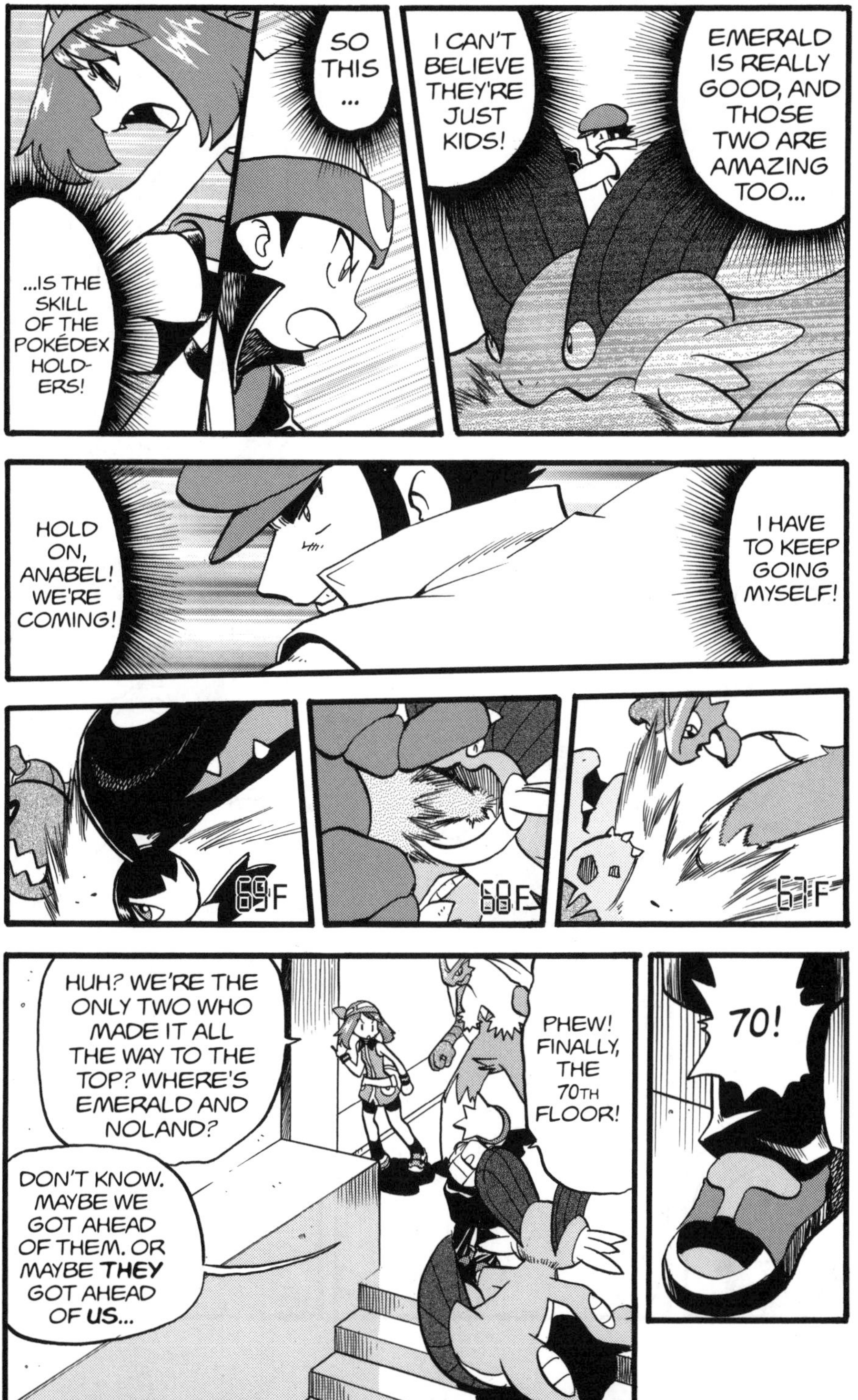
EMERALD IS REALLY GOOD, AND THOSE TWO ARE AMAZING TOO...
I CAN'T BELIEVE THEY'RE JUST KIDS!
SO THIS...
...IS THE SKILL OF THE POKÉDEX HOLDERS!
I HAVE TO KEEP GOING MYSELF!
HOLD ON, ANABEL! WE'RE COMING!
67F
68F
69F
70!
PHEW! FINALLY, THE 70TH FLOOR!
HUH? WE'RE THE ONLY TWO WHO MADE IT ALL THE WAY TO THE TOP? WHERE'S EMERALD AND NOLAND?
DON'T KNOW. MAYBE WE GOT AHEAD OF THEM. OR MAYBE **THEY** GOT AHEAD OF **US**...

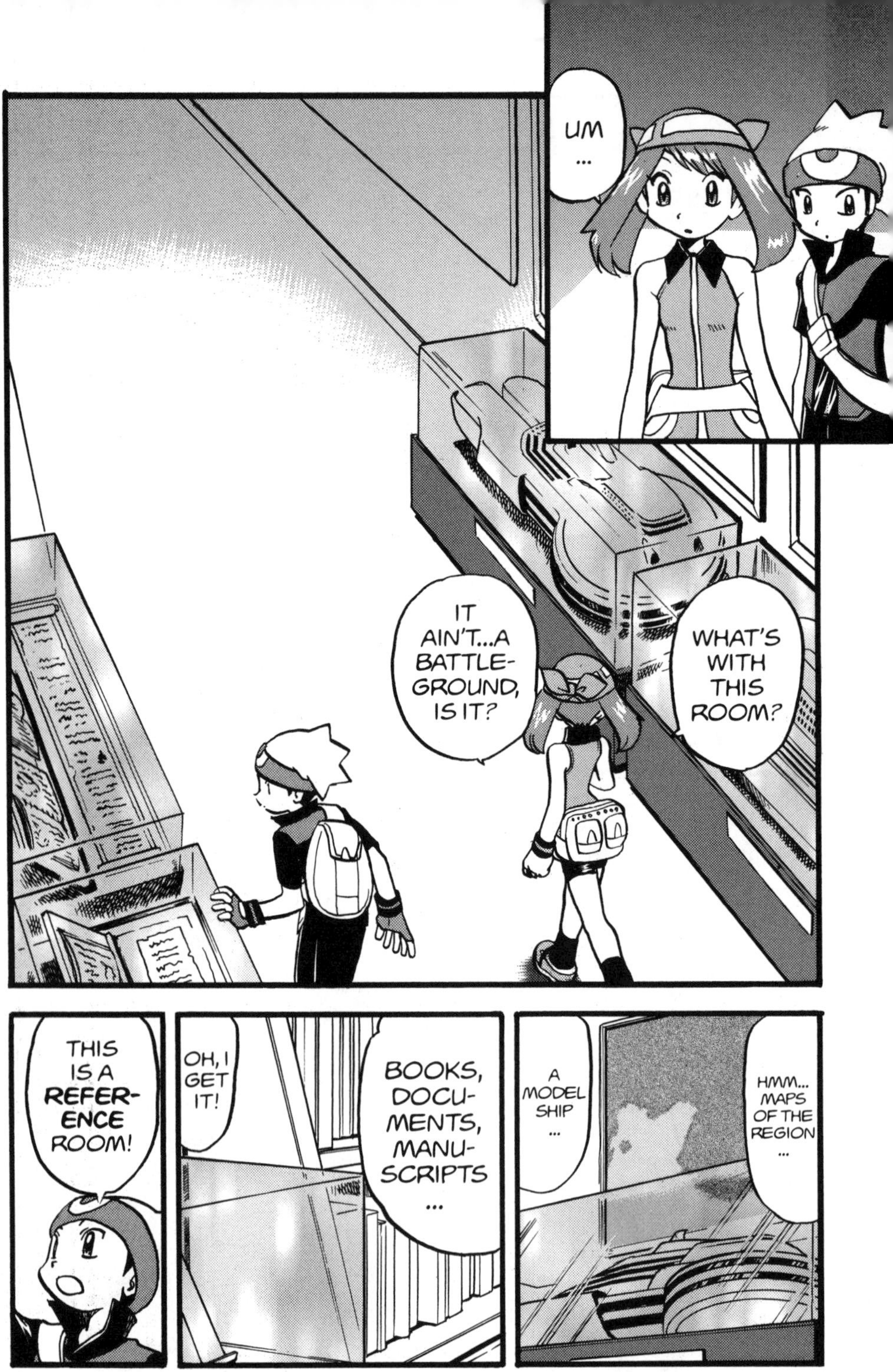
UM ...
WHAT'S WITH THIS ROOM?
IT AIN'T...A BATTLE-GROUND, IS IT?
HMM... MAPS OF THE REGION ...
A MODEL SHIP ...
BOOKS, DOCU-MENTS, MANU-SCRIPTS ...
OH, I GET IT!
THIS IS A **REFER-ENCE** ROOM!

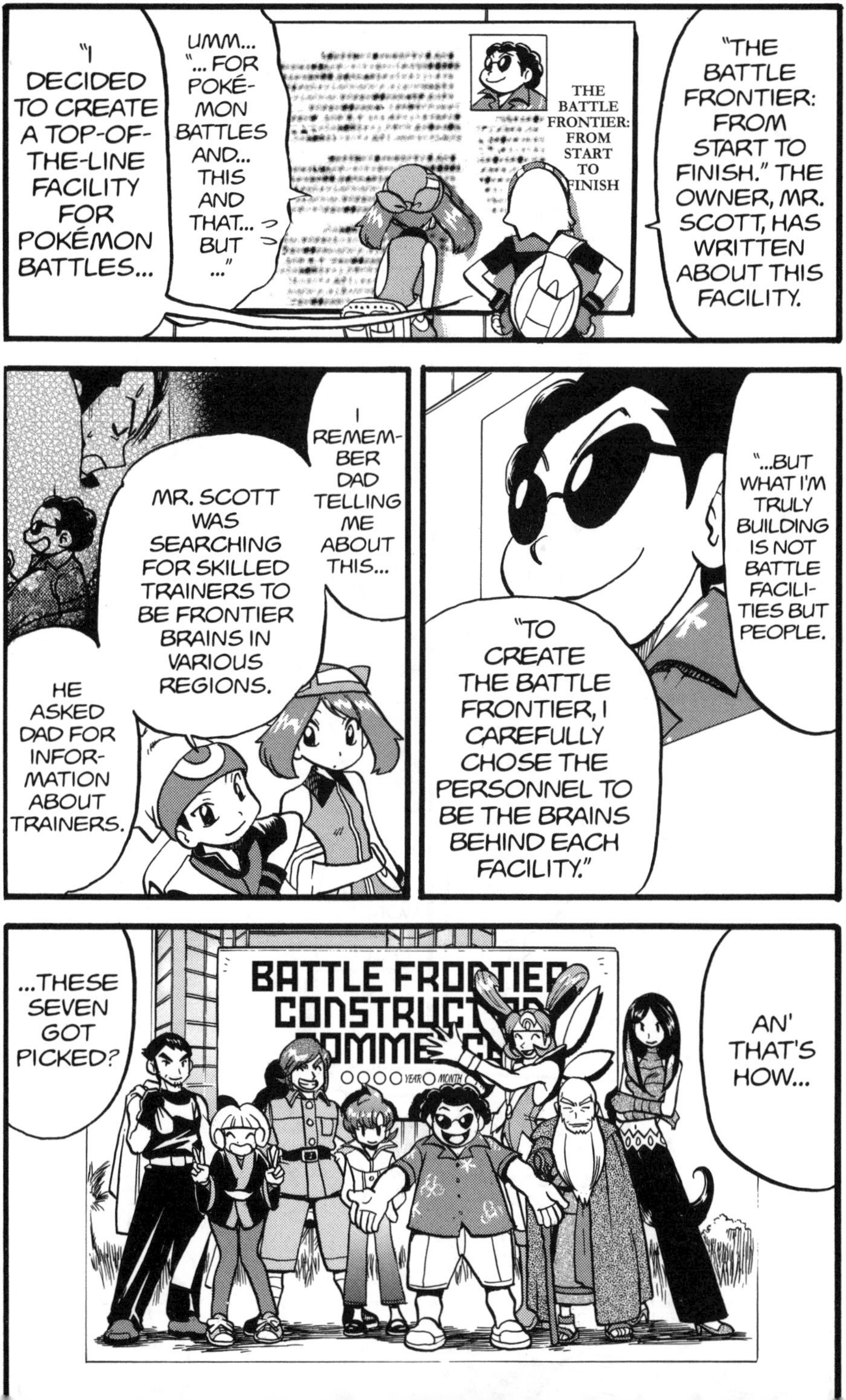
"THE BATTLE FRONTIER: FROM START TO FINISH." THE OWNER, MR. SCOTT, HAS WRITTEN ABOUT THIS FACILITY.
THE BATTLE FRONTIER: FROM START TO FINISH
UMM... "... FOR POKÉMON BATTLES AND... THIS AND THAT... BUT ..."
"I DECIDED TO CREATE A TOP-OF-THE-LINE FACILITY FOR POKÉMON BATTLES...
"...BUT WHAT I'M TRULY BUILDING IS NOT BATTLE FACILITIES BUT PEOPLE.
"TO CREATE THE BATTLE FRONTIER, I CAREFULLY CHOSE THE PERSONNEL TO BE THE BRAINS BEHIND EACH FACILITY."
I REMEMBER DAD TELLING ME ABOUT THIS...
MR. SCOTT WAS SEARCHING FOR SKILLED TRAINERS TO BE FRONTIER BRAINS IN VARIOUS REGIONS.
HE ASKED DAD FOR INFORMATION ABOUT TRAINERS.
AN' THAT'S HOW...
...THESE SEVEN GOT PICKED?

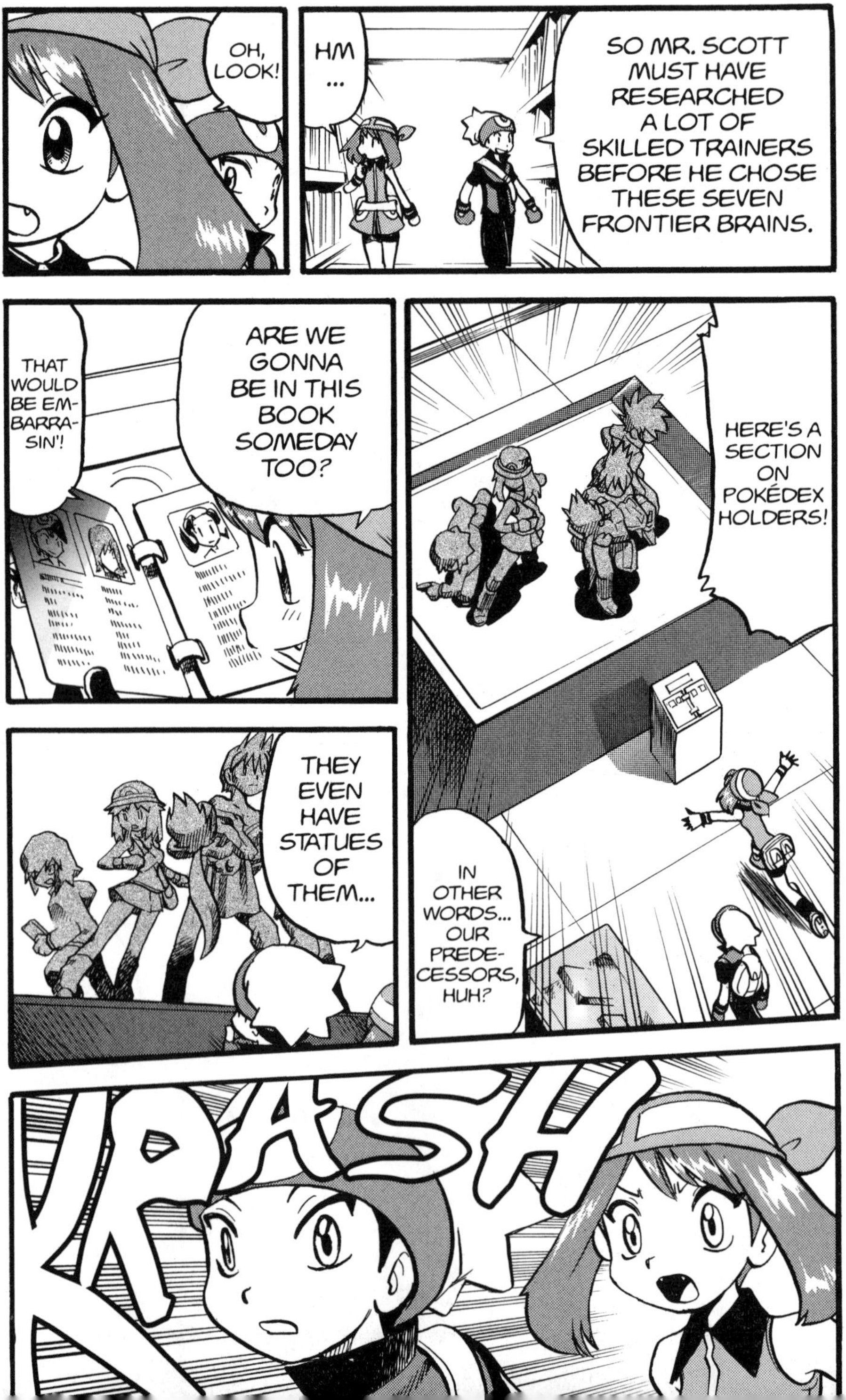
SO MR. SCOTT MUST HAVE RESEARCHED A LOT OF SKILLED TRAINERS BEFORE HE CHOSE THESE SEVEN FRONTIER BRAINS.
HM ...
OH, LOOK!
HERE'S A SECTION ON POKÉDEX HOLDERS!
IN OTHER WORDS... OUR PREDE-CESSORS, HUH?
ARE WE GONNA BE IN THIS BOOK SOMEDAY TOO?
THAT WOULD BE EM-BARRA-SIN'!
THEY EVEN HAVE STATUES OF THEM...
KRASH

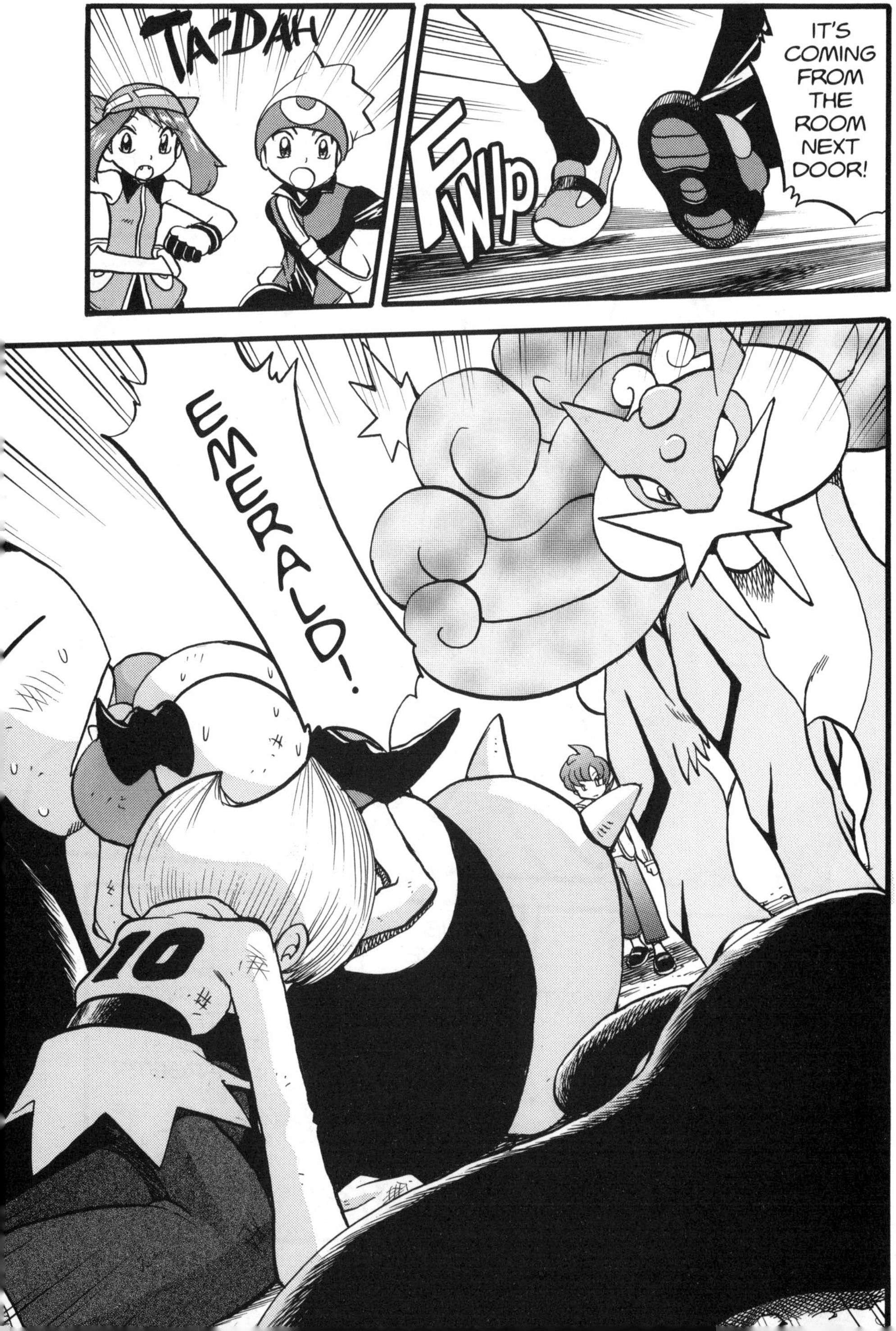
IT'S COMING FROM THE ROOM NEXT DOOR!
FWIP
TA-DAH
EMERALD!!

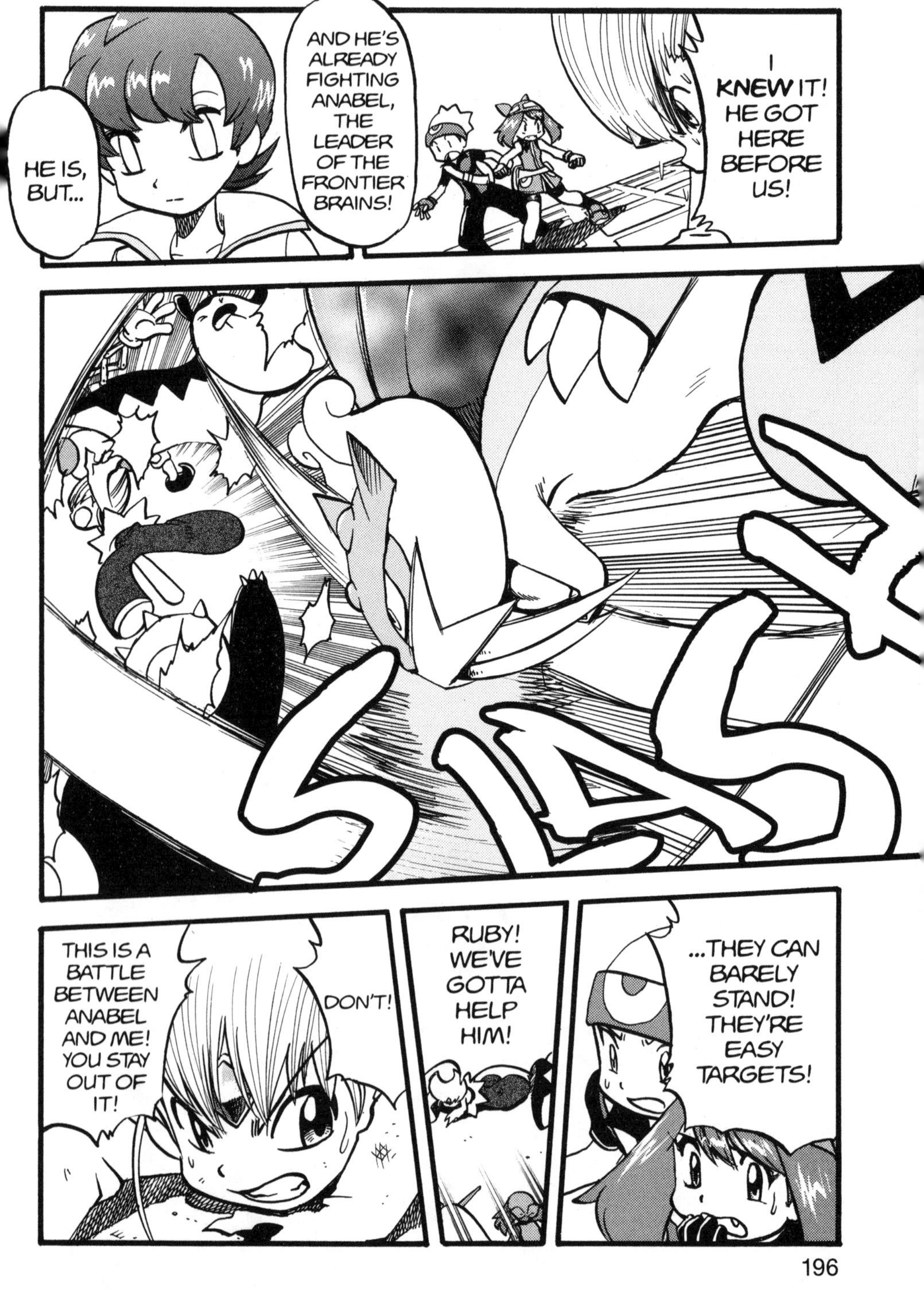
I KNEW IT! HE GOT HERE BEFORE US!
AND HE'S ALREADY FIGHTING ANABEL, THE LEADER OF THE FRONTIER BRAINS!
HE IS, BUT...
SLASH
...THEY CAN BARELY STAND! THEY'RE EASY TARGETS!
RUBY! WE'VE GOTTA HELP HIM!
DON'T!
THIS IS A BATTLE BETWEEN ANABEL AND ME! YOU STAY OUT OF IT!

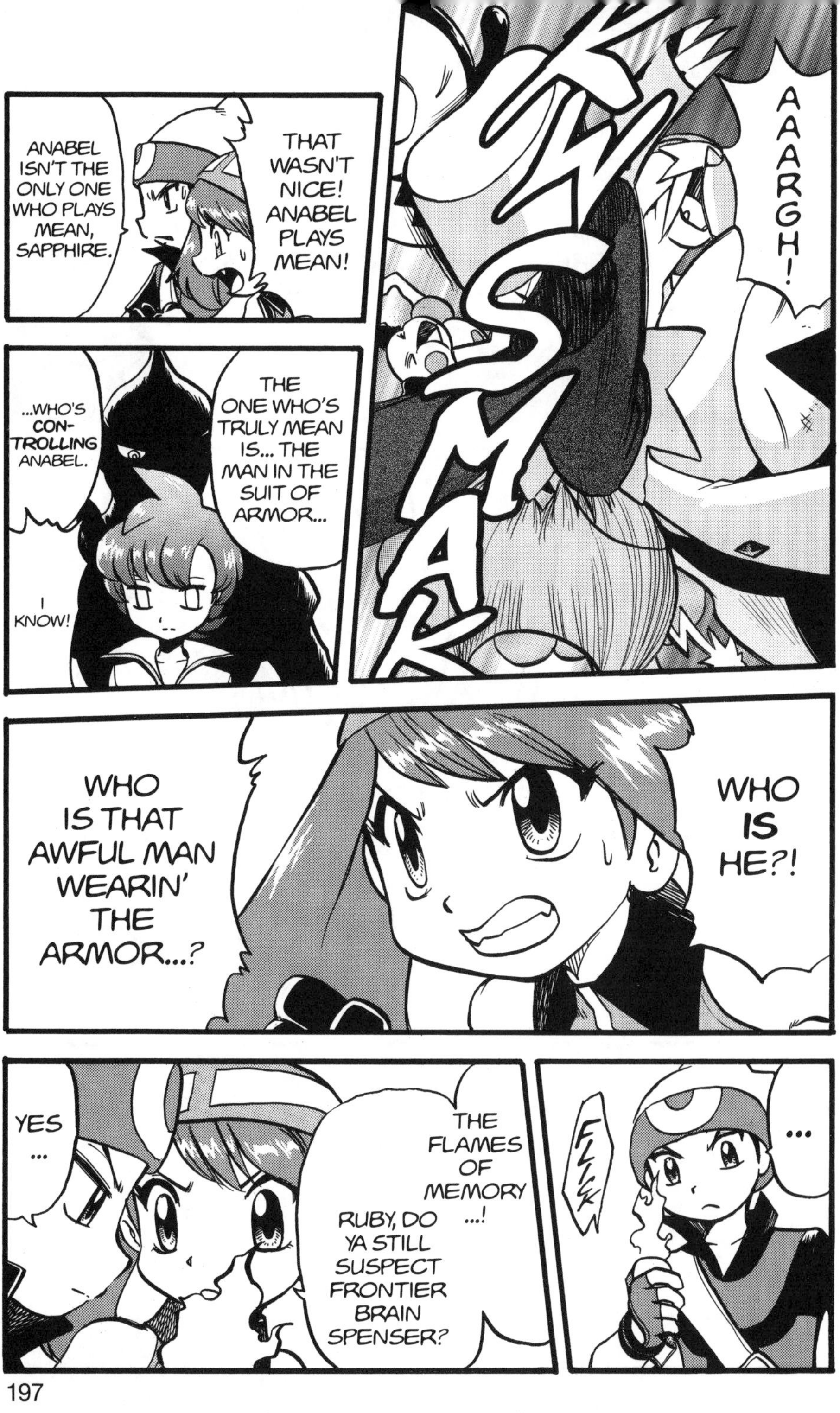
AAAARGH!
THAT WASN'T NICE! ANABEL PLAYS MEAN!
ANABEL ISN'T THE ONLY ONE WHO PLAYS MEAN, SAPPHIRE.
THE ONE WHO'S TRULY MEAN IS... THE MAN IN THE SUIT OF ARMOR...
...WHO'S **CONTROLLING** ANABEL.
I KNOW!
WHO IS THAT AWFUL MAN WEARIN' THE ARMOR...?
WHO **IS** HE?!
FLICK
...
THE FLAMES OF MEMORY ...!
RUBY, DO YA STILL SUSPECT FRONTIER BRAIN SPENSER?
YES ...

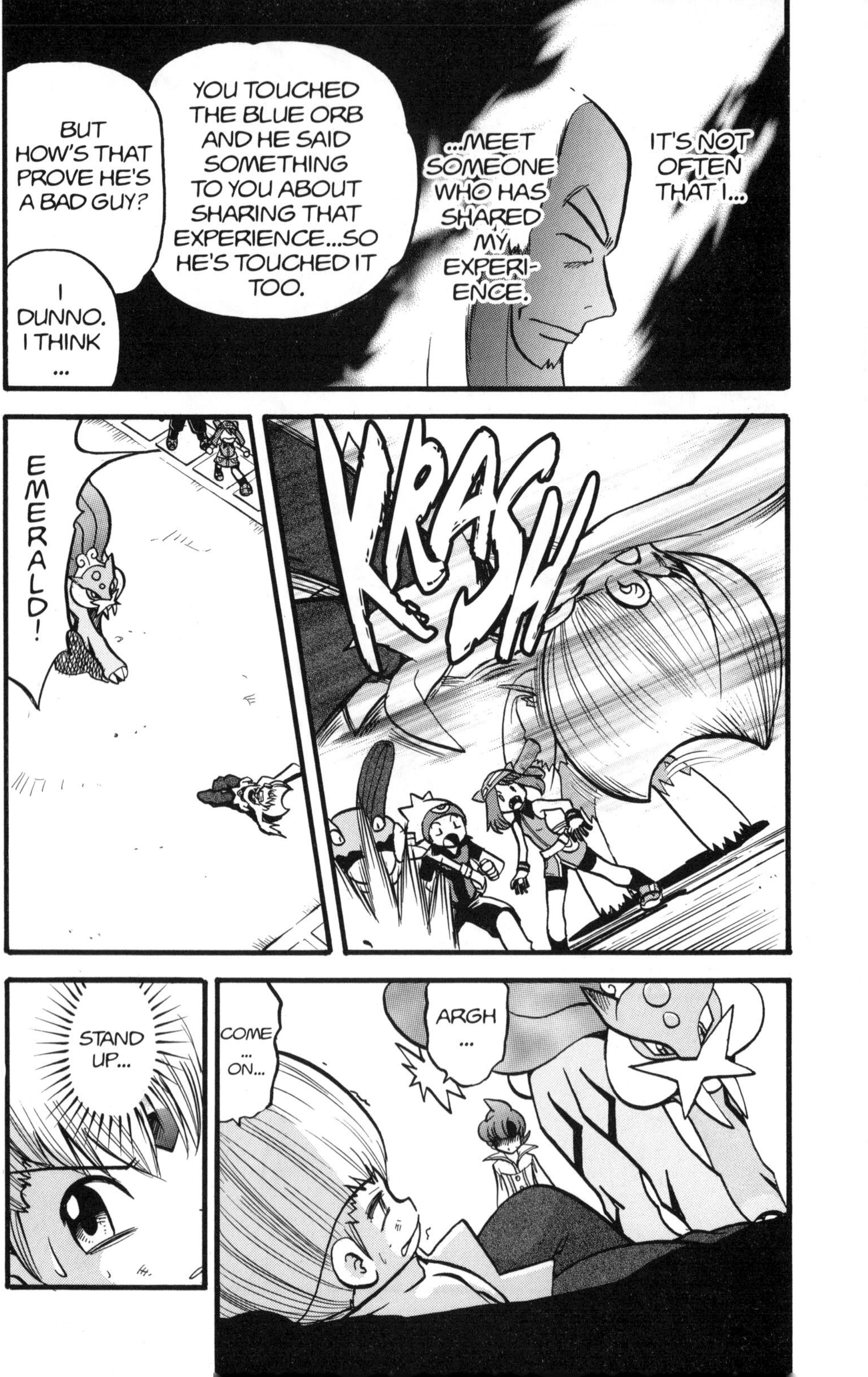
IT'S NOT OFTEN THAT I...
...MEET SOMEONE WHO HAS SHARED MY EXPERI-ENCE.
YOU TOUCHED THE BLUE ORB AND HE SAID SOMETHING TO YOU ABOUT SHARING THAT EXPERIENCE...SO HE'S TOUCHED IT TOO.
BUT HOW'S THAT PROVE HE'S A BAD GUY?
I DUNNO. I THINK ...
KRASH
EMERALD!
ARGH ...
COME ... ON...
STAND UP...

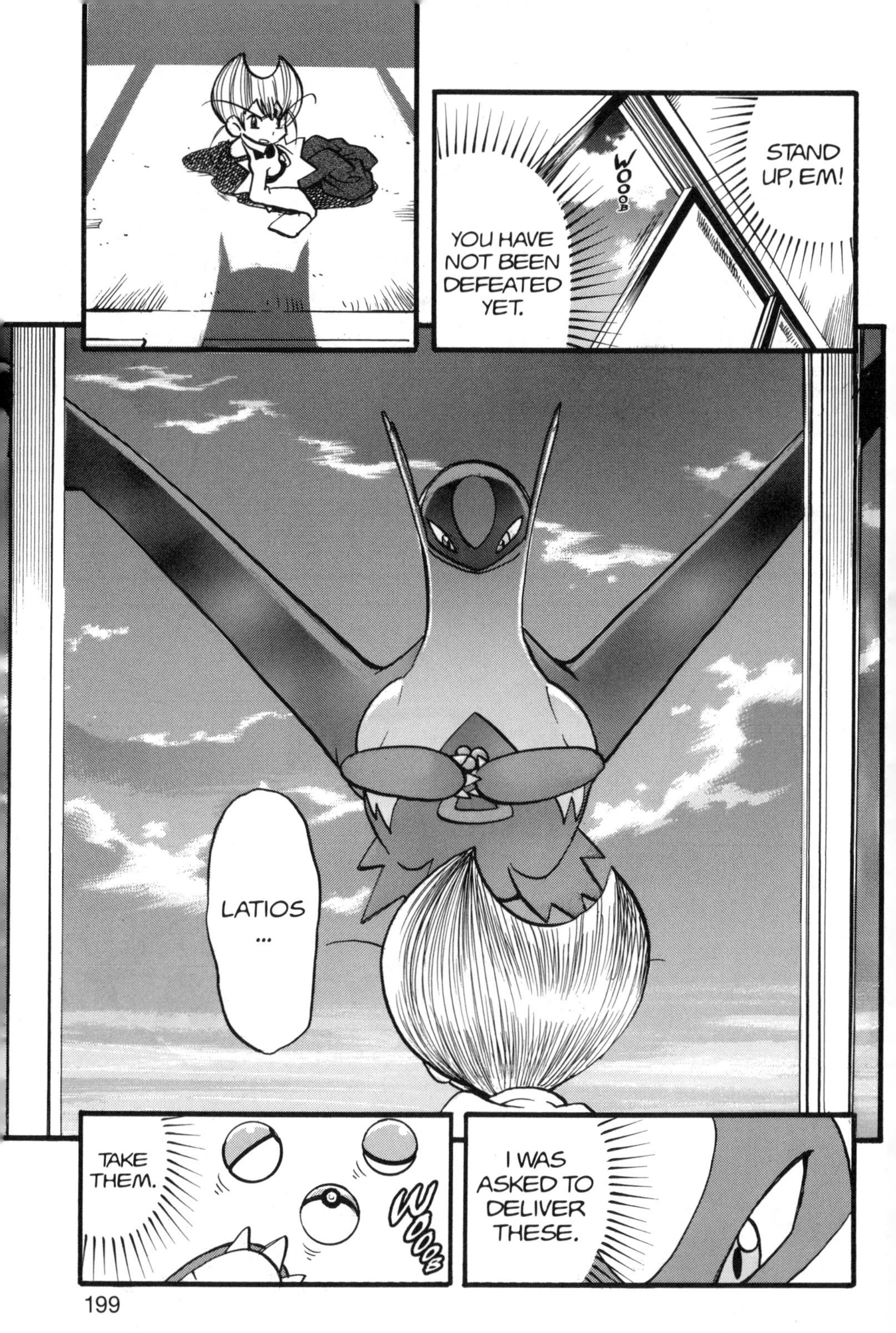
STAND UP, EM!
WOOOB
YOU HAVE NOT BEEN DEFEATED YET.
LATIOS ...
I WAS ASKED TO DELIVER THESE.
TAKE THEM.
WOOOB

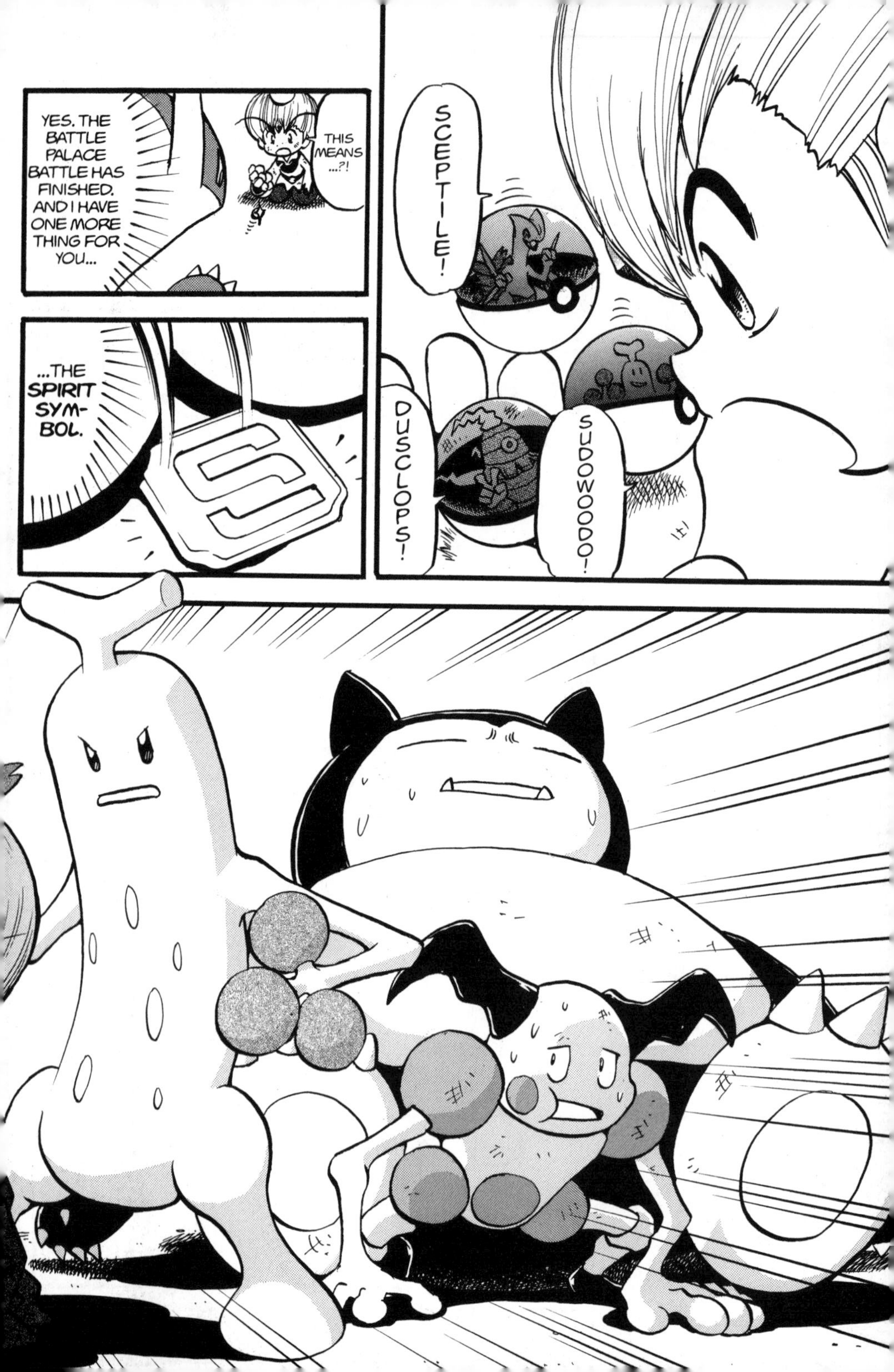
SCEPTILE!
SUDOWOODO!
DUSCLOPS!
THIS MEANS ...?!
YES. THE BATTLE PALACE BATTLE HAS FINISHED. AND I HAVE ONE MORE THING FOR YOU...
...THE SPIRIT SYMBOL.

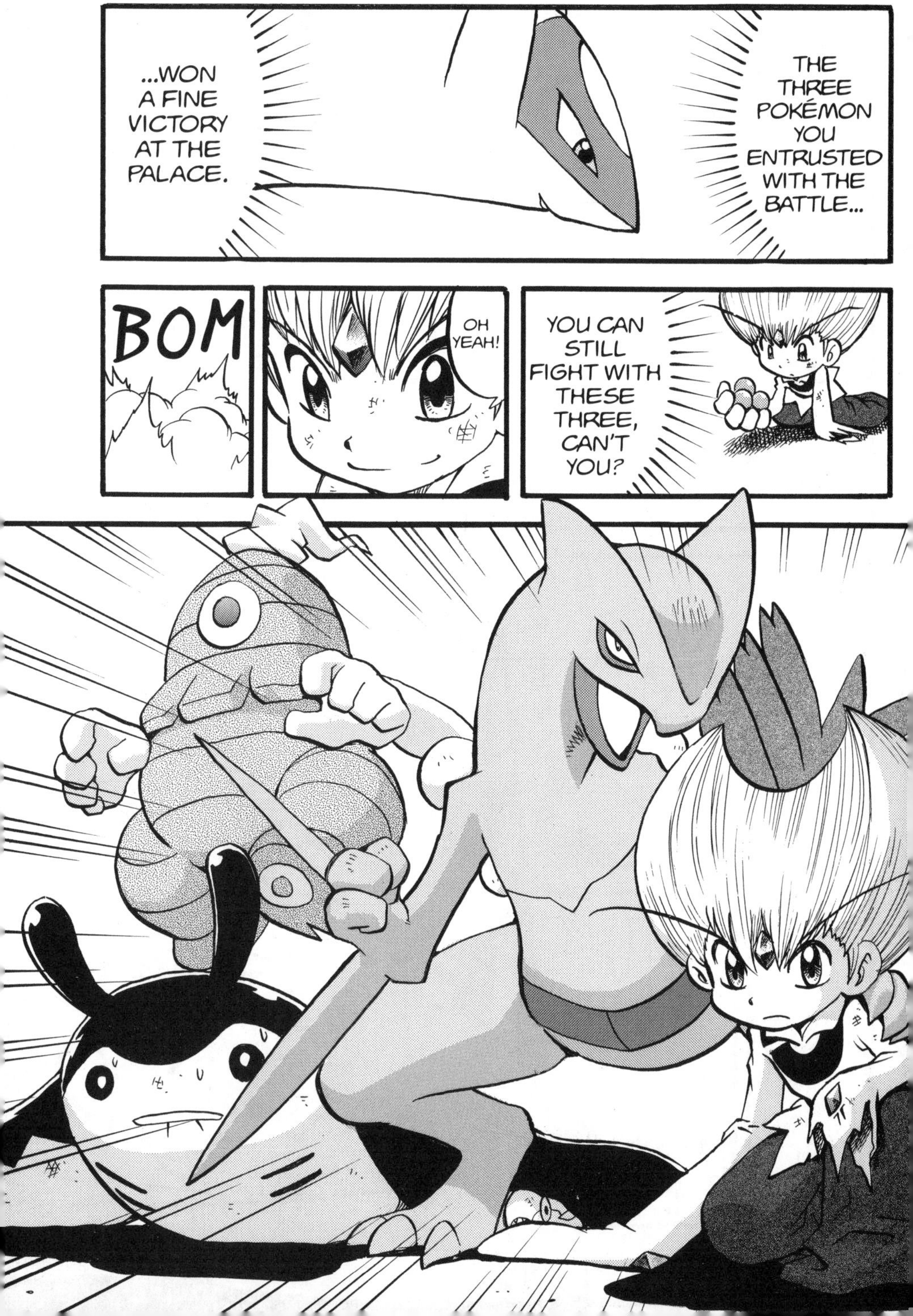
THE THREE POKÉMON YOU ENTRUSTED WITH THE BATTLE...
...WON A FINE VICTORY AT THE PALACE.
YOU CAN STILL FIGHT WITH THESE THREE, CAN'T YOU?
OH YEAH!
BOM

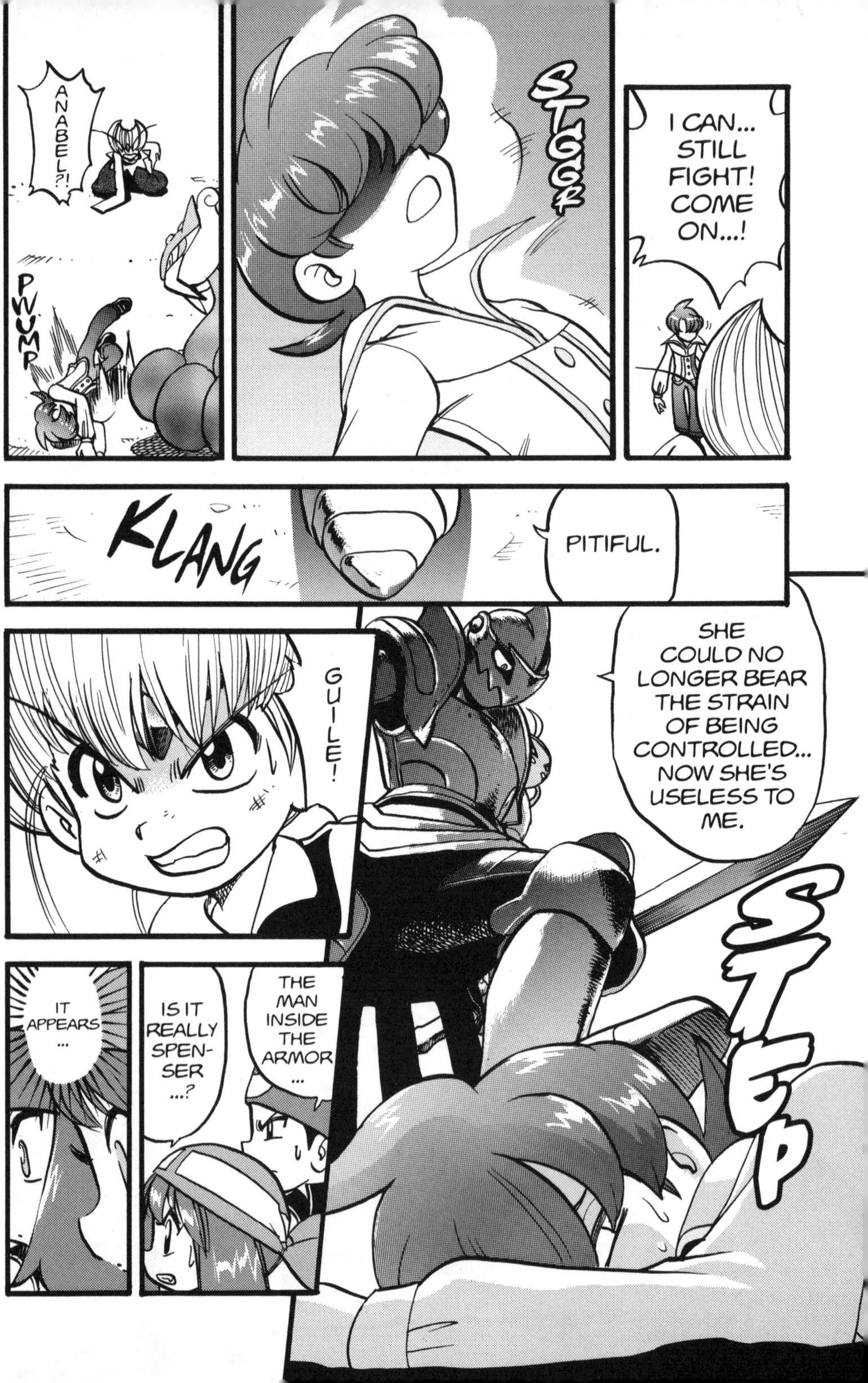
I CAN... STILL FIGHT! COME ON...!
STGGR
ANABEL?!
PWUMP
PITIFUL.
KLANG
SHE COULD NO LONGER BEAR THE STRAIN OF BEING CONTROLLED... NOW SHE'S USELESS TO ME.
STEP
GUILE!
THE MAN INSIDE THE ARMOR...
IS IT REALLY SPEN-SER...?
IT APPEARS...

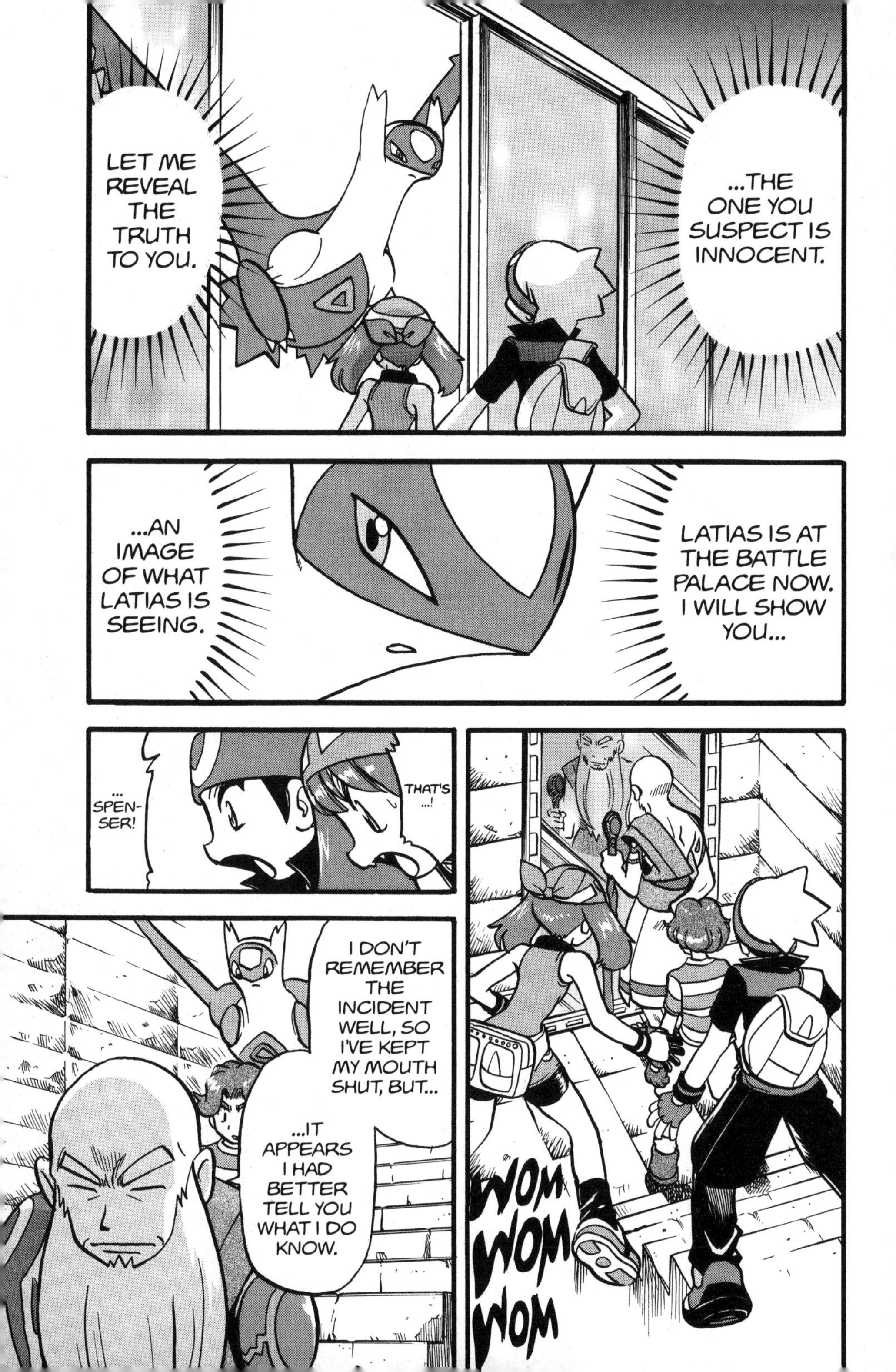
...THE ONE YOU SUSPECT IS INNOCENT.
LET ME REVEAL THE TRUTH TO YOU.
LATIAS IS AT THE BATTLE PALACE NOW. I WILL SHOW YOU...
...AN IMAGE OF WHAT LATIAS IS SEEING.
WOM WOM WOM WOM
THAT'S ...!
... SPEN-SER!
I DON'T REMEMBER THE INCIDENT WELL, SO I'VE KEPT MY MOUTH SHUT, BUT...
...IT APPEARS I HAD BETTER TELL YOU WHAT I DO KNOW.

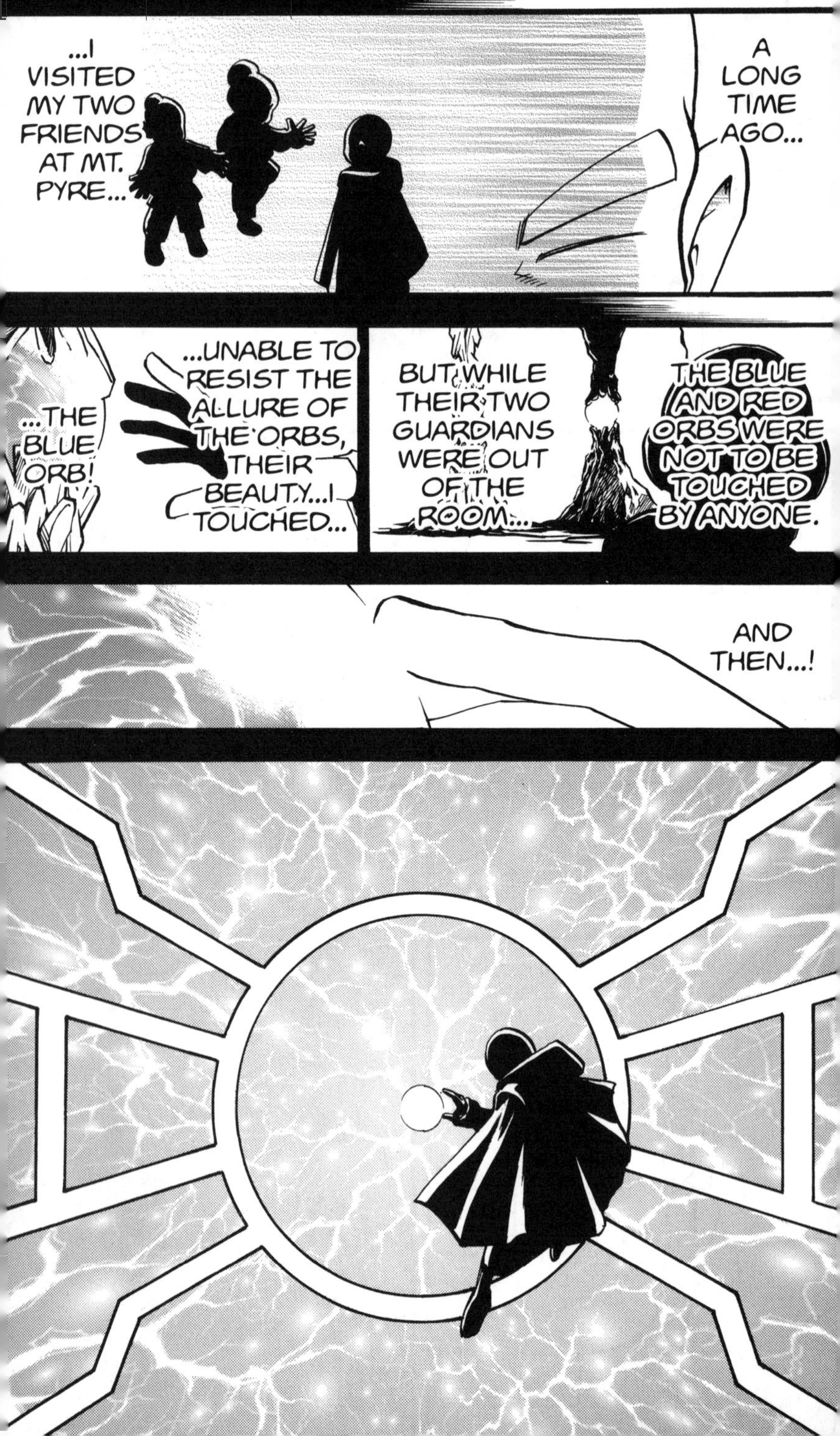
A LONG TIME AGO...
...I VISITED MY TWO FRIENDS AT MT. PYRE...
THE BLUE AND RED ORBS WERE NOT TO BE TOUCHED BY ANYONE.
BUT WHILE THEIR TWO GUARDIANS WERE OUT OF THE ROOM...
...UNABLE TO RESIST THE ALLURE OF THE ORBS, THEIR BEAUTY...I TOUCHED...
...THE BLUE ORB!
AND THEN...!

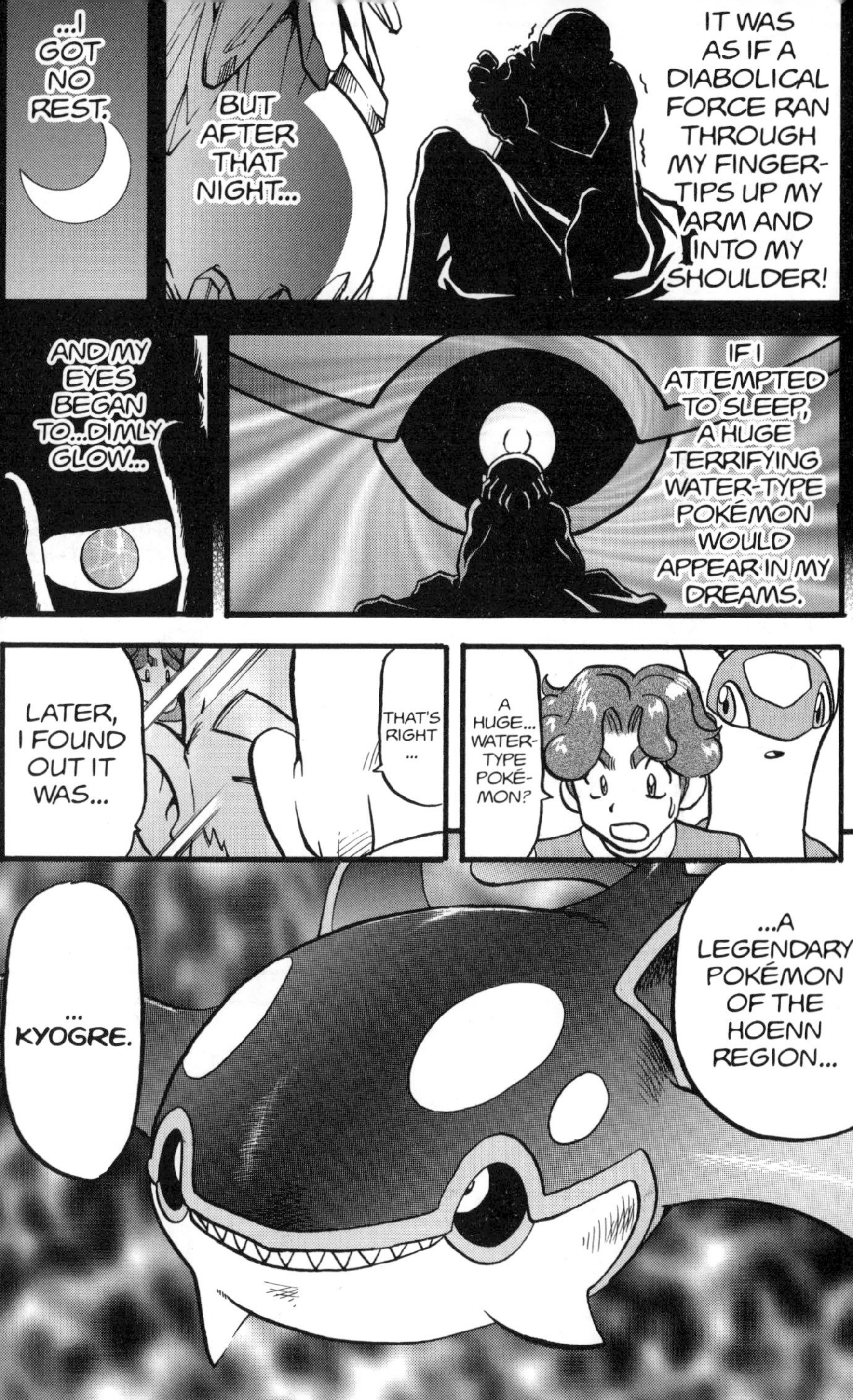
IT WAS AS IF A DIABOLICAL FORCE RAN THROUGH MY FINGER-TIPS UP MY ARM AND INTO MY SHOULDER!
BUT AFTER THAT NIGHT...
...I GOT NO REST.
IF I ATTEMPTED TO SLEEP, A HUGE TERRIFYING WATER-TYPE POKÉMON WOULD APPEAR IN MY DREAMS.
AND MY EYES BEGAN TO...DIMLY GLOW...
A HUGE... WATER-TYPE POKÉMON?
THAT'S RIGHT ...
LATER, I FOUND OUT IT WAS...
...A LEGENDARY POKÉMON OF THE HOENN REGION...
... KYOGRE.

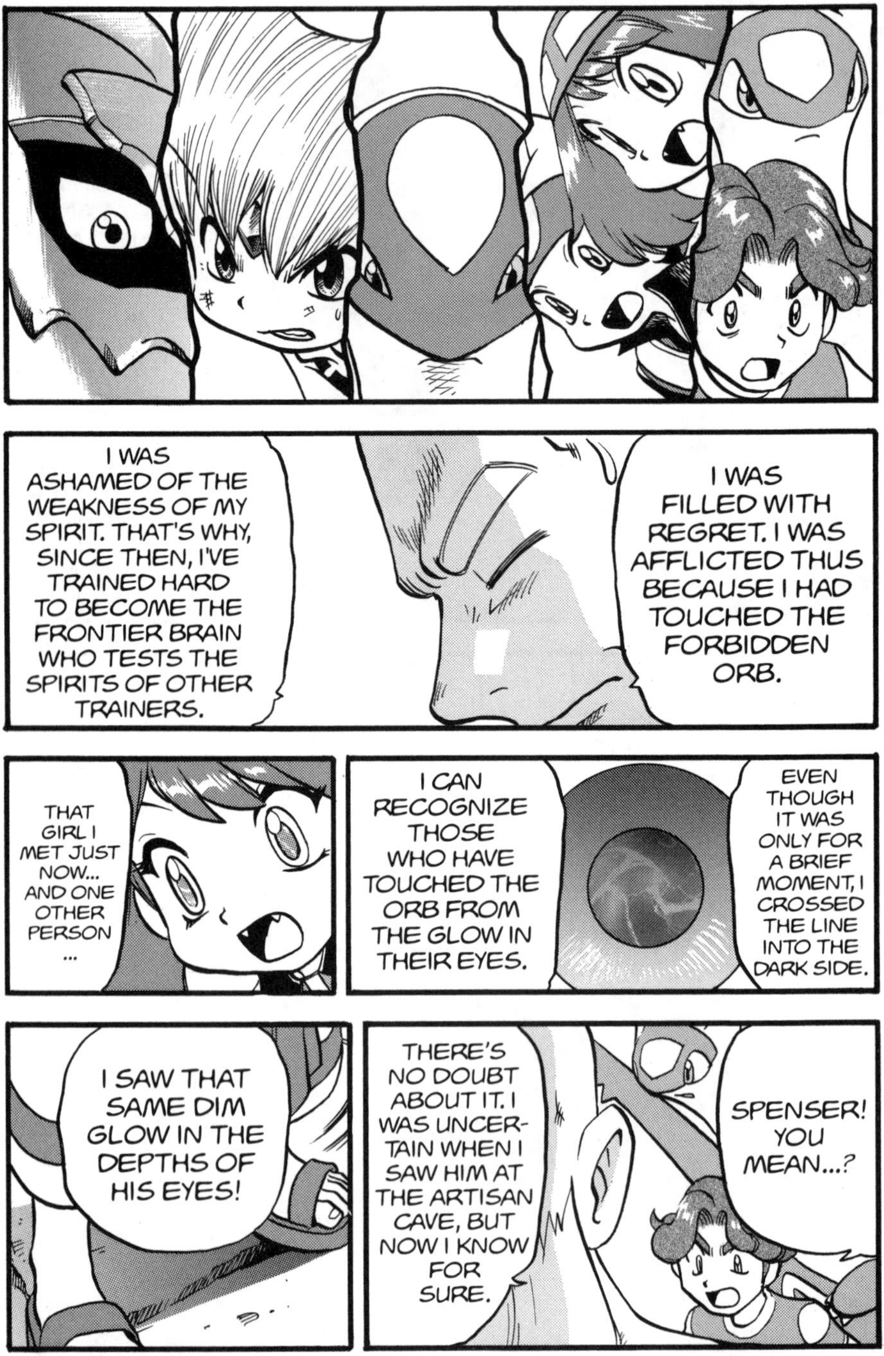
I WAS FILLED WITH REGRET. I WAS AFFLICTED THUS BECAUSE I HAD TOUCHED THE FORBIDDEN ORB.
I WAS ASHAMED OF THE WEAKNESS OF MY SPIRIT. THAT'S WHY, SINCE THEN, I'VE TRAINED HARD TO BECOME THE FRONTIER BRAIN WHO TESTS THE SPIRITS OF OTHER TRAINERS.
EVEN THOUGH IT WAS ONLY FOR A BRIEF MOMENT, I CROSSED THE LINE INTO THE DARK SIDE.
I CAN RECOGNIZE THOSE WHO HAVE TOUCHED THE ORB FROM THE GLOW IN THEIR EYES.
THAT GIRL I MET JUST NOW... AND ONE OTHER PERSON...
SPENSER! YOU MEAN...?
THERE'S NO DOUBT ABOUT IT. I WAS UNCERTAIN WHEN I SAW HIM AT THE ARTISAN CAVE, BUT NOW I KNOW FOR SURE.
I SAW THAT SAME DIM GLOW IN THE DEPTHS OF HIS EYES!

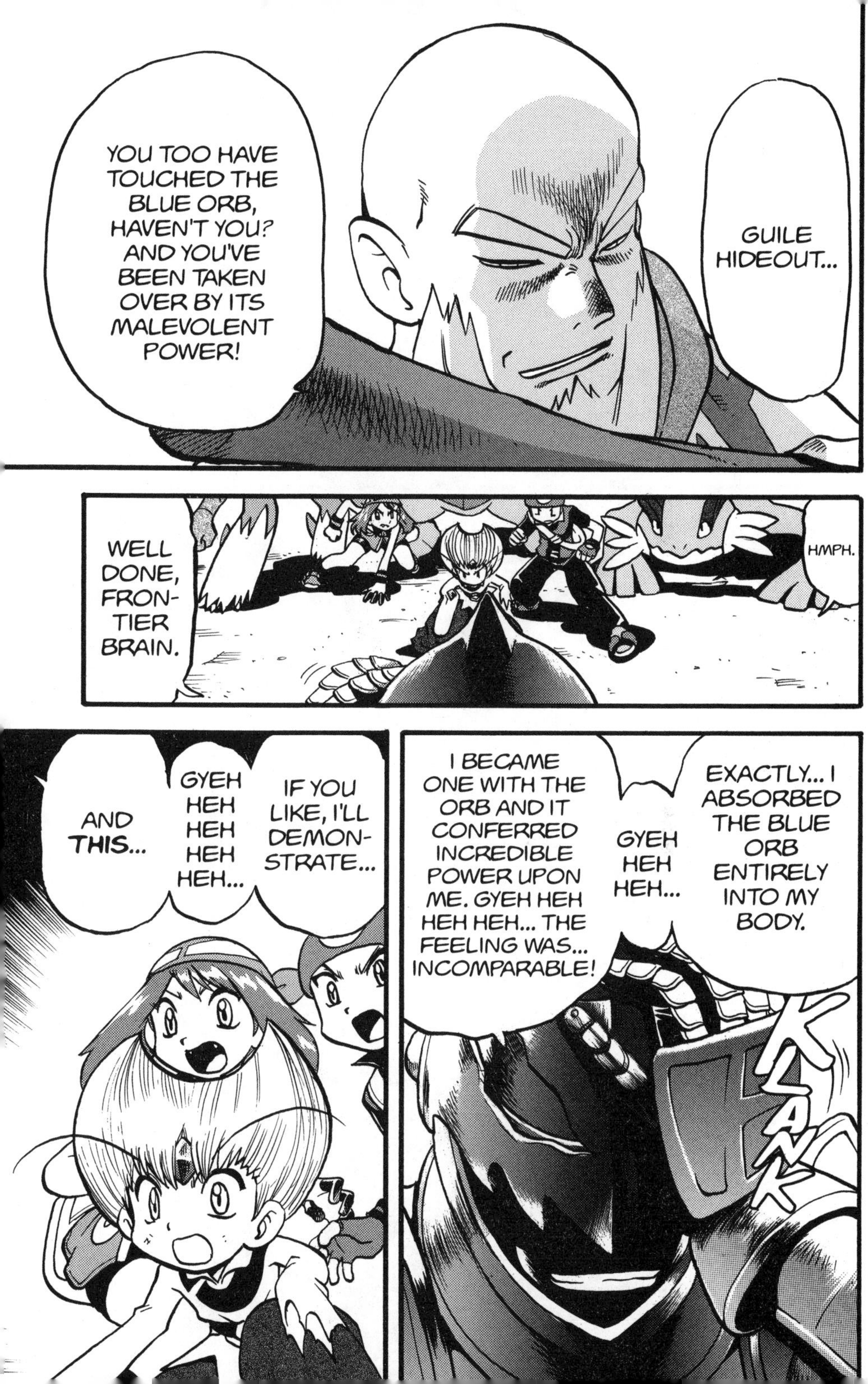
GUILE HIDEOUT...
YOU TOO HAVE TOUCHED THE BLUE ORB, HAVEN'T YOU? AND YOU'VE BEEN TAKEN OVER BY ITS MALEVOLENT POWER!
HMPH.
WELL DONE, FRONTIER BRAIN.
EXACTLY... I ABSORBED THE BLUE ORB ENTIRELY INTO MY BODY.
GYEH HEH HEH...
I BECAME ONE WITH THE ORB AND IT CONFERRED INCREDIBLE POWER UPON ME. GYEH HEH HEH HEH... THE FEELING WAS... INCOMPARABLE!
KLANK
IF YOU LIKE, I'LL DEMONSTRATE...
GYEH HEH HEH HEH HEH...
AND THIS...

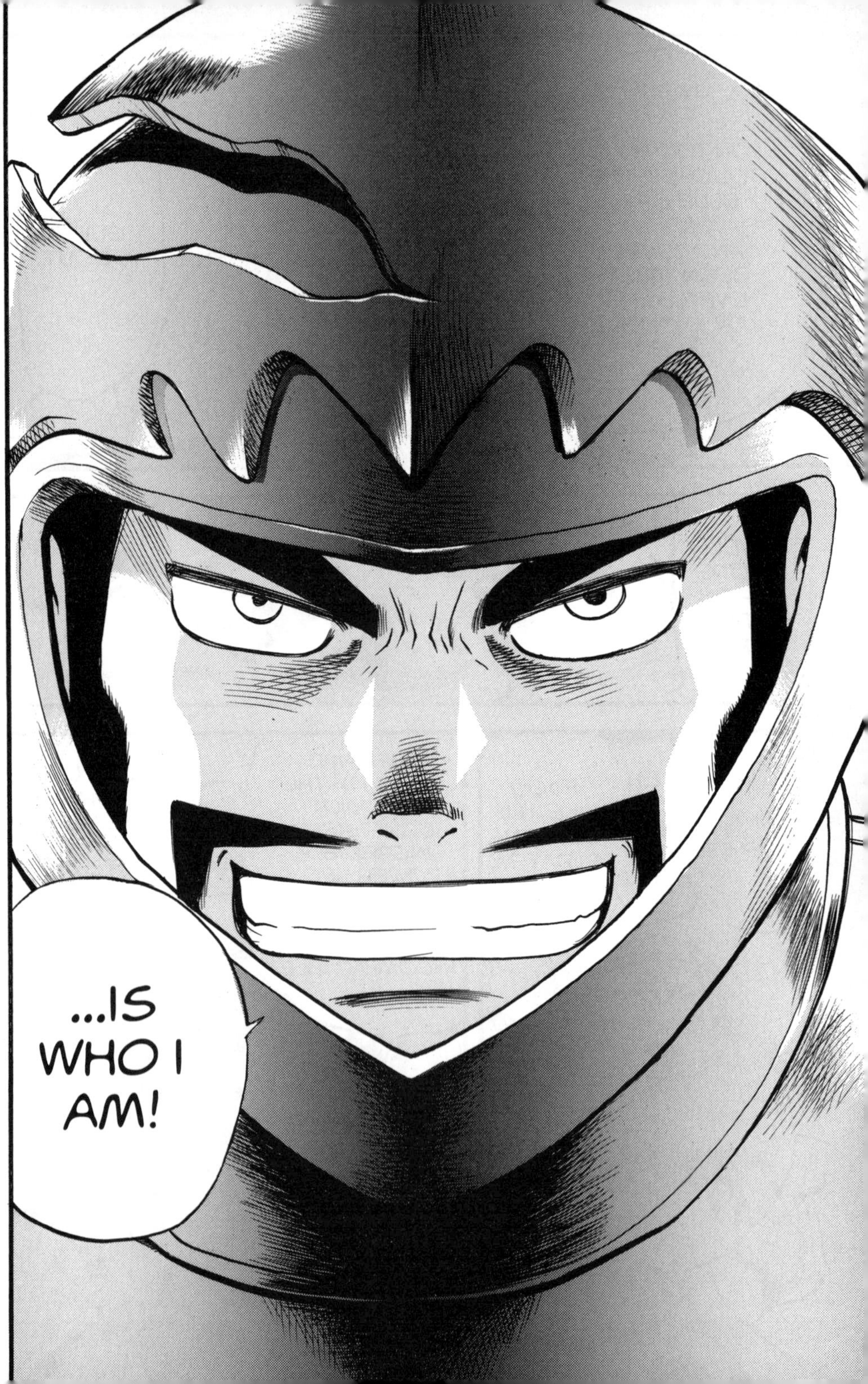
...IS WHO I AM!

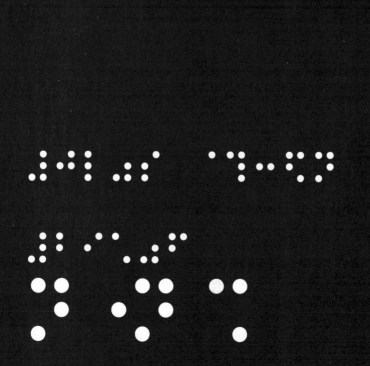

Message from
Hidenori Kusaka

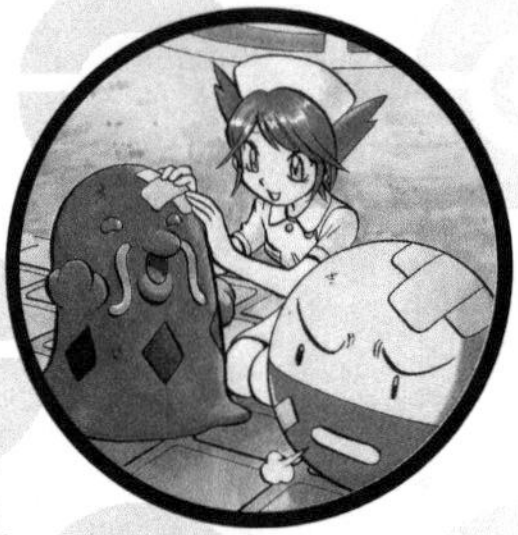

I played *Pokémon Ruby/Sapphire* to complete the National Pokédex for *Platinum*. I was filling in the Pokédex using the dual-slot mode and Pal Park, but I still couldn't complete it, so I dragged out the GameCube games, including *Pokémon Box: Ruby & Sapphire* and *Pokémon Colosseum*. For Lugia, I snagged Shadow Lugia, purified it, sent it to my GBA and then challenged myself on *Pokémon XD: Gale of Darkness* again so I could send the data to *Platinum*. It was a reunion with the Pokémon I raised...not just in my memories but in reality too. That's what makes Pokémon so much fun!

–2008

Message from
Satoshi Yamamoto

This is the final volume of the Emerald story arc! As I first read the script for the end of this story, I began to shake with excitement. I got goose bumps on my skin and tears in my eyes. I think everyone should read it. I worked extra hard on the chapters for this volume. If you're a new reader to the series who is thinking about starting from this volume, I advise you to go back and start with volume 1. I can assure you, you'll enjoy this one a million times better!

–2008

The Final Battle, Part 1

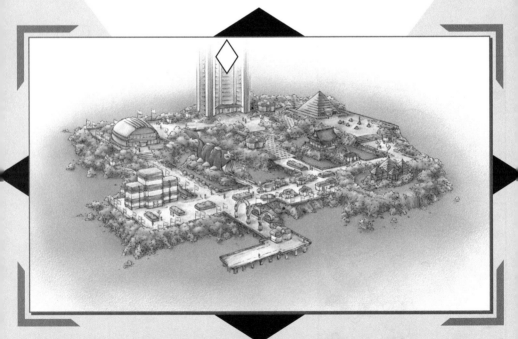

POKÉMON ADVENTURES·THE SIXTH CHAPTER·EMERALD

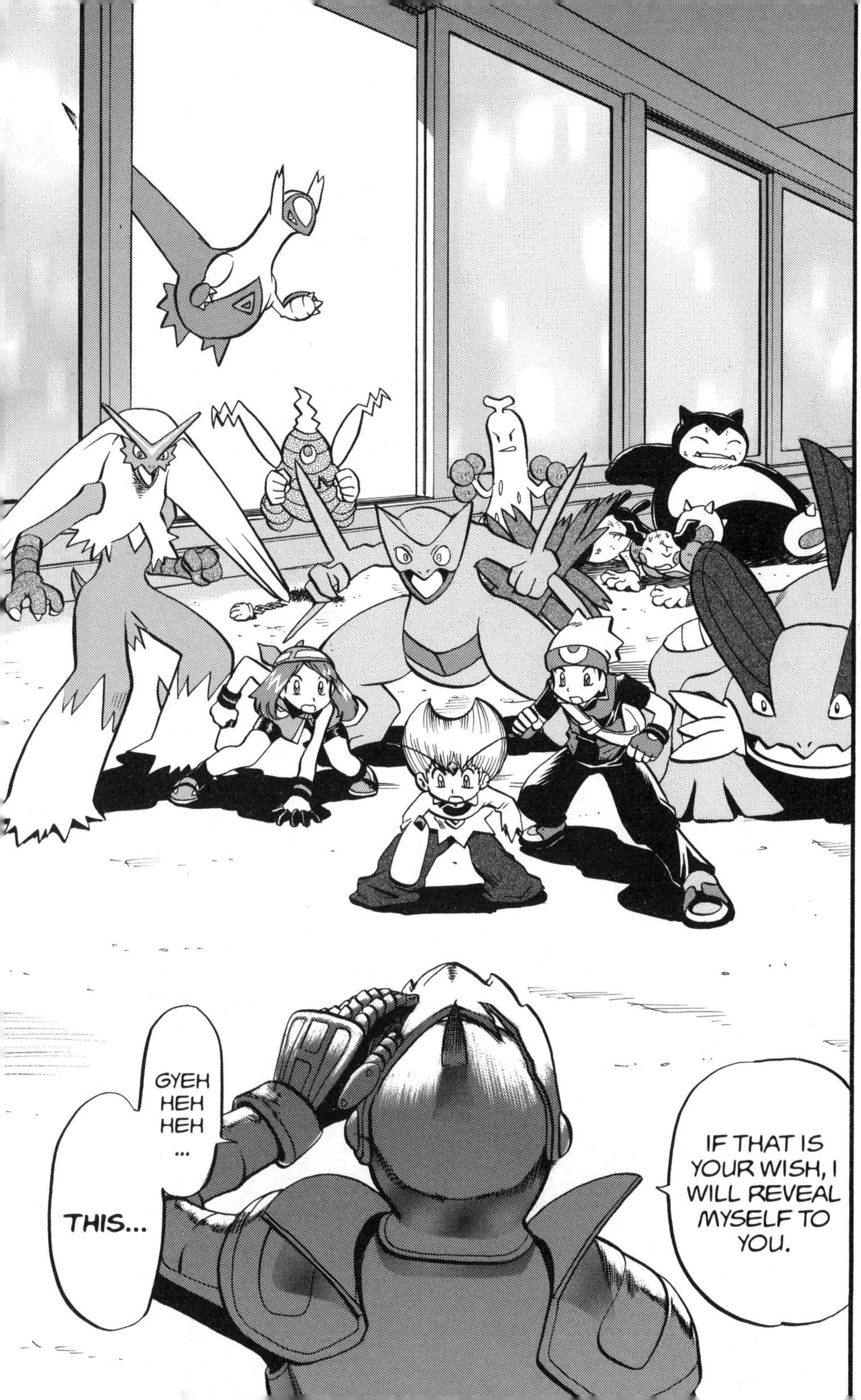
IF THAT IS YOUR WISH, I WILL REVEAL MYSELF TO YOU.
GYEH HEH HEH ...
THIS...

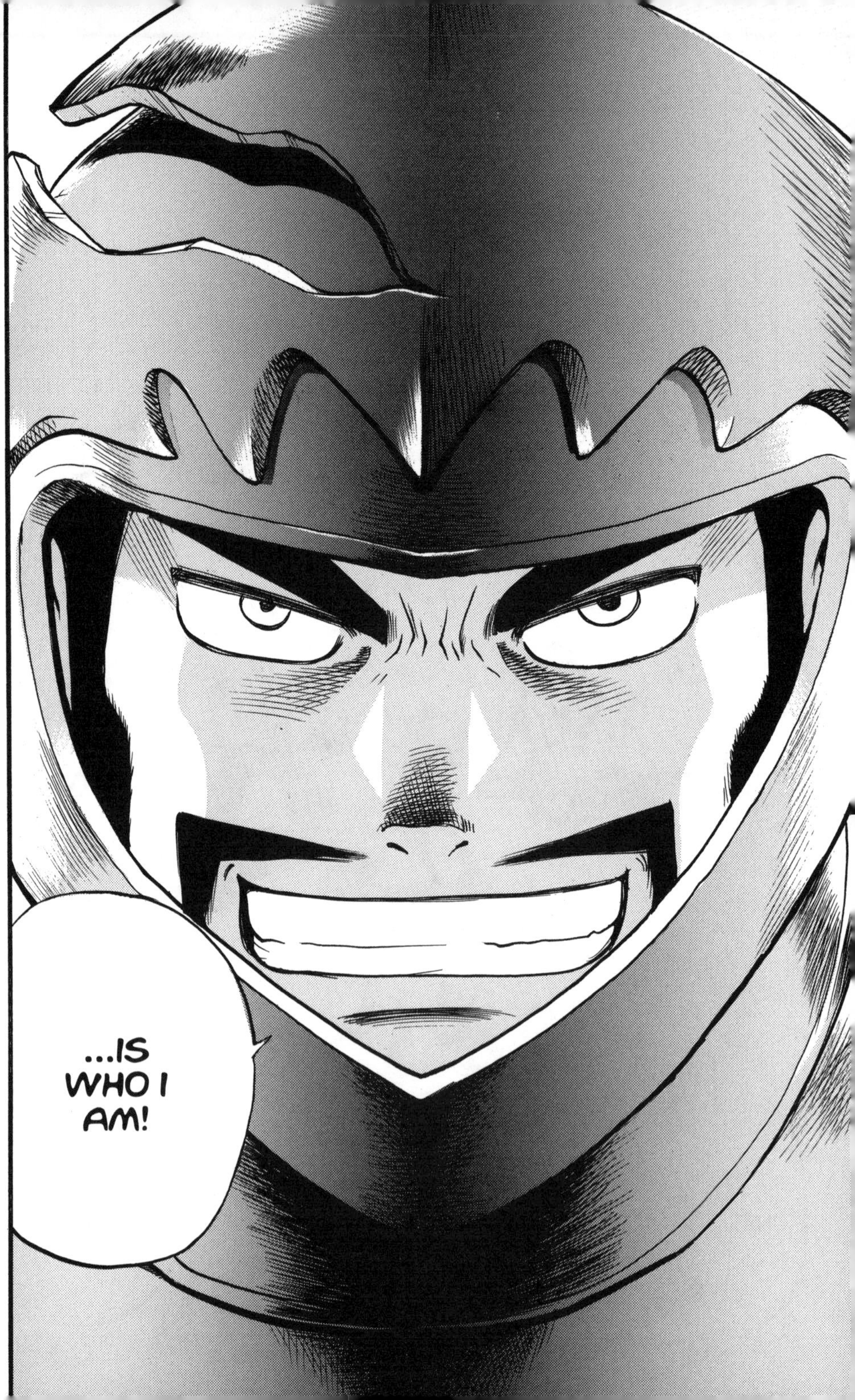
...IS WHO I AM!

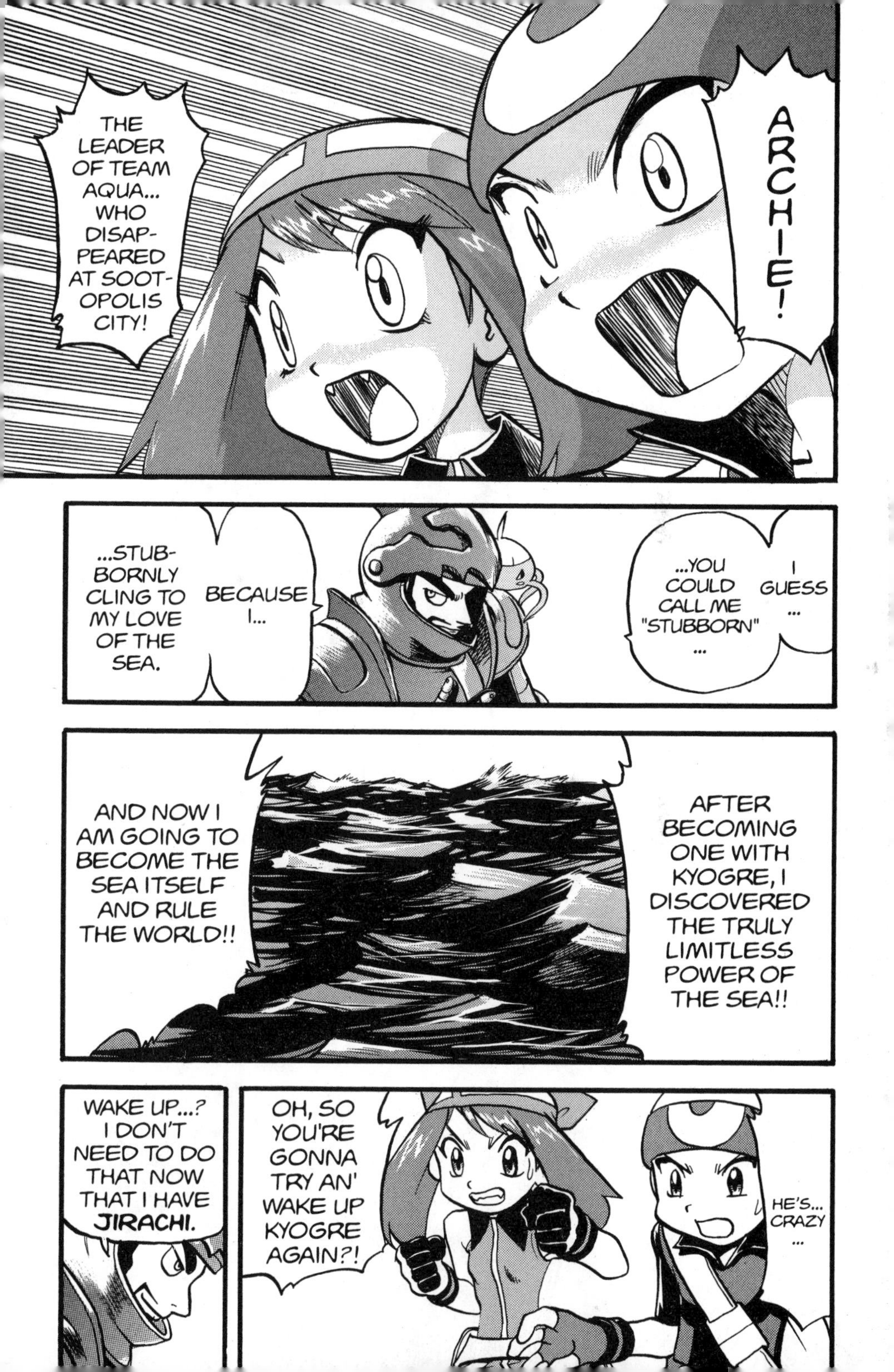
ARCHIE!
THE LEADER OF TEAM AQUA... WHO DISAPPEARED AT SOOTOPOLIS CITY!
I GUESS...
...YOU COULD CALL ME "STUBBORN"...
BECAUSE I...
...STUBBORNLY CLING TO MY LOVE OF THE SEA.
AFTER BECOMING ONE WITH KYOGRE, I DISCOVERED THE TRULY LIMITLESS POWER OF THE SEA!!
AND NOW I AM GOING TO BECOME THE SEA ITSELF AND RULE THE WORLD!!
OH, SO YOU'RE GONNA TRY AN' WAKE UP KYOGRE AGAIN?!
HE'S... CRAZY...
WAKE UP...? I DON'T NEED TO DO THAT NOW THAT I HAVE **JIRACHI**.

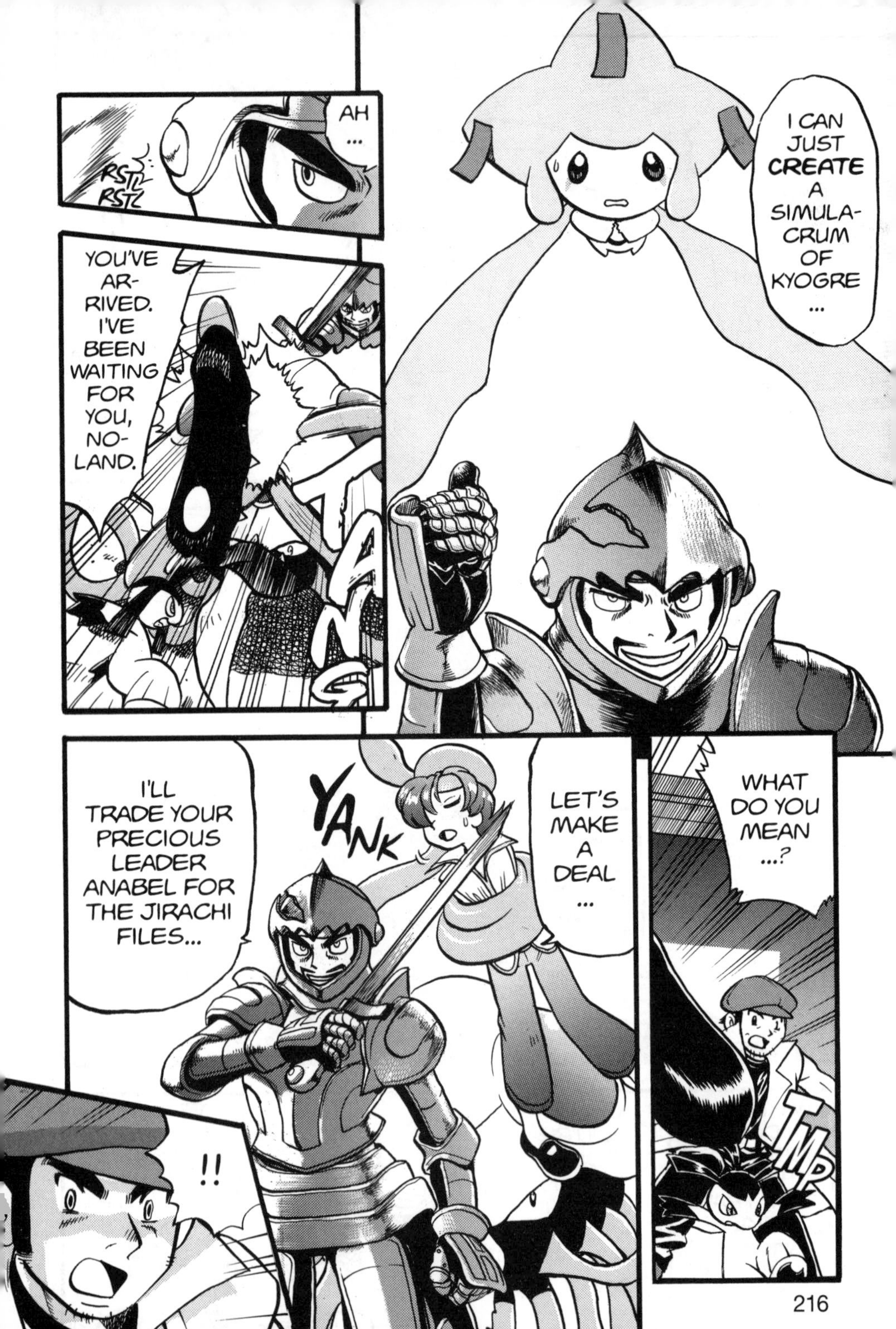

I CAN JUST **CREATE** A SIMULA-CRUM OF KYOGRE ...
AH ...
RSTL RSTL
YOU'VE AR-RIVED. I'VE BEEN WAITING FOR YOU, NO-LAND.
WHAT DO YOU MEAN ...?
TMP
LET'S MAKE A DEAL ...
YANK
I'LL TRADE YOUR PRECIOUS LEADER ANABEL FOR THE JIRACHI FILES...
!!

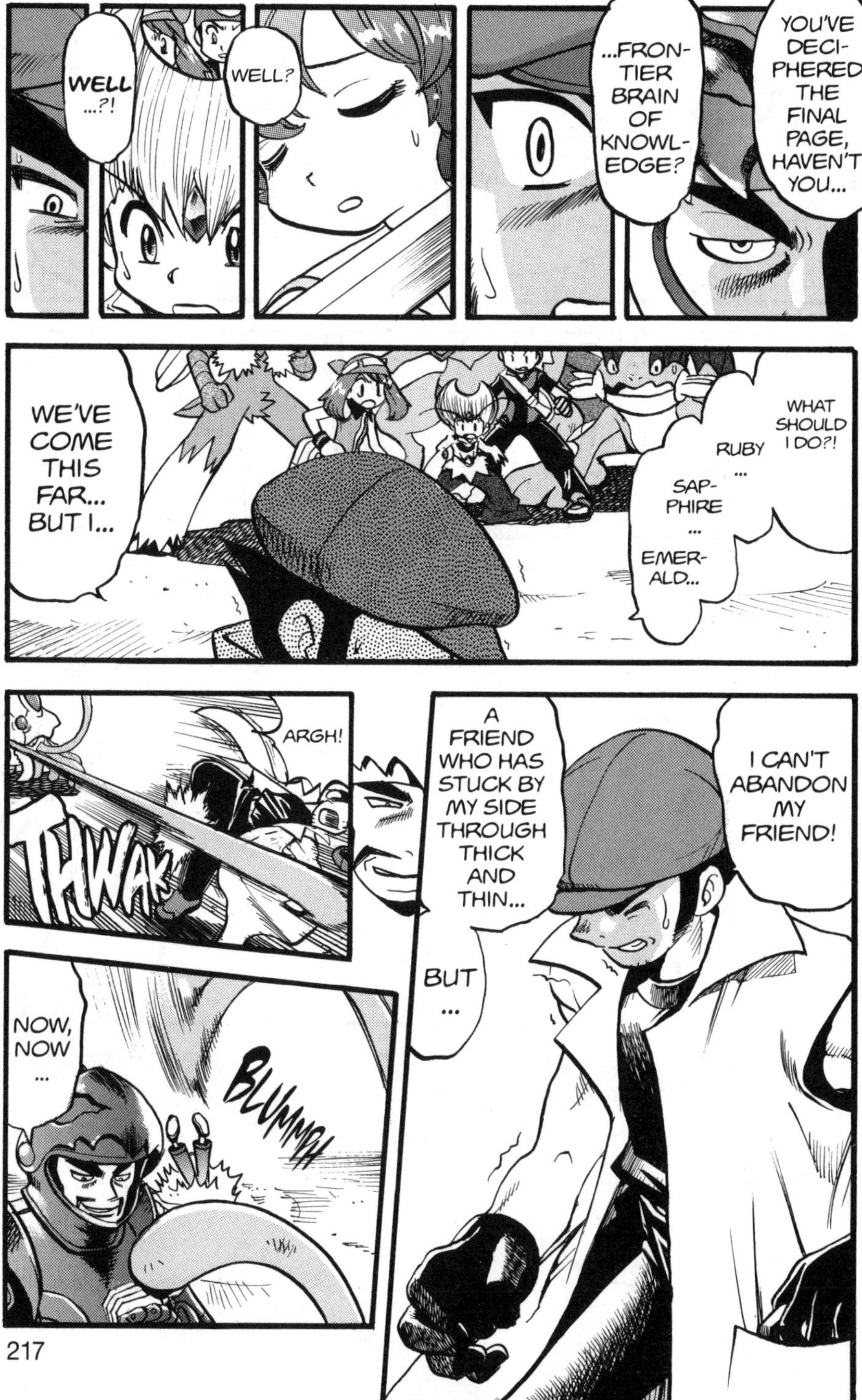
YOU'VE DECI-PHERED THE FINAL PAGE, HAVEN'T YOU...
...FRON-TIER BRAIN OF KNOWL-EDGE?
WELL?
WELL ...?!
RUBY ... SAP-PHIRE ... EMER-ALD... WHAT SHOULD I DO?!
WE'VE COME THIS FAR... BUT I...
I CAN'T ABANDON MY FRIEND!
A FRIEND WHO HAS STUCK BY MY SIDE THROUGH THICK AND THIN...
BUT ...
ARGH!
THWAK
NOW, NOW ...
BLUMMPH

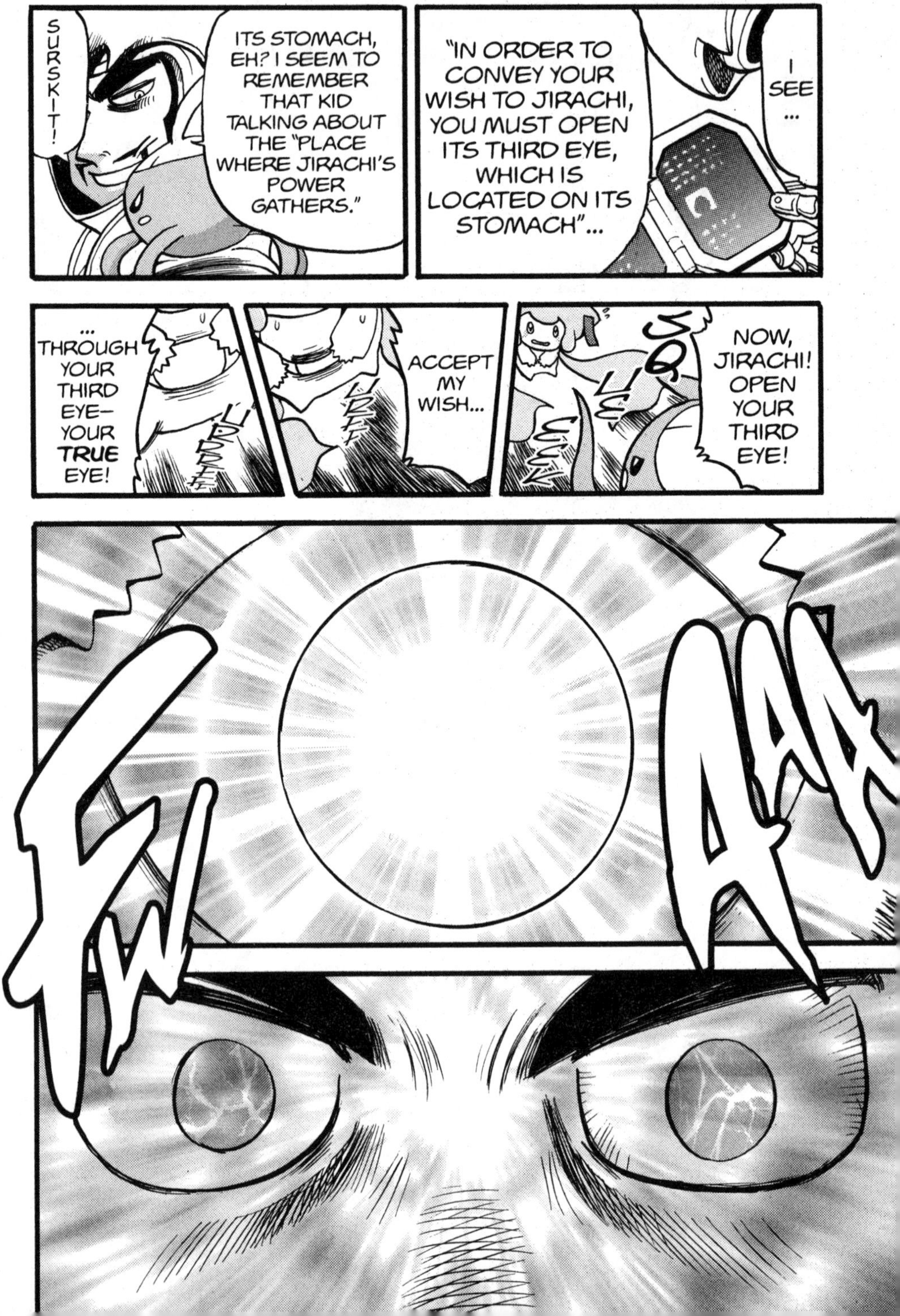
I SEE ...
"IN ORDER TO CONVEY YOUR WISH TO JIRACHI, YOU MUST OPEN ITS THIRD EYE, WHICH IS LOCATED ON ITS STOMACH"...
ITS STOMACH, EH? I SEEM TO REMEMBER THAT KID TALKING ABOUT THE "PLACE WHERE JIRACHI'S POWER GATHERS."
SURSKIT!
NOW, JIRACHI! OPEN YOUR THIRD EYE!
ACCEPT MY WISH...
...THROUGH YOUR THIRD EYE— YOUR TRUE EYE!
FWAAA

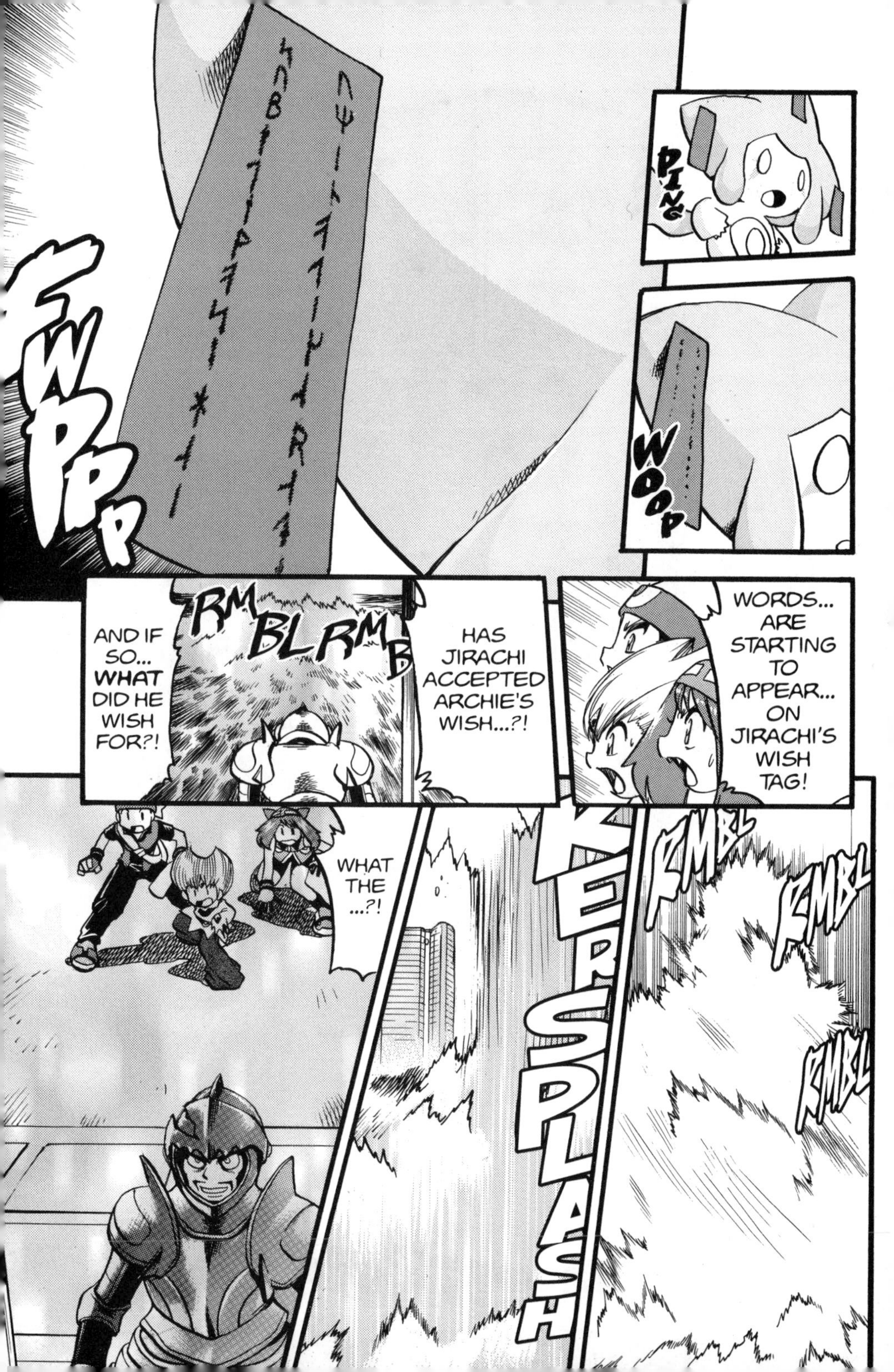
PING
WOOP
FWPPP
WORDS... ARE STARTING TO APPEAR... ON JIRACHI'S WISH TAG!
HAS JIRACHI ACCEPTED ARCHIE'S WISH...?!
RMBLRMB
AND IF SO... **WHAT** DID HE WISH FOR?!
RMBL
RMBL
RMBL
KERSPLASH
WHAT THE ...?!

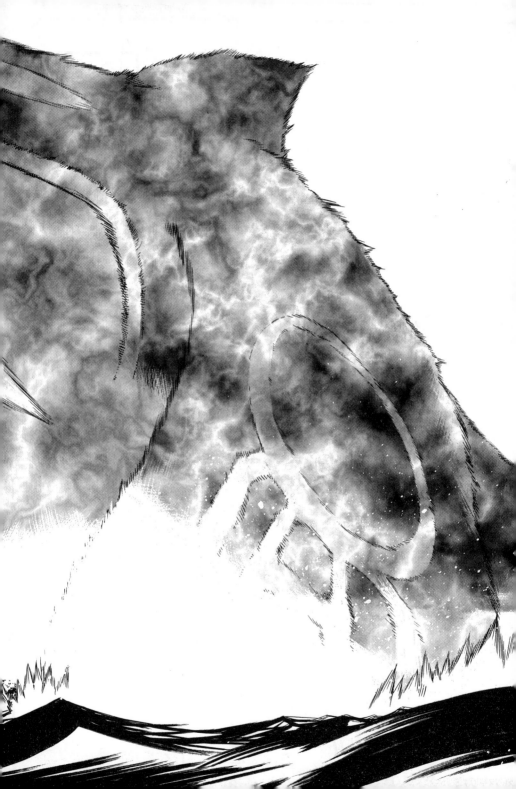

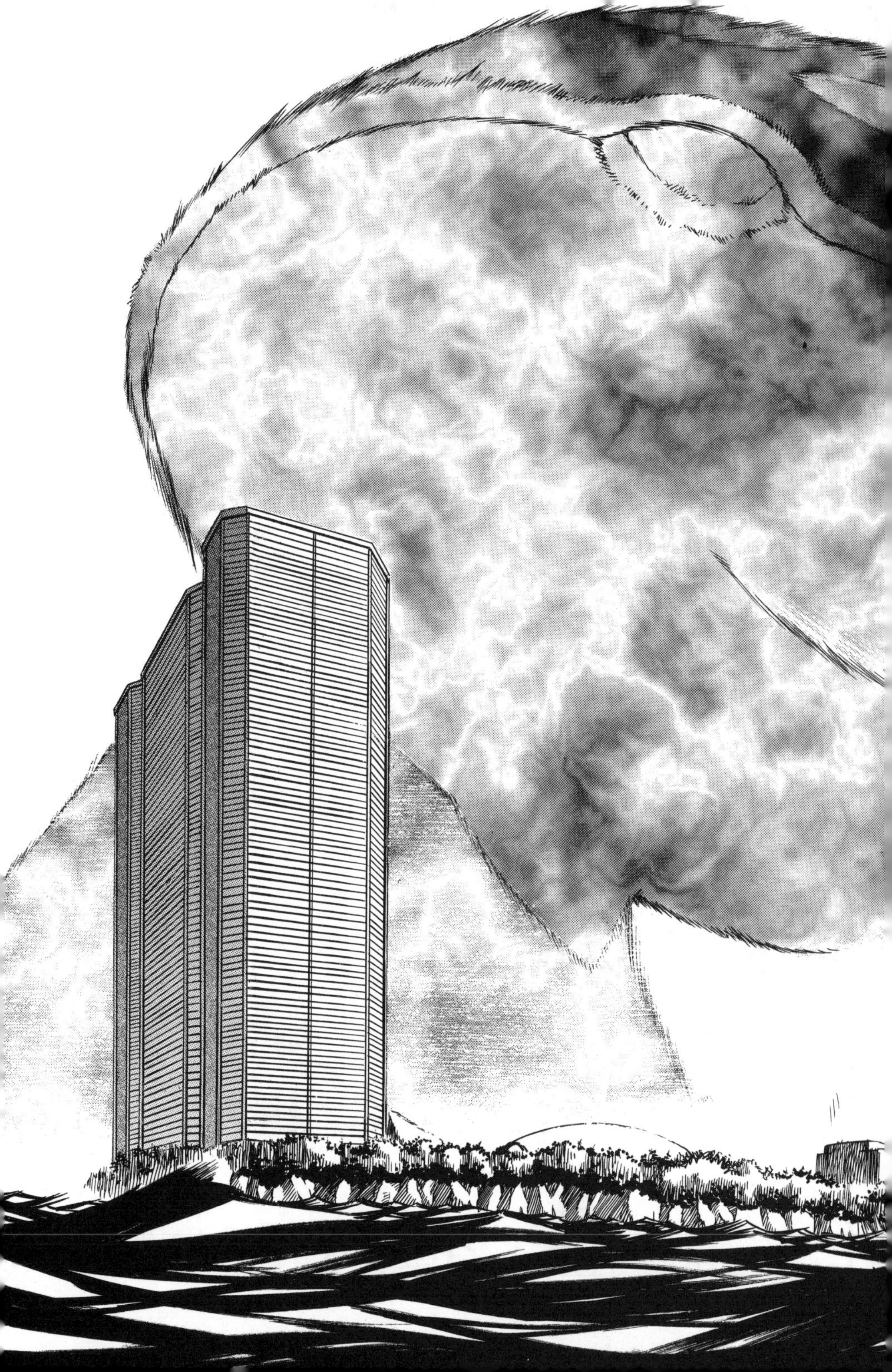

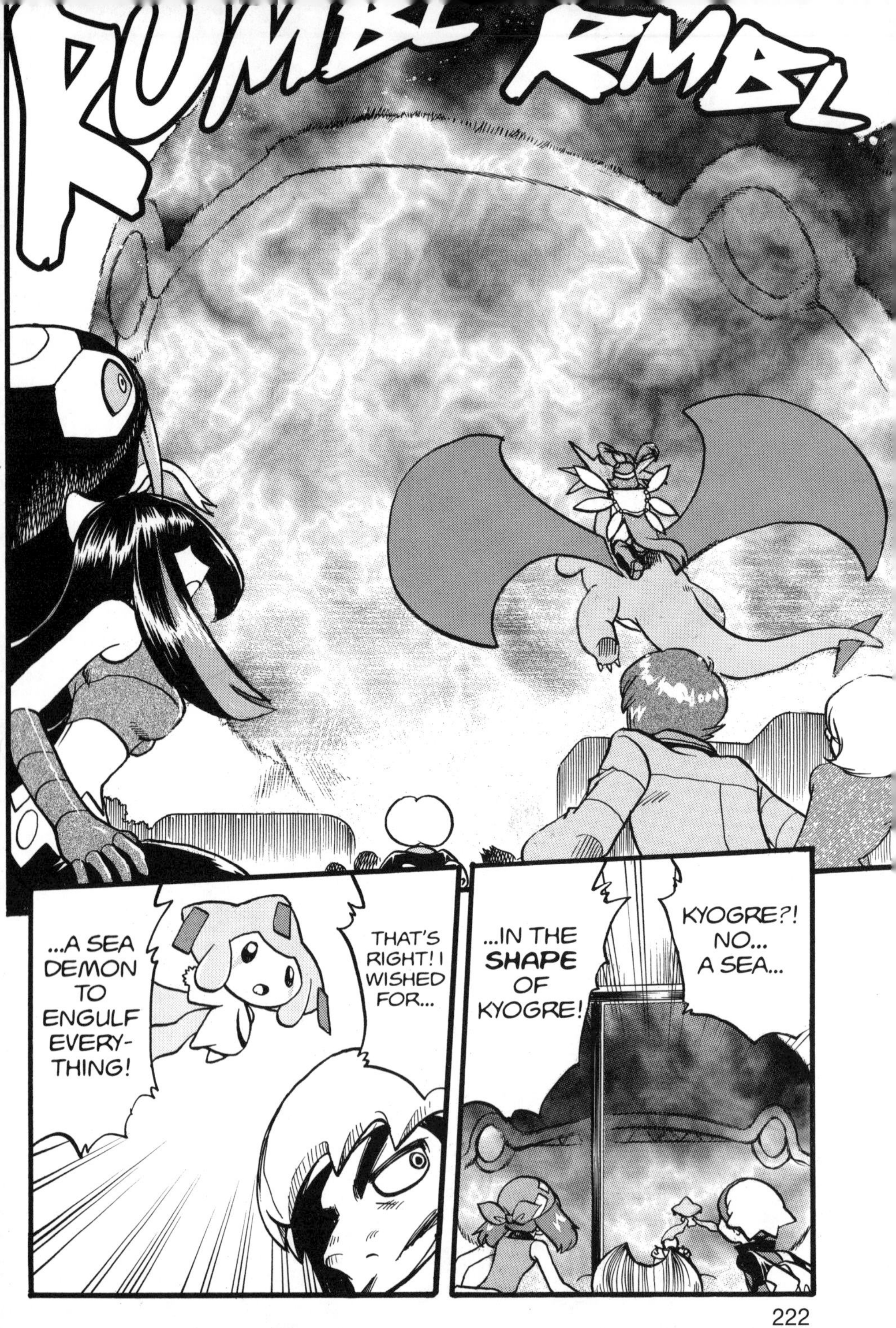
RUMBL RMBL
KYOGRE?! NO... A SEA...
...IN THE SHAPE OF KYOGRE!
THAT'S RIGHT! I WISHED FOR...
...A SEA DEMON TO ENGULF EVERY-THING!

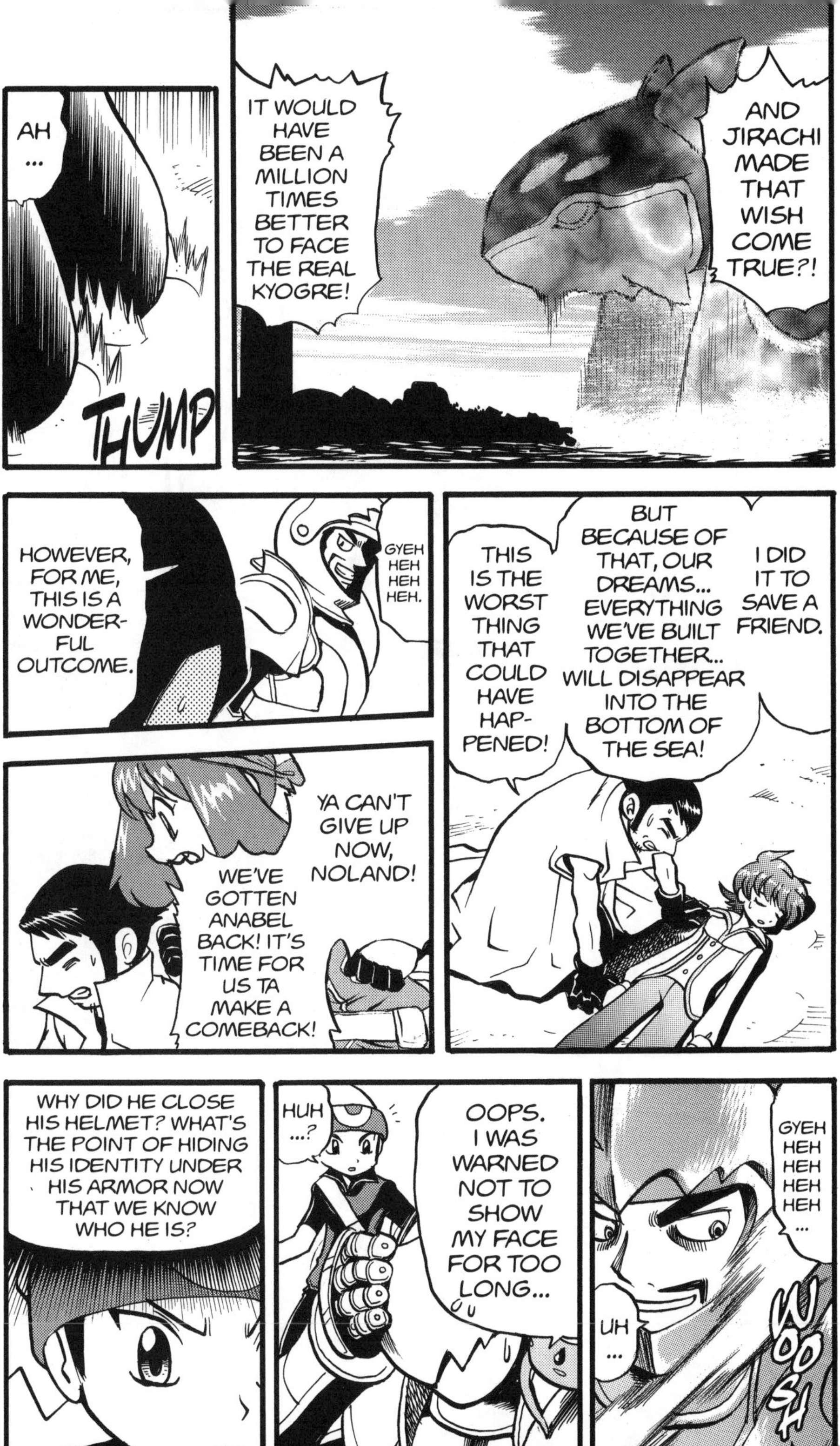
AND JIRACHI MADE THAT WISH COME TRUE?!
IT WOULD HAVE BEEN A MILLION TIMES BETTER TO FACE THE REAL KYOGRE!
AH ...
THUMP
I DID IT TO SAVE A FRIEND.
BUT BECAUSE OF THAT, OUR DREAMS... EVERYTHING WE'VE BUILT TOGETHER... WILL DISAPPEAR INTO THE BOTTOM OF THE SEA!
THIS IS THE WORST THING THAT COULD HAVE HAP-PENED!
GYEH HEH HEH HEH.
HOWEVER, FOR ME, THIS IS A WONDER-FUL OUTCOME.
YA CAN'T GIVE UP NOW, NOLAND!
WE'VE GOTTEN ANABEL BACK! IT'S TIME FOR US TA MAKE A COMEBACK!
GYEH HEH HEH HEH HEH ...
WOOSH
UH ...
OOPS. I WAS WARNED NOT TO SHOW MY FACE FOR TOO LONG...
HUH ...?
WHY DID HE CLOSE HIS HELMET? WHAT'S THE POINT OF HIDING HIS IDENTITY UNDER HIS ARMOR NOW THAT WE KNOW WHO HE IS?

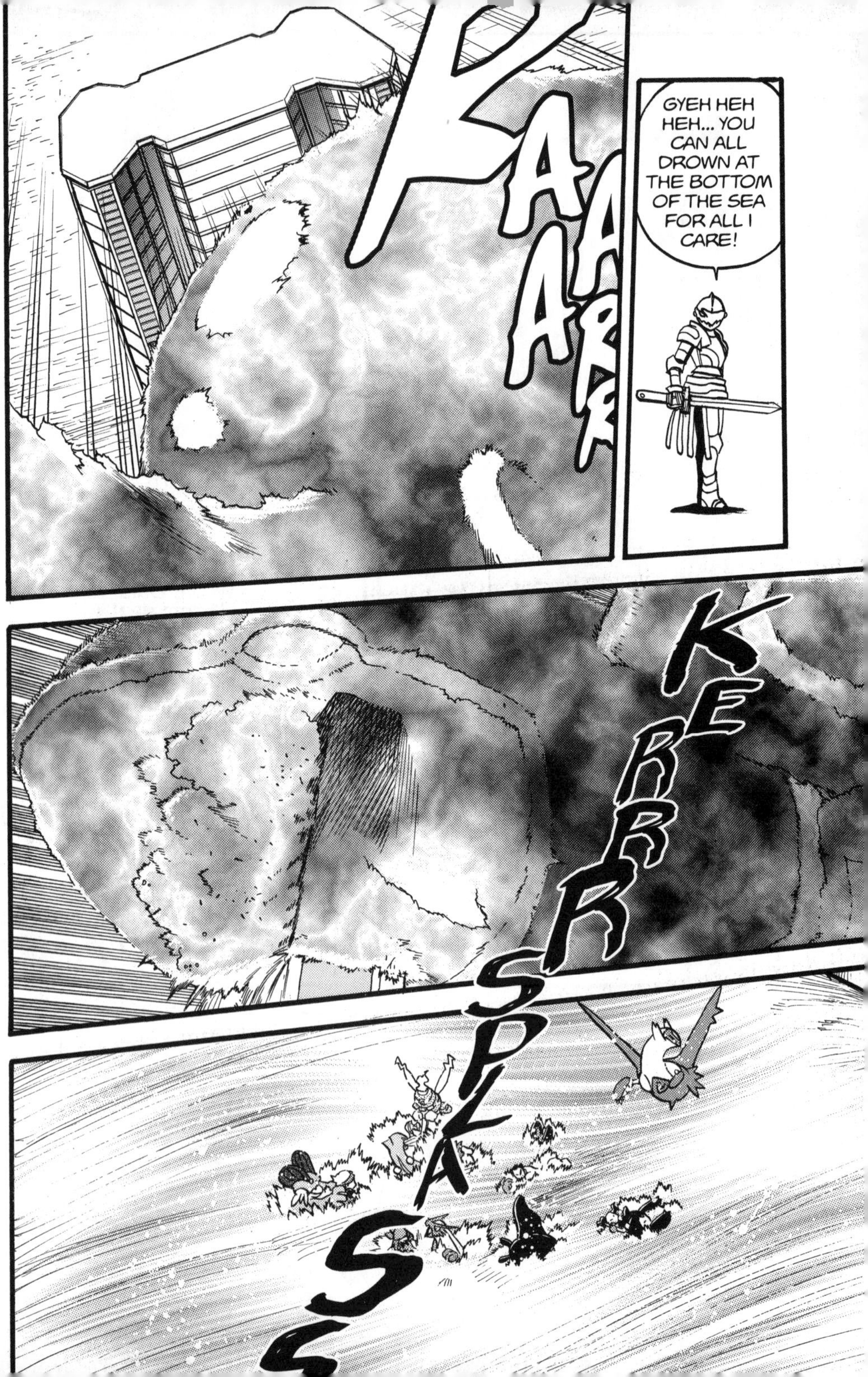
GYEH HEH HEH... YOU CAN ALL DROWN AT THE BOTTOM OF THE SEA FOR ALL I CARE!
KAAARR
KERRRR
SPLASS

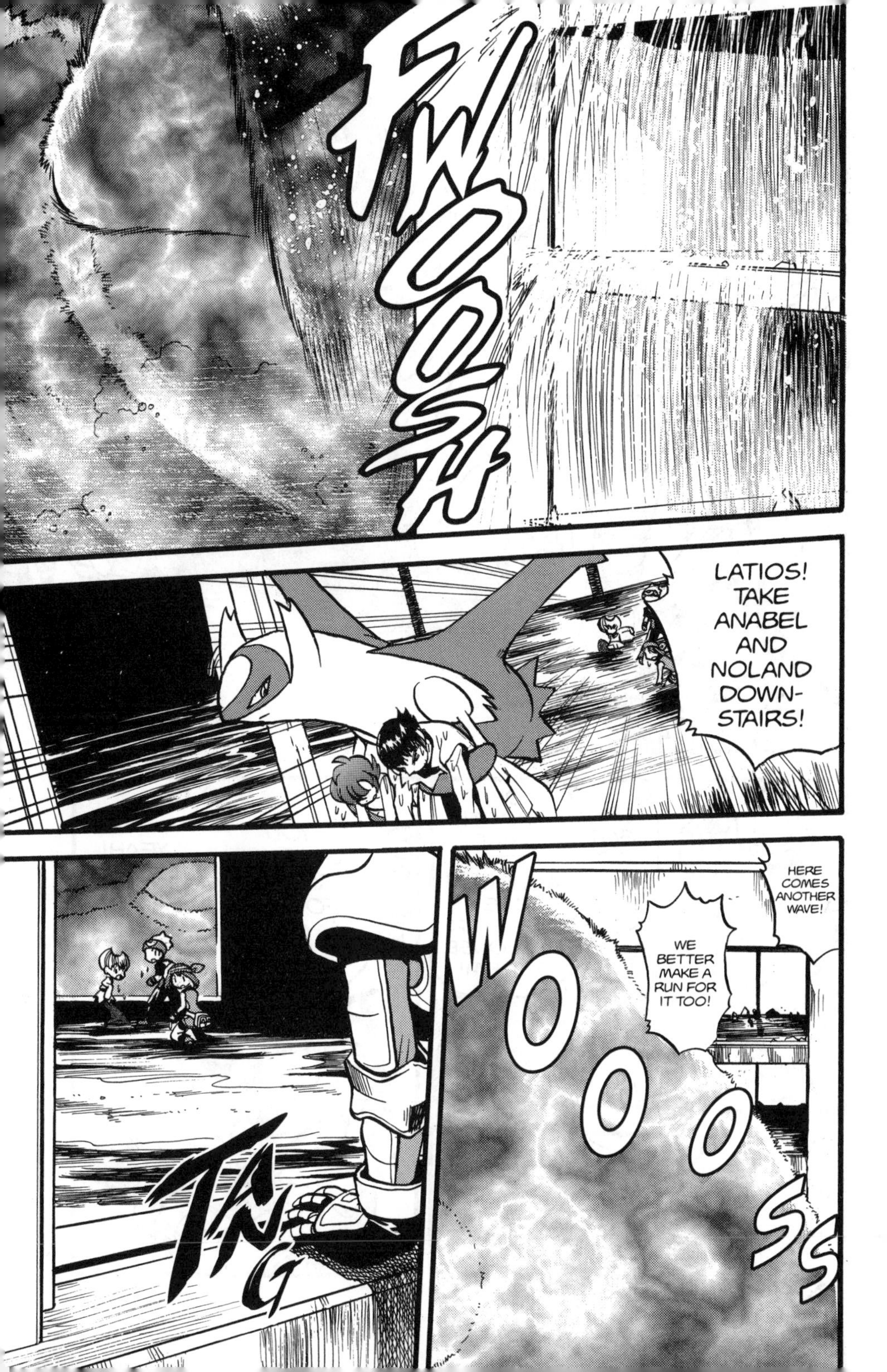
FWOOSH
LATIOS! TAKE ANABEL AND NOLAND DOWNSTAIRS!
HERE COMES ANOTHER WAVE!
WE BETTER MAKE A RUN FOR IT TOO!
WOOOOSS
TNG

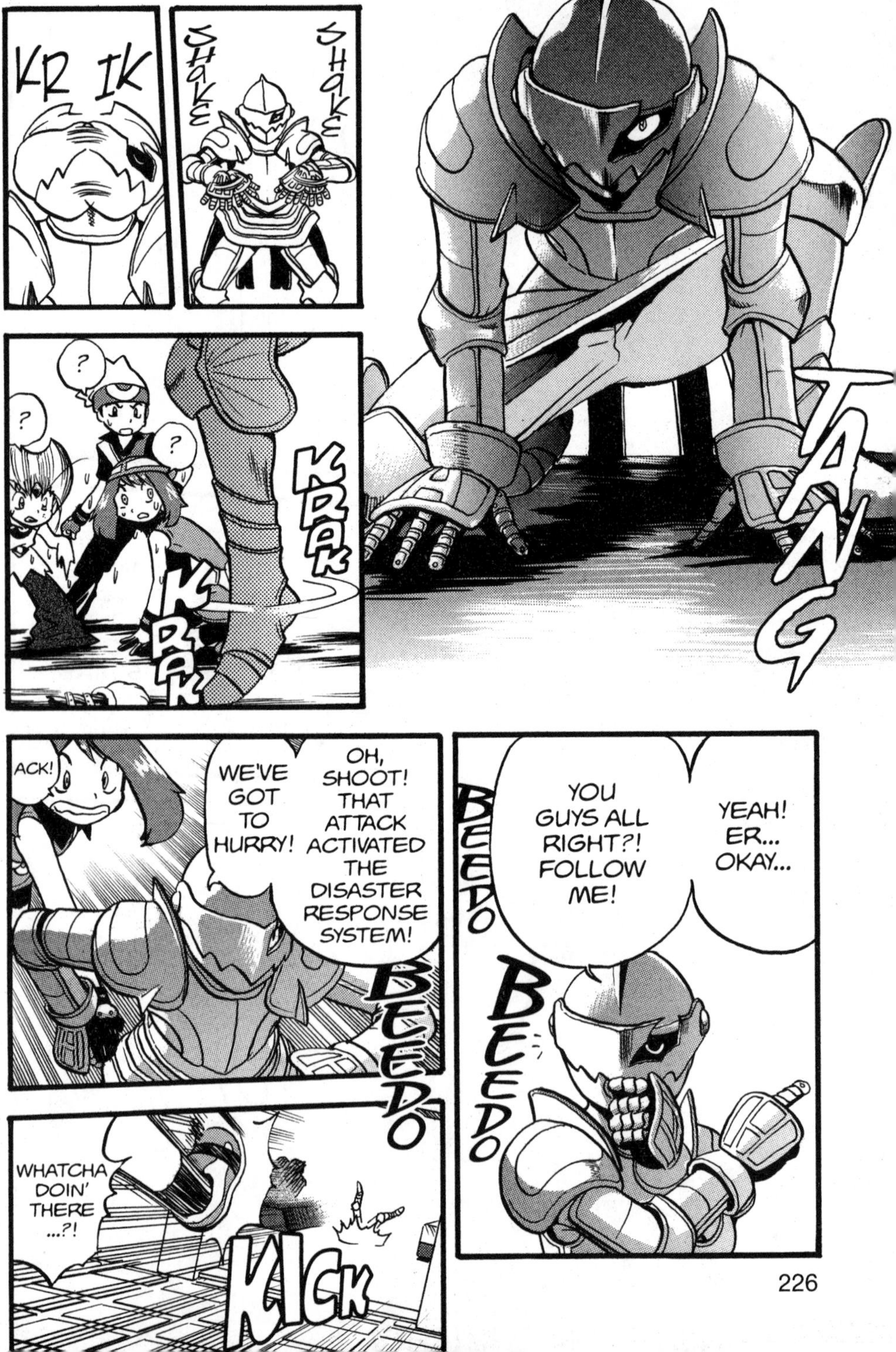
TANG
SHAKE SHAKE
KR IK
KRAK KRAK
?
?
?
YEAH! ER... OKAY...
YOU GUYS ALL RIGHT?! FOLLOW ME!
BEEDO BEEDO
OH, SHOOT! THAT ATTACK ACTIVATED THE DISASTER RESPONSE SYSTEM!
WE'VE GOT TO HURRY!
ACK!
BEEDO BEEDO
WHATCHA DOIN' THERE ...?!
KICK

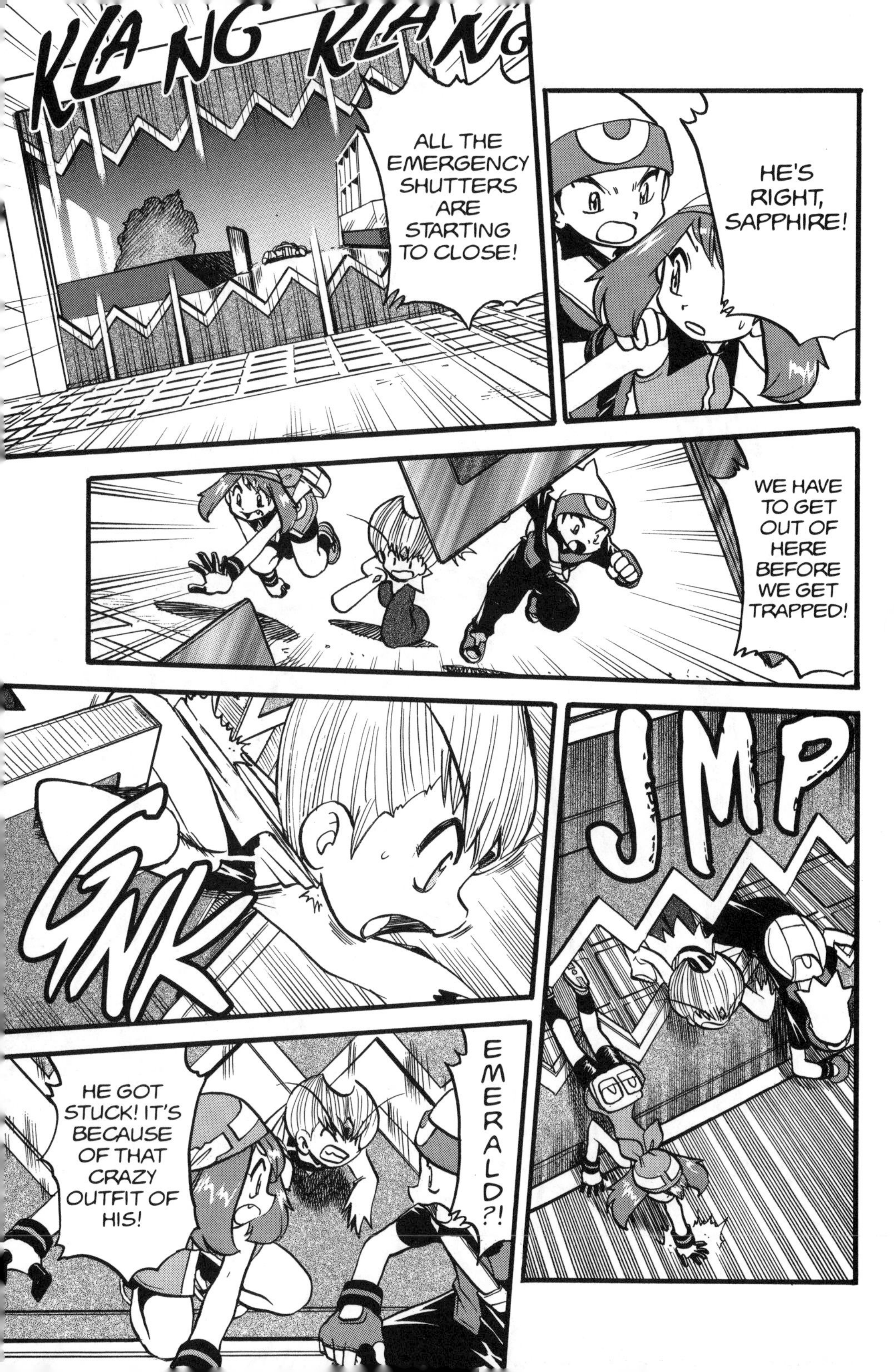
HE'S RIGHT, SAPPHIRE!
KLANG KLANG
ALL THE EMERGENCY SHUTTERS ARE STARTING TO CLOSE!
WE HAVE TO GET OUT OF HERE BEFORE WE GET TRAPPED!
JMP
GNK
EMERALD?!
HE GOT STUCK! IT'S BECAUSE OF THAT CRAZY OUTFIT OF HIS!

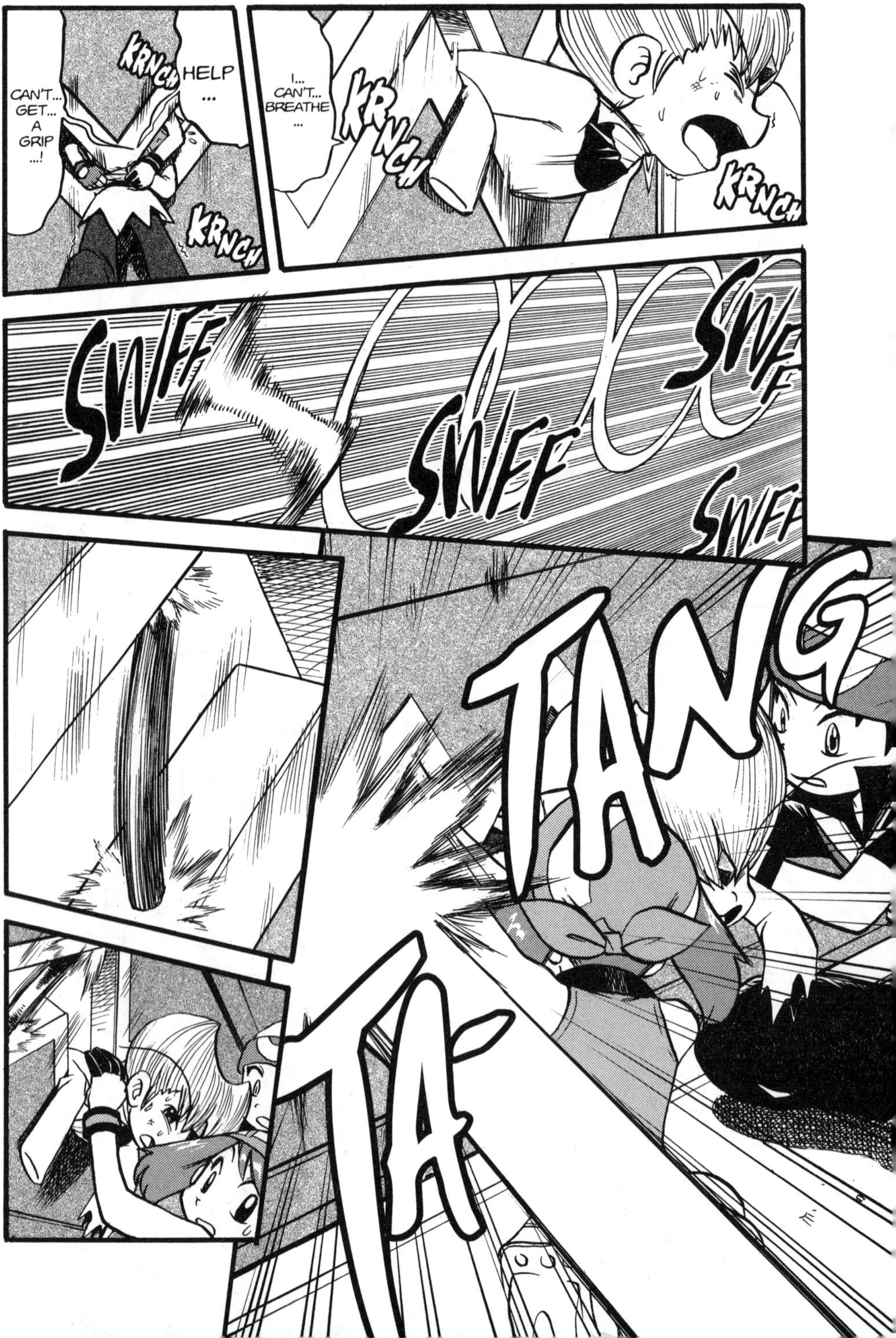
KRNCH
I... CAN'T... BREATHE ...
KRNCH
HELP ...
KRNCH
CAN'T... GET... A GRIP ...!
KRNCH
SWFF
SWFF
SWFF
SWFF
TANG
TA

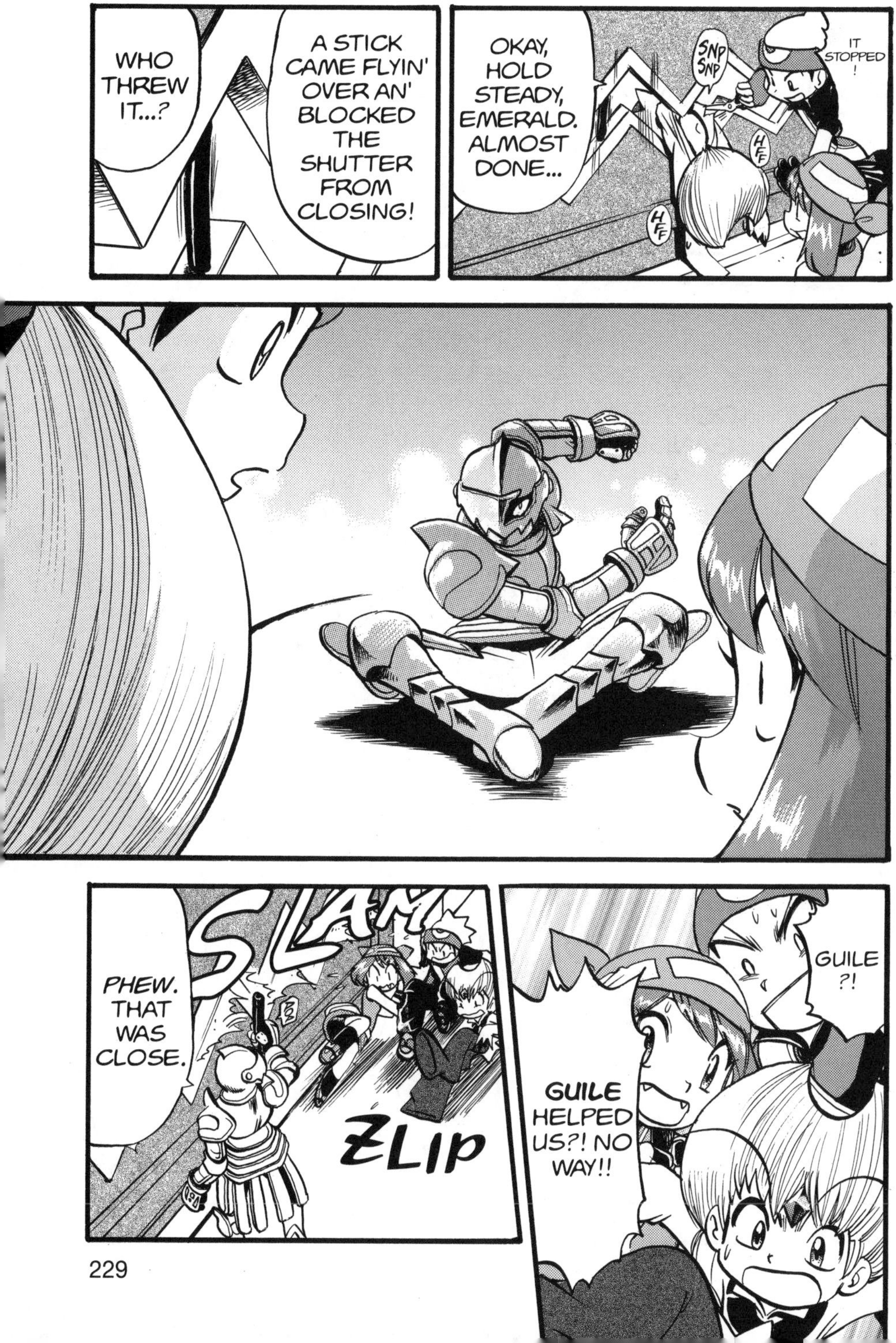
OKAY, HOLD STEADY, EMERALD. ALMOST DONE...
SNP SNP
IT STOPPED!
HFF
HFF
A STICK CAME FLYIN' OVER AN' BLOCKED THE SHUTTER FROM CLOSING!
WHO THREW IT...?
GUILE ?!
GUILE HELPED US?! NO WAY!!
SLAM
PHEW. THAT WAS CLOSE.
ZLIP

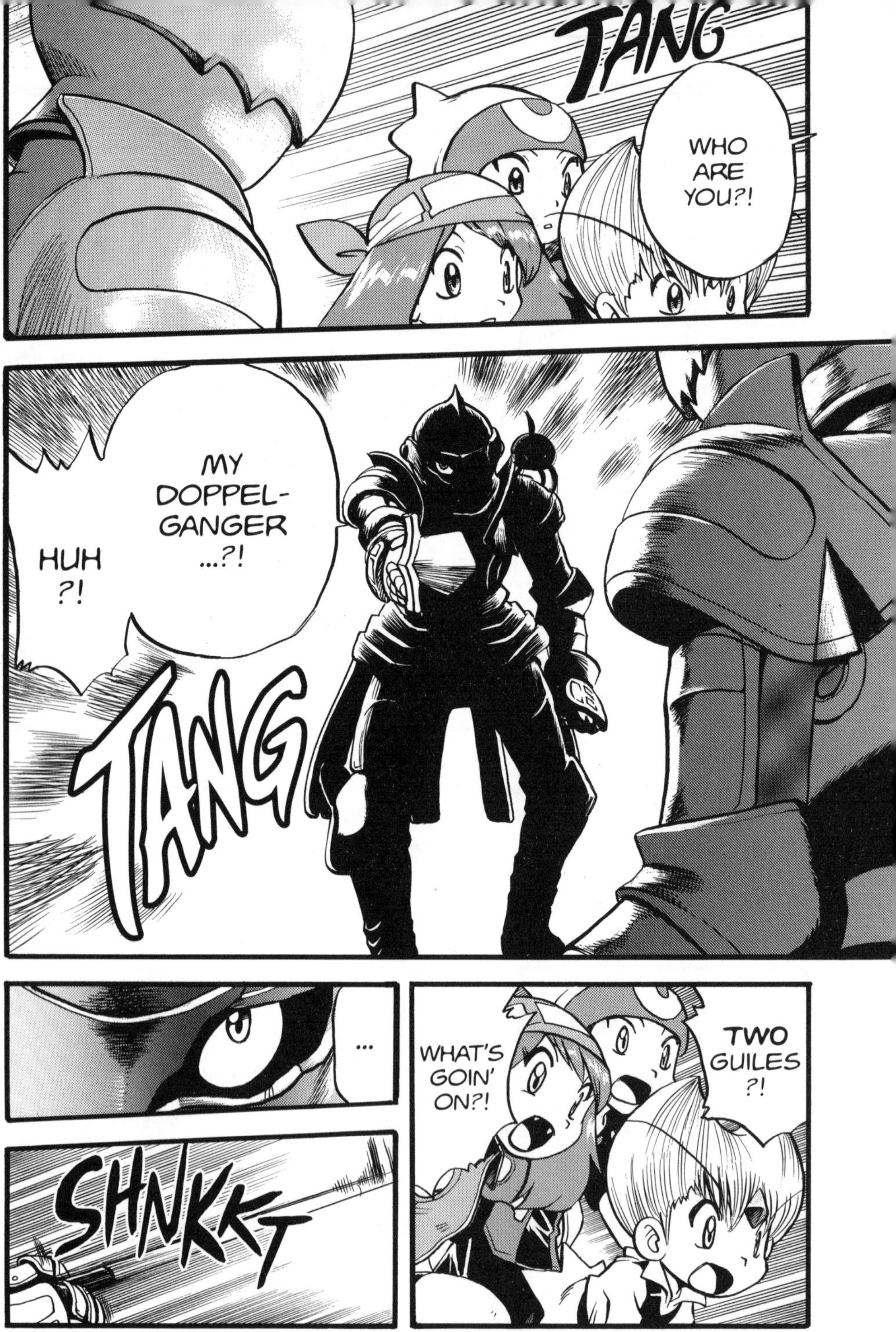
TANG
WHO ARE YOU?!
MY DOPPEL-GANGER ...?!
HUH ?!
TANG
TWO GUILES ?!
WHAT'S GOIN' ON?!
...
SHNKKT

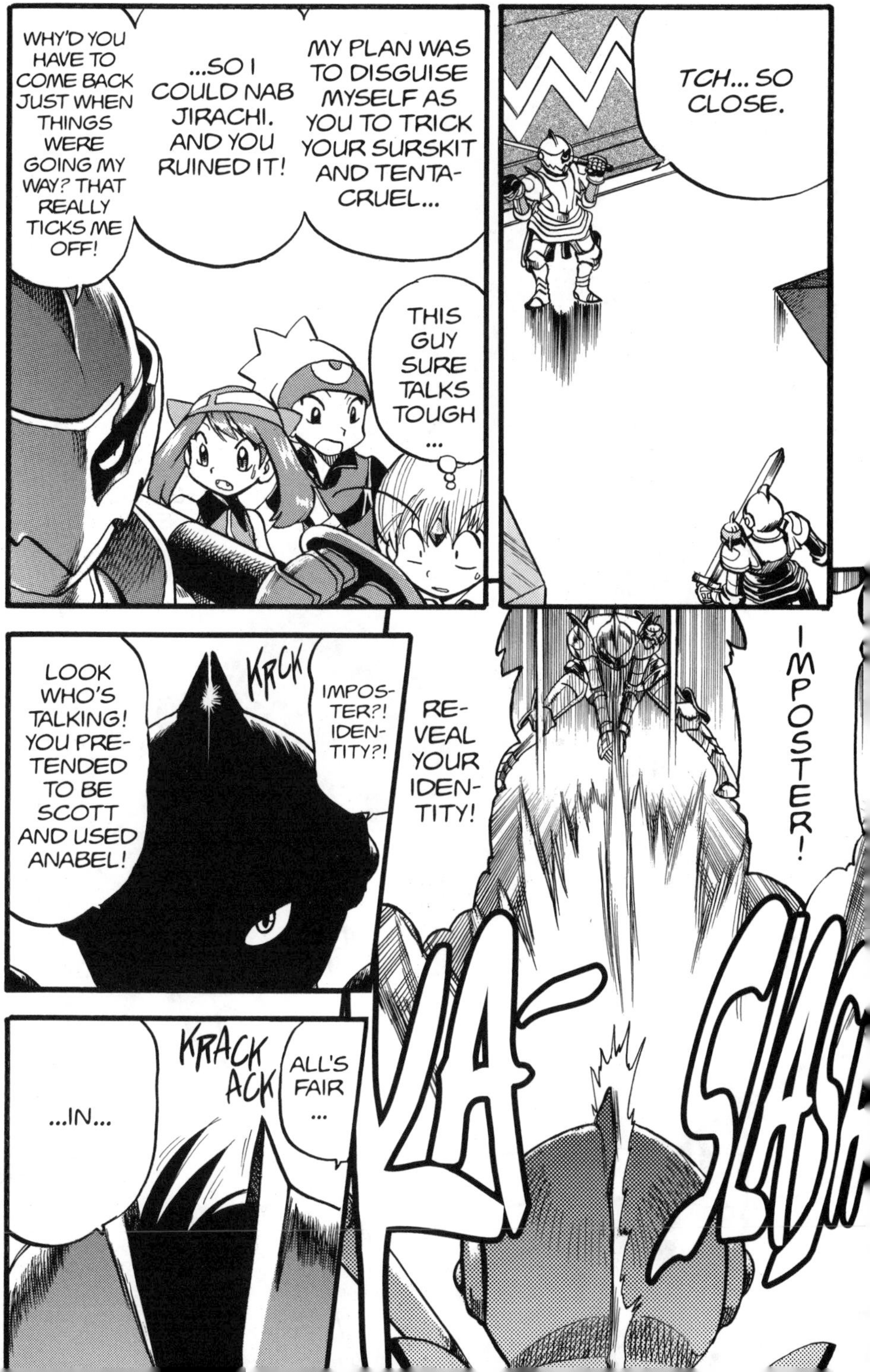
TCH... SO CLOSE.
MY PLAN WAS TO DISGUISE MYSELF AS YOU TO TRICK YOUR SURSKIT AND TENTA-CRUEL...
...SO I COULD NAB JIRACHI. AND YOU RUINED IT!
WHY'D YOU HAVE TO COME BACK JUST WHEN THINGS WERE GOING MY WAY? THAT REALLY TICKS ME OFF!
THIS GUY SURE TALKS TOUGH...
IMPOSTER!
REVEAL YOUR IDENTITY!
IMPOSTER?! IDENTITY?!
KRCK
LOOK WHO'S TALKING! YOU PRETENDED TO BE SCOTT AND USED ANABEL!
ALL'S FAIR...
KRACK ACK
...IN...

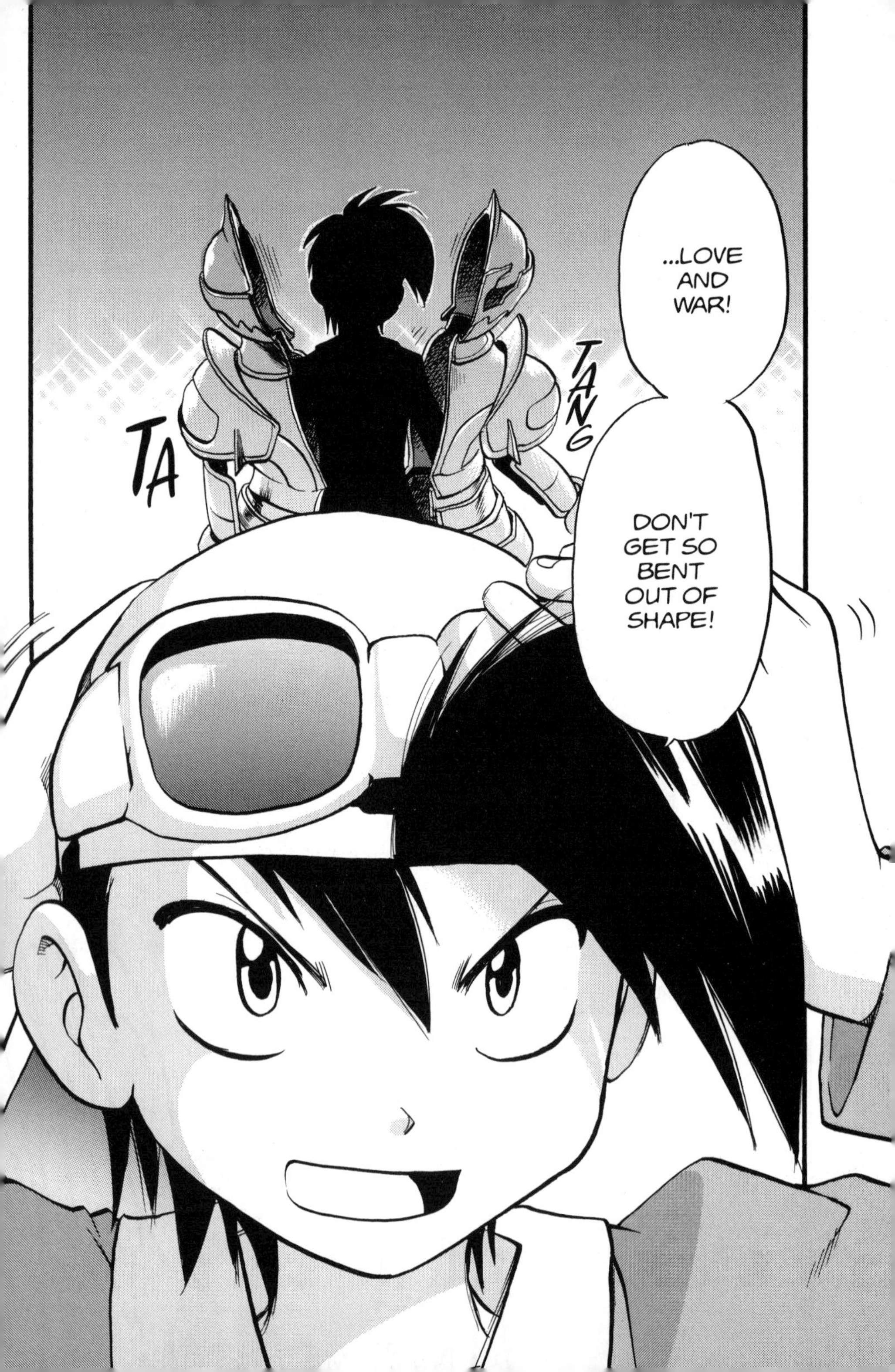
...LOVE AND WAR!
TANG
TA
DON'T GET SO BENT OUT OF SHAPE!

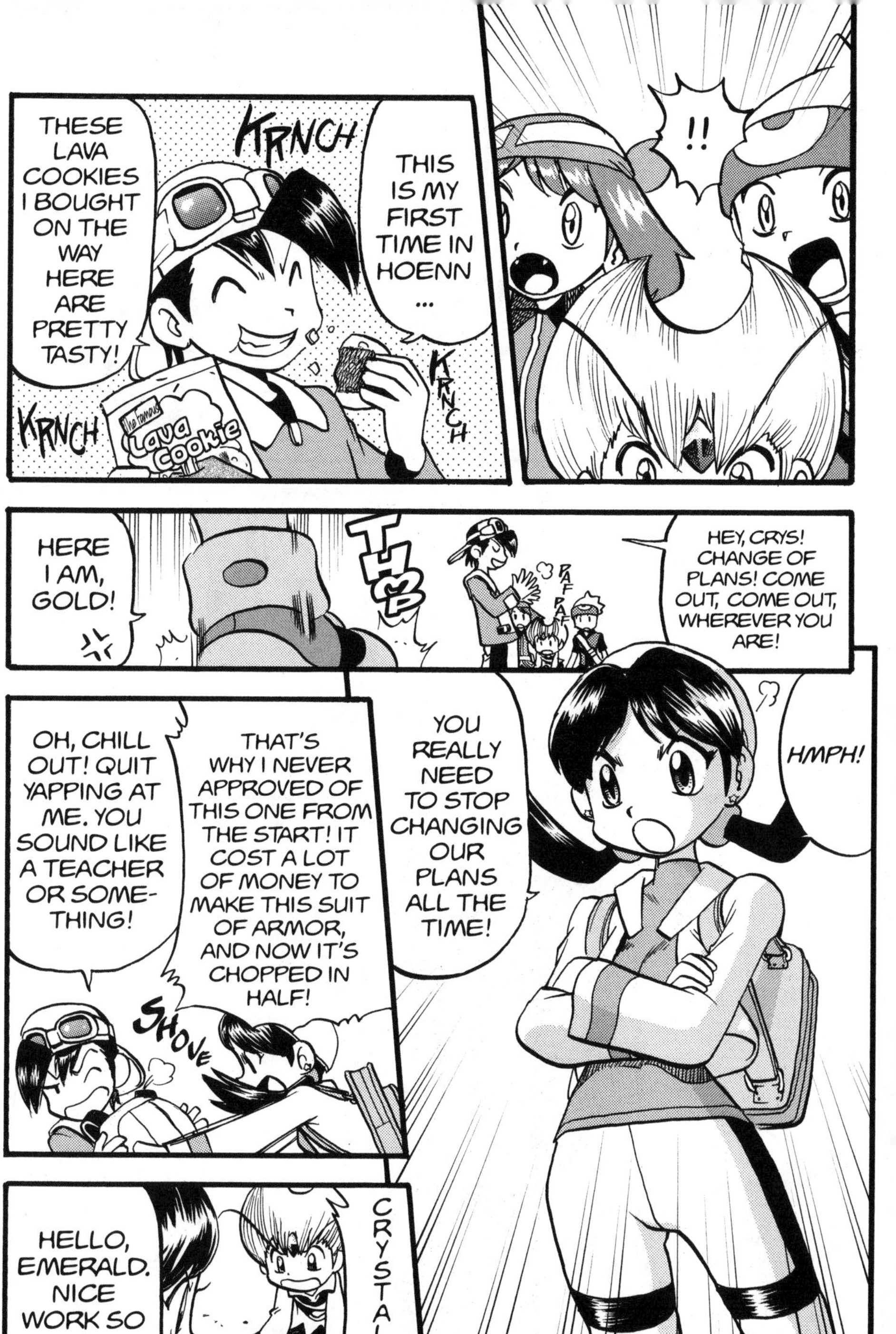
!!
KRNCH
THIS IS MY FIRST TIME IN HOENN ...
THESE LAVA COOKIES I BOUGHT ON THE WAY HERE ARE PRETTY TASTY!
KRNCH
KRNCH
The Famous Lava Cookie
HEY, CRYS! CHANGE OF PLANS! COME OUT, COME OUT, WHEREVER YOU ARE!
PAF PAF
THB
HERE I AM, GOLD!
HMPH!
YOU REALLY NEED TO STOP CHANGING OUR PLANS ALL THE TIME!
THAT'S WHY I NEVER APPROVED OF THIS ONE FROM THE START! IT COST A LOT OF MONEY TO MAKE THIS SUIT OF ARMOR, AND NOW IT'S CHOPPED IN HALF!
OH, CHILL OUT! QUIT YAPPING AT ME. YOU SOUND LIKE A TEACHER OR SOME-THING!
SHOVE
CRYSTAL?
HELLO, EMERALD. NICE WORK SO FAR!

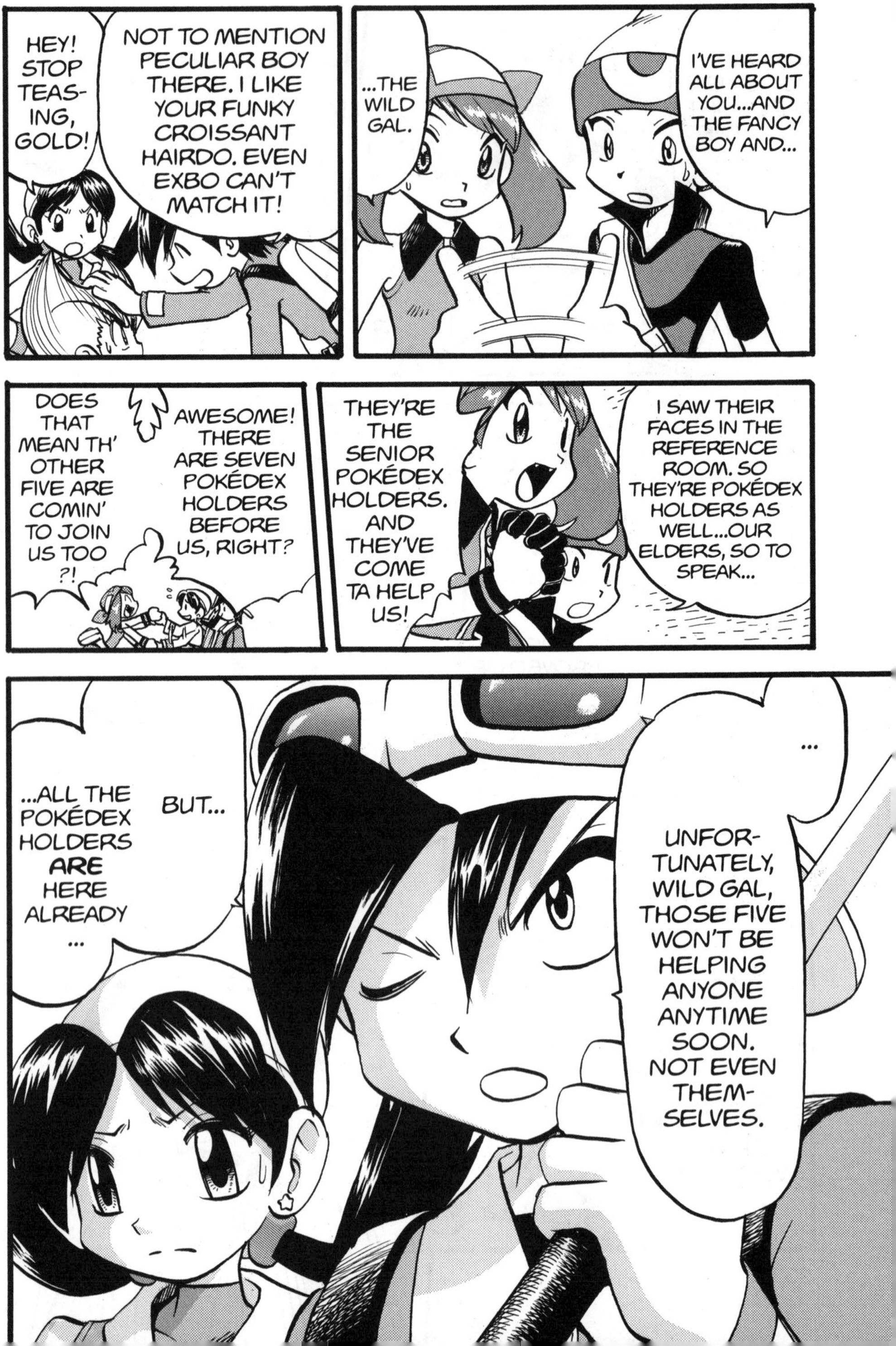
I'VE HEARD ALL ABOUT YOU...AND THE FANCY BOY AND...
...THE WILD GAL.
NOT TO MENTION PECULIAR BOY THERE. I LIKE YOUR FUNKY CROISSANT HAIRDO. EVEN EXBO CAN'T MATCH IT!
HEY! STOP TEAS-ING, GOLD!
I SAW THEIR FACES IN THE REFERENCE ROOM. SO THEY'RE POKÉDEX HOLDERS AS WELL...OUR ELDERS, SO TO SPEAK...
THEY'RE THE SENIOR POKÉDEX HOLDERS. AND THEY'VE COME TA HELP US!
AWESOME! THERE ARE SEVEN POKÉDEX HOLDERS BEFORE US, RIGHT?
DOES THAT MEAN TH' OTHER FIVE ARE COMIN' TO JOIN US TOO?!
...
UNFOR-TUNATELY, WILD GAL, THOSE FIVE WON'T BE HELPING ANYONE ANYTIME SOON. NOT EVEN THEM-SELVES.
BUT...
...ALL THE POKÉDEX HOLDERS **ARE** HERE ALREADY...

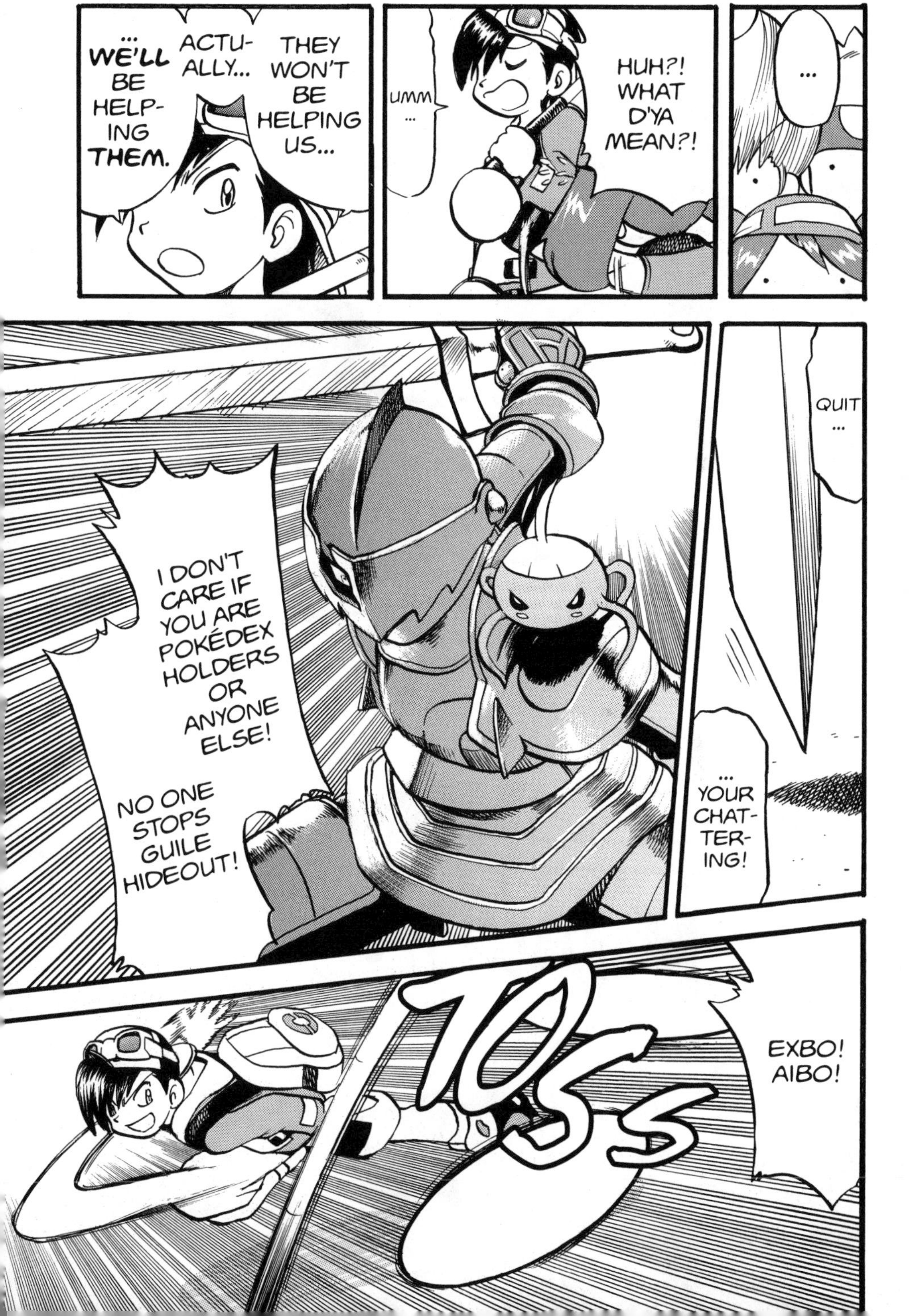
...
HUH?! WHAT D'YA MEAN?!
UMM ...
THEY WON'T BE HELPING US...
ACTU-ALLY...
... **WE'LL** BE HELP-ING **THEM.**
QUIT ...
... YOUR CHAT-TER-ING!
I DON'T CARE IF YOU ARE POKÉDEX HOLDERS OR ANYONE ELSE!
NO ONE STOPS GUILE HIDEOUT!
EXBO! AIBO!
TOSS

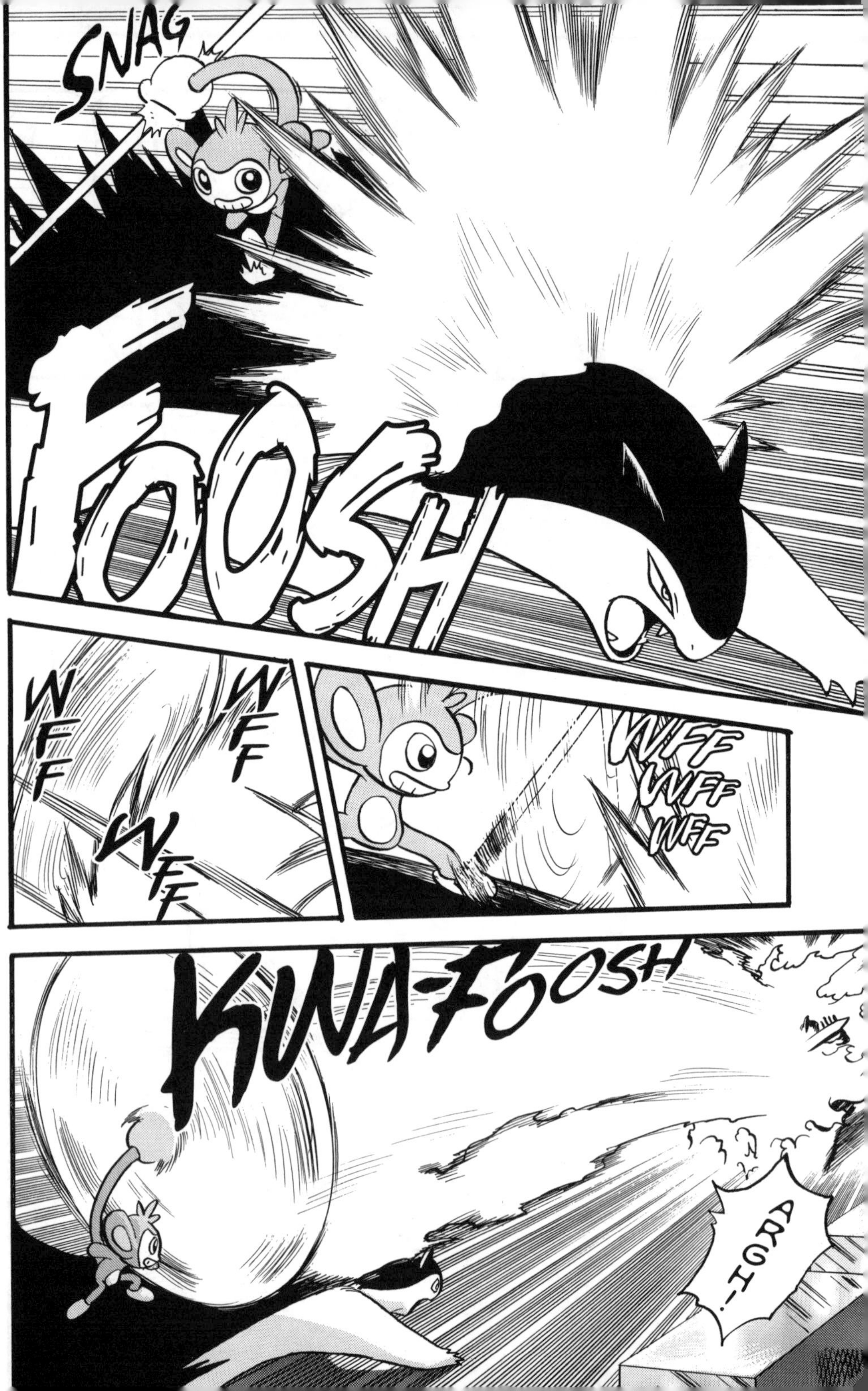
SNAG
FOOSH
WFF WFF WFF
WFF
WFF
WFF
KWA-FOOSH
ARGH--!

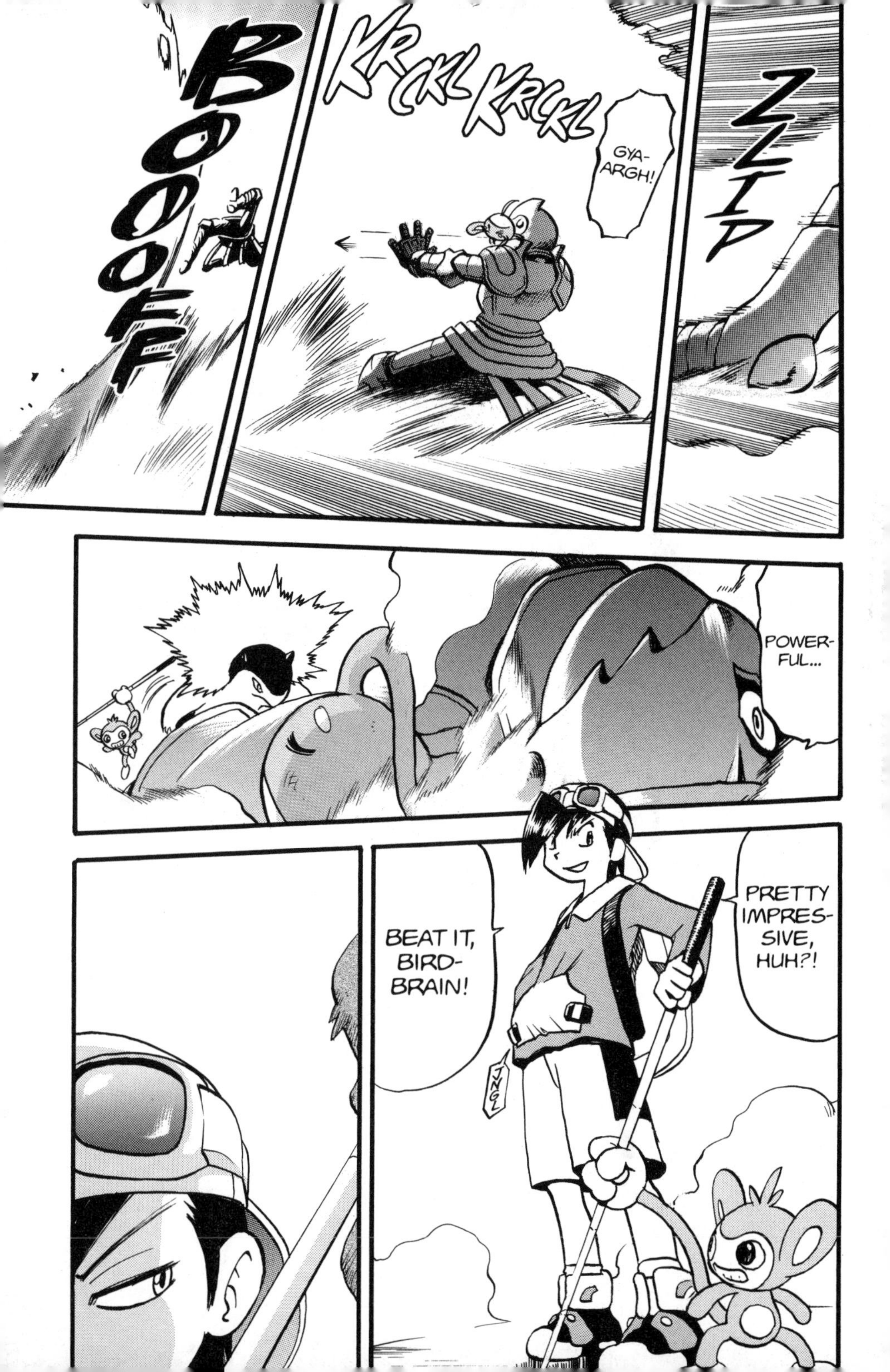
ZZIP
KRCKL KRCKL
GYA-ARGH!
BOOOOFF
POWER-FUL...
PRETTY IMPRES-SIVE, HUH?!
BEAT IT, BIRD-BRAIN!
JNGL

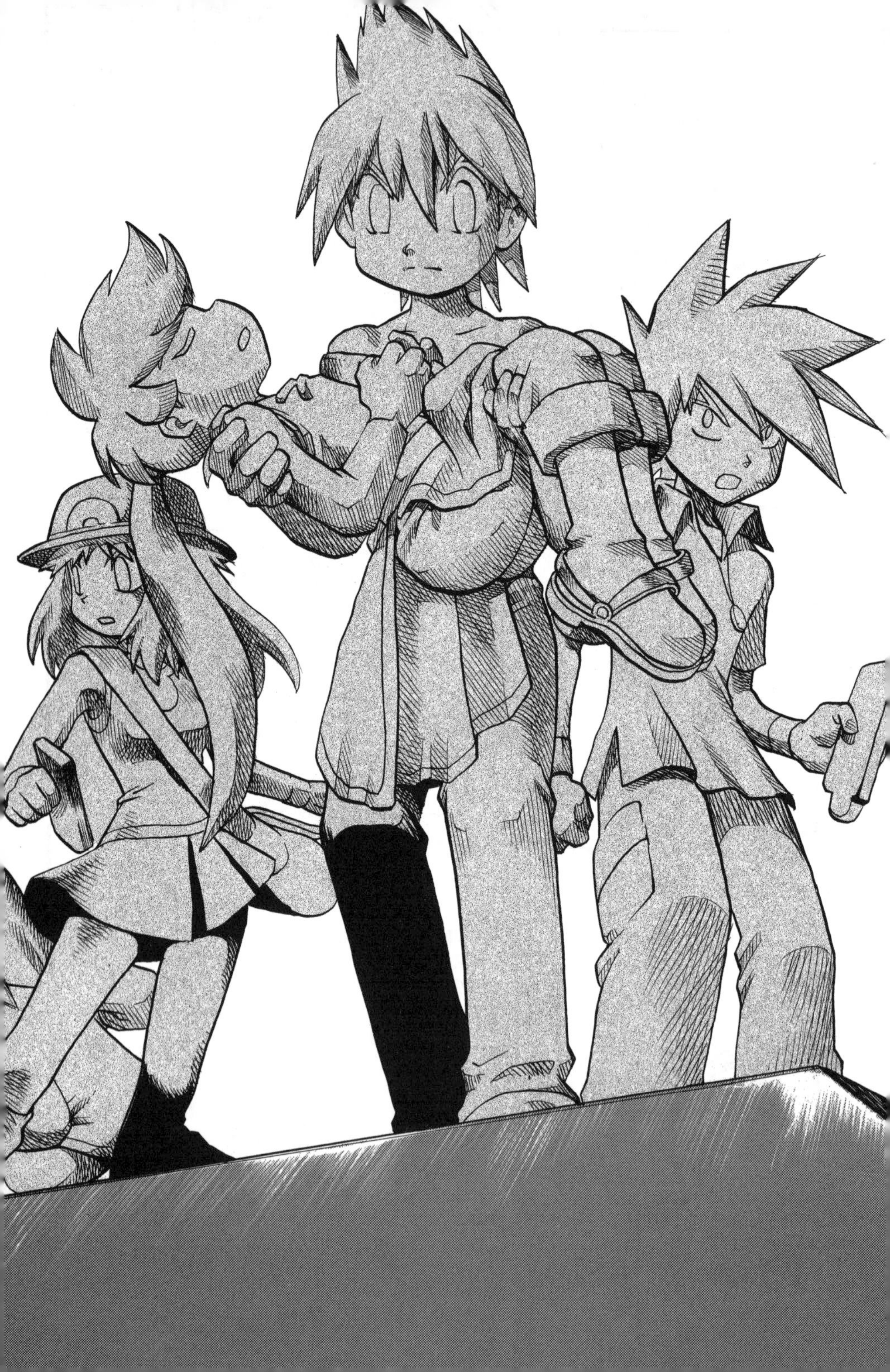

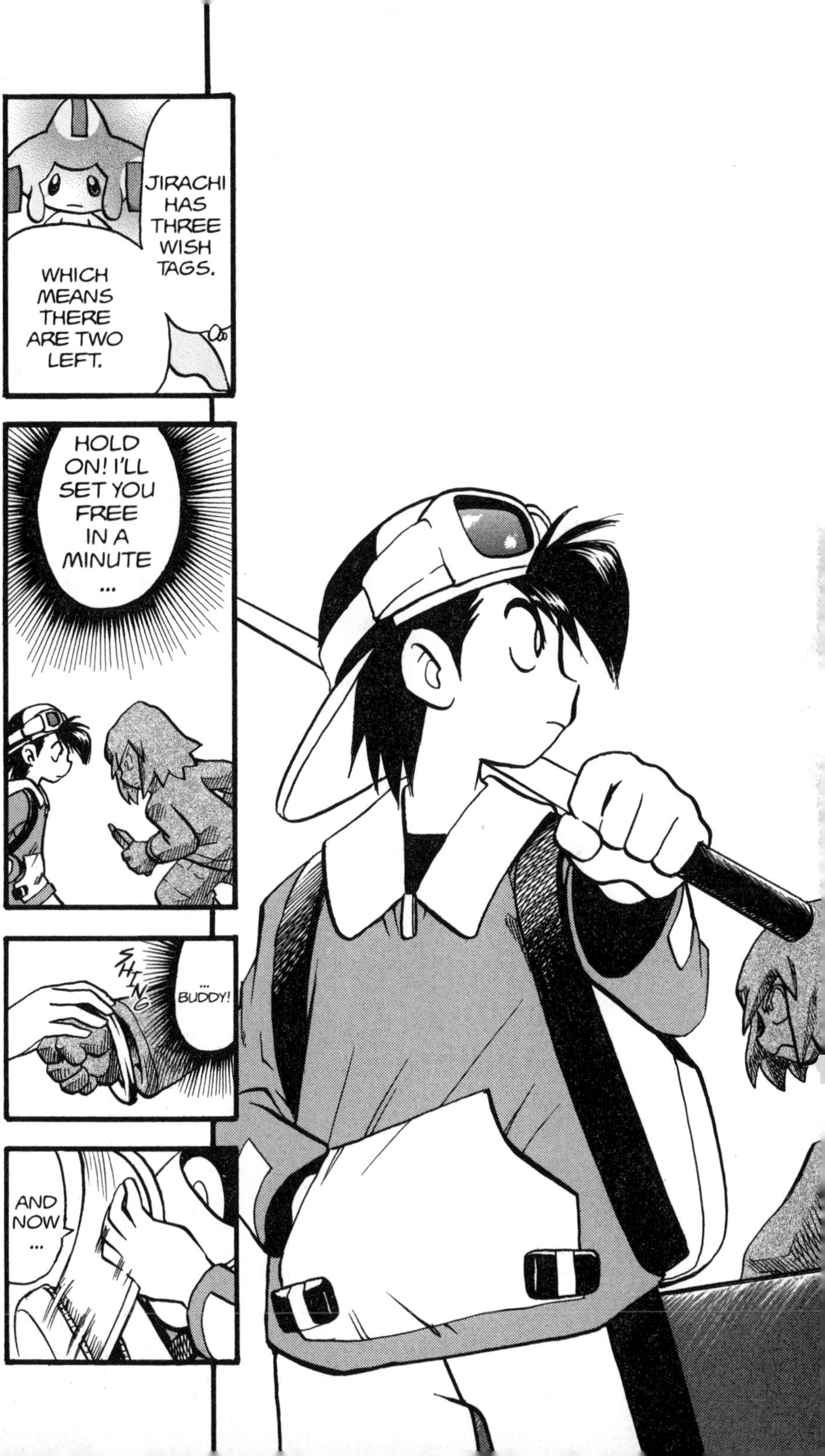
JIRACHI HAS THREE WISH TAGS.
WHICH MEANS THERE ARE TWO LEFT.
HOLD ON! I'LL SET YOU FREE IN A MINUTE ...
... BUDDY!
SHING
AND NOW ...

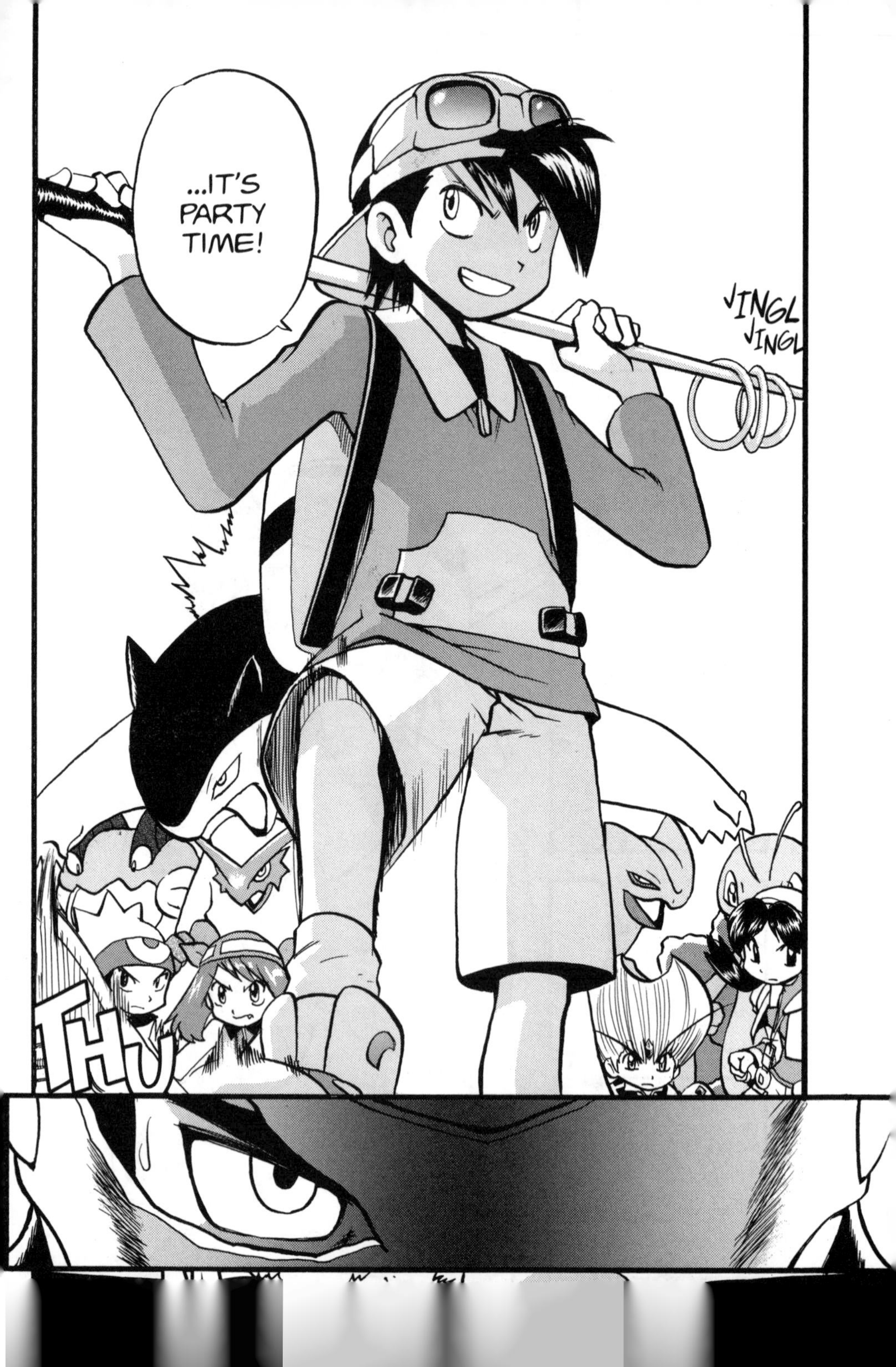
...IT'S PARTY TIME!
JINGL
JINGL
THU

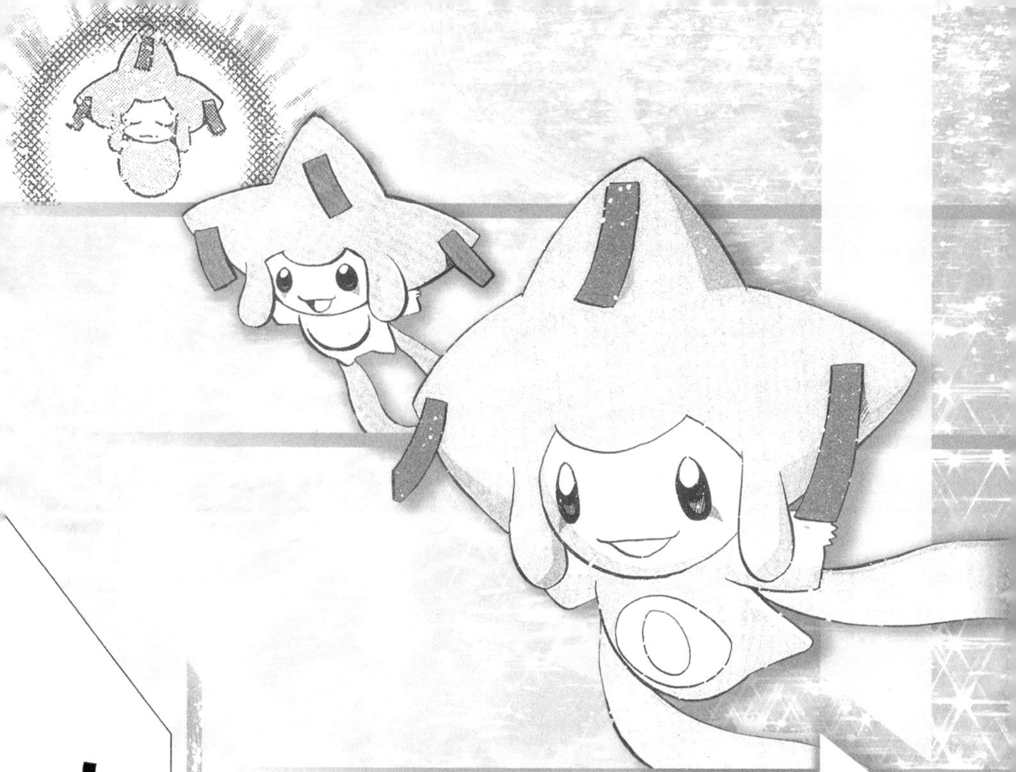

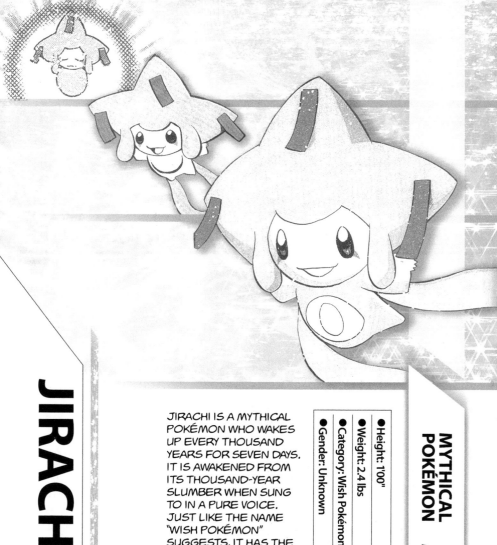

MYTHICAL POKÉMON JIRACHI 1

- Height: 1'00"
- Weight: 2.4 lbs
- Category: Wish Pokémon
- Gender: Unknown

JIRACHI IS A MYTHICAL POKÉMON WHO WAKES UP EVERY THOUSAND YEARS FOR SEVEN DAYS. IT IS AWAKENED FROM ITS THOUSAND-YEAR SLUMBER WHEN SUNG TO IN A PURE VOICE. JUST LIKE THE NAME "WISH POKÉMON" SUGGESTS, IT HAS THE POWER TO MAKE ANY WISH COME TRUE. THE WISHER MUST LOOK INTO JIRACHI'S THIRD EYE (TRUE EYE) LOCATED ON ITS STOMACH TO CONVEY THEIR WISH. THE TAGS HANGING FROM ITS HEAD ARE WISH TAGS WHERE THE WISHES WILL BE INSCRIBED.

JIRACHI

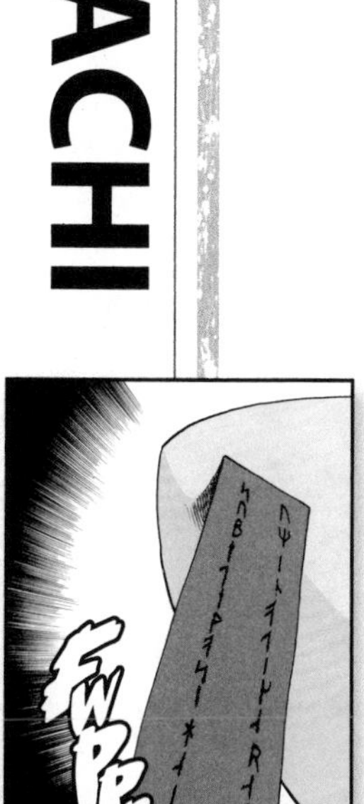
FWPP

329

The Final Battle, Part 2

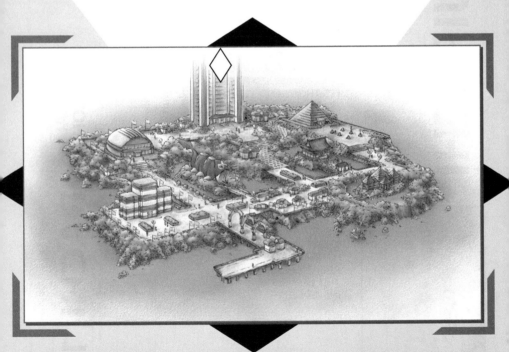

POKÉMON ADVENTURES·THE SIXTH CHAPTER·EMERALD

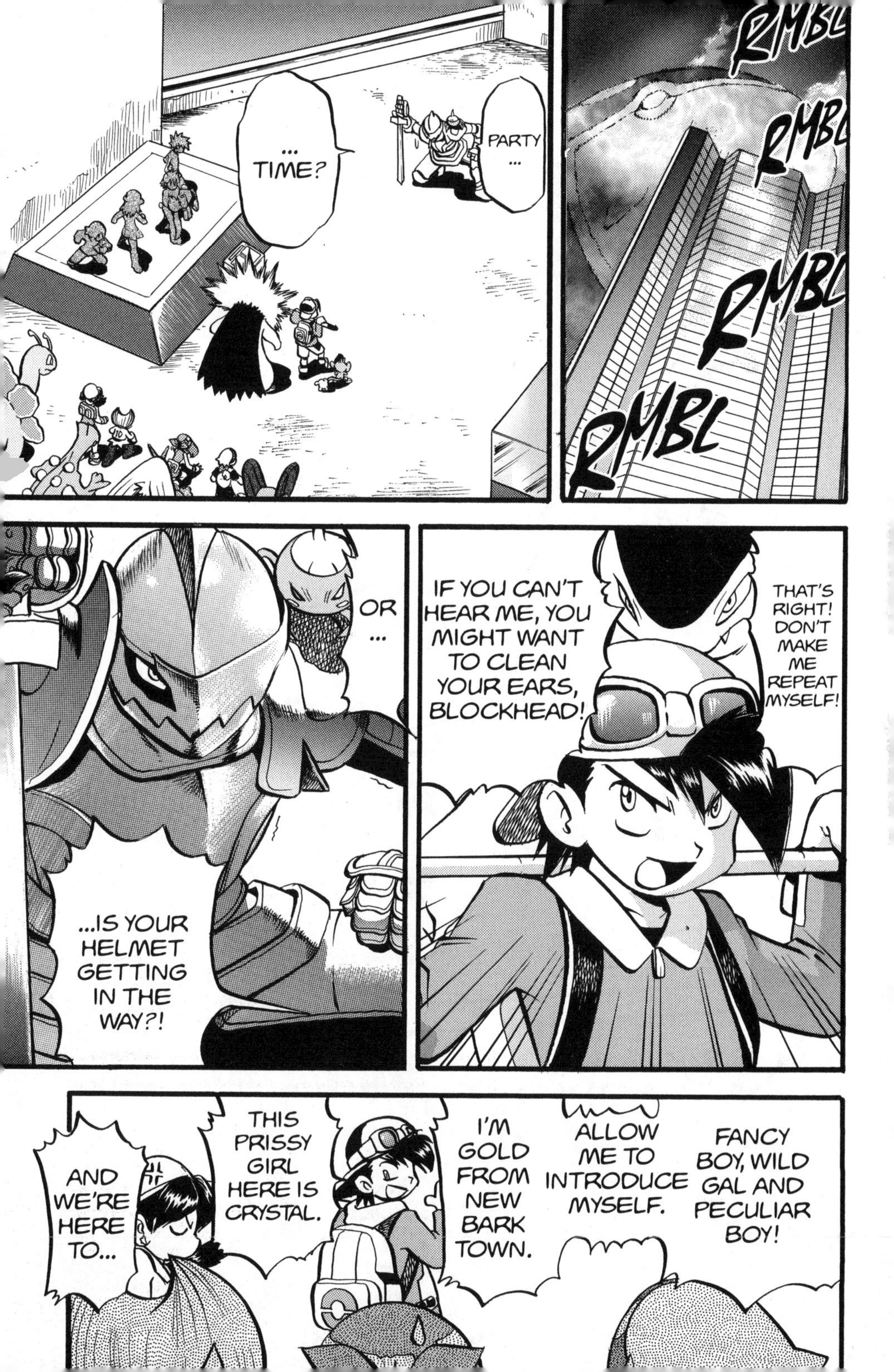
RMBL
RMBL
RMBL
RMBL
PARTY ...
... TIME?
THAT'S RIGHT! DON'T MAKE ME REPEAT MYSELF!
IF YOU CAN'T HEAR ME, YOU MIGHT WANT TO CLEAN YOUR EARS, BLOCKHEAD!
OR ...
...IS YOUR HELMET GETTING IN THE WAY?!
FANCY BOY, WILD GAL AND PECULIAR BOY!
ALLOW ME TO INTRODUCE MYSELF.
I'M GOLD FROM NEW BARK TOWN.
THIS PRISSY GIRL HERE IS CRYSTAL.
AND WE'RE HERE TO...

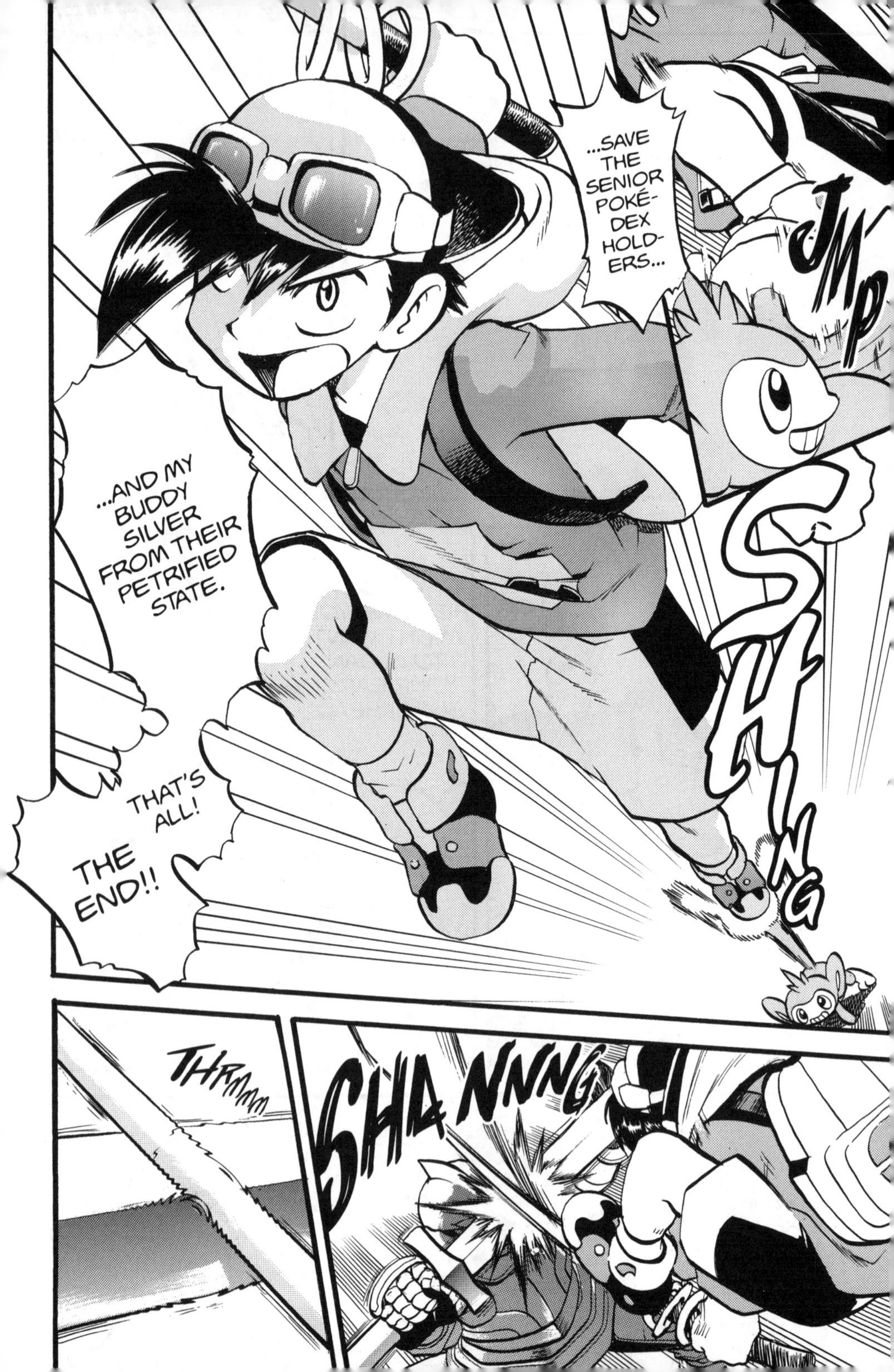

...SAVE THE SENIOR POKÉ-DEX HOLD-ERS...
JMP
...AND MY BUDDY SILVER FROM THEIR PETRIFIED STATE.
SHING
THAT'S ALL!
THE END!!
SHANNNG
THRMMM

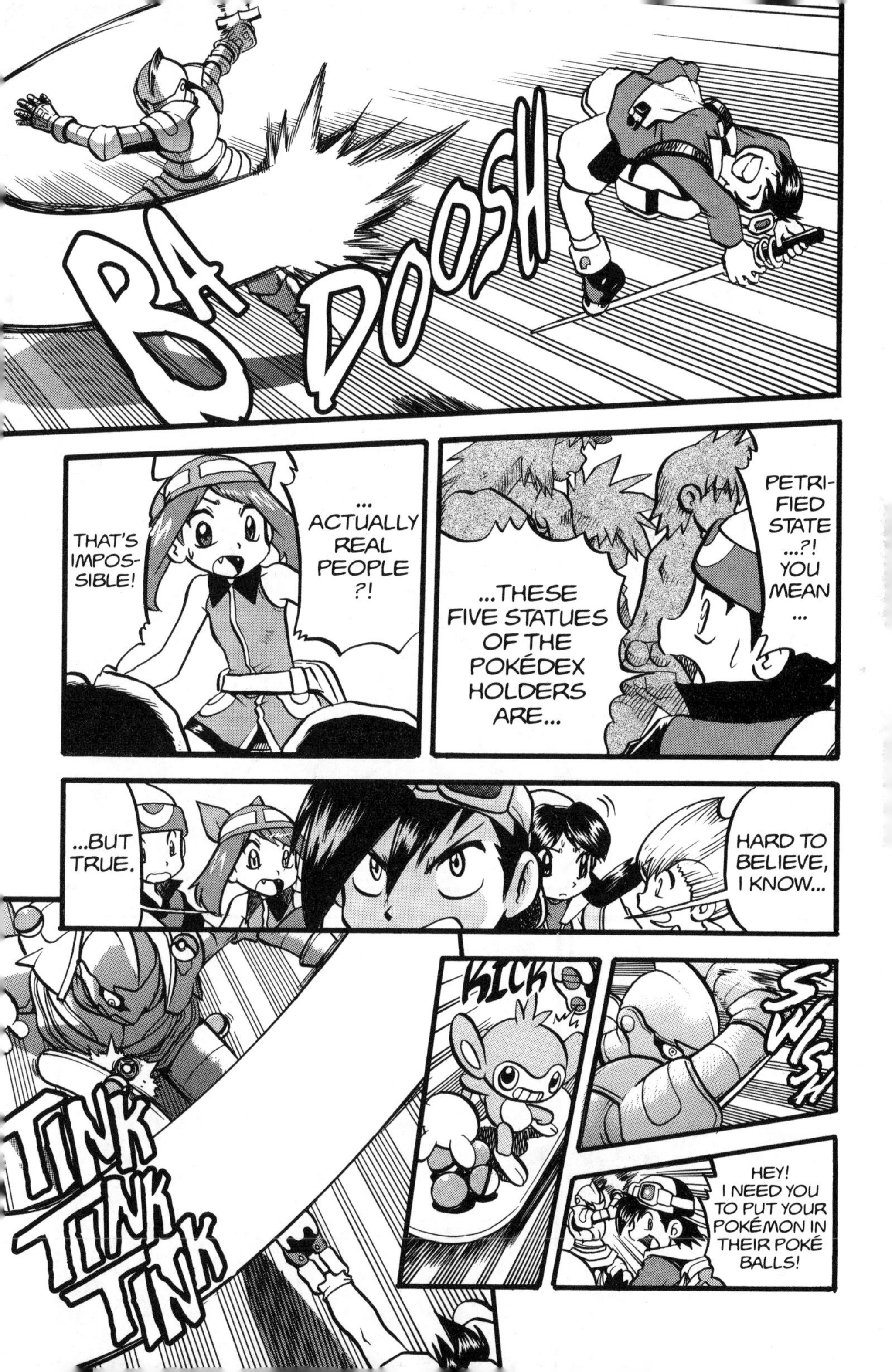
BA DOOSH
PETRI-FIED STATE ...?! YOU MEAN ...
...THESE FIVE STATUES OF THE POKÉDEX HOLDERS ARE...
... ACTUALLY REAL PEOPLE ?!
THAT'S IMPOS-SIBLE!
HARD TO BELIEVE, I KNOW...
...BUT TRUE.
SWISH
HEY! I NEED YOU TO PUT YOUR POKÉMON IN THEIR POKÉ BALLS!
KICK
TINK TINK TINK

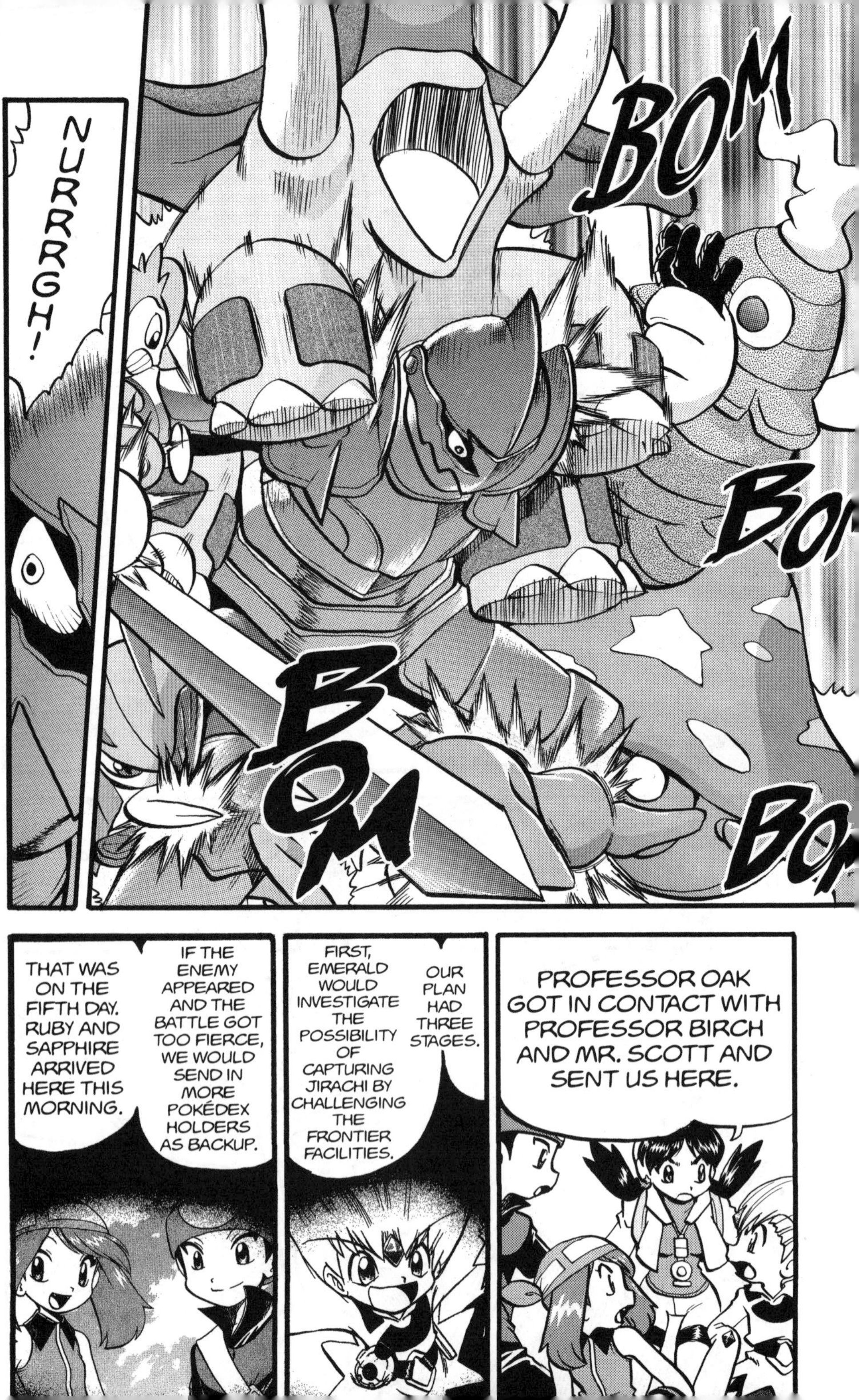
BOM
BO
BO
BOM
NURRRGH!
PROFESSOR OAK GOT IN CONTACT WITH PROFESSOR BIRCH AND MR. SCOTT AND SENT US HERE.
OUR PLAN HAD THREE STAGES.
FIRST, EMERALD WOULD INVESTIGATE THE POSSIBILITY OF CAPTURING JIRACHI BY CHALLENGING THE FRONTIER FACILITIES.
IF THE ENEMY APPEARED AND THE BATTLE GOT TOO FIERCE, WE WOULD SEND IN MORE POKÉDEX HOLDERS AS BACKUP.
THAT WAS ON THE FIFTH DAY. RUBY AND SAPPHIRE ARRIVED HERE THIS MORNING.

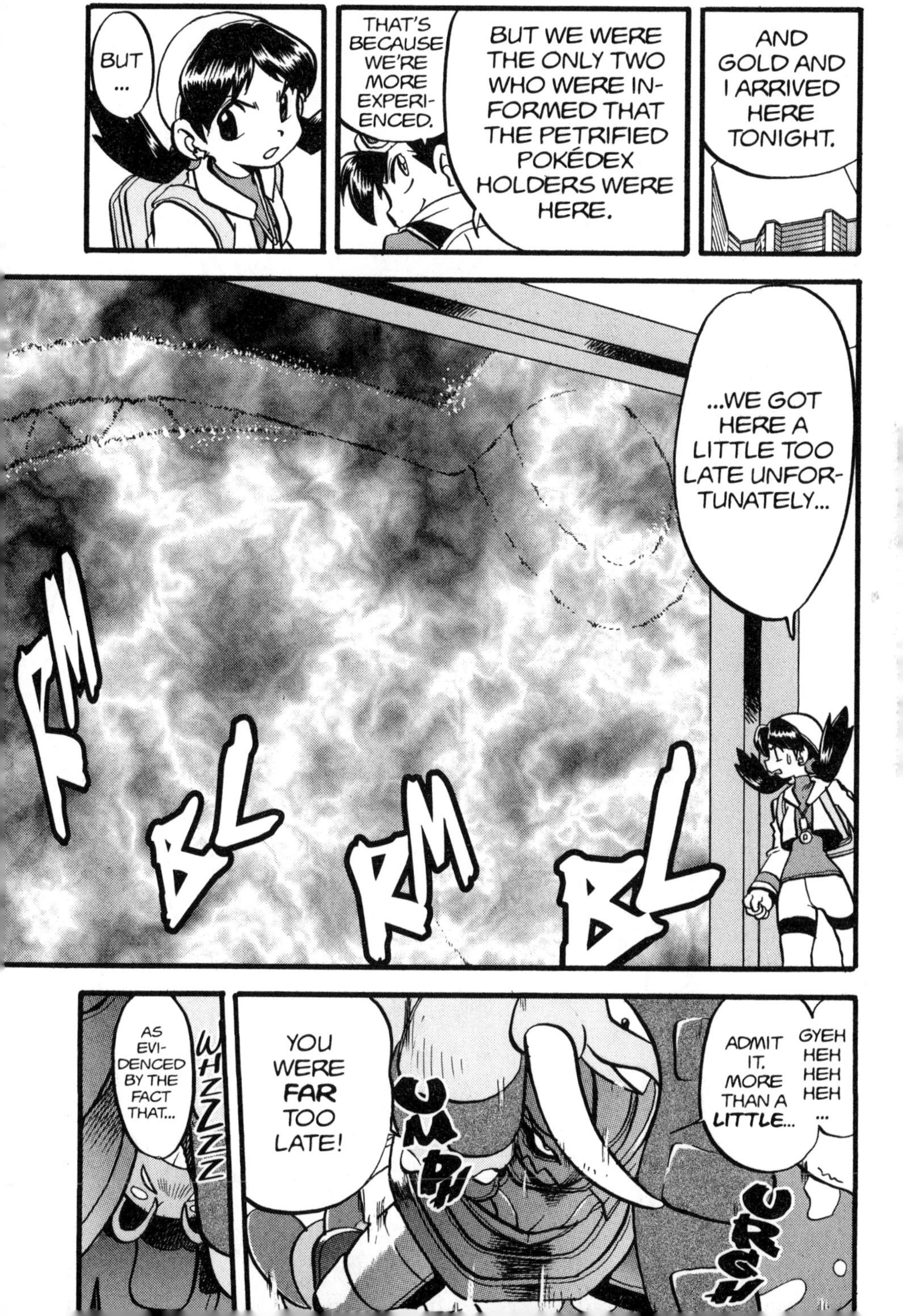
AND GOLD AND I ARRIVED HERE TONIGHT.
BUT WE WERE THE ONLY TWO WHO WERE INFORMED THAT THE PETRIFIED POKÉDEX HOLDERS WERE HERE.
THAT'S BECAUSE WE'RE MORE EXPERIENCED.
BUT ...
...WE GOT HERE A LITTLE TOO LATE UNFORTUNATELY...
RM BL RM BL
GYEH HEH HEH HEH ...
ADMIT IT. MORE THAN A **LITTLE**...
URGH
UMPH
YOU WERE **FAR** TOO LATE!
WHZZZZ
AS EVIDENCED BY THE FACT THAT...

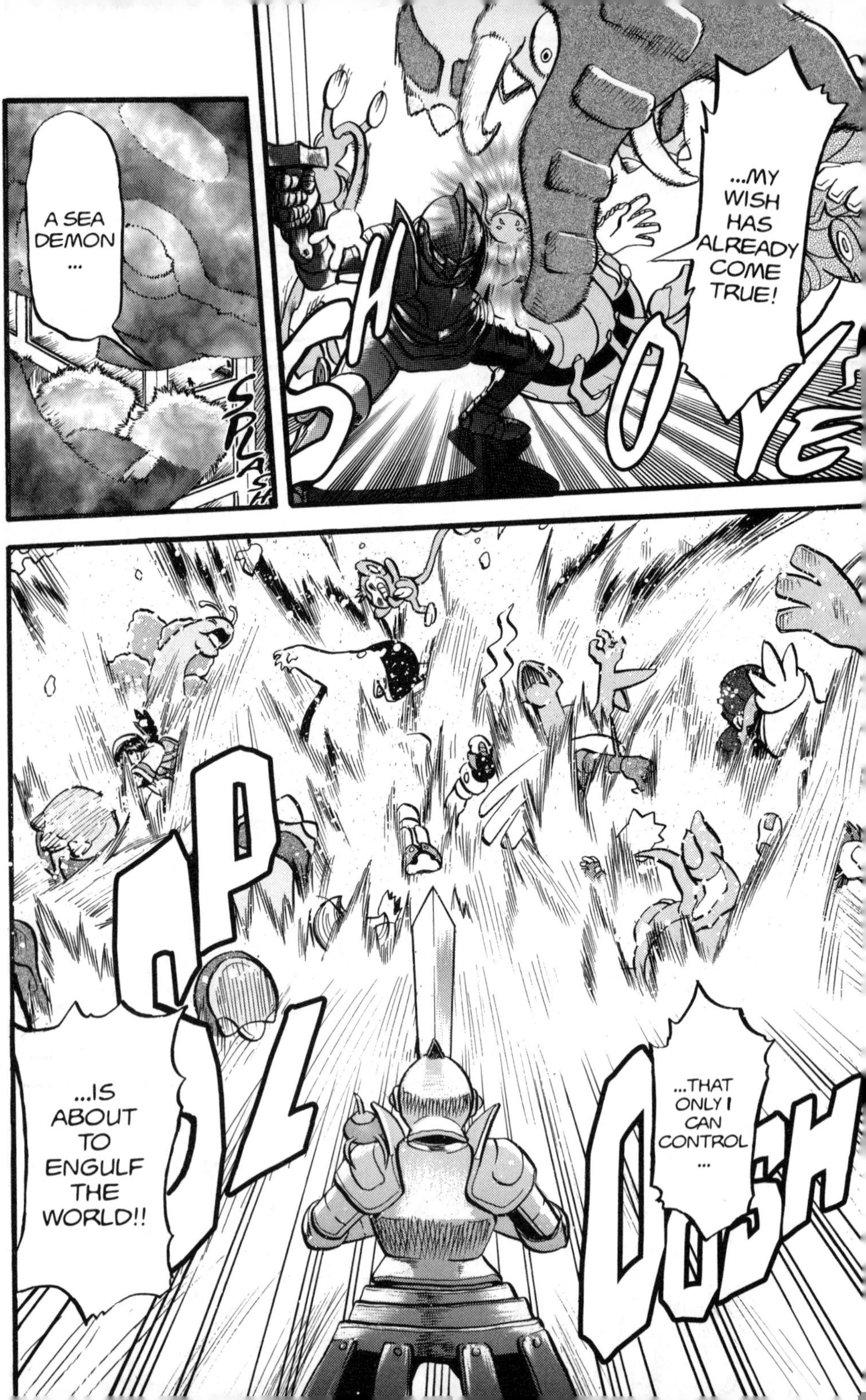
...MY WISH HAS ALREADY COME TRUE!
A SEA DEMON ...
SPLASH
...THAT ONLY I CAN CONTROL ...
...IS ABOUT TO ENGULF THE WORLD!!

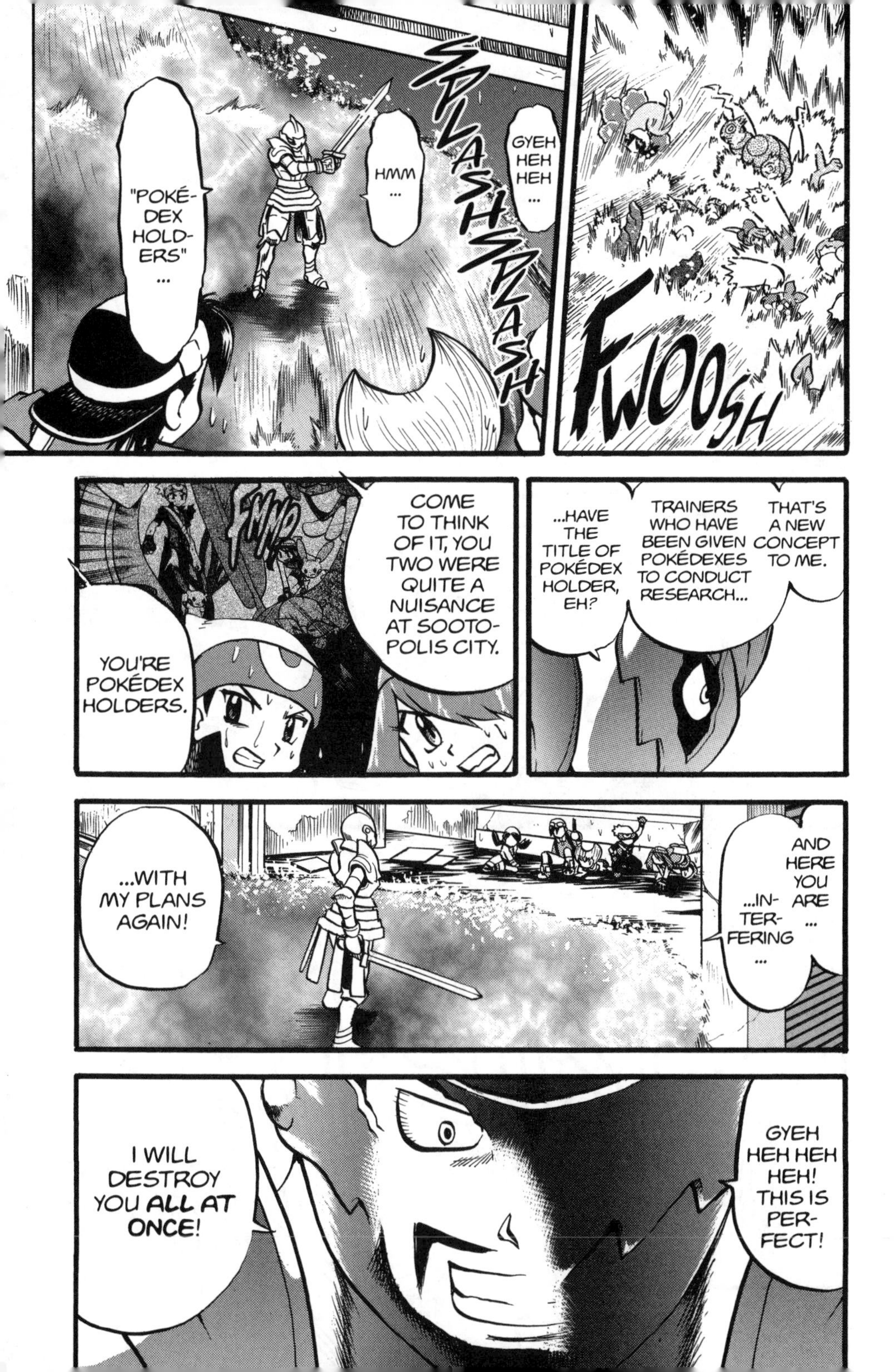
FWOOSH
GYEH HEH HEH ...
SPLASHSPLASH
HMM ...
"POKÉDEX HOLDERS" ...
THAT'S A NEW CONCEPT TO ME.
TRAINERS WHO HAVE BEEN GIVEN POKÉDEXES TO CONDUCT RESEARCH...
...HAVE THE TITLE OF POKÉDEX HOLDER, EH?
COME TO THINK OF IT, YOU TWO WERE QUITE A NUISANCE AT SOOTOPOLIS CITY.
YOU'RE POKÉDEX HOLDERS.
AND HERE YOU ARE ...
...INTERFERING ...
...WITH MY PLANS AGAIN!
GYEH HEH HEH HEH! THIS IS PERFECT!
I WILL DESTROY YOU **ALL AT ONCE**!

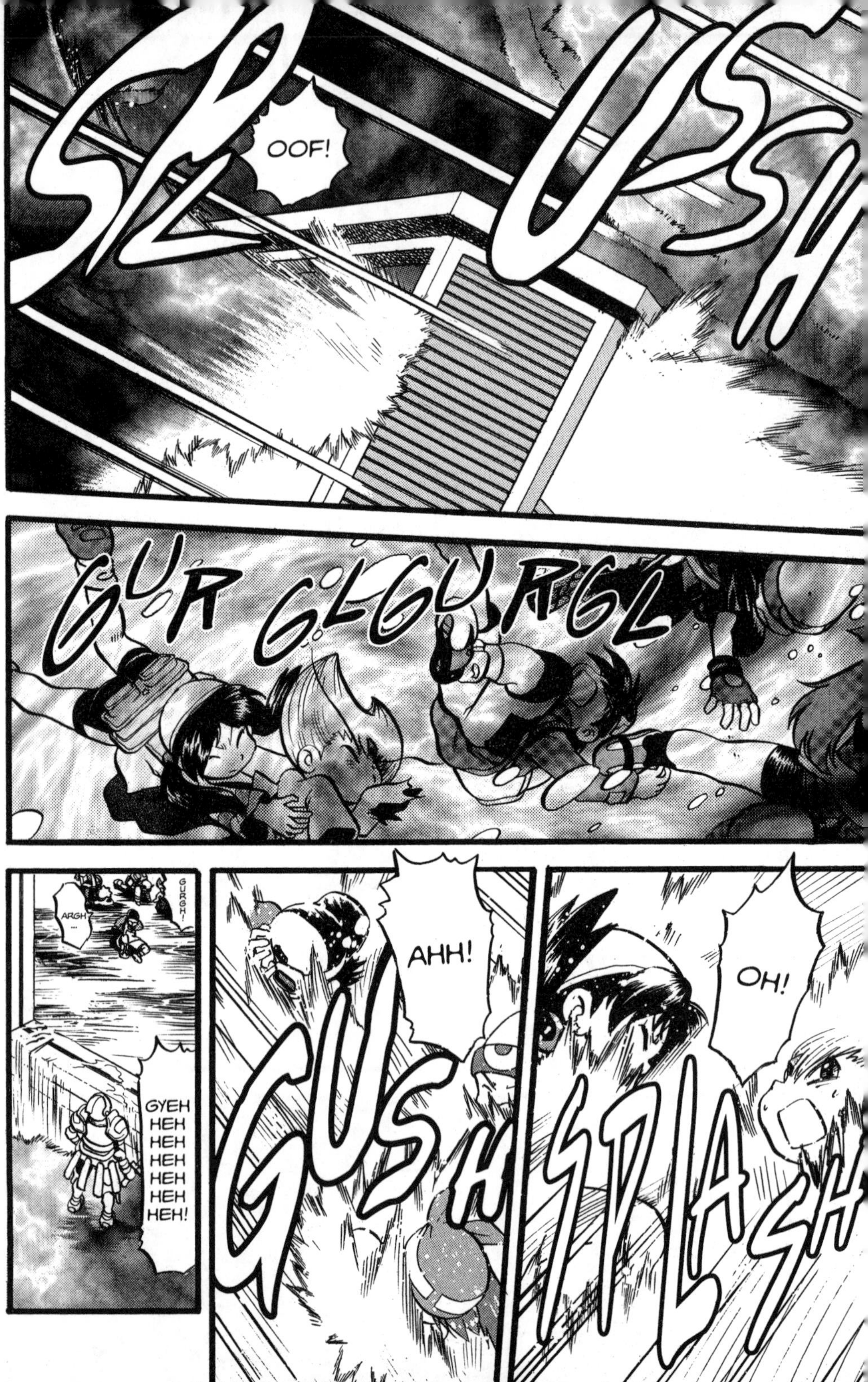
SPLUSH
OOF!
GURGL GURGL
OH!
SPLASH
AHH!
GUSH
GURGH!
ARGH...
GYEH HEH HEH HEH HEH HEH HEH!

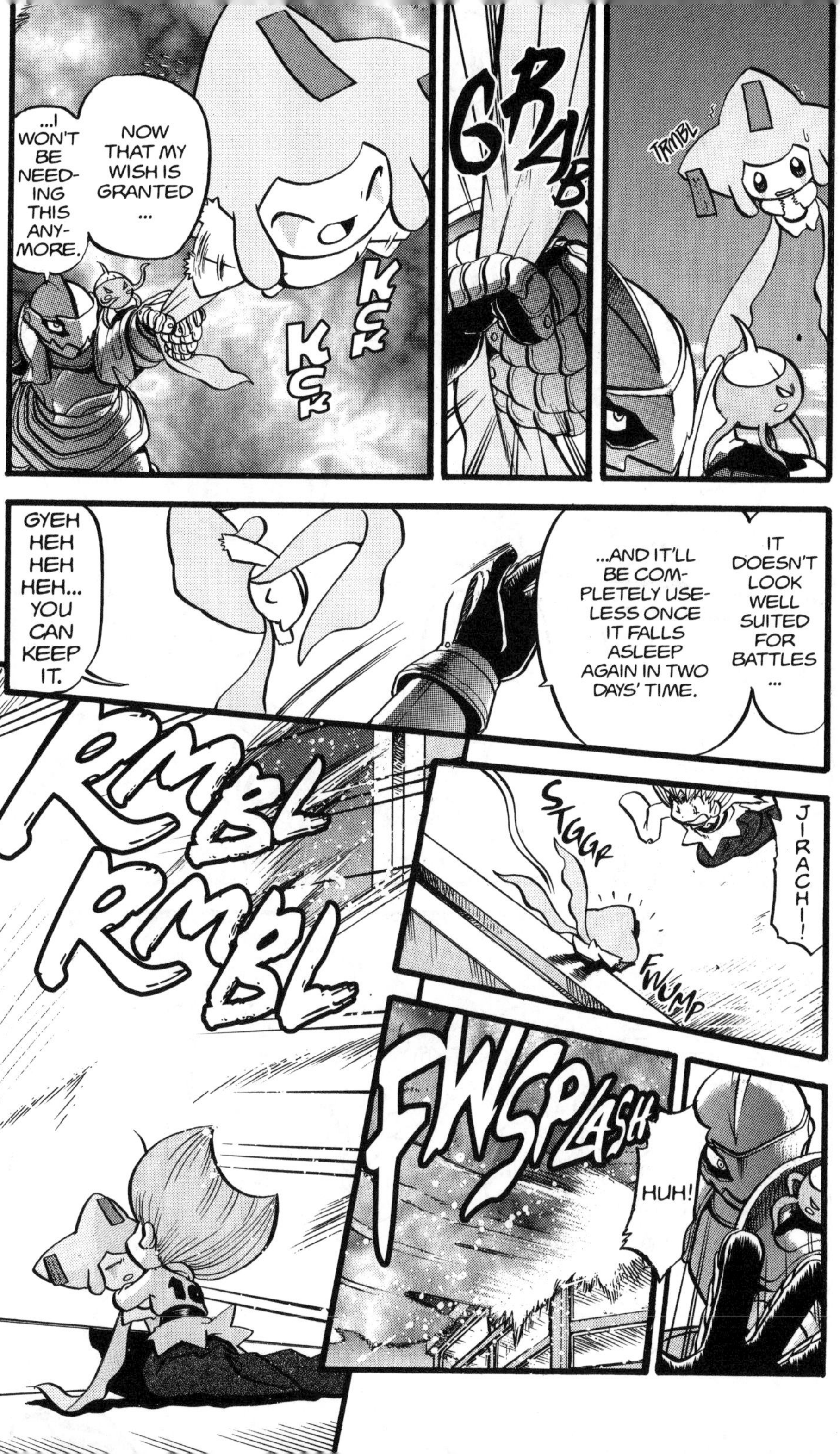
TRMBL
GRAB
NOW THAT MY WISH IS GRANTED...
...I WON'T BE NEEDING THIS ANYMORE.
KCK
KCK
KCK
IT DOESN'T LOOK WELL SUITED FOR BATTLES...
...AND IT'LL BE COMPLETELY USELESS ONCE IT FALLS ASLEEP AGAIN IN TWO DAYS' TIME.
GYEH HEH HEH HEH... YOU CAN KEEP IT.
JIRACHI!
SKGGR
FWUMP
RMBL
RMBL
HUH!
FWSPLASH

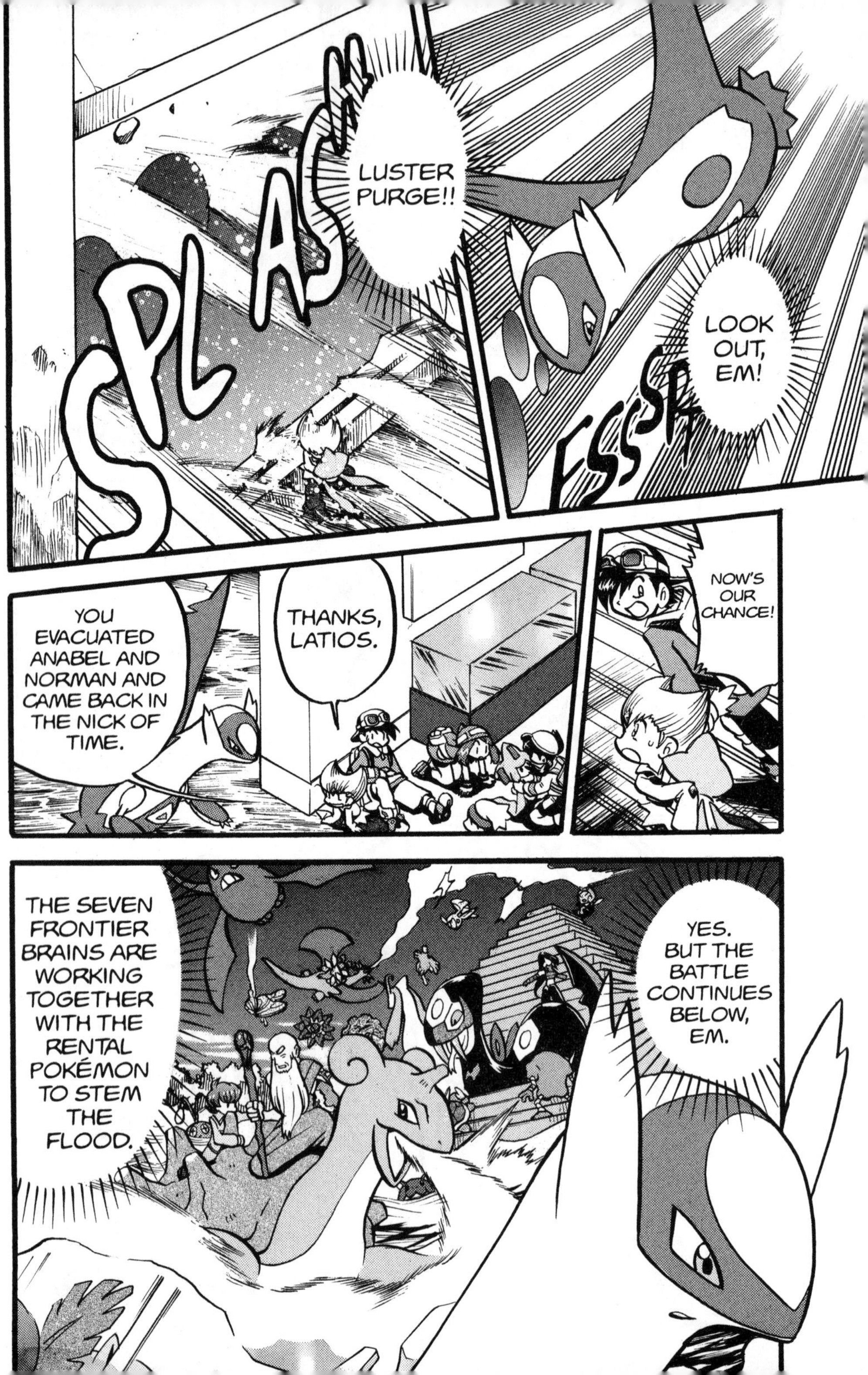

LOOK OUT, EM!
FSSSH
LUSTER PURGE!!
SPLASH
NOW'S OUR CHANCE!
THANKS, LATIOS.
YOU EVACUATED ANABEL AND NORMAN AND CAME BACK IN THE NICK OF TIME.
THE SEVEN FRONTIER BRAINS ARE WORKING TOGETHER WITH THE RENTAL POKÉMON TO STEM THE FLOOD.
YES. BUT THE BATTLE CONTINUES BELOW, EM.

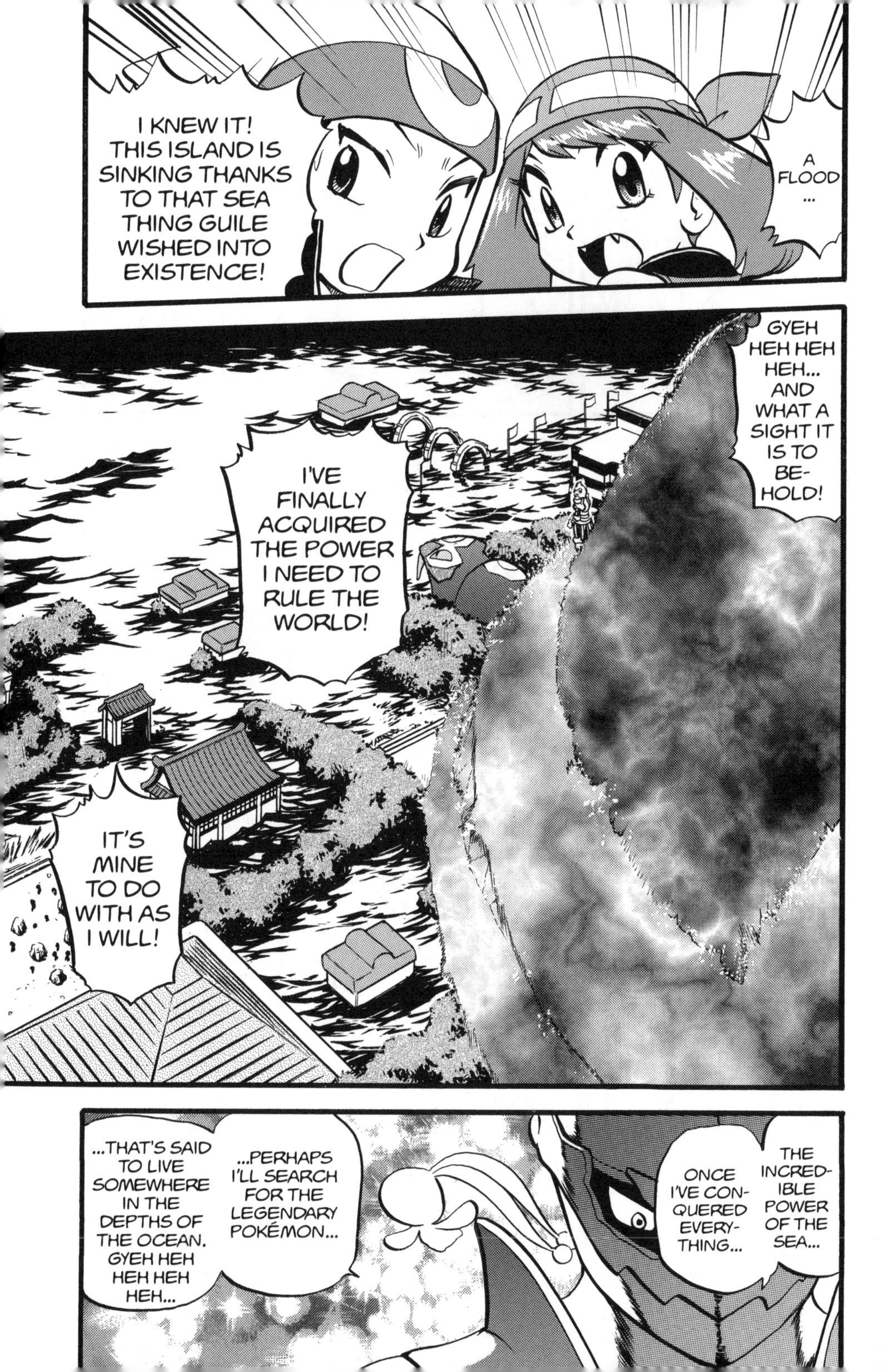
A FLOOD ...
I KNEW IT! THIS ISLAND IS SINKING THANKS TO THAT SEA THING GUILE WISHED INTO EXISTENCE!
GYEH HEH HEH HEH... AND WHAT A SIGHT IT IS TO BE-HOLD!
I'VE FINALLY ACQUIRED THE POWER I NEED TO RULE THE WORLD!
IT'S MINE TO DO WITH AS I WILL!
THE INCRED-IBLE POWER OF THE SEA...
ONCE I'VE CON-QUERED EVERY-THING...
...PERHAPS I'LL SEARCH FOR THE LEGENDARY POKÉMON...
...THAT'S SAID TO LIVE SOMEWHERE IN THE DEPTHS OF THE OCEAN. GYEH HEH HEH HEH HEH HEH...

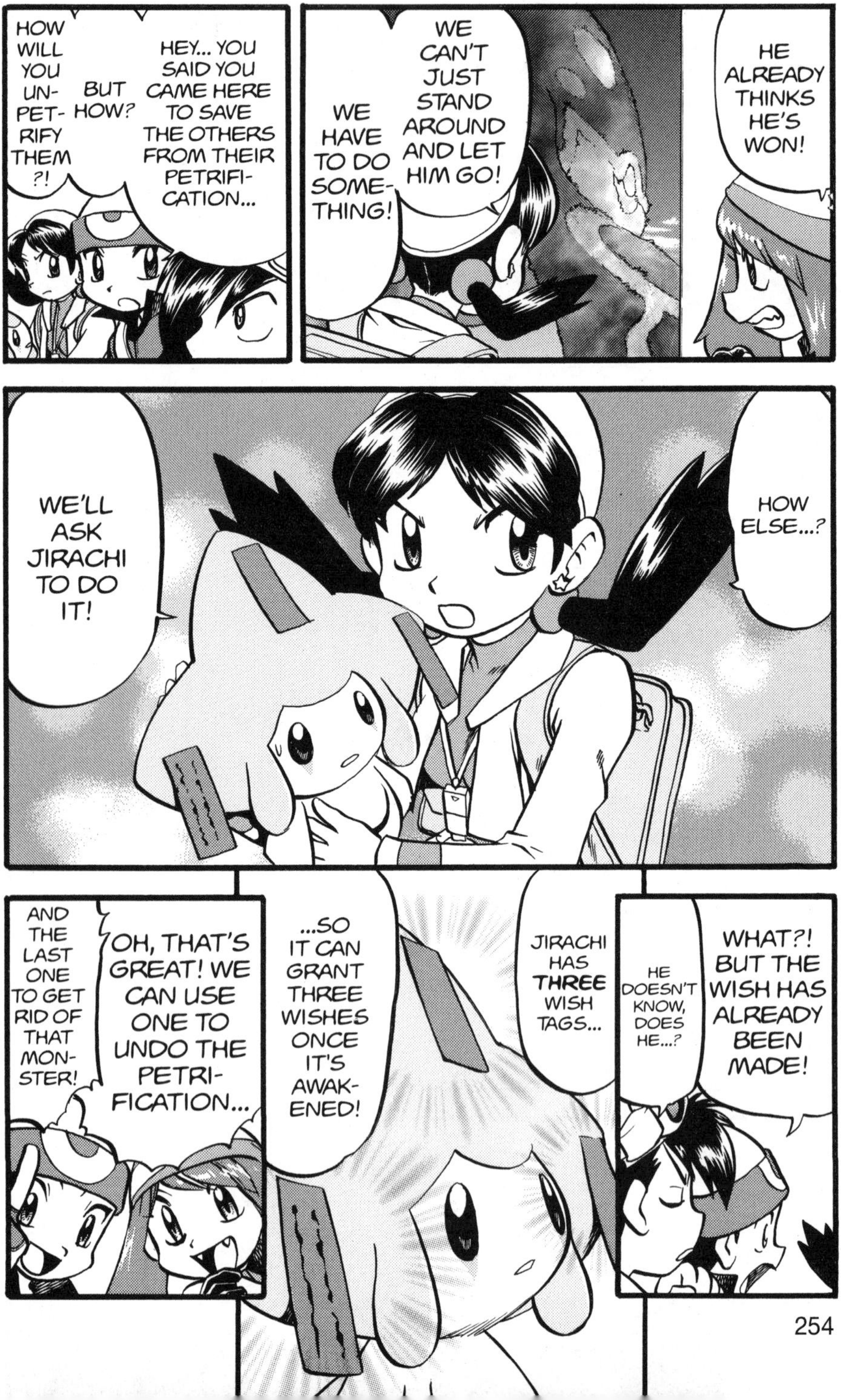
HE ALREADY THINKS HE'S WON!
WE CAN'T JUST STAND AROUND AND LET HIM GO!
WE HAVE TO DO SOME-THING!
HEY... YOU SAID YOU CAME HERE TO SAVE THE OTHERS FROM THEIR PETRIFI-CATION...
BUT HOW?
HOW WILL YOU UN-PET-RIFY THEM?!
HOW ELSE...?
WE'LL ASK JIRACHI TO DO IT!
WHAT?! BUT THE WISH HAS ALREADY BEEN MADE!
HE DOESN'T KNOW, DOES HE...?
JIRACHI HAS **THREE** WISH TAGS...
...SO IT CAN GRANT THREE WISHES ONCE IT'S AWAK-ENED!
OH, THAT'S GREAT! WE CAN USE ONE TO UNDO THE PETRI-FICATION...
AND THE LAST ONE TO GET RID OF THAT MON-STER!

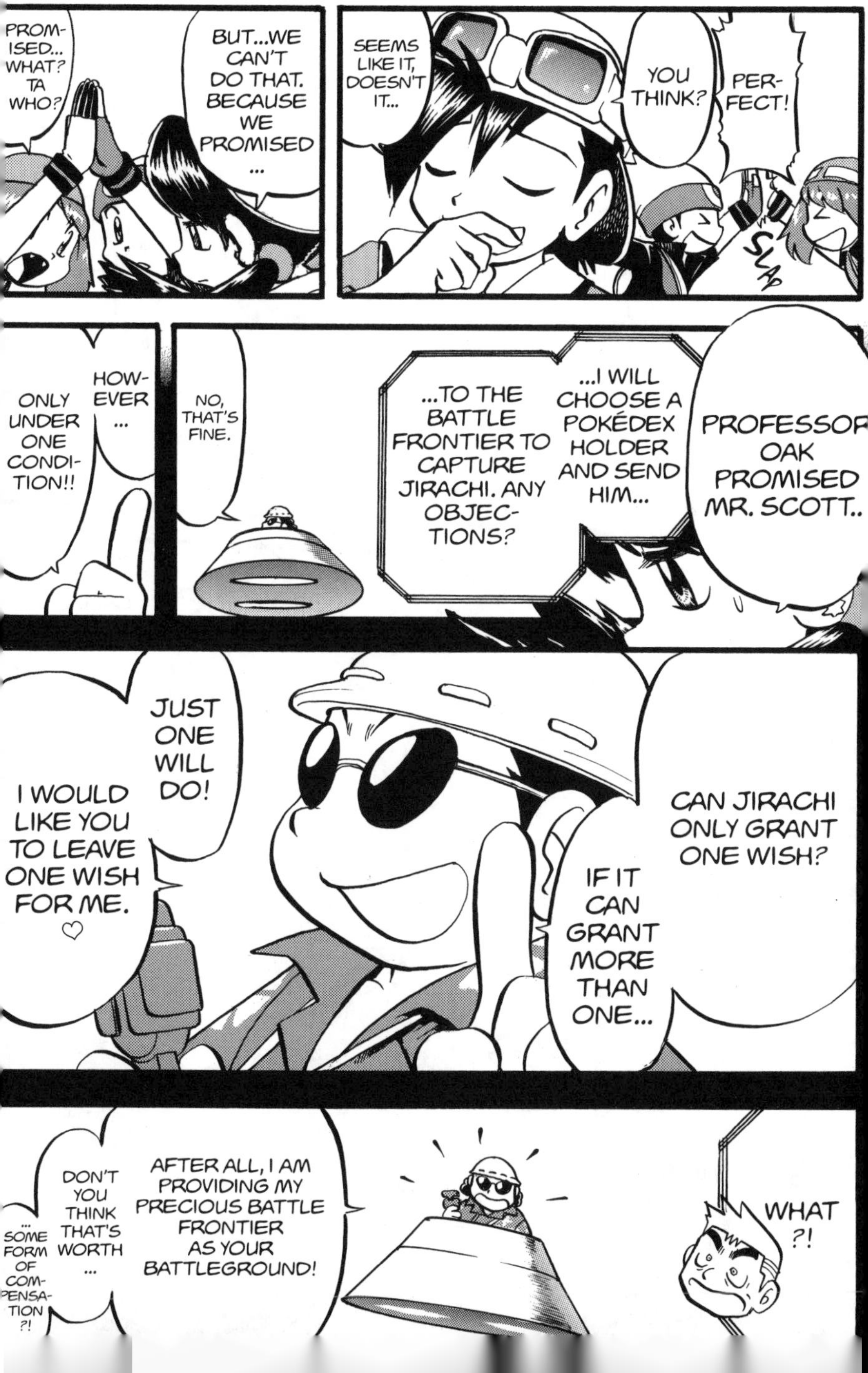
PER-FECT!
YOU THINK?
SEEMS LIKE IT, DOESN'T IT...
SLAP
BUT...WE CAN'T DO THAT. BECAUSE WE PROMISED ...
PROM-ISED... WHAT? TA WHO?
PROFESSOR OAK PROMISED MR. SCOTT..
...I WILL CHOOSE A POKÉDEX HOLDER AND SEND HIM...
...TO THE BATTLE FRONTIER TO CAPTURE JIRACHI. ANY OBJEC-TIONS?
NO, THAT'S FINE.
HOW-EVER ...
ONLY UNDER ONE CONDI-TION!!
CAN JIRACHI ONLY GRANT ONE WISH?
IF IT CAN GRANT MORE THAN ONE...
JUST ONE WILL DO!
I WOULD LIKE YOU TO LEAVE ONE WISH FOR ME. ♡
WHAT?!
AFTER ALL, I AM PROVIDING MY PRECIOUS BATTLE FRONTIER AS YOUR BATTLEGROUND!
DON'T YOU THINK THAT'S WORTH ...
... SOME FORM OF COM-PENSA-TION ?!

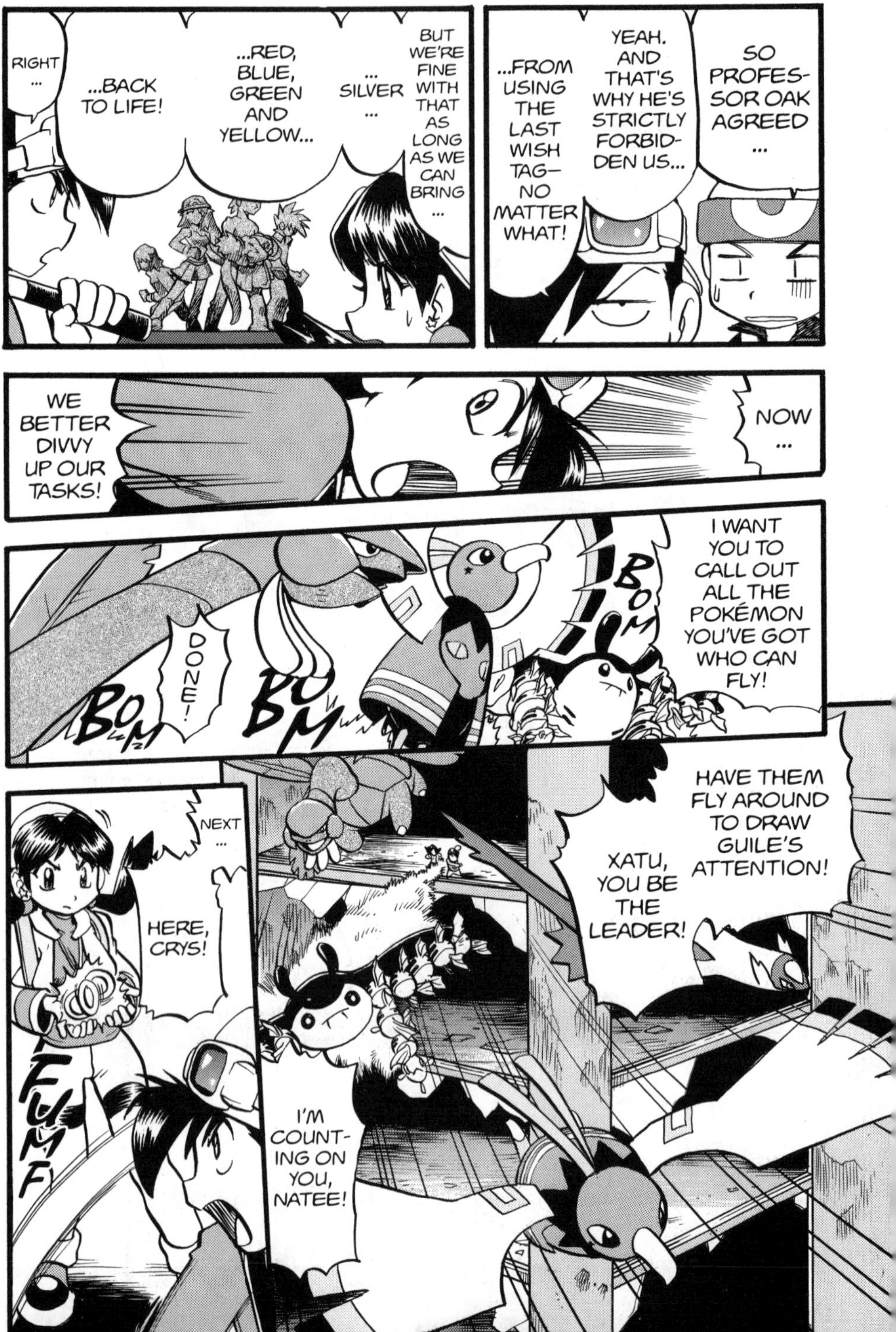
SO PROFESSOR OAK AGREED...
YEAH. AND THAT'S WHY HE'S STRICTLY FORBIDDEN US...
...FROM USING THE LAST WISH TAG—NO MATTER WHAT!
BUT WE'RE FINE WITH THAT AS LONG AS WE CAN BRING...
...SILVER...
...RED, BLUE, GREEN AND YELLOW...
...BACK TO LIFE!
RIGHT...
NOW...
WE BETTER DIVVY UP OUR TASKS!
I WANT YOU TO CALL OUT ALL THE POKÉMON YOU'VE GOT WHO CAN FLY!
BOM
DONE!
BOM
HAVE THEM FLY AROUND TO DRAW GUILE'S ATTENTION!
XATU, YOU BE THE LEADER!
I'M COUNTING ON YOU, NATEE!
NEXT...
HERE, CRYS!
FUMF

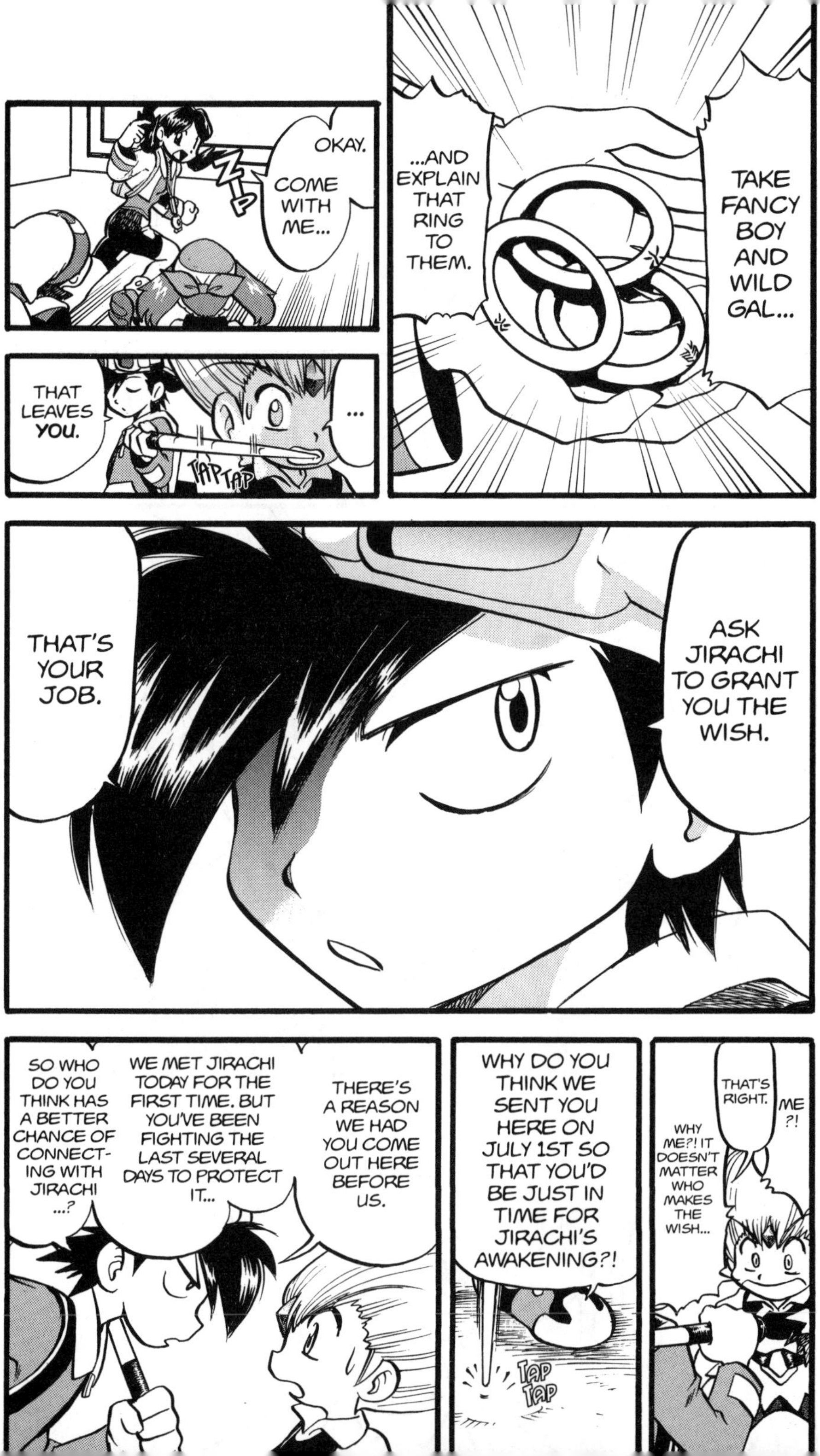
TAKE FANCY BOY AND WILD GAL...
...AND EXPLAIN THAT RING TO THEM.
OKAY.
COME WITH ME...
ZAP
...
THAT LEAVES YOU.
TAP TAP
ASK JIRACHI TO GRANT YOU THE WISH.
THAT'S YOUR JOB.
ME?!
THAT'S RIGHT.
WHY ME?! IT DOESN'T MATTER WHO MAKES THE WISH...
WHY DO YOU THINK WE SENT YOU HERE ON JULY 1ST SO THAT YOU'D BE JUST IN TIME FOR JIRACHI'S AWAKENING?!
TAP TAP
THERE'S A REASON WE HAD YOU COME OUT HERE BEFORE US.
WE MET JIRACHI TODAY FOR THE FIRST TIME. BUT YOU'VE BEEN FIGHTING THE LAST SEVERAL DAYS TO PROTECT IT...
SO WHO DO YOU THINK HAS A BETTER CHANCE OF CONNECTING WITH JIRACHI ...?

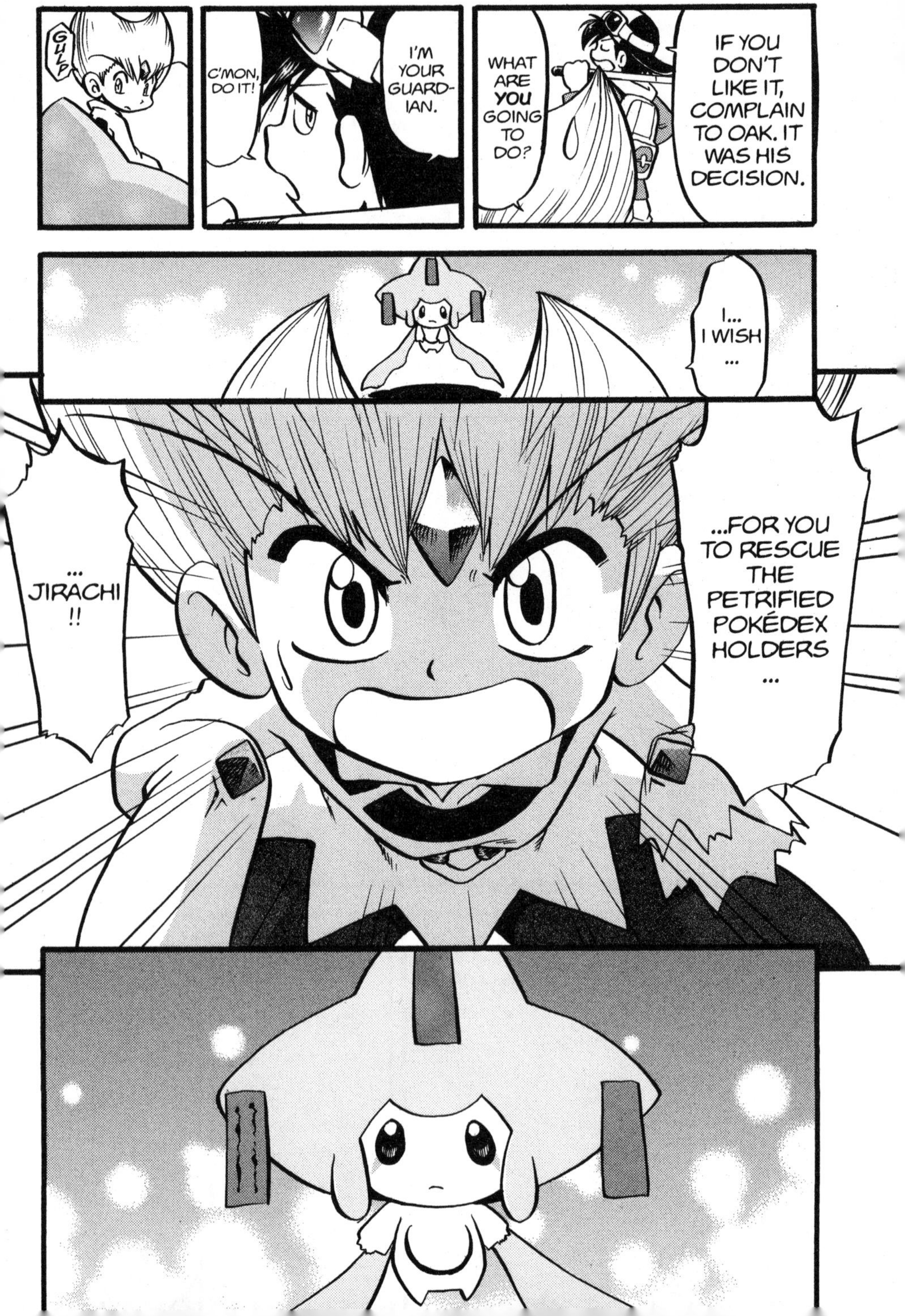
IF YOU DON'T LIKE IT, COMPLAIN TO OAK. IT WAS HIS DECISION.
WHAT ARE YOU GOING TO DO?
I'M YOUR GUARD-IAN.
C'MON, DO IT!
GULP
I... I WISH...
...FOR YOU TO RESCUE THE PETRIFIED POKÉDEX HOLDERS...
...JIRACHI!!

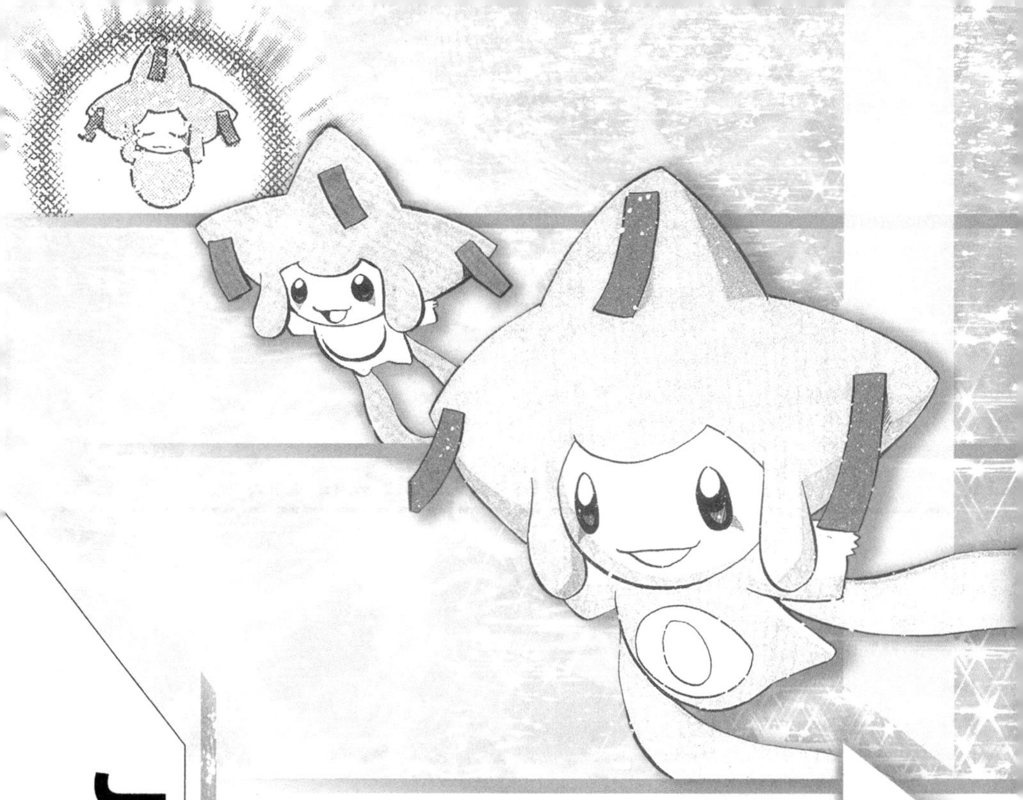

JIRACHI

MYTHICAL POKÉMON JIRACHI 2

- Type: Steel/Psychic
- Ability: Serene Grace
- Pokédex Number Hoenn: 201/National: 385

AFTER AWAKENING FOR SEVEN DAYS (OR SOONER ONCE ALL ITS WISH TAGS HAVE BEEN USED), JIRACHI WILL GO BACK TO SLEEP FOR ANOTHER THOUSAND YEARS. A TOUGH CRYSTAL-LIKE PROTECTIVE SUBSTANCE SURROUNDS ITS BODY WHILE JIRACHI IS ASLEEP; WHEN ENDANGERED, JIRACHI IS ALSO CAPABLE OF FIGHTING WHILE ASLEEP. DOOM DESIRE IS JIRACHI'S SIGNATURE ATTACK.

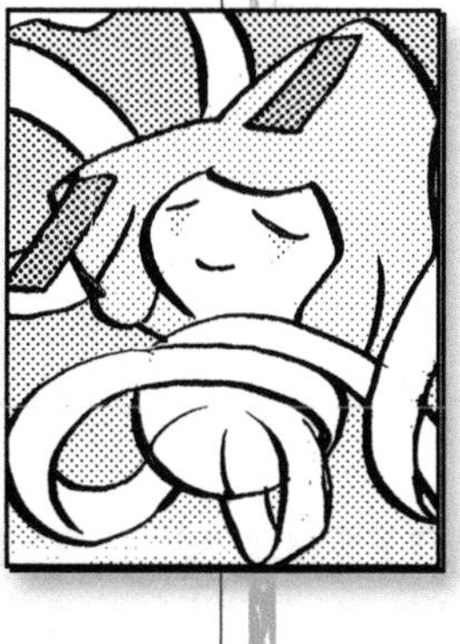

330

The Final Battle, Part 3

● S K B ● G L

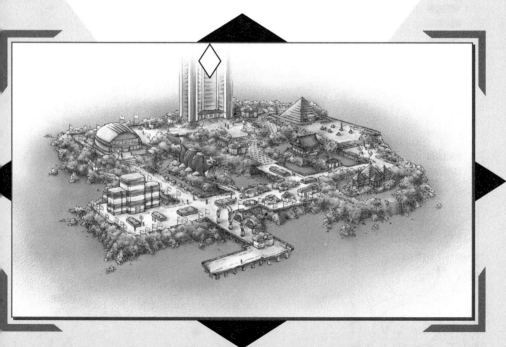

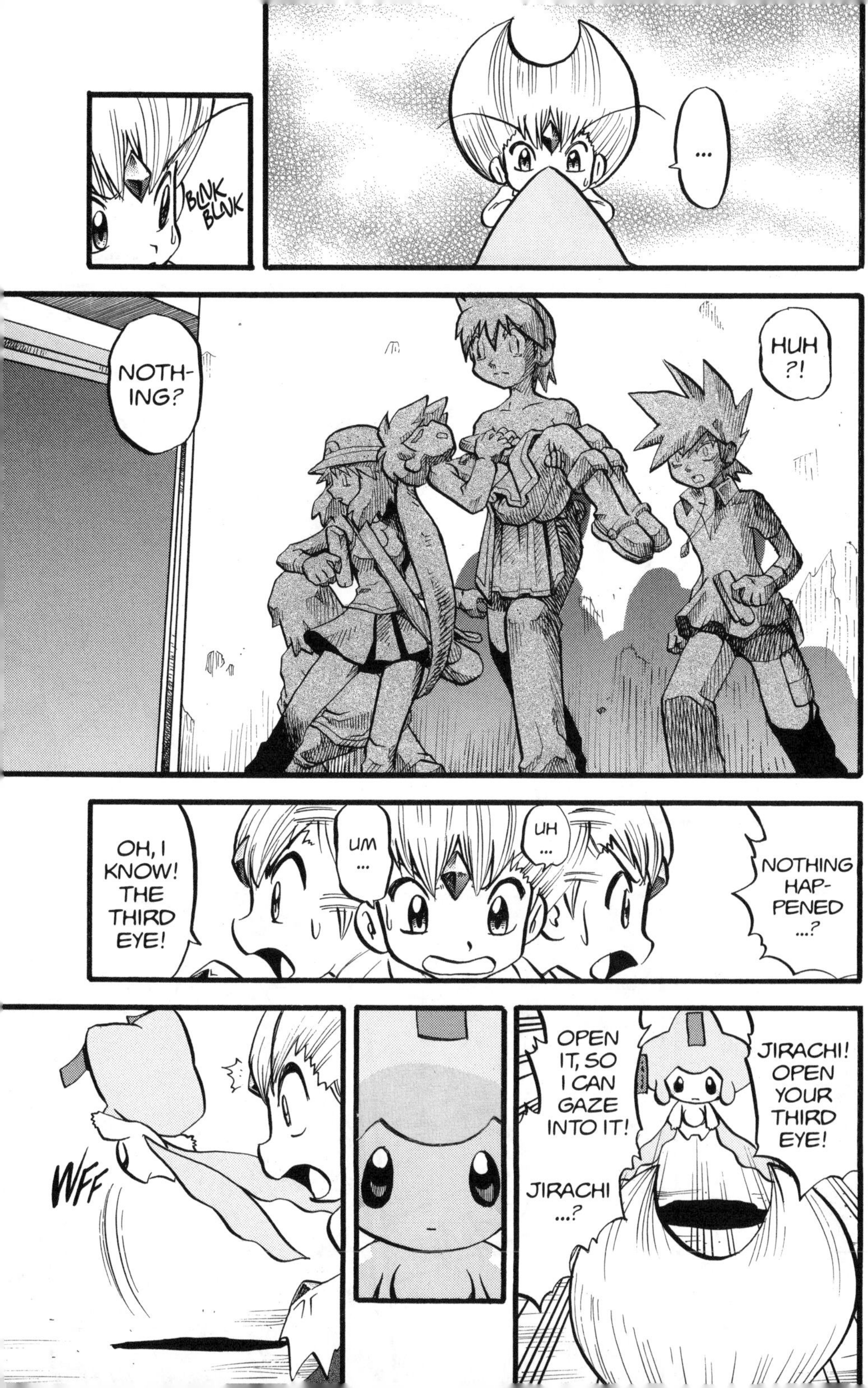
...
BLINK BLINK
HUH ?!
NOTH-ING?
NOTHING HAP-PENED ...?
UH ...
UM ...
OH, I KNOW! THE THIRD EYE!
JIRACHI! OPEN YOUR THIRD EYE!
OPEN IT, SO I CAN GAZE INTO IT!
JIRACHI ...?
WFF

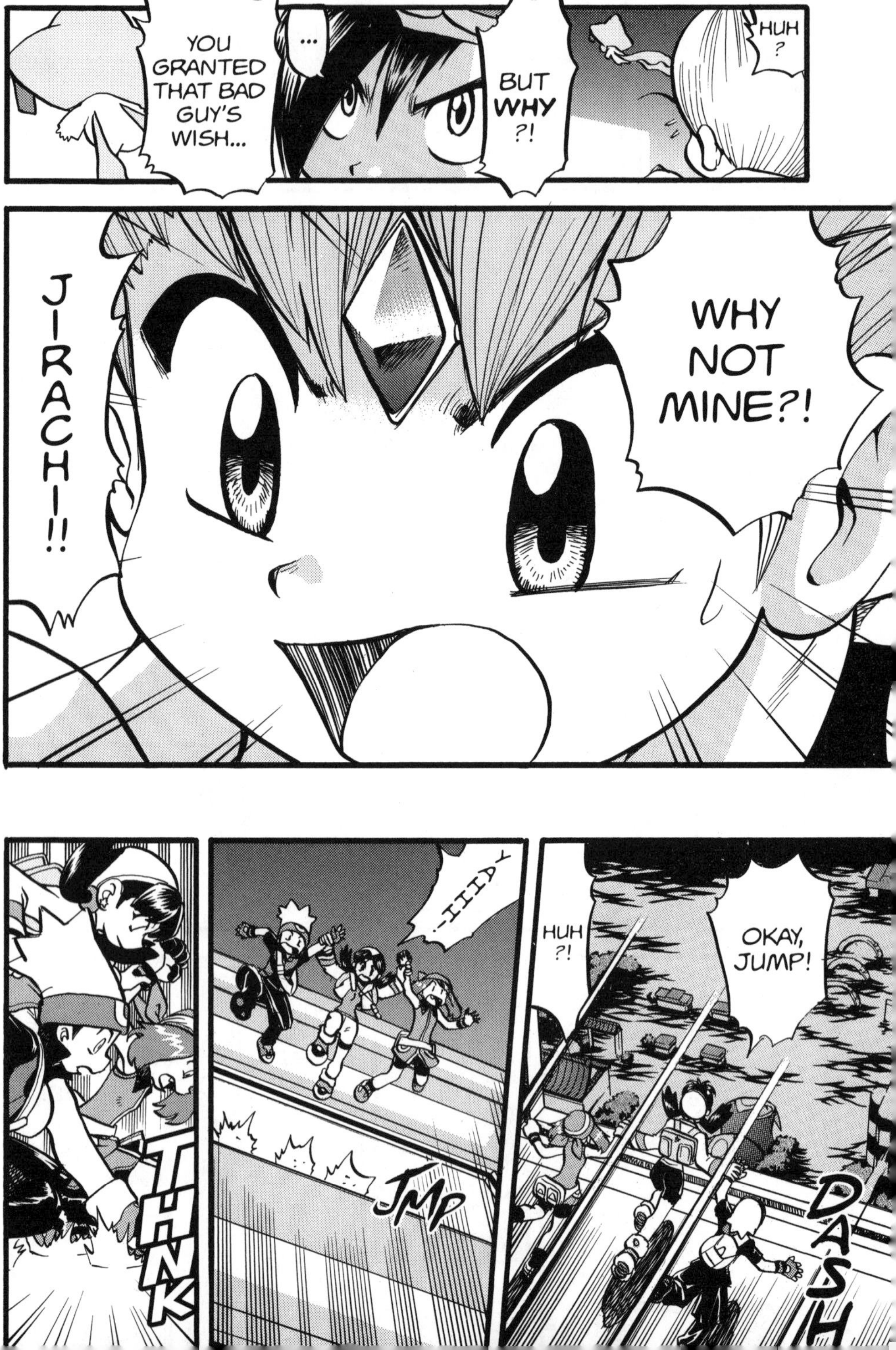
HUH ?
BUT WHY ?!
...
YOU GRANTED THAT BAD GUY'S WISH...
WHY NOT MINE?!
JIRACHI!!
OKAY, JUMP!
HUH ?!
DASH
JMP
THNK

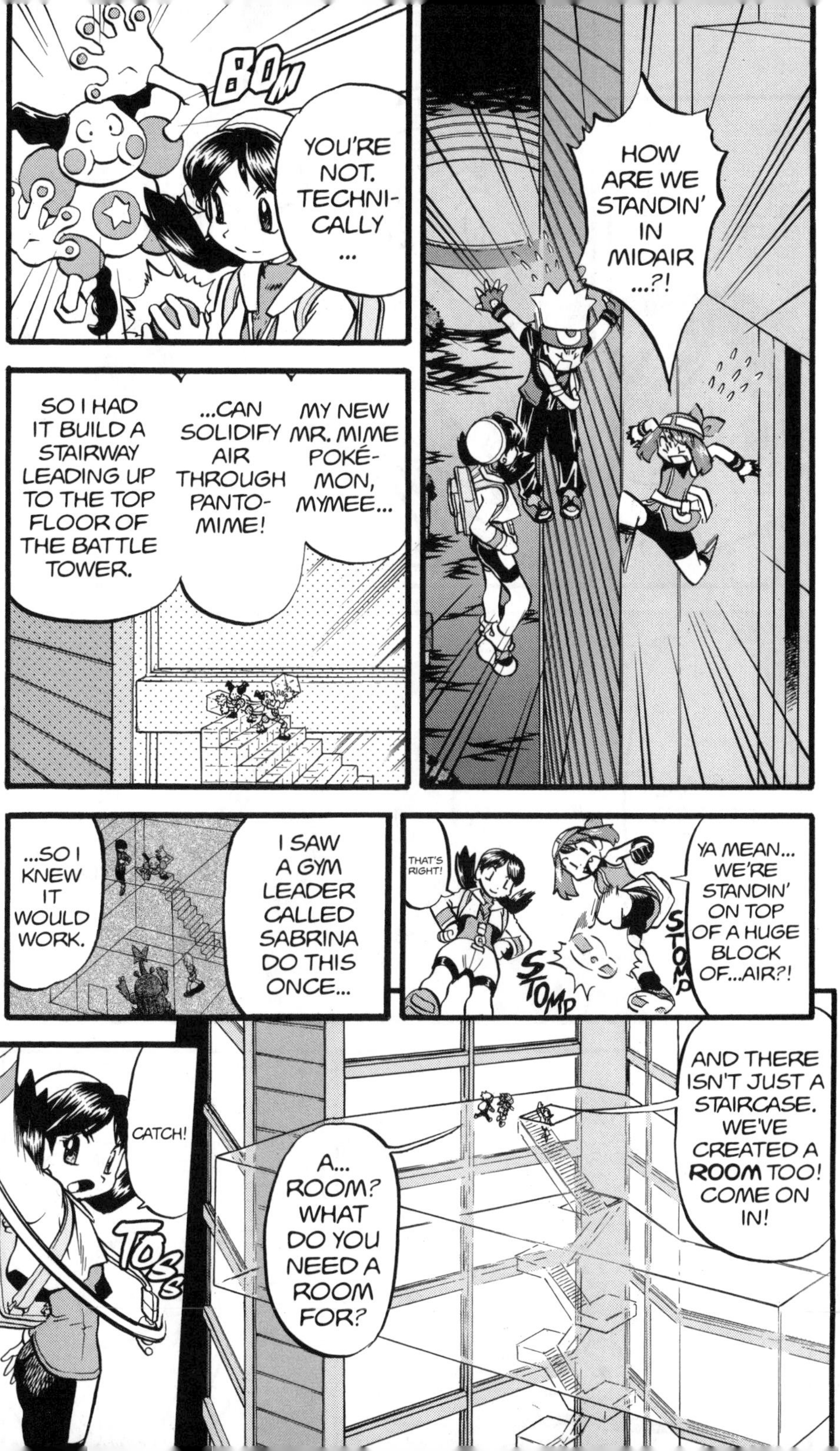
HOW ARE WE STANDIN' IN MIDAIR ...?!
BOM
YOU'RE NOT. TECHNICALLY ...
MY NEW MR. MIME POKÉMON, MYMEE...
...CAN SOLIDIFY AIR THROUGH PANTOMIME!
SO I HAD IT BUILD A STAIRWAY LEADING UP TO THE TOP FLOOR OF THE BATTLE TOWER.
YA MEAN... WE'RE STANDIN' ON TOP OF A HUGE BLOCK OF...AIR?!
STOMP
STOMP
THAT'S RIGHT!
I SAW A GYM LEADER CALLED SABRINA DO THIS ONCE...
...SO I KNEW IT WOULD WORK.
AND THERE ISN'T JUST A STAIRCASE. WE'VE CREATED A **ROOM** TOO! COME ON IN!
A... ROOM? WHAT DO YOU NEED A ROOM FOR?
CATCH!
TOSS

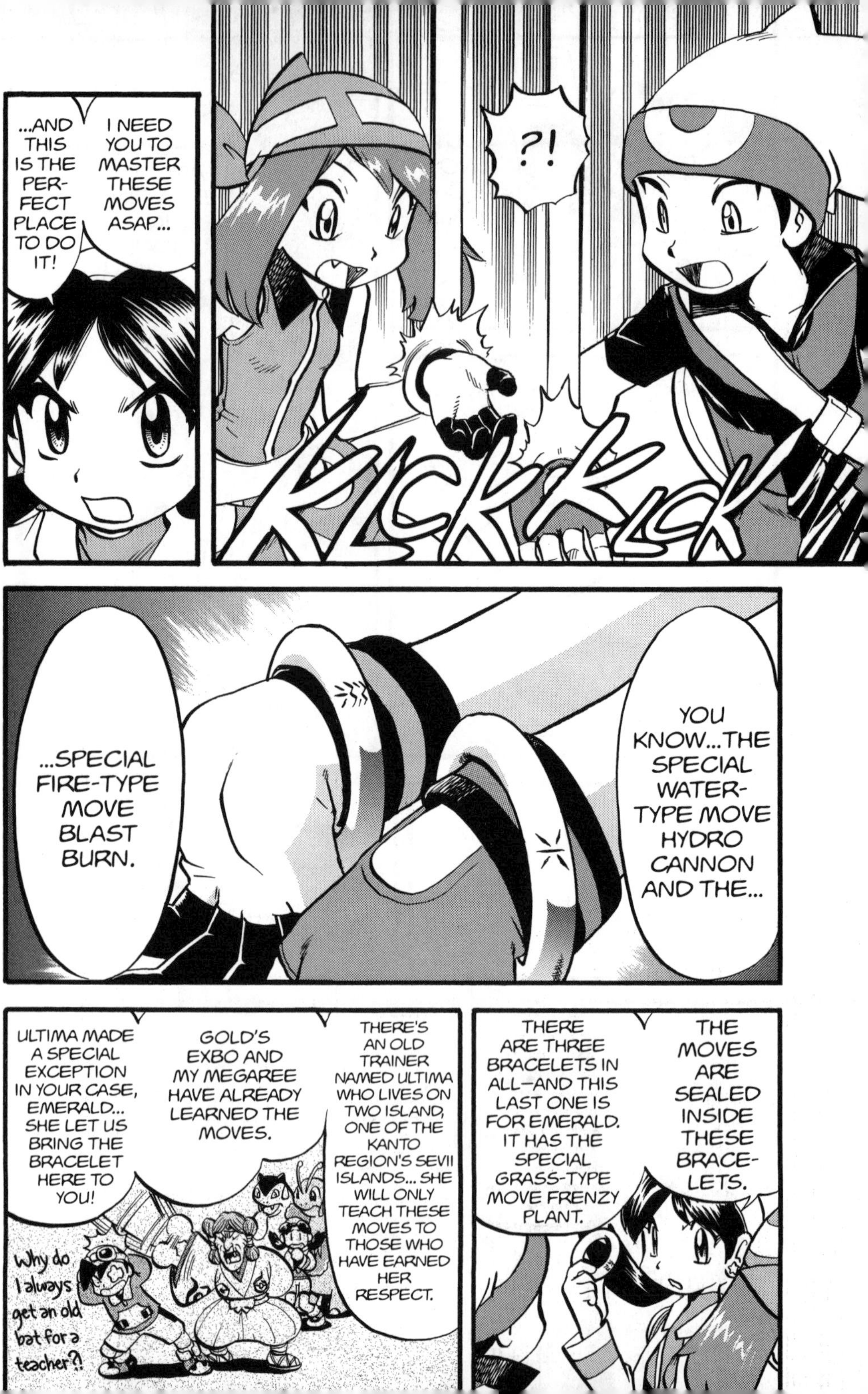
?!
KICK KICK
I NEED YOU TO MASTER THESE MOVES ASAP...
...AND THIS IS THE PERFECT PLACE TO DO IT!
YOU KNOW...THE SPECIAL WATER-TYPE MOVE HYDRO CANNON AND THE...
...SPECIAL FIRE-TYPE MOVE BLAST BURN.
THE MOVES ARE SEALED INSIDE THESE BRACELETS.
THERE ARE THREE BRACELETS IN ALL—AND THIS LAST ONE IS FOR EMERALD. IT HAS THE SPECIAL GRASS-TYPE MOVE FRENZY PLANT.
THERE'S AN OLD TRAINER NAMED ULTIMA WHO LIVES ON TWO ISLAND, ONE OF THE KANTO REGION'S SEVII ISLANDS... SHE WILL ONLY TEACH THESE MOVES TO THOSE WHO HAVE EARNED HER RESPECT.
GOLD'S EXBO AND MY MEGAREE HAVE ALREADY LEARNED THE MOVES.
ULTIMA MADE A SPECIAL EXCEPTION IN YOUR CASE, EMERALD... SHE LET US BRING THE BRACELET HERE TO YOU!
Why do I always get an old bat for a teacher?!

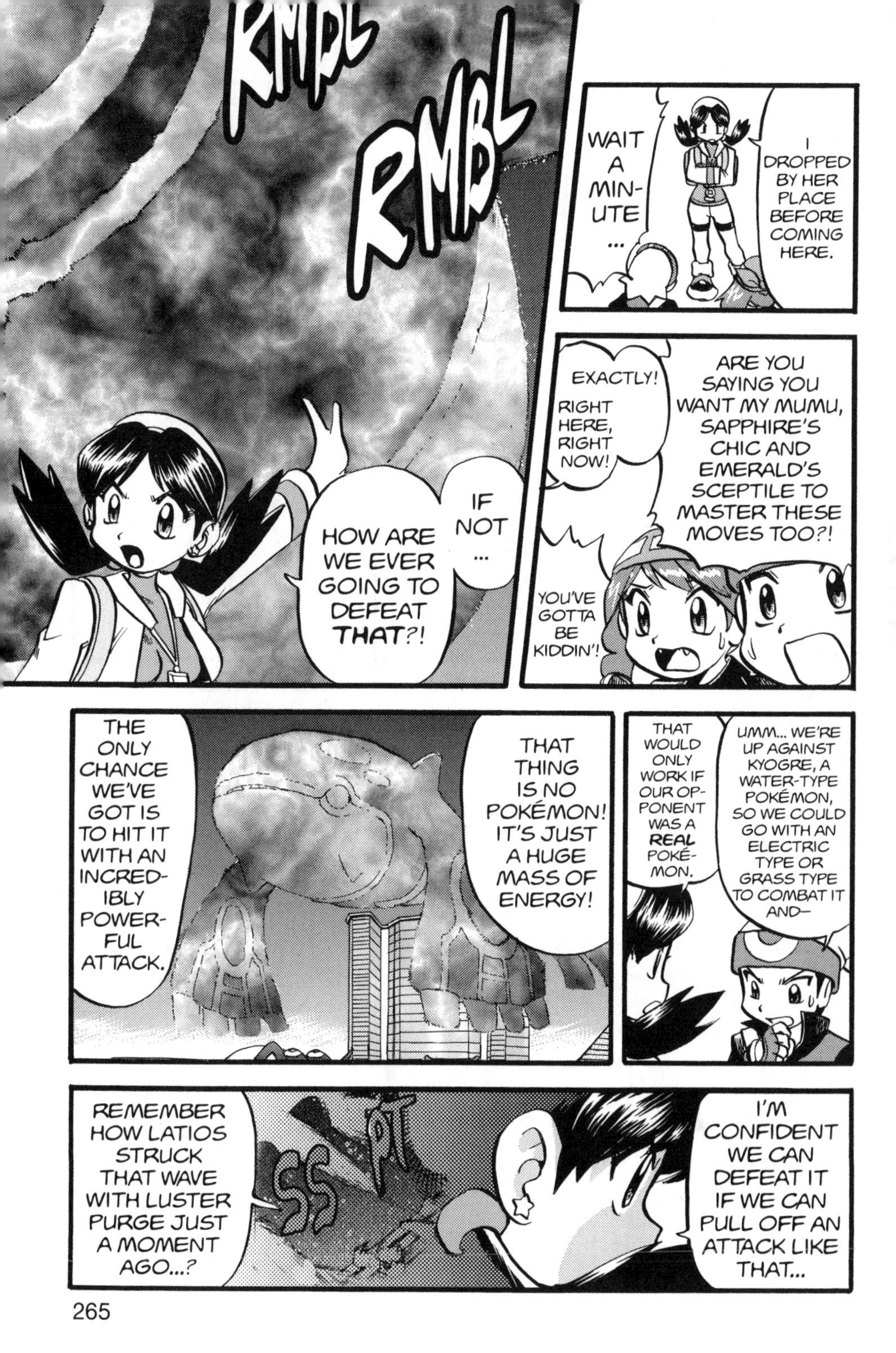
I DROPPED BY HER PLACE BEFORE COMING HERE.
WAIT A MIN-UTE...
ARE YOU SAYING YOU WANT MY MUMU, SAPPHIRE'S CHIC AND EMERALD'S SCEPTILE TO MASTER THESE MOVES TOO?!
EXACTLY!
RIGHT HERE, RIGHT NOW!
YOU'VE GOTTA BE KIDDIN'!
RMBL
RMBL
IF NOT...
HOW ARE WE EVER GOING TO DEFEAT THAT?!
UMM... WE'RE UP AGAINST KYOGRE, A WATER-TYPE POKÉMON, SO WE COULD GO WITH AN ELECTRIC TYPE OR GRASS TYPE TO COMBAT IT AND—
THAT WOULD ONLY WORK IF OUR OP-PONENT WAS A REAL POKÉ-MON.
THAT THING IS NO POKÉMON! IT'S JUST A HUGE MASS OF ENERGY!
THE ONLY CHANCE WE'VE GOT IS TO HIT IT WITH AN INCRED-IBLY POWER-FUL ATTACK.
I'M CONFIDENT WE CAN DEFEAT IT IF WE CAN PULL OFF AN ATTACK LIKE THAT...
REMEMBER HOW LATIOS STRUCK THAT WAVE WITH LUSTER PURGE JUST A MOMENT AGO...?

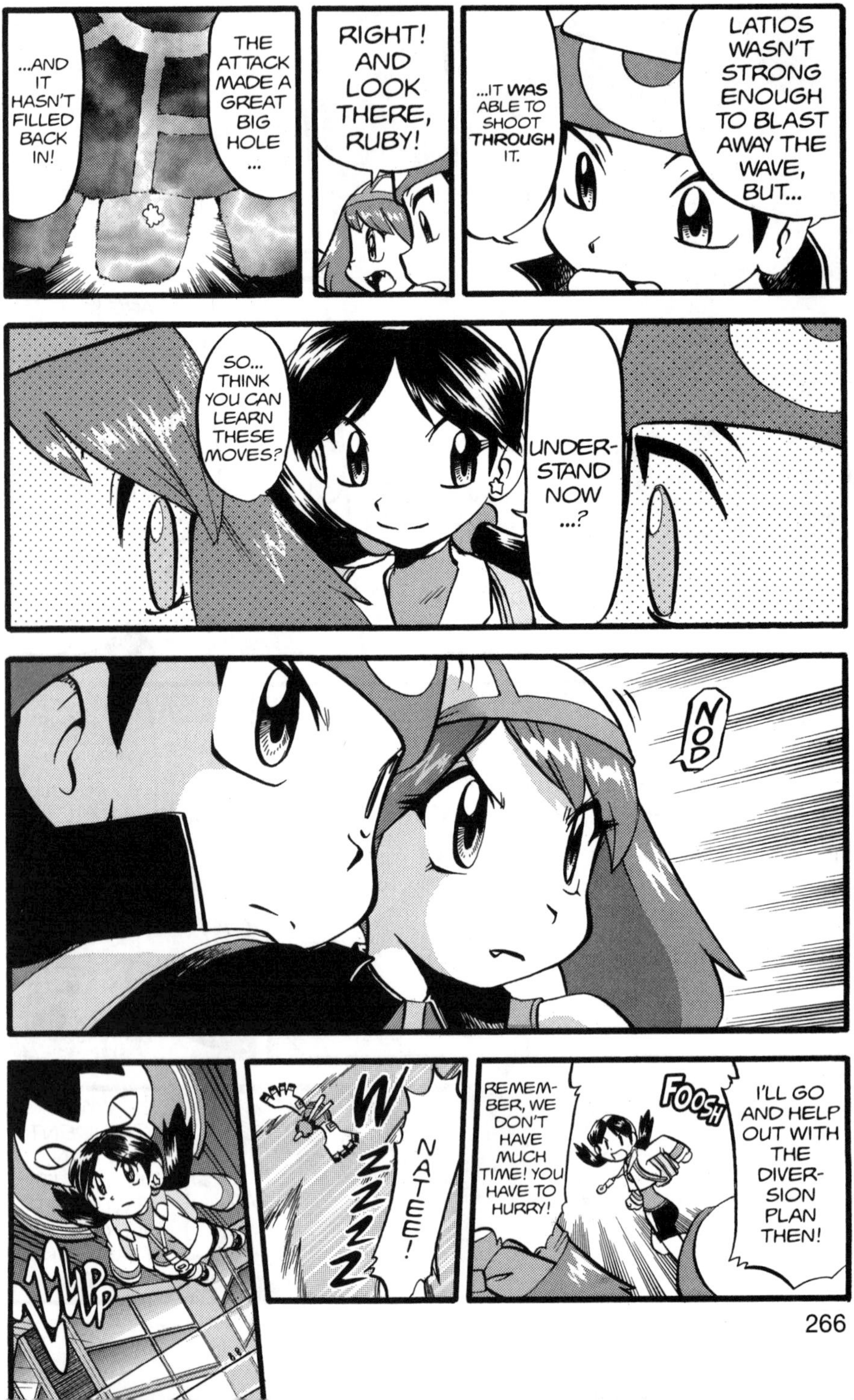
LATIOS WASN'T STRONG ENOUGH TO BLAST AWAY THE WAVE, BUT...
...IT **WAS** ABLE TO SHOOT **THROUGH** IT.
RIGHT! AND LOOK THERE, RUBY!
THE ATTACK MADE A GREAT BIG HOLE...
...AND IT HASN'T FILLED BACK IN!
UNDER-STAND NOW...?
SO... THINK YOU CAN LEARN THESE MOVES?
NOD
I'LL GO AND HELP OUT WITH THE DIVER-SION PLAN THEN!
FOOSH
REMEM-BER, WE DON'T HAVE MUCH TIME! YOU HAVE TO HURRY!
NATEE!
WZZZZZ
ZZIPP

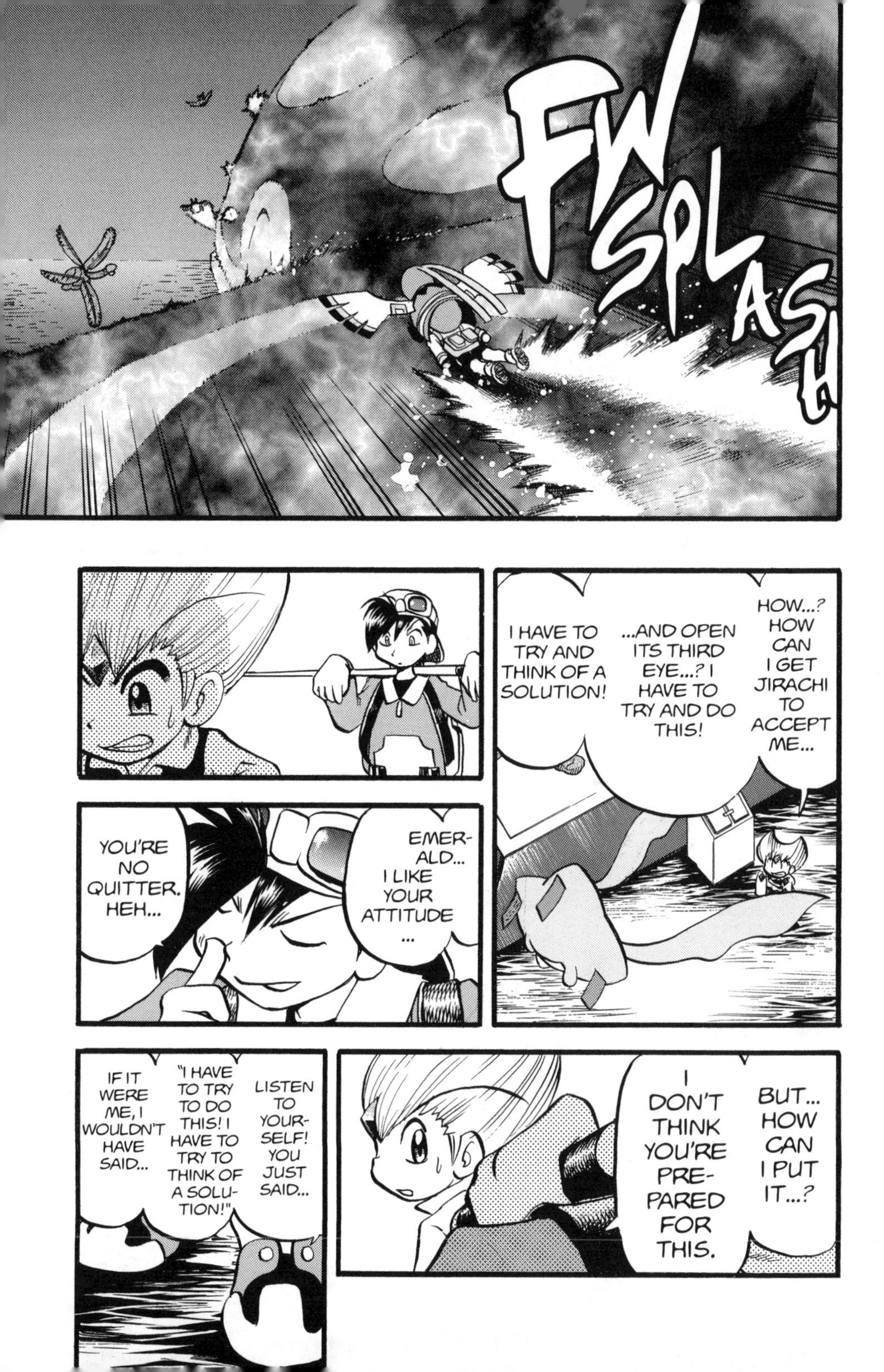
FW
SPLASH
HOW...? HOW CAN I GET JIRACHI TO ACCEPT ME...
...AND OPEN ITS THIRD EYE...? I HAVE TO TRY AND DO THIS!
I HAVE TO TRY AND THINK OF A SOLUTION!
EMERALD... I LIKE YOUR ATTITUDE...
YOU'RE NO QUITTER. HEH...
BUT... HOW CAN I PUT IT...?
I DON'T THINK YOU'RE PREPARED FOR THIS.
LISTEN TO YOURSELF! YOU JUST SAID...
"I HAVE TO TRY TO DO THIS! I HAVE TO TRY TO THINK OF A SOLUTION!"
IF IT WERE ME, I WOULDN'T HAVE SAID...

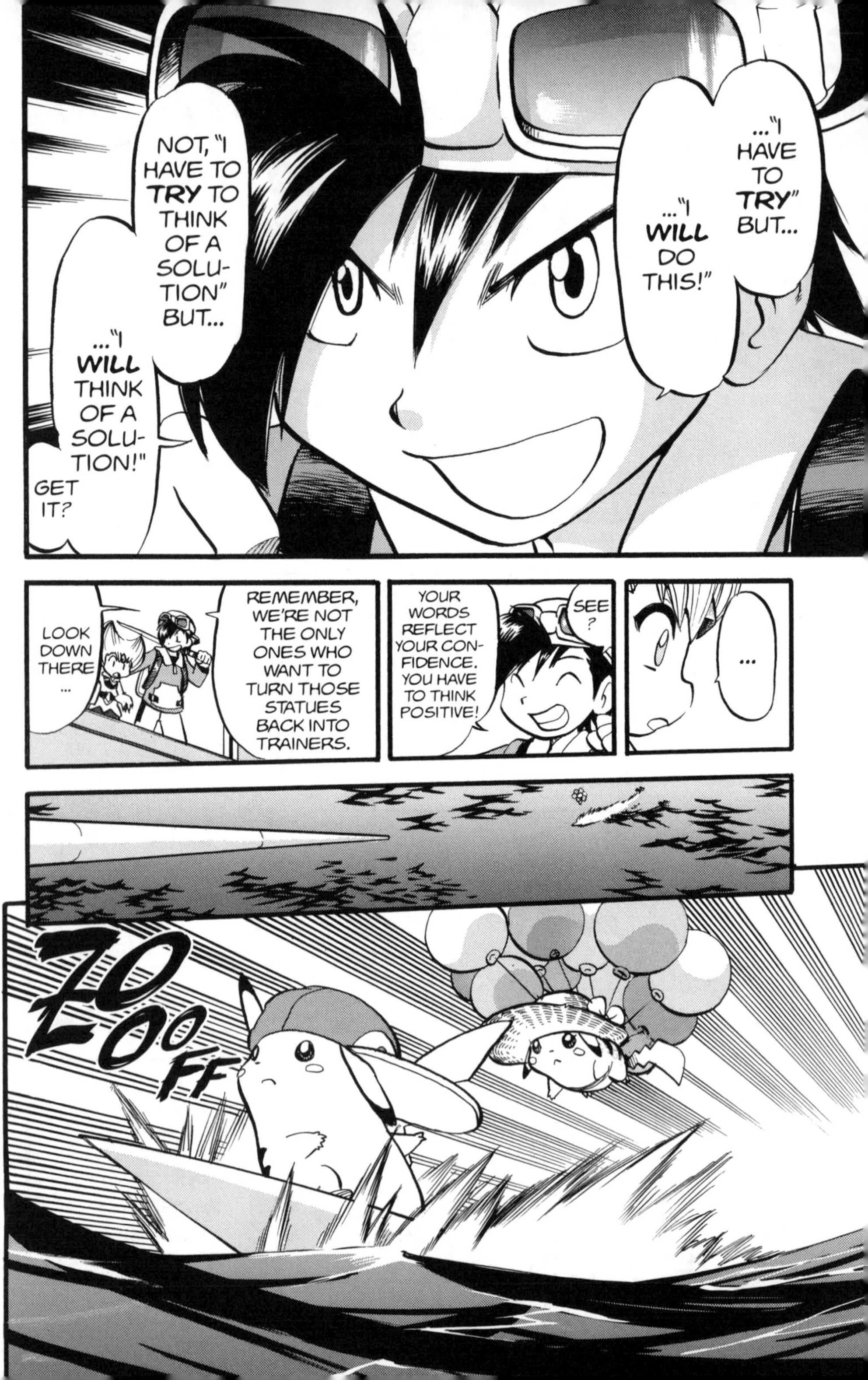
..."I HAVE TO TRY" BUT...
..."I WILL DO THIS!"
NOT, "I HAVE TO TRY TO THINK OF A SOLUTION" BUT...
..."I WILL THINK OF A SOLUTION!"
GET IT?
...
SEE?
YOUR WORDS REFLECT YOUR CONFIDENCE. YOU HAVE TO THINK POSITIVE!
REMEMBER, WE'RE NOT THE ONLY ONES WHO WANT TO TURN THOSE STATUES BACK INTO TRAINERS.
LOOK DOWN THERE ...
ZOOOFF

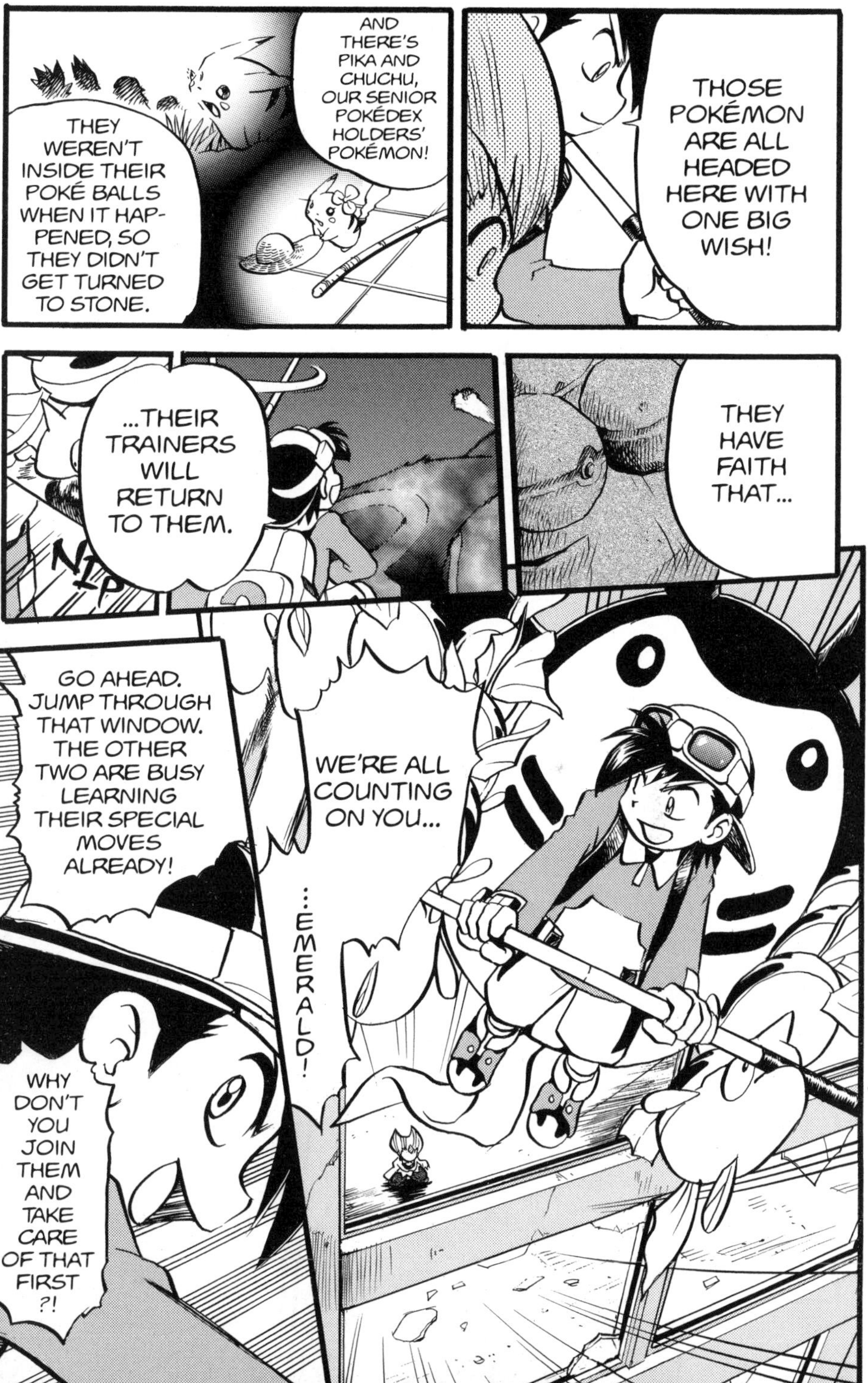
THOSE POKÉMON ARE ALL HEADED HERE WITH ONE BIG WISH!
AND THERE'S PIKA AND CHUCHU, OUR SENIOR POKÉDEX HOLDERS' POKÉMON!
THEY WEREN'T INSIDE THEIR POKÉ BALLS WHEN IT HAPPENED, SO THEY DIDN'T GET TURNED TO STONE.
THEY HAVE FAITH THAT...
...THEIR TRAINERS WILL RETURN TO THEM.
NIP
WE'RE ALL COUNTING ON YOU...
...EMERALD!
GO AHEAD. JUMP THROUGH THAT WINDOW. THE OTHER TWO ARE BUSY LEARNING THEIR SPECIAL MOVES ALREADY!
WHY DON'T YOU JOIN THEM AND TAKE CARE OF THAT FIRST?!

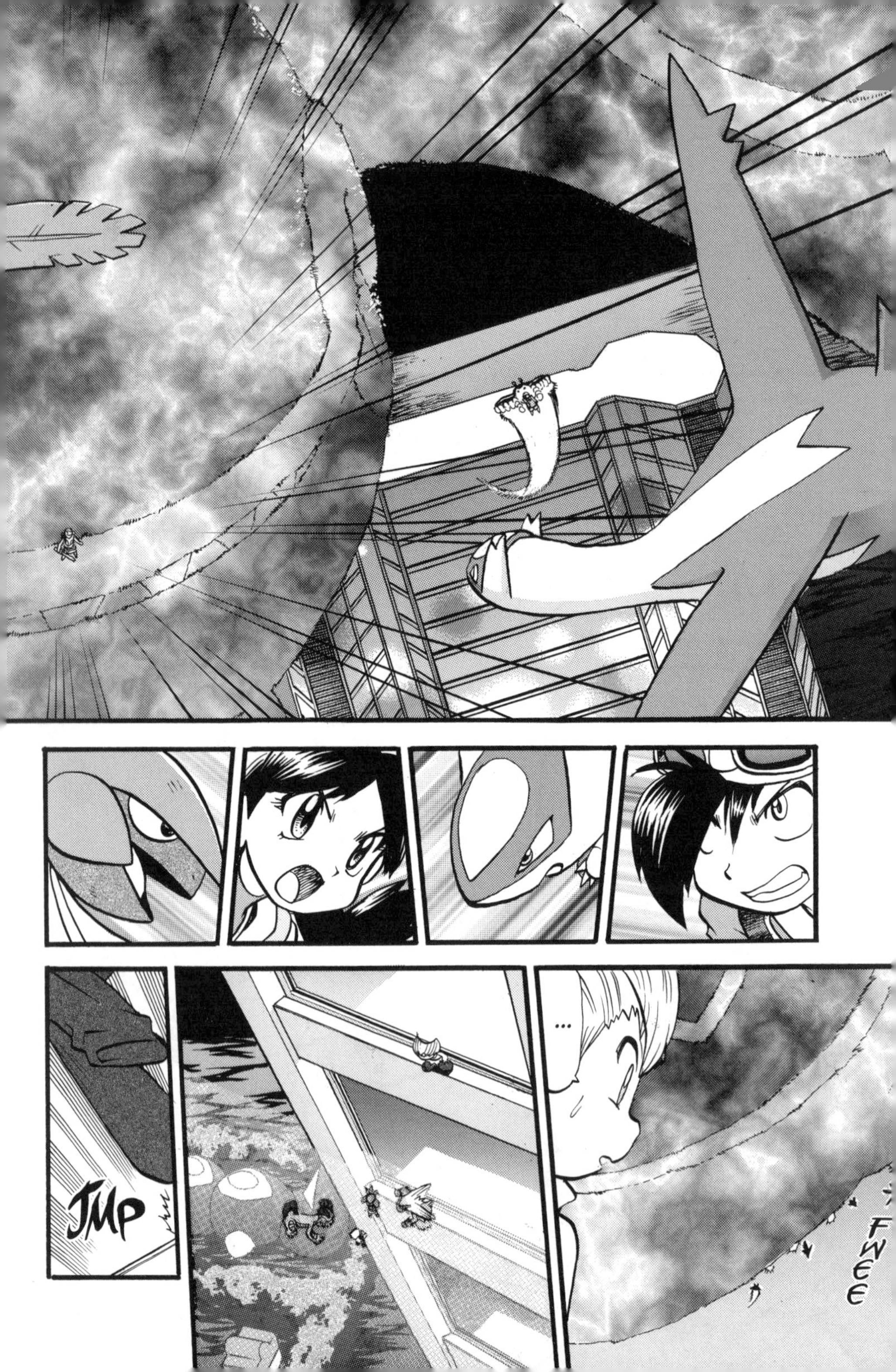
FWEE
...
JMP

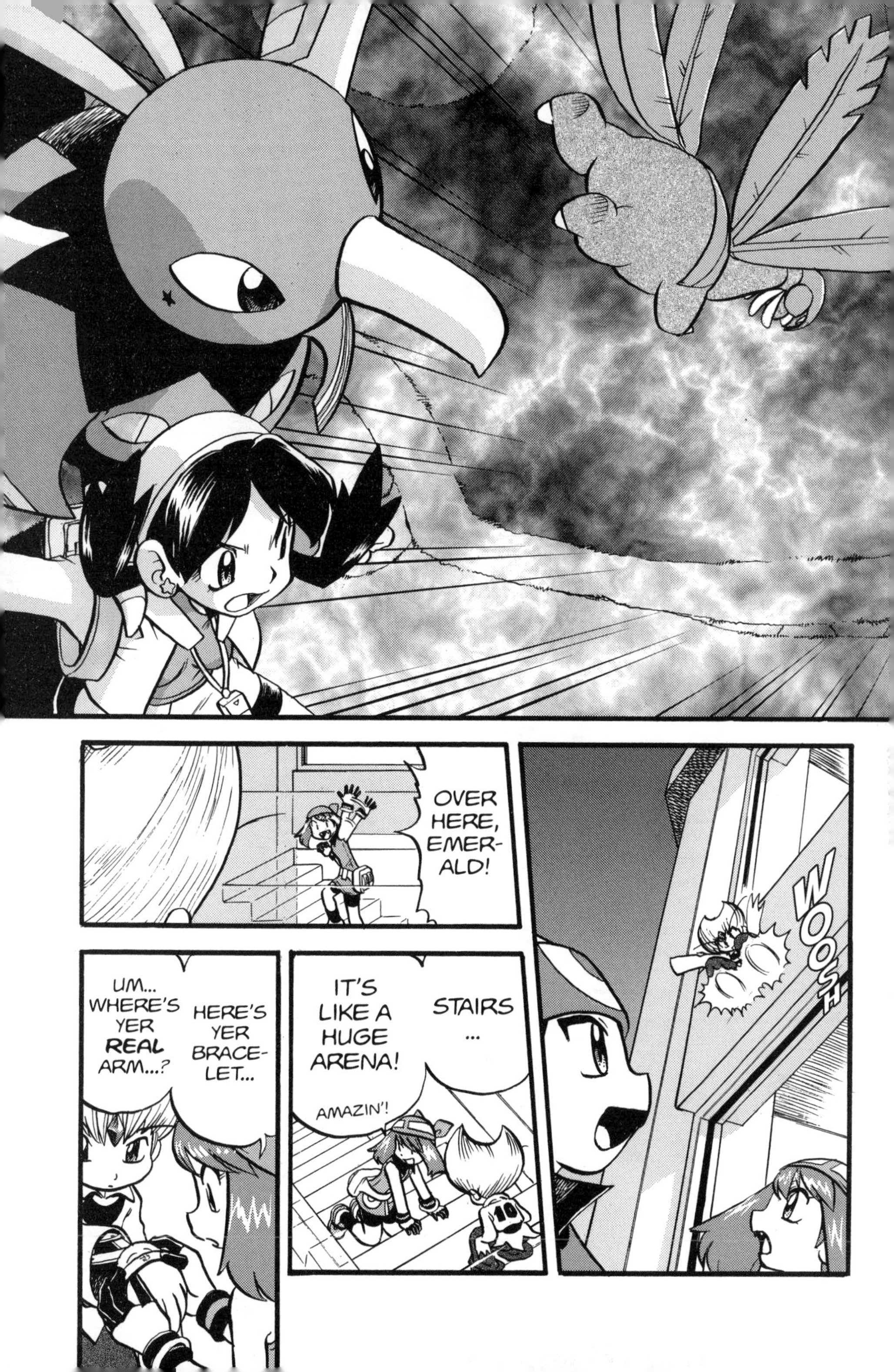
WOOSH
OVER HERE, EMERALD!
STAIRS ...
IT'S LIKE A HUGE ARENA!
AMAZIN'!
HERE'S YER BRACELET...
UM... WHERE'S YER **REAL** ARM...?

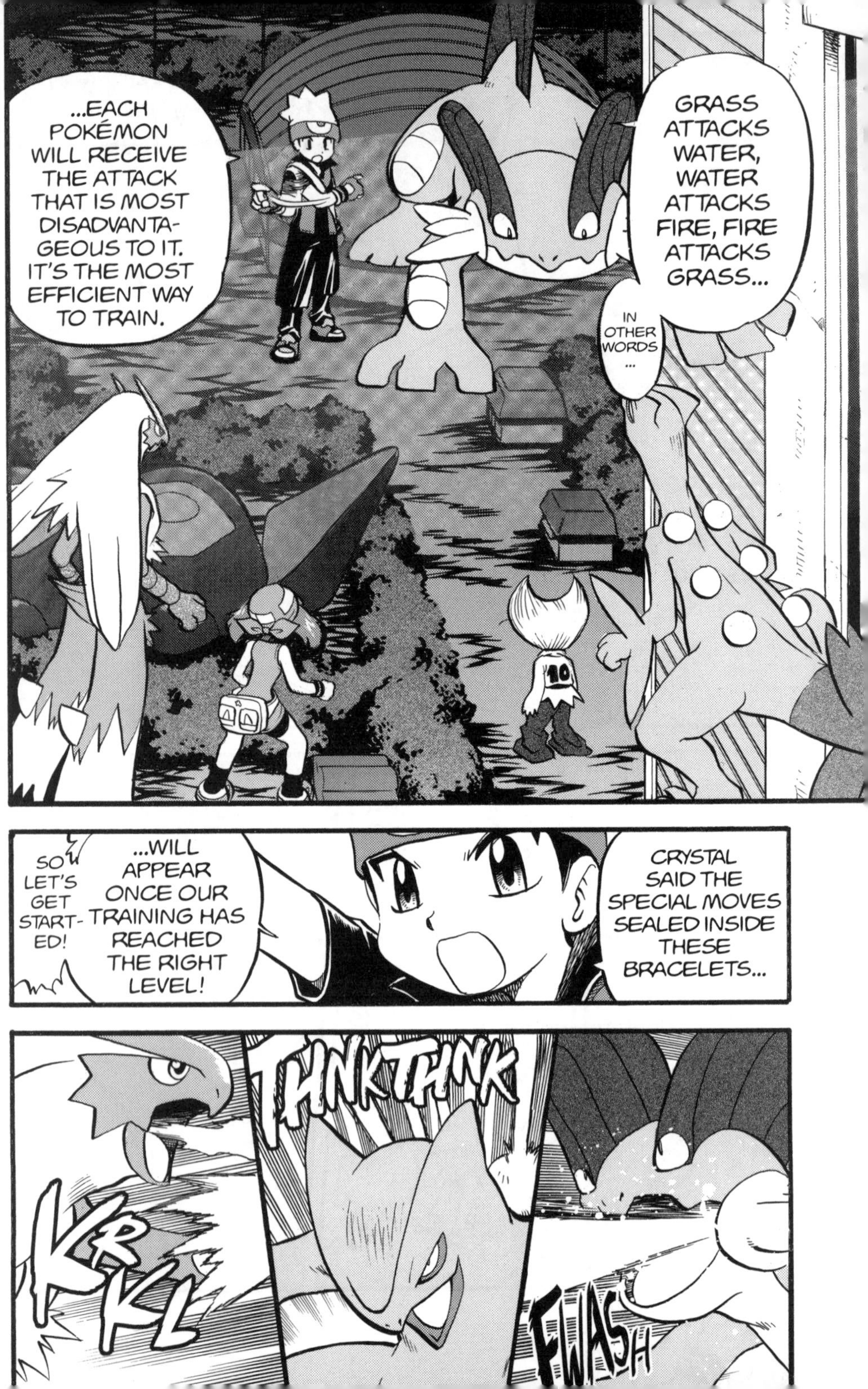
GRASS ATTACKS WATER, WATER ATTACKS FIRE, FIRE ATTACKS GRASS...
IN OTHER WORDS...
...EACH POKÉMON WILL RECEIVE THE ATTACK THAT IS MOST DISADVANTA-GEOUS TO IT. IT'S THE MOST EFFICIENT WAY TO TRAIN.
CRYSTAL SAID THE SPECIAL MOVES SEALED INSIDE THESE BRACELETS...
...WILL APPEAR ONCE OUR TRAINING HAS REACHED THE RIGHT LEVEL!
SO LET'S GET START-ED!
FWASH
THNKTHINK
KRKL

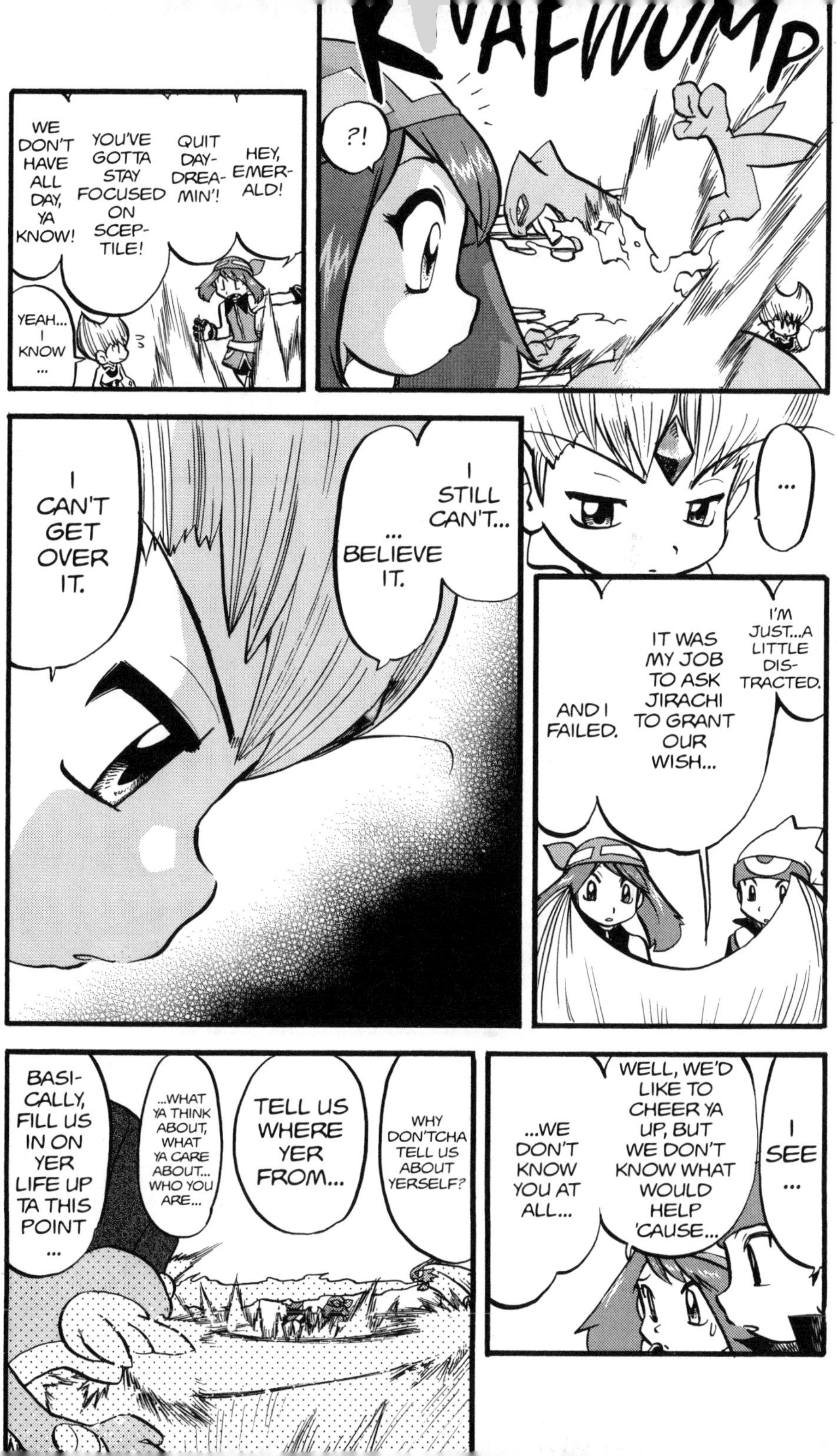
KWAFWUMP
?!
HEY, EMERALD!
QUIT DAYDREAMIN'!
YOU'VE GOTTA STAY FOCUSED ON SCEPTILE!
WE DON'T HAVE ALL DAY, YA KNOW!
YEAH... I KNOW...
...
I'M JUST...A LITTLE DISTRACTED.
IT WAS MY JOB TO ASK JIRACHI TO GRANT OUR WISH...
AND I FAILED.
I STILL CAN'T... ... BELIEVE IT.
I CAN'T GET OVER IT.
I SEE...
WELL, WE'D LIKE TO CHEER YA UP, BUT WE DON'T KNOW WHAT WOULD HELP 'CAUSE...
...WE DON'T KNOW YOU AT ALL...
WHY DON'TCHA TELL US ABOUT YERSELF?
TELL US WHERE YER FROM...
...WHAT YA THINK ABOUT, WHAT YA CARE ABOUT... WHO YOU ARE...
BASICALLY, FILL US IN ON YER LIFE UP TA THIS POINT...

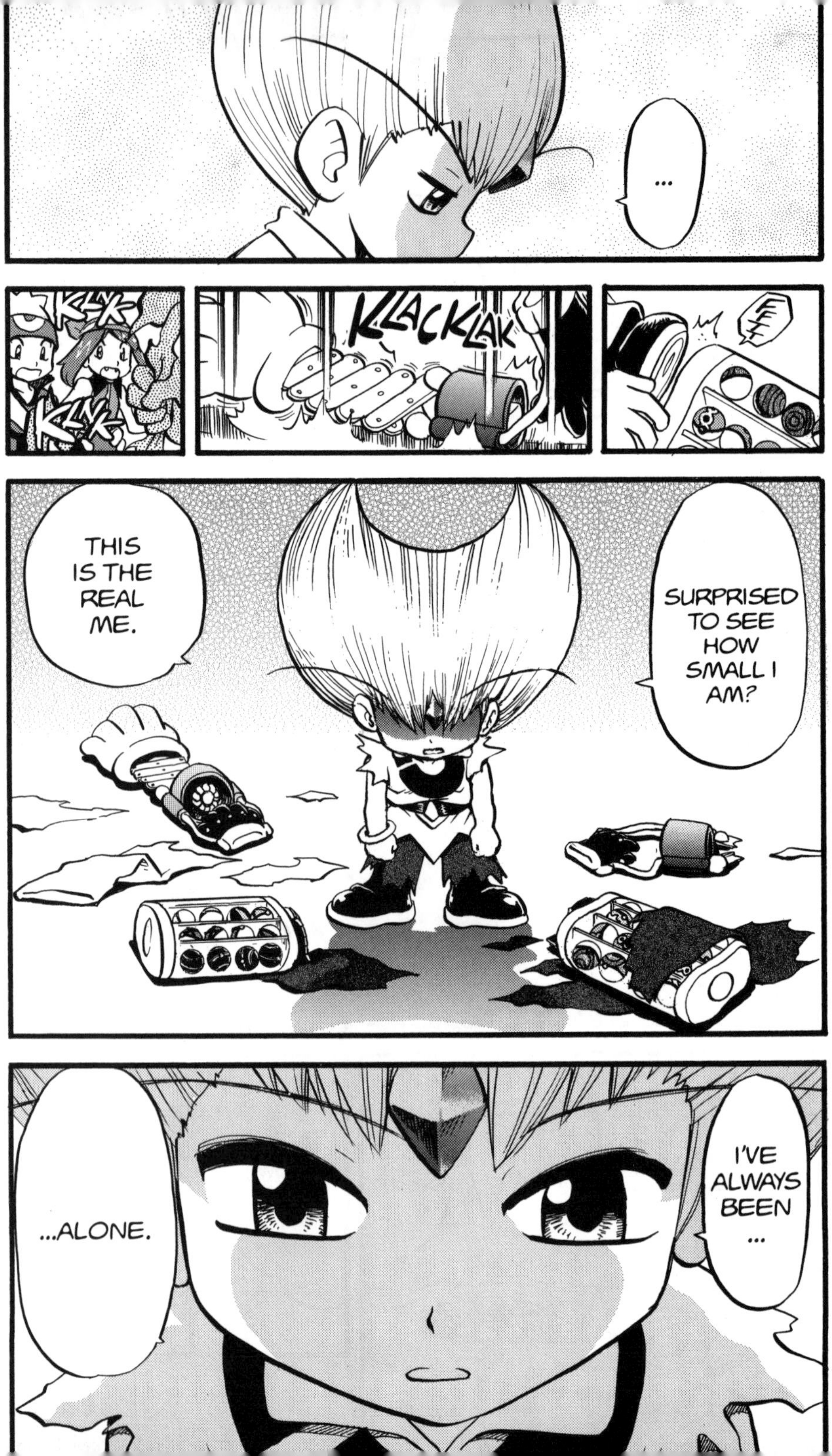
...
KLACKLAK
KLNK
KLNK
SURPRISED TO SEE HOW SMALL I AM?
THIS IS THE REAL ME.
I'VE ALWAYS BEEN ...
...ALONE.

GOLD

A SHARP-TONGUED BUT KINDHEARTED POKÉMON TRAINER FROM JOHTO. RECENTLY, GOLD CAME TO ACCEPT THAT, AS ONE OF THE POKÉDEX HOLDERS, HE IS FATED TO FIGHT THE MASK OF ICE AND OPPOSE HIS EVIL SCHEMES. GOLD GIVES THE IMPRESSION THAT HE'S SELF-CENTERED, BUT HE IS UNABLE TO IGNORE PEOPLE AND POKÉMON IN NEED. THE HOME HE SHARES WITH MANY POKÉMON HAS BEEN DUBBED THE "POKÉMON HOUSE." GOLD IS KNOWN AS THE "HATCHER."

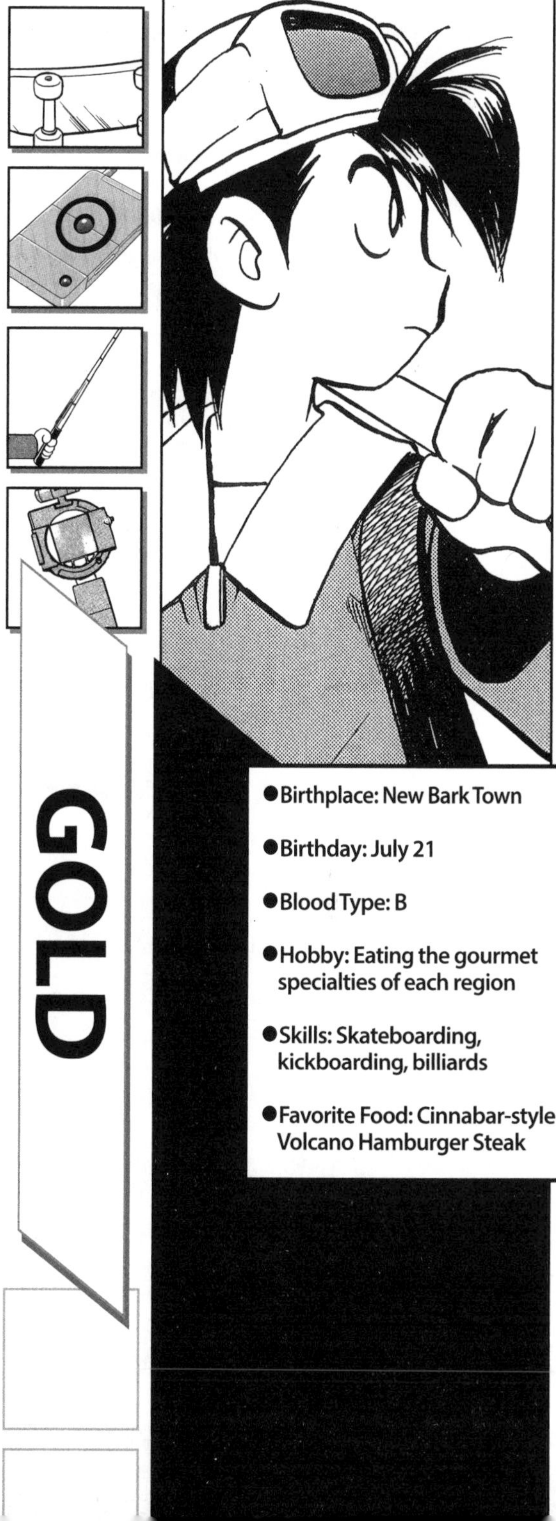

- Birthplace: New Bark Town
- Birthday: July 21
- Blood Type: B
- Hobby: Eating the gourmet specialties of each region
- Skills: Skateboarding, kickboarding, billiards
- Favorite Food: Cinnabar-style Volcano Hamburger Steak

331

The Final Battle, Part 4

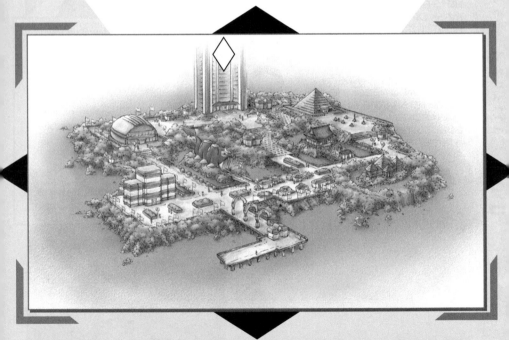

POKÉMON ADVENTURES·THE SIXTH CHAPTER·EMERALD

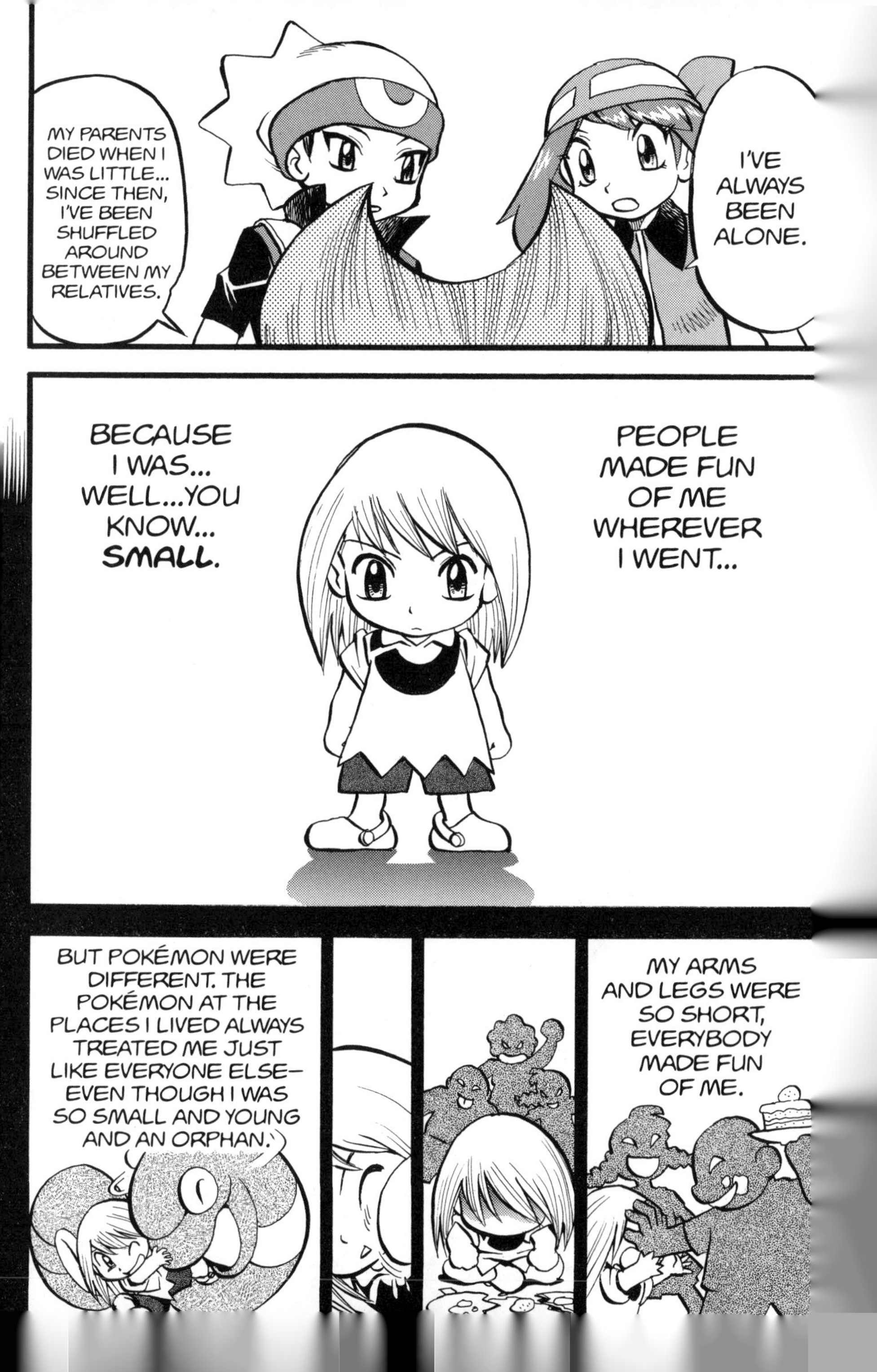
I'VE ALWAYS BEEN ALONE.
MY PARENTS DIED WHEN I WAS LITTLE... SINCE THEN, I'VE BEEN SHUFFLED AROUND BETWEEN MY RELATIVES.
PEOPLE MADE FUN OF ME WHEREVER I WENT...
BECAUSE I WAS... WELL...YOU KNOW... **SMALL.**
MY ARMS AND LEGS WERE SO SHORT, EVERYBODY MADE FUN OF ME.
BUT POKÉMON WERE DIFFERENT. THE POKÉMON AT THE PLACES I LIVED ALWAYS TREATED ME JUST LIKE EVERYONE ELSE—EVEN THOUGH I WAS SO SMALL AND YOUNG AND AN ORPHAN.

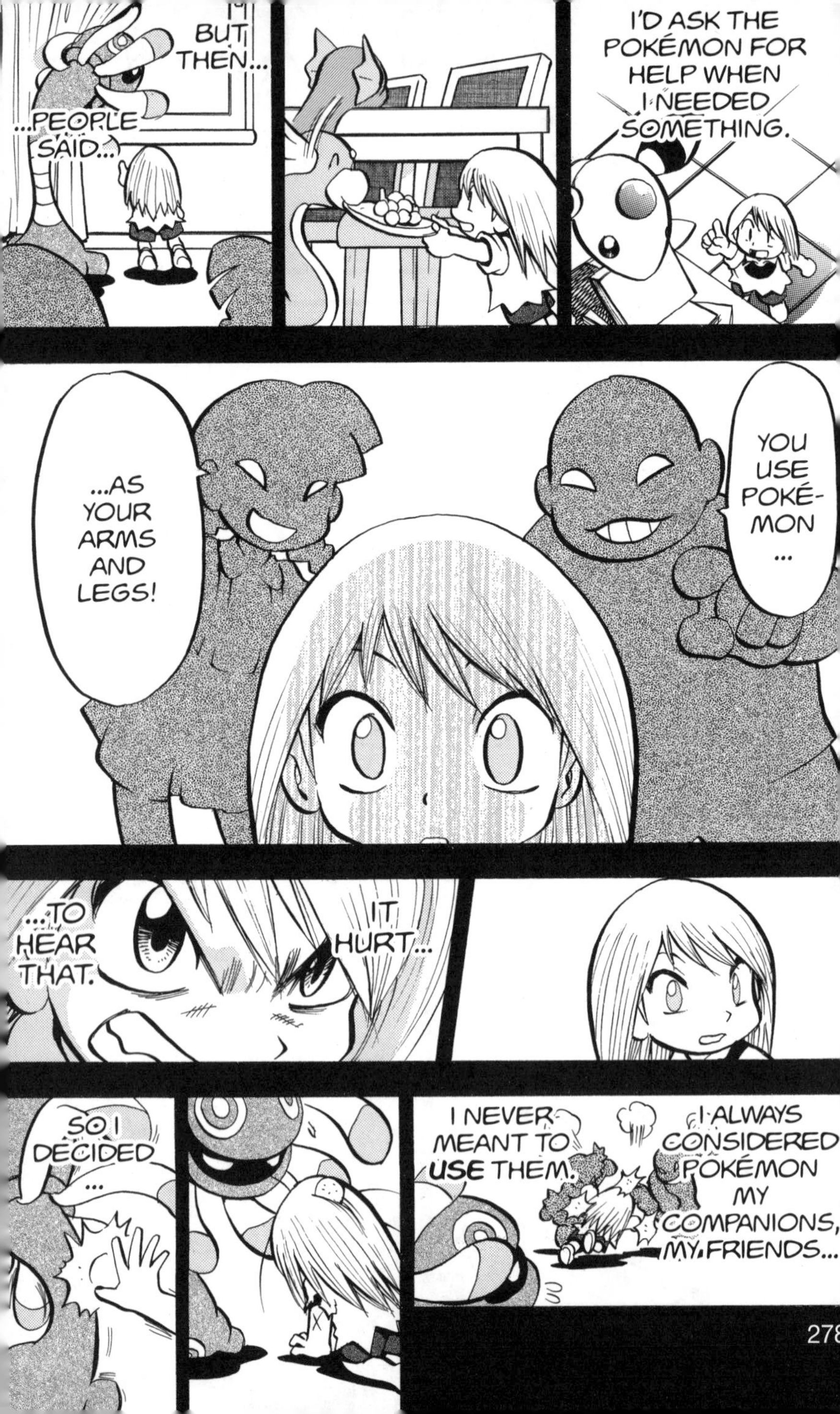
I'D ASK THE POKÉMON FOR HELP WHEN I NEEDED SOMETHING.
BUT THEN...
...PEOPLE SAID...
YOU USE POKÉMON...
...AS YOUR ARMS AND LEGS!
IT HURT...
...TO HEAR THAT.
I ALWAYS CONSIDERED POKÉMON MY COMPANIONS, MY FRIENDS...
I NEVER MEANT TO USE THEM.
SO I DECIDED...

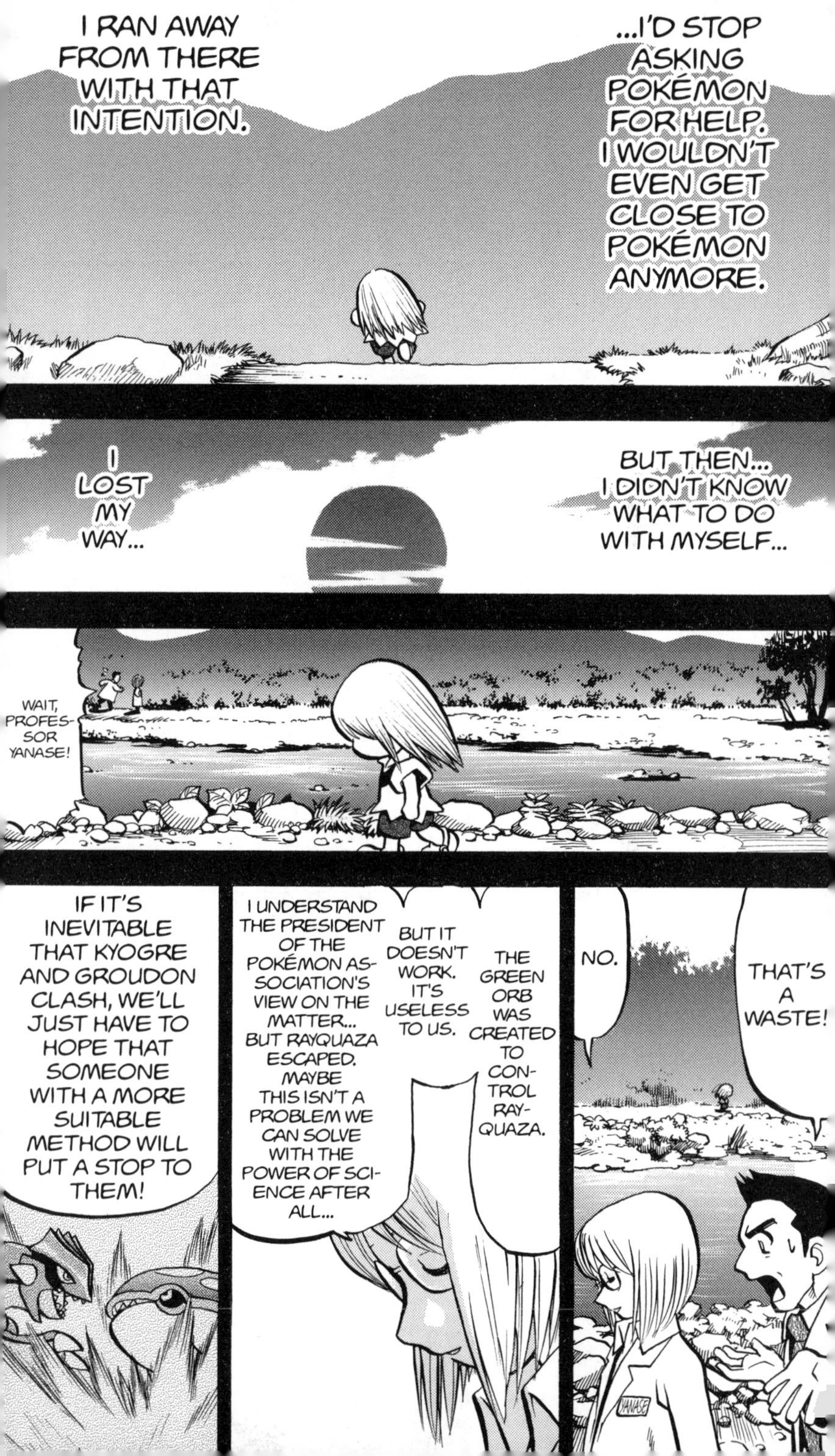

...I'D STOP ASKING POKÉMON FOR HELP. I WOULDN'T EVEN GET CLOSE TO POKÉMON ANYMORE.
I RAN AWAY FROM THERE WITH THAT INTENTION.
BUT THEN... I DIDN'T KNOW WHAT TO DO WITH MYSELF...
I LOST MY WAY...
WAIT, PROFES-SOR YANASE!
THAT'S A WASTE!
NO.
YANASE
THE GREEN ORB WAS CREATED TO CON-TROL RAY-QUAZA.
BUT IT DOESN'T WORK. IT'S USELESS TO US.
I UNDERSTAND THE PRESIDENT OF THE POKÉMON AS-SOCIATION'S VIEW ON THE MATTER... BUT RAYQUAZA ESCAPED. MAYBE THIS ISN'T A PROBLEM WE CAN SOLVE WITH THE POWER OF SCI-ENCE AFTER ALL...
IF IT'S INEVITABLE THAT KYOGRE AND GROUDON CLASH, WE'LL JUST HAVE TO HOPE THAT SOMEONE WITH A MORE SUITABLE METHOD WILL PUT A STOP TO THEM!

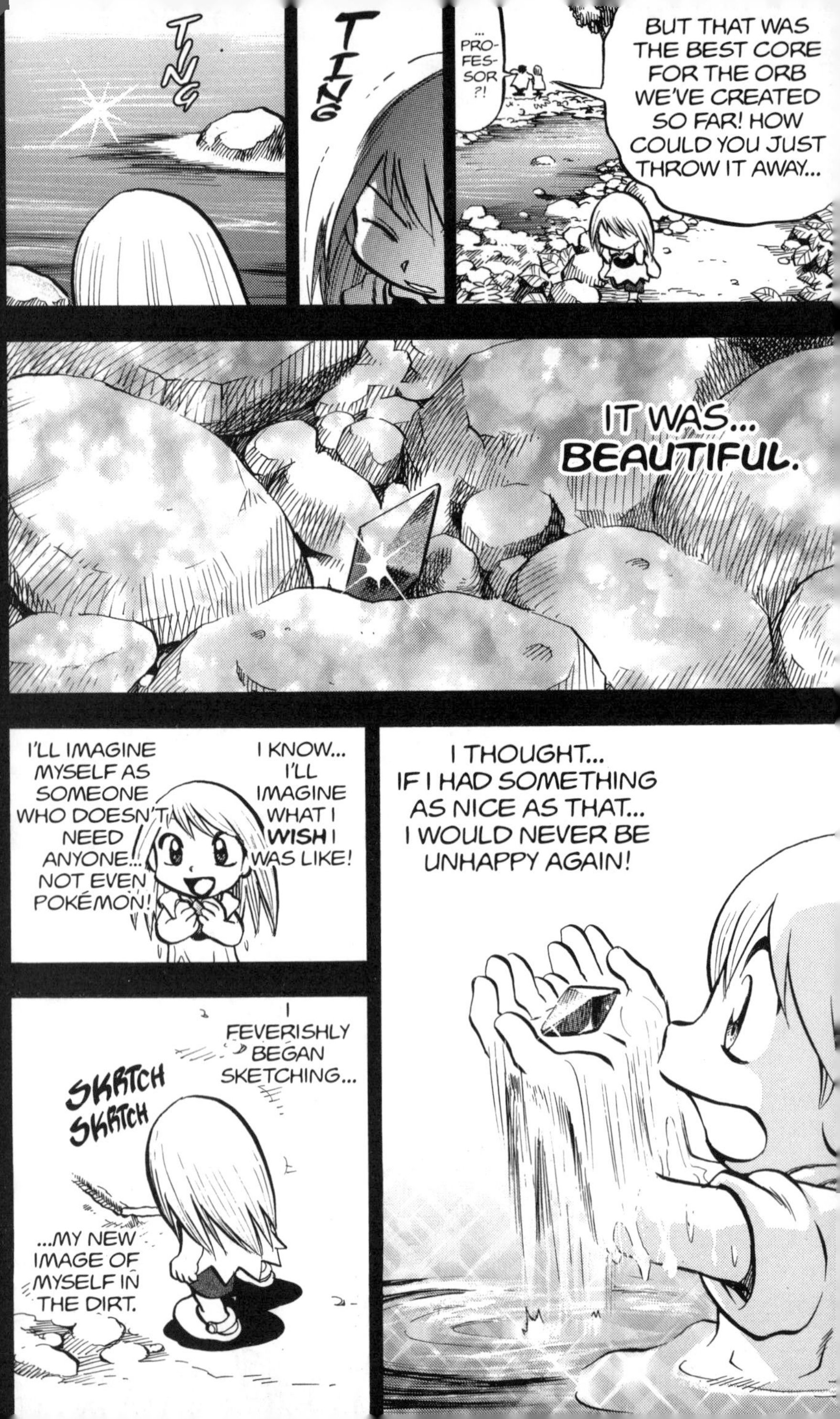
BUT THAT WAS THE BEST CORE FOR THE ORB WE'VE CREATED SO FAR! HOW COULD YOU JUST THROW IT AWAY...
...PROFESSOR?!
TING
TING
IT WAS... BEAUTIFUL.
I THOUGHT... IF I HAD SOMETHING AS NICE AS THAT... I WOULD NEVER BE UNHAPPY AGAIN!
I KNOW... I'LL IMAGINE WHAT I WISH I WAS LIKE!
I'LL IMAGINE MYSELF AS SOMEONE WHO DOESN'T NEED ANYONE... NOT EVEN POKÉMON!
I FEVERISHLY BEGAN SKETCHING...
SKRTCH SKRTCH
...MY NEW IMAGE OF MYSELF IN THE DIRT.

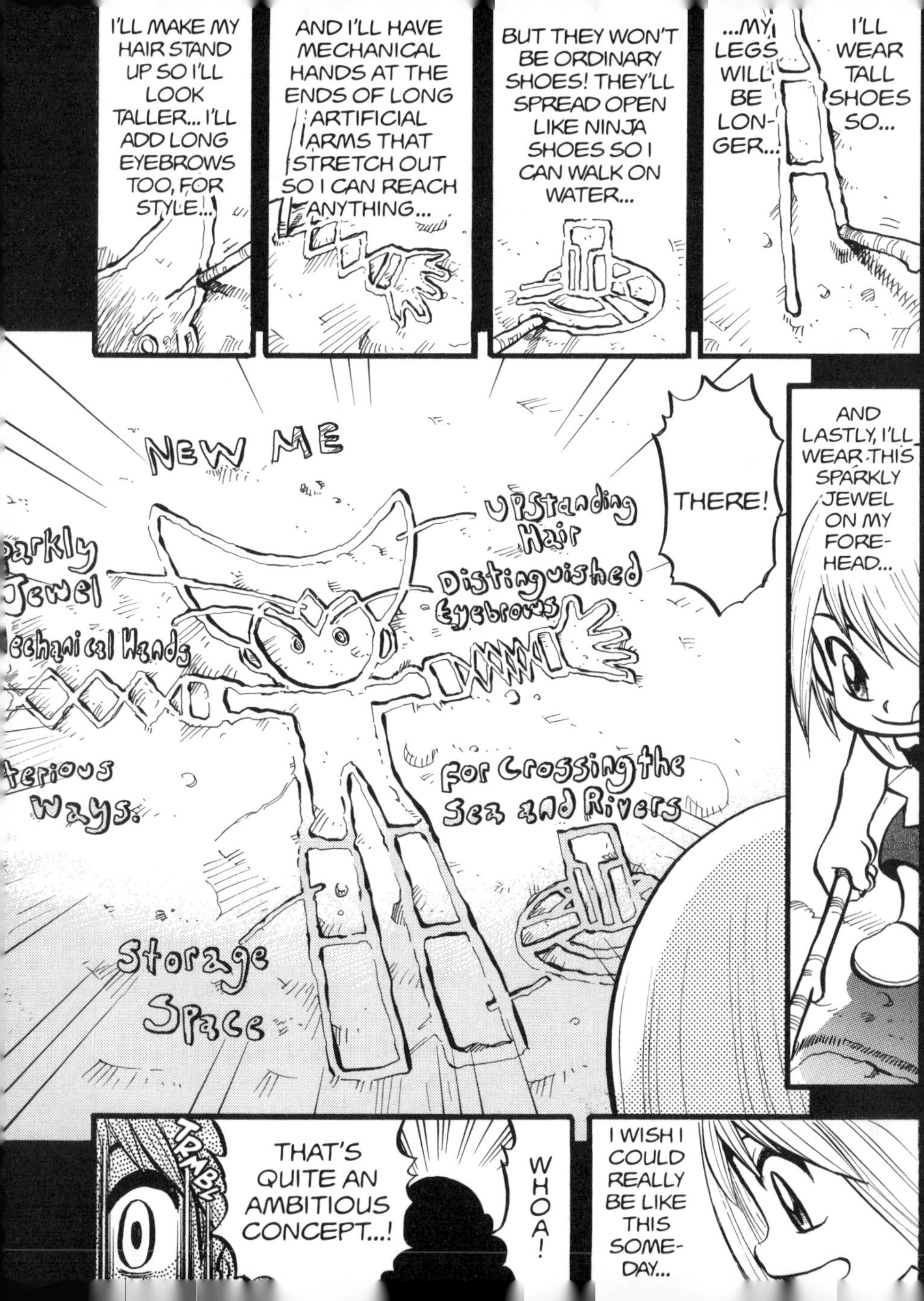

I'LL WEAR TALL SHOES SO...
...MY LEGS WILL BE LONGER...
BUT THEY WON'T BE ORDINARY SHOES! THEY'LL SPREAD OPEN LIKE NINJA SHOES SO I CAN WALK ON WATER...
AND I'LL HAVE MECHANICAL HANDS AT THE ENDS OF LONG ARTIFICIAL ARMS THAT STRETCH OUT SO I CAN REACH ANYTHING...
I'LL MAKE MY HAIR STAND UP SO I'LL LOOK TALLER... I'LL ADD LONG EYEBROWS TOO, FOR STYLE...
AND LASTLY, I'LL WEAR THIS SPARKLY JEWEL ON MY FOREHEAD...
THERE!
NEW ME
Upstanding Hair
Distinguished Eyebrows
parkly Jewel
echanical Hands
terious Ways.
For Crossing the Sea and Rivers
Storage Space
I WISH I COULD REALLY BE LIKE THIS SOMEDAY...
WHOA!
THAT'S QUITE AN AMBITIOUS CONCEPT...!
TRMBL

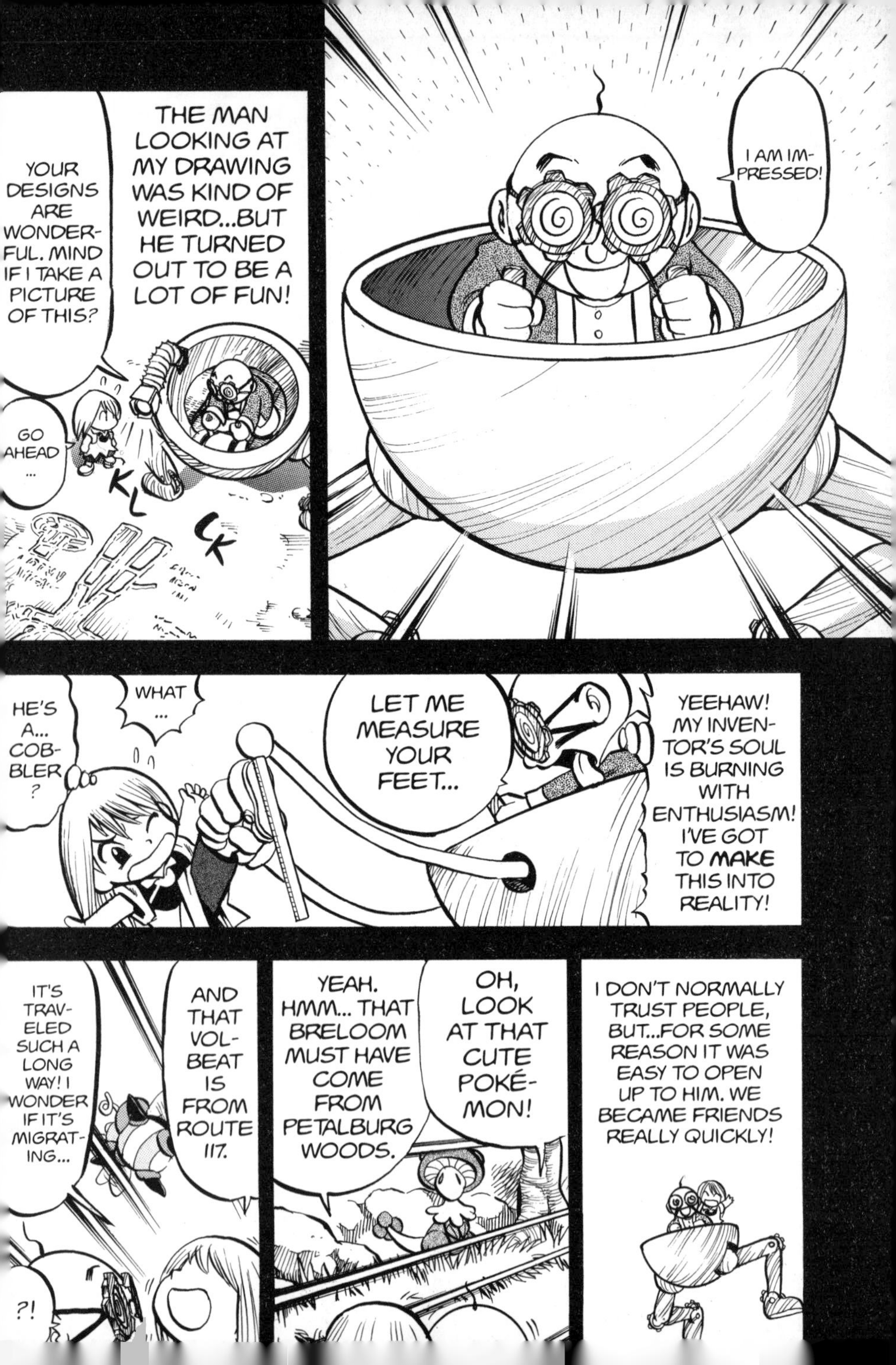
I AM IMPRESSED!
THE MAN LOOKING AT MY DRAWING WAS KIND OF WEIRD...BUT HE TURNED OUT TO BE A LOT OF FUN!
YOUR DESIGNS ARE WONDERFUL. MIND IF I TAKE A PICTURE OF THIS?
GO AHEAD ...
KL
CK
YEEHAW! MY INVENTOR'S SOUL IS BURNING WITH ENTHUSIASM! I'VE GOT TO **MAKE** THIS INTO REALITY!
LET ME MEASURE YOUR FEET...
WHAT ...
HE'S A... COBBLER ?
I DON'T NORMALLY TRUST PEOPLE, BUT...FOR SOME REASON IT WAS EASY TO OPEN UP TO HIM. WE BECAME FRIENDS REALLY QUICKLY!
OH, LOOK AT THAT CUTE POKÉMON!
YEAH. HMM... THAT BRELOOM MUST HAVE COME FROM PETALBURG WOODS.
AND THAT VOLBEAT IS FROM ROUTE 117.
IT'S TRAVELED SUCH A LONG WAY! I WONDER IF IT'S MIGRATING...
?!

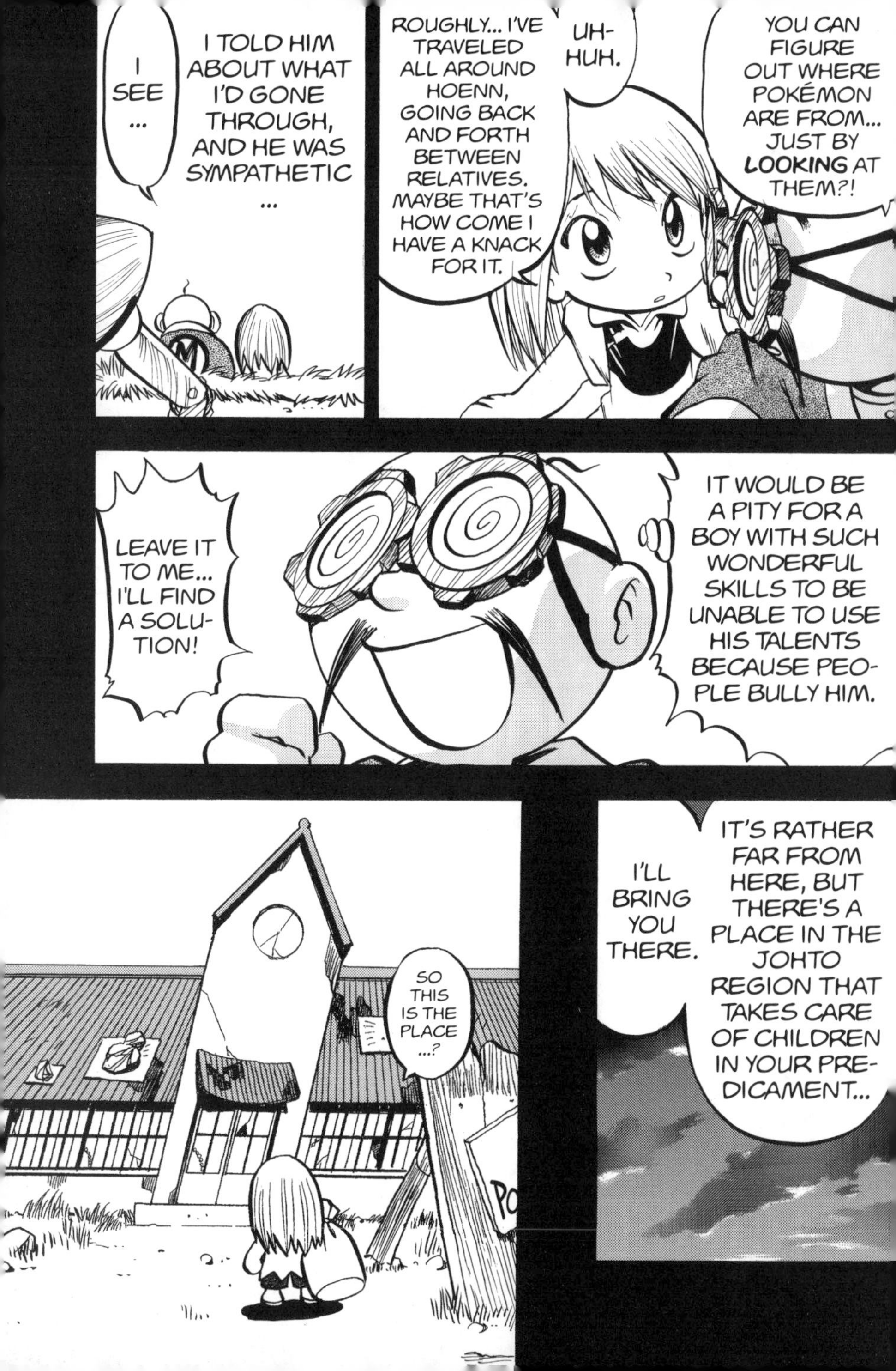
YOU CAN FIGURE OUT WHERE POKÉMON ARE FROM... JUST BY **LOOKING** AT THEM?!
UH-HUH.
ROUGHLY... I'VE TRAVELED ALL AROUND HOENN, GOING BACK AND FORTH BETWEEN RELATIVES. MAYBE THAT'S HOW COME I HAVE A KNACK FOR IT.
I TOLD HIM ABOUT WHAT I'D GONE THROUGH, AND HE WAS SYMPATHETIC...
I SEE...
IT WOULD BE A PITY FOR A BOY WITH SUCH WONDERFUL SKILLS TO BE UNABLE TO USE HIS TALENTS BECAUSE PEOPLE BULLY HIM.
LEAVE IT TO ME... I'LL FIND A SOLUTION!
IT'S RATHER FAR FROM HERE, BUT THERE'S A PLACE IN THE JOHTO REGION THAT TAKES CARE OF CHILDREN IN YOUR PREDICAMENT...
I'LL BRING YOU THERE.
SO THIS IS THE PLACE...?

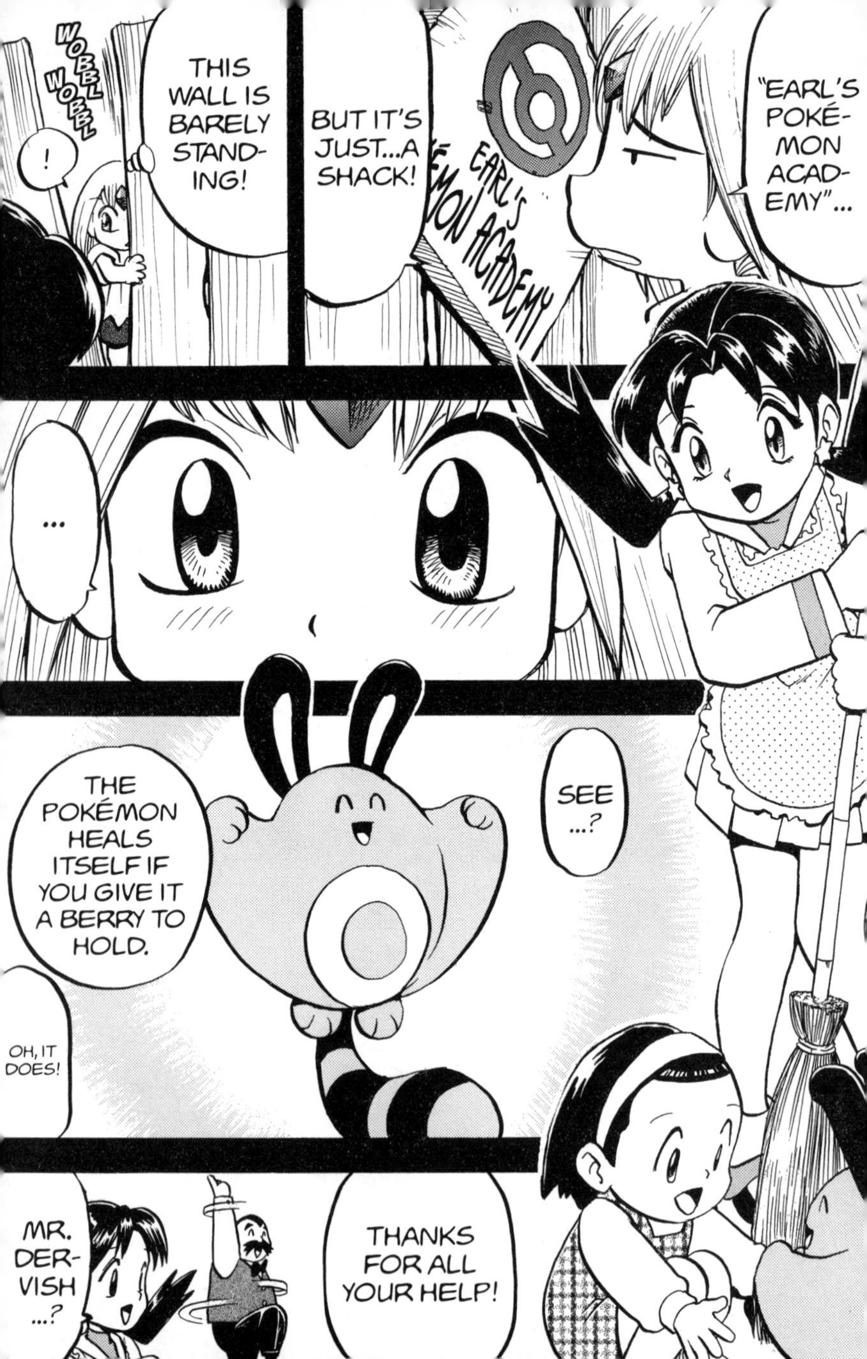
"EARL'S POKÉ-MON ACAD-EMY"...
EARL'S
MON ACADEMY
BUT IT'S JUST...A SHACK!
THIS WALL IS BARELY STAND-ING!
WOBBL WOBBL
!
...
SEE ...?
THE POKÉMON HEALS ITSELF IF YOU GIVE IT A BERRY TO HOLD.
OH, IT DOES!
THANKS FOR ALL YOUR HELP!
MR. DER-VISH ...?

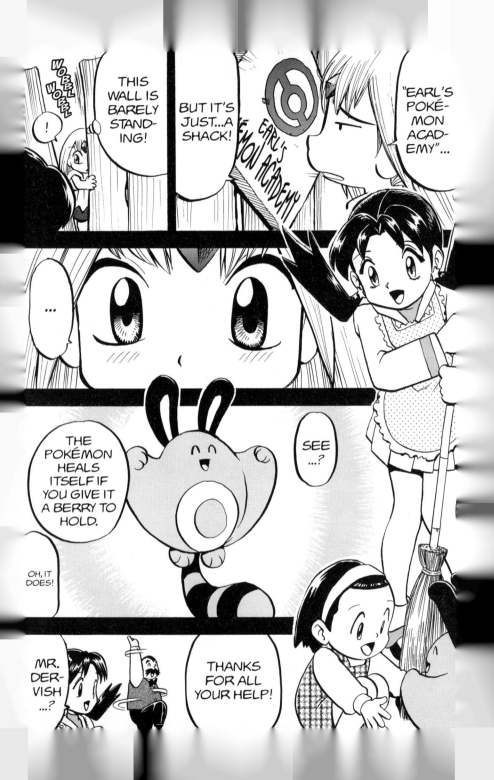

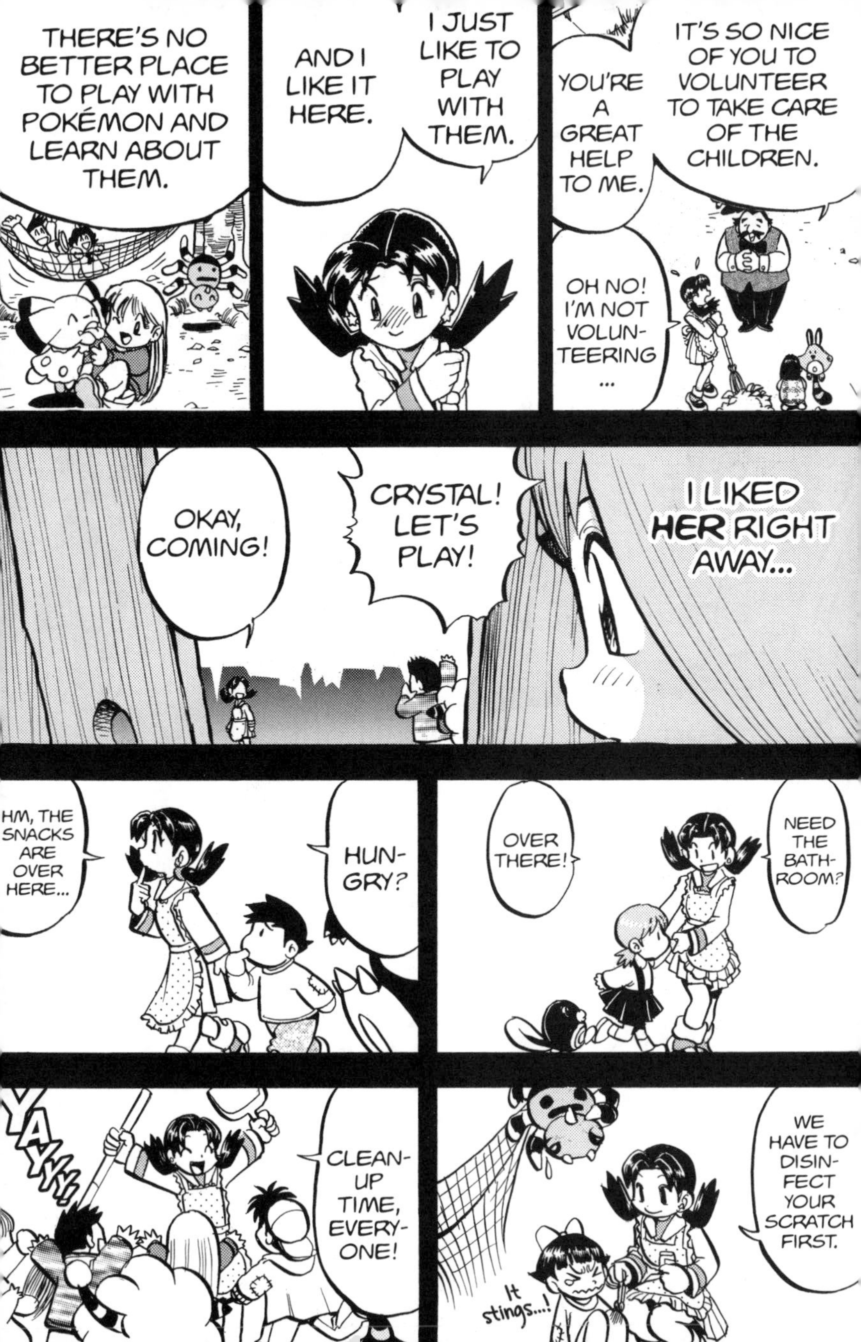
IT'S SO NICE OF YOU TO VOLUNTEER TO TAKE CARE OF THE CHILDREN.
YOU'RE A GREAT HELP TO ME.
OH NO! I'M NOT VOLUN-TEERING ...
I JUST LIKE TO PLAY WITH THEM.
AND I LIKE IT HERE.
THERE'S NO BETTER PLACE TO PLAY WITH POKÉMON AND LEARN ABOUT THEM.
I LIKED **HER** RIGHT AWAY...
CRYSTAL! LET'S PLAY!
OKAY, COMING!
NEED THE BATH-ROOM?
OVER THERE!
HUN-GRY?
HM, THE SNACKS ARE OVER HERE...
WE HAVE TO DISIN-FECT YOUR SCRATCH FIRST.
It stings...!
CLEAN-UP TIME, EVERY-ONE!
YAYY!

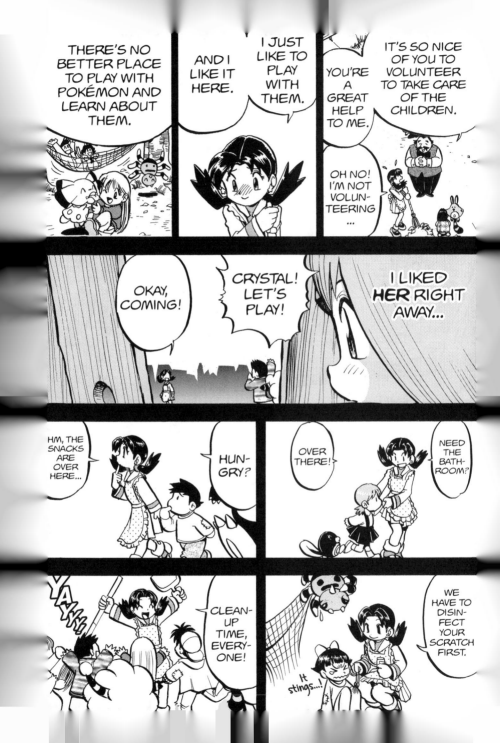

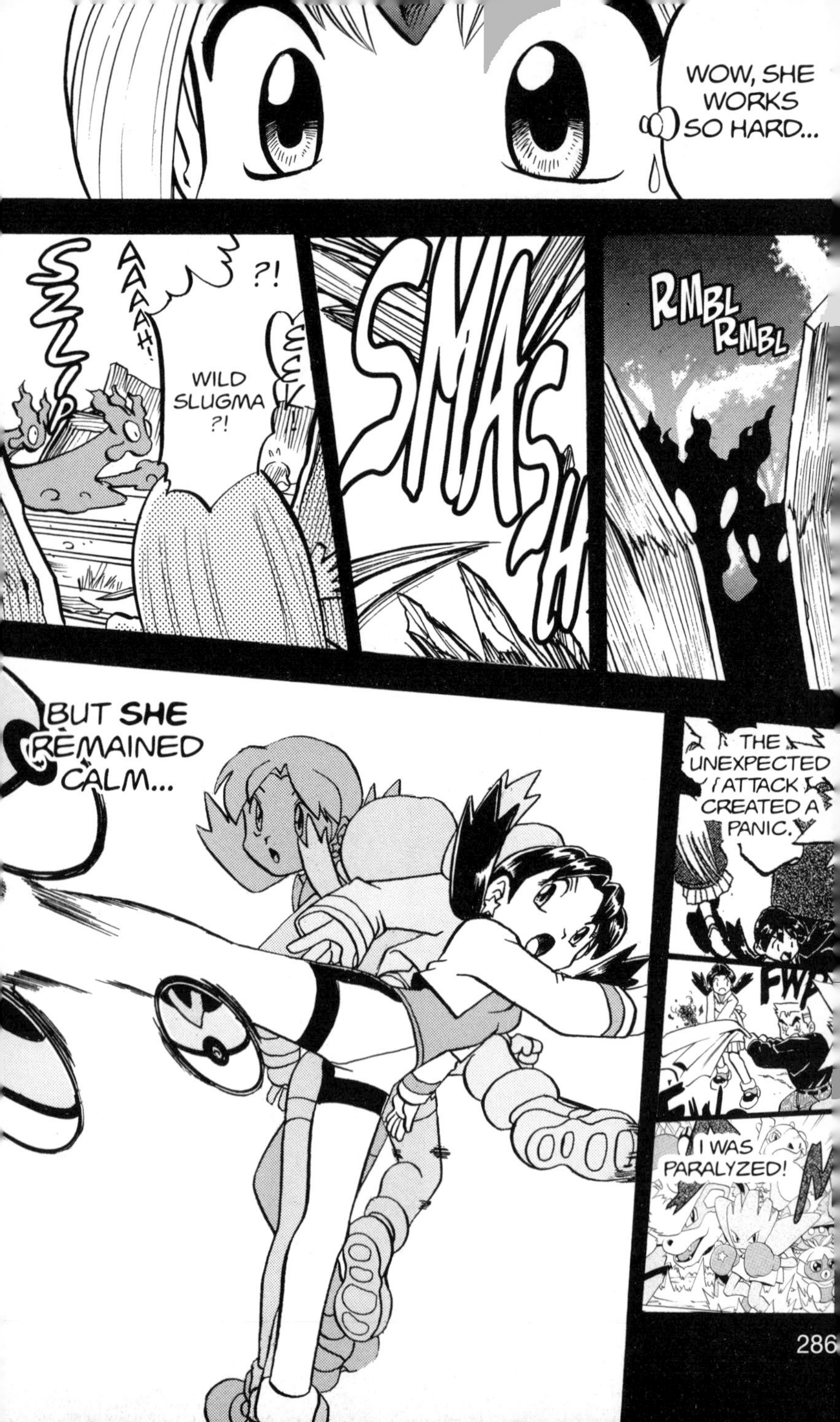
WOW, SHE WORKS SO HARD...
RMBL RMBL
SMASH
?!
EEEK
AAAAH!
WILD SLUGMA ?!
THE UNEXPECTED ATTACK CREATED A PANIC.
I WAS PARALYZED!
BUT SHE REMAINED CALM...

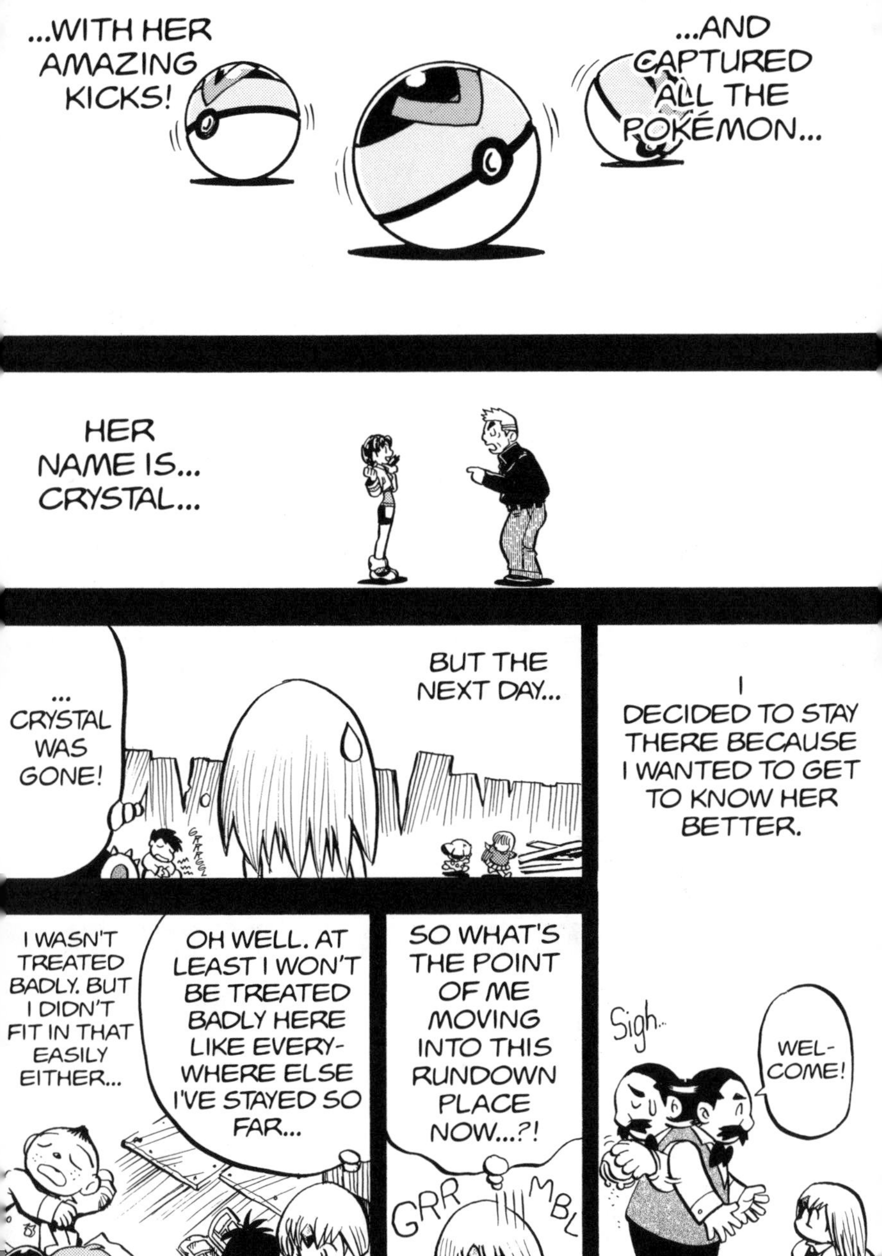
...AND CAPTURED ALL THE POKÉMON...
...WITH HER AMAZING KICKS!
HER NAME IS... CRYSTAL...
I DECIDED TO STAY THERE BECAUSE I WANTED TO GET TO KNOW HER BETTER.
BUT THE NEXT DAY...
...CRYSTAL WAS GONE!
WEL-COME!
Sigh...
SO WHAT'S THE POINT OF ME MOVING INTO THIS RUNDOWN PLACE NOW...?!
GRR
MBL
OH WELL. AT LEAST I WON'T BE TREATED BADLY HERE LIKE EVERYWHERE ELSE I'VE STAYED SO FAR...
I WASN'T TREATED BADLY. BUT I DIDN'T FIT IN THAT EASILY EITHER...

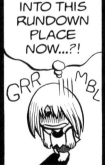

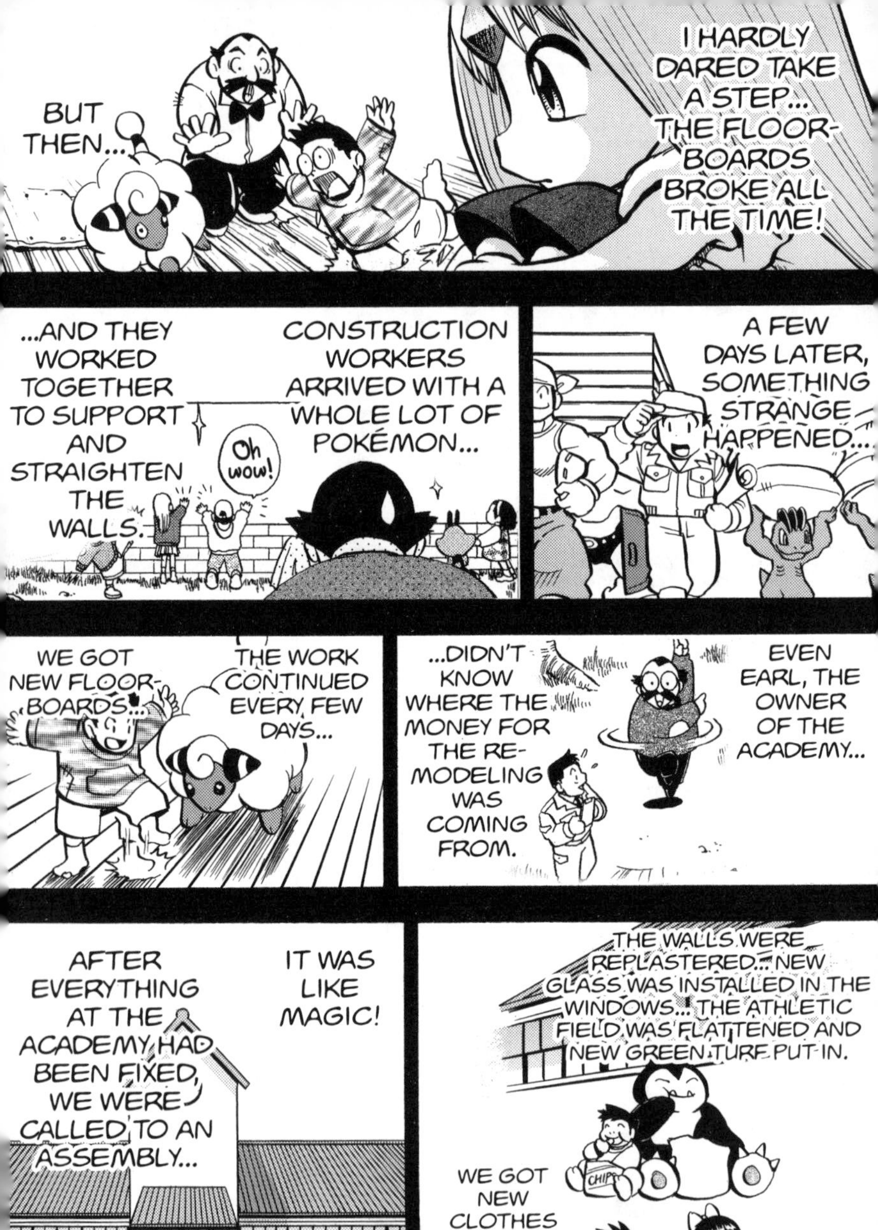
I HARDLY DARED TAKE A STEP... THE FLOOR-BOARDS BROKE ALL THE TIME!
BUT THEN...
A FEW DAYS LATER, SOMETHING STRANGE HAPPENED...
CONSTRUCTION WORKERS ARRIVED WITH A WHOLE LOT OF POKÉMON...
...AND THEY WORKED TOGETHER TO SUPPORT AND STRAIGHTEN THE WALLS.
Oh wow!
EVEN EARL, THE OWNER OF THE ACADEMY...
...DIDN'T KNOW WHERE THE MONEY FOR THE RE-MODELING WAS COMING FROM.
THE WORK CONTINUED EVERY FEW DAYS...
WE GOT NEW FLOOR-BOARDS...
THE WALLS WERE REPLASTERED... NEW GLASS WAS INSTALLED IN THE WINDOWS... THE ATHLETIC FIELD WAS FLATTENED AND NEW GREEN TURF PUT IN.
WE GOT NEW CLOTHES AND ALL THE FOOD WE COULD EAT.
IT WAS LIKE MAGIC!
AFTER EVERYTHING AT THE ACADEMY HAD BEEN FIXED, WE WERE CALLED TO AN ASSEMBLY...

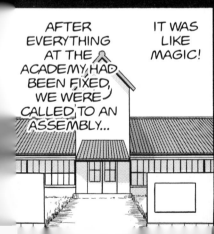

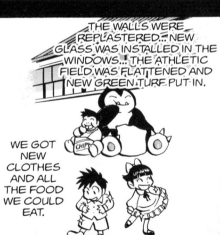

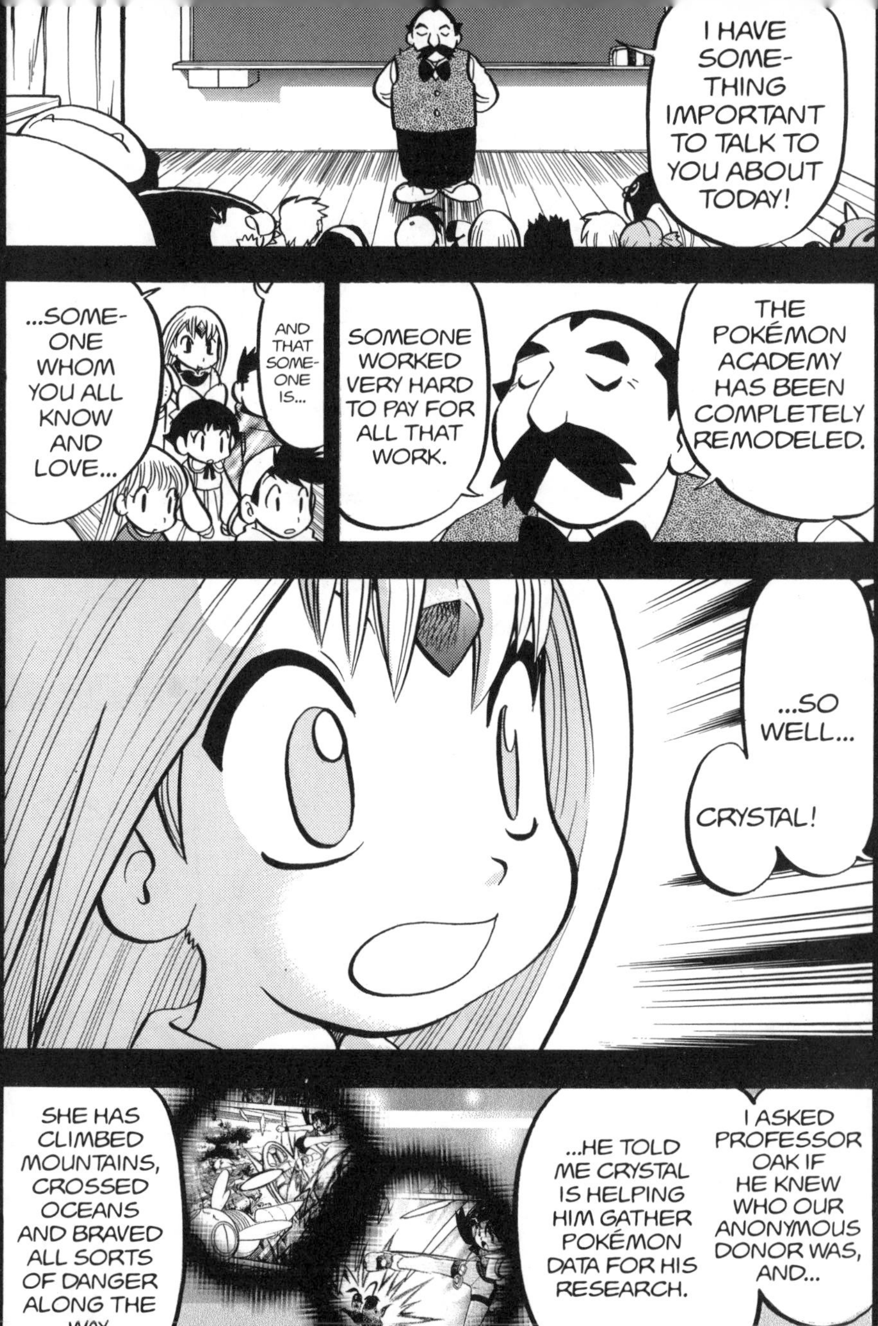
I HAVE SOMETHING IMPORTANT TO TALK TO YOU ABOUT TODAY!
THE POKÉMON ACADEMY HAS BEEN COMPLETELY REMODELED.
SOMEONE WORKED VERY HARD TO PAY FOR ALL THAT WORK.
AND THAT SOMEONE IS...
...SOMEONE WHOM YOU ALL KNOW AND LOVE...
...SO WELL...
CRYSTAL!
I ASKED PROFESSOR OAK IF HE KNEW WHO OUR ANONYMOUS DONOR WAS, AND...
...HE TOLD ME CRYSTAL IS HELPING HIM GATHER POKÉMON DATA FOR HIS RESEARCH.
SHE HAS CLIMBED MOUNTAINS, CROSSED OCEANS AND BRAVED ALL SORTS OF DANGER ALONG THE WAY.

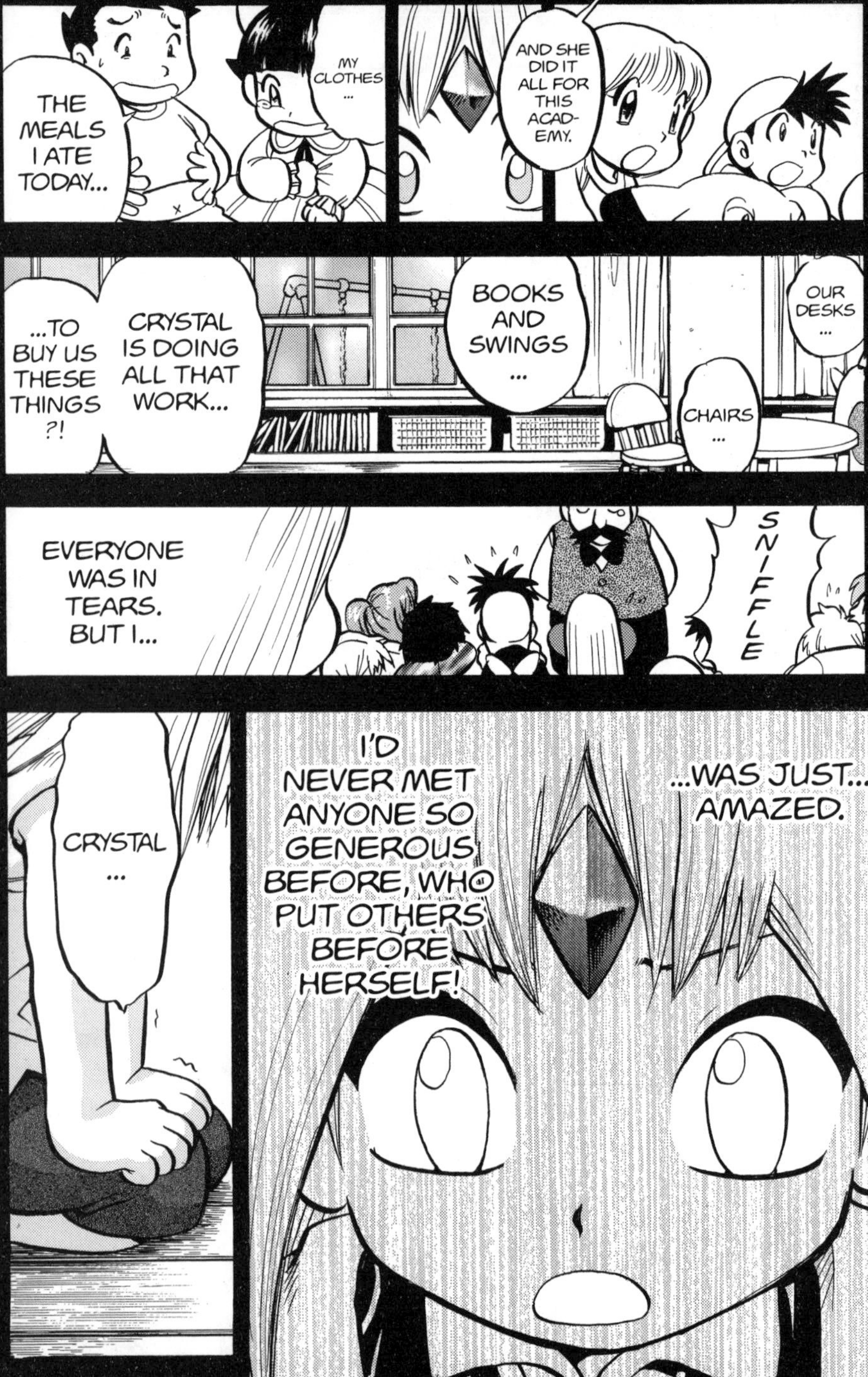
AND SHE DID IT ALL FOR THIS ACAD-EMY.
MY CLOTHES ...
THE MEALS I ATE TODAY...
OUR DESKS ...
CHAIRS ...
BOOKS AND SWINGS ...
CRYSTAL IS DOING ALL THAT WORK...
...TO BUY US THESE THINGS ?!
SNIFFLE
EVERYONE WAS IN TEARS. BUT I...
...WAS JUST... AMAZED.
I'D NEVER MET ANYONE SO GENEROUS BEFORE, WHO PUT OTHERS BEFORE HERSELF!
CRYSTAL ...

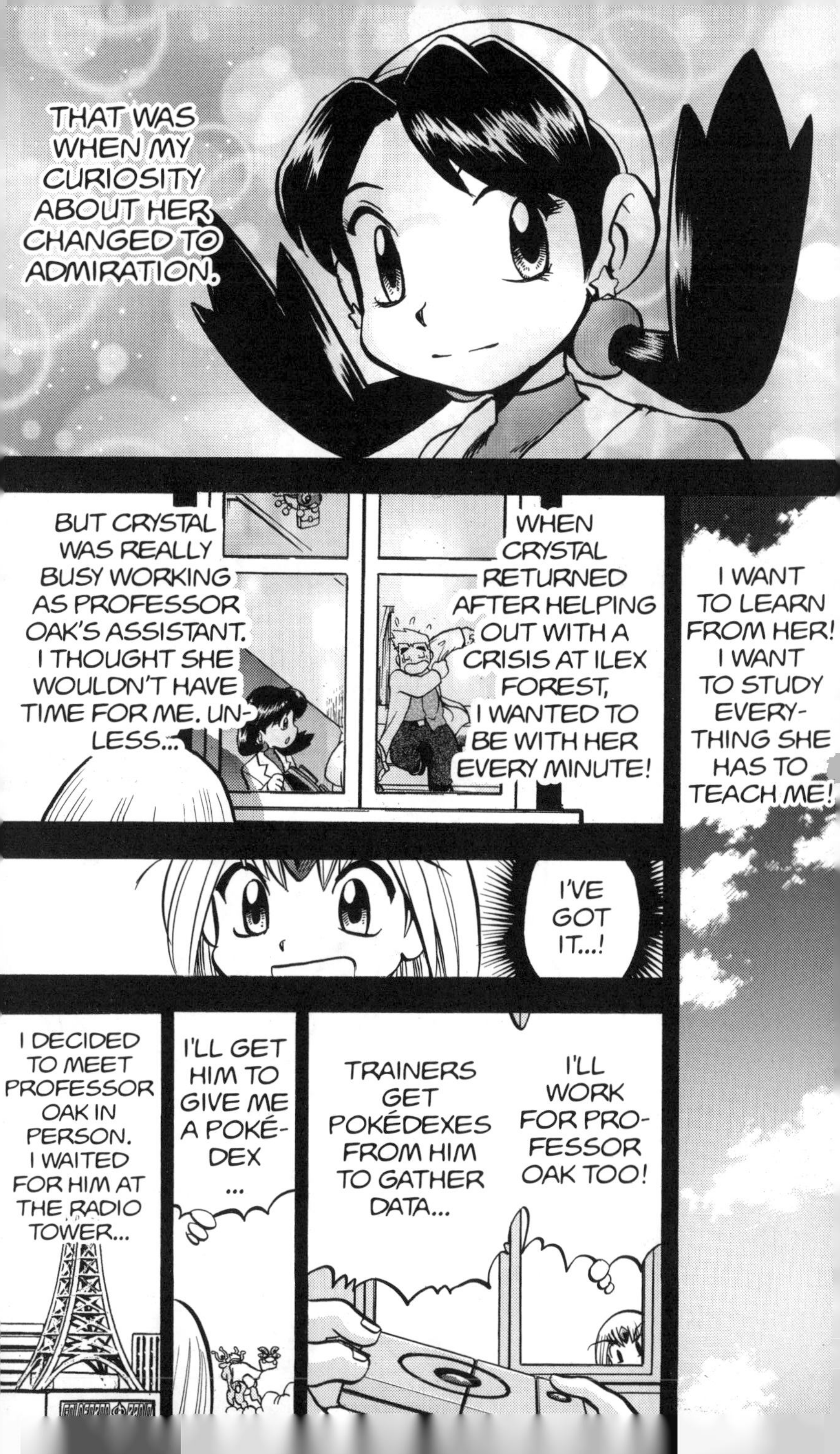
THAT WAS WHEN MY CURIOSITY ABOUT HER CHANGED TO ADMIRATION.
I WANT TO LEARN FROM HER! I WANT TO STUDY EVERY-THING SHE HAS TO TEACH ME!
WHEN CRYSTAL RETURNED AFTER HELPING OUT WITH A CRISIS AT ILEX FOREST, I WANTED TO BE WITH HER EVERY MINUTE!
BUT CRYSTAL WAS REALLY BUSY WORKING AS PROFESSOR OAK'S ASSISTANT. I THOUGHT SHE WOULDN'T HAVE TIME FOR ME. UN-LESS...
I'VE GOT IT...!
I'LL WORK FOR PRO-FESSOR OAK TOO!
TRAINERS GET POKÉDEXES FROM HIM TO GATHER DATA...
I'LL GET HIM TO GIVE ME A POKÉ-DEX ...
I DECIDED TO MEET PROFESSOR OAK IN PERSON. I WAITED FOR HIM AT THE RADIO TOWER...

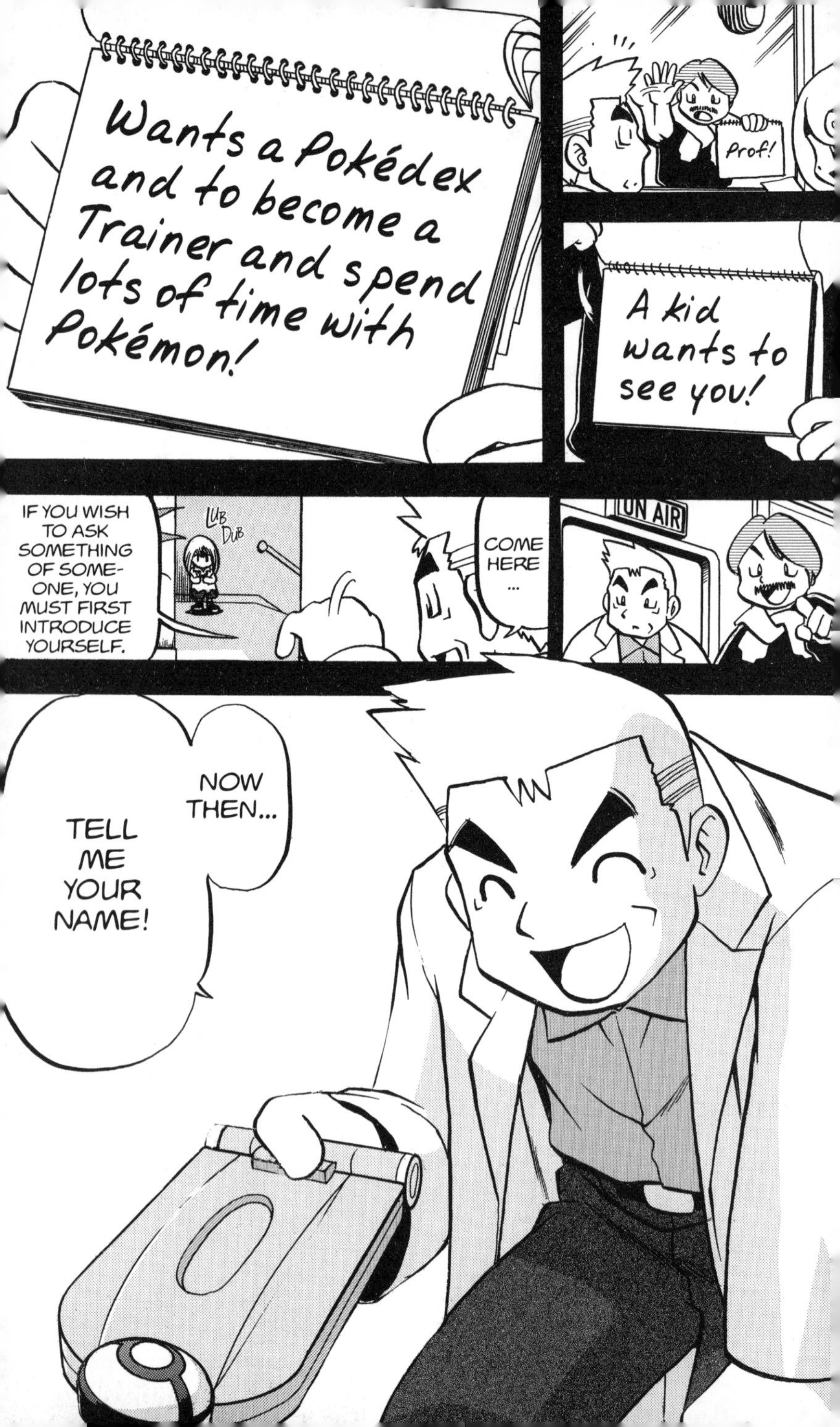
Prof!
A kid wants to see you!
Wants a Pokédex and to become a Trainer and spend lots of time with Pokémon!
ON AIR
COME HERE ...
IF YOU WISH TO ASK SOMETHING OF SOME-ONE, YOU MUST FIRST INTRODUCE YOURSELF.
LUB DUB
NOW THEN...
TELL ME YOUR NAME!

POKÉMON EMERALD

CHARACTER PROFILE / CRYSTAL

PROFESSOR OAK GAVE CRYSTAL A POKÉDEX AND ASKED HER TO FILL IT WITH DATA ABOUT POKÉMON. SHE IS KNOWN AS THE "CATCHER." CRYSTAL IS A KIND GIRL WHO TAKES CARE OF EVERYONE. SHE IS DEVOTED TO HER VOLUNTEER WORK AT EARL'S POKÉMON ACADEMY, BUT SHE CAN ALSO BE A WORKAHOLIC WHEN IT COMES TO CAPTURING POKÉMON WITH HER TEAM. SHE IS CURRENTLY WORKING AT PROFESSOR OAK'S LABORATORY AS HIS ASSISTANT.

CRYSTAL

- ●Birthplace: Violet City
- ●Birthday: April 30
- ●Blood Type: A
- ●Family: Mother
- ●Skill: Apricorn picking
- ●Hobby: Reading

332

The Final Battle, Part 5

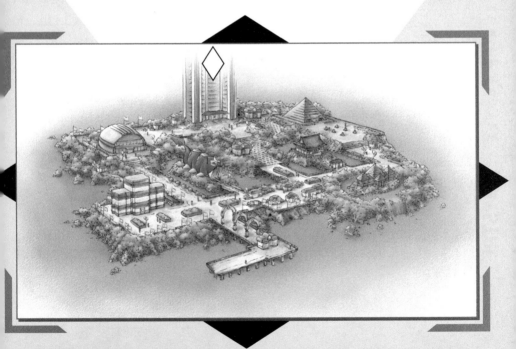

POKÉMON ADVENTURES·THE SIXTH CHAPTER·EMERALD

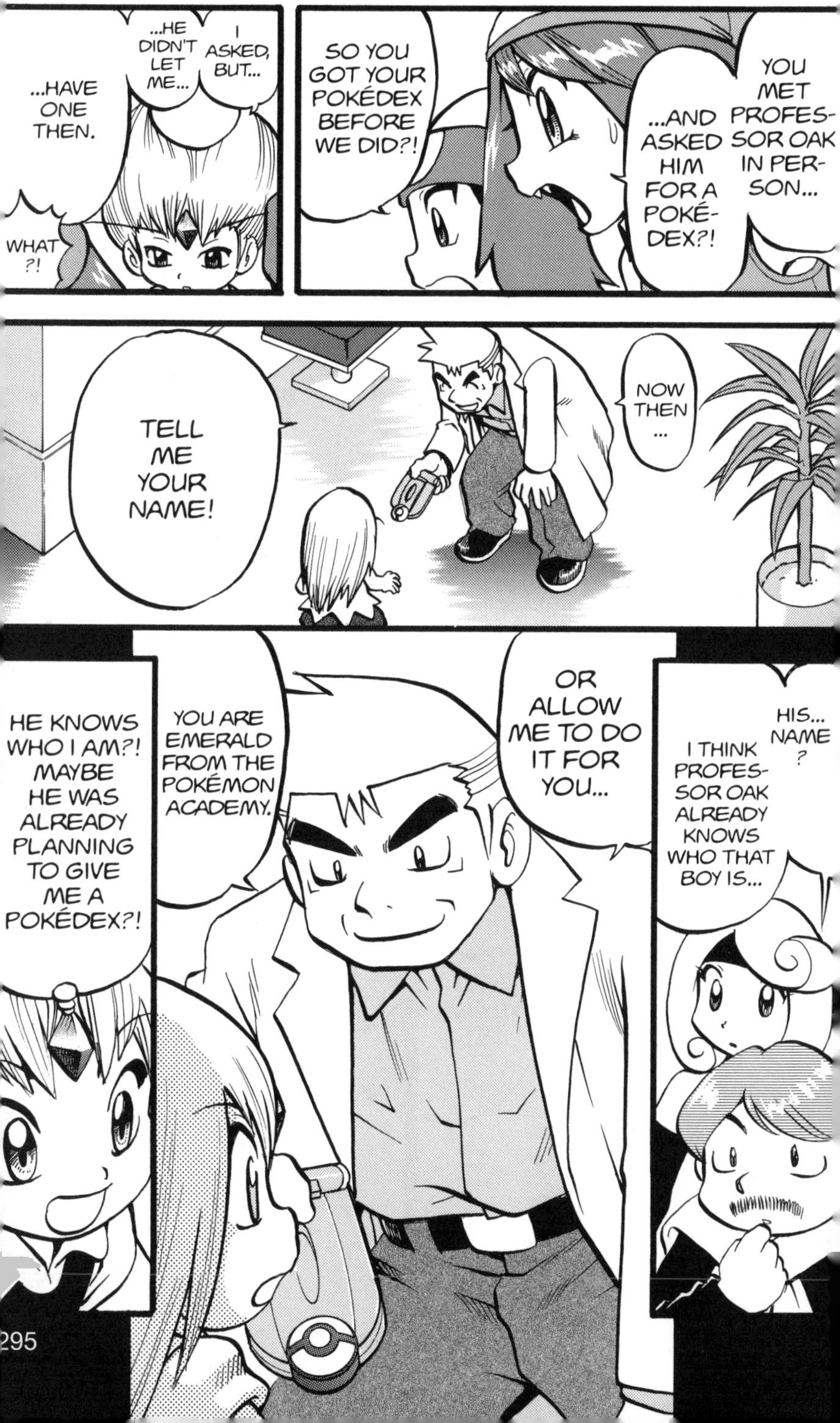
YOU MET PROFESSOR OAK IN PERSON...
...AND ASKED HIM FOR A POKÉDEX?!
SO YOU GOT YOUR POKÉDEX BEFORE WE DID?!
I ASKED, BUT...
...HE DIDN'T LET ME...
...HAVE ONE THEN.
WHAT?!
NOW THEN...
TELL ME YOUR NAME!
HIS... NAME?
I THINK PROFESSOR OAK ALREADY KNOWS WHO THAT BOY IS...
OR ALLOW ME TO DO IT FOR YOU...
YOU ARE EMERALD FROM THE POKÉMON ACADEMY.
HE KNOWS WHO I AM?! MAYBE HE WAS ALREADY PLANNING TO GIVE ME A POKÉDEX?!

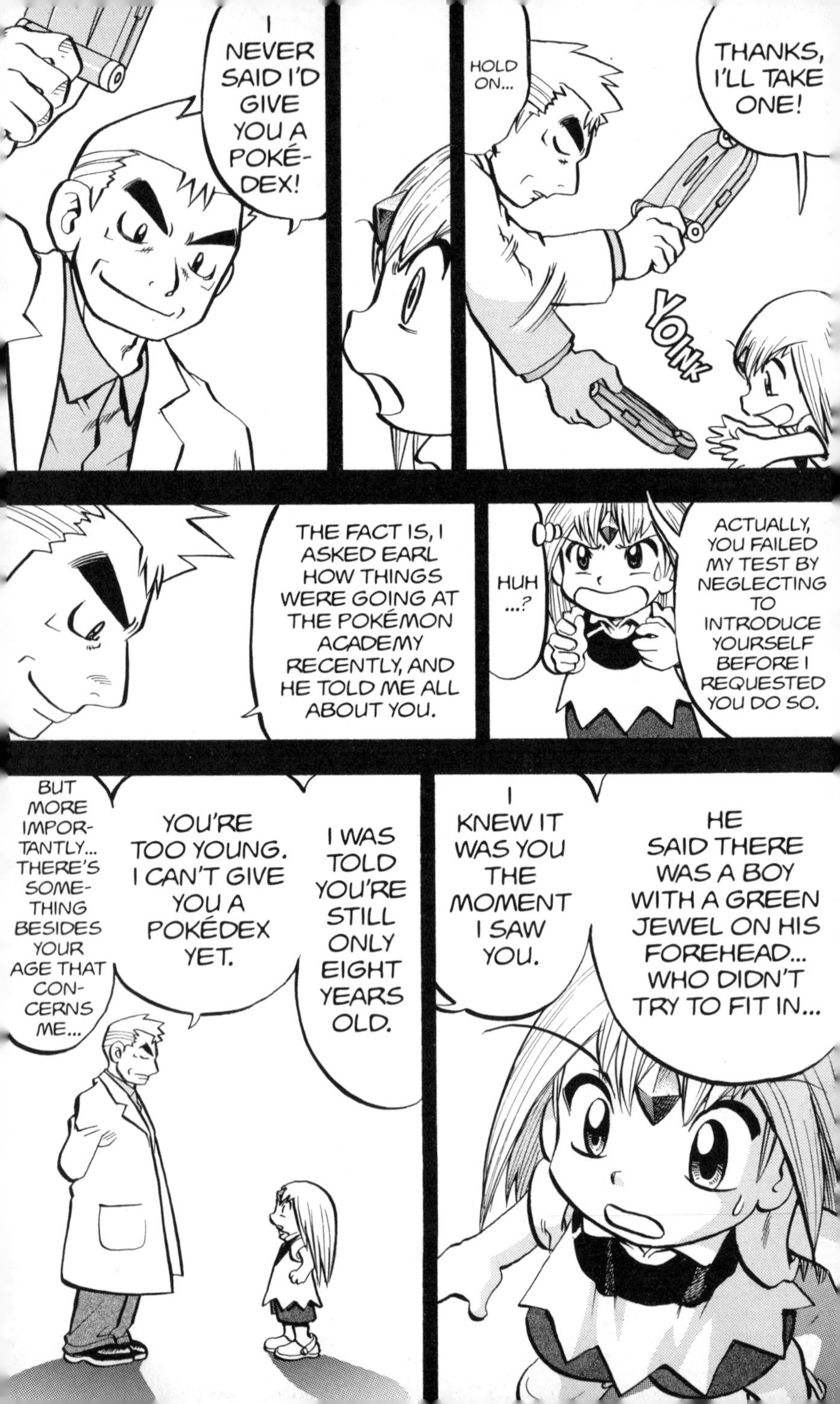
THANKS, I'LL TAKE ONE!
HOLD ON...
YOINK
I NEVER SAID I'D GIVE YOU A POKÉDEX!
ACTUALLY, YOU FAILED MY TEST BY NEGLECTING TO INTRODUCE YOURSELF BEFORE I REQUESTED YOU DO SO.
HUH ...?
THE FACT IS, I ASKED EARL HOW THINGS WERE GOING AT THE POKÉMON ACADEMY RECENTLY, AND HE TOLD ME ALL ABOUT YOU.
HE SAID THERE WAS A BOY WITH A GREEN JEWEL ON HIS FOREHEAD... WHO DIDN'T TRY TO FIT IN...
I KNEW IT WAS YOU THE MOMENT I SAW YOU.
I WAS TOLD YOU'RE STILL ONLY EIGHT YEARS OLD.
YOU'RE TOO YOUNG. I CAN'T GIVE YOU A POKÉDEX YET.
BUT MORE IMPORTANTLY... THERE'S SOMETHING BESIDES YOUR AGE THAT CONCERNS ME...

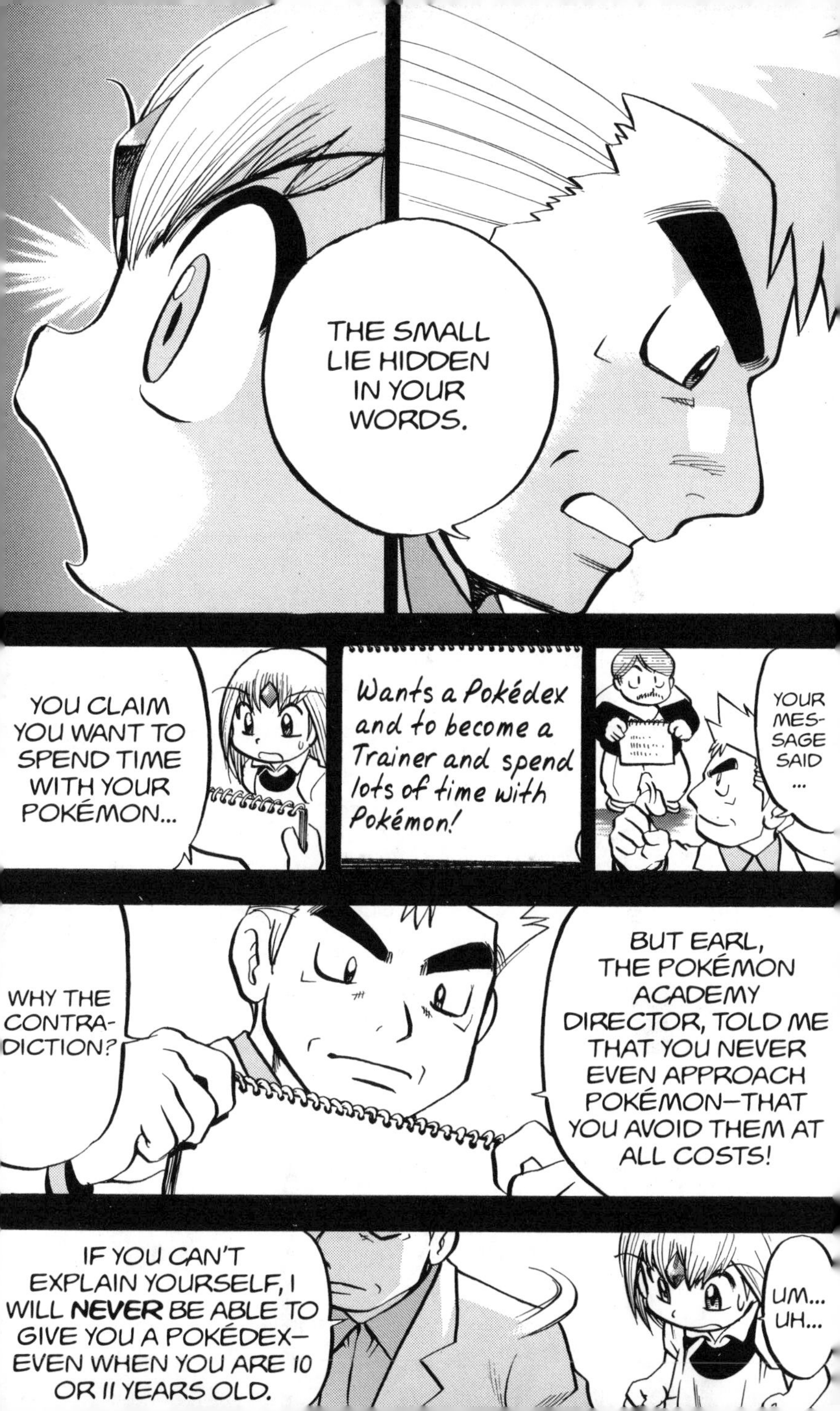
THE SMALL LIE HIDDEN IN YOUR WORDS.
YOUR MESSAGE SAID...
Wants a Pokédex and to become a Trainer and spend lots of time with Pokémon!
YOU CLAIM YOU WANT TO SPEND TIME WITH YOUR POKÉMON...
BUT EARL, THE POKÉMON ACADEMY DIRECTOR, TOLD ME THAT YOU NEVER EVEN APPROACH POKÉMON—THAT YOU AVOID THEM AT ALL COSTS!
WHY THE CONTRADICTION?
IF YOU CAN'T EXPLAIN YOURSELF, I WILL **NEVER** BE ABLE TO GIVE YOU A POKÉDEX—EVEN WHEN YOU ARE 10 OR 11 YEARS OLD.
UM... UH...

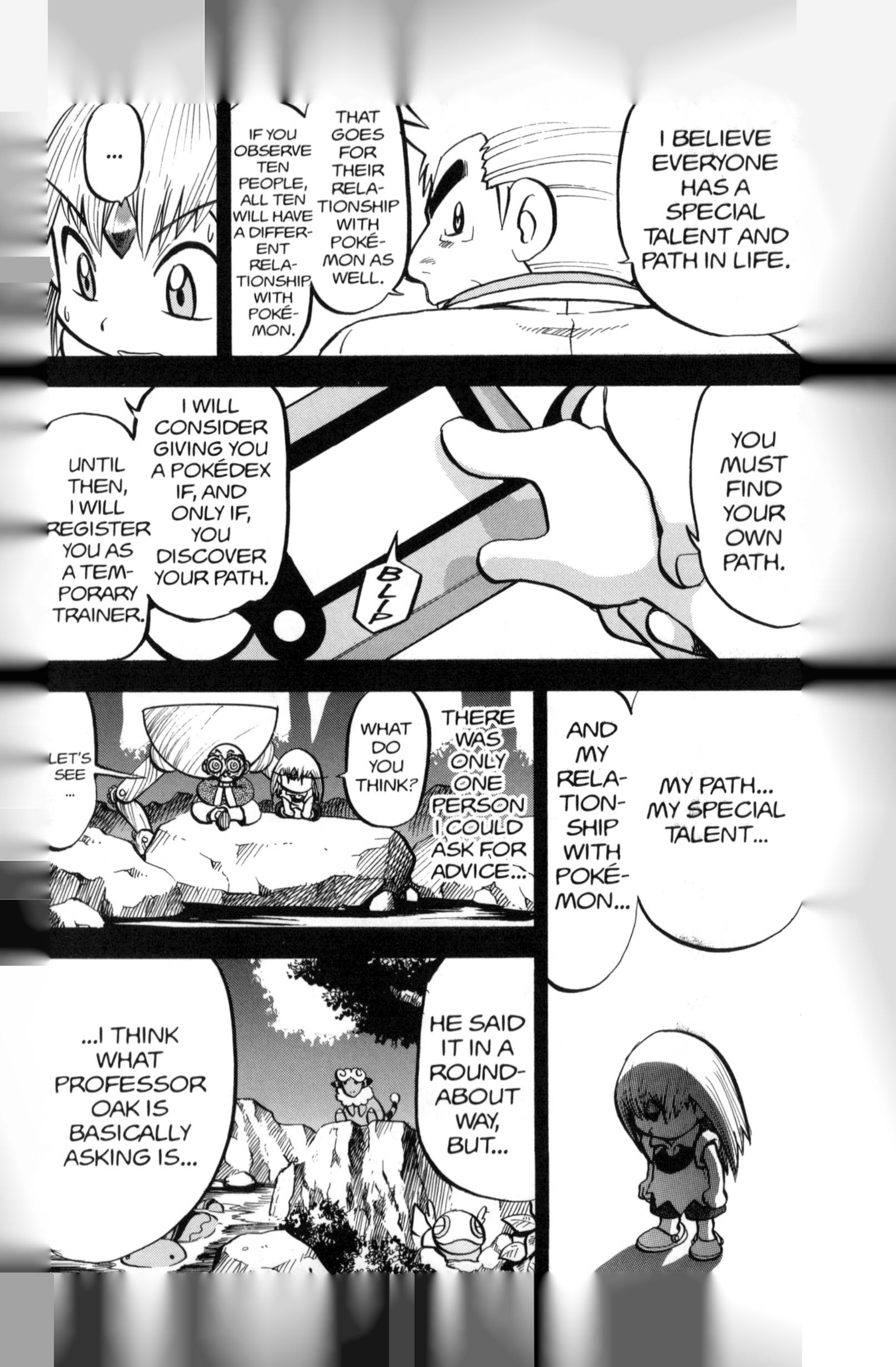
I BELIEVE EVERYONE HAS A SPECIAL TALENT AND PATH IN LIFE.
THAT GOES FOR THEIR RELATIONSHIP WITH POKÉMON AS WELL.
IF YOU OBSERVE TEN PEOPLE, ALL TEN WILL HAVE A DIFFERENT RELATIONSHIP WITH POKÉMON.
...
YOU MUST FIND YOUR OWN PATH.
BLIP
I WILL CONSIDER GIVING YOU A POKÉDEX IF, AND ONLY IF, YOU DISCOVER YOUR PATH.
UNTIL THEN, I WILL REGISTER YOU AS A TEMPORARY TRAINER.
MY PATH... MY SPECIAL TALENT...
AND MY RELATIONSHIP WITH POKÉMON...
THERE WAS ONLY ONE PERSON I COULD ASK FOR ADVICE...
WHAT DO YOU THINK?
LET'S SEE ...
HE SAID IT IN A ROUNDABOUT WAY, BUT...
...I THINK WHAT PROFESSOR OAK IS BASICALLY ASKING IS...

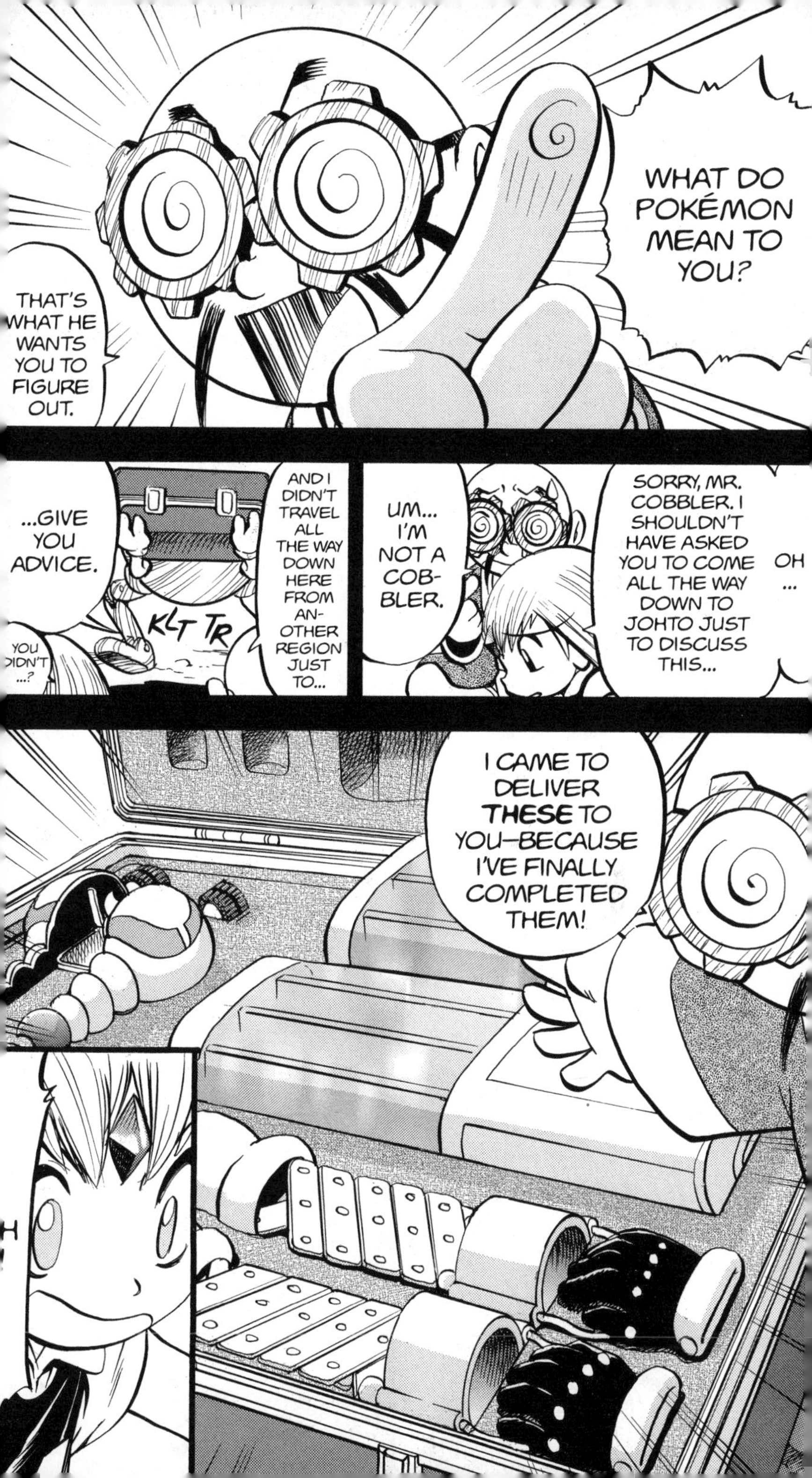
WHAT DO POKÉMON MEAN TO YOU?
THAT'S WHAT HE WANTS YOU TO FIGURE OUT.
SORRY, MR. COBBLER. I SHOULDN'T HAVE ASKED YOU TO COME ALL THE WAY DOWN TO JOHTO JUST TO DISCUSS THIS...
OH ...
UM... I'M NOT A COB-BLER.
AND I DIDN'T TRAVEL ALL THE WAY DOWN HERE FROM AN-OTHER REGION JUST TO...
...GIVE YOU ADVICE.
KLT TR
YOU DIDN'T ...?
I CAME TO DELIVER **THESE** TO YOU—BECAUSE I'VE FINALLY COMPLETED THEM!

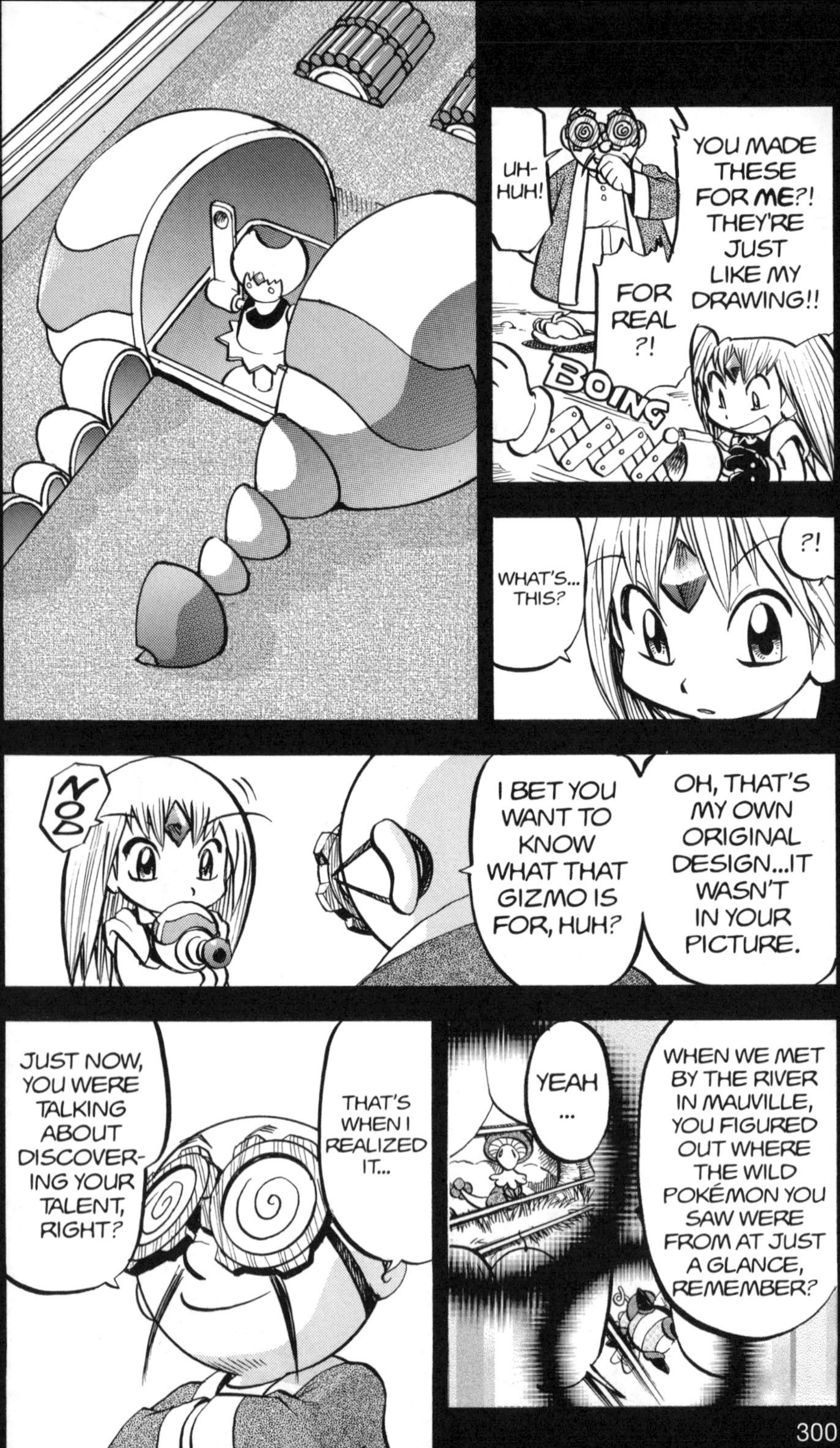
YOU MADE THESE FOR ME?! THEY'RE JUST LIKE MY DRAWING!!
UH-HUH!
FOR REAL ?!
BOING
?!
WHAT'S... THIS?
OH, THAT'S MY OWN ORIGINAL DESIGN...IT WASN'T IN YOUR PICTURE.
I BET YOU WANT TO KNOW WHAT THAT GIZMO IS FOR, HUH?
NOD
WHEN WE MET BY THE RIVER IN MAUVILLE, YOU FIGURED OUT WHERE THE WILD POKÉMON YOU SAW WERE FROM AT JUST A GLANCE, REMEMBER?
YEAH ...
THAT'S WHEN I REALIZED IT...
JUST NOW, YOU WERE TALKING ABOUT DISCOVER-ING YOUR TALENT, RIGHT?

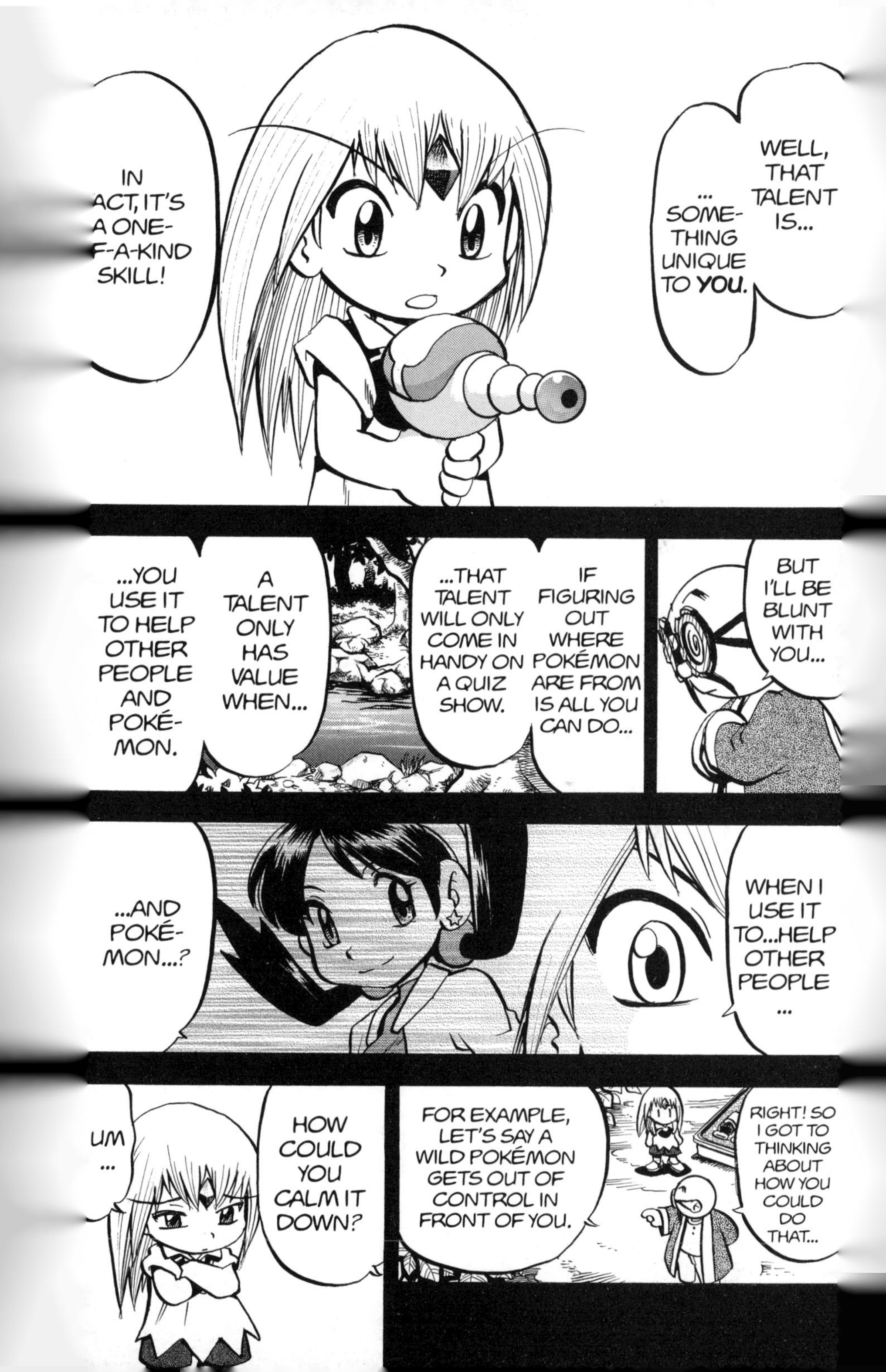
WELL, THAT TALENT IS...
...SOMETHING UNIQUE TO **YOU**.
IN ACT, IT'S A ONE-F-A-KIND SKILL!
BUT I'LL BE BLUNT WITH YOU...
IF FIGURING OUT WHERE POKÉMON ARE FROM IS ALL YOU CAN DO...
...THAT TALENT WILL ONLY COME IN HANDY ON A QUIZ SHOW.
A TALENT ONLY HAS VALUE WHEN...
...YOU USE IT TO HELP OTHER PEOPLE AND POKÉMON.
WHEN I USE IT TO...HELP OTHER PEOPLE...
...AND POKÉMON...?
RIGHT! SO I GOT TO THINKING ABOUT HOW YOU COULD DO THAT...
FOR EXAMPLE, LET'S SAY A WILD POKÉMON GETS OUT OF CONTROL IN FRONT OF YOU.
HOW COULD YOU CALM IT DOWN?
UM...

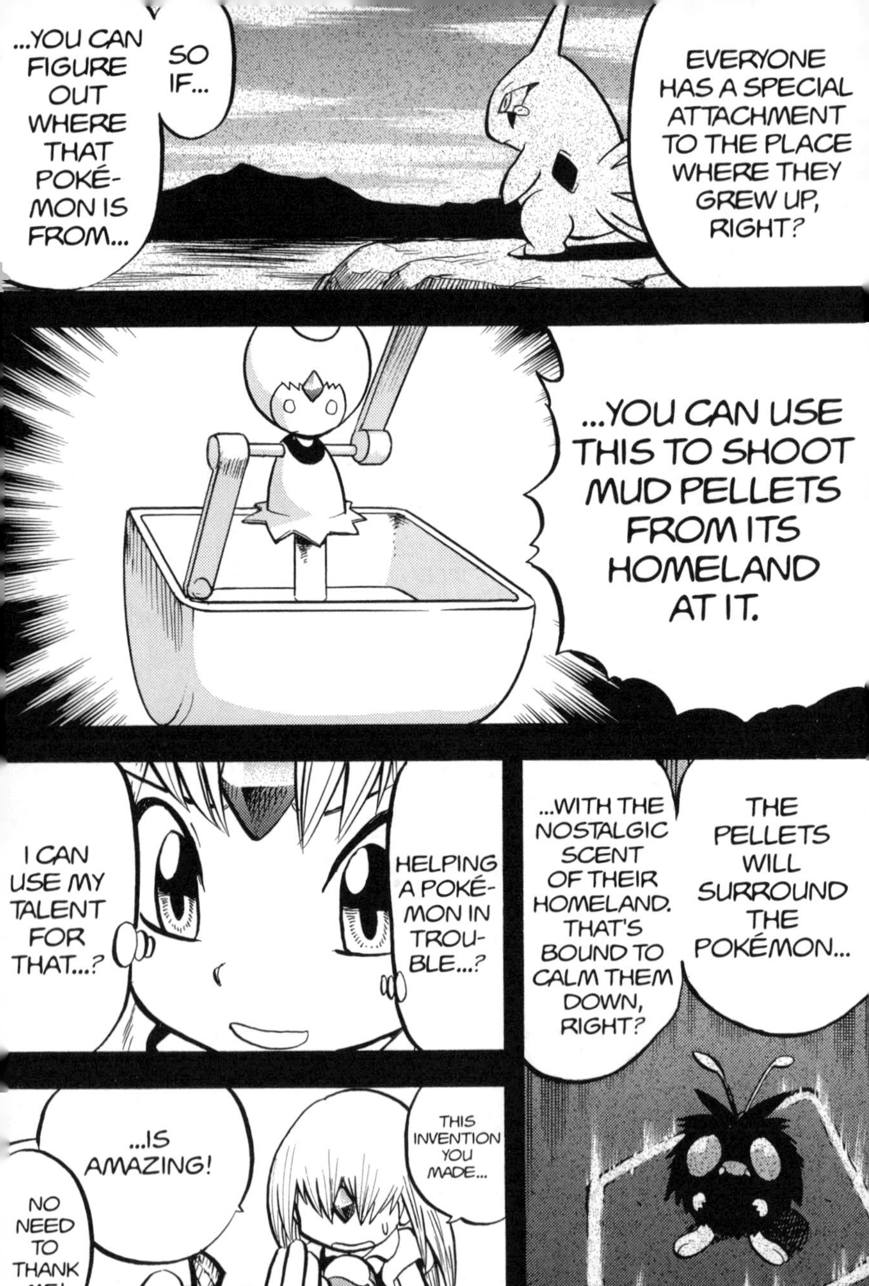
EVERYONE HAS A SPECIAL ATTACHMENT TO THE PLACE WHERE THEY GREW UP, RIGHT?
SO IF...
...YOU CAN FIGURE OUT WHERE THAT POKÉMON IS FROM...
...YOU CAN USE THIS TO SHOOT MUD PELLETS FROM ITS HOMELAND AT IT.
THE PELLETS WILL SURROUND THE POKÉMON...
...WITH THE NOSTALGIC SCENT OF THEIR HOMELAND. THAT'S BOUND TO CALM THEM DOWN, RIGHT?
HELPING A POKÉMON IN TROUBLE...?
I CAN USE MY TALENT FOR THAT...?
THIS INVENTION YOU MADE...
...IS AMAZING!
NO NEED TO THANK ME!

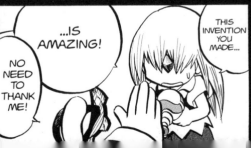

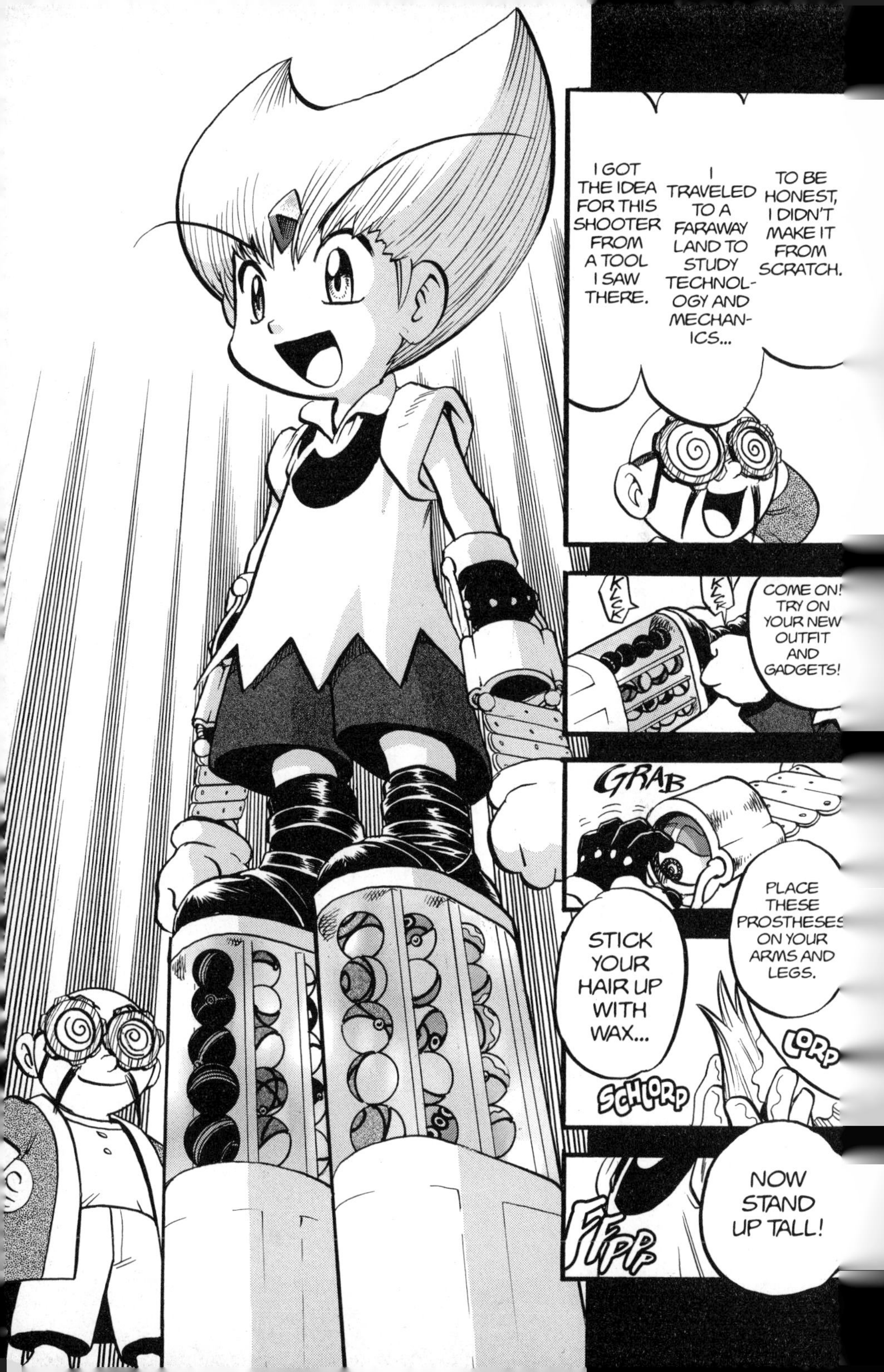
TO BE HONEST, I DIDN'T MAKE IT FROM SCRATCH.
I TRAVELED TO A FARAWAY LAND TO STUDY TECHNOLOGY AND MECHANICS...
I GOT THE IDEA FOR THIS SHOOTER FROM A TOOL I SAW THERE.
KLCK
KLCK
COME ON! TRY ON YOUR NEW OUTFIT AND GADGETS!
GRAB
PLACE THESE PROSTHESES ON YOUR ARMS AND LEGS.
STICK YOUR HAIR UP WITH WAX...
LORP
SCHLORP
NOW STAND UP TALL!

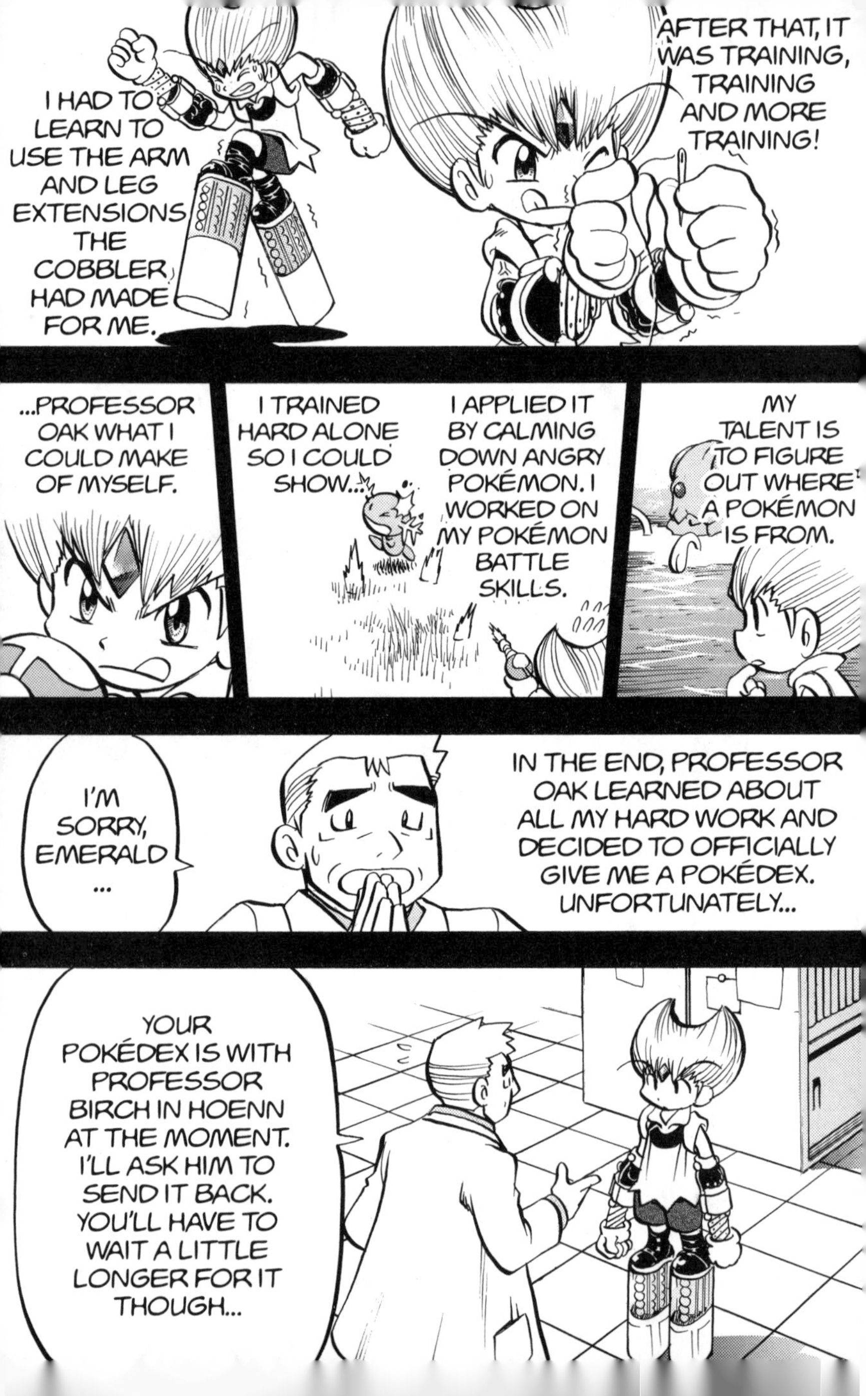
AFTER THAT, IT WAS TRAINING, TRAINING AND MORE TRAINING!
I HAD TO LEARN TO USE THE ARM AND LEG EXTENSIONS THE COBBLER HAD MADE FOR ME.
MY TALENT IS TO FIGURE OUT WHERE A POKÉMON IS FROM.
I APPLIED IT BY CALMING DOWN ANGRY POKÉMON. I WORKED ON MY POKÉMON BATTLE SKILLS.
I TRAINED HARD ALONE SO I COULD SHOW...
...PROFESSOR OAK WHAT I COULD MAKE OF MYSELF.
IN THE END, PROFESSOR OAK LEARNED ABOUT ALL MY HARD WORK AND DECIDED TO OFFICIALLY GIVE ME A POKÉDEX. UNFORTUNATELY...
I'M SORRY, EMERALD ...
YOUR POKÉDEX IS WITH PROFESSOR BIRCH IN HOENN AT THE MOMENT. I'LL ASK HIM TO SEND IT BACK. YOU'LL HAVE TO WAIT A LITTLE LONGER FOR IT THOUGH...

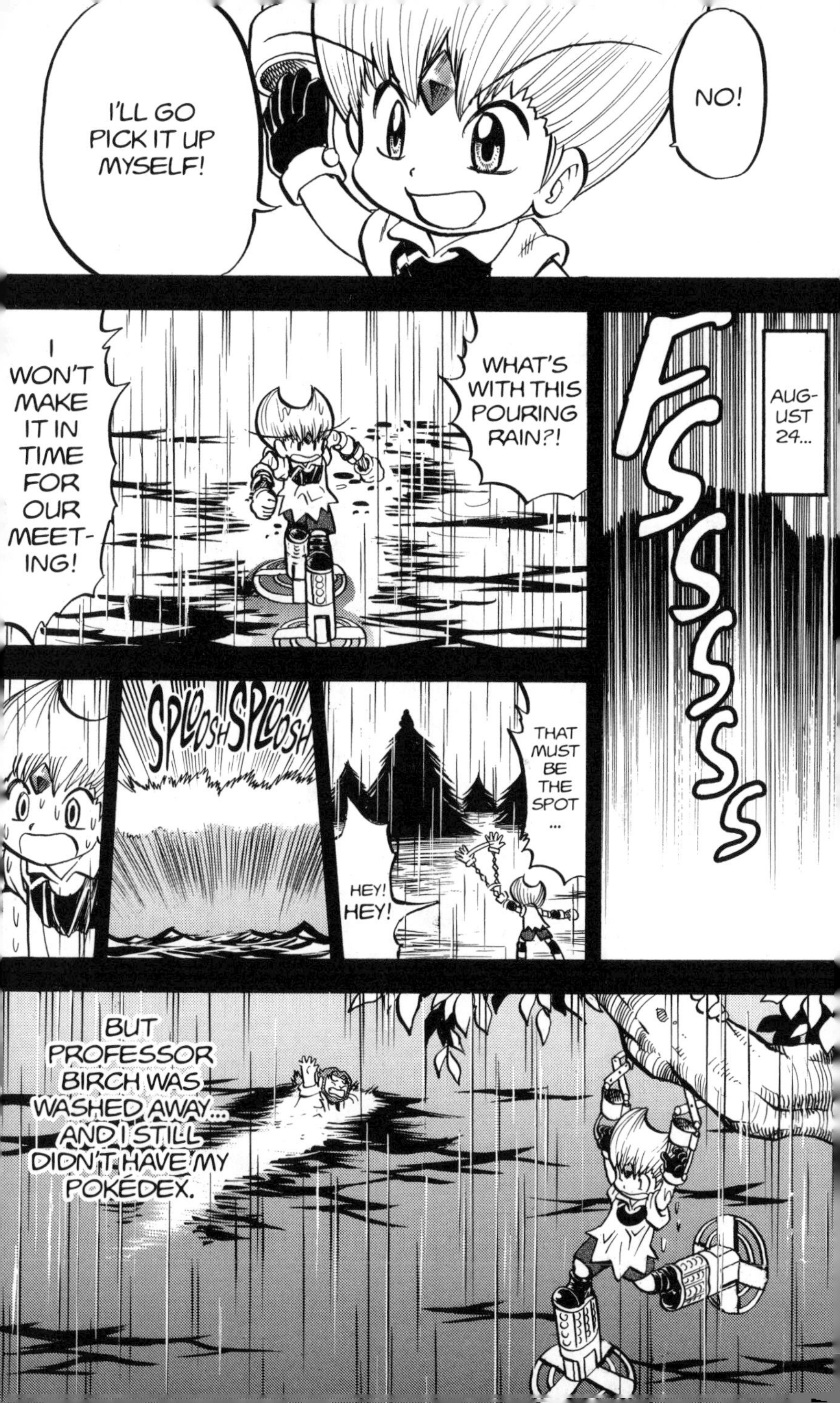
NO!
I'LL GO PICK IT UP MYSELF!
AUGUST 24...
FSSSSSS
WHAT'S WITH THIS POURING RAIN?!
I WON'T MAKE IT IN TIME FOR OUR MEETING!
THAT MUST BE THE SPOT...
HEY! HEY!
SPLOOSH SPLOOSH
BUT PROFESSOR BIRCH WAS WASHED AWAY... AND I STILL DIDN'T HAVE MY POKÉDEX.

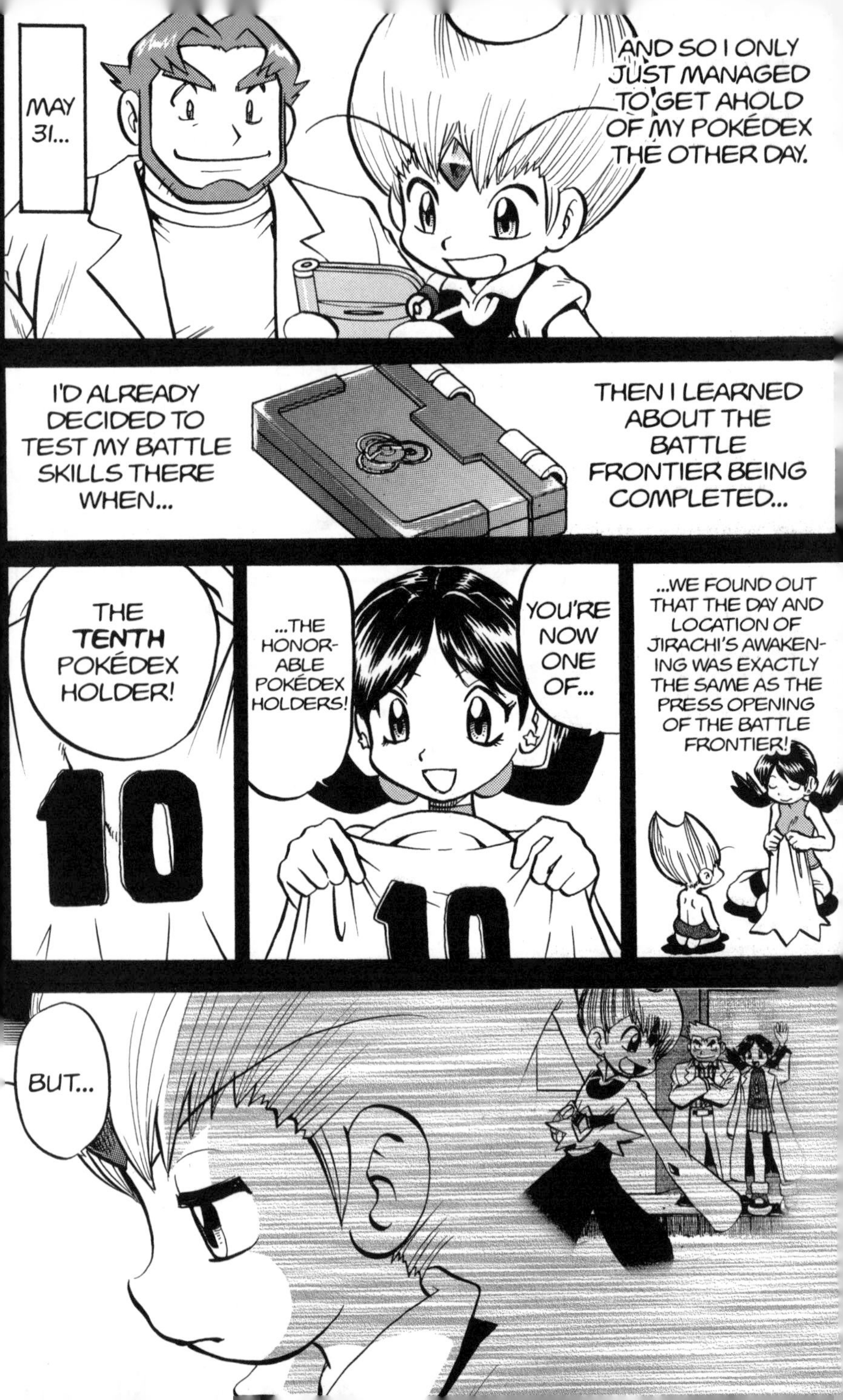
AND SO I ONLY JUST MANAGED TO GET AHOLD OF MY POKÉDEX THE OTHER DAY.
MAY 31...
THEN I LEARNED ABOUT THE BATTLE FRONTIER BEING COMPLETED...
I'D ALREADY DECIDED TO TEST MY BATTLE SKILLS THERE WHEN...
...WE FOUND OUT THAT THE DAY AND LOCATION OF JIRACHI'S AWAKENING WAS EXACTLY THE SAME AS THE PRESS OPENING OF THE BATTLE FRONTIER!
YOU'RE NOW ONE OF...
...THE HONORABLE POKÉDEX HOLDERS!
THE **TENTH** POKÉDEX HOLDER!
10
BUT...

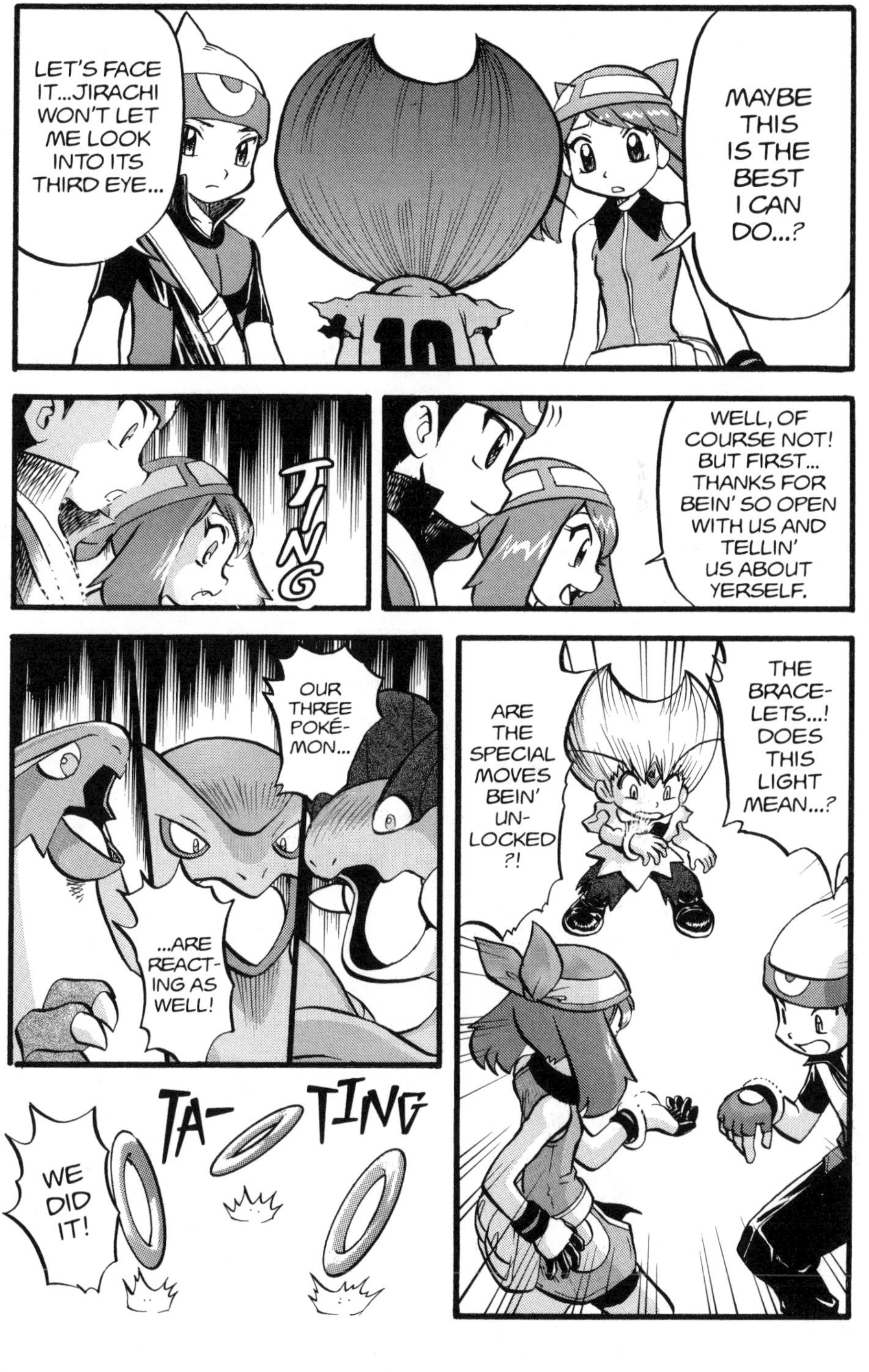
MAYBE THIS IS THE BEST I CAN DO...?
LET'S FACE IT...JIRACHI WON'T LET ME LOOK INTO ITS THIRD EYE...
WELL, OF COURSE NOT! BUT FIRST... THANKS FOR BEIN' SO OPEN WITH US AND TELLIN' US ABOUT YERSELF.
TING
THE BRACE-LETS...! DOES THIS LIGHT MEAN...?
ARE THE SPECIAL MOVES BEIN' UN-LOCKED?!
OUR THREE POKÉ-MON...
...ARE REACT-ING AS WELL!
TA-TING
WE DID IT!

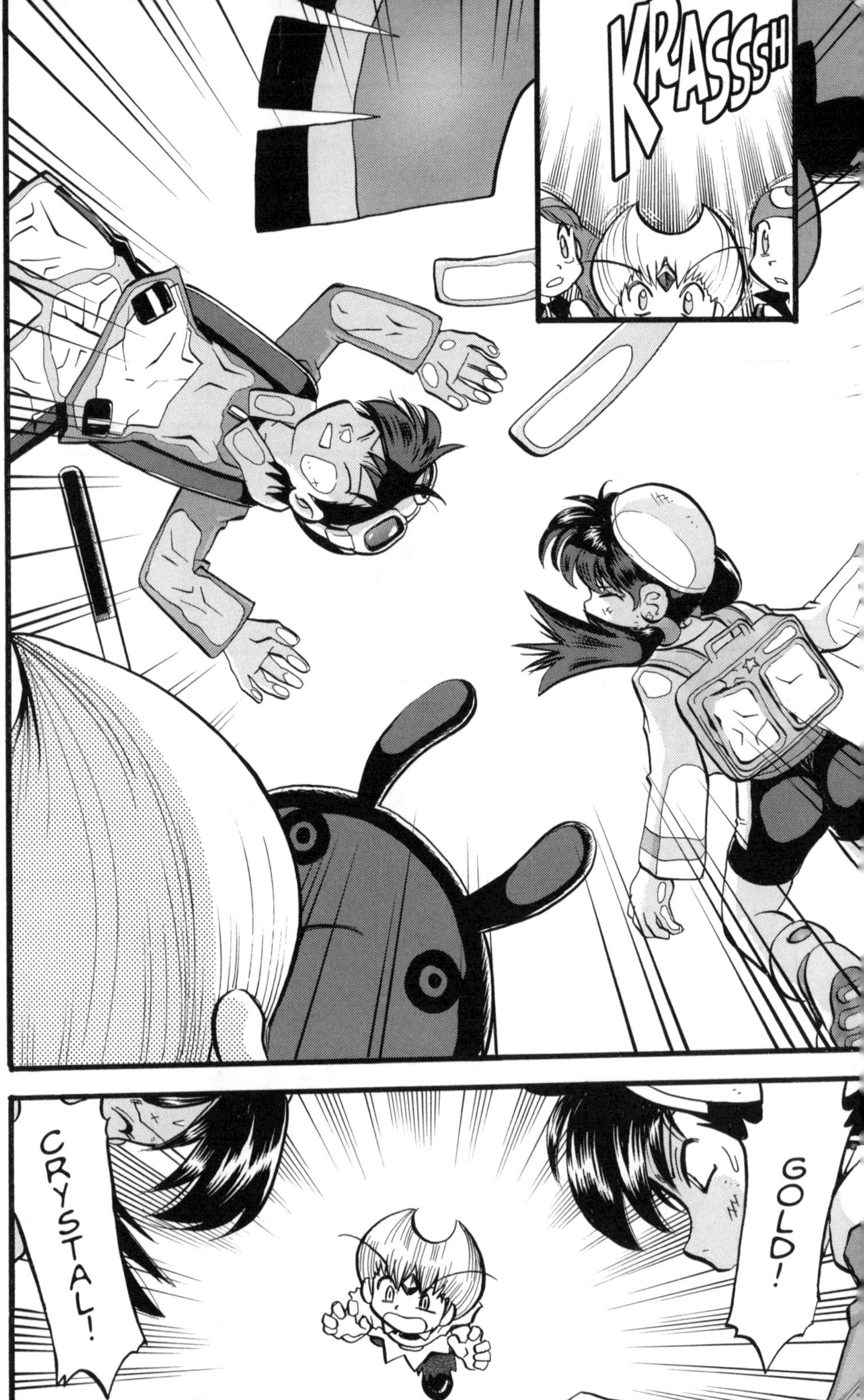
KRASSSH
GOLD!
CRYSTAL!

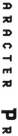

C H A R A C T E R   P R O F I L E   RUBY

THE POKÉDEX HOLDER WHO HAS WON EVERY POKÉMON CONTEST IN THE HOENN REGION. ORIGINALLY FROM JOHTO, HE MOVED TO HOENN WITH HIS MOTHER WHEN HIS FATHER BECAME THE PETALBURG CITY GYM LEADER. WHILE COMPETING IN THE POKÉMON CONTESTS HE LOVES, RUBY LEARNED OF A CRISIS THAT WAS TEARING HOENN APART AND DECIDED TO BATTLE TO HELP SAVE THE POPULACE, EVEN THOUGH HE ALWAYS CLAIMED TO HATE POKÉMON BATTLES BEFORE. HE SEEMS TO HAVE INHERITED THE POKÉMON BATTLE SKILLS OF HIS FATHER, NORMAN. ("BEAUTY IS BEST" IS STILL HIS MOTTO THOUGH.)

RUBY

- Birthplace: Goldenrod City
- Birthday: July 2
- Blood Type: O
- Skills: Sewing, making Pokéblocks
- Family: Father (Norman), mother
- Prizes Won: Every Pokémon Contest in Hoenn (Five Category × Four Cities)

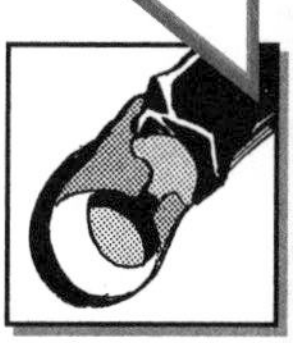

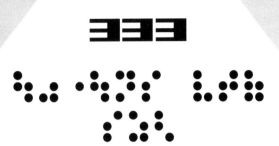

333

The Final Battle, Part 6

SKB GL

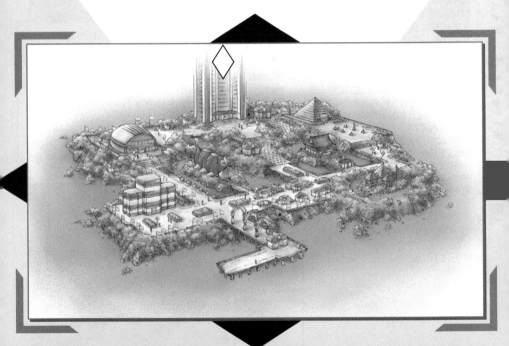

POKÉMON ADVENTURES·THE SIXTH CHAPTER·EMERALD

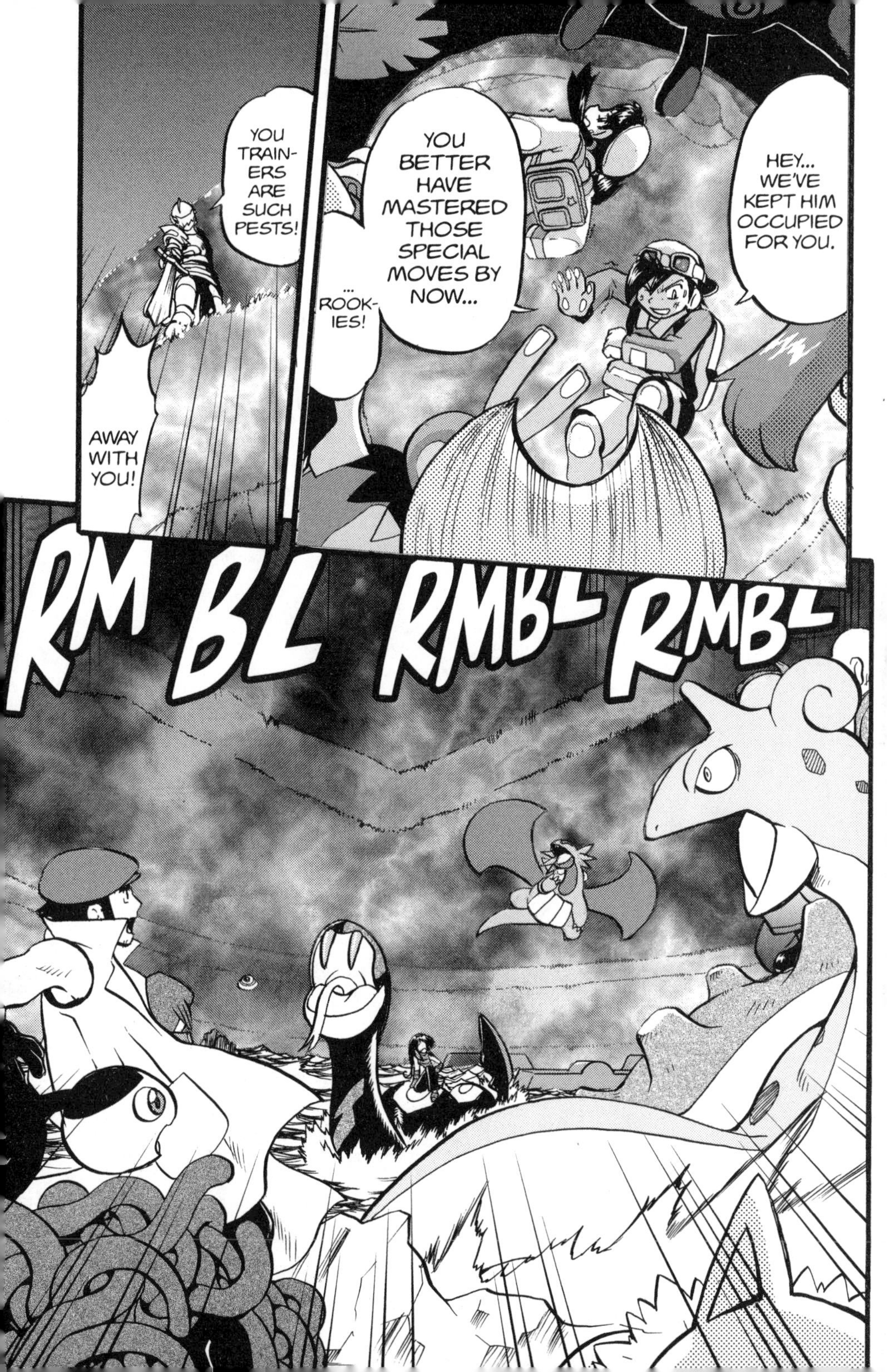
HEY... WE'VE KEPT HIM OCCUPIED FOR YOU.
YOU BETTER HAVE MASTERED THOSE SPECIAL MOVES BY NOW...
... ROOK-IES!
YOU TRAIN-ERS ARE SUCH PESTS!
AWAY WITH YOU!
RM BL RMBL RMBL

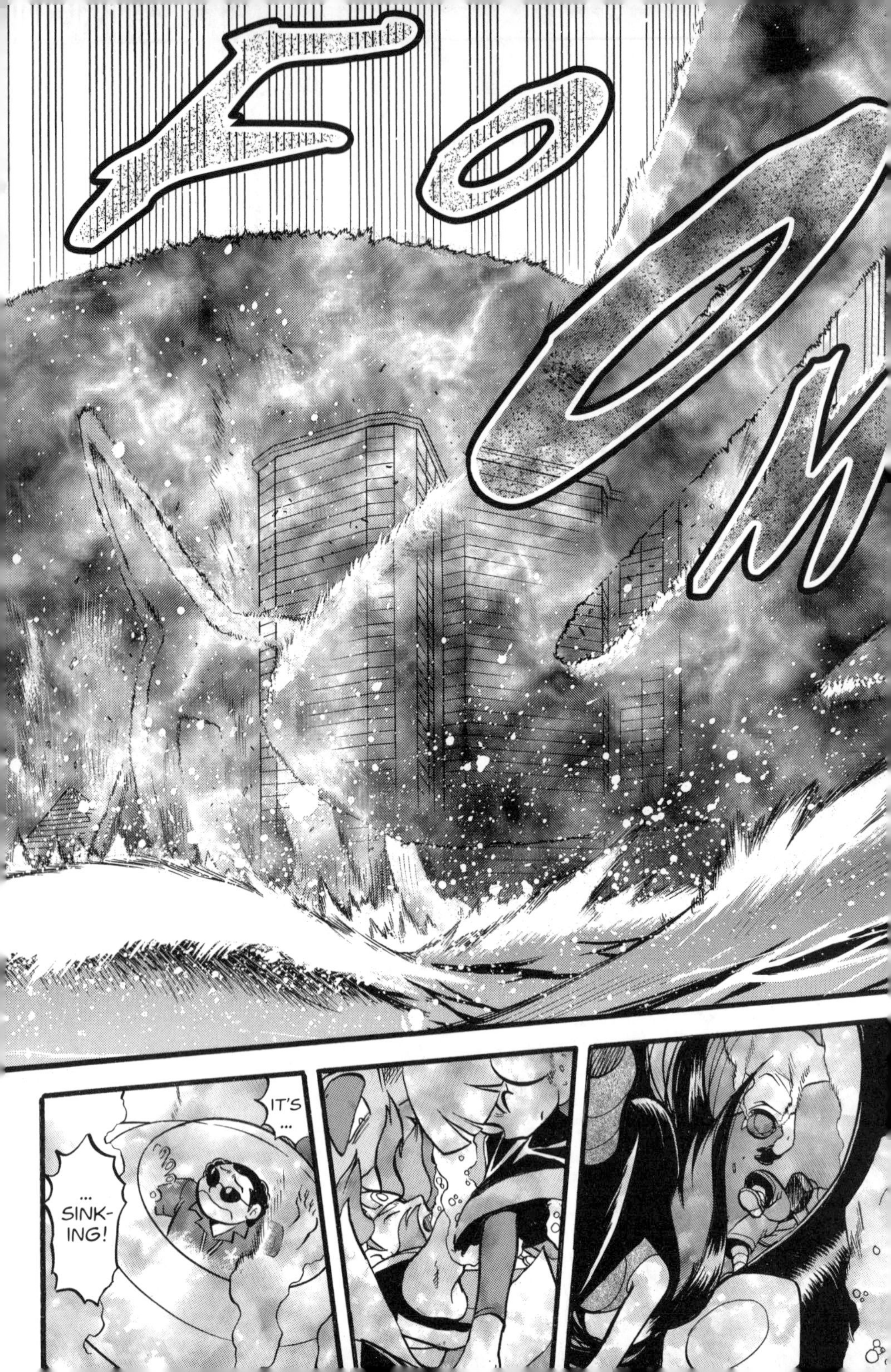
IT'S ...
... SINK-ING!

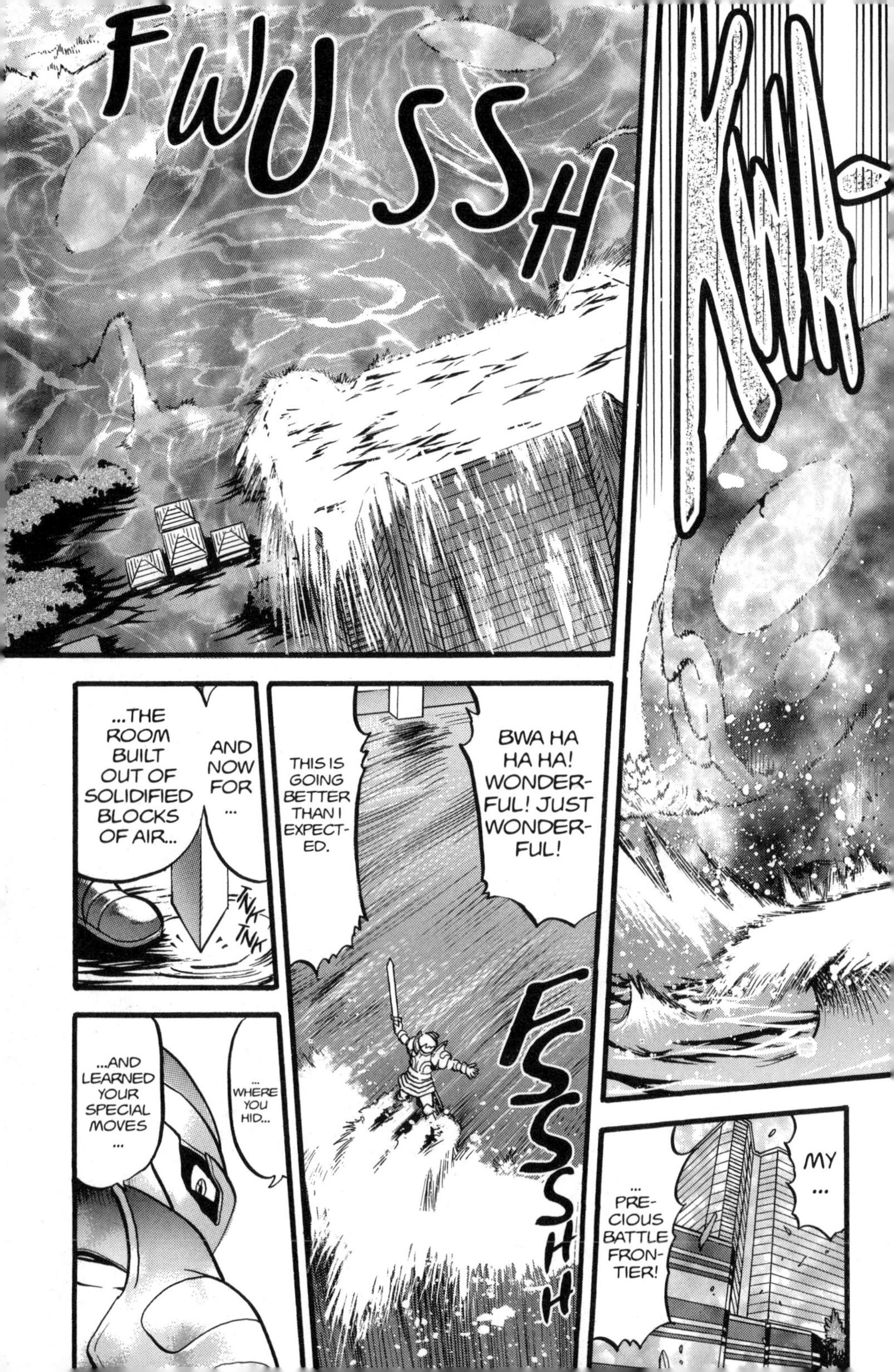

FWUSSH
BWA HA HA HA! WONDERFUL! JUST WONDERFUL!
THIS IS GOING BETTER THAN I EXPECTED.
FSSSHH
AND NOW FOR ...
...THE ROOM BUILT OUT OF SOLIDIFIED BLOCKS OF AIR...
TNK TNK
... WHERE YOU HID...
...AND LEARNED YOUR SPECIAL MOVES ...
MY ...
... PRECIOUS BATTLE FRONTIER!

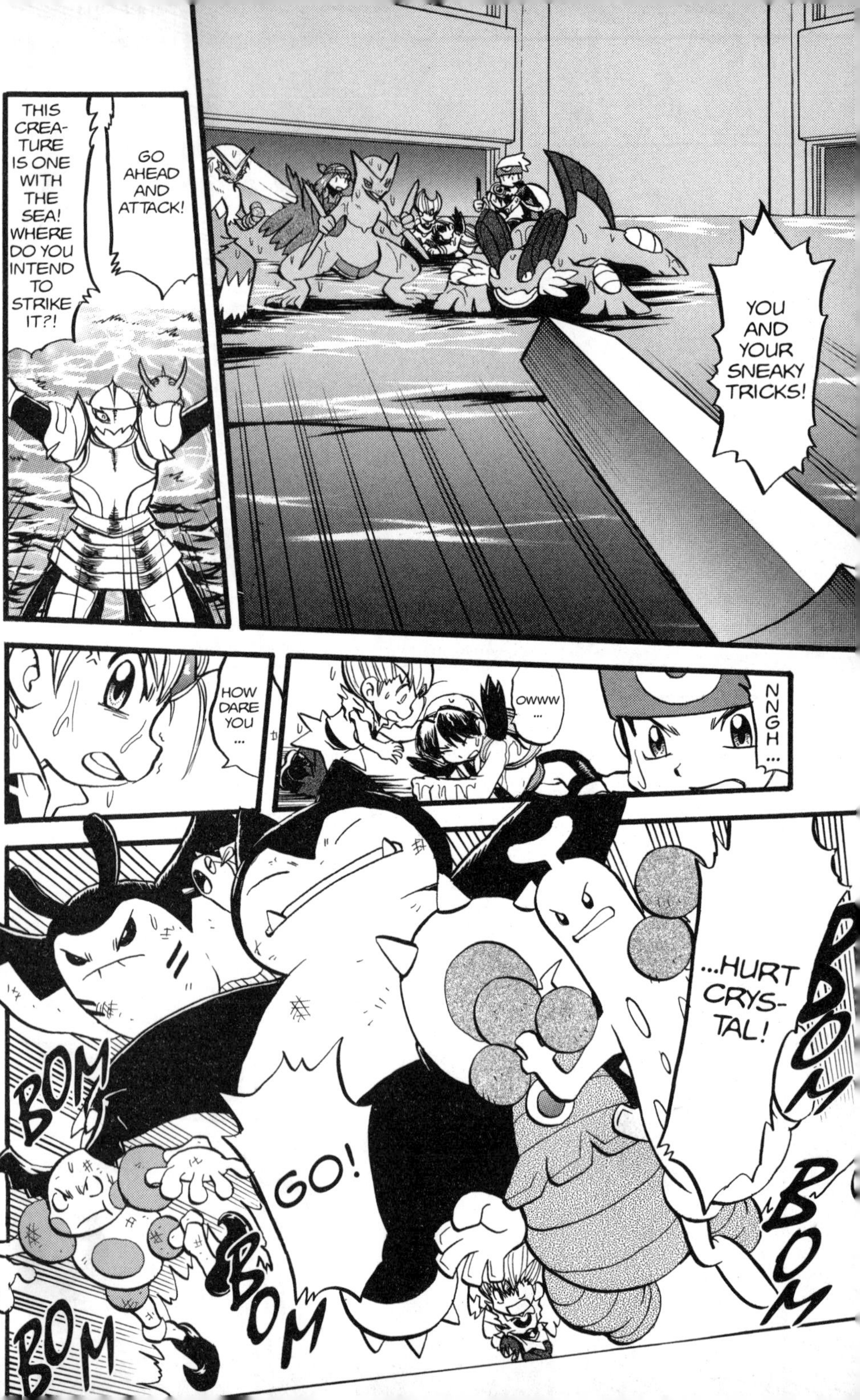
YOU AND YOUR SNEAKY TRICKS!
GO AHEAD AND ATTACK!
THIS CREA-TURE IS ONE WITH THE SEA! WHERE DO YOU INTEND TO STRIKE IT?!
NNGH...
OWWW...
HOW DARE YOU...
BOM
...HURT CRYS-TAL!
BOM
BOM
GO!
BOM
BOM
BOM

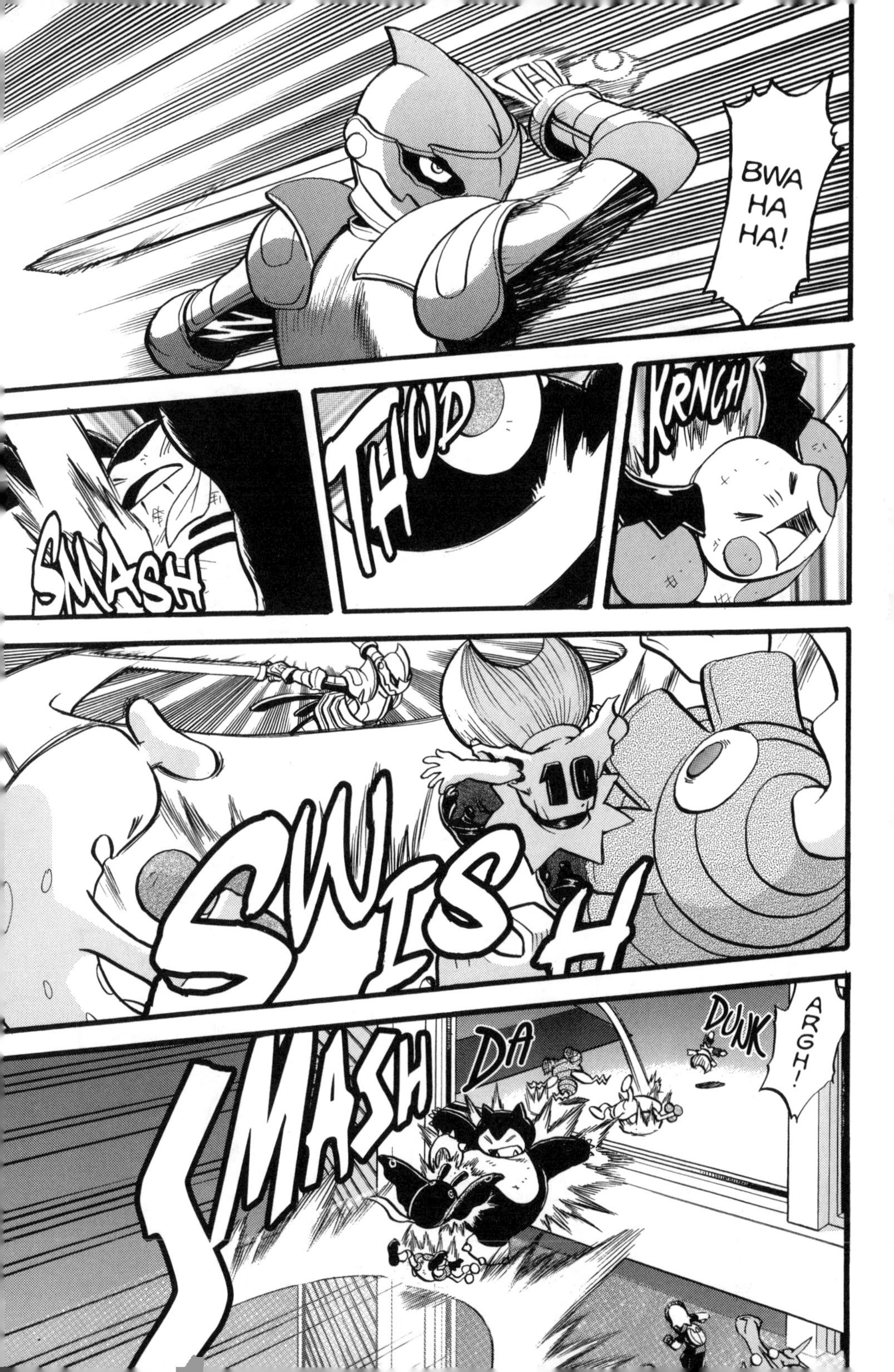
BWA HA HA HA!
KRNCH
THUD
SMASH
SWISH
ARGH!
DUNK
DA
SMASH

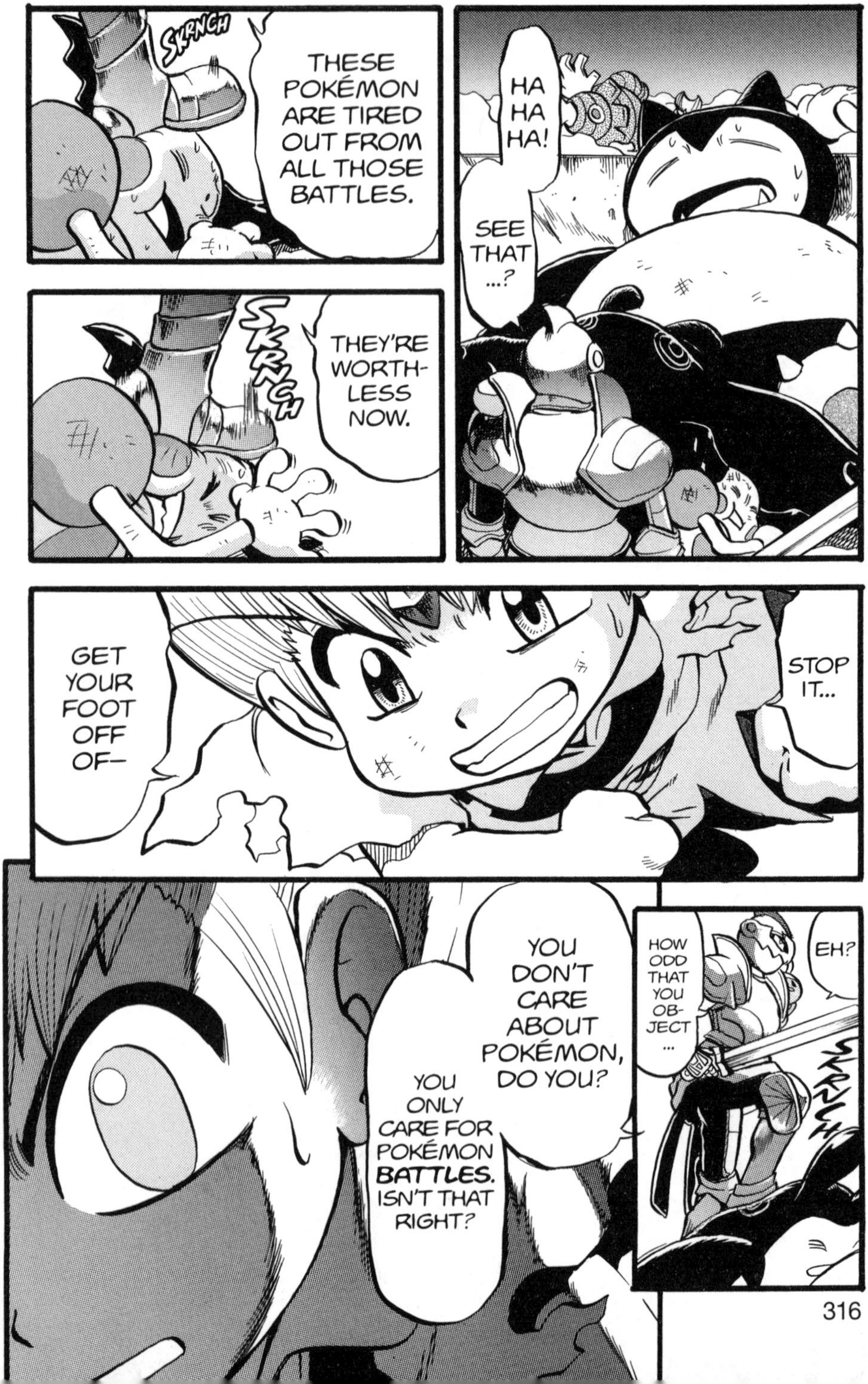
HA HA HA!
SEE THAT ...?
SKRNCH
THESE POKÉMON ARE TIRED OUT FROM ALL THOSE BATTLES.
SKRNCH
THEY'RE WORTHLESS NOW.
STOP IT...
GET YOUR FOOT OFF OF–
EH?
HOW ODD THAT YOU OBJECT ...
SKRNCH
YOU DON'T CARE ABOUT POKÉMON, DO YOU?
YOU ONLY CARE FOR POKÉMON **BATTLES.** ISN'T THAT RIGHT?

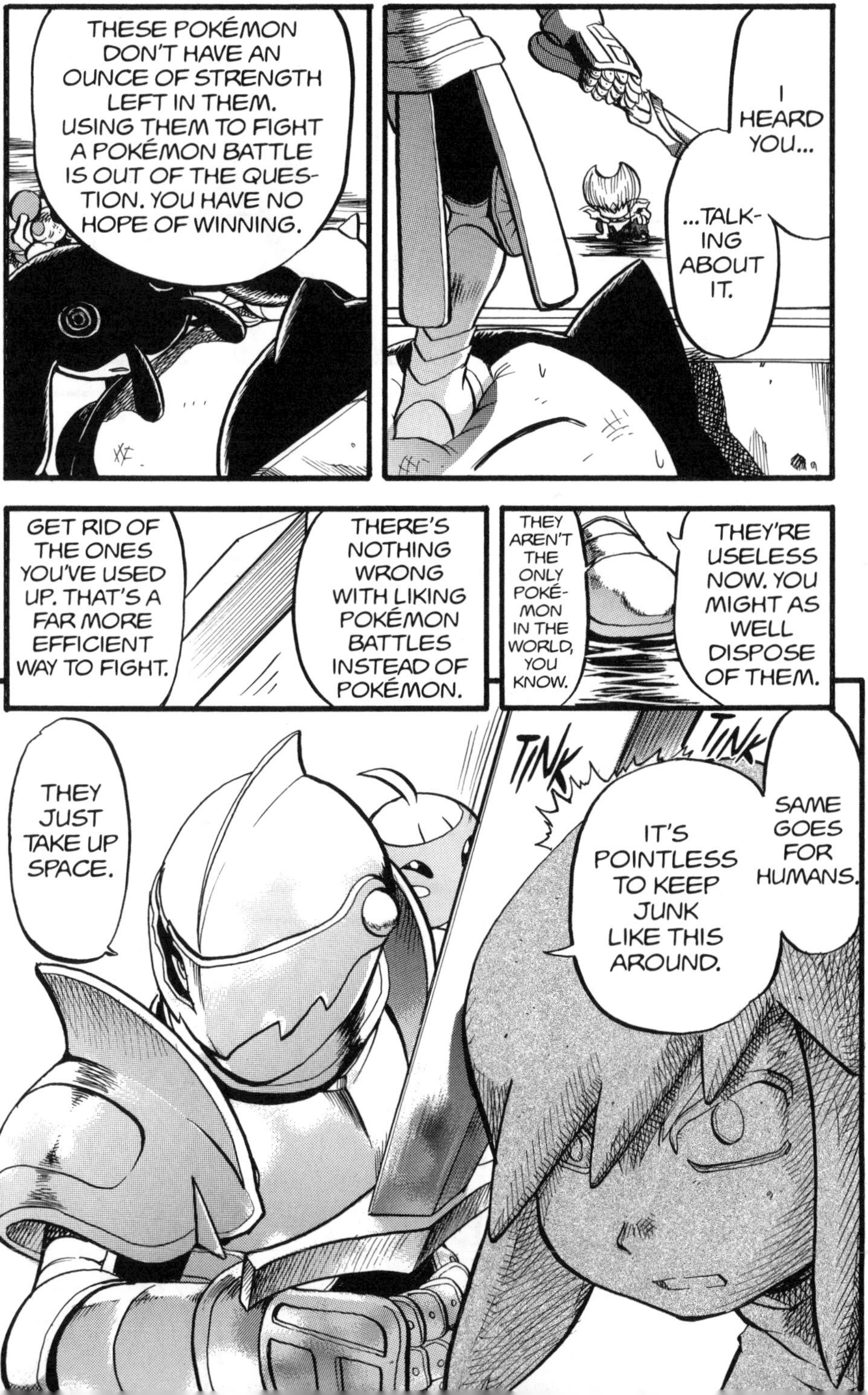
I HEARD YOU...
...TALKING ABOUT IT.
THESE POKÉMON DON'T HAVE AN OUNCE OF STRENGTH LEFT IN THEM. USING THEM TO FIGHT A POKÉMON BATTLE IS OUT OF THE QUESTION. YOU HAVE NO HOPE OF WINNING.
THEY'RE USELESS NOW. YOU MIGHT AS WELL DISPOSE OF THEM.
THEY AREN'T THE ONLY POKÉMON IN THE WORLD, YOU KNOW.
THERE'S NOTHING WRONG WITH LIKING POKÉMON BATTLES INSTEAD OF POKÉMON.
GET RID OF THE ONES YOU'VE USED UP. THAT'S A FAR MORE EFFICIENT WAY TO FIGHT.
SAME GOES FOR HUMANS.
TINK
TINK
IT'S POINTLESS TO KEEP JUNK LIKE THIS AROUND.
THEY JUST TAKE UP SPACE.

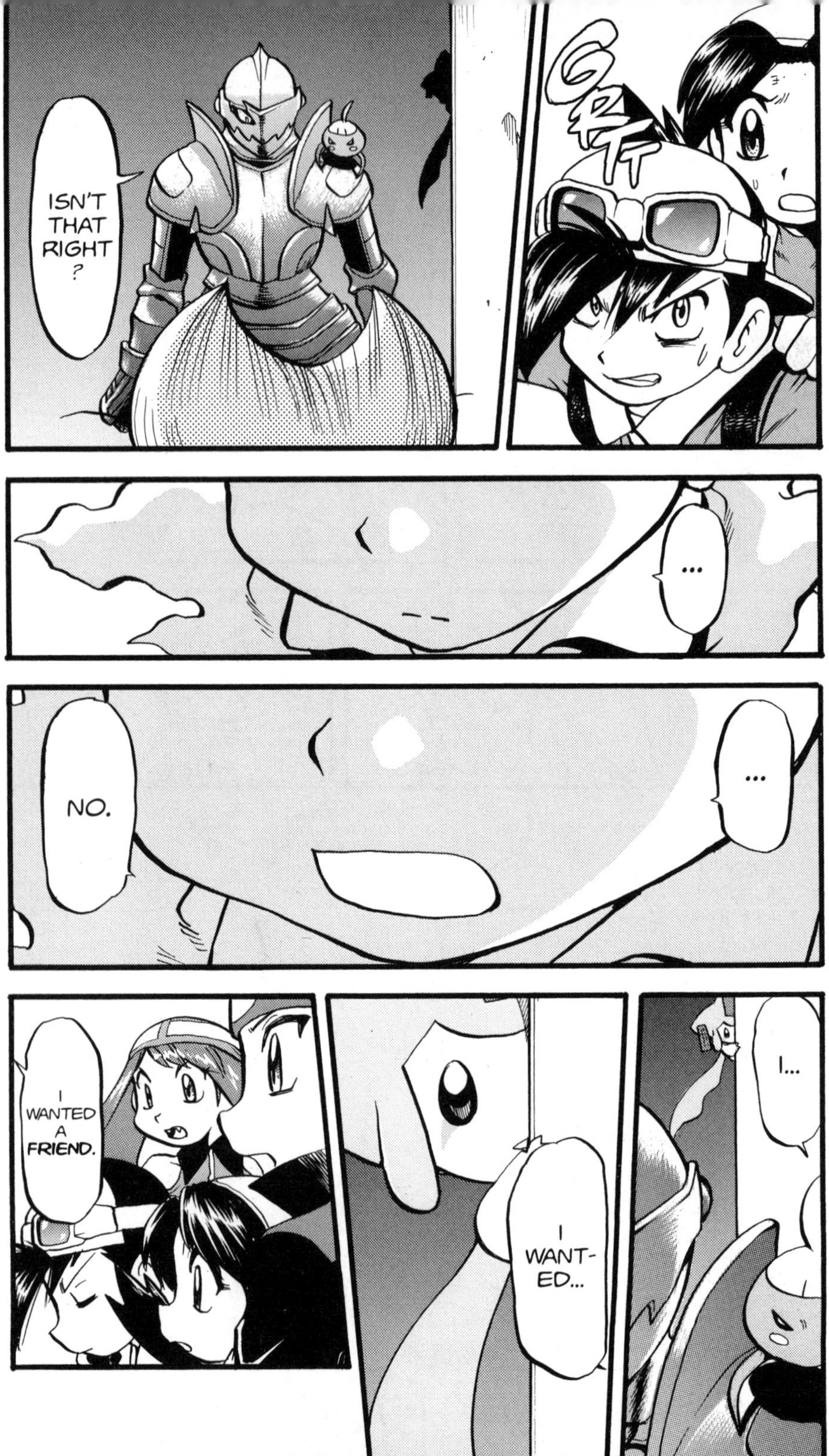
GRTT
ISN'T THAT RIGHT?
...
...
NO.
I...
I WANT-ED...
I WANTED A **FRIEND**.

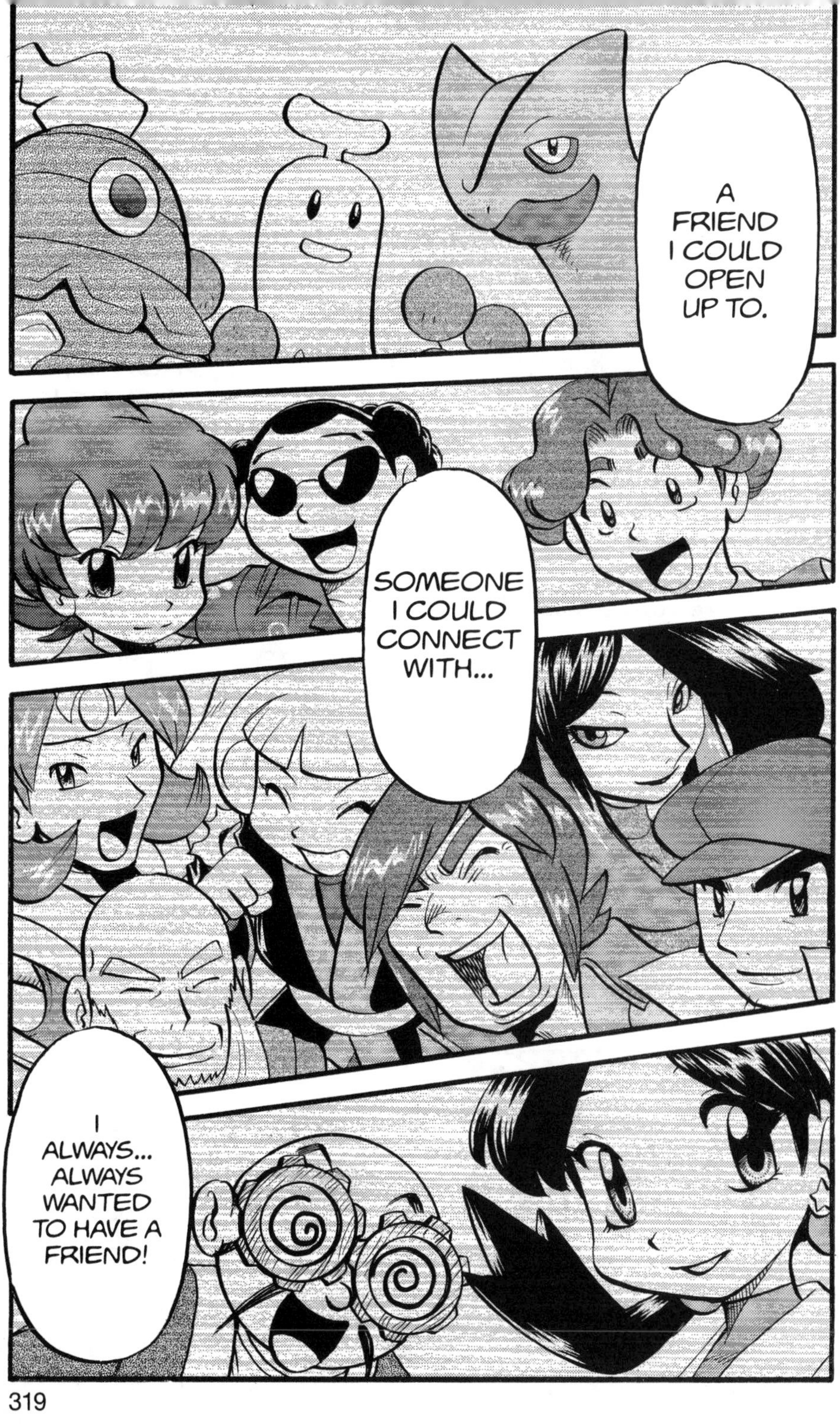
A FRIEND I COULD OPEN UP TO.
SOMEONE I COULD CONNECT WITH...
I ALWAYS... ALWAYS WANTED TO HAVE A FRIEND!

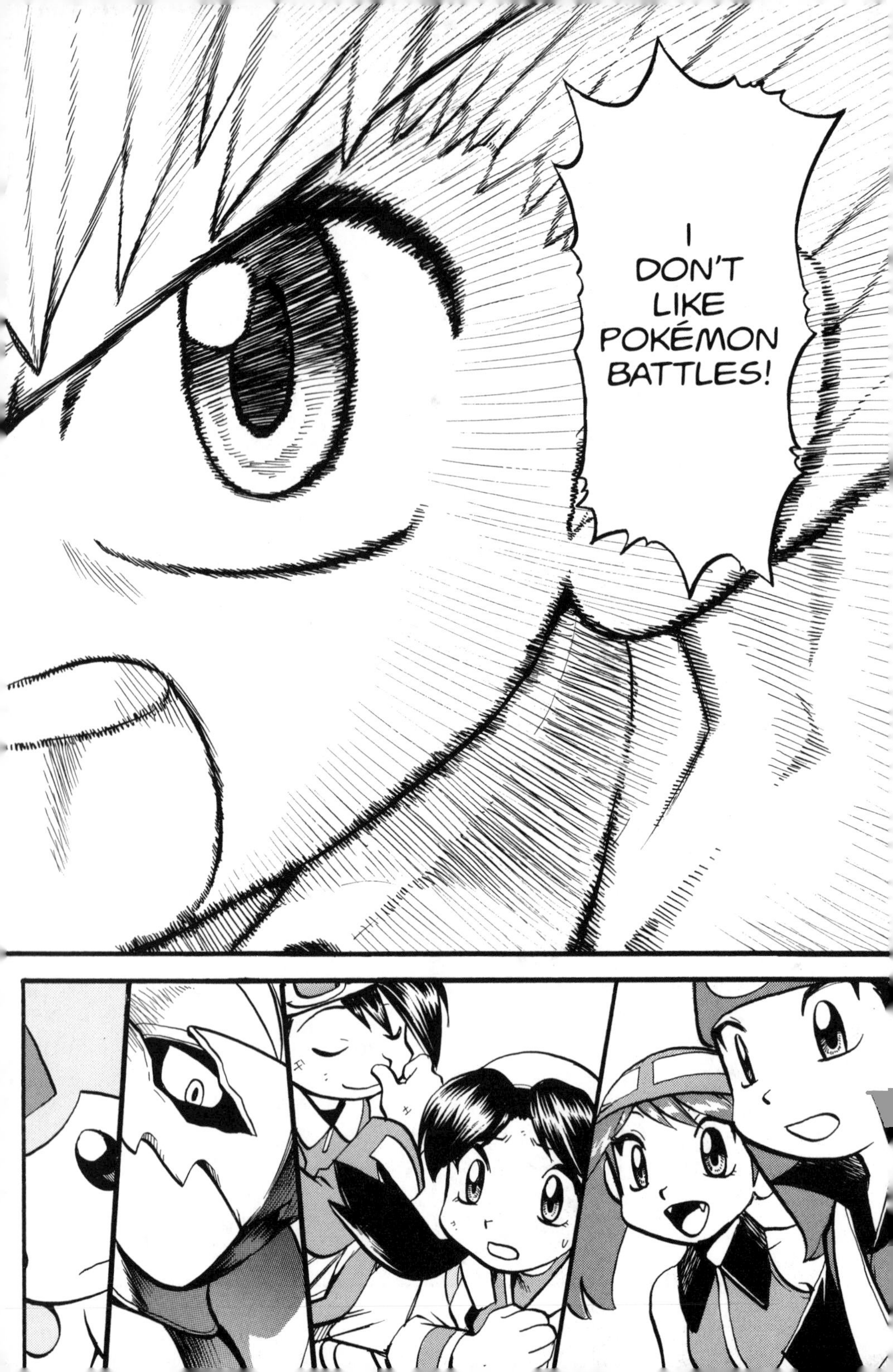
I DON'T LIKE POKÉMON BATTLES!

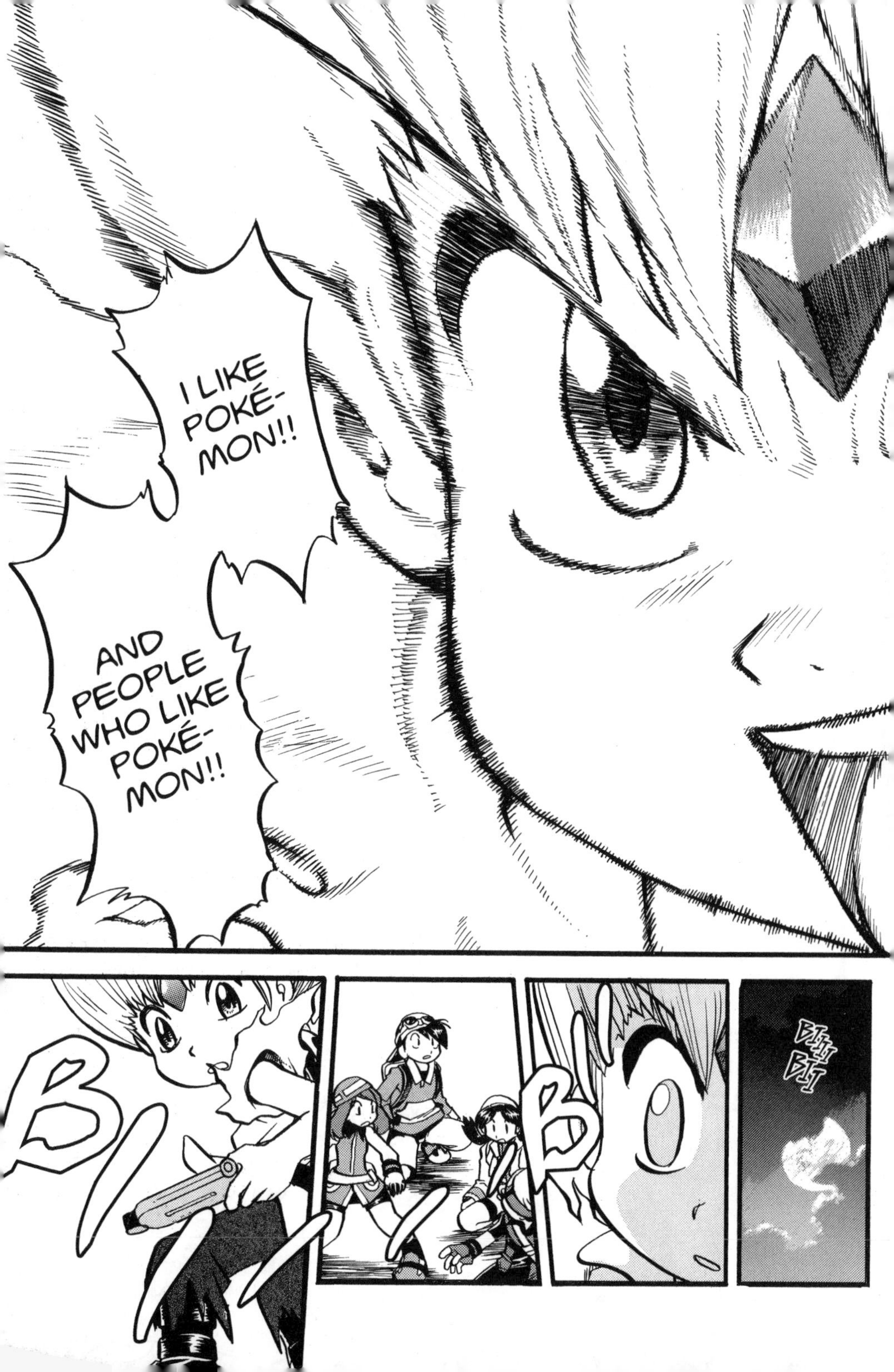
I LIKE POKÉ-MON!!
AND PEOPLE WHO LIKE POKÉ-MON!!
BIII BII
B
BI

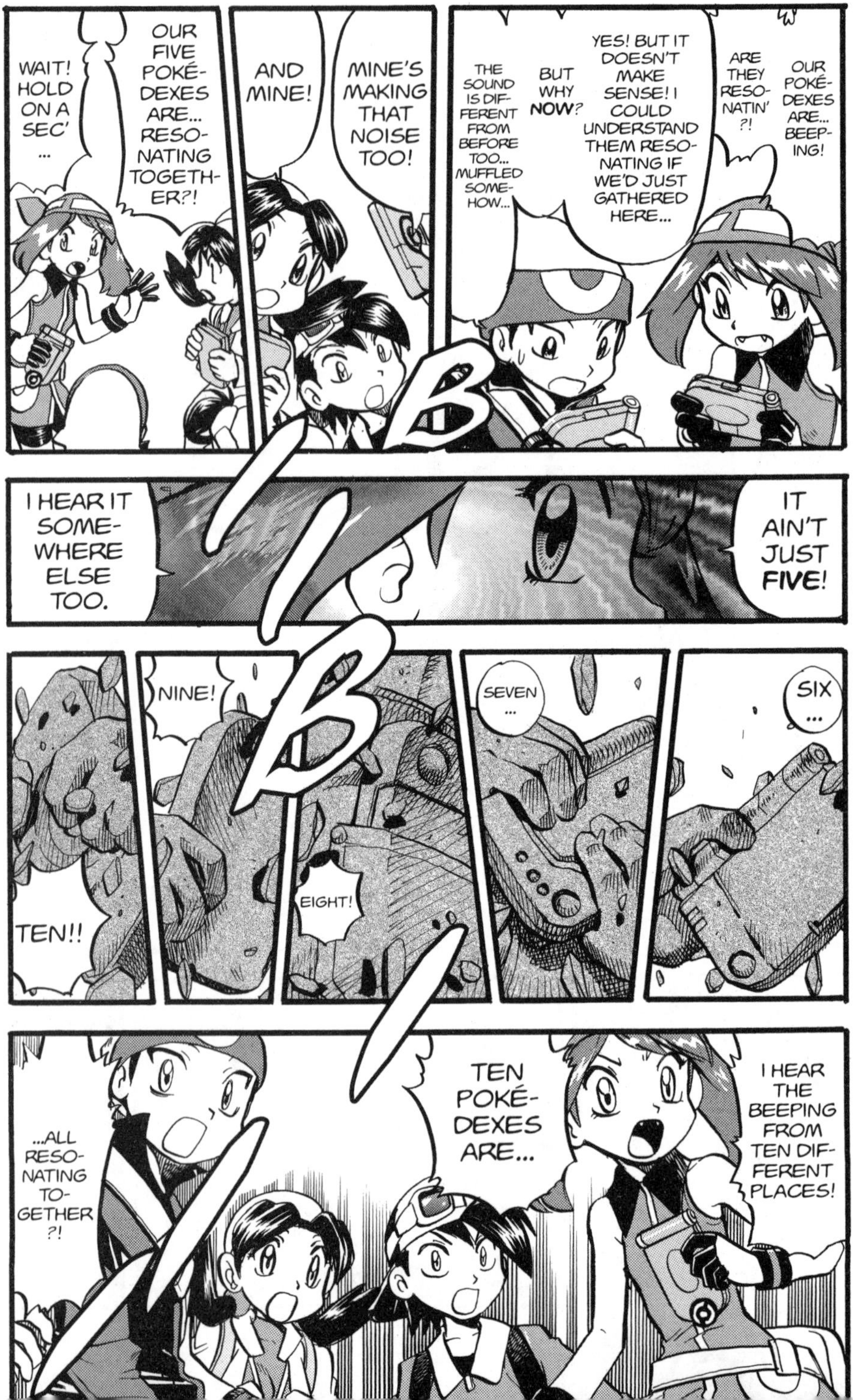
OUR POKÉDEXES ARE... BEEPING!
ARE THEY RESONATIN'?!
YES! BUT IT DOESN'T MAKE SENSE! I COULD UNDERSTAND THEM RESONATING IF WE'D JUST GATHERED HERE...
BUT WHY **NOW**?
THE SOUND IS DIFFERENT FROM BEFORE TOO... MUFFLED SOMEHOW...
MINE'S MAKING THAT NOISE TOO!
AND MINE!
OUR FIVE POKÉDEXES ARE... RESONATING TOGETHER?!
WAIT! HOLD ON A SEC'...
BIBI
IT AIN'T JUST **FIVE**!
I HEAR IT SOMEWHERE ELSE TOO.
SIX...
SEVEN...
EIGHT!
NINE!
TEN!!
I HEAR THE BEEPING FROM TEN DIFFERENT PLACES!
TEN POKÉDEXES ARE...
...ALL RESONATING TOGETHER?!

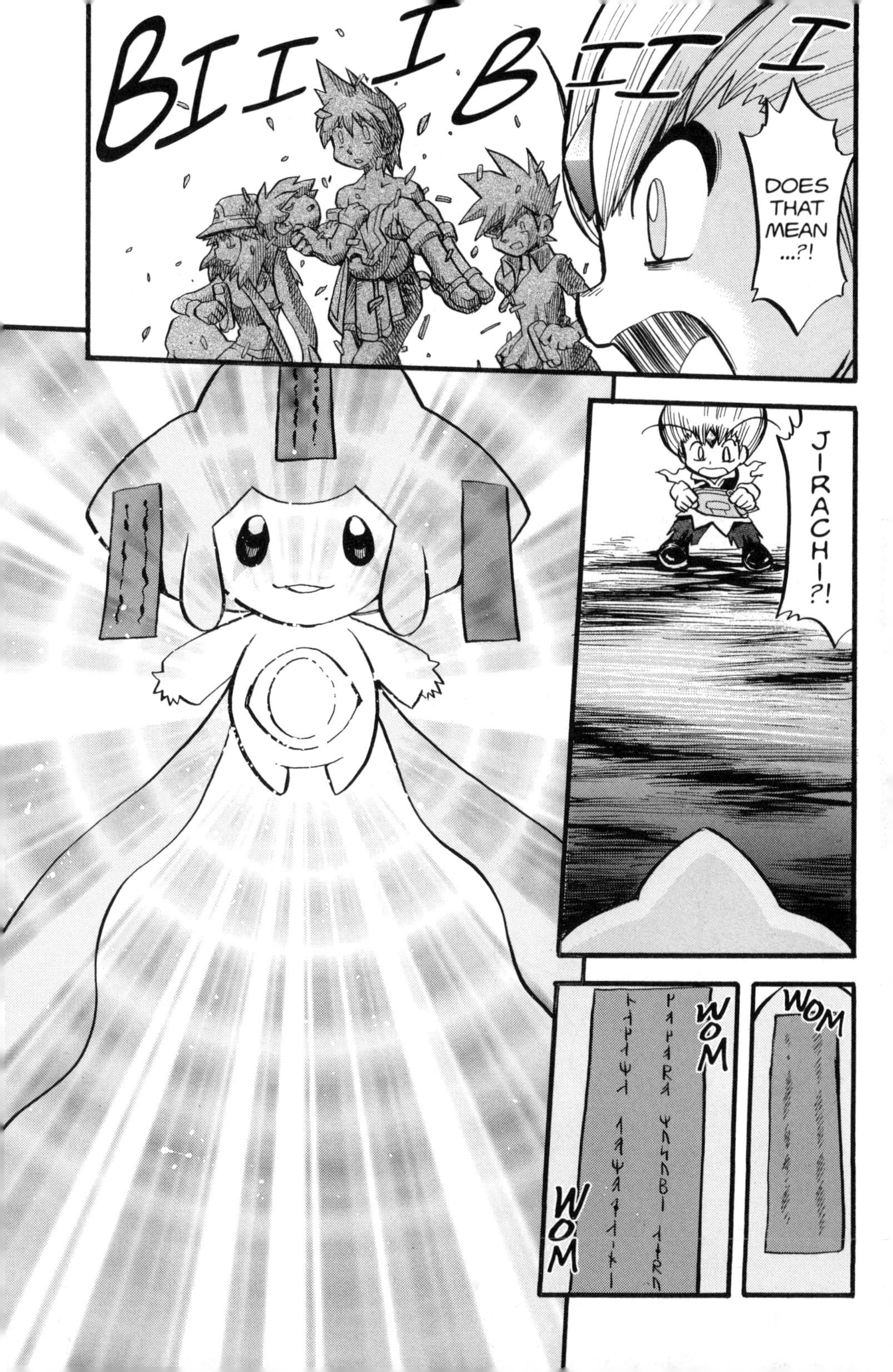
BIII BIII
DOES THAT MEAN ...?!
JIRACHI?!
WOM
WOM
WOM

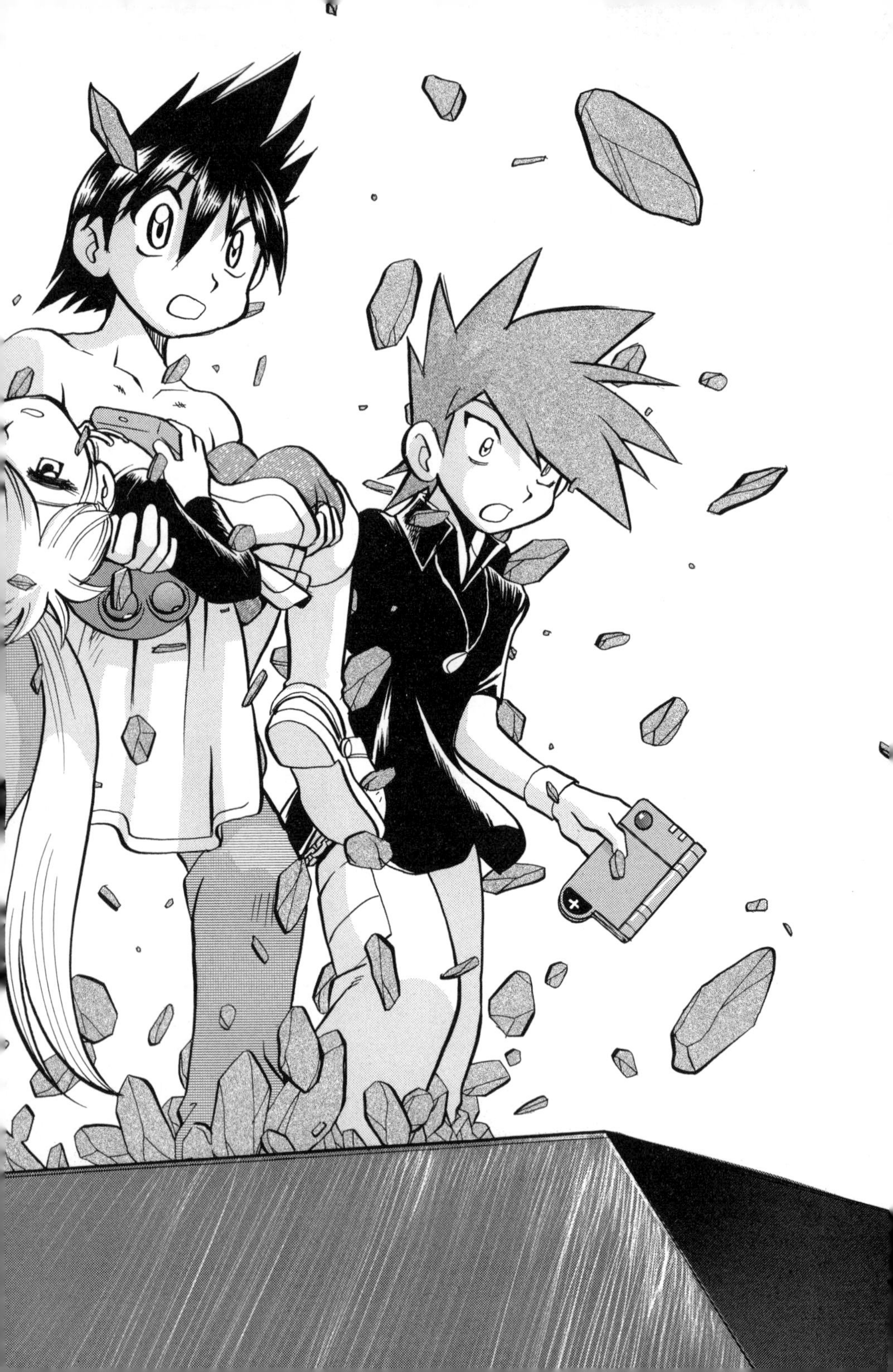

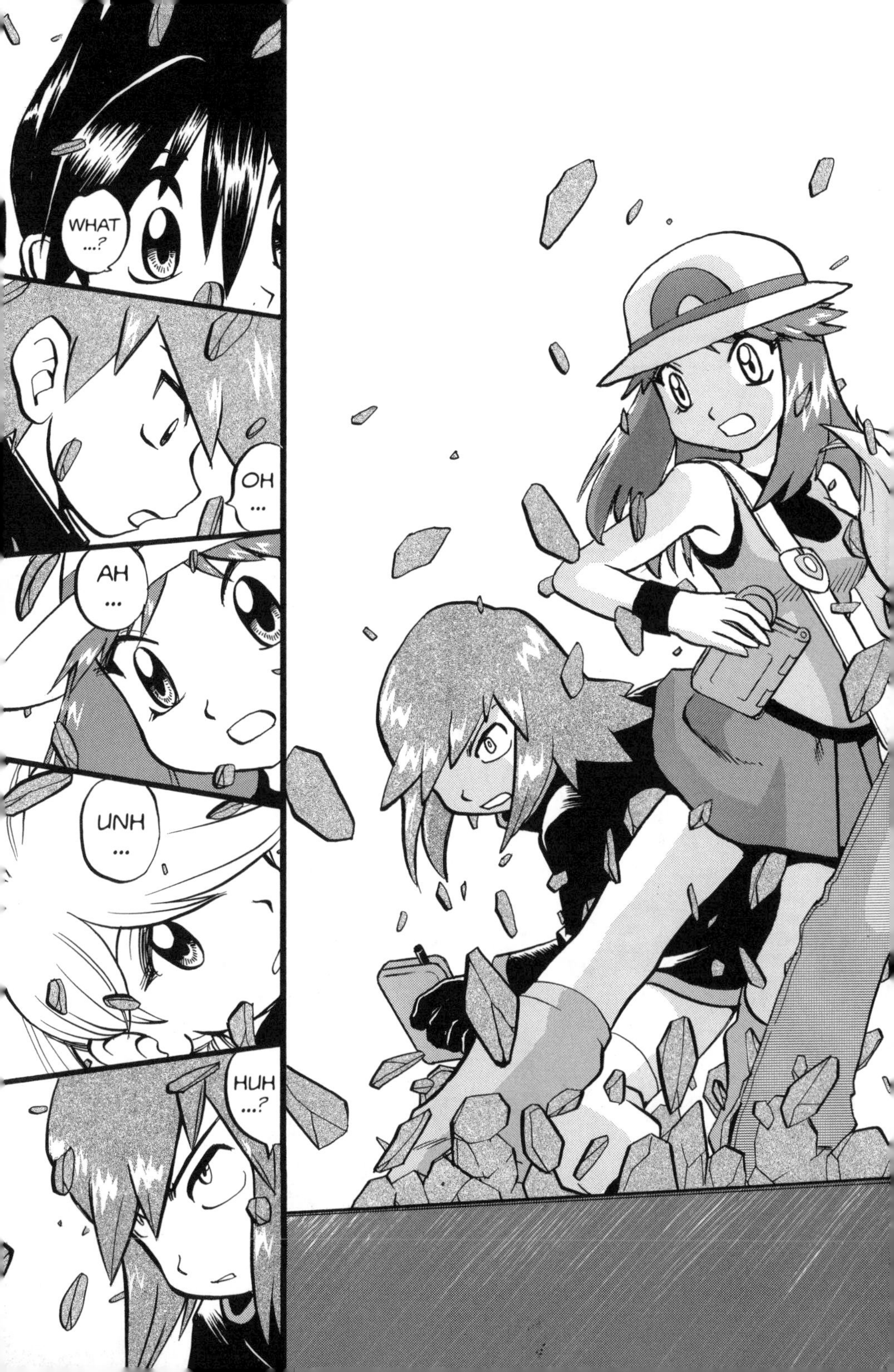
WHAT ...?
OH ...
AH ...
UNH ...
HUH ...?

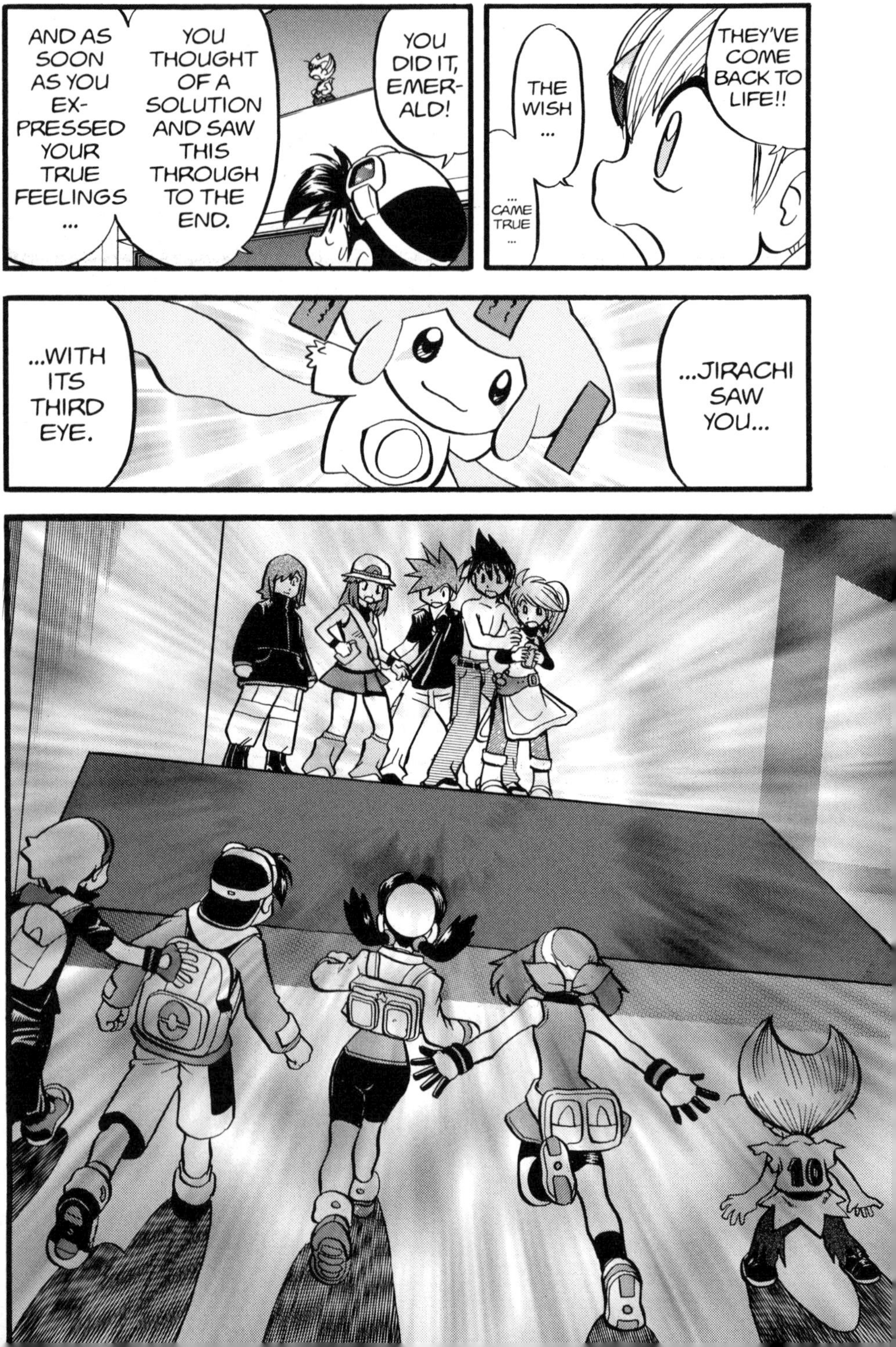
THEY'VE COME BACK TO LIFE!!
THE WISH...
...CAME TRUE...
YOU DID IT, EMERALD!
AND AS SOON AS YOU EX-PRESSED YOUR TRUE FEELINGS...
YOU THOUGHT OF A SOLUTION AND SAW THIS THROUGH TO THE END.
...JIRACHI SAW YOU...
...WITH ITS THIRD EYE.
10

CHARACTER PROFILE

SAPPHIRE

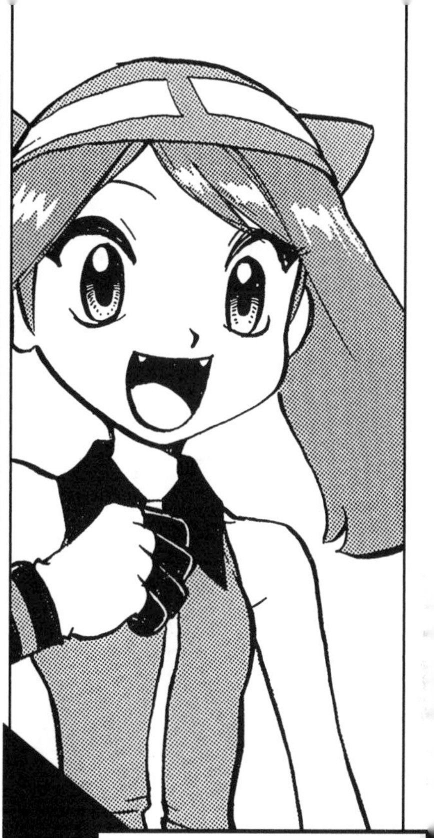

SAPPHIRE

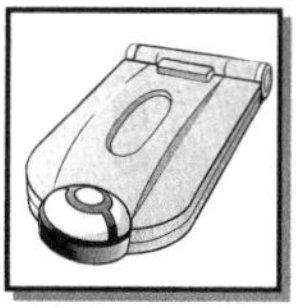

THE DAUGHTER OF POKÉMON RESEARCHER PROFESSOR BIRCH, WHO IS RENOWNED FOR HIS FIELDWORK. HAVING SPENT HER CHILDHOOD PLAYING IN THE FORESTS, FIELDS AND MOUNTAINS HELPING HER FATHER WITH HIS WORK, SHE HAS ACQUIRED A WILD AND FREE NATURE. HER EYES, EARS AND NOSE ARE EXTREMELY SENSITIVE, ENABLING HER TO SENSE THINGS ORDINARY PEOPLE CANNOT. SHE ALSO HAS A WIDE KNOWLEDGE OF BERRIES AND AN UNCANNY ABILITY TO DIAGNOSE A SICK POKÉMON AND EVALUATE ITS HEALTH. WHILE ATTEMPTING TO DEFEAT ALL THE POKÉMON GYMS, SHE LEARNED ABOUT THE AWAKENING OF LEGENDARY POKÉMON THAT WERE CAUSING HAVOC. WITH RUBY, SHE FOUGHT TO SAVE THE WORLD. ALTHOUGH SHE APPEARS WILD AT HEART, SHE IS ACTUALLY QUITE EMOTIONALLY VULNERABLE.

- Birthplace: Littleroot Town
- Birthday: September 20
- Blood Type: O
- Skills: Tree and cliff climbing
- Family: Father (Birch), mother
- Prizes Won: Defeated every Pokémon Gym in Hoenn

334

The Final Battle, Part 7

POKÉMON ADVENTURES•THE SIXTH CHAPTER•EMERALD

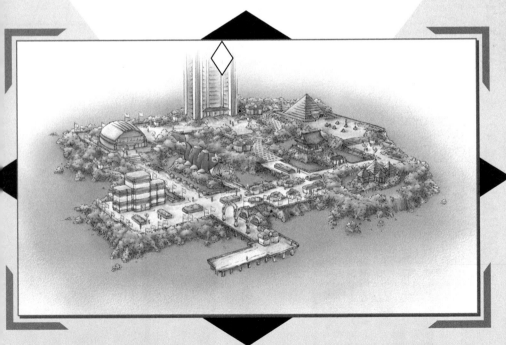

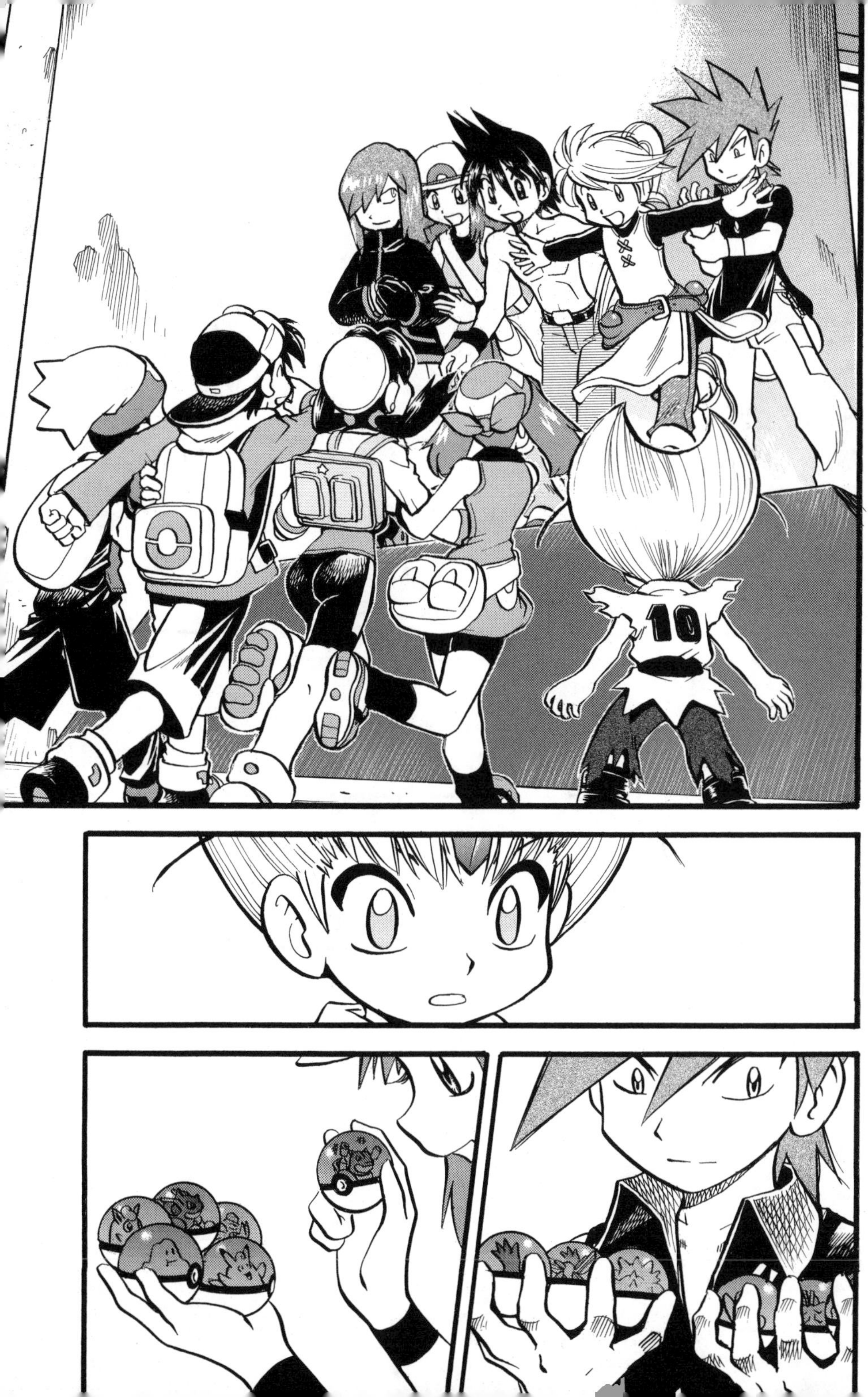
10

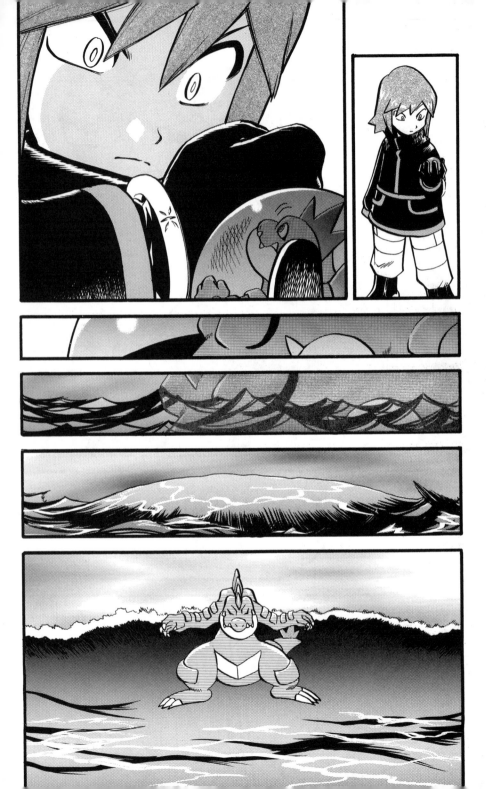

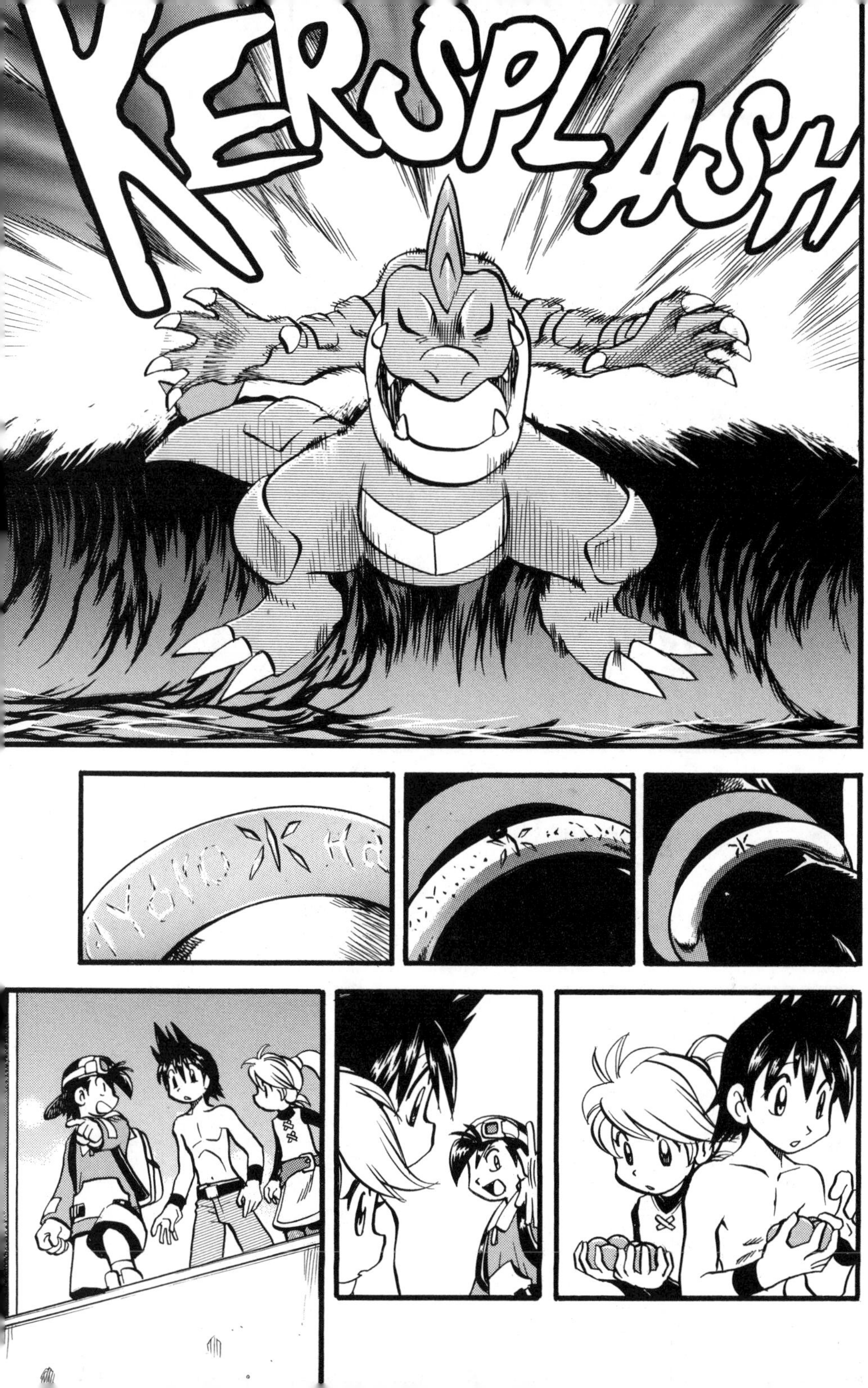
KERSPLASH

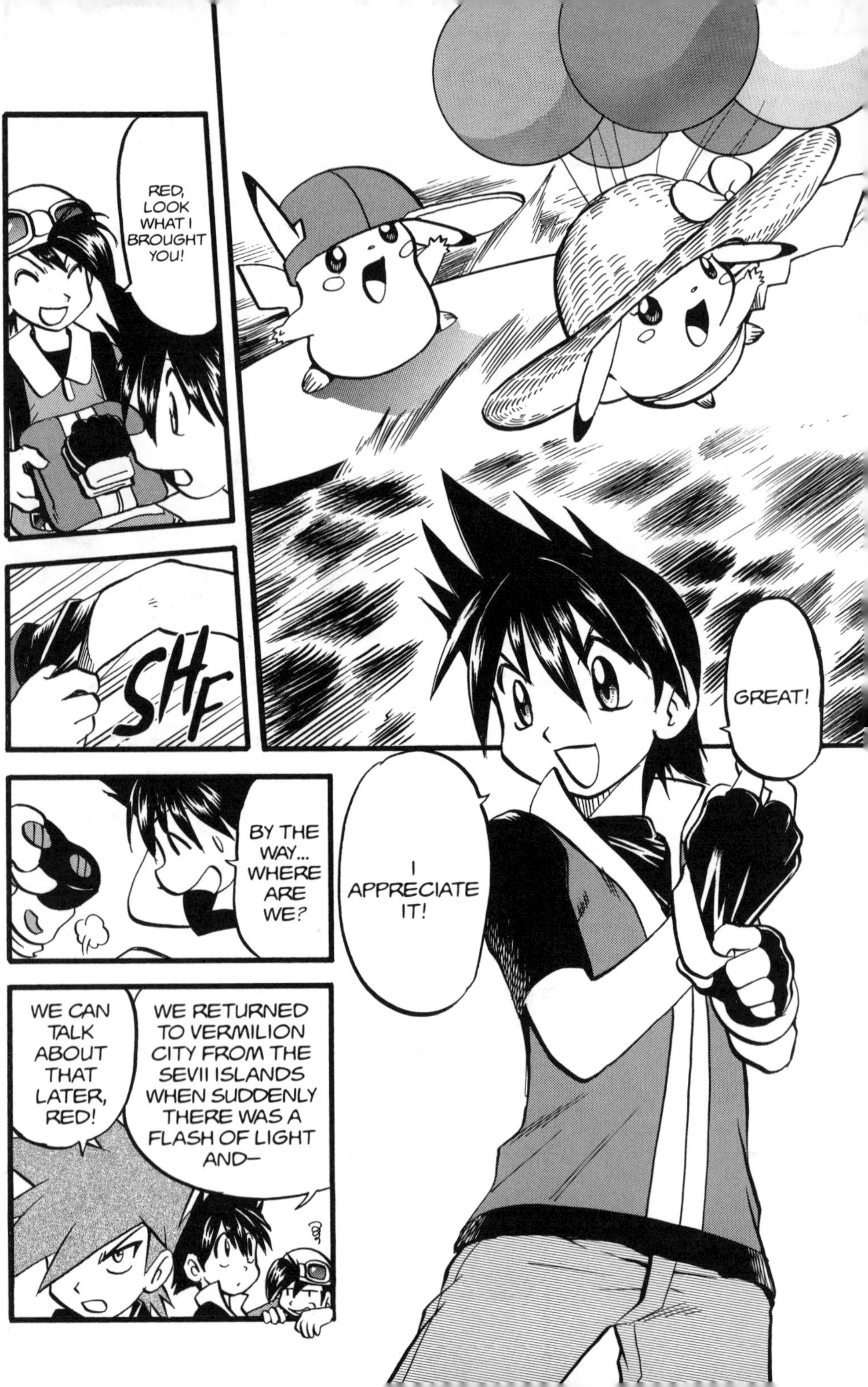
RED, LOOK WHAT I BROUGHT YOU!
SHF
GREAT!
I APPRECIATE IT!
BY THE WAY... WHERE ARE WE?
WE RETURNED TO VERMILION CITY FROM THE SEVII ISLANDS WHEN SUDDENLY THERE WAS A FLASH OF LIGHT AND—
WE CAN TALK ABOUT THAT LATER, RED!

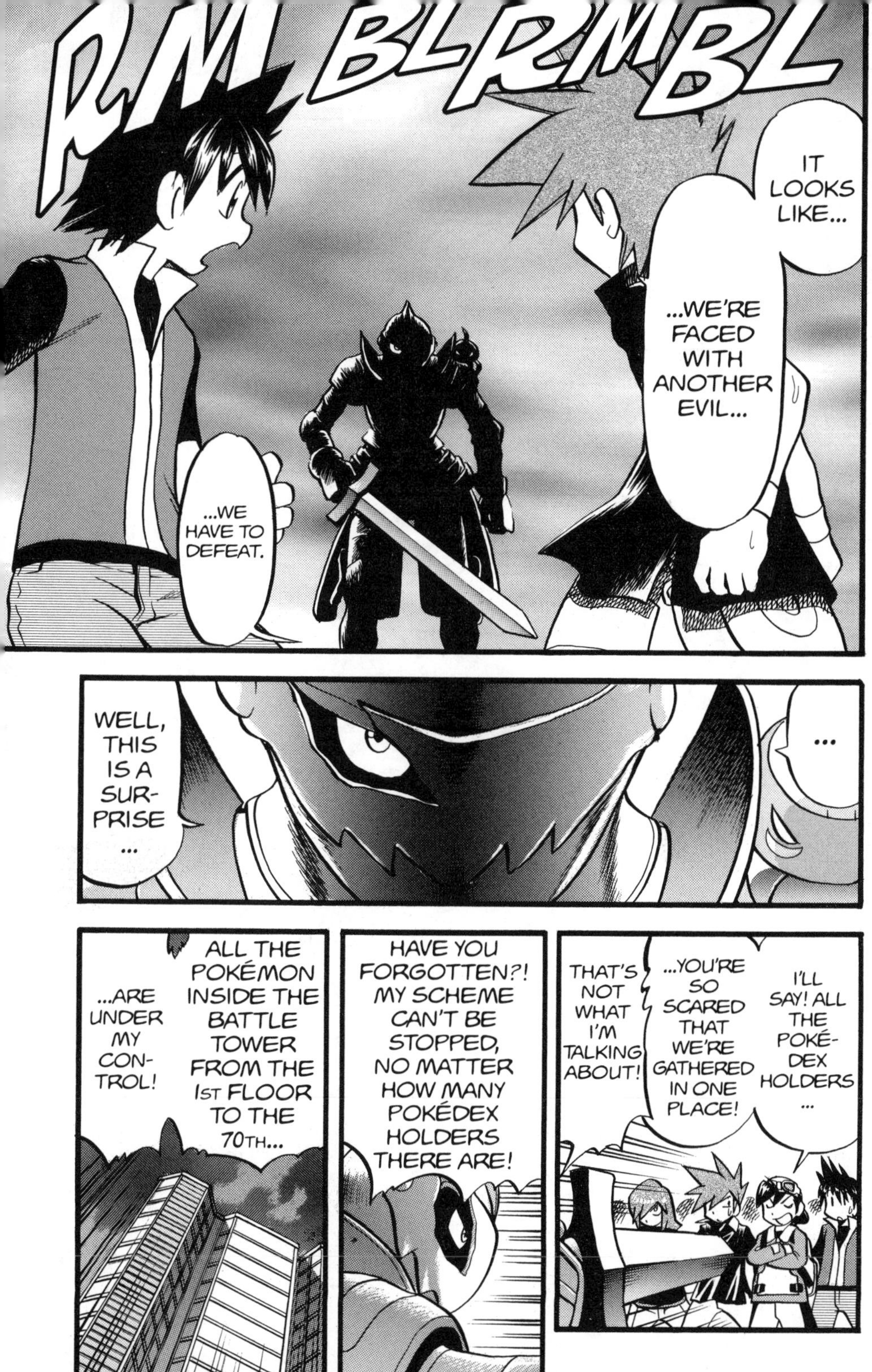
RMBLRMBL
IT LOOKS LIKE...
...WE'RE FACED WITH ANOTHER EVIL...
...WE HAVE TO DEFEAT.
...
WELL, THIS IS A SURPRISE...
I'LL SAY! ALL THE POKÉDEX HOLDERS...
...YOU'RE SO SCARED THAT WE'RE GATHERED IN ONE PLACE!
THAT'S NOT WHAT I'M TALKING ABOUT!
HAVE YOU FORGOTTEN?! MY SCHEME CAN'T BE STOPPED, NO MATTER HOW MANY POKÉDEX HOLDERS THERE ARE!
ALL THE POKÉMON INSIDE THE BATTLE TOWER FROM THE 1ST FLOOR TO THE 70TH...
...ARE UNDER MY CONTROL!

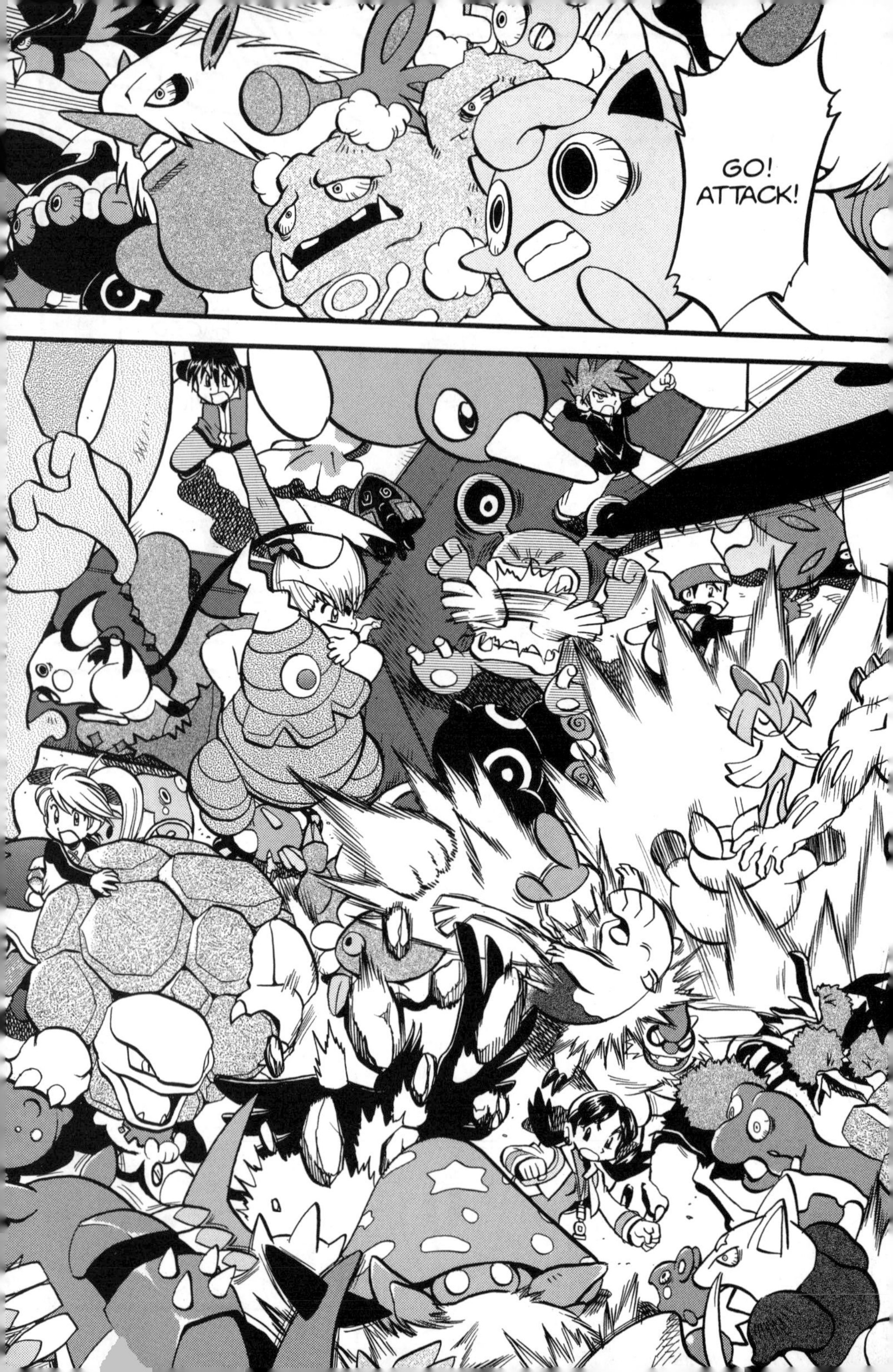
GO! ATTACK!

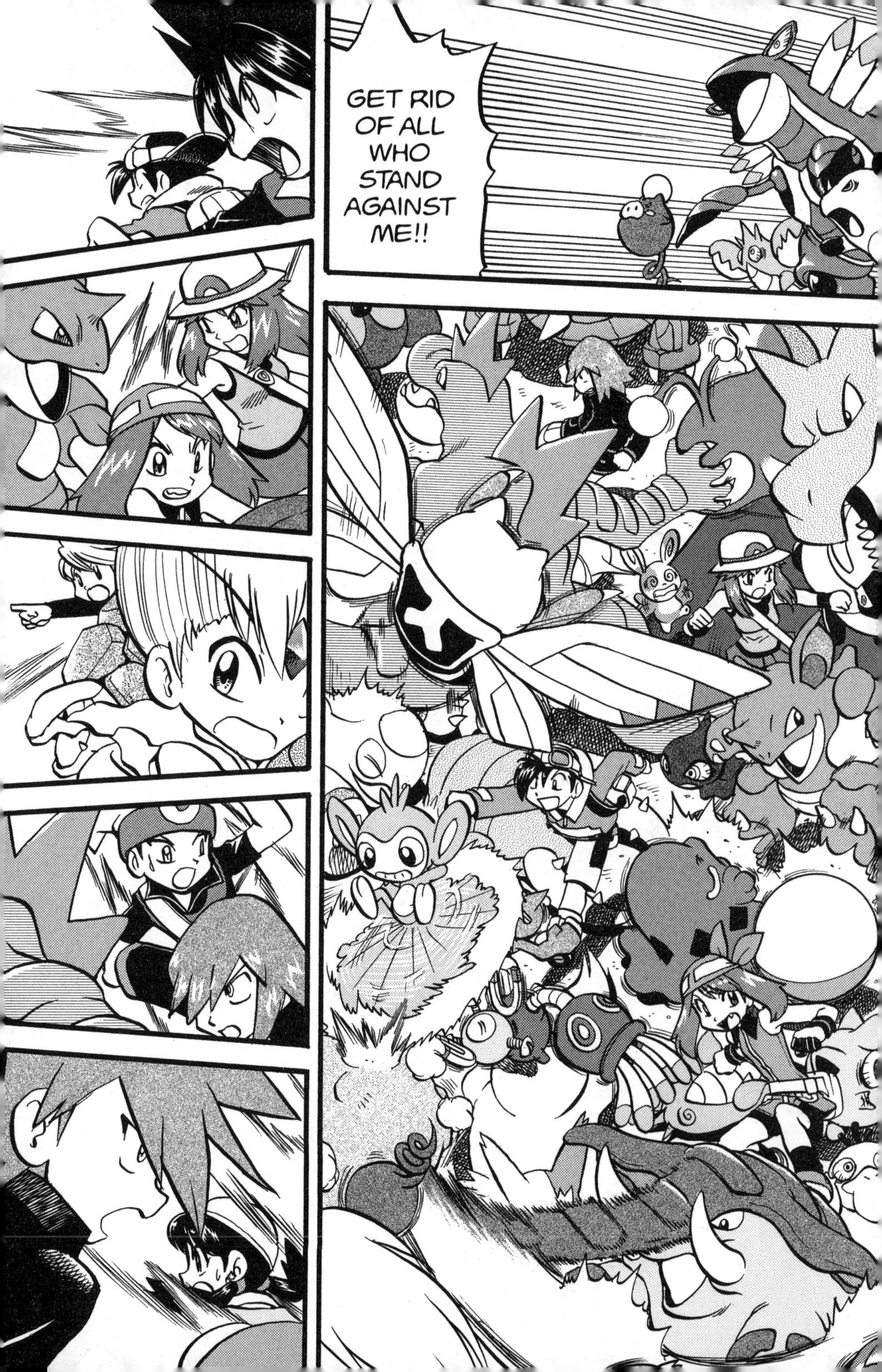
GET RID OF ALL WHO STAND AGAINST ME!!

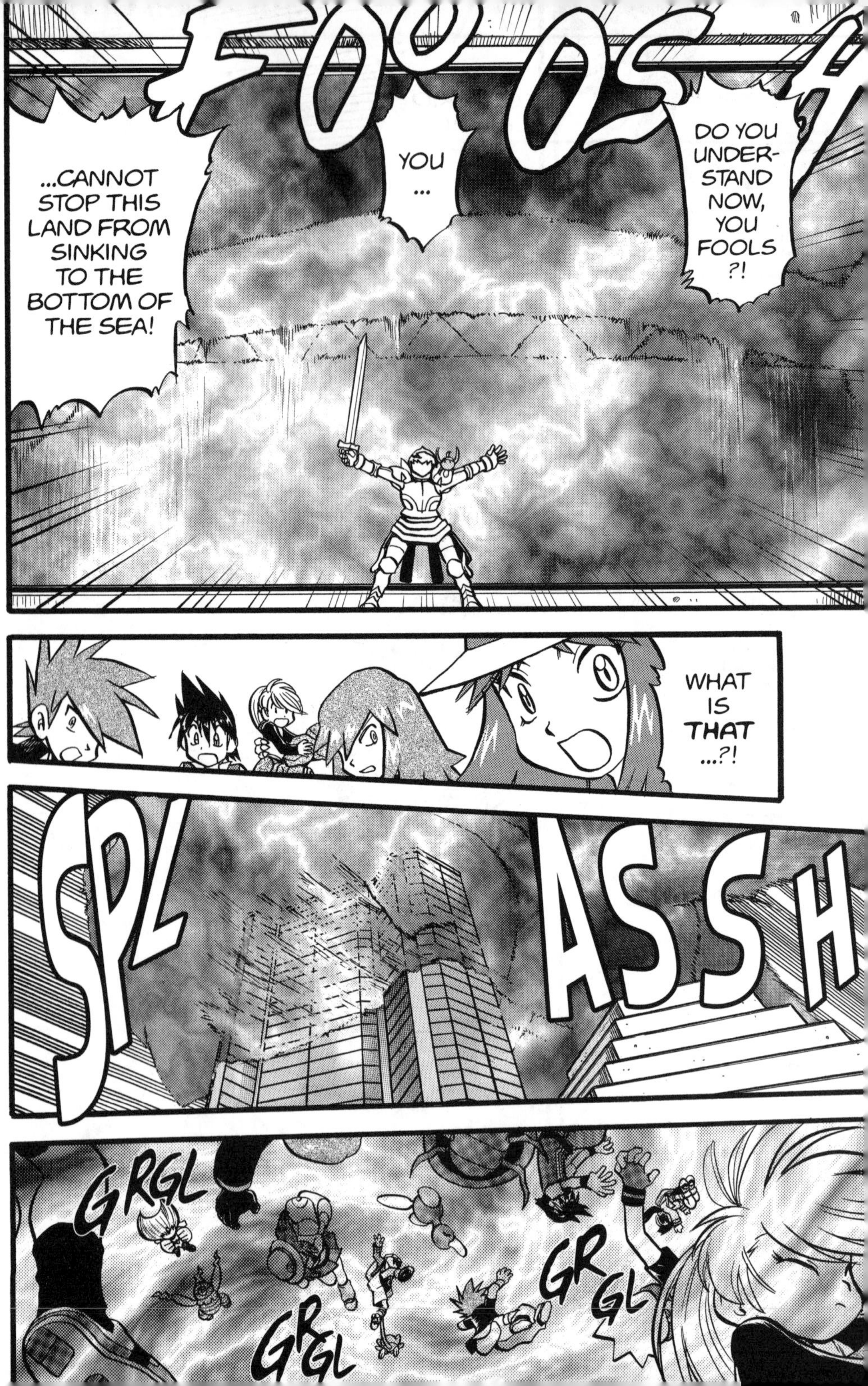
FOOOOSH
DO YOU UNDERSTAND NOW, YOU FOOLS ?!
YOU ...
...CANNOT STOP THIS LAND FROM SINKING TO THE BOTTOM OF THE SEA!
WHAT IS THAT ...?!
SPLASSH
GRGL
GRGL
GRGL

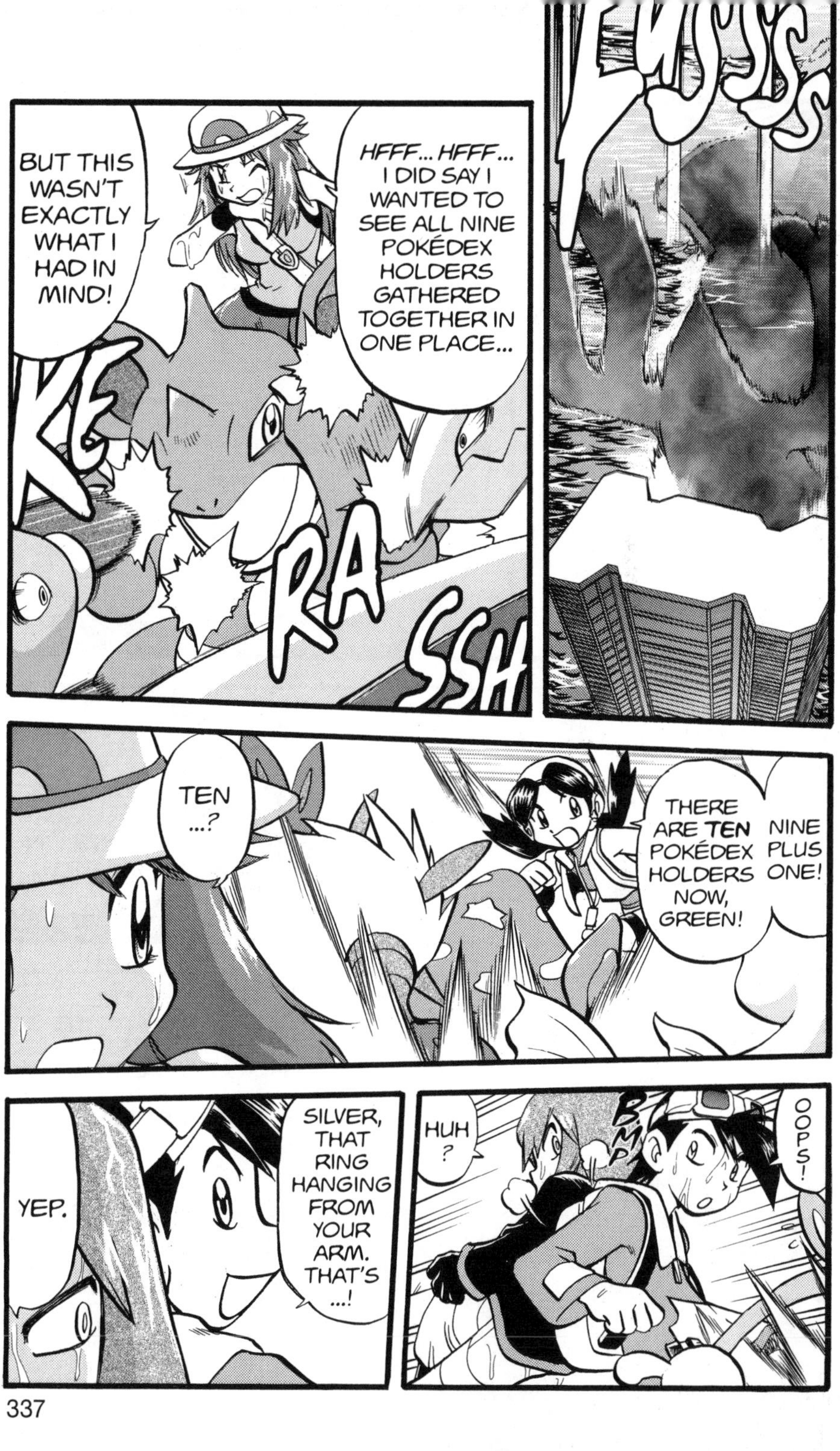
HFFF... HFFF... I DID SAY I WANTED TO SEE ALL NINE POKÉDEX HOLDERS GATHERED TOGETHER IN ONE PLACE...
BUT THIS WASN'T EXACTLY WHAT I HAD IN MIND!
KE
RA
SSH
THERE ARE **TEN** POKÉDEX HOLDERS NOW, GREEN!
NINE PLUS ONE!
TEN ...?
OOPS!
BMP
HUH ?
SILVER, THAT RING HANGING FROM YOUR ARM. THAT'S ...!
YEP.

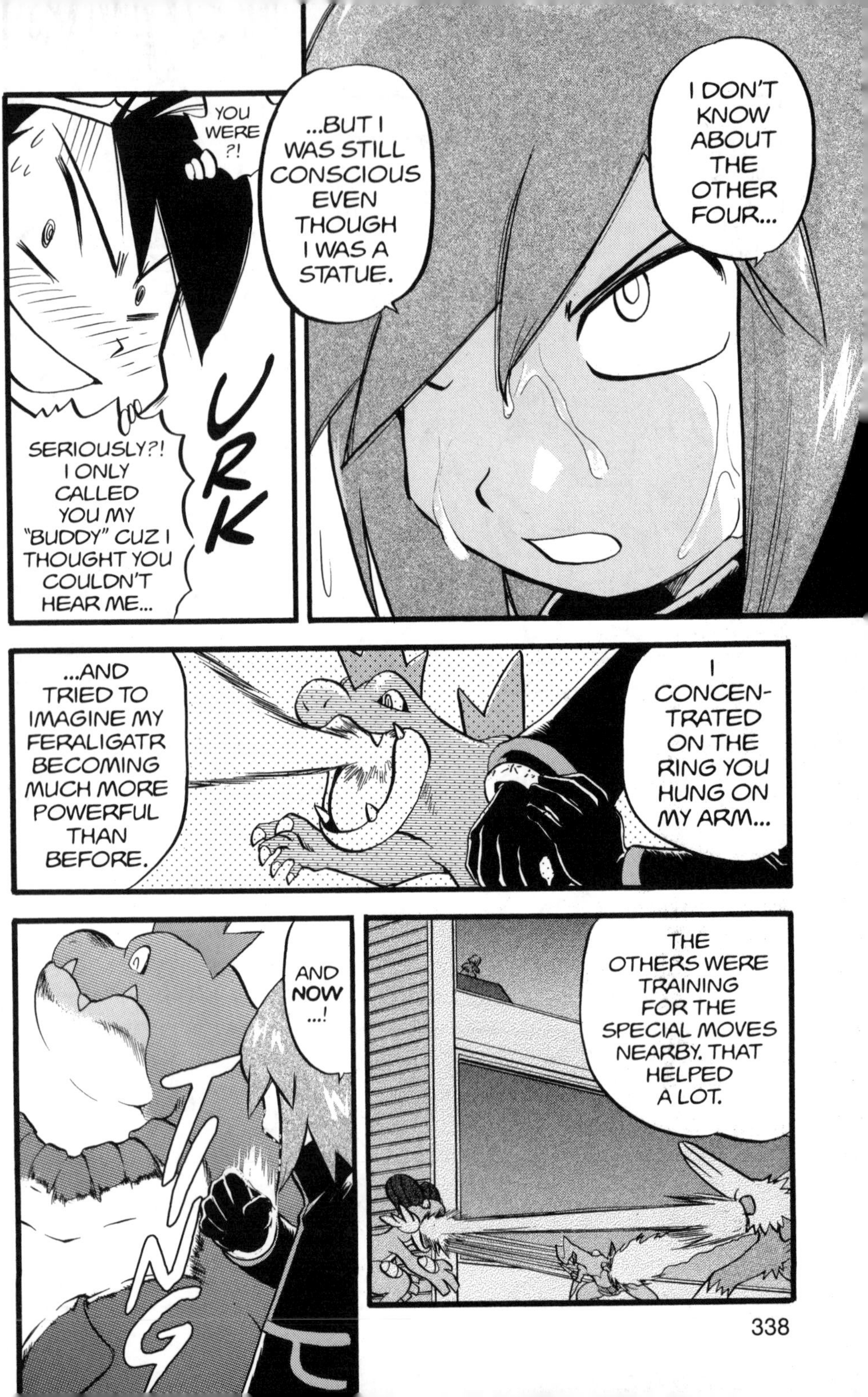
I DON'T KNOW ABOUT THE OTHER FOUR...
...BUT I WAS STILL CONSCIOUS EVEN THOUGH I WAS A STATUE.
YOU WERE?!
URK
SERIOUSLY?! I ONLY CALLED YOU MY "BUDDY" CUZ I THOUGHT YOU COULDN'T HEAR ME...
I CONCENTRATED ON THE RING YOU HUNG ON MY ARM...
...AND TRIED TO IMAGINE MY FERALIGATR BECOMING MUCH MORE POWERFUL THAN BEFORE.
THE OTHERS WERE TRAINING FOR THE SPECIAL MOVES NEARBY. THAT HELPED A LOT.
AND **NOW**...!
TING

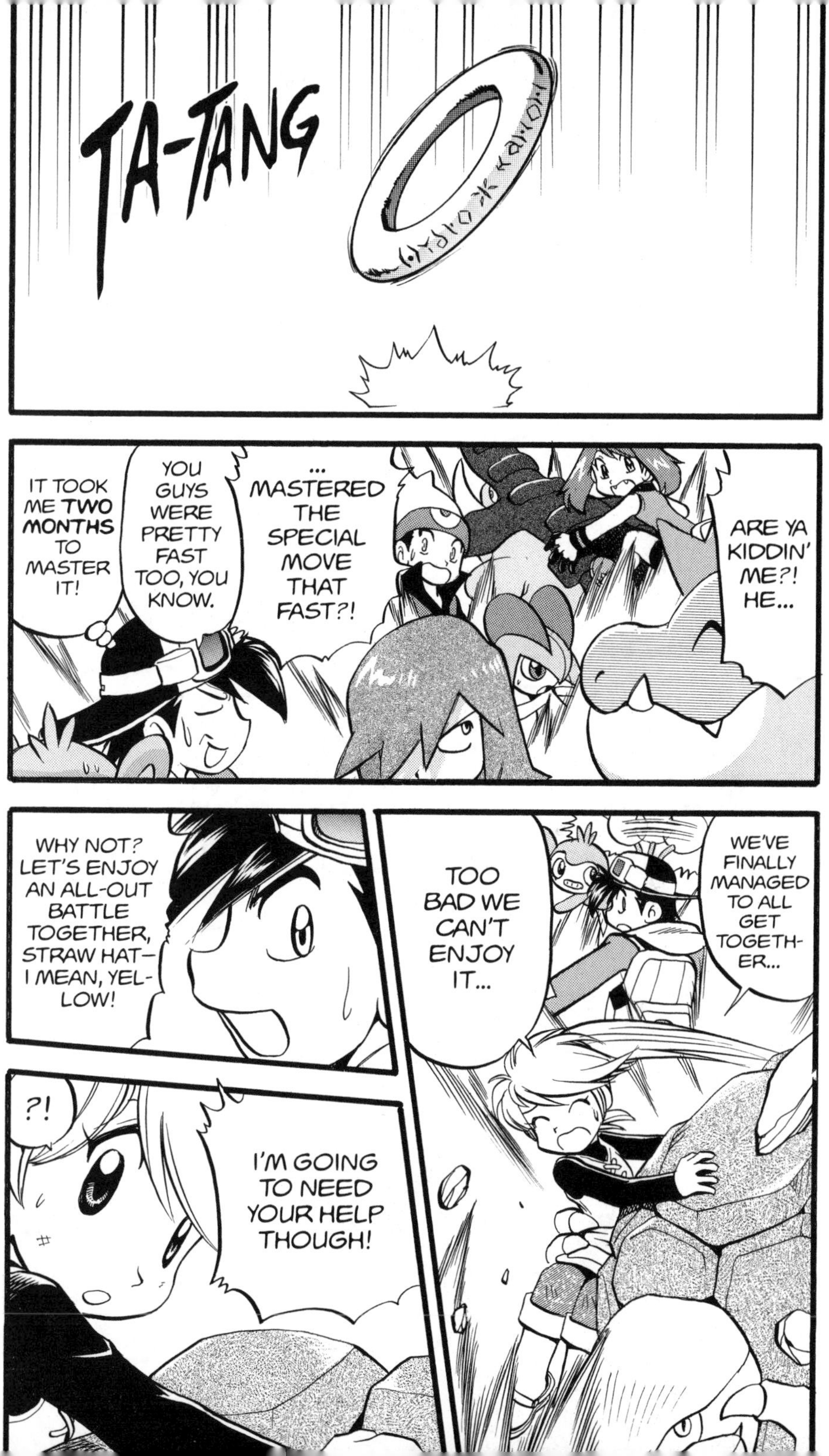
TA-TANG
ARE YA KIDDIN' ME?! HE...
... MASTERED THE SPECIAL MOVE THAT FAST?!
YOU GUYS WERE PRETTY FAST TOO, YOU KNOW.
IT TOOK ME **TWO MONTHS** TO MASTER IT!
WE'VE FINALLY MANAGED TO ALL GET TOGETH-ER...
TOO BAD WE CAN'T ENJOY IT...
WHY NOT? LET'S ENJOY AN ALL-OUT BATTLE TOGETHER, STRAW HAT— I MEAN, YEL-LOW!
?!
I'M GOING TO NEED YOUR HELP THOUGH!

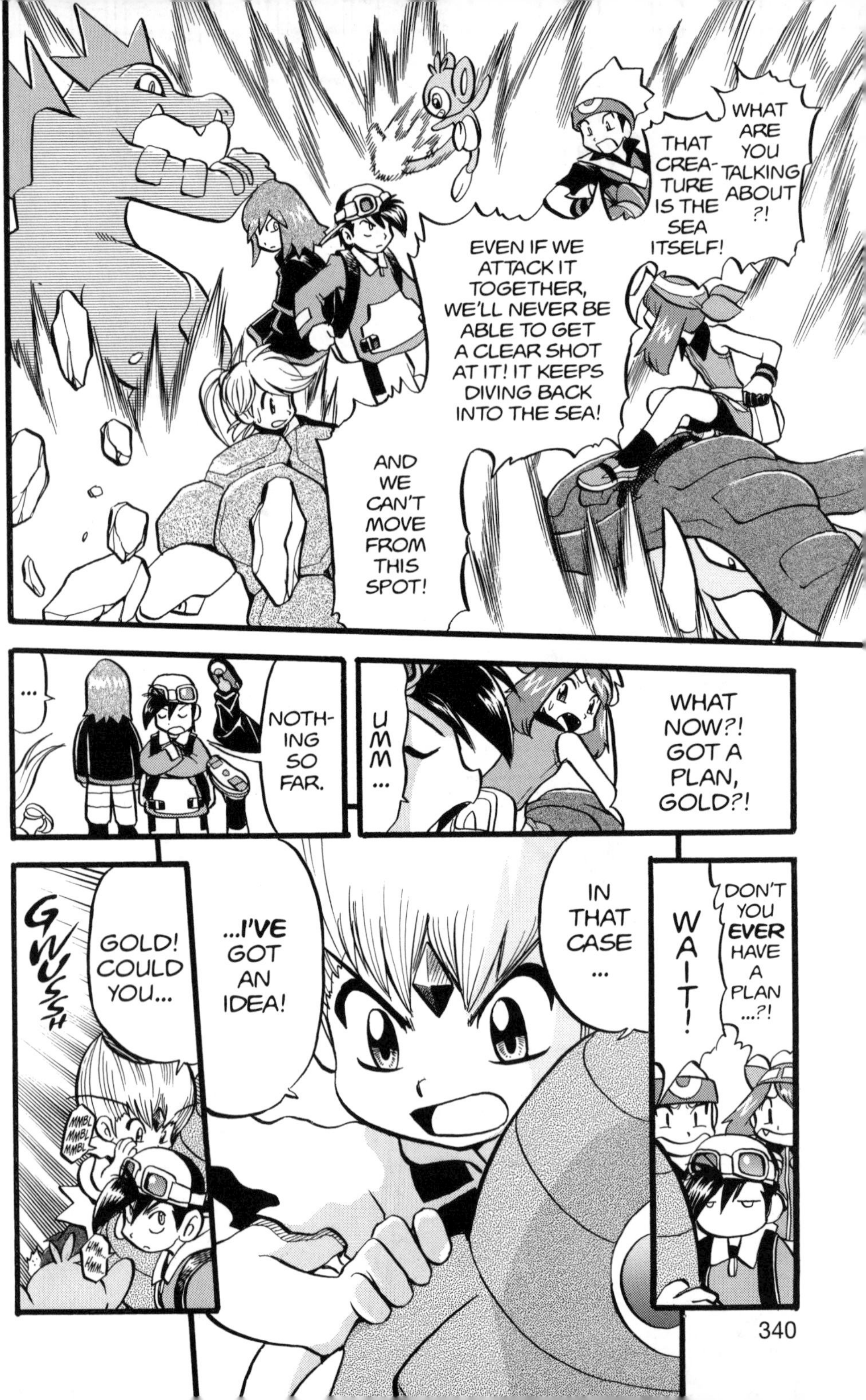
WHAT ARE YOU TALKING ABOUT?!
THAT CREATURE IS THE SEA ITSELF!
EVEN IF WE ATTACK IT TOGETHER, WE'LL NEVER BE ABLE TO GET A CLEAR SHOT AT IT! IT KEEPS DIVING BACK INTO THE SEA!
AND WE CAN'T MOVE FROM THIS SPOT!
WHAT NOW?! GOT A PLAN, GOLD?!
UMM...
NOTHING SO FAR.
...
DON'T YOU **EVER** HAVE A PLAN...?!
WAIT!
IN THAT CASE...
...**I'VE** GOT AN IDEA!
GWUSSH
GOLD! COULD YOU...
MMBL MMBL MMBL
HMM... HMM...

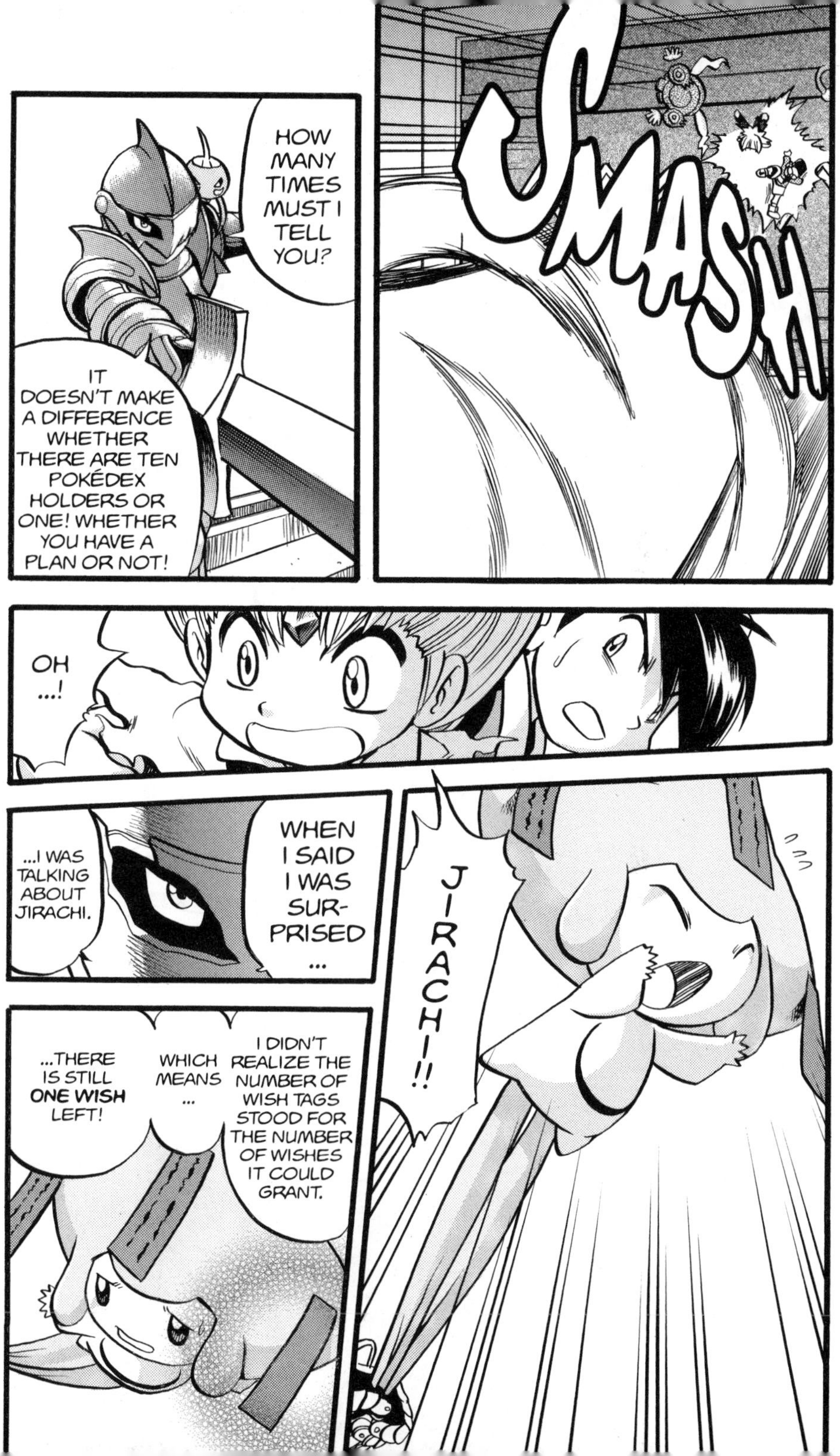
SMASH
HOW MANY TIMES MUST I TELL YOU?
IT DOESN'T MAKE A DIFFERENCE WHETHER THERE ARE TEN POKÉDEX HOLDERS OR ONE! WHETHER YOU HAVE A PLAN OR NOT!
OH ...!
JIRACHI!!
WHEN I SAID I WAS SURPRISED ...
...I WAS TALKING ABOUT JIRACHI.
I DIDN'T REALIZE THE NUMBER OF WISH TAGS STOOD FOR THE NUMBER OF WISHES IT COULD GRANT.
WHICH MEANS ...
...THERE IS STILL **ONE WISH** LEFT!

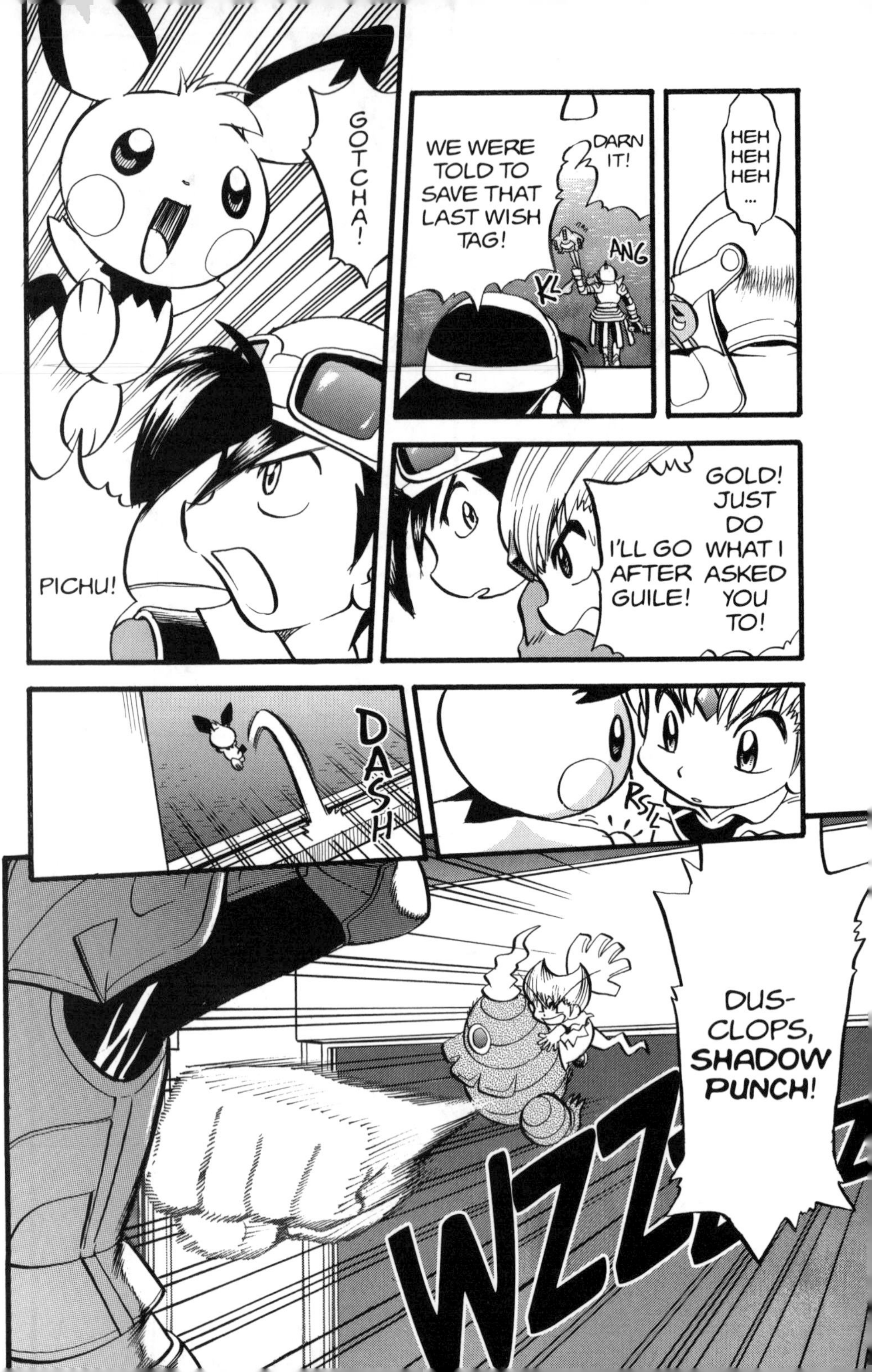
HEH HEH HEH ...
WE WERE TOLD TO SAVE THAT LAST WISH TAG!
DARN IT!
ANG
KL
GOLD! JUST DO WHAT I ASKED YOU TO!
I'LL GO AFTER GUILE!
GOTCHA!
PICHU!
RSTL
DASH
DUS-CLOPS, SHADOW PUNCH!
WZZ

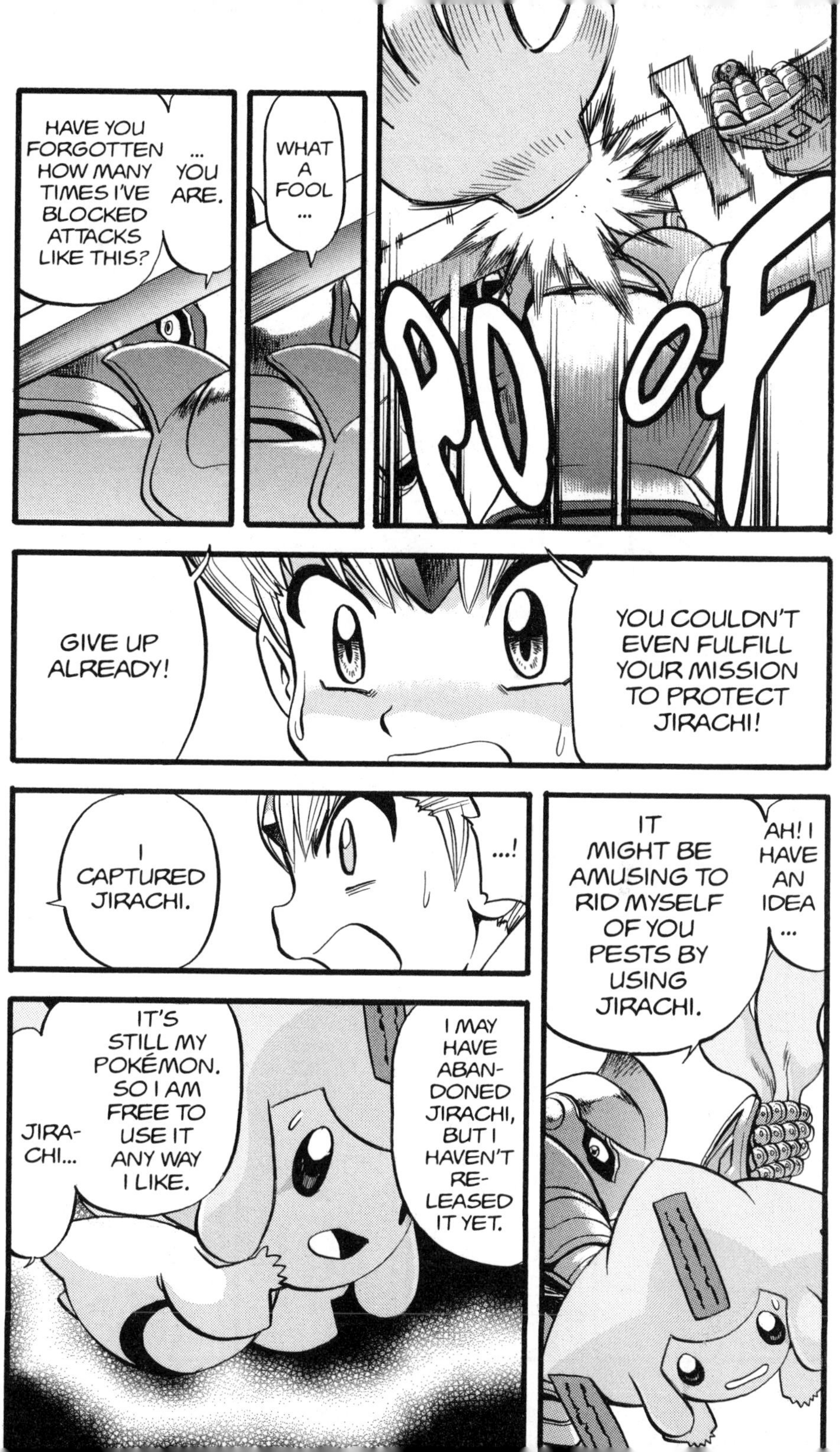
POOF
WHAT A FOOL ...
... YOU ARE.
HAVE YOU FORGOTTEN HOW MANY TIMES I'VE BLOCKED ATTACKS LIKE THIS?
YOU COULDN'T EVEN FULFILL YOUR MISSION TO PROTECT JIRACHI!
GIVE UP ALREADY!
AH! I HAVE AN IDEA ...
IT MIGHT BE AMUSING TO RID MYSELF OF YOU PESTS BY USING JIRACHI.
...!
I CAPTURED JIRACHI.
I MAY HAVE ABAN-DONED JIRACHI, BUT I HAVEN'T RE-LEASED IT YET.
IT'S STILL MY POKÉMON. SO I AM FREE TO USE IT ANY WAY I LIKE.
JIRA-CHI...

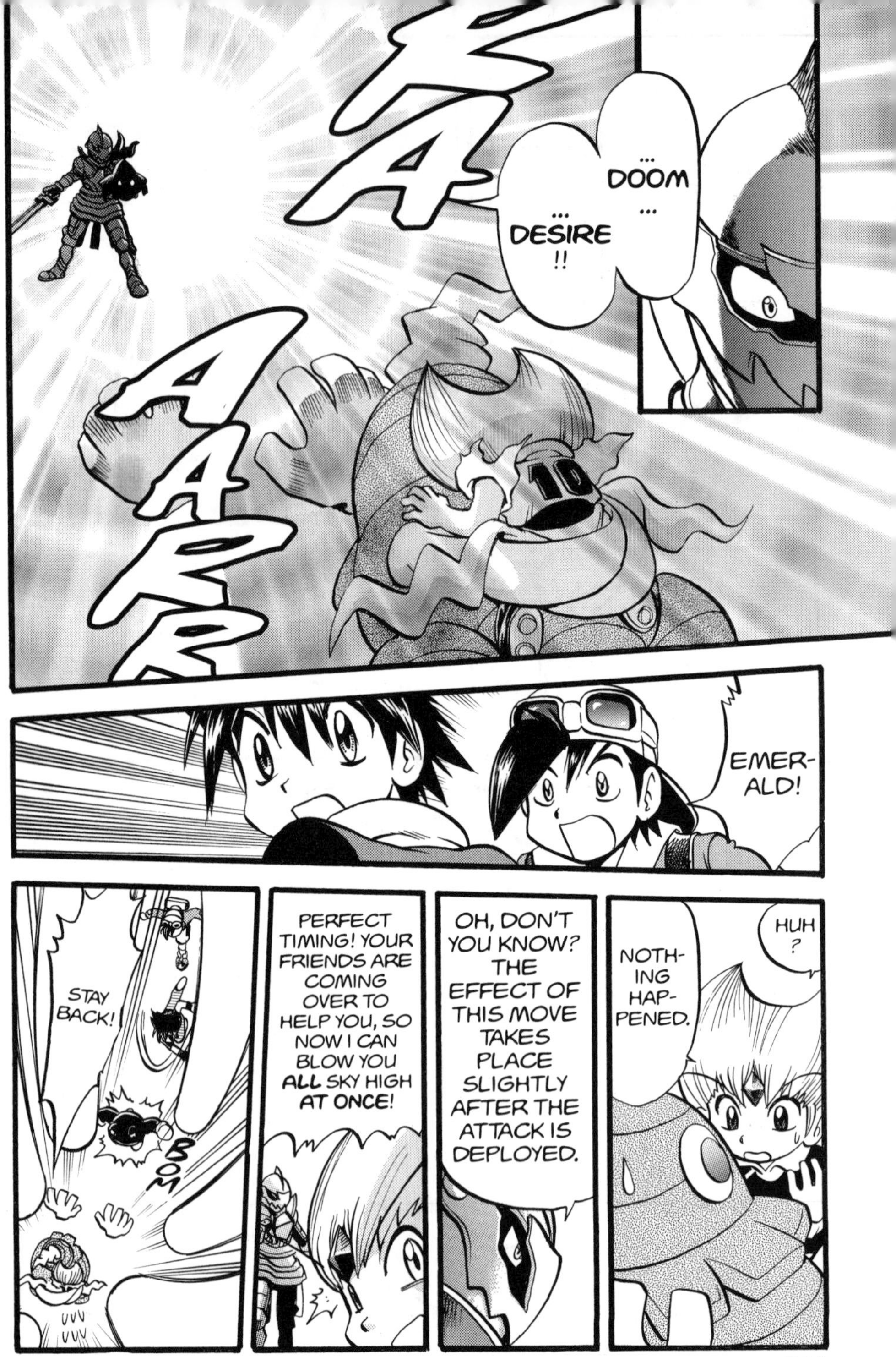
...DOOM... ...DESIRE!!
KA
AARR
EMER-ALD!
HUH?
NOTH-ING HAP-PENED.
OH, DON'T YOU KNOW? THE EFFECT OF THIS MOVE TAKES PLACE SLIGHTLY AFTER THE ATTACK IS DEPLOYED.
PERFECT TIMING! YOUR FRIENDS ARE COMING OVER TO HELP YOU, SO NOW I CAN BLOW YOU **ALL** SKY HIGH **AT ONCE**!
STAY BACK!
BOM

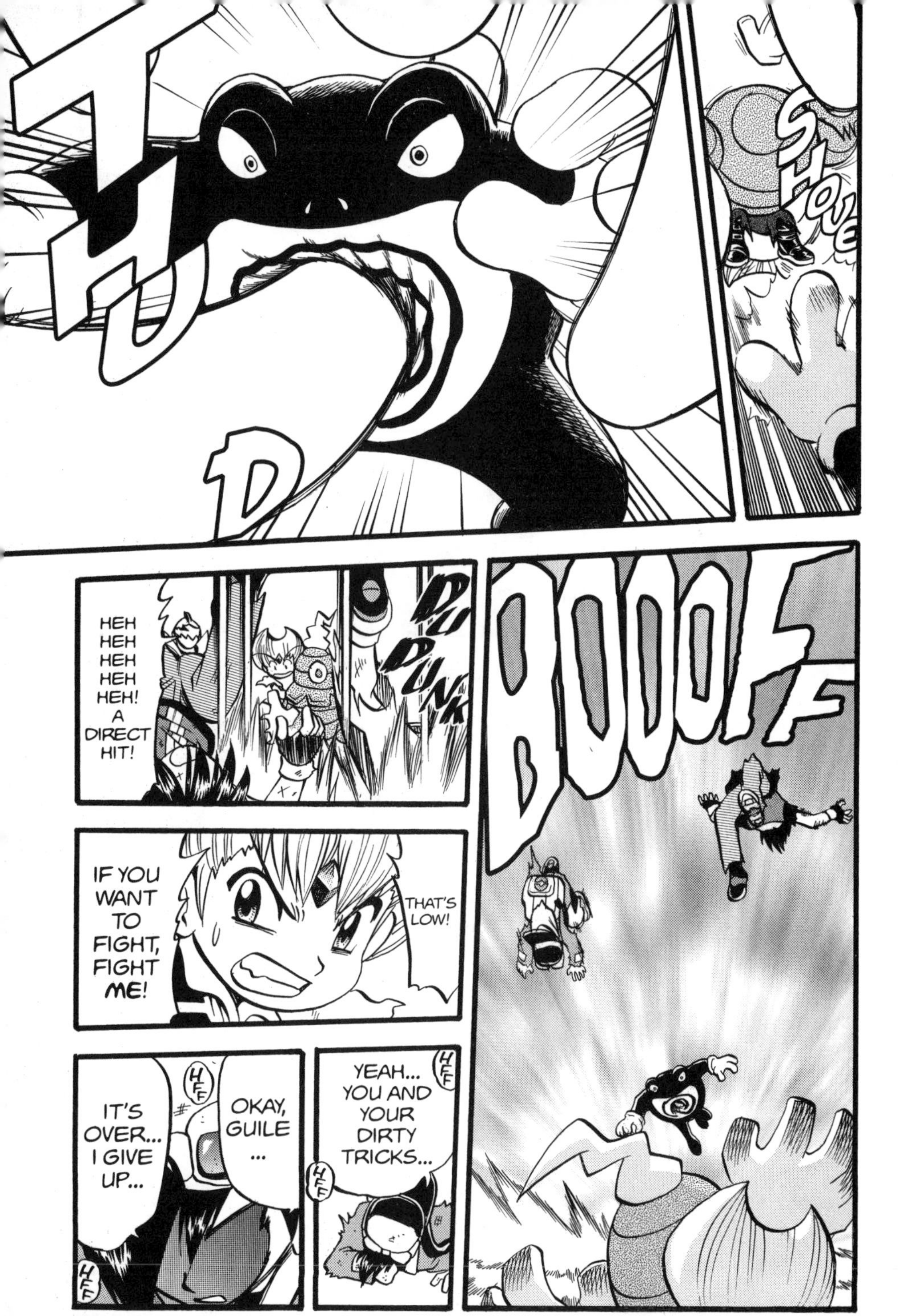
SHOVE
THUD
BOOOF
DUDUNK
HEH HEH HEH HEH HEH! A DIRECT HIT!
THAT'S LOW!
IF YOU WANT TO FIGHT, FIGHT ME!
HFF
YEAH... YOU AND YOUR DIRTY TRICKS...
HFF
HFF
OKAY, GUILE...
IT'S OVER... I GIVE UP...
HFF

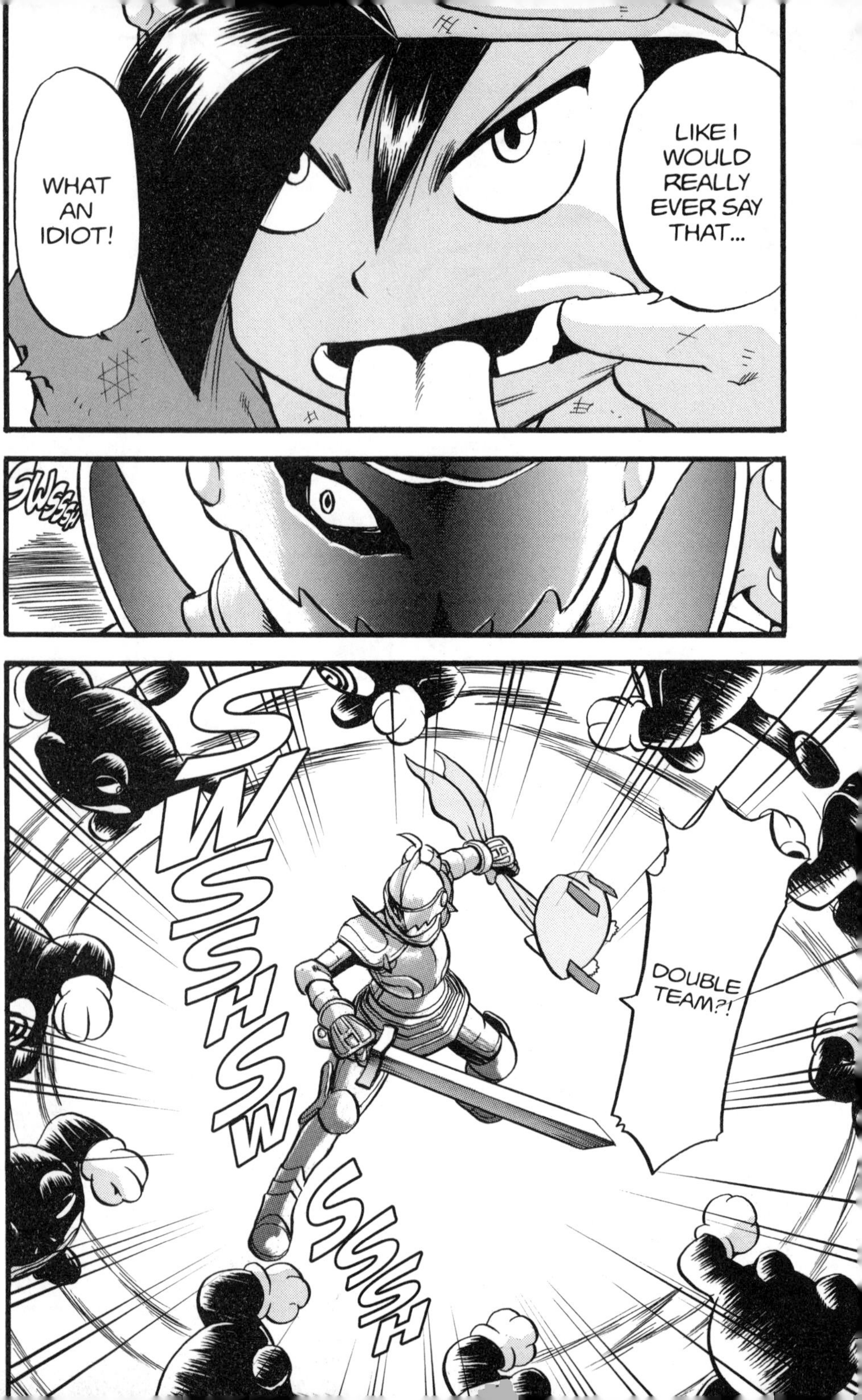
LIKE I WOULD REALLY EVER SAY THAT...
WHAT AN IDIOT!
SWSSSH
DOUBLE TEAM?!
SWSSHSW
SSSH

CHARACTER PROFILE

SILVER

SILVER

SILVER IS A TRAINER WHO SEARCHED LONG AND HARD TO FIND HIS ROOTS. HE WAS KIDNAPPED BY THE INFAMOUS MASKED MAN AS A CHILD, SO THE STORY OF HIS ORIGIN REMAINED A MYSTERY FOR QUITE SOME TIME, BUT HE WAS FINALLY REUNITED WITH HIS FATHER, GIOVANNI. AS A HIGHLY SKILLED TRAINER, HE EXCELS IN POKÉMON BATTLES AND IS ESPECIALLY KNOWL-EDGEABLE ABOUT TRADING POKÉMON. THUS, HE IS KNOWN AS THE "EXCHANGER." HE HAS LEARNED TO FACE DIFFICULT CHALLENGES WITH COURAGE AND DIGNITY.

- Birthplace: Viridian City
- Birthday: December 24 (discovered after his reunion with Giovanni)
- Blood Type: AB
- Family: Father (Giovanni)

335

The Final Battle, Part 8

POKÉMON ADVENTURES·THE SIXTH CHAPTER·EMERALD

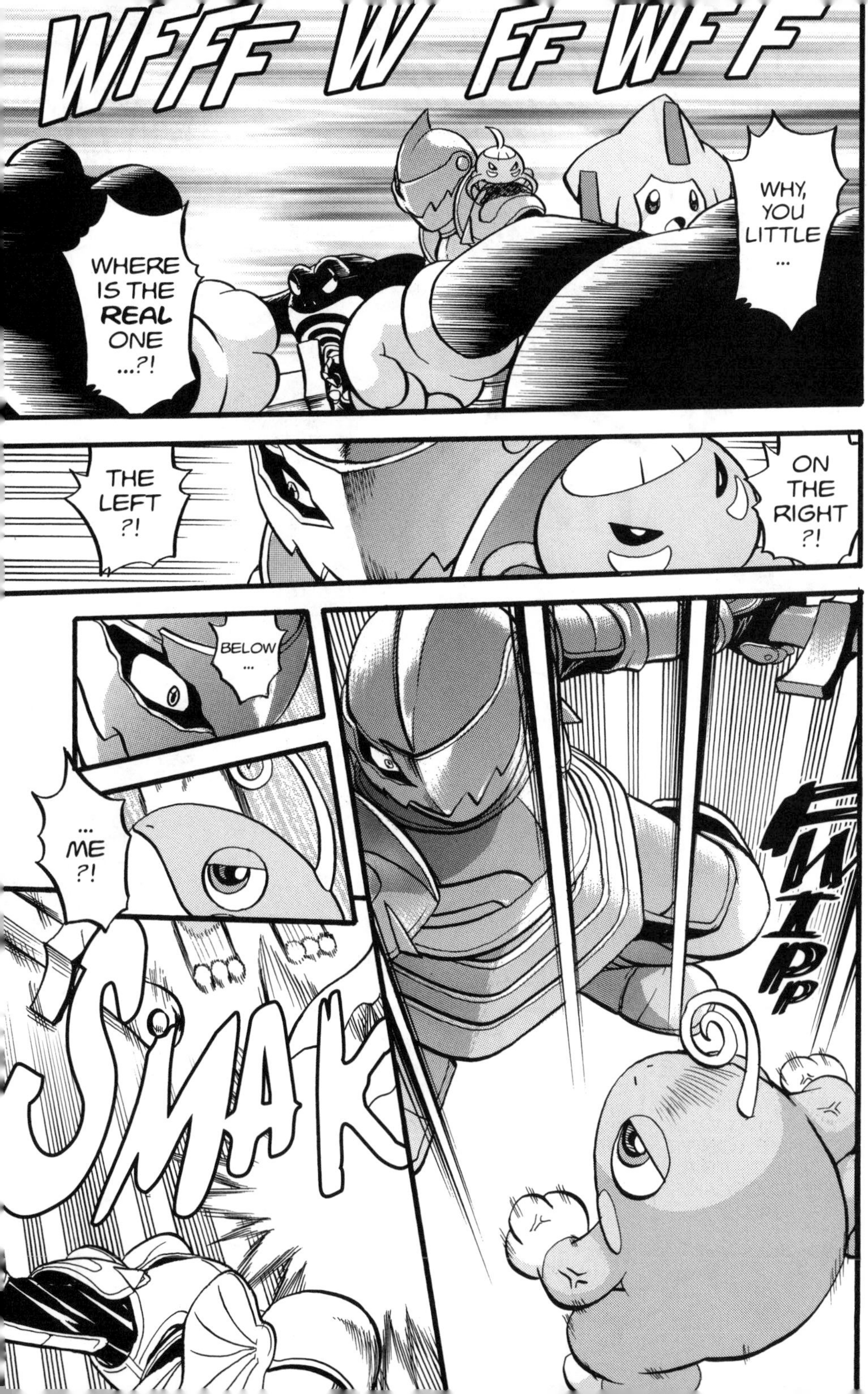
WFFF W FF WF F
WHY, YOU LITTLE ...
WHERE IS THE **REAL** ONE ...?!
ON THE RIGHT ?!
THE LEFT ?!
FWIPP
SMAK
BELOW ...
... ME ?!

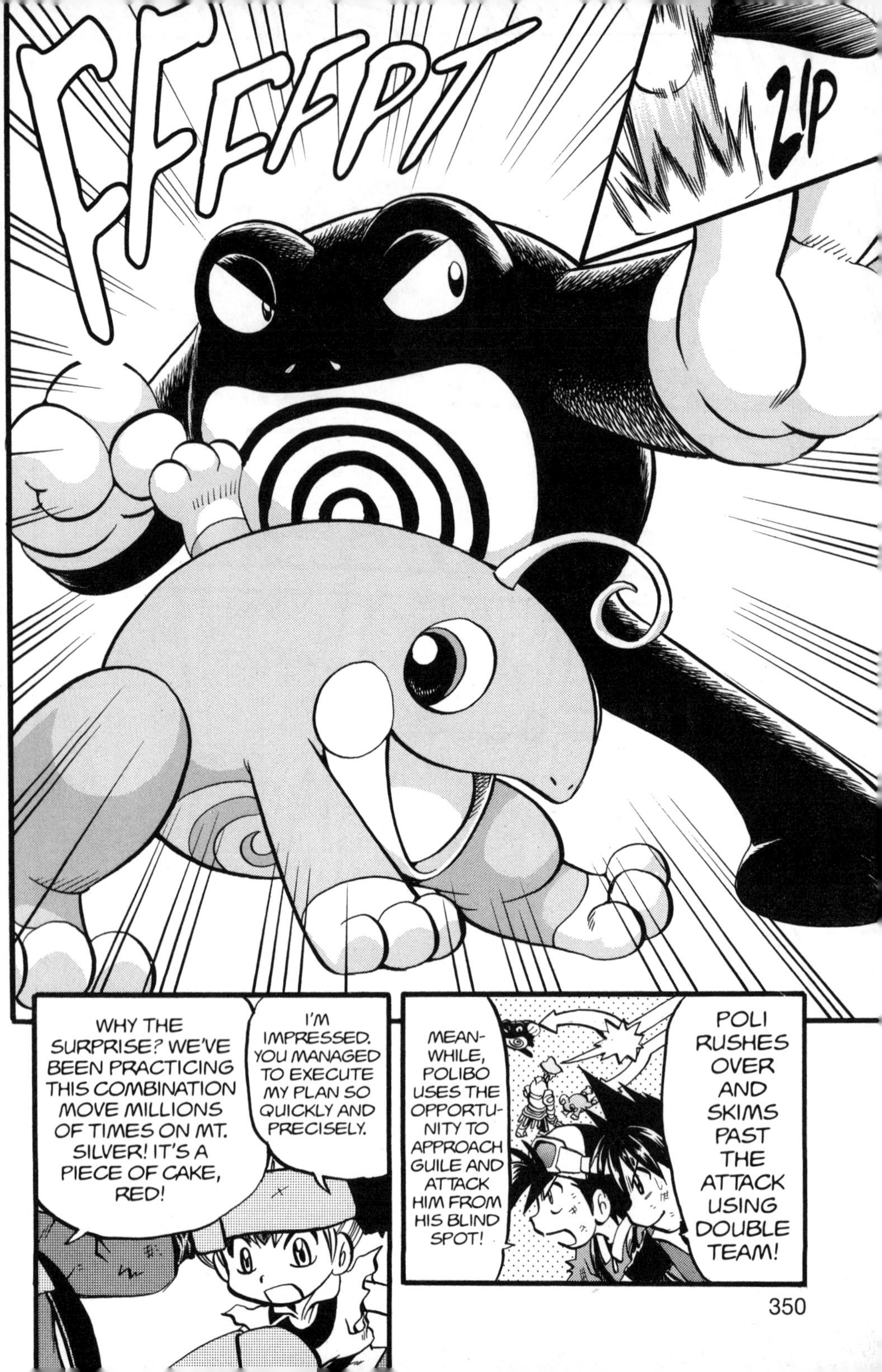
ZIP
FFFPT
POLI RUSHES OVER AND SKIMS PAST THE ATTACK USING DOUBLE TEAM!
MEAN-WHILE, POLIBO USES THE OPPORTU-NITY TO APPROACH GUILE AND ATTACK HIM FROM HIS BLIND SPOT!
I'M IMPRESSED. YOU MANAGED TO EXECUTE MY PLAN SO QUICKLY AND PRECISELY.
WHY THE SURPRISE? WE'VE BEEN PRACTICING THIS COMBINATION MOVE MILLIONS OF TIMES ON MT. SILVER! IT'S A PIECE OF CAKE, RED!

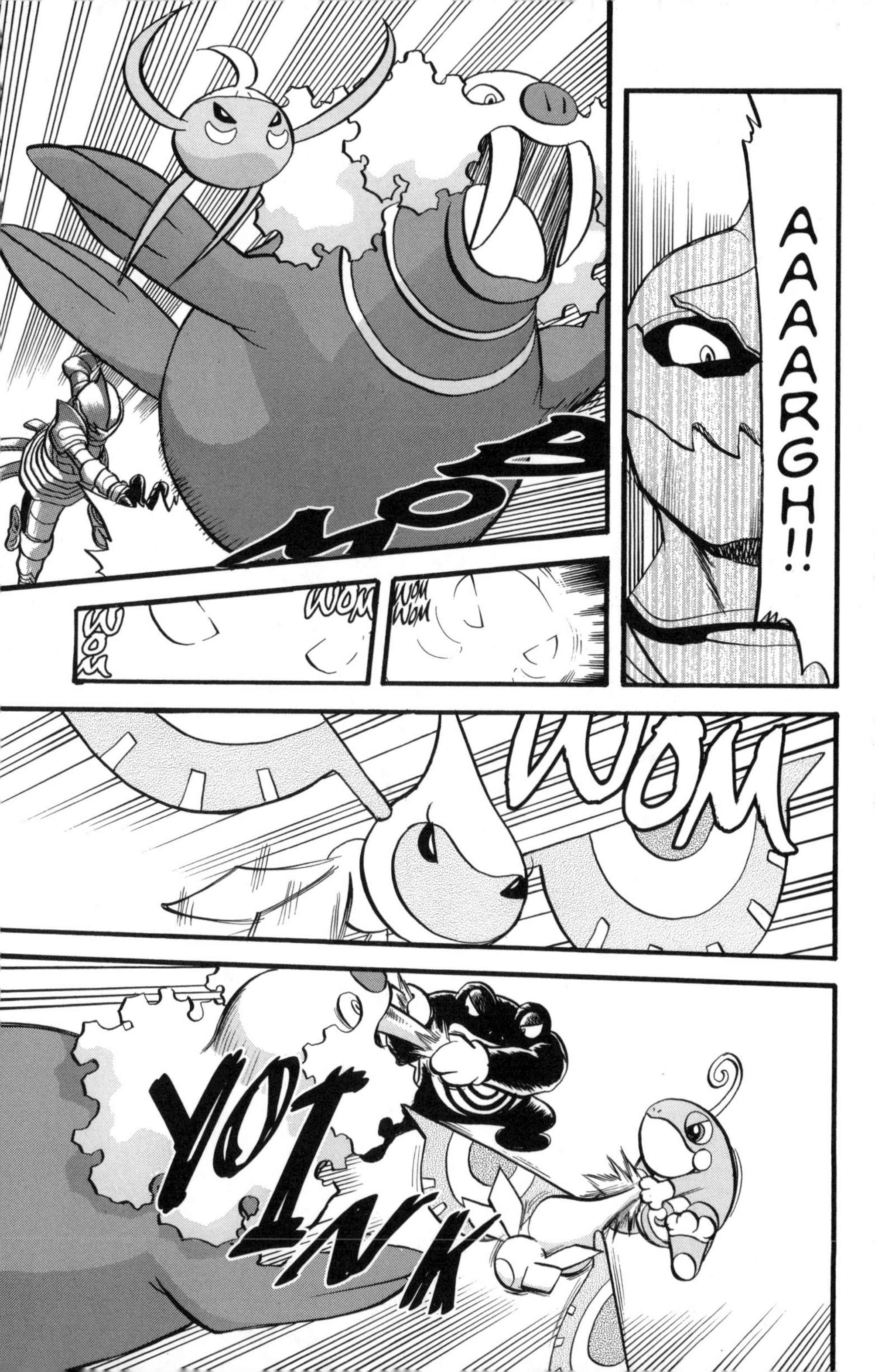
AAAARGH!!
WOM
WOM
WOM
WOM
WOM
WOM
YOINK

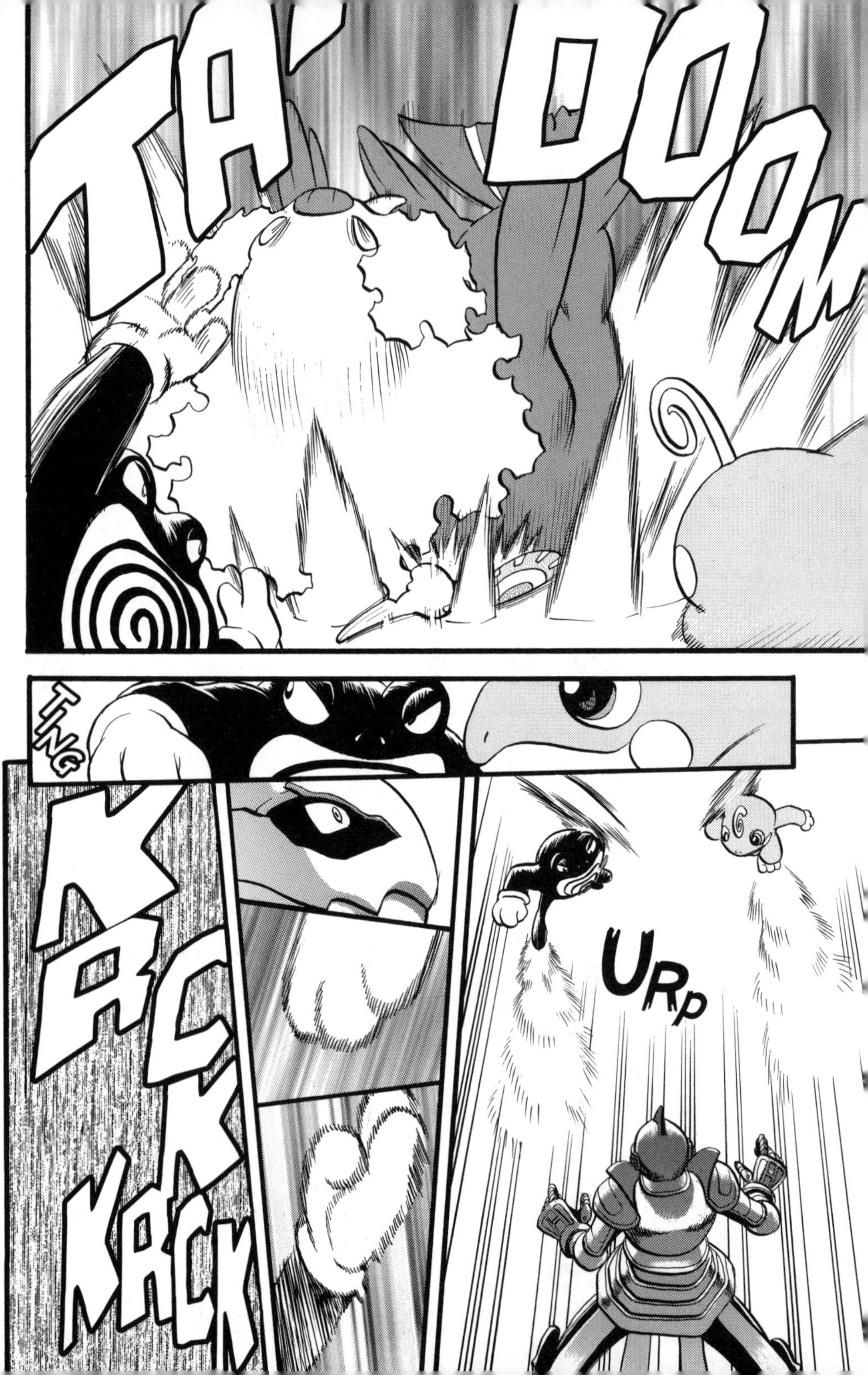
TA'DOOM
TING
URp
KACK
KACK

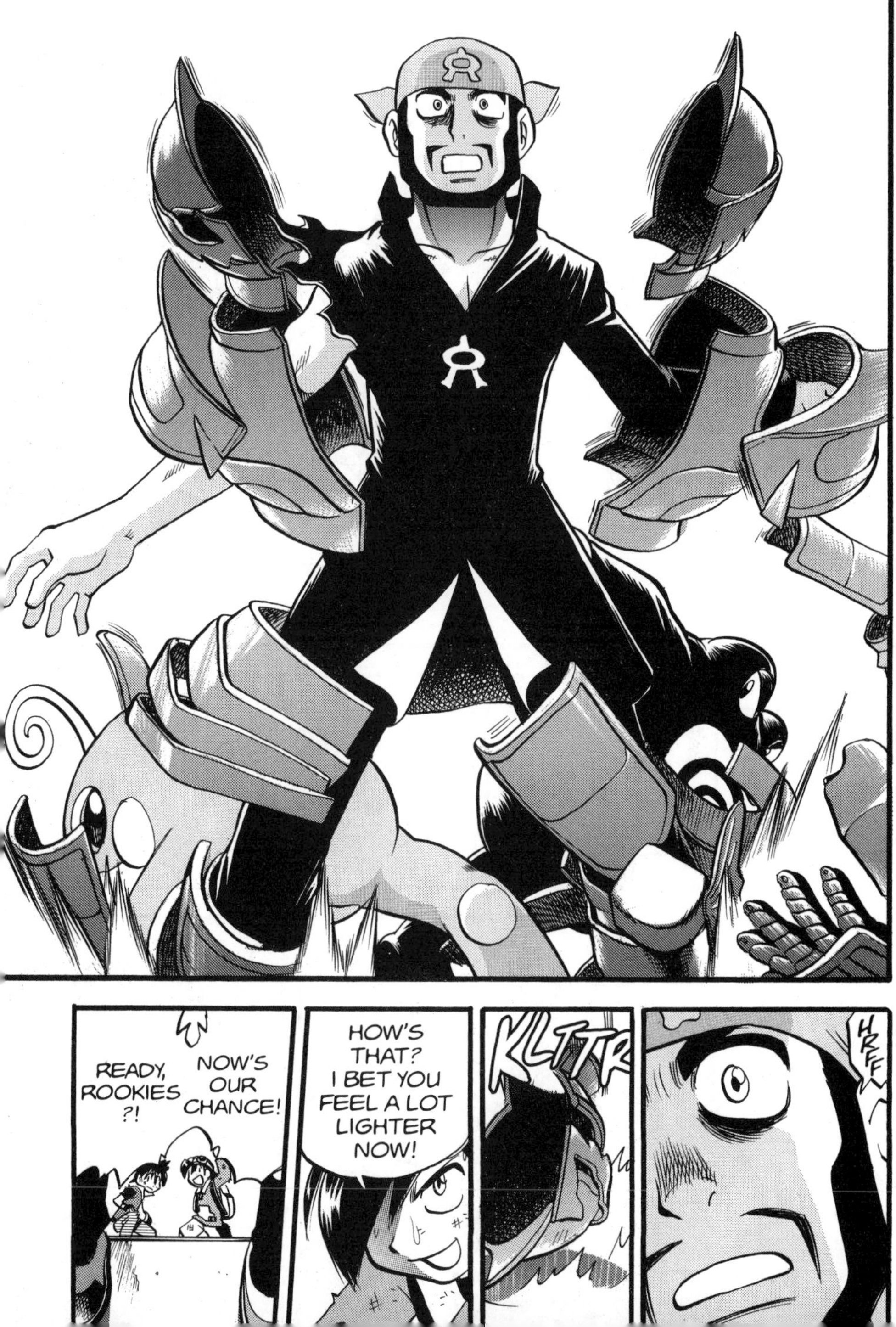
HRFF
KLTTR
HOW'S THAT? I BET YOU FEEL A LOT LIGHTER NOW!
NOW'S OUR CHANCE!
READY, ROOKIES ?!

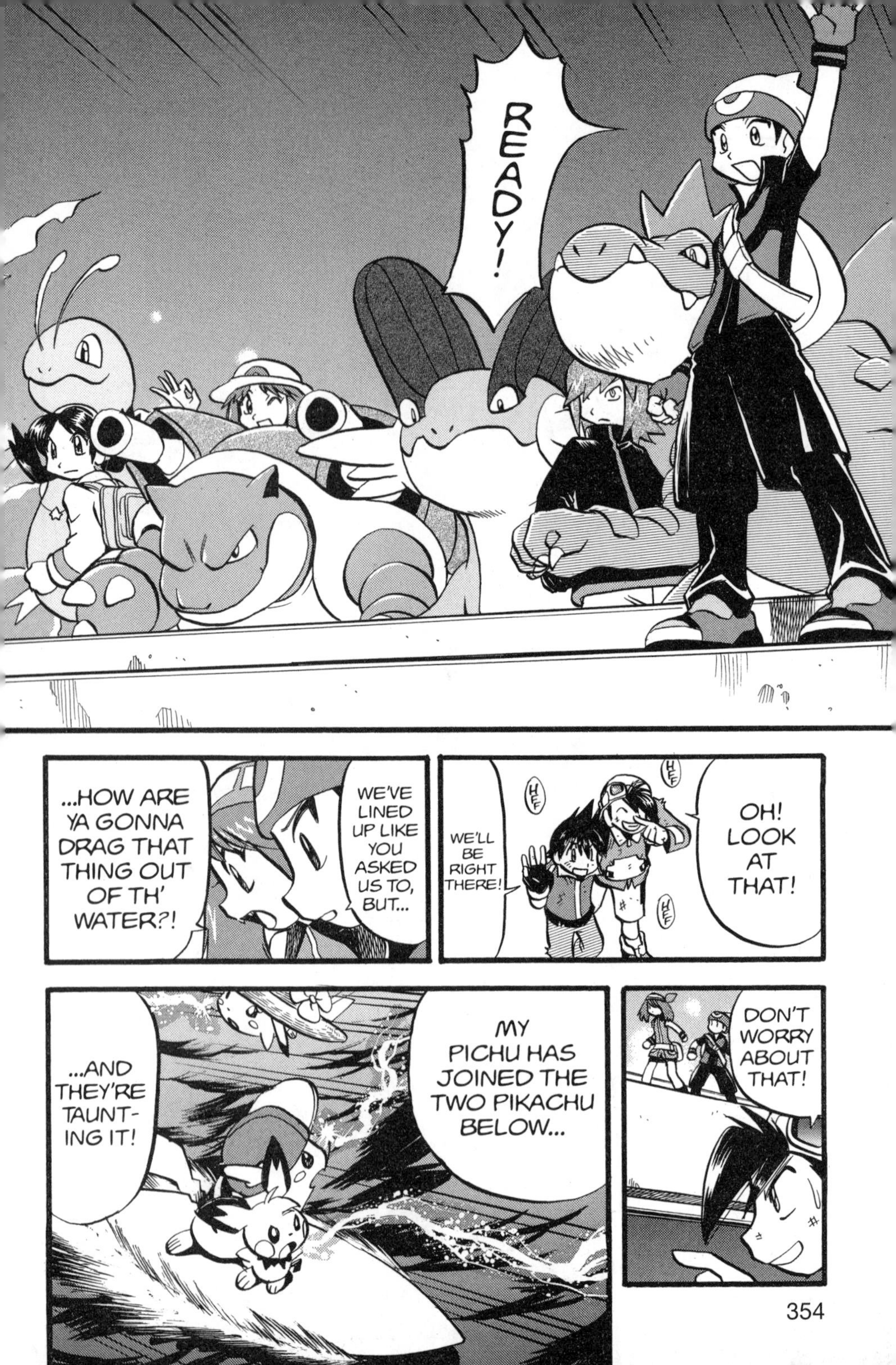
READY!
OH! LOOK AT THAT!
HFF
WE'LL BE RIGHT THERE!
HFF
HFF
WE'VE LINED UP LIKE YOU ASKED US TO, BUT...
...HOW ARE YA GONNA DRAG THAT THING OUT OF TH' WATER?!
DON'T WORRY ABOUT THAT!
MY PICHU HAS JOINED THE TWO PIKACHU BELOW...
...AND THEY'RE TAUNT-ING IT!

READY!

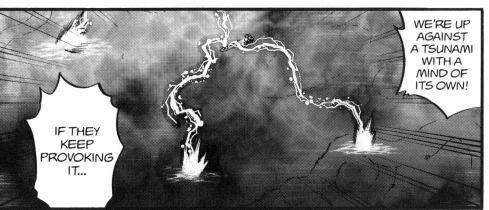

WE'RE UP AGAINST A TSUNAMI WITH A MIND OF ITS OWN!

IF THEY KEEP PROVOKING IT...

BUBBL

BUBBL

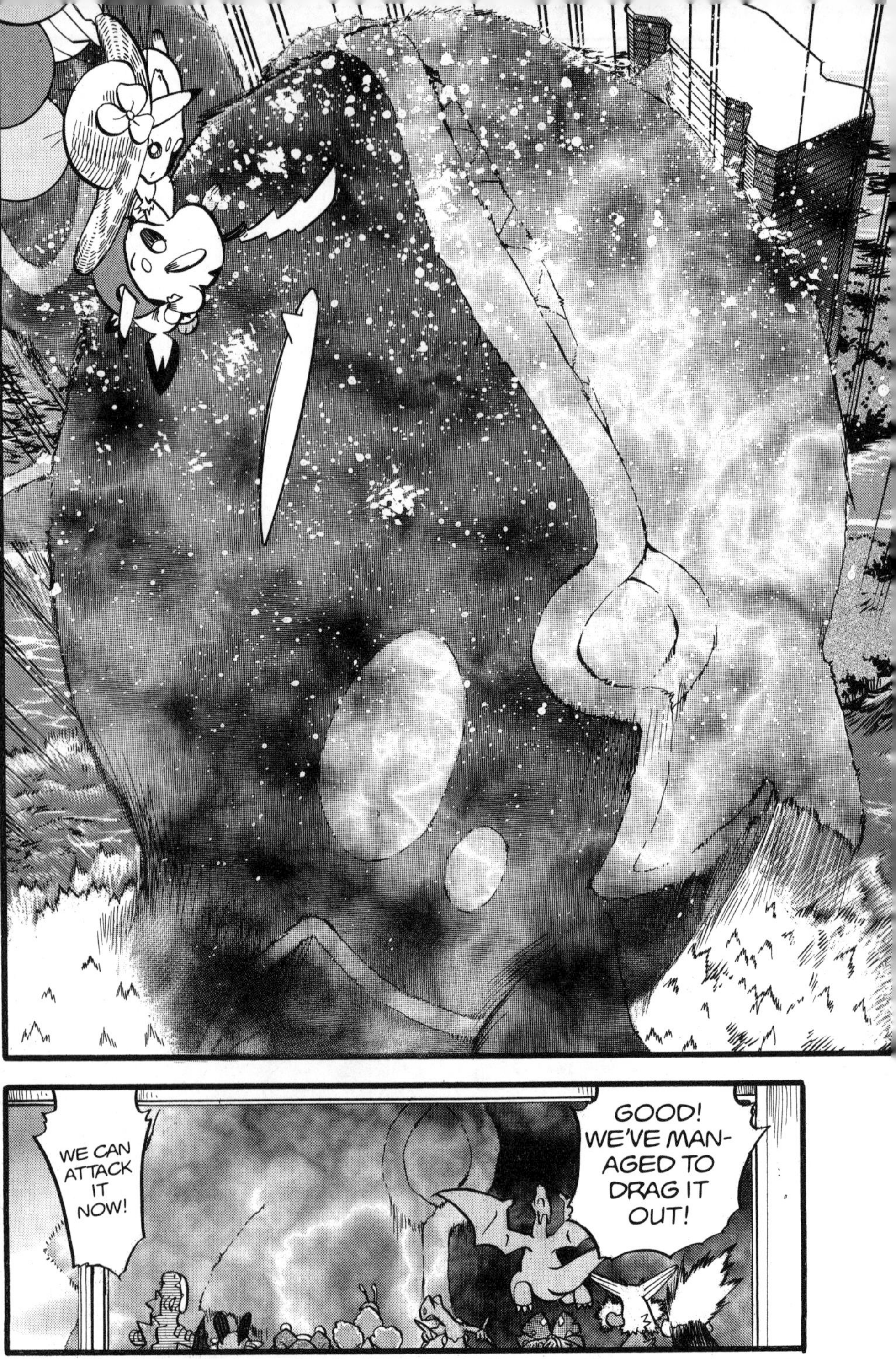
GOOD! WE'VE MAN-AGED TO DRAG IT OUT!
WE CAN ATTACK IT NOW!

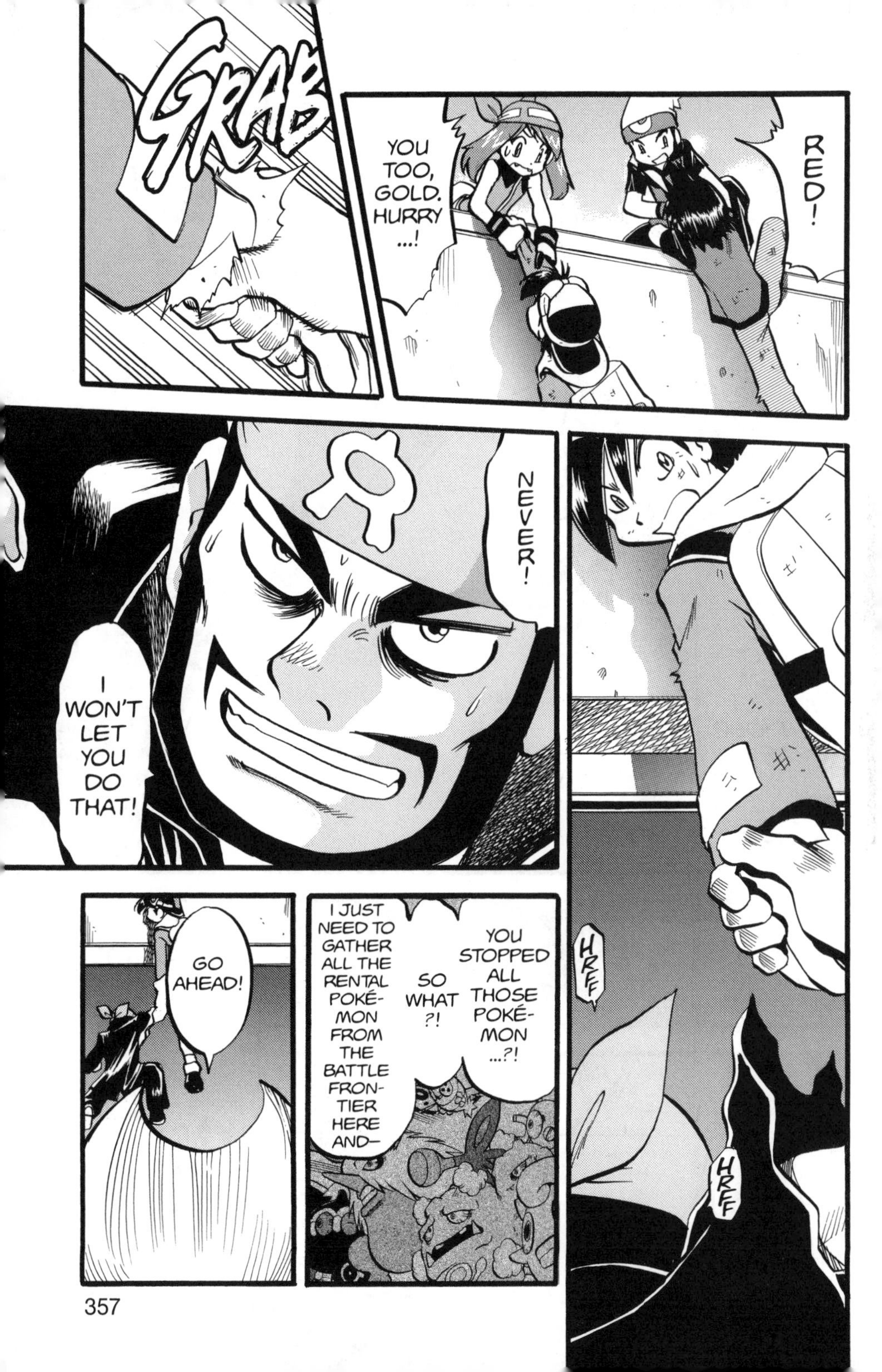
RED!
YOU TOO, GOLD. HURRY ...!
GRAB
HRFF
HRFF
NEVER!
I WON'T LET YOU DO THAT!
YOU STOPPED ALL THOSE POKÉMON ...?!
SO WHAT?!
I JUST NEED TO GATHER ALL THE RENTAL POKÉMON FROM THE BATTLE FRONTIER HERE AND—
GO AHEAD!

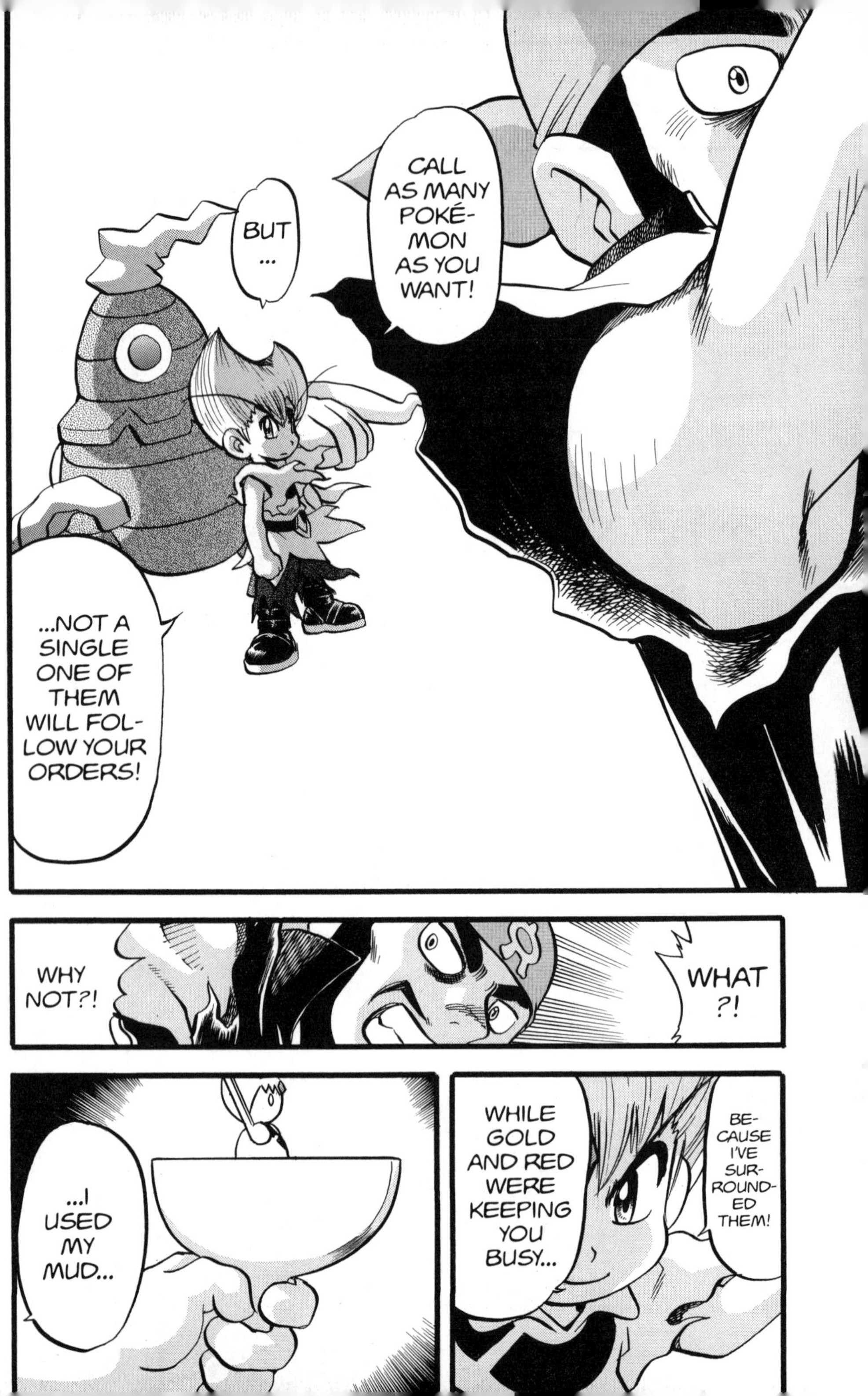
CALL AS MANY POKÉMON AS YOU WANT!
BUT ...
...NOT A SINGLE ONE OF THEM WILL FOLLOW YOUR ORDERS!
WHAT?!
WHY NOT?!
BECAUSE I'VE SURROUNDED THEM!
WHILE GOLD AND RED WERE KEEPING YOU BUSY...
...I USED MY MUD...

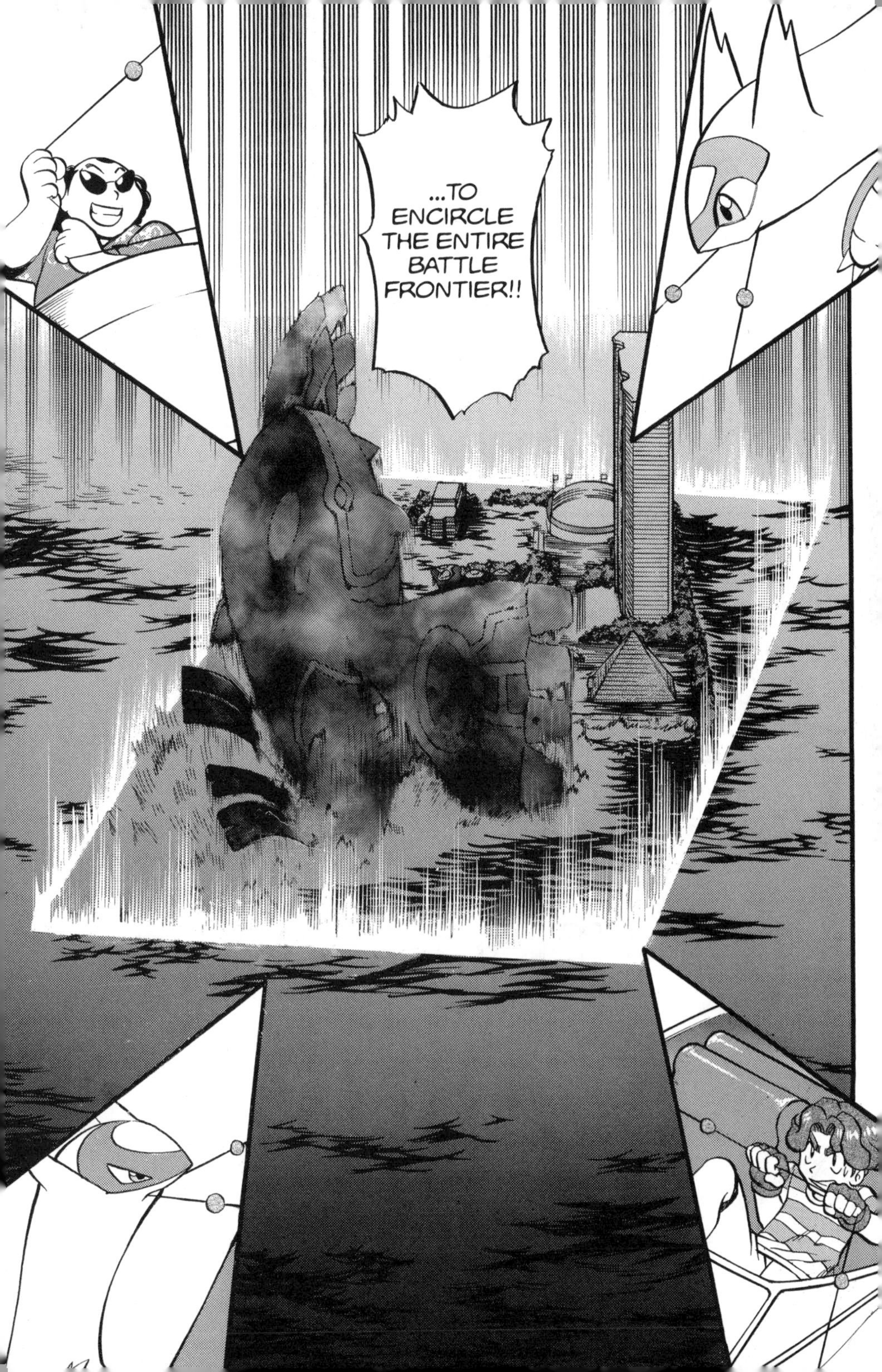
...TO ENCIRCLE THE ENTIRE BATTLE FRONTIER!!

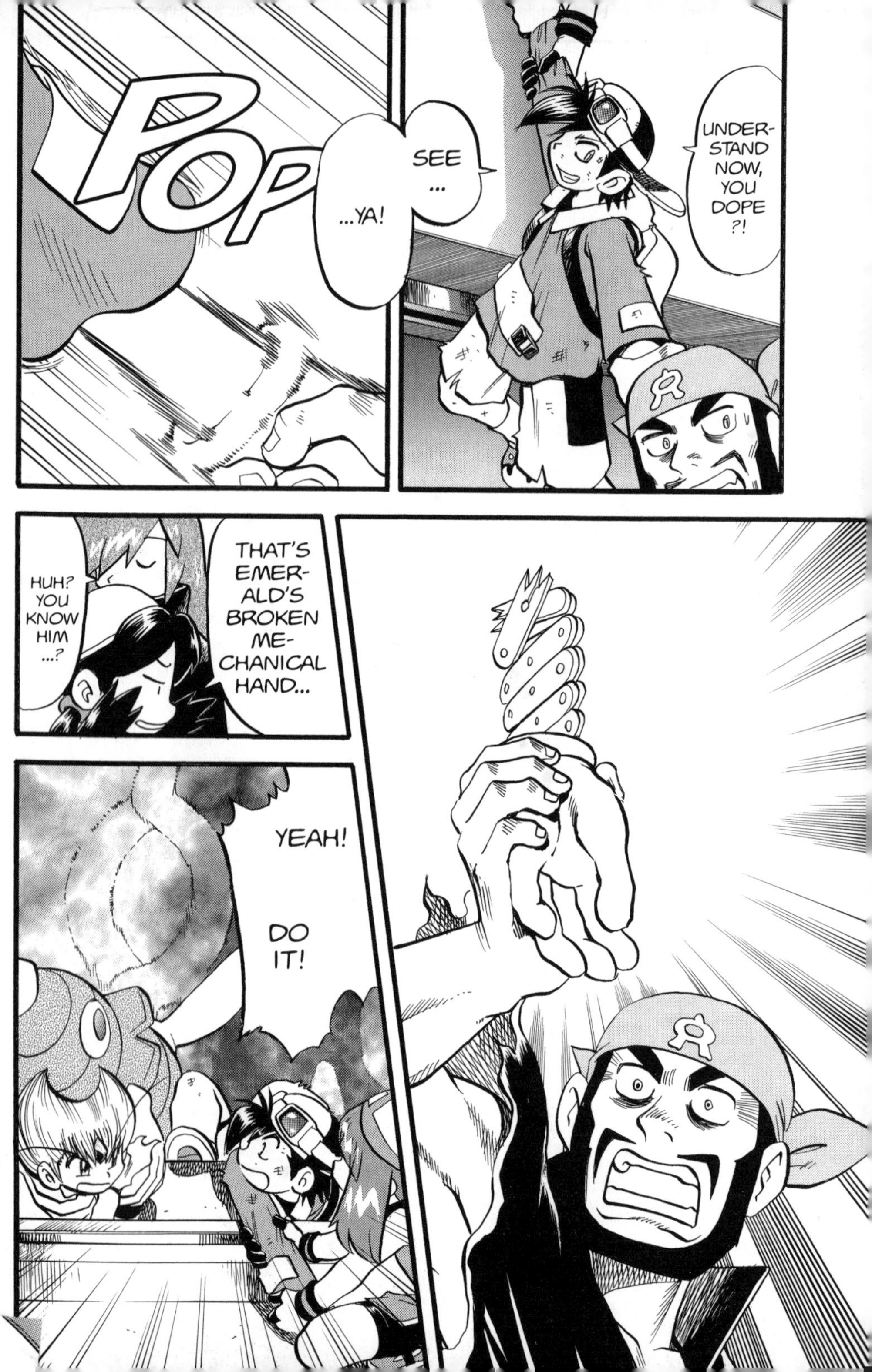
UNDER-STAND NOW, YOU DOPE?!
SEE... ...YA!
POP
THAT'S EMER-ALD'S BROKEN ME-CHANICAL HAND...
HUH? YOU KNOW HIM...?
YEAH!
DO IT!

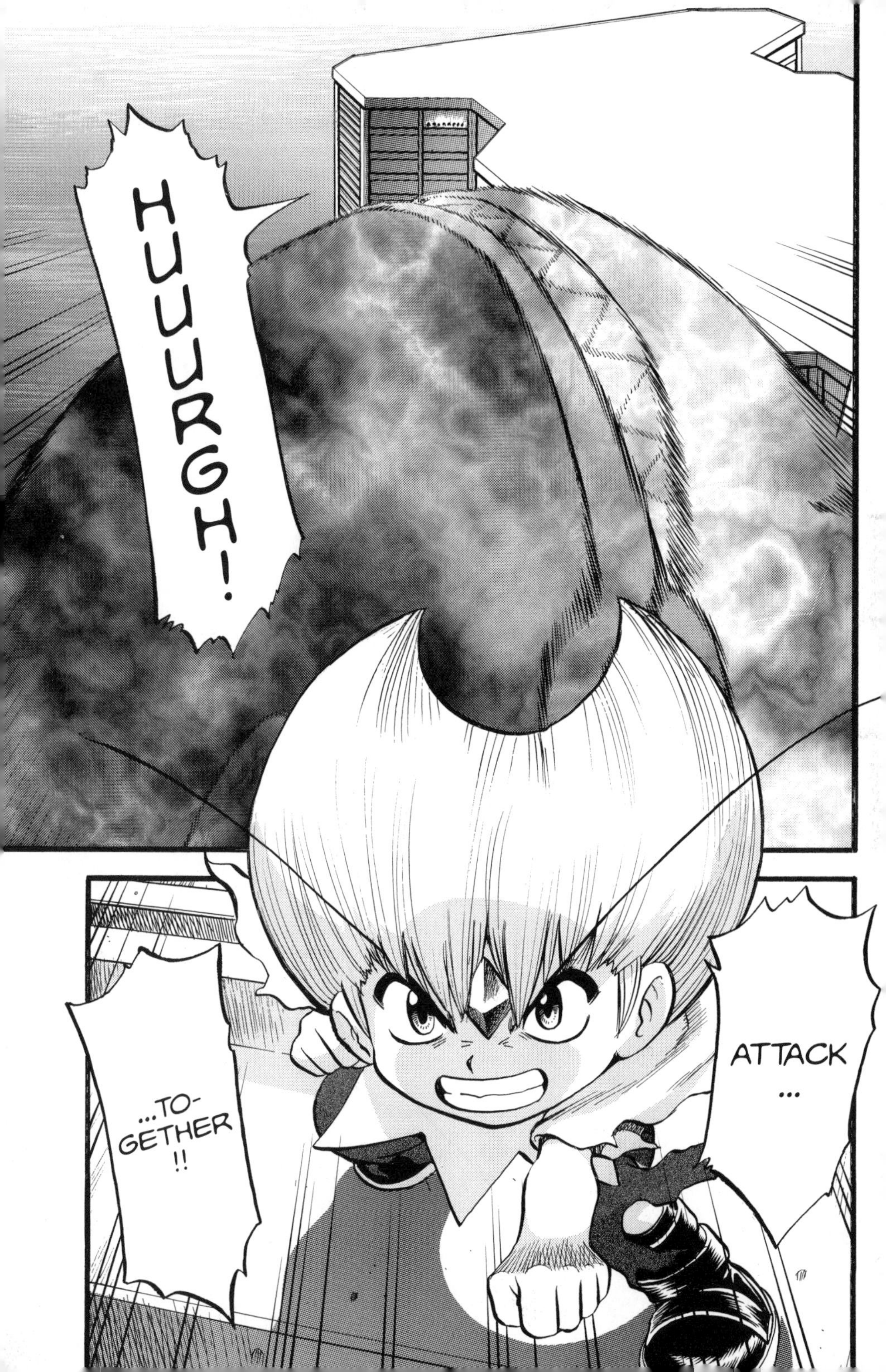
HUUURGH!
ATTACK ...
...TO-GETHER !!

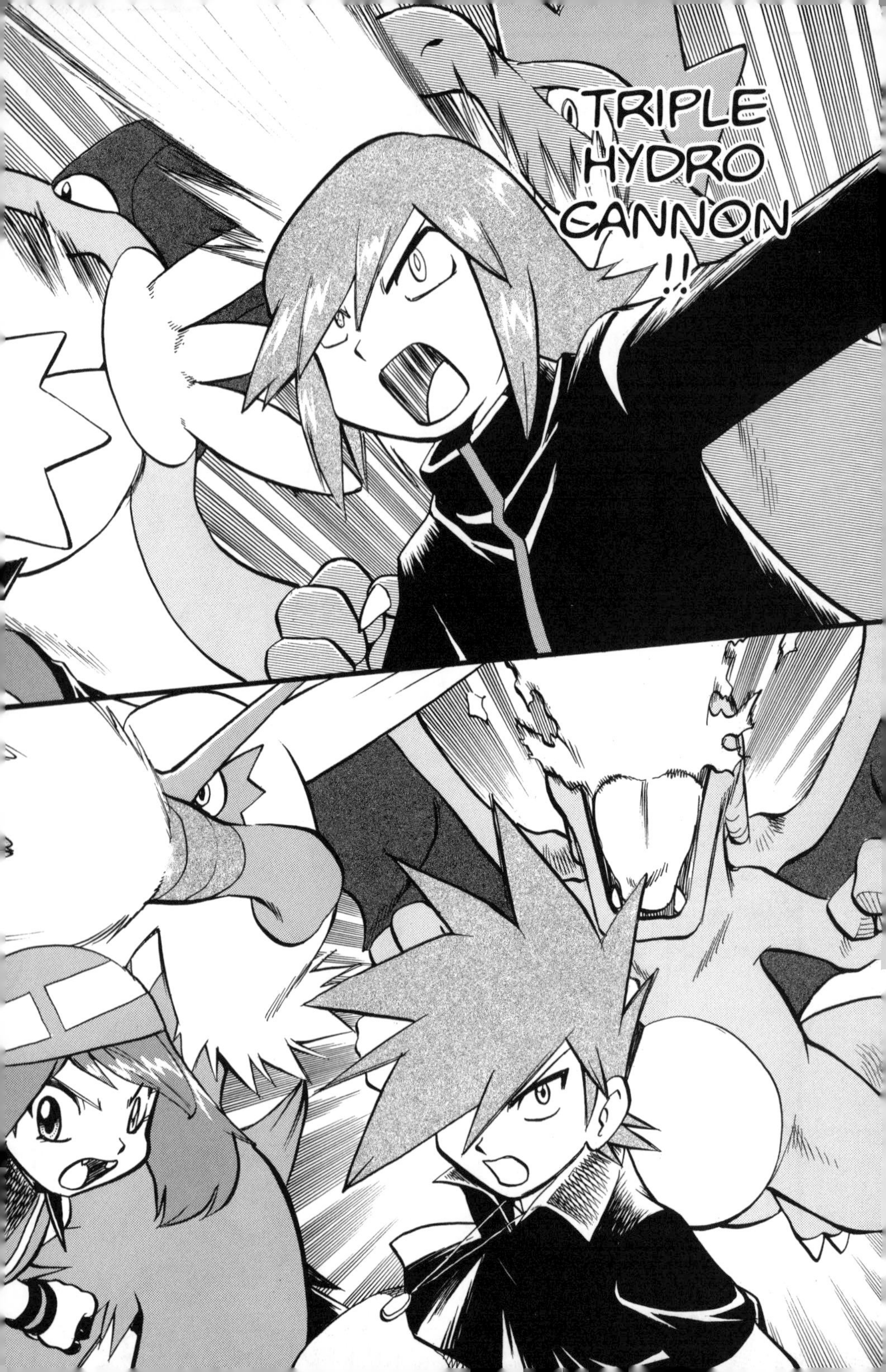
TRIPLE HYDRO CANNON !!

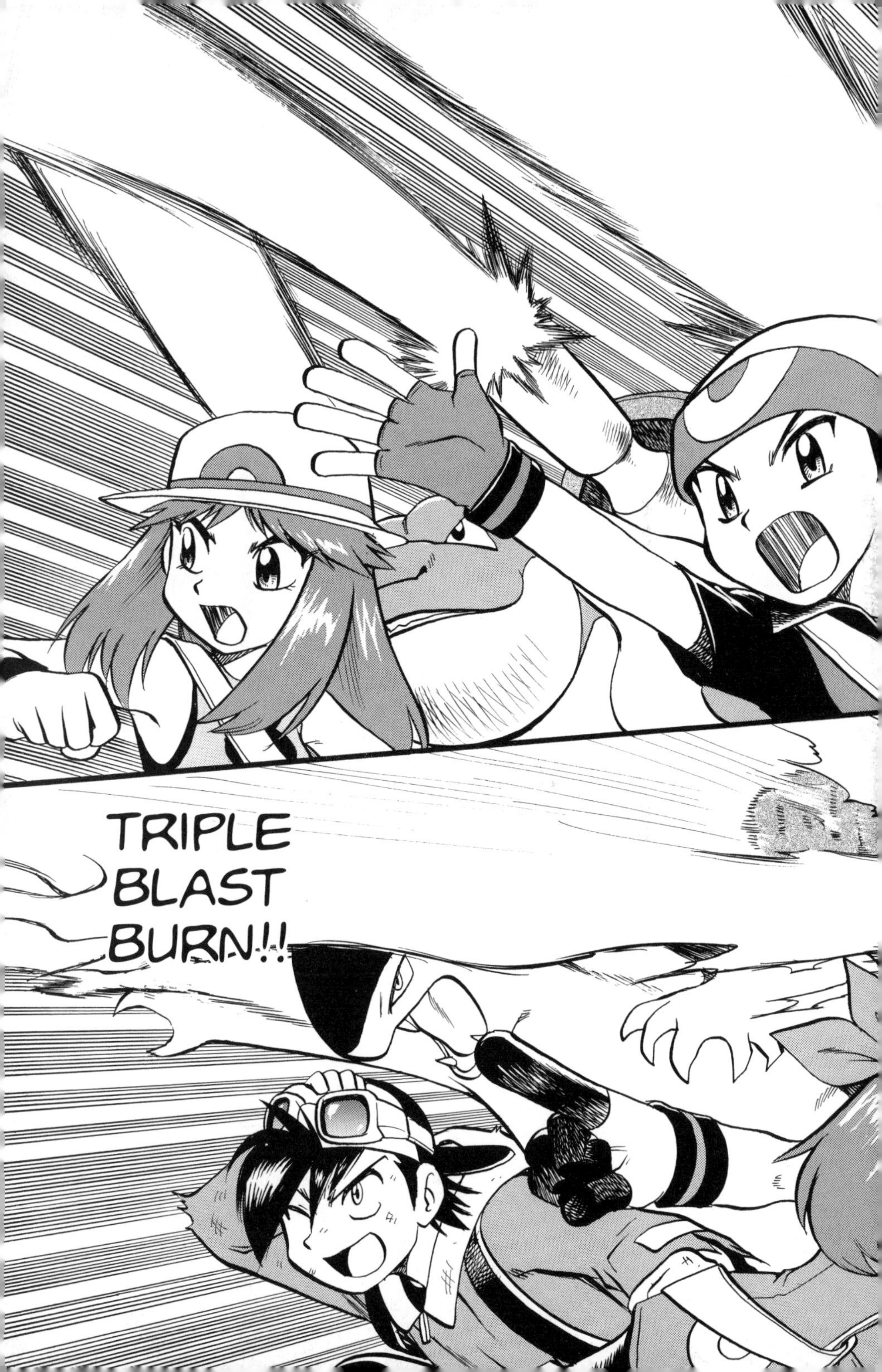
TRIPLE BLAST BURN!!

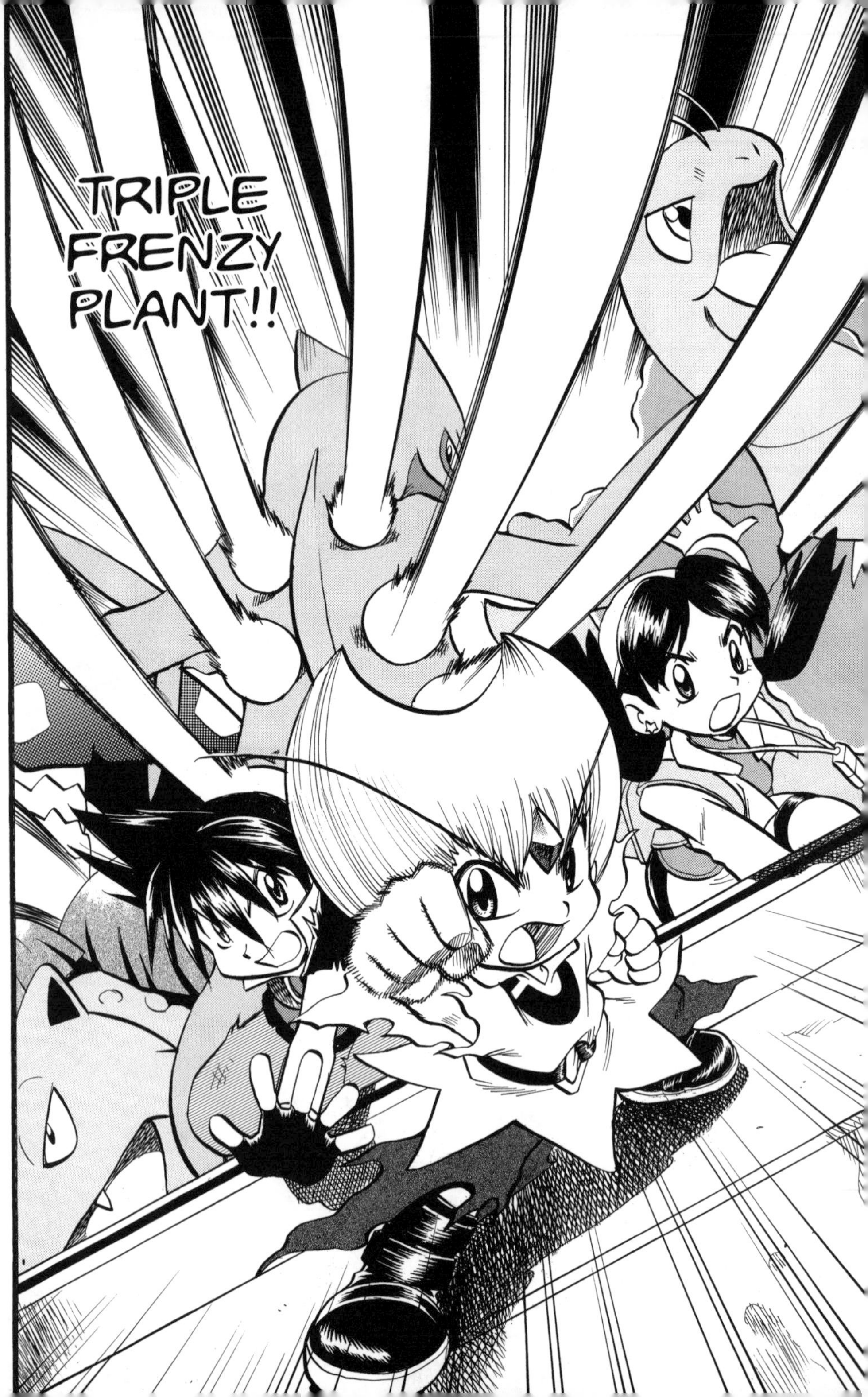
TRIPLE FRENZY PLANT!!

The Final Battle, Part 9

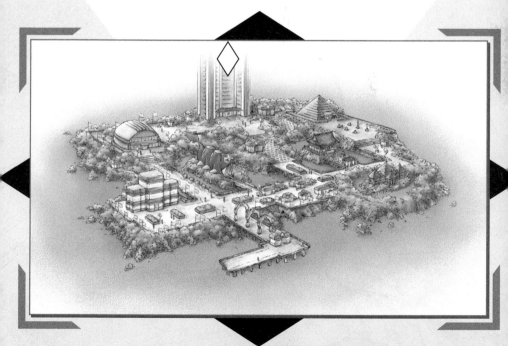

POKÉMON ADVENTURES·THE SIXTH CHAPTER·EMERALD

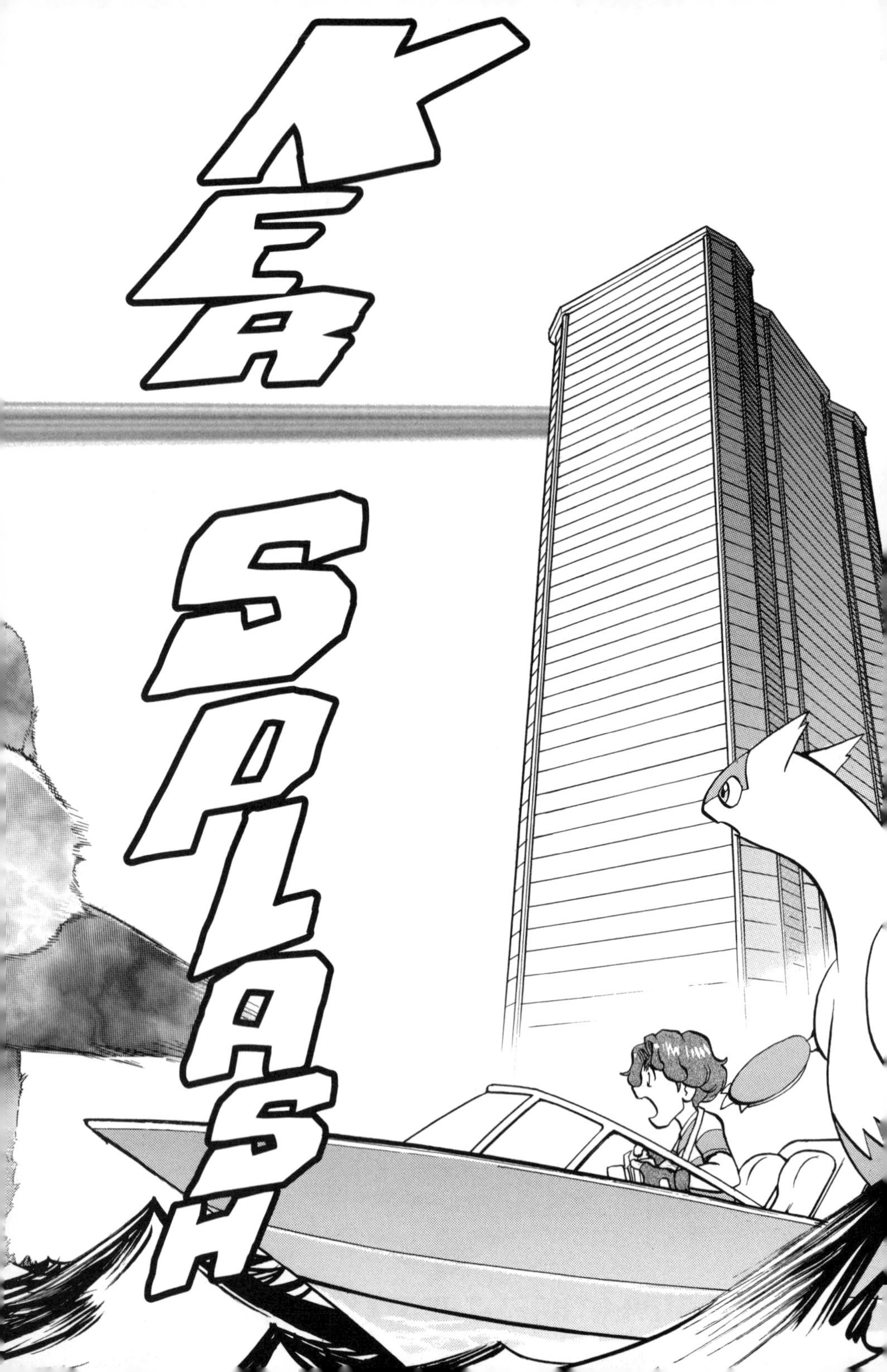
KER
SPLASH

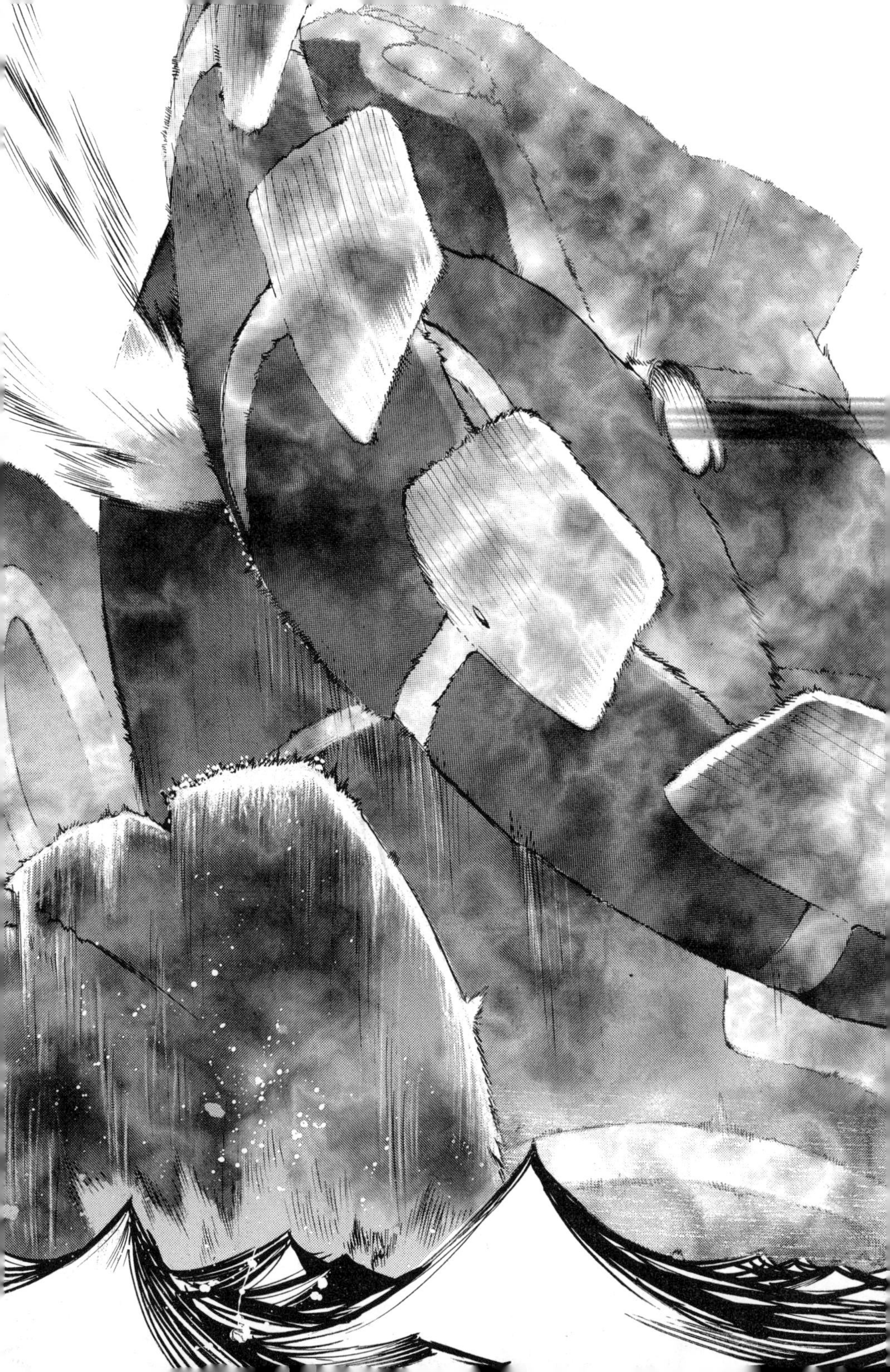

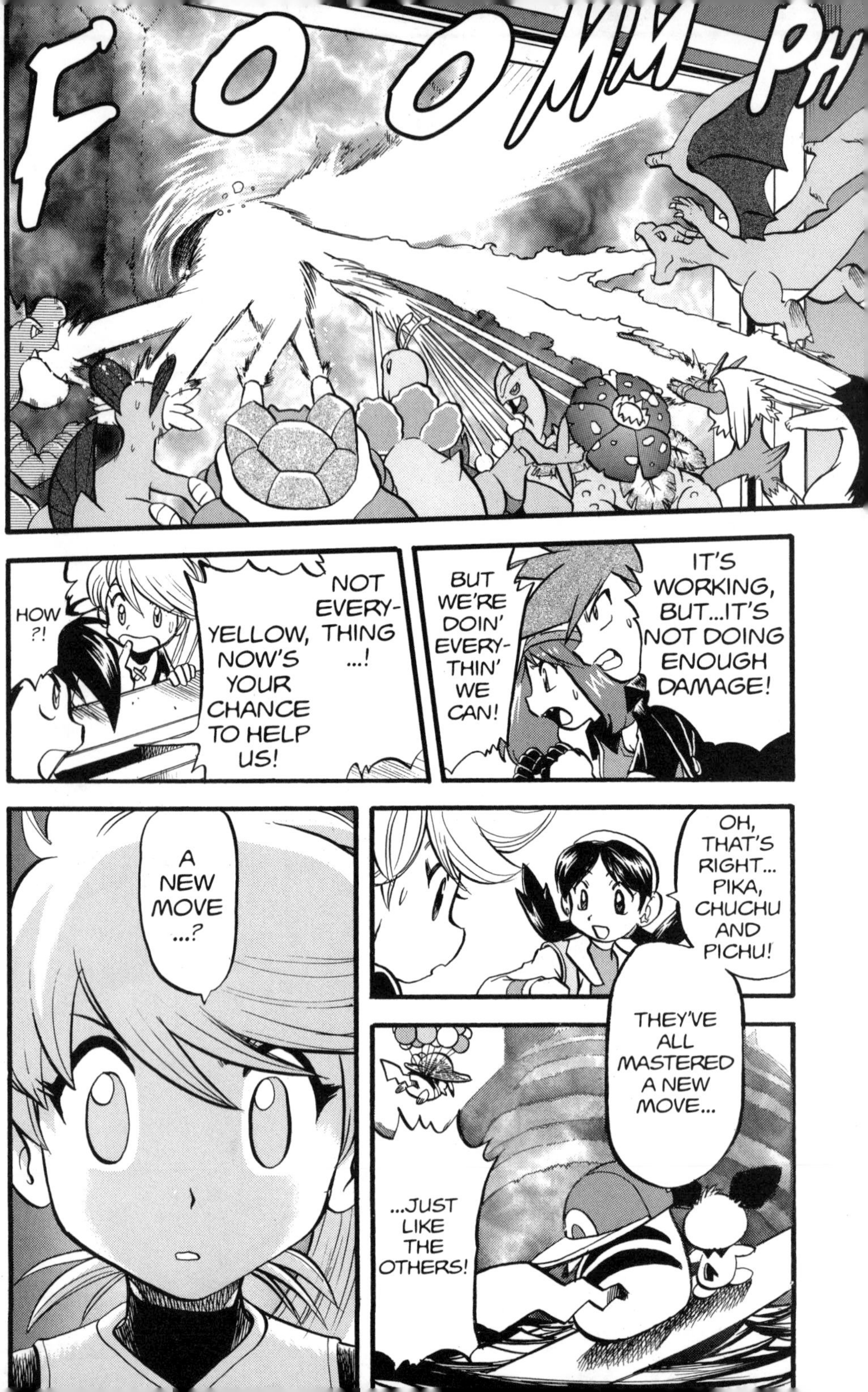
FOOMMPH
IT'S WORKING, BUT...IT'S NOT DOING ENOUGH DAMAGE!
BUT WE'RE DOIN' EVERY-THIN' WE CAN!
NOT EVERY-THING...!
YELLOW, NOW'S YOUR CHANCE TO HELP US!
HOW?!
OH, THAT'S RIGHT... PIKA, CHUCHU AND PICHU!
THEY'VE ALL MASTERED A NEW MOVE...
...JUST LIKE THE OTHERS!
A NEW MOVE...?

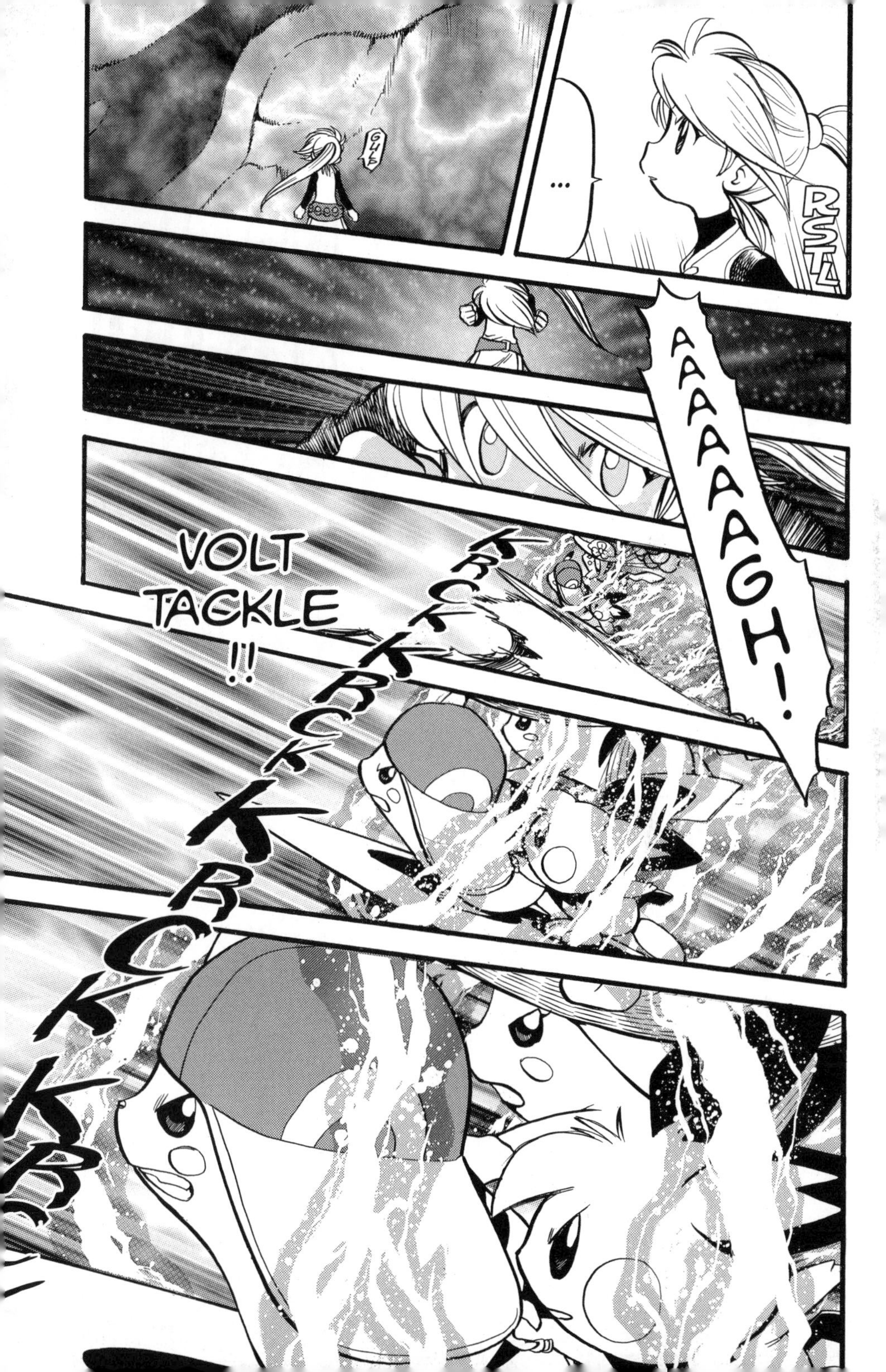
...
RSTL
GULP
AAAAAAAGH!
VOLT TACKLE!!
KRCK KRCK KRCK KKR

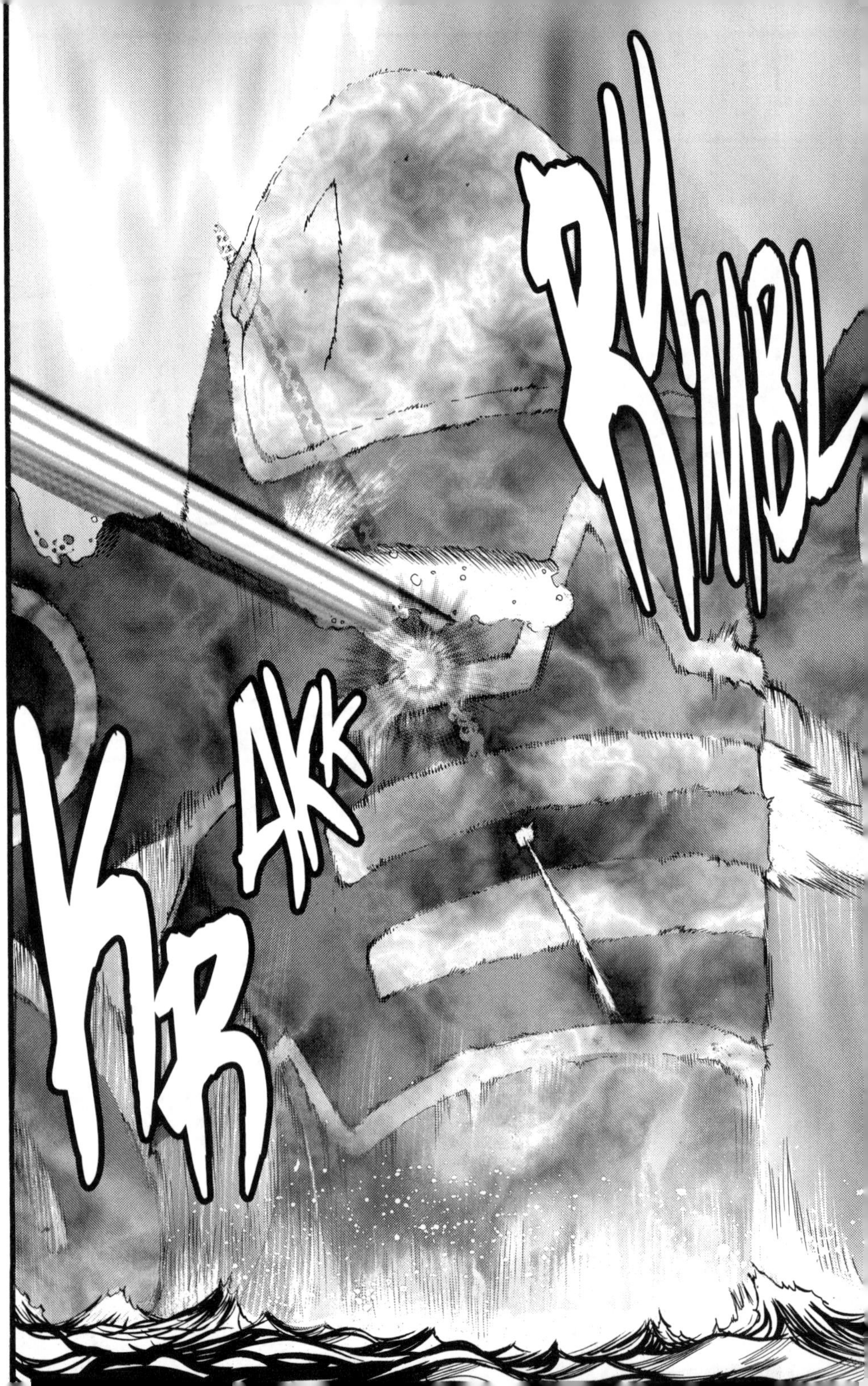
RUMBL
KRAKK

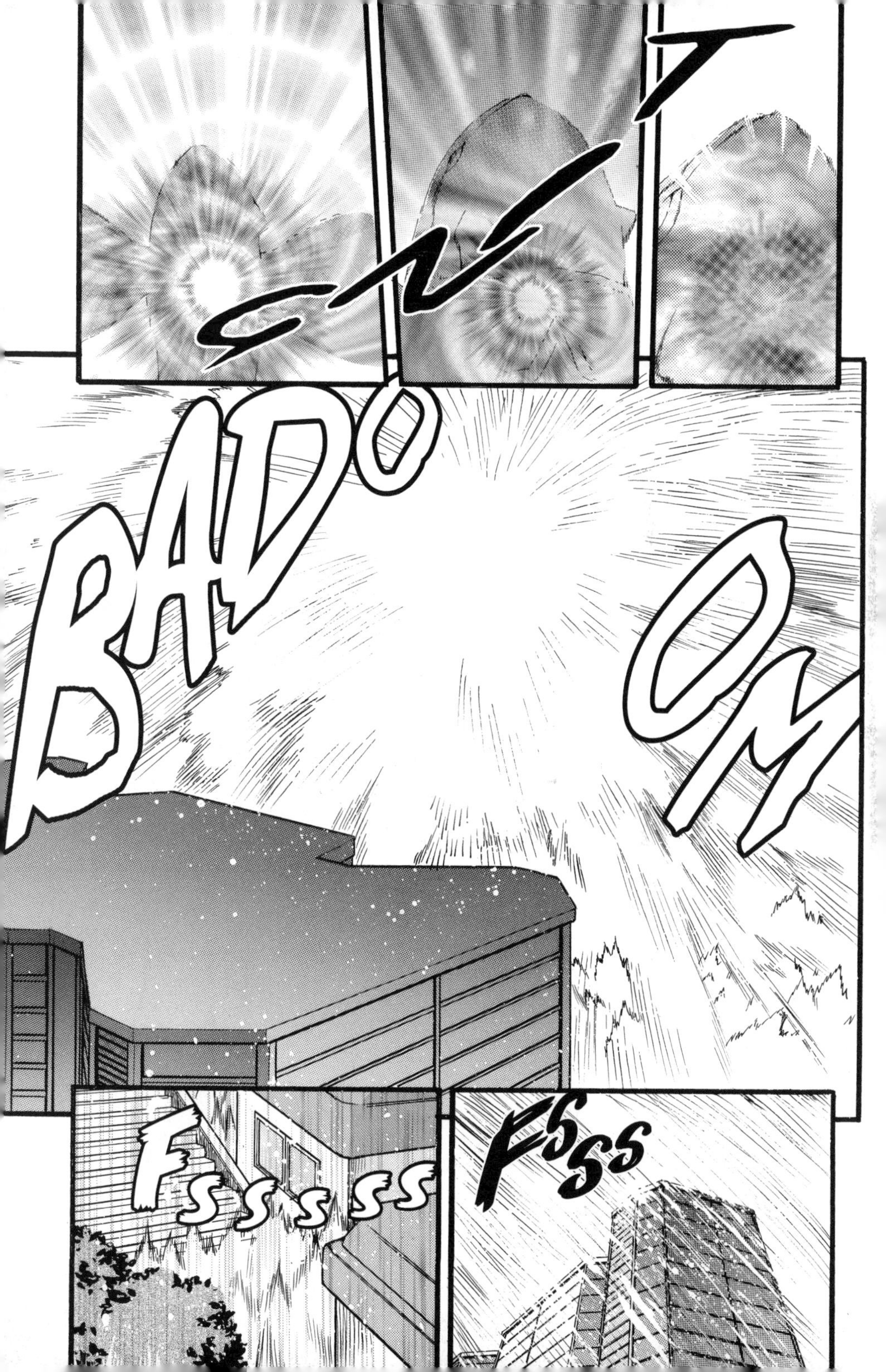
SNIT
BADOOM
FSSS
FSSSSS

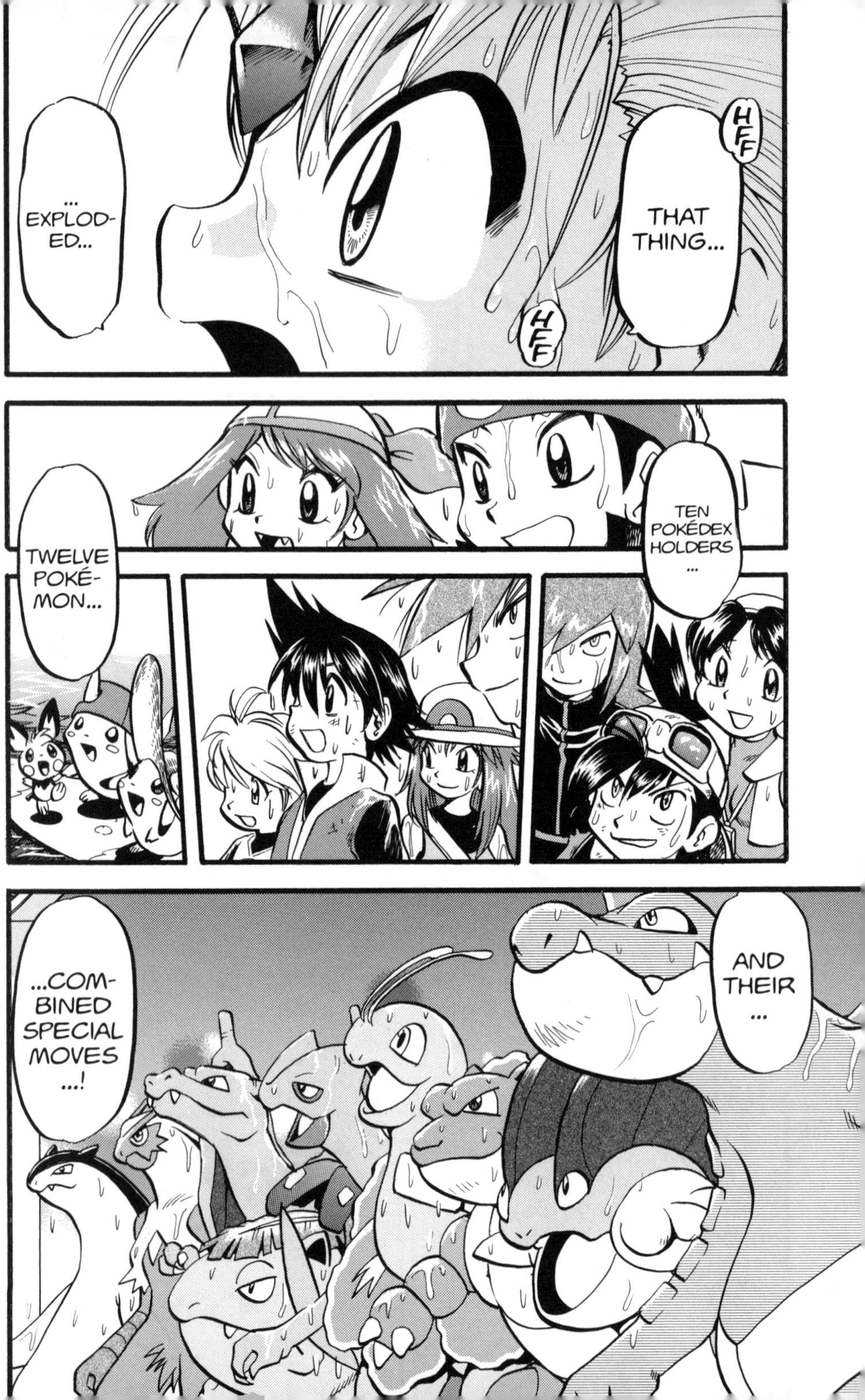
HFF
THAT THING...
HFF
...EXPLOD-ED...
TEN POKÉDEX HOLDERS ...
TWELVE POKÉ-MON...
AND THEIR ...
...COM-BINED SPECIAL MOVES ...!

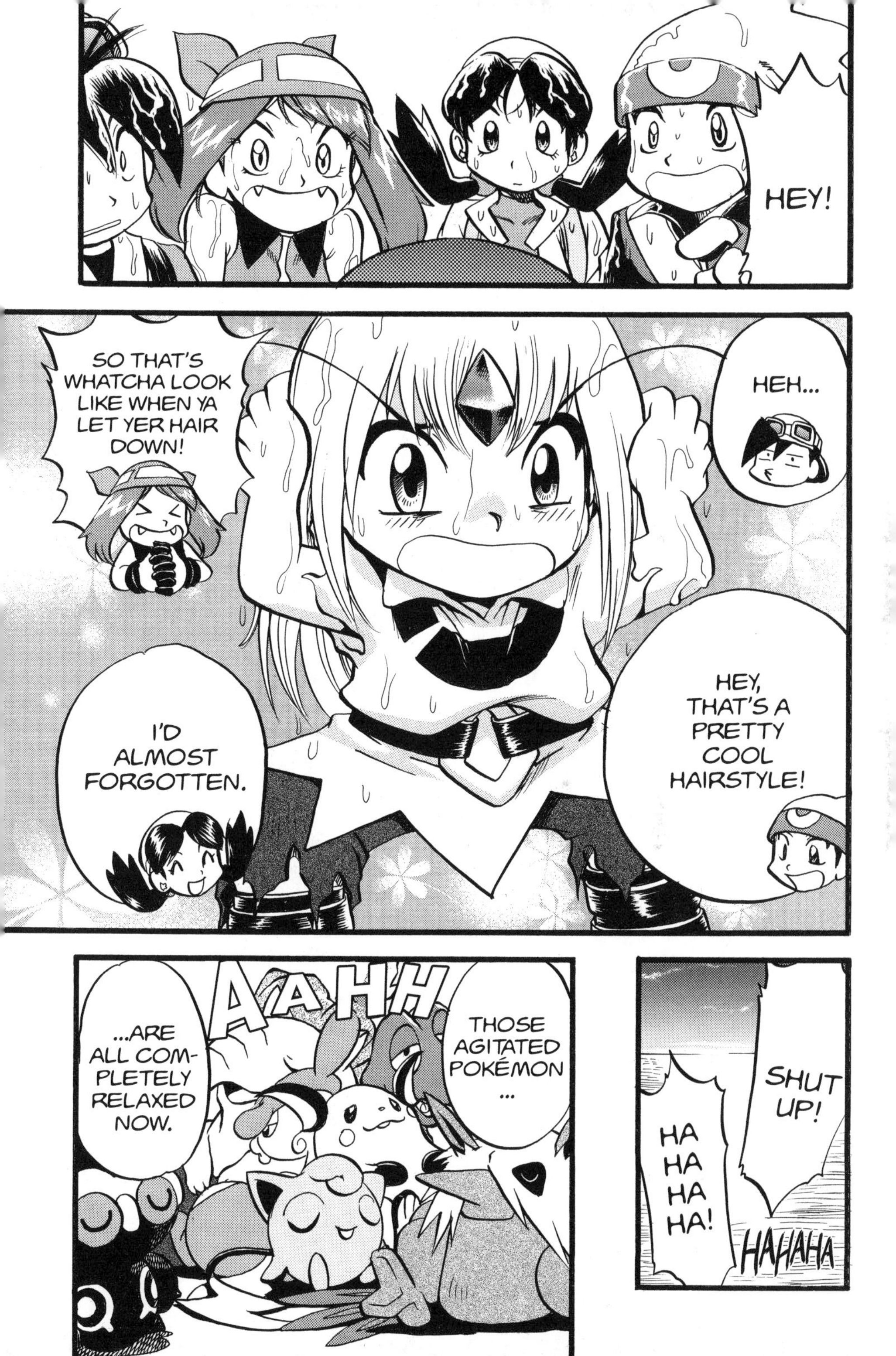
HEY!
HEH...
SO THAT'S WHATCHA LOOK LIKE WHEN YA LET YER HAIR DOWN!
HEY, THAT'S A PRETTY COOL HAIRSTYLE!
I'D ALMOST FORGOTTEN.
SHUT UP!
HA HA HA HA!
HAHAHA
THOSE AGITATED POKÉMON ...
AAHH
...ARE ALL COM-PLETELY RELAXED NOW.

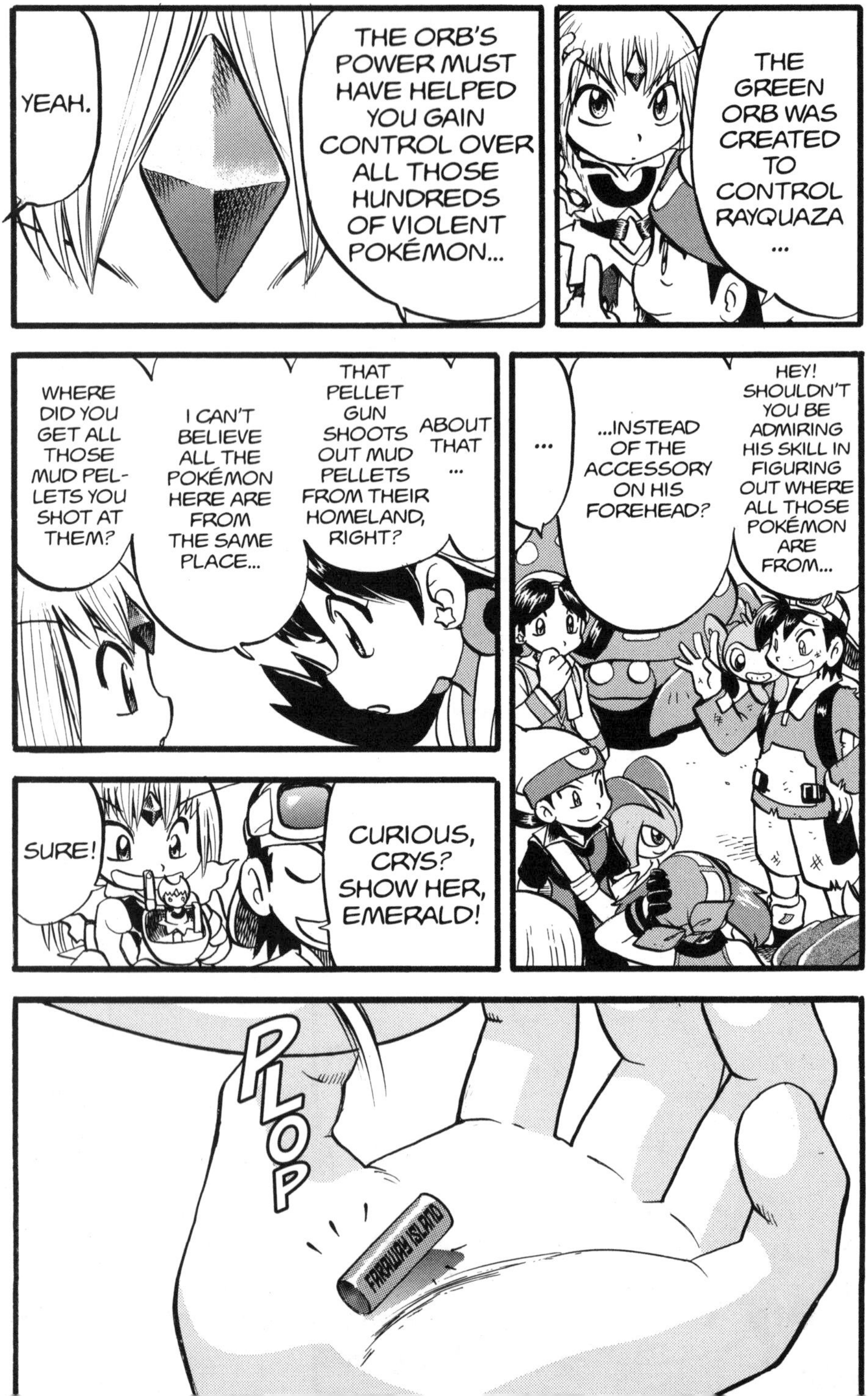
THE GREEN ORB WAS CREATED TO CONTROL RAYQUAZA ...
THE ORB'S POWER MUST HAVE HELPED YOU GAIN CONTROL OVER ALL THOSE HUNDREDS OF VIOLENT POKÉMON...
YEAH.
HEY! SHOULDN'T YOU BE ADMIRING HIS SKILL IN FIGURING OUT WHERE ALL THOSE POKÉMON ARE FROM...
...INSTEAD OF THE ACCESSORY ON HIS FOREHEAD?
...
ABOUT THAT ...
THAT PELLET GUN SHOOTS OUT MUD PELLETS FROM THEIR HOMELAND, RIGHT?
I CAN'T BELIEVE ALL THE POKÉMON HERE ARE FROM THE SAME PLACE...
WHERE DID YOU GET ALL THOSE MUD PEL-LETS YOU SHOT AT THEM?
CURIOUS, CRYS? SHOW HER, EMERALD!
SURE!
PLOP
FARAWAY ISLAND

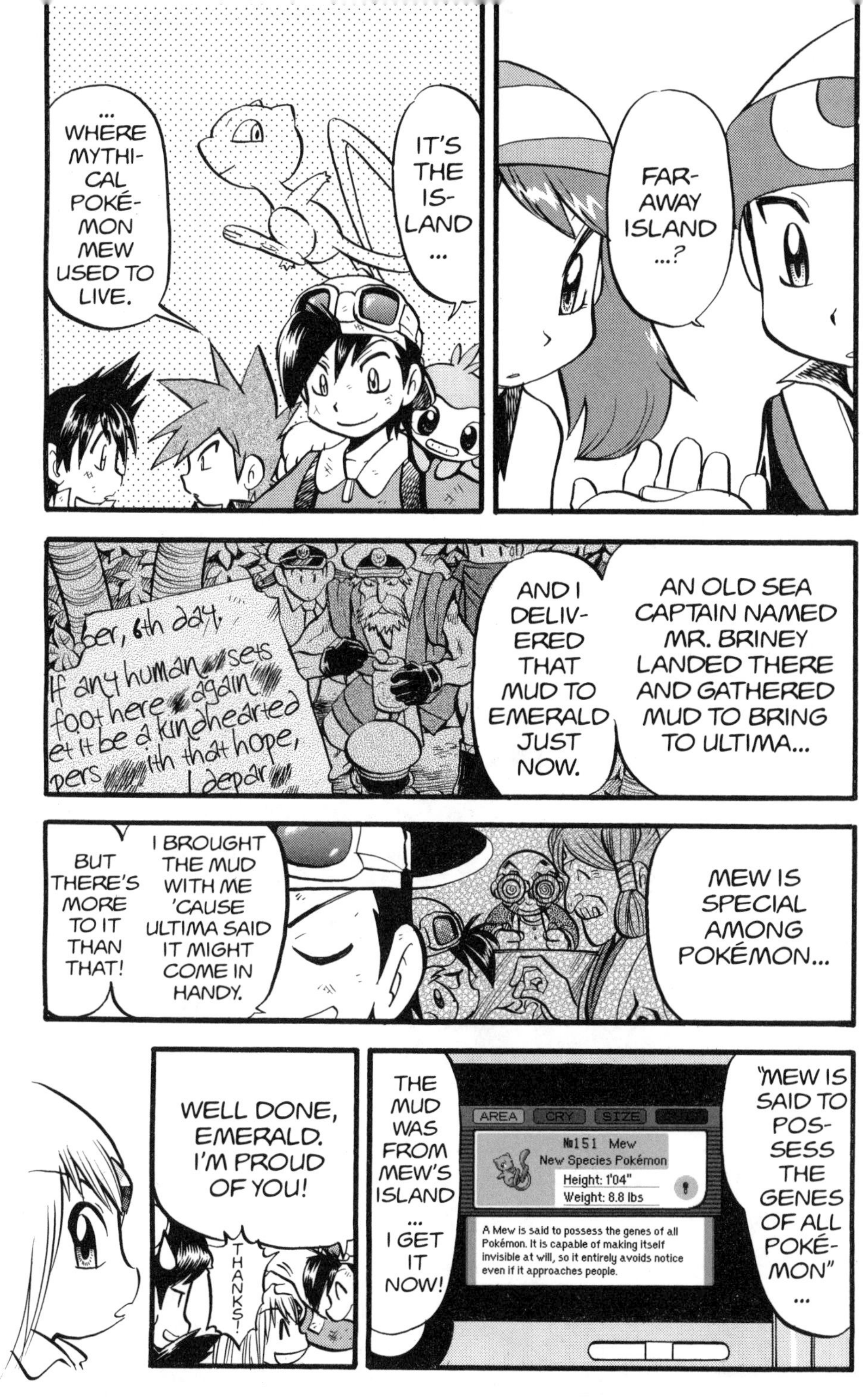
FARAWAY ISLAND ...?
IT'S THE ISLAND ...
... WHERE MYTHICAL POKÉMON MEW USED TO LIVE.
AN OLD SEA CAPTAIN NAMED MR. BRINEY LANDED THERE AND GATHERED MUD TO BRING TO ULTIMA...
AND I DELIVERED THAT MUD TO EMERALD JUST NOW.
ber, 6th day,
If any human sets
foot here again
et it be a kindhearted
pers ith that hope,
I depar
MEW IS SPECIAL AMONG POKÉMON...
I BROUGHT THE MUD WITH ME 'CAUSE ULTIMA SAID IT MIGHT COME IN HANDY.
BUT THERE'S MORE TO IT THAN THAT!
"MEW IS SAID TO POSSESS THE GENES OF ALL POKÉMON" ...
AREA
CRY
SIZE
№151 Mew
New Species Pokémon
Height: 1'04"
Weight: 8.8 lbs
A Mew is said to possess the genes of all Pokémon. It is capable of making itself invisible at will, so it entirely avoids notice even if it approaches people.
THE MUD WAS FROM MEW'S ISLAND ... I GET IT NOW!
WELL DONE, EMERALD. I'M PROUD OF YOU!
THANKS!

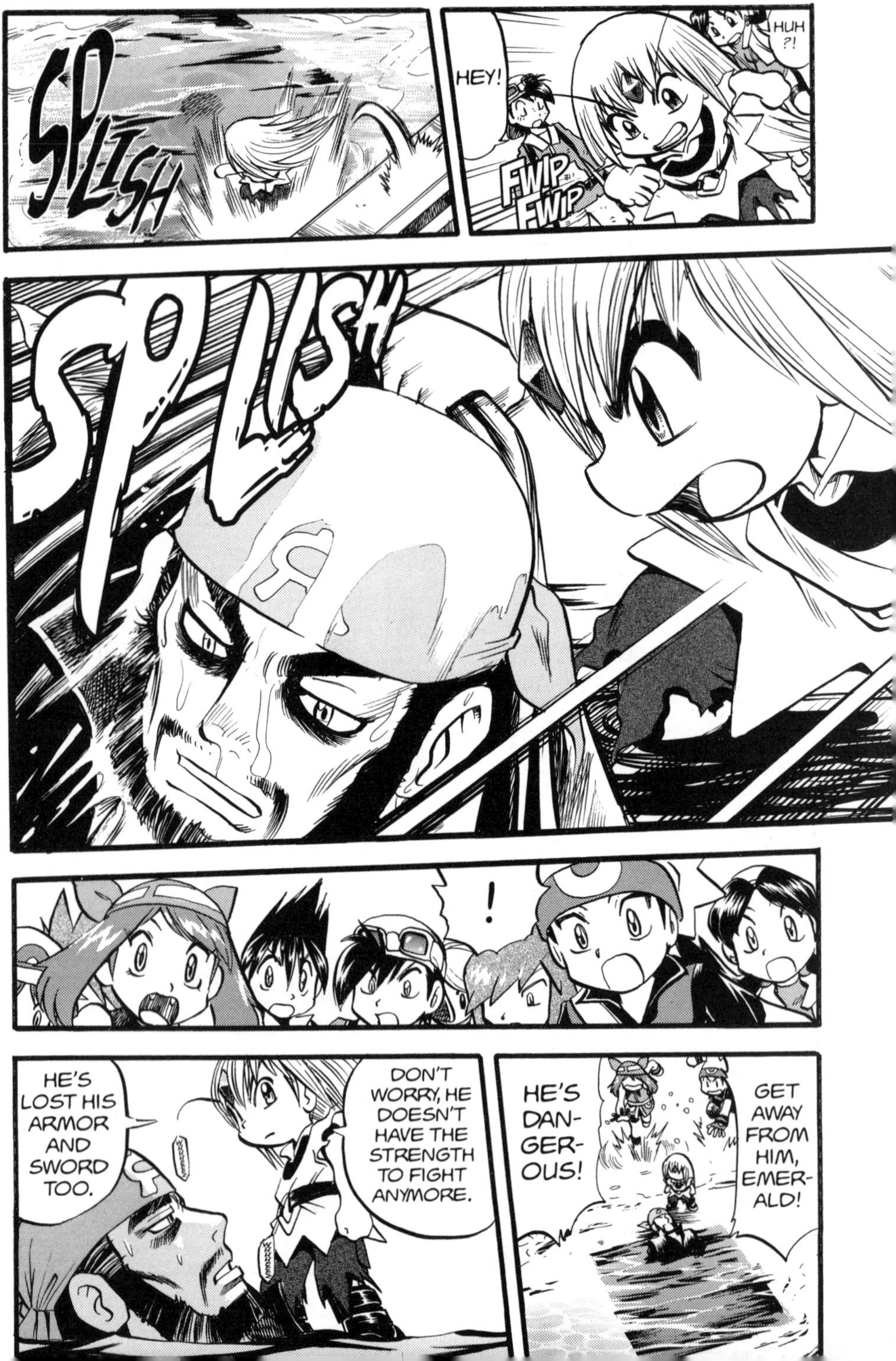
HUH ?!
HEY!
FWIP FWIP
SPLISH
SPLISH
!
GET AWAY FROM HIM, EMERALD!
HE'S DANGEROUS!
DON'T WORRY, HE DOESN'T HAVE THE STRENGTH TO FIGHT ANYMORE.
HE'S LOST HIS ARMOR AND SWORD TOO.

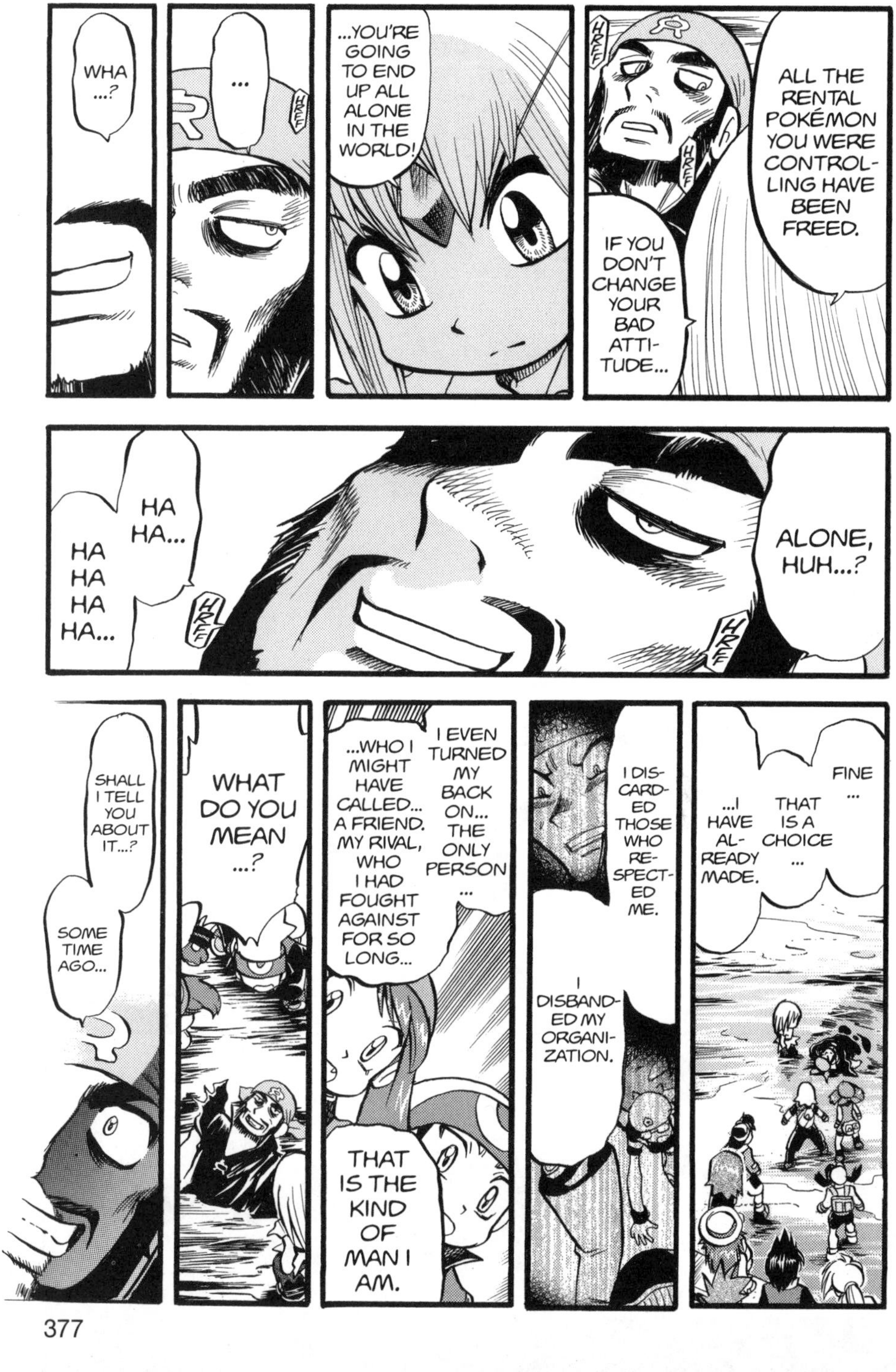
HRFF
ALL THE RENTAL POKÉMON YOU WERE CONTROLLING HAVE BEEN FREED.
HRFF
IF YOU DON'T CHANGE YOUR BAD ATTITUDE...
...YOU'RE GOING TO END UP ALL ALONE IN THE WORLD!
...
HRFF
WHA ...?
ALONE, HUH...?
HRFF
HA HA...
HA HA HA HA...
HRFF
FINE ...
THAT IS A CHOICE ...
...I HAVE ALREADY MADE.
I DISCARDED THOSE WHO RESPECTED ME.
I DISBANDED MY ORGANIZATION.
I EVEN TURNED MY BACK ON... THE ONLY PERSON ...
...WHO I MIGHT HAVE CALLED... A FRIEND. MY RIVAL, WHO I HAD FOUGHT AGAINST FOR SO LONG...
THAT IS THE KIND OF MAN I AM.
WHAT DO YOU MEAN ...?
SHALL I TELL YOU ABOUT IT...?
SOME TIME AGO...

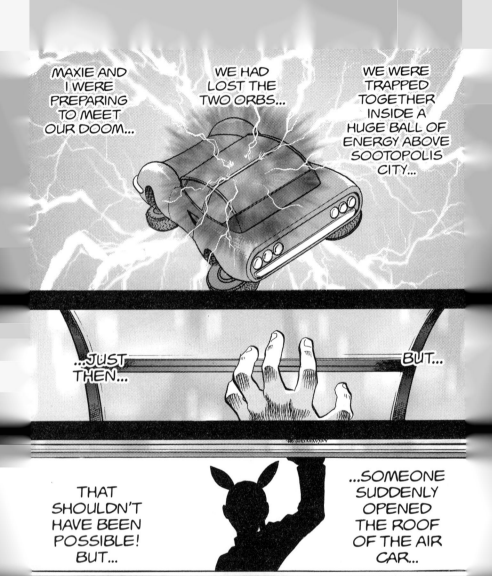

WE WERE TRAPPED TOGETHER INSIDE A HUGE BALL OF ENERGY ABOVE SOOTOPOLIS CITY...
WE HAD LOST THE TWO ORBS...
MAXIE AND I WERE PREPARING TO MEET OUR DOOM...
BUT...
...JUST THEN...
...SOMEONE SUDDENLY OPENED THE ROOF OF THE AIR CAR...
THAT SHOULDN'T HAVE BEEN POSSIBLE! BUT...

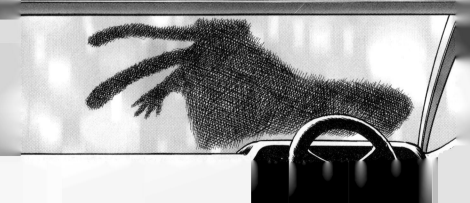

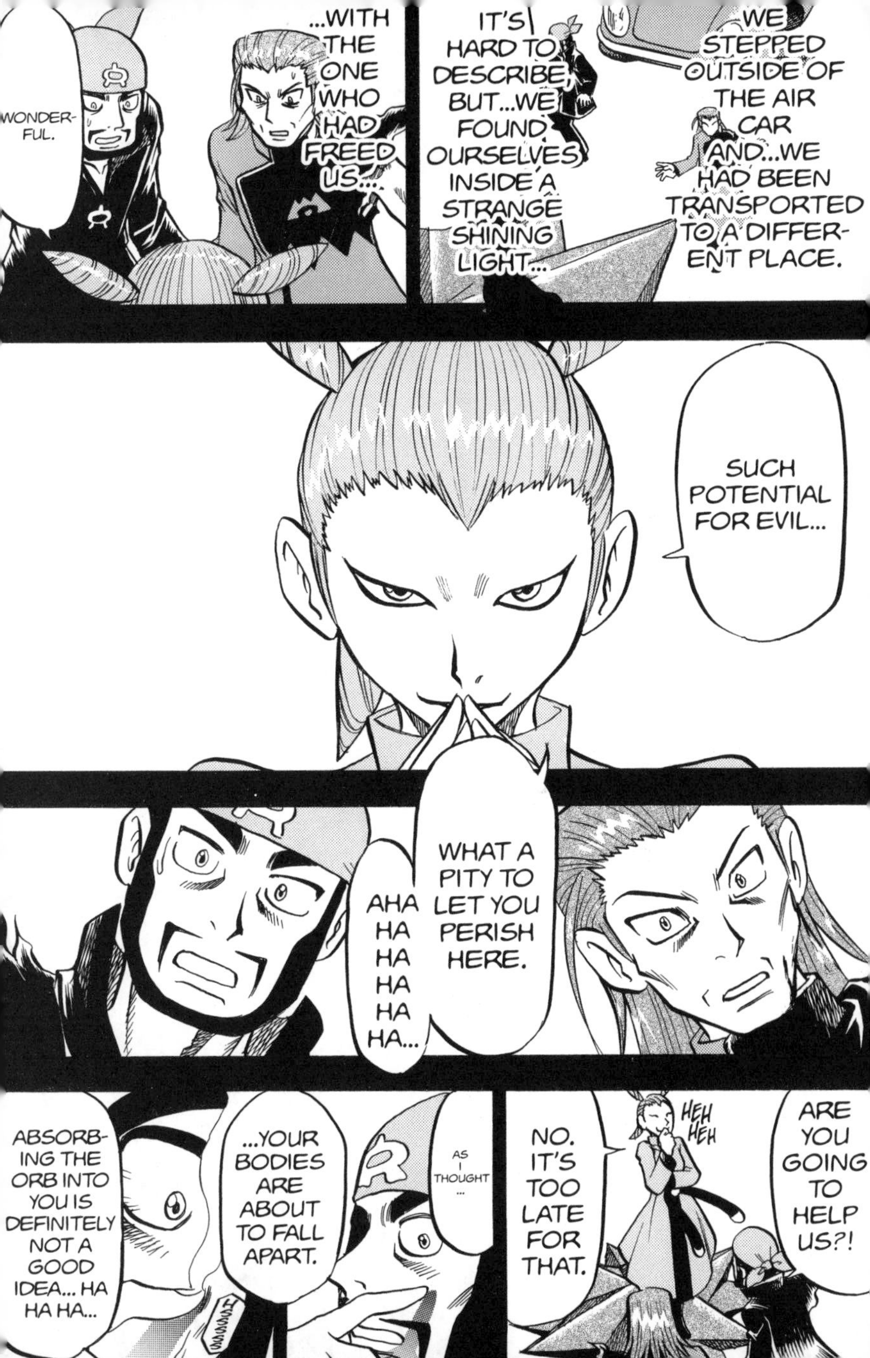
WE STEPPED OUTSIDE OF THE AIR CAR AND...WE HAD BEEN TRANSPORTED TO A DIFFERENT PLACE.
IT'S HARD TO DESCRIBE, BUT...WE FOUND OURSELVES INSIDE A STRANGE SHINING LIGHT...
...WITH THE ONE WHO HAD FREED US...
WONDERFUL.
SUCH POTENTIAL FOR EVIL...
WHAT A PITY TO LET YOU PERISH HERE.
AHA HA HA HA HA HA...
ARE YOU GOING TO HELP US?!
HEH HEH
NO. IT'S TOO LATE FOR THAT.
AS I THOUGHT...
...YOUR BODIES ARE ABOUT TO FALL APART.
ABSORBING THE ORB INTO YOU IS DEFINITELY NOT A GOOD IDEA... HA HA HA...

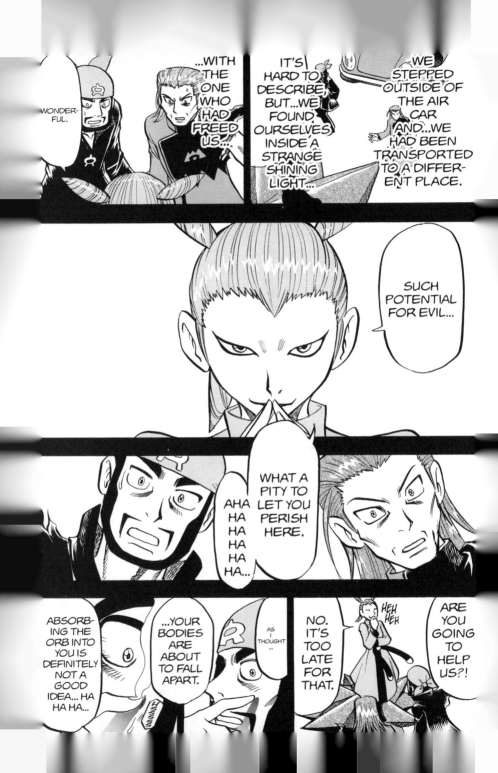

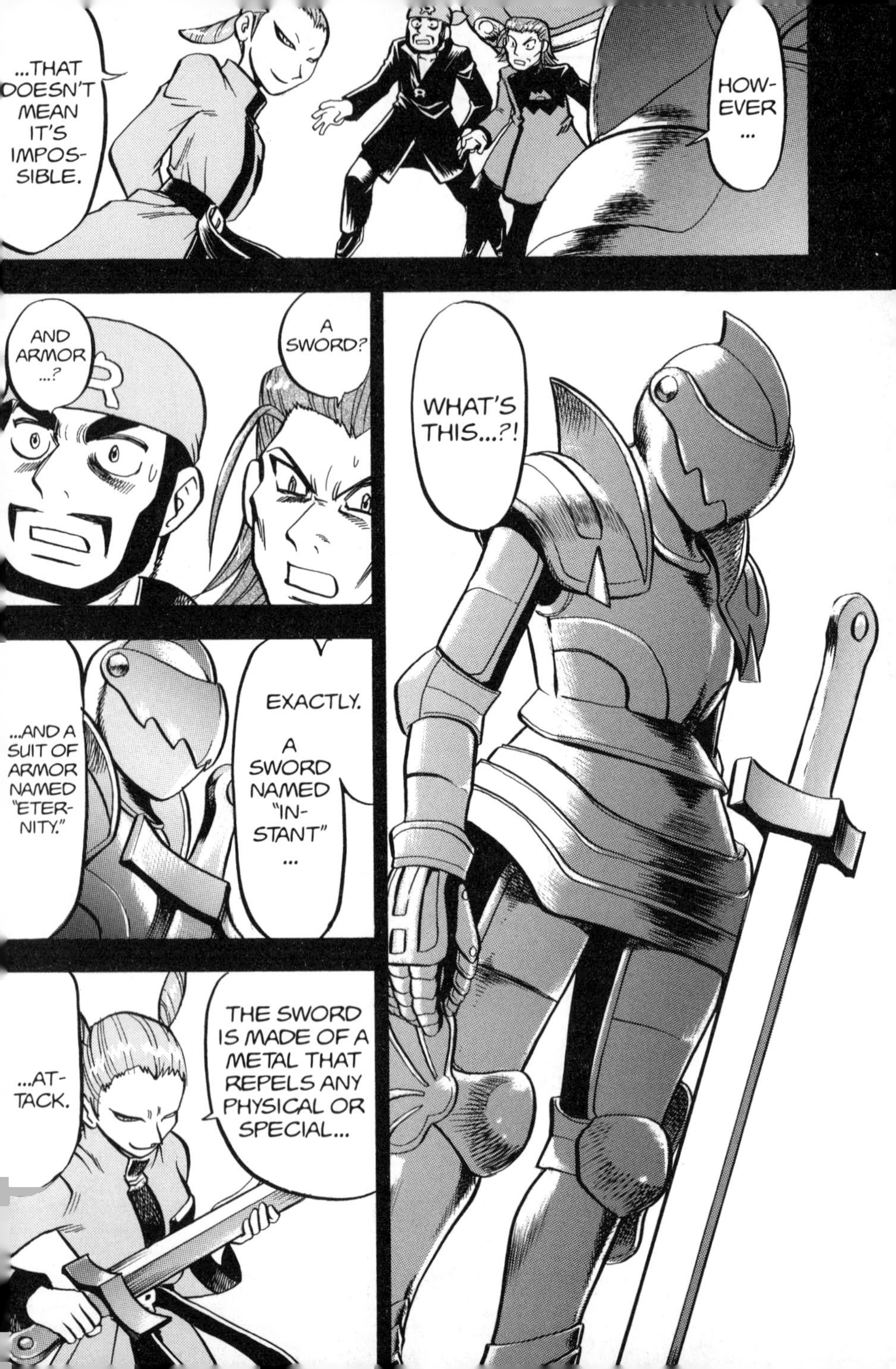
HOW-EVER...
...THAT DOESN'T MEAN IT'S IMPOSSIBLE.
WHAT'S THIS...?!
A SWORD?
AND ARMOR...?
EXACTLY.
A SWORD NAMED "INSTANT"...
...AND A SUIT OF ARMOR NAMED "ETERNITY."
THE SWORD IS MADE OF A METAL THAT REPELS ANY PHYSICAL OR SPECIAL...
...ATTACK.

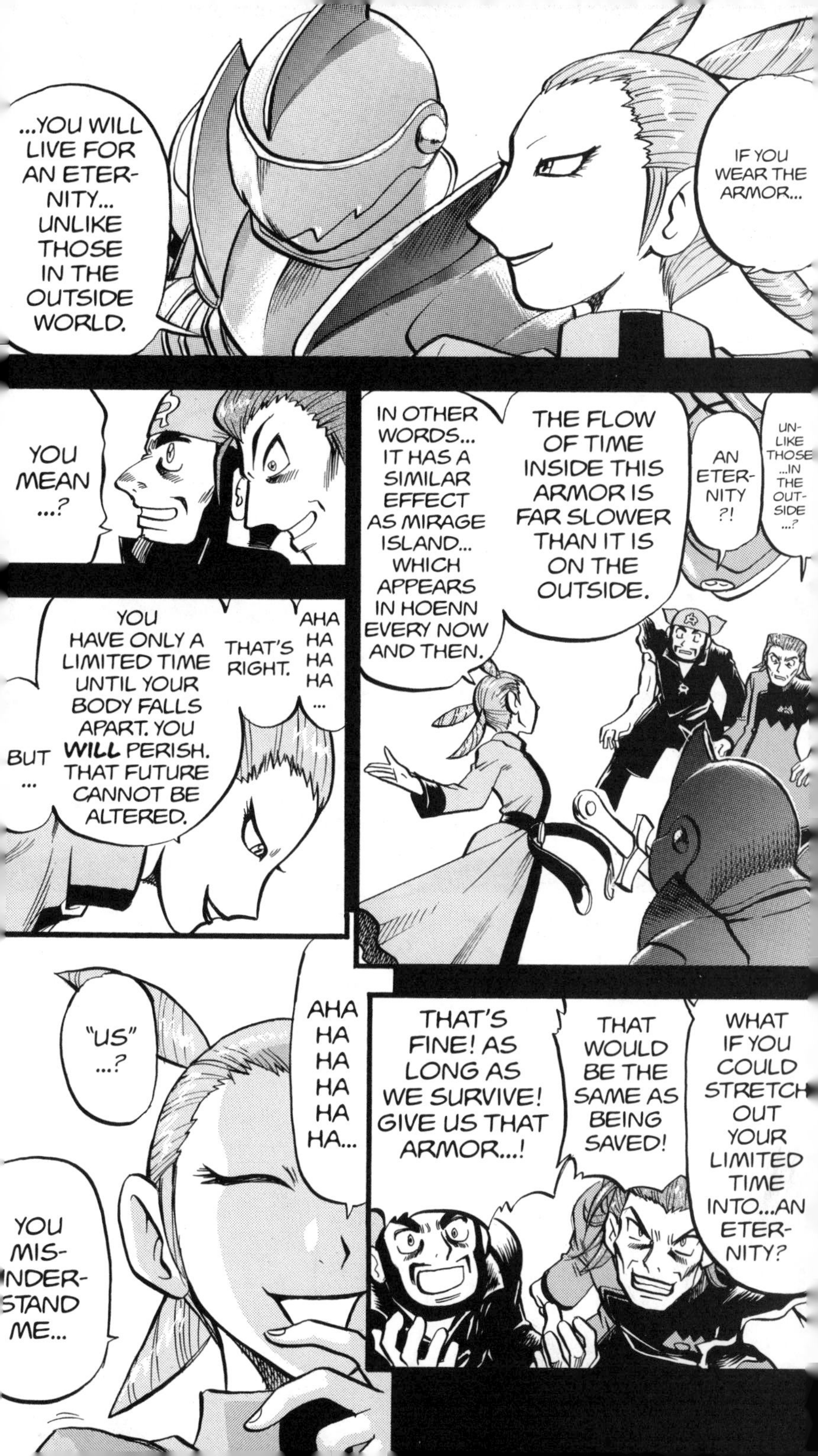
IF YOU WEAR THE ARMOR...
...YOU WILL LIVE FOR AN ETERNITY... UNLIKE THOSE IN THE OUTSIDE WORLD.
UNLIKE THOSE ...IN THE OUTSIDE ...?
AN ETERNITY ?!
THE FLOW OF TIME INSIDE THIS ARMOR IS FAR SLOWER THAN IT IS ON THE OUTSIDE.
IN OTHER WORDS... IT HAS A SIMILAR EFFECT AS MIRAGE ISLAND... WHICH APPEARS IN HOENN EVERY NOW AND THEN.
YOU MEAN ...?
AHA HA HA HA ...
THAT'S RIGHT.
YOU HAVE ONLY A LIMITED TIME UNTIL YOUR BODY FALLS APART. YOU **WILL** PERISH. THAT FUTURE CANNOT BE ALTERED.
BUT ...
WHAT IF YOU COULD STRETCH OUT YOUR LIMITED TIME INTO...AN ETERNITY?
THAT WOULD BE THE SAME AS BEING SAVED!
THAT'S FINE! AS LONG AS WE SURVIVE! GIVE US THAT ARMOR...!
AHA HA HA HA HA HA...
"US" ...?
YOU MISUNDERSTAND ME...

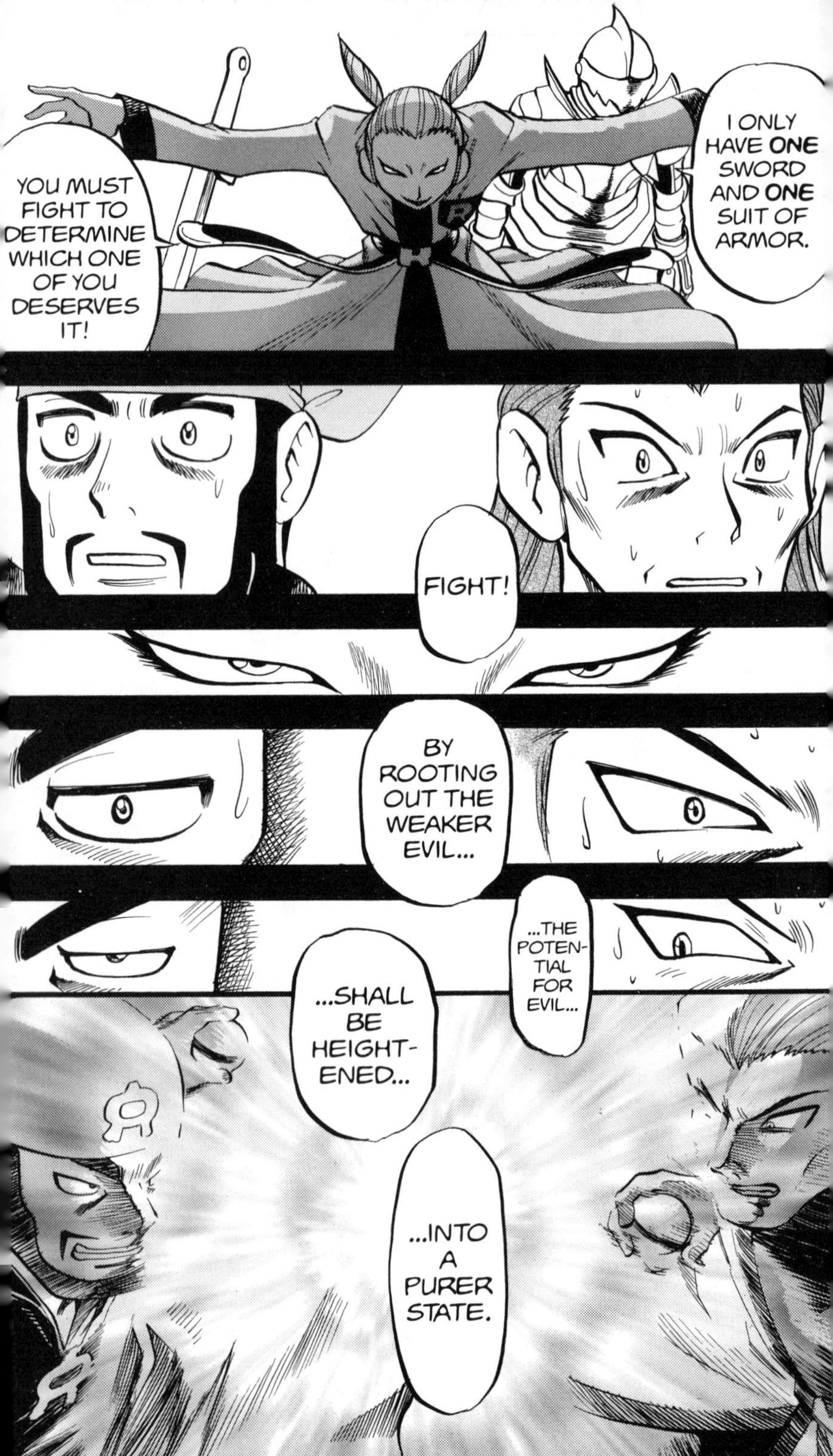
I ONLY HAVE ONE SWORD AND ONE SUIT OF ARMOR.
YOU MUST FIGHT TO DETERMINE WHICH ONE OF YOU DESERVES IT!
FIGHT!
BY ROOTING OUT THE WEAKER EVIL...
...THE POTENTIAL FOR EVIL...
...SHALL BE HEIGHTENED...
...INTO A PURER STATE.

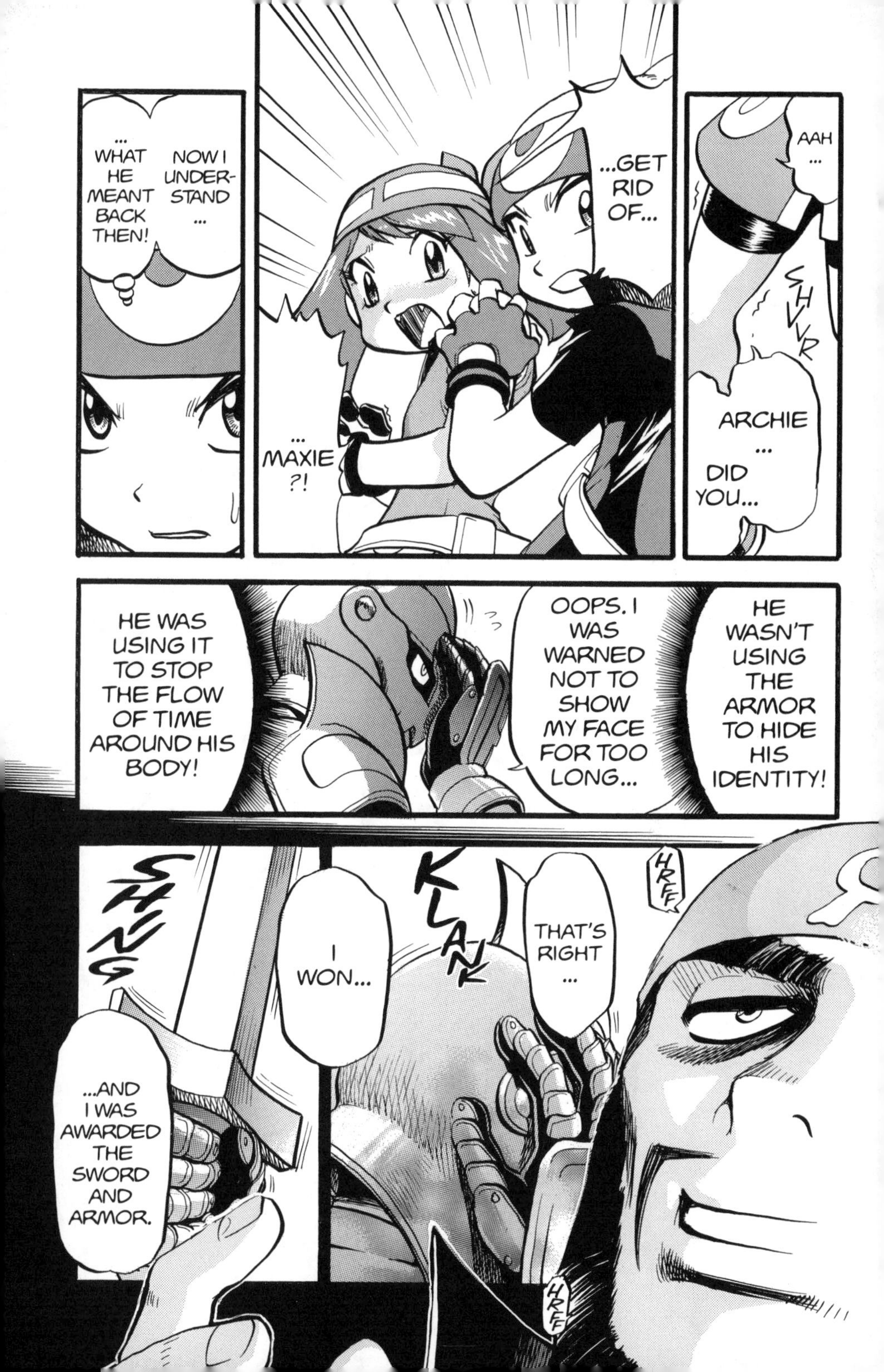
AAH ...
SHVVR
ARCHIE ... DID YOU...
...GET RID OF...
... MAXIE ?!
NOW I UNDERSTAND ...
... WHAT HE MEANT BACK THEN!
HE WASN'T USING THE ARMOR TO HIDE HIS IDENTITY!
OOPS. I WAS WARNED NOT TO SHOW MY FACE FOR TOO LONG...
HE WAS USING IT TO STOP THE FLOW OF TIME AROUND HIS BODY!
HRFF
THAT'S RIGHT ...
KLANK
I WON...
SHING
...AND I WAS AWARDED THE SWORD AND ARMOR.
HRFF

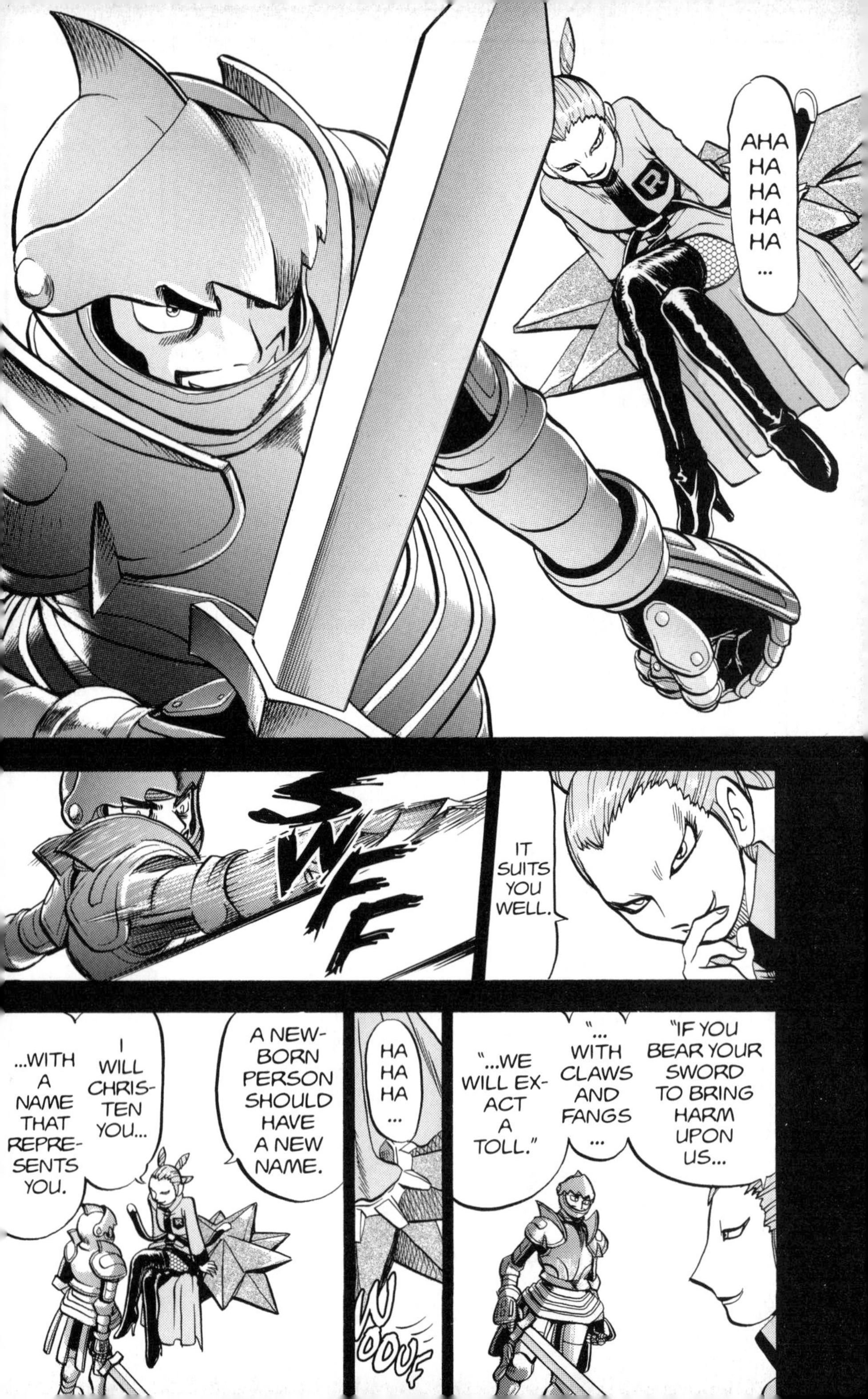
AHA HA HA HA HA ...
IT SUITS YOU WELL.
SWFF
"IF YOU BEAR YOUR SWORD TO BRING HARM UPON US...
"... WITH CLAWS AND FANGS ...
"...WE WILL EXACT A TOLL."
HA HA HA ...
A NEWBORN PERSON SHOULD HAVE A NEW NAME.
I WILL CHRISTEN YOU...
...WITH A NAME THAT REPRESENTS YOU.

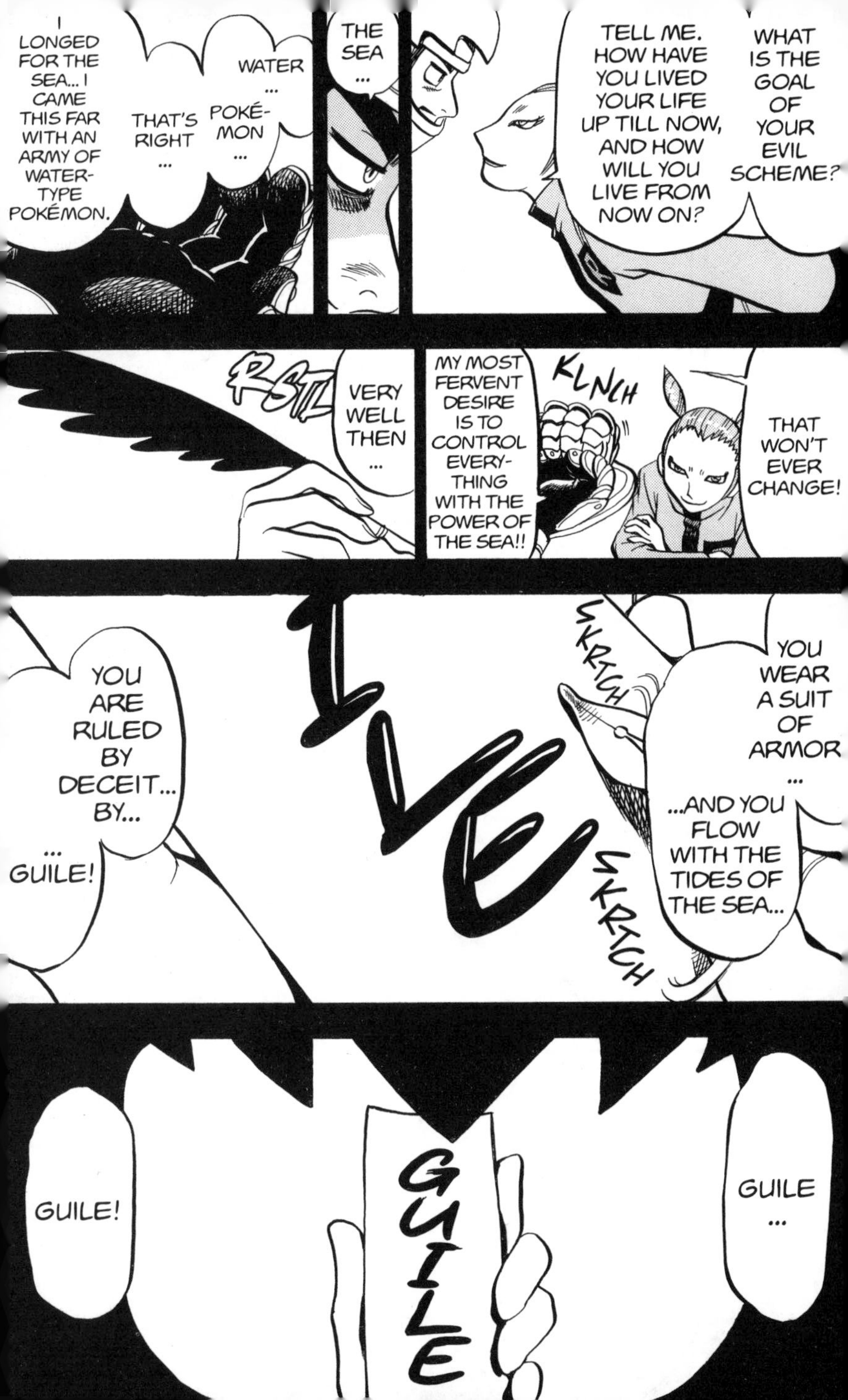
WHAT IS THE GOAL OF YOUR EVIL SCHEME?
TELL ME. HOW HAVE YOU LIVED YOUR LIFE UP TILL NOW, AND HOW WILL YOU LIVE FROM NOW ON?
THE SEA ...
WATER ... POKÉMON ...
THAT'S RIGHT ...
I LONGED FOR THE SEA... I CAME THIS FAR WITH AN ARMY OF WATER-TYPE POKÉMON.
THAT WON'T EVER CHANGE!
KLNCH
MY MOST FERVENT DESIRE IS TO CONTROL EVERY-THING WITH THE POWER OF THE SEA!!
VERY WELL THEN ...
RSTL
YOU WEAR A SUIT OF ARMOR ...
...AND YOU FLOW WITH THE TIDES OF THE SEA...
SKRTCH
SKRTCH
YOU ARE RULED BY DECEIT... BY...
... GUILE!
GUILE ...
GUILE
GUILE!

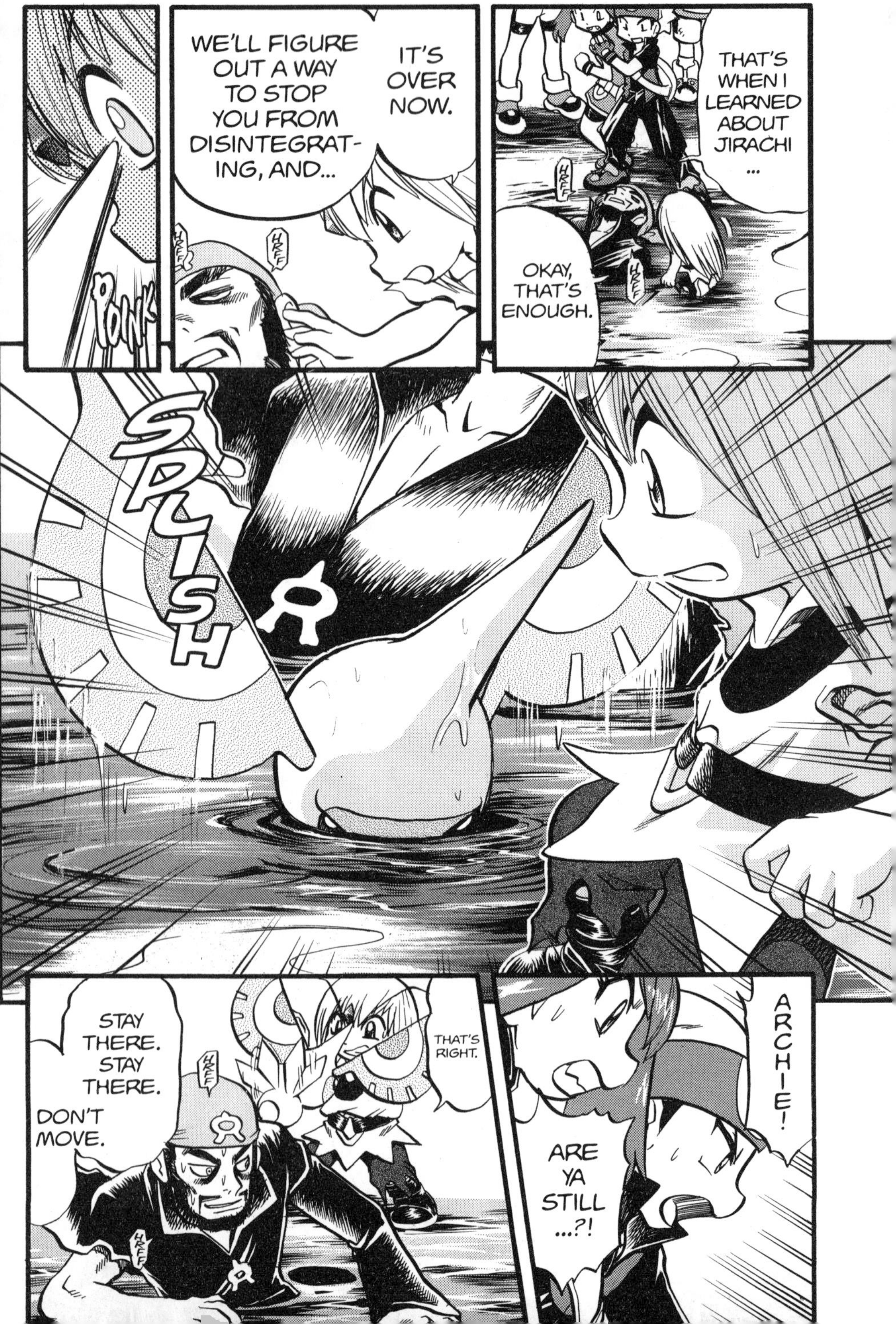
THAT'S WHEN I LEARNED ABOUT JIRACHI ...
HRFF
HRFF
OKAY, THAT'S ENOUGH.
IT'S OVER NOW.
WE'LL FIGURE OUT A WAY TO STOP YOU FROM DISINTEGRAT-ING, AND...
HRFF
HRFF
POINK
SPLISH
ARCHIE!
ARE YA STILL ...?!
THAT'S RIGHT.
STAY THERE. STAY THERE.
HRFF
DON'T MOVE.
HRFF

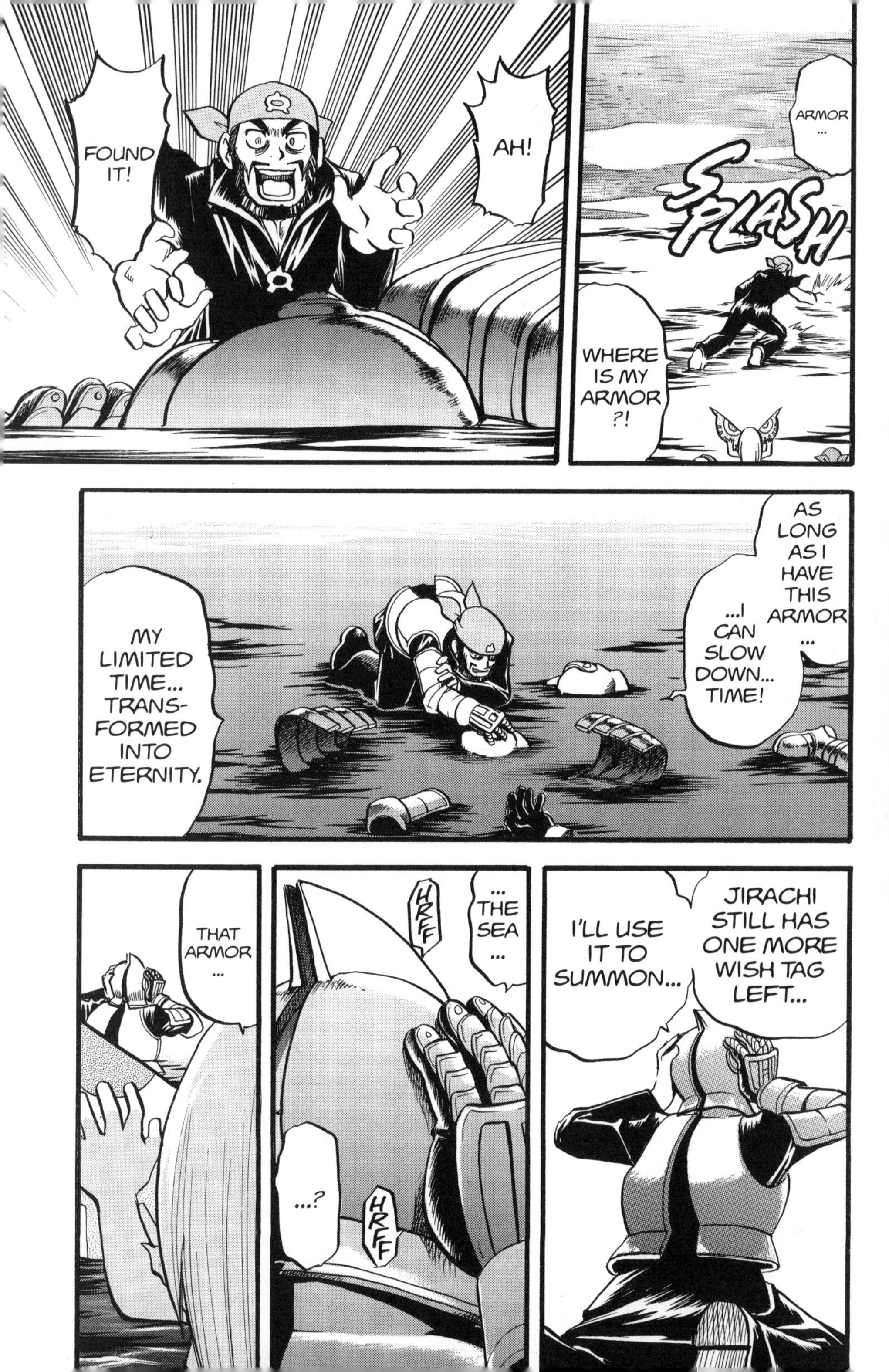
ARMOR ...
SPLASH
WHERE IS MY ARMOR ?!
AH!
FOUND IT!
AS LONG AS I HAVE THIS ARMOR ...
...I CAN SLOW DOWN... TIME!
MY LIMITED TIME... TRANS-FORMED INTO ETERNITY.
JIRACHI STILL HAS ONE MORE WISH TAG LEFT...
I'LL USE IT TO SUMMON...
... THE SEA ...
HRFF
...?
HRFF
THAT ARMOR ...

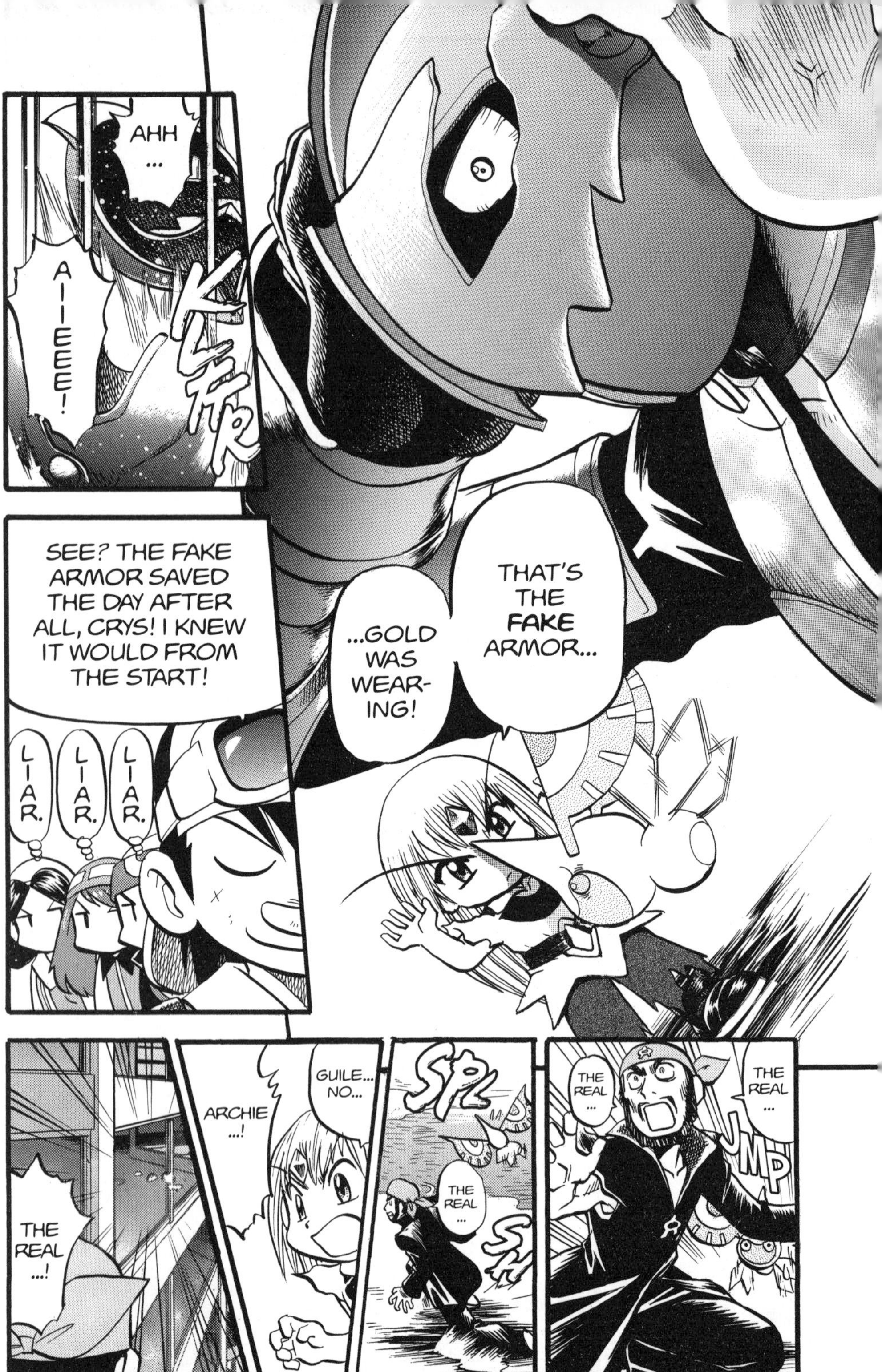
AHH ...
A-IIEEEE!
THAT'S THE FAKE ARMOR...
...GOLD WAS WEAR-ING!
SEE? THE FAKE ARMOR SAVED THE DAY AFTER ALL, CRYS! I KNEW IT WOULD FROM THE START!
LIAR.
LIAR.
LIAR.
THE REAL ...
JMP
THE REAL ...
SPL
THE REAL ...
SH
GUILE... NO...
ARCHIE ...!
THE REAL ...!

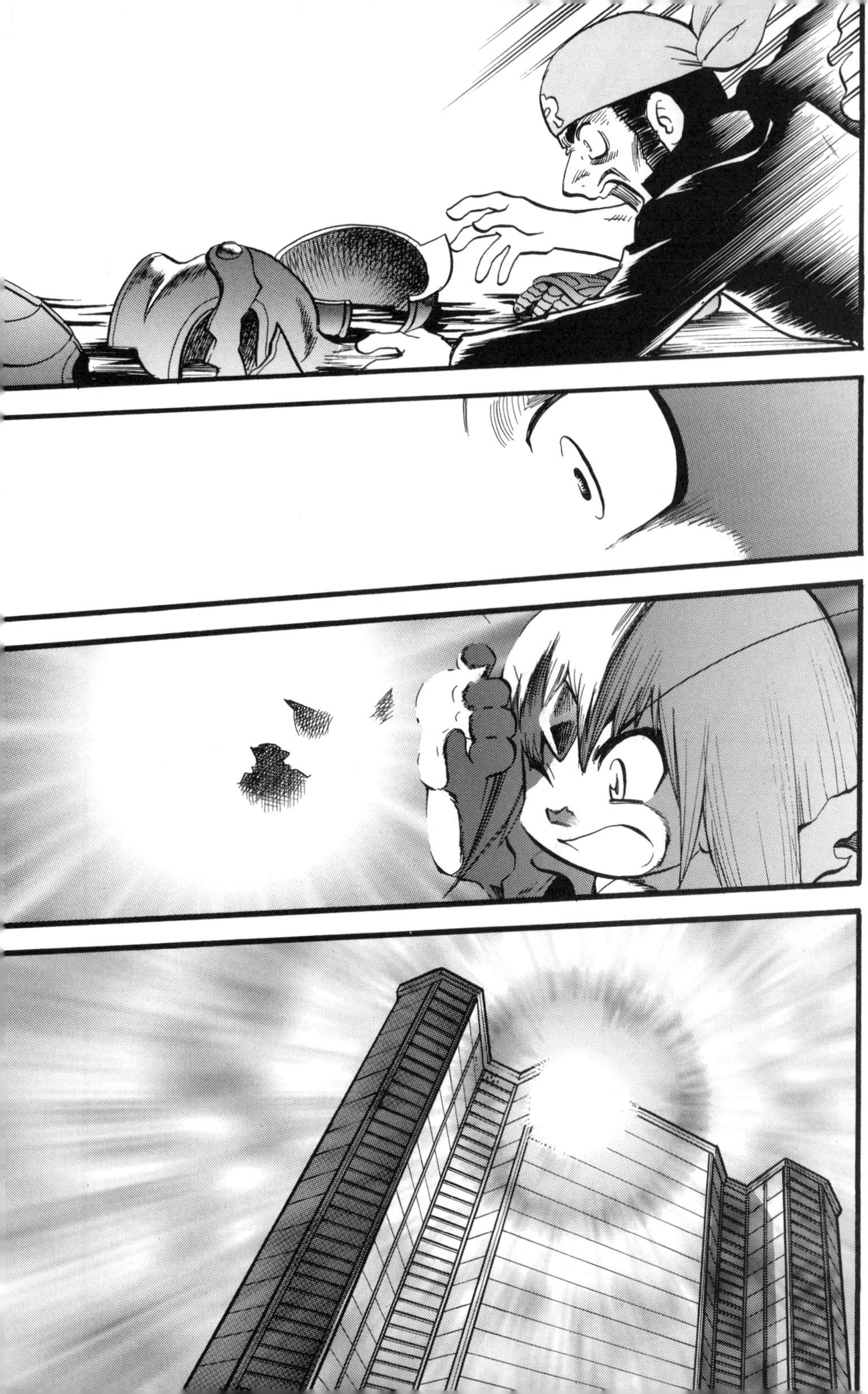

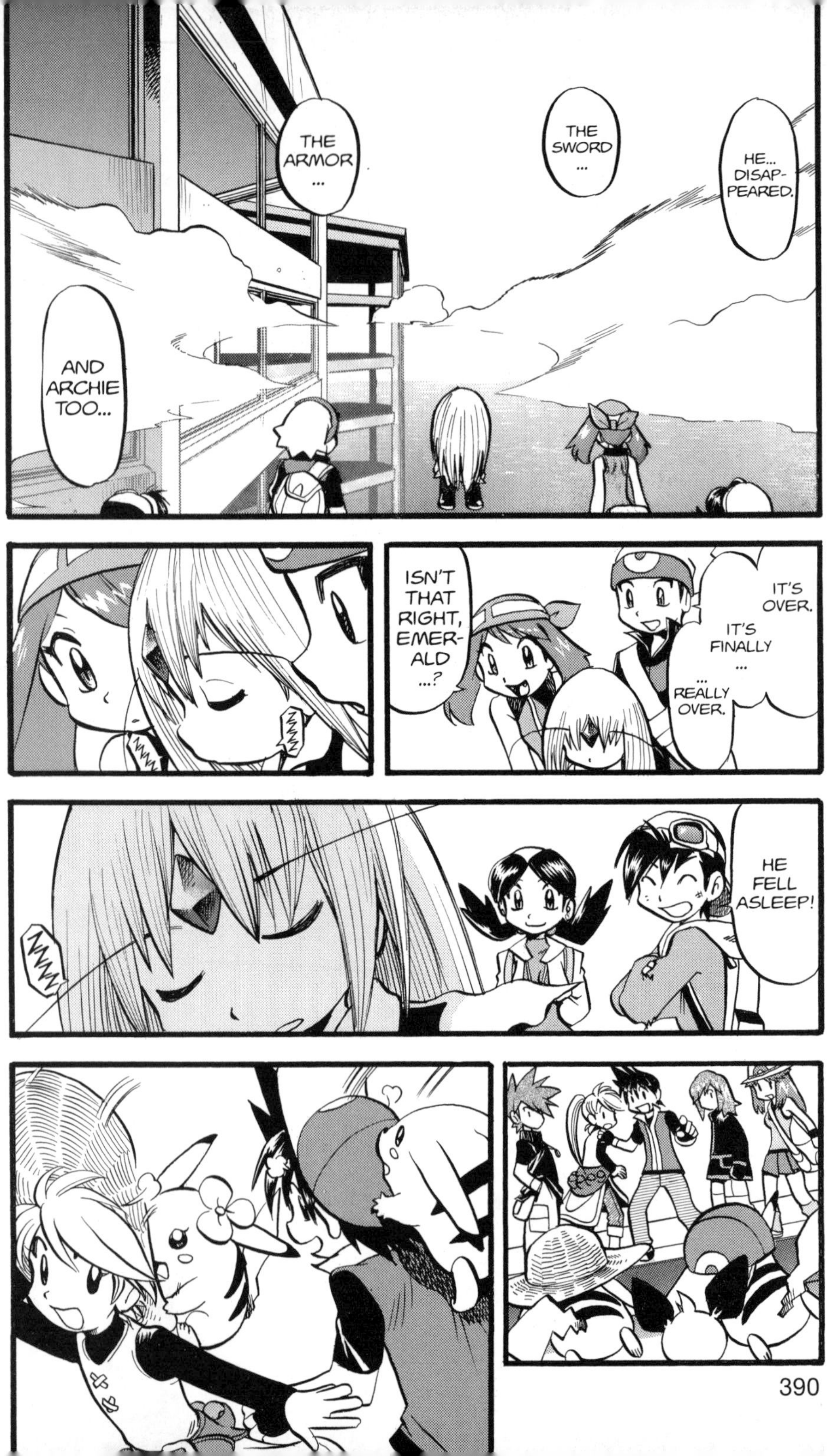
HE... DISAP-PEARED.
THE SWORD...
THE ARMOR...
AND ARCHIE TOO...
IT'S OVER.
IT'S FINALLY...
...REALLY OVER.
ISN'T THAT RIGHT, EMER-ALD...?
HE FELL ASLEEP!

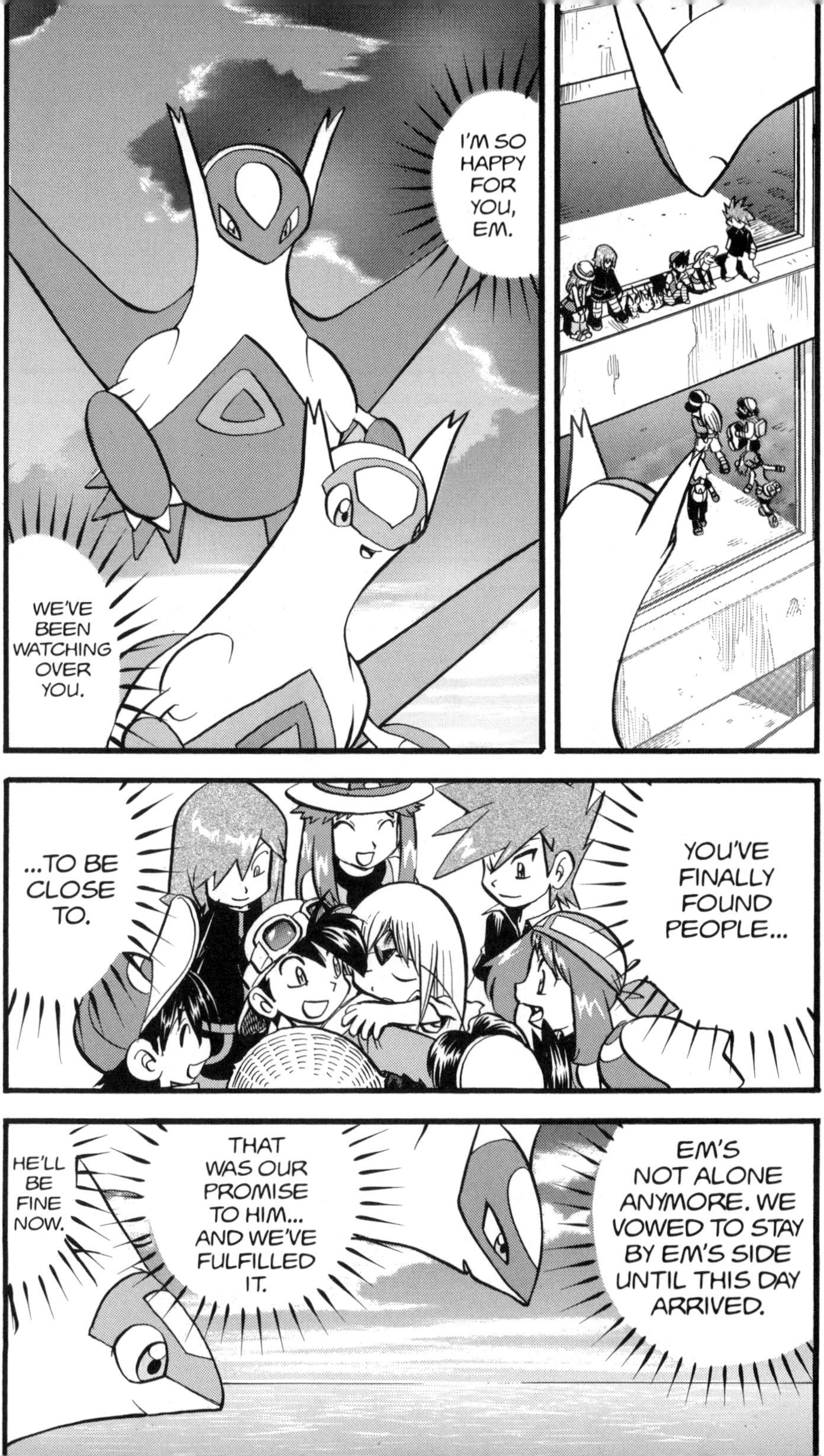
I'M SO HAPPY FOR YOU, EM.
WE'VE BEEN WATCHING OVER YOU.
YOU'VE FINALLY FOUND PEOPLE...
...TO BE CLOSE TO.
EM'S NOT ALONE ANYMORE. WE VOWED TO STAY BY EM'S SIDE UNTIL THIS DAY ARRIVED.
THAT WAS OUR PROMISE TO HIM... AND WE'VE FULFILLED IT.
HE'LL BE FINE NOW.

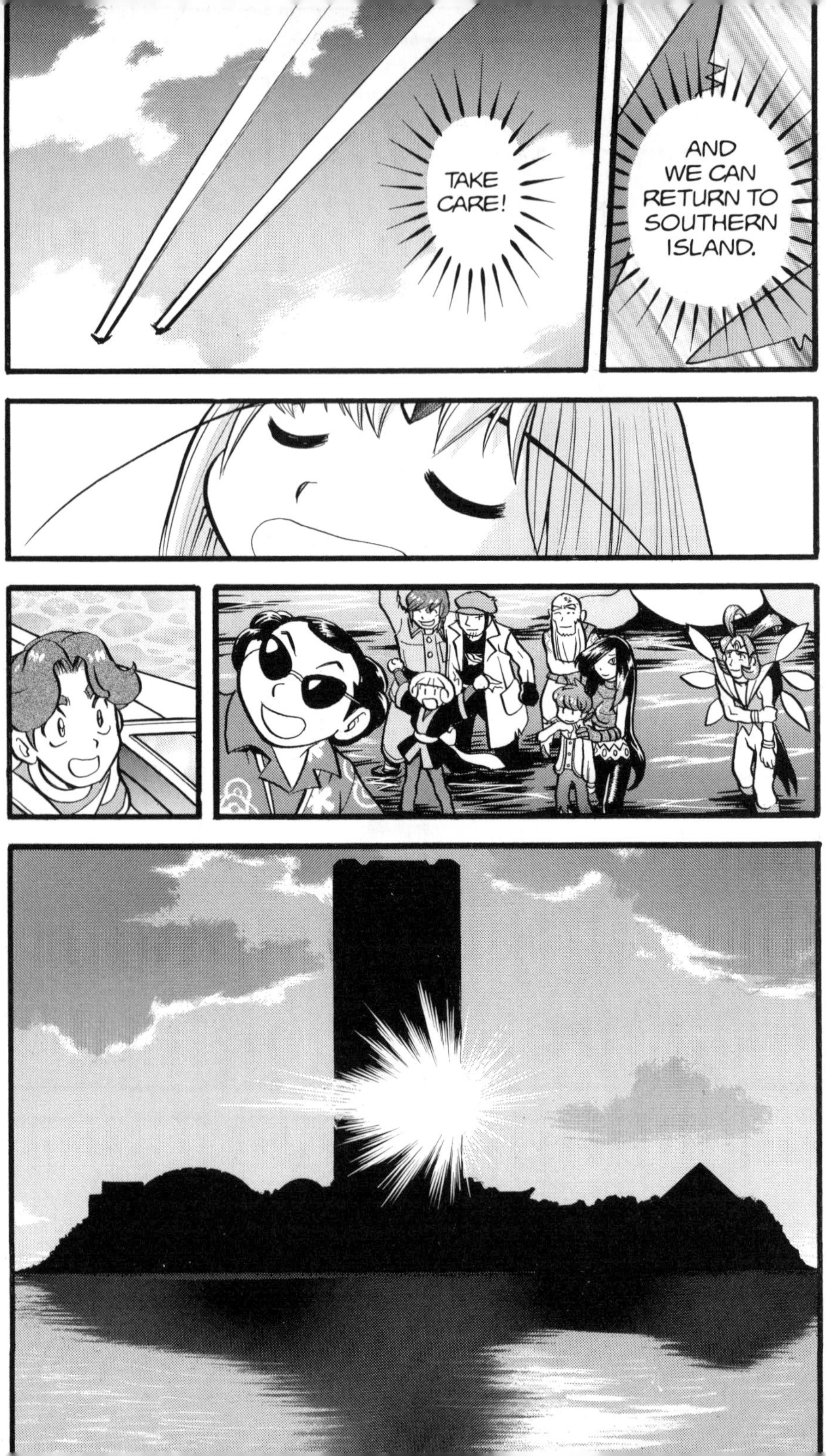
AND WE CAN RETURN TO SOUTHERN ISLAND.
TAKE CARE!

337

Epilogue

POKÉMON ADVENTURES·THE SIXTH CHAPTER·EMERALD

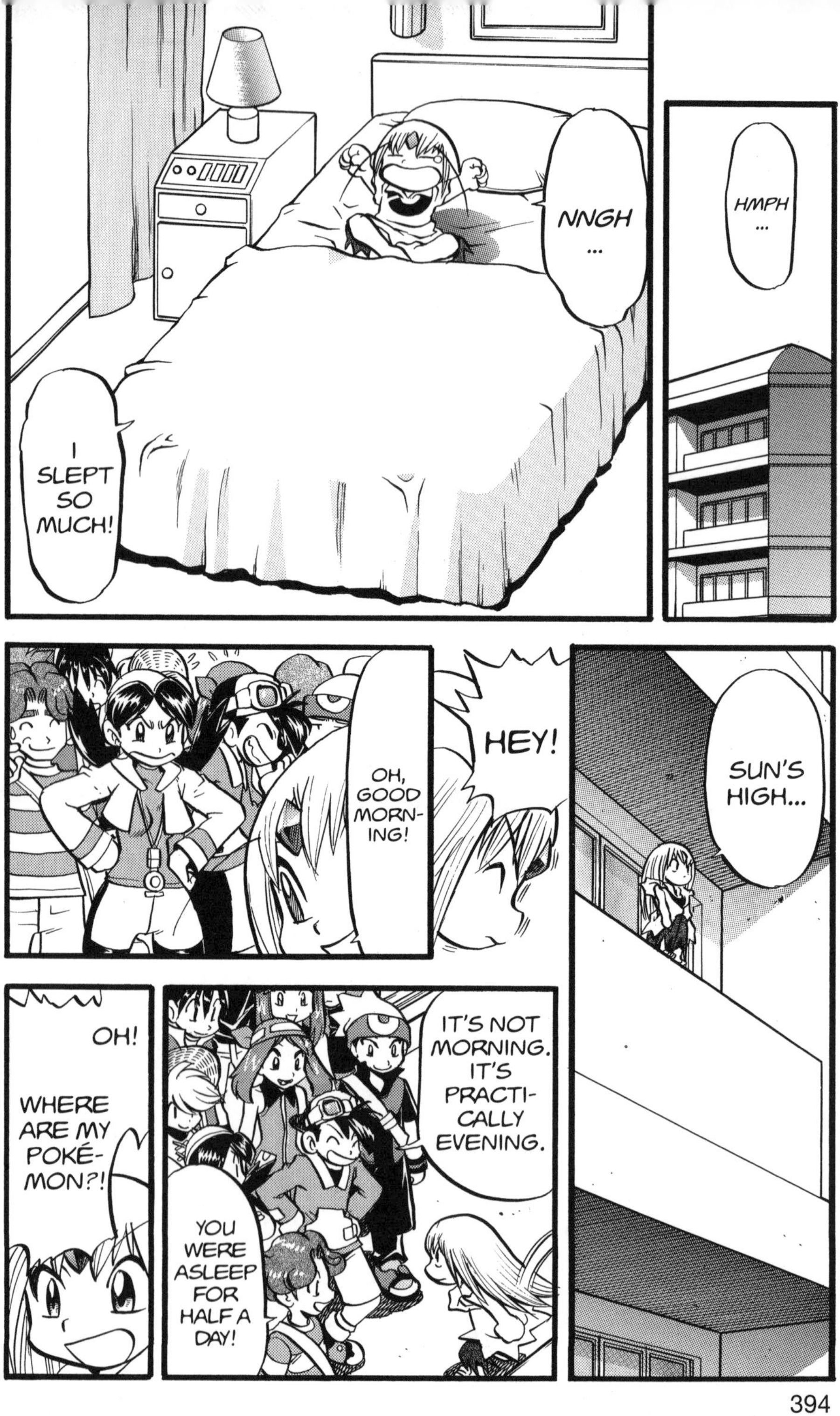
HMPH…
NNGH…
I SLEPT SO MUCH!
SUN'S HIGH…
HEY!
OH, GOOD MORNING!
IT'S NOT MORNING. IT'S PRACTICALLY EVENING.
YOU WERE ASLEEP FOR HALF A DAY!
OH!
WHERE ARE MY POKÉMON?!

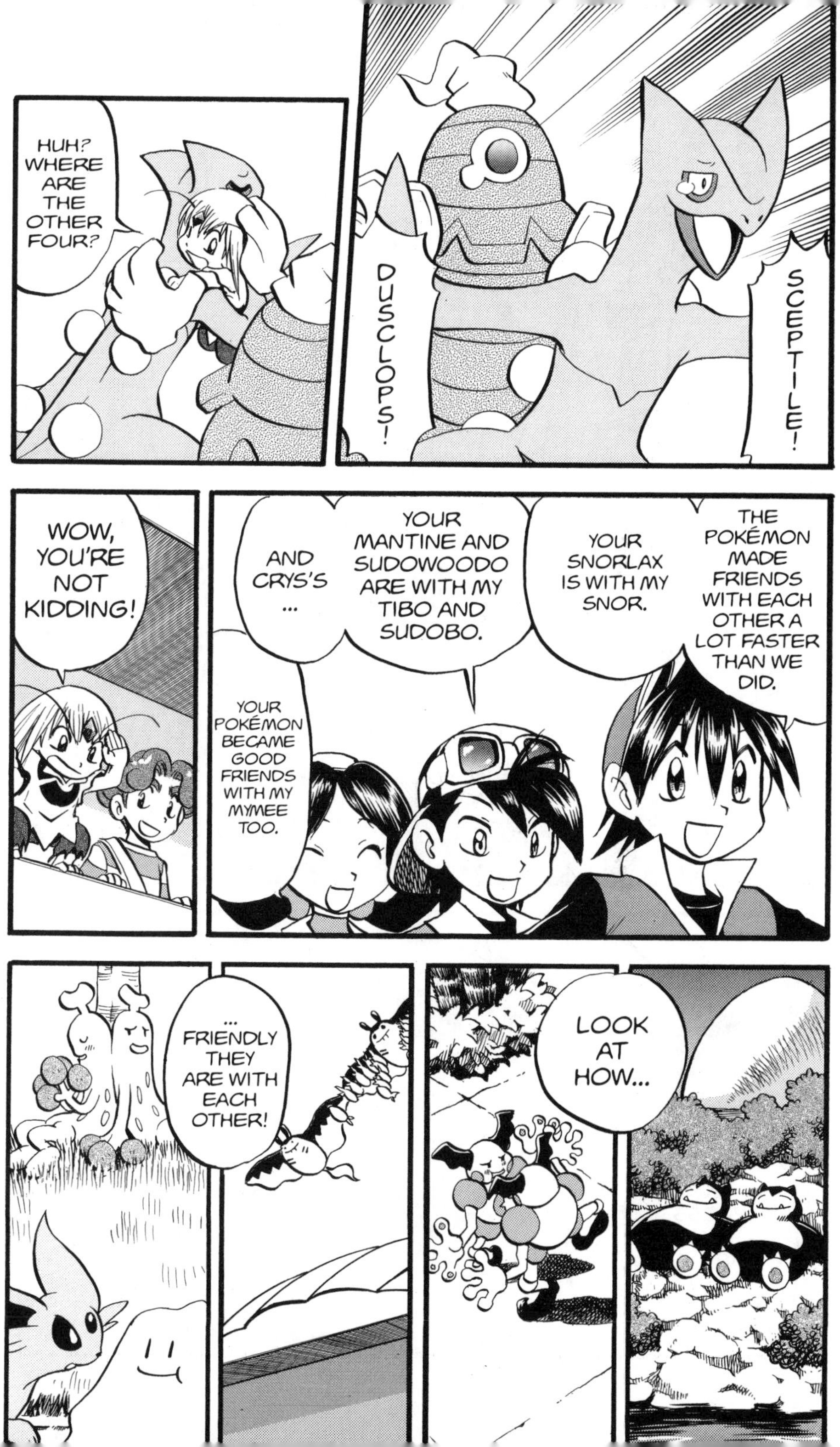
SCEPTILE!
DUSCLOPS!
HUH? WHERE ARE THE OTHER FOUR?
THE POKÉMON MADE FRIENDS WITH EACH OTHER A LOT FASTER THAN WE DID.
YOUR SNORLAX IS WITH MY SNOR.
YOUR MANTINE AND SUDOWOODO ARE WITH MY TIBO AND SUDOBO.
AND CRYS'S ...
YOUR POKÉMON BECAME GOOD FRIENDS WITH MY MYMEE TOO.
WOW, YOU'RE NOT KIDDING!
LOOK AT HOW...
... FRIENDLY THEY ARE WITH EACH OTHER!

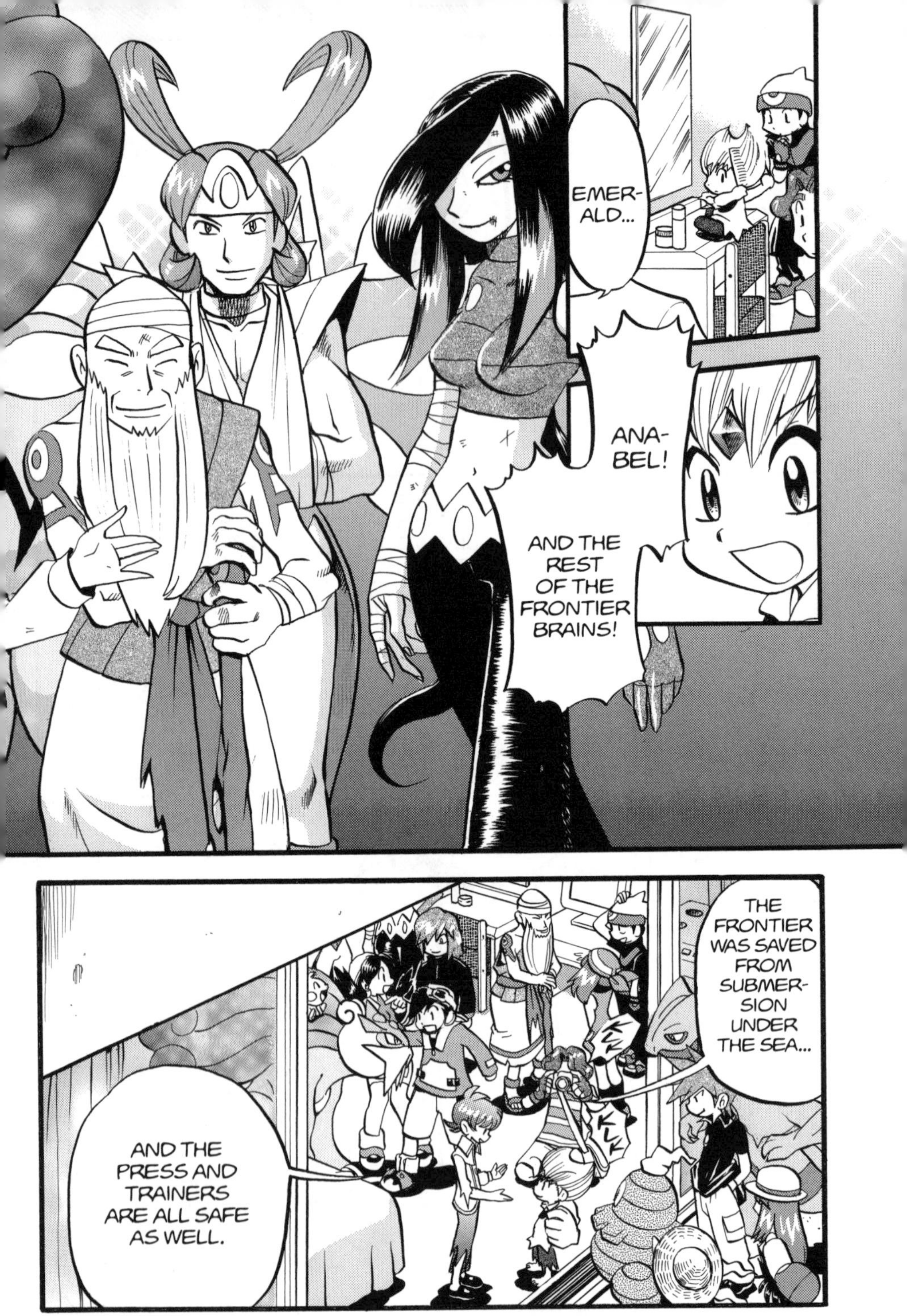
EMER-
ALD...
ANA-
BEL!
AND THE
REST
OF THE
FRONTIER
BRAINS!
THE
FRONTIER
WAS SAVED
FROM
SUBMER-
SION
UNDER
THE SEA...
AND THE
PRESS AND
TRAINERS
ARE ALL SAFE
AS WELL.

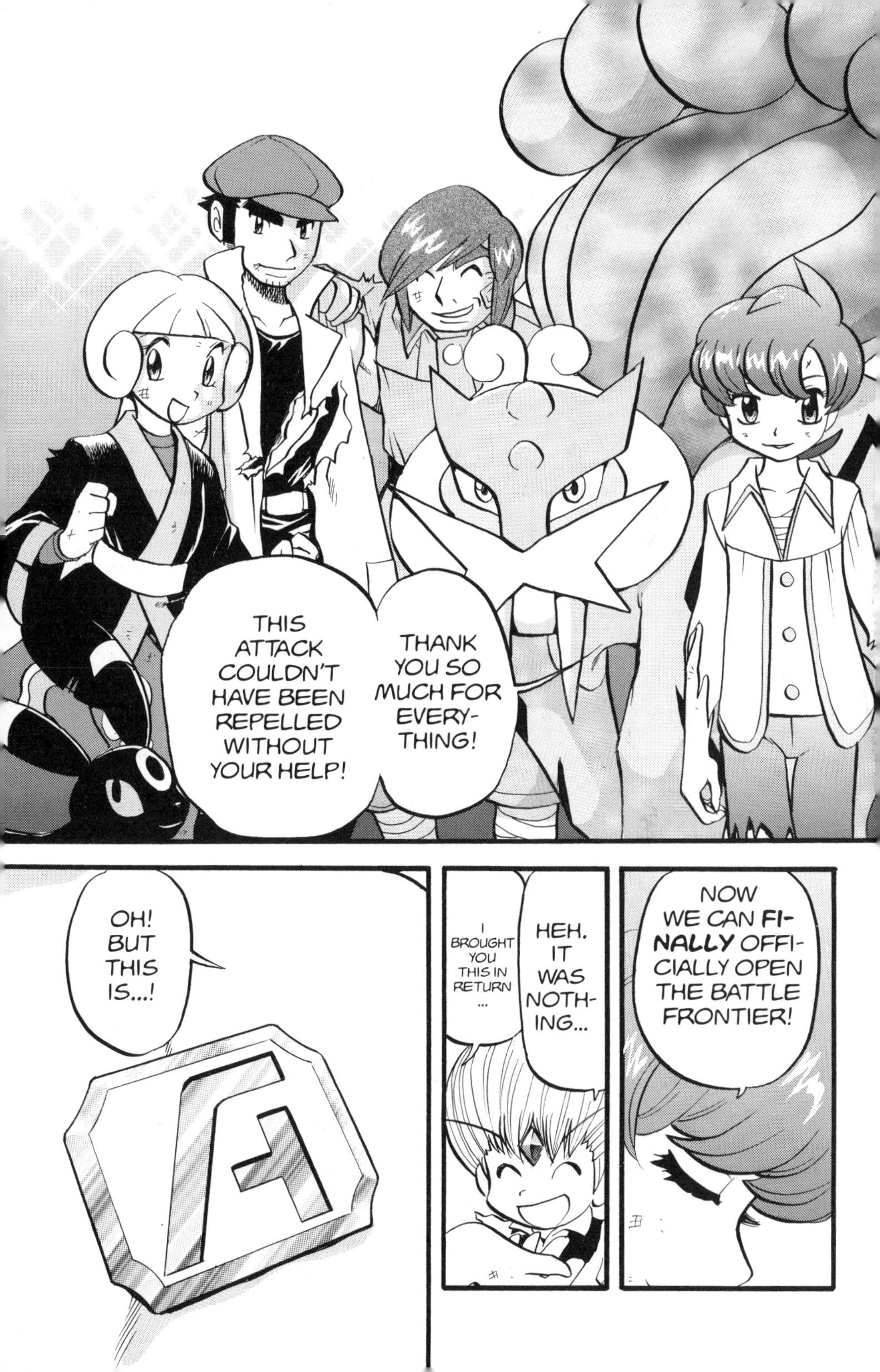
THANK YOU SO MUCH FOR EVERY-THING!
THIS ATTACK COULDN'T HAVE BEEN REPELLED WITHOUT YOUR HELP!
NOW WE CAN **FI-NALLY** OFFI-CIALLY OPEN THE BATTLE FRONTIER!
HEH. IT WAS NOTH-ING...
I BROUGHT YOU THIS IN RETURN...
OH! BUT THIS IS...!

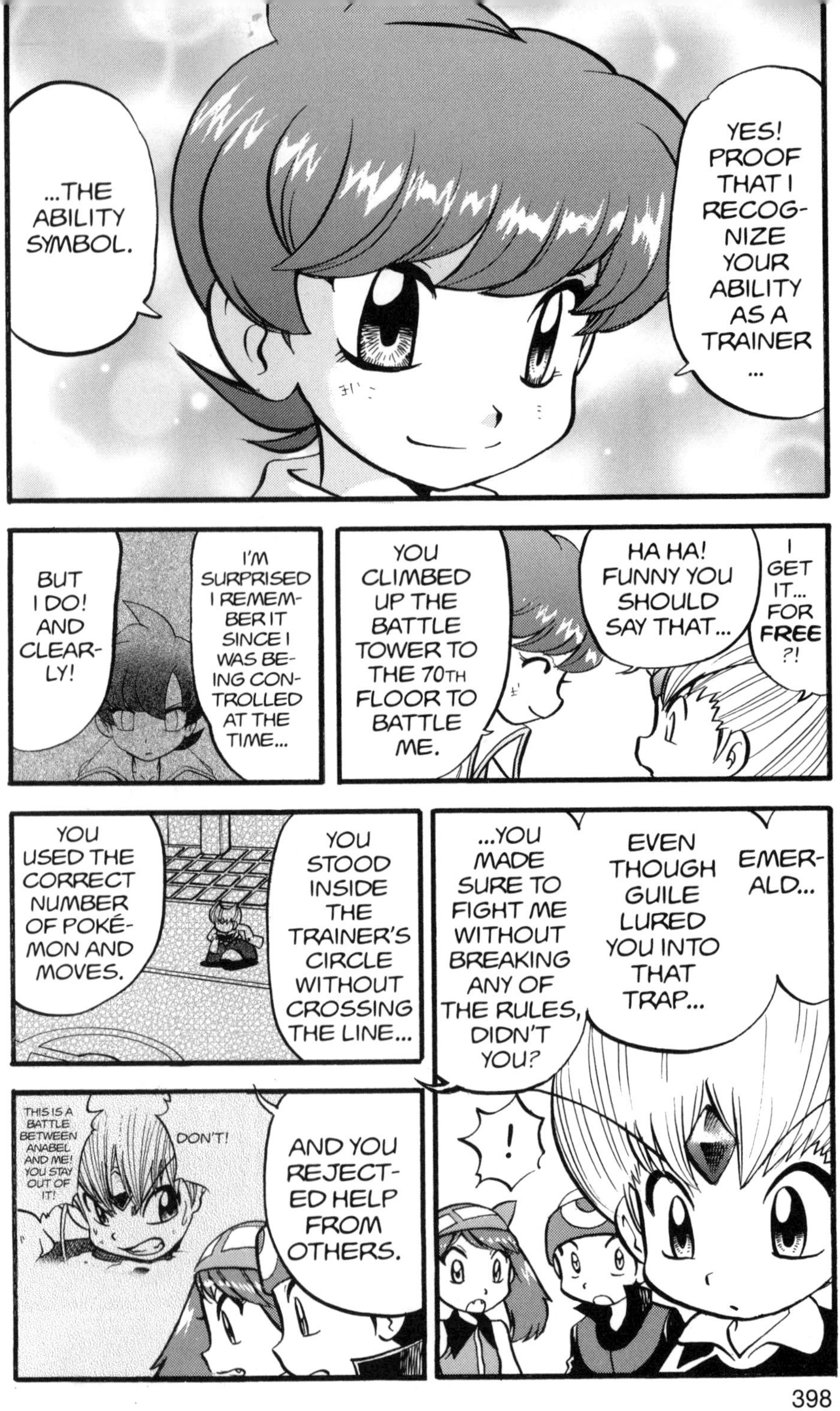
YES! PROOF THAT I RECOGNIZE YOUR ABILITY AS A TRAINER ...
...THE ABILITY SYMBOL.
I GET IT... FOR **FREE**?!
HA HA! FUNNY YOU SHOULD SAY THAT...
YOU CLIMBED UP THE BATTLE TOWER TO THE 70TH FLOOR TO BATTLE ME.
I'M SURPRISED I REMEMBER IT SINCE I WAS BEING CONTROLLED AT THE TIME...
BUT I DO! AND CLEARLY!
EMERALD...
EVEN THOUGH GUILE LURED YOU INTO THAT TRAP...
...YOU MADE SURE TO FIGHT ME WITHOUT BREAKING ANY OF THE RULES, DIDN'T YOU?
YOU STOOD INSIDE THE TRAINER'S CIRCLE WITHOUT CROSSING THE LINE...
YOU USED THE CORRECT NUMBER OF POKÉMON AND MOVES.
!
AND YOU REJECTED HELP FROM OTHERS.
DON'T!
THIS IS A BATTLE BETWEEN ANABEL AND ME! YOU STAY OUT OF IT!

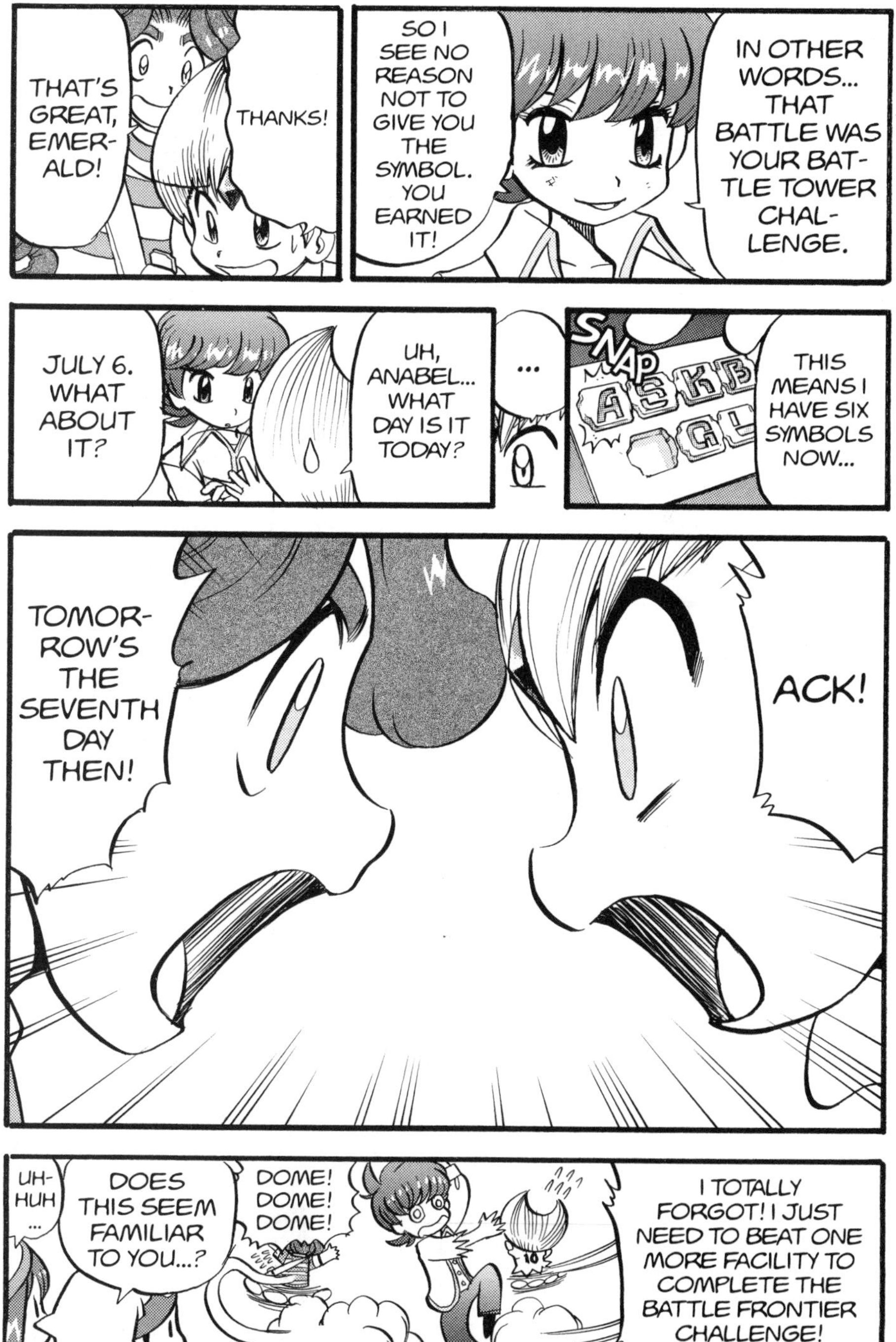
IN OTHER WORDS... THAT BATTLE WAS YOUR BATTLE TOWER CHALLENGE.
SO I SEE NO REASON NOT TO GIVE YOU THE SYMBOL. YOU EARNED IT!
THAT'S GREAT, EMERALD!
THANKS!
THIS MEANS I HAVE SIX SYMBOLS NOW...
SNAP
...
UH, ANABEL... WHAT DAY IS IT TODAY?
JULY 6. WHAT ABOUT IT?
TOMORROW'S THE SEVENTH DAY THEN!
ACK!
I TOTALLY FORGOT! I JUST NEED TO BEAT ONE MORE FACILITY TO COMPLETE THE BATTLE FRONTIER CHALLENGE!
DOME! DOME! DOME!
DOES THIS SEEM FAMILIAR TO YOU...?
UH-HUH ...

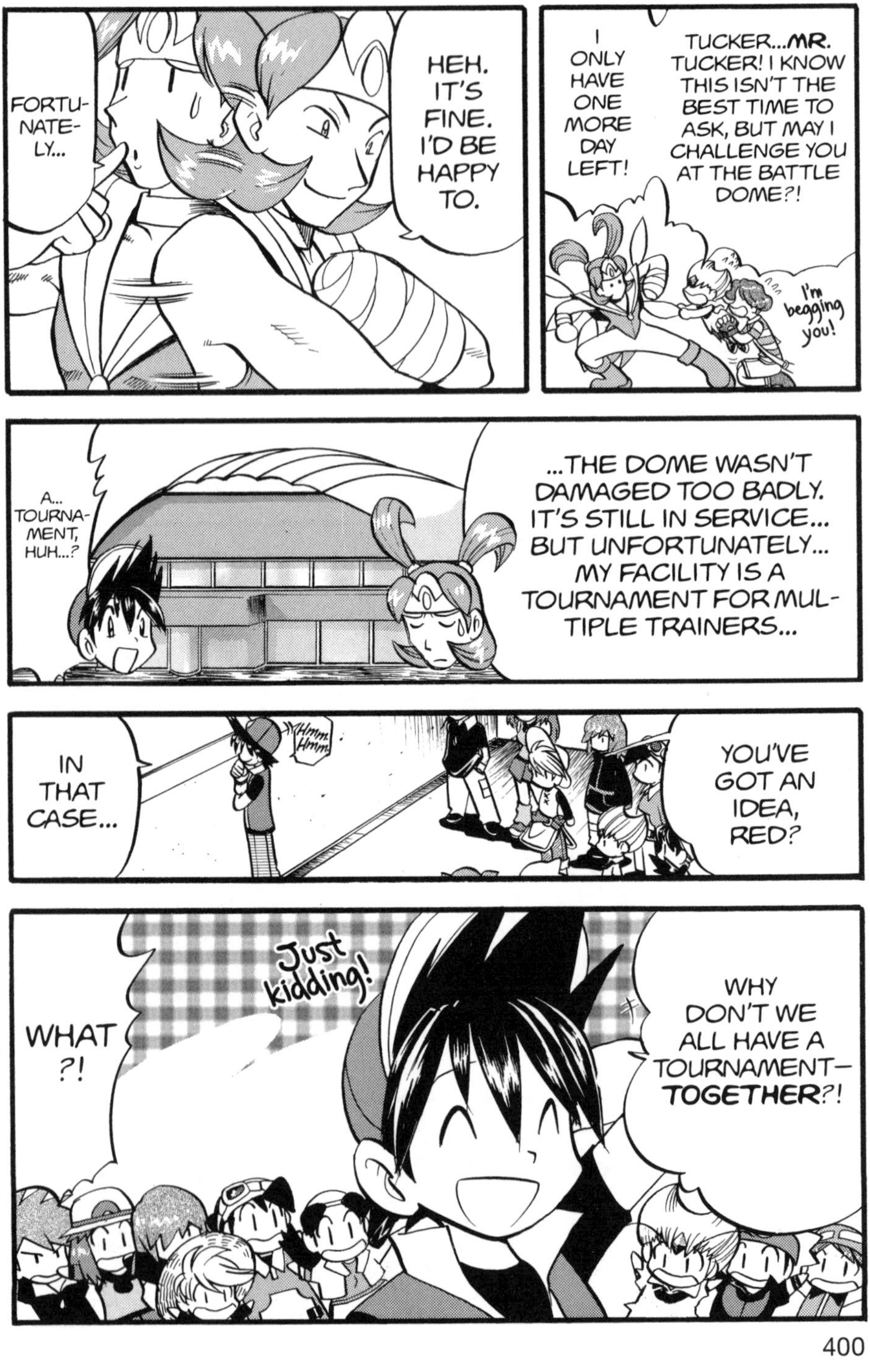
TUCKER...MR. TUCKER! I KNOW THIS ISN'T THE BEST TIME TO ASK, BUT MAY I CHALLENGE YOU AT THE BATTLE DOME?!
I ONLY HAVE ONE MORE DAY LEFT!
I'm begging you!
HEH. IT'S FINE. I'D BE HAPPY TO.
FORTUNATELY...
...THE DOME WASN'T DAMAGED TOO BADLY. IT'S STILL IN SERVICE... BUT UNFORTUNATELY... MY FACILITY IS A TOURNAMENT FOR MULTIPLE TRAINERS...
A... TOURNAMENT, HUH...?
YOU'VE GOT AN IDEA, RED?
Hmm. Hmm.
IN THAT CASE...
WHY DON'T WE ALL HAVE A TOURNAMENT—TOGETHER?!
Just kidding!
WHAT?!

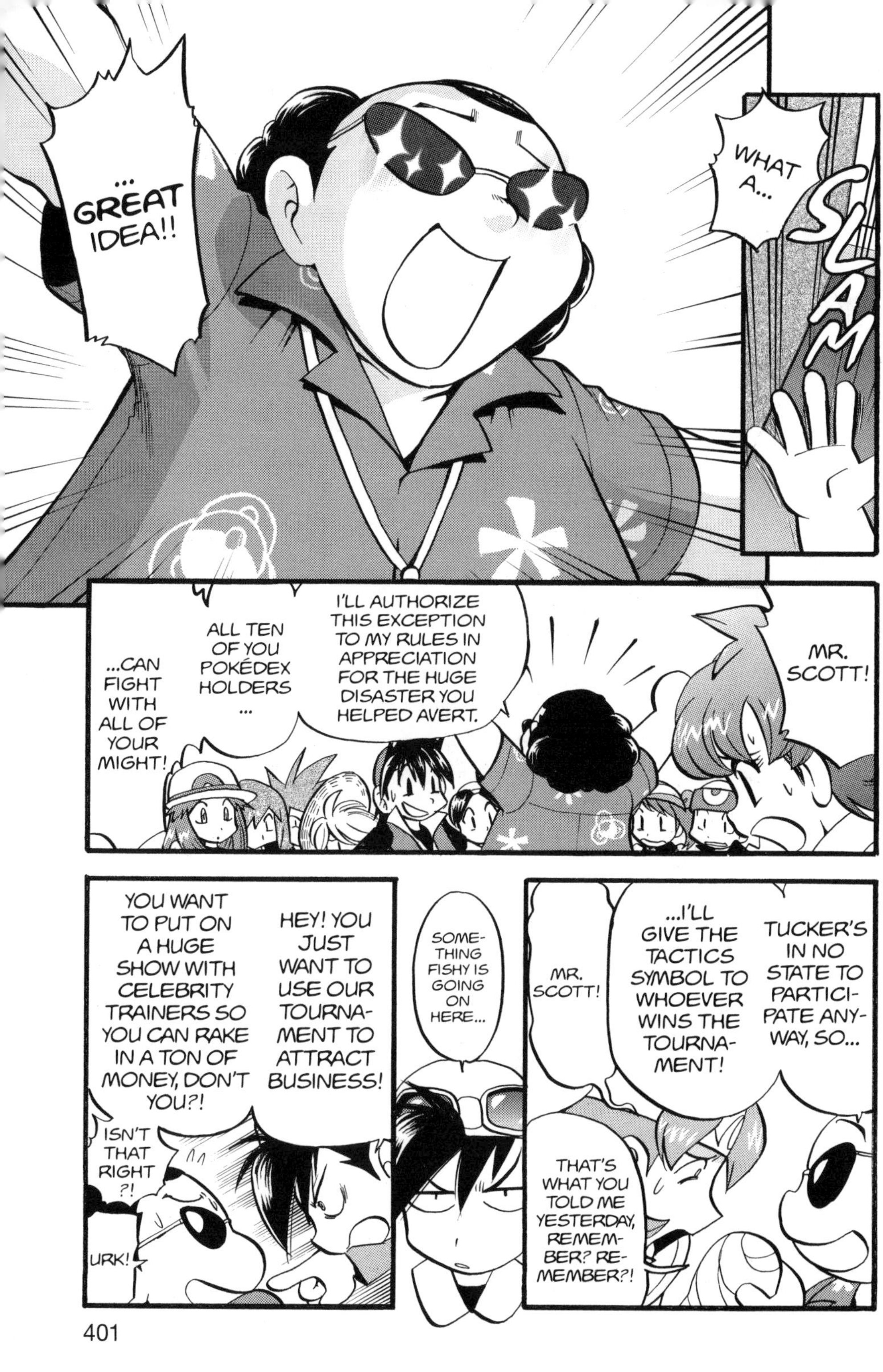

WHAT A...
SLAM
...GREAT IDEA!!
MR. SCOTT!
I'LL AUTHORIZE THIS EXCEPTION TO MY RULES IN APPRECIATION FOR THE HUGE DISASTER YOU HELPED AVERT.
ALL TEN OF YOU POKÉDEX HOLDERS ...
...CAN FIGHT WITH ALL OF YOUR MIGHT!
TUCKER'S IN NO STATE TO PARTICI-PATE ANY-WAY, SO...
...I'LL GIVE THE TACTICS SYMBOL TO WHOEVER WINS THE TOURNA-MENT!
MR. SCOTT!
THAT'S WHAT YOU TOLD ME YESTERDAY, REMEM-BER? RE-MEMBER?!
SOME-THING FISHY IS GOING ON HERE...
HEY! YOU JUST WANT TO USE OUR TOURNA-MENT TO ATTRACT BUSINESS!
YOU WANT TO PUT ON A HUGE SHOW WITH CELEBRITY TRAINERS SO YOU CAN RAKE IN A TON OF MONEY, DON'T YOU?!
ISN'T THAT RIGHT ?!
URK!

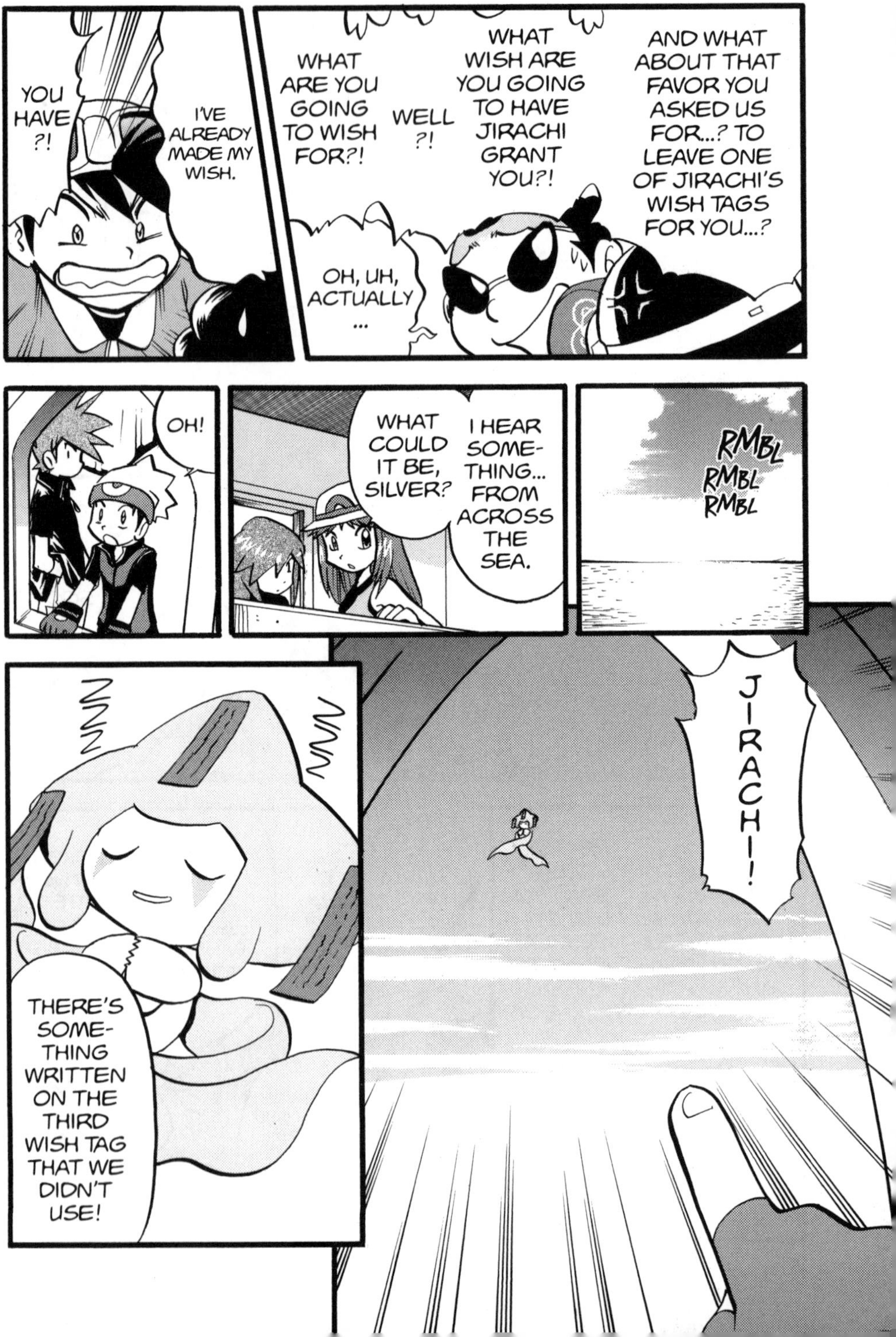
AND WHAT ABOUT THAT FAVOR YOU ASKED US FOR...? TO LEAVE ONE OF JIRACHI'S WISH TAGS FOR YOU...?
WHAT WISH ARE YOU GOING TO HAVE JIRACHI GRANT YOU?!
WELL ?!
WHAT ARE YOU GOING TO WISH FOR?!
OH, UH, ACTUALLY ...
I'VE ALREADY MADE MY WISH.
YOU HAVE ?!
RMBL RMBL RMBL
I HEAR SOME-THING... FROM ACROSS THE SEA.
WHAT COULD IT BE, SILVER?
OH!
JIRACHI!
THERE'S SOME-THING WRITTEN ON THE THIRD WISH TAG THAT WE DIDN'T USE!

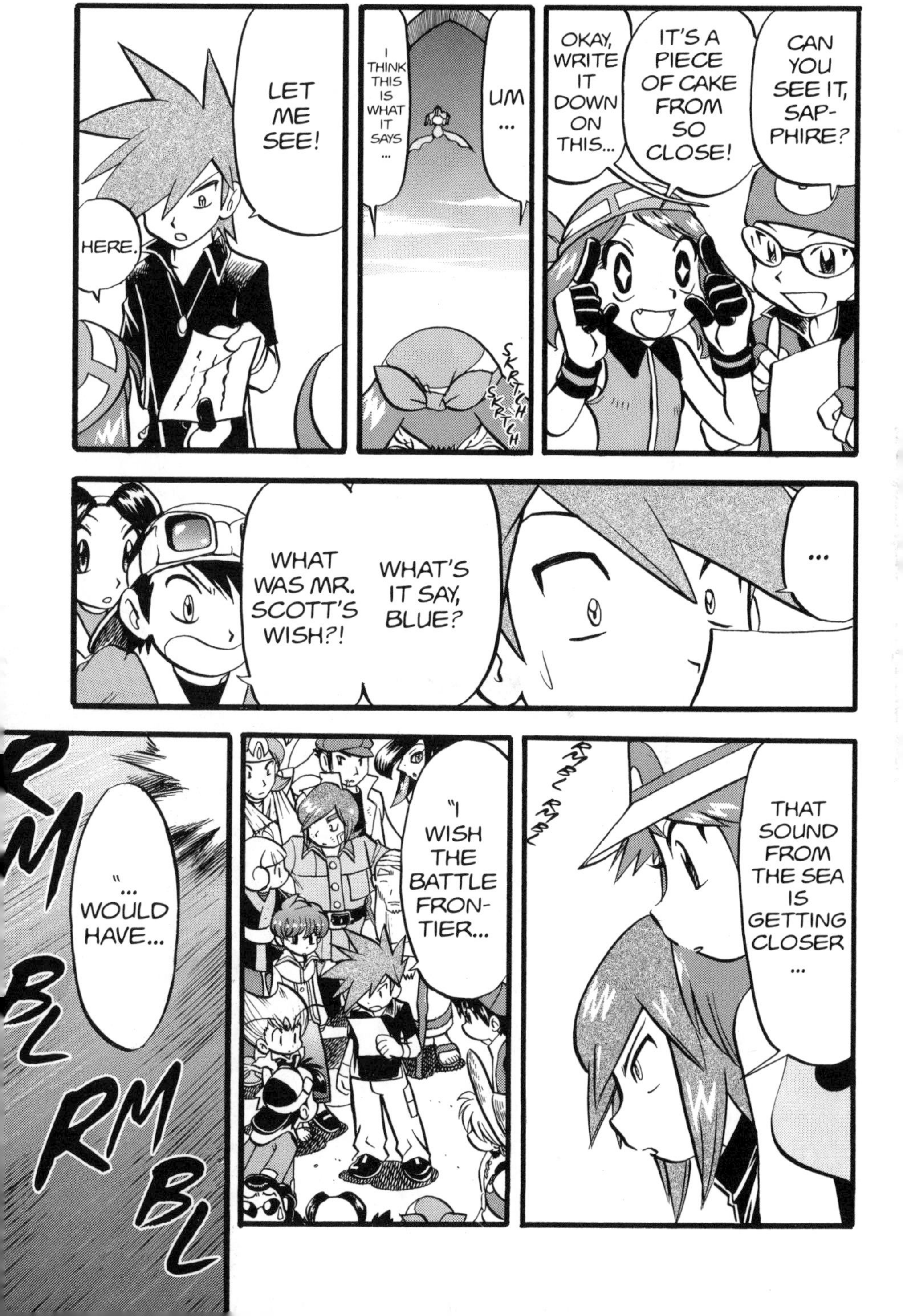
CAN YOU SEE IT, SAPPHIRE?
IT'S A PIECE OF CAKE FROM SO CLOSE!
OKAY, WRITE IT DOWN ON THIS...
UM...
I THINK THIS IS WHAT IT SAYS...
SKRTCH SKRTCH
LET ME SEE!
HERE.
...
WHAT'S IT SAY, BLUE?
WHAT WAS MR. SCOTT'S WISH?!
RMBL RMBL
THAT SOUND FROM THE SEA IS GETTING CLOSER...
"I WISH THE BATTLE FRONTIER...
"...WOULD HAVE...
RMBL RMBL

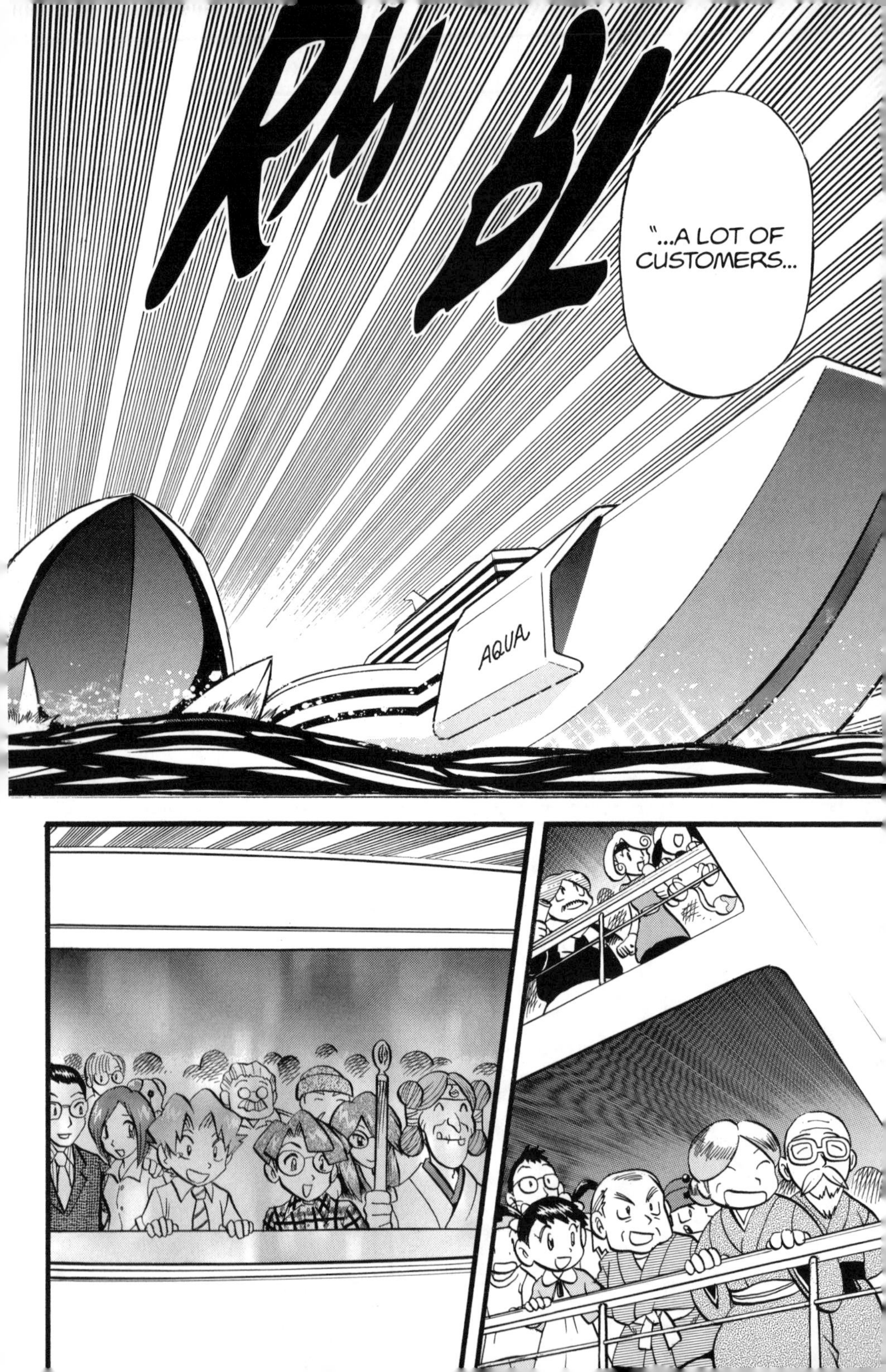
"...A LOT OF CUSTOMERS...
AQUA

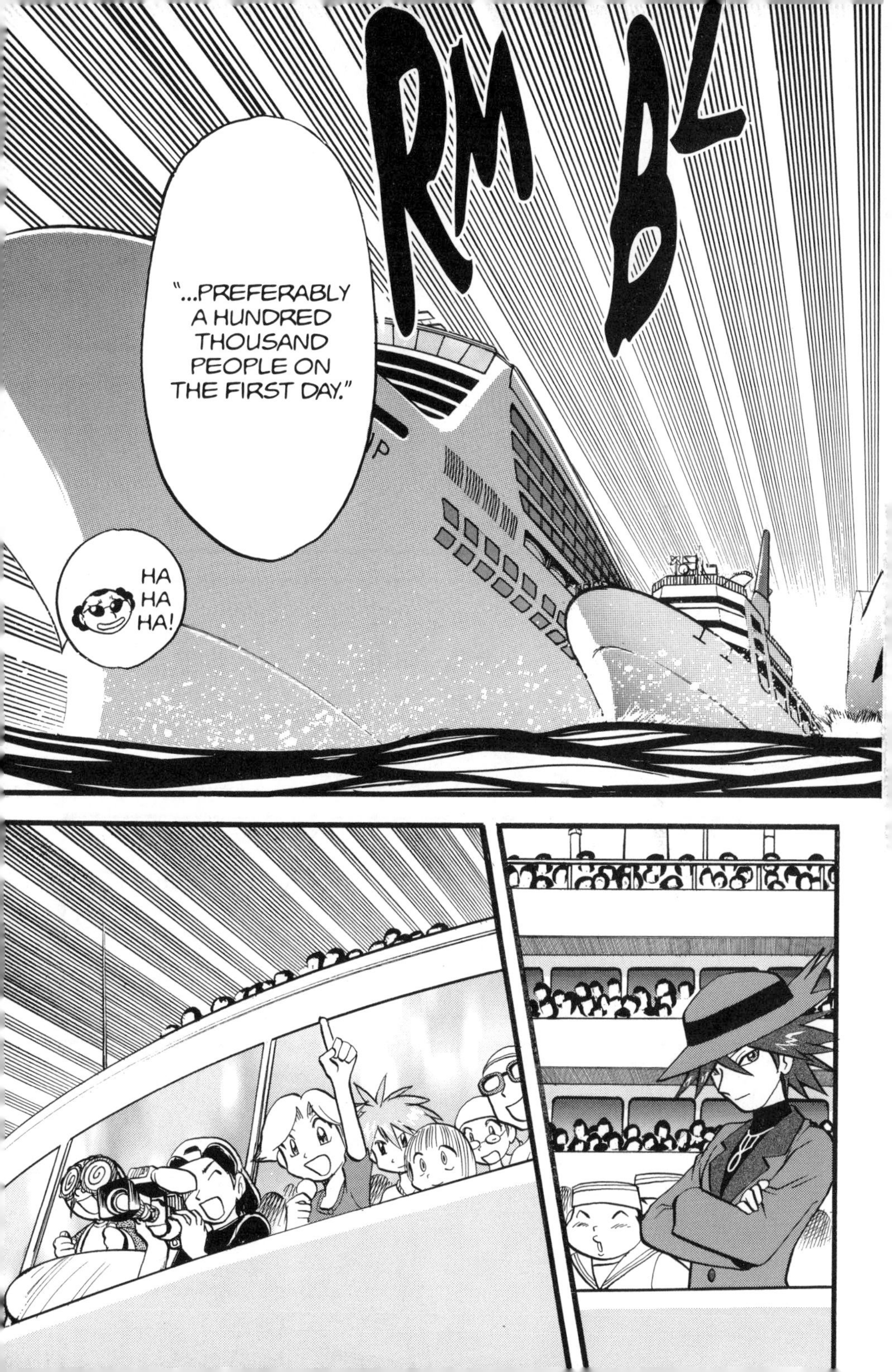
"...PREFERABLY A HUNDRED THOUSAND PEOPLE ON THE FIRST DAY."
HA HA HA!

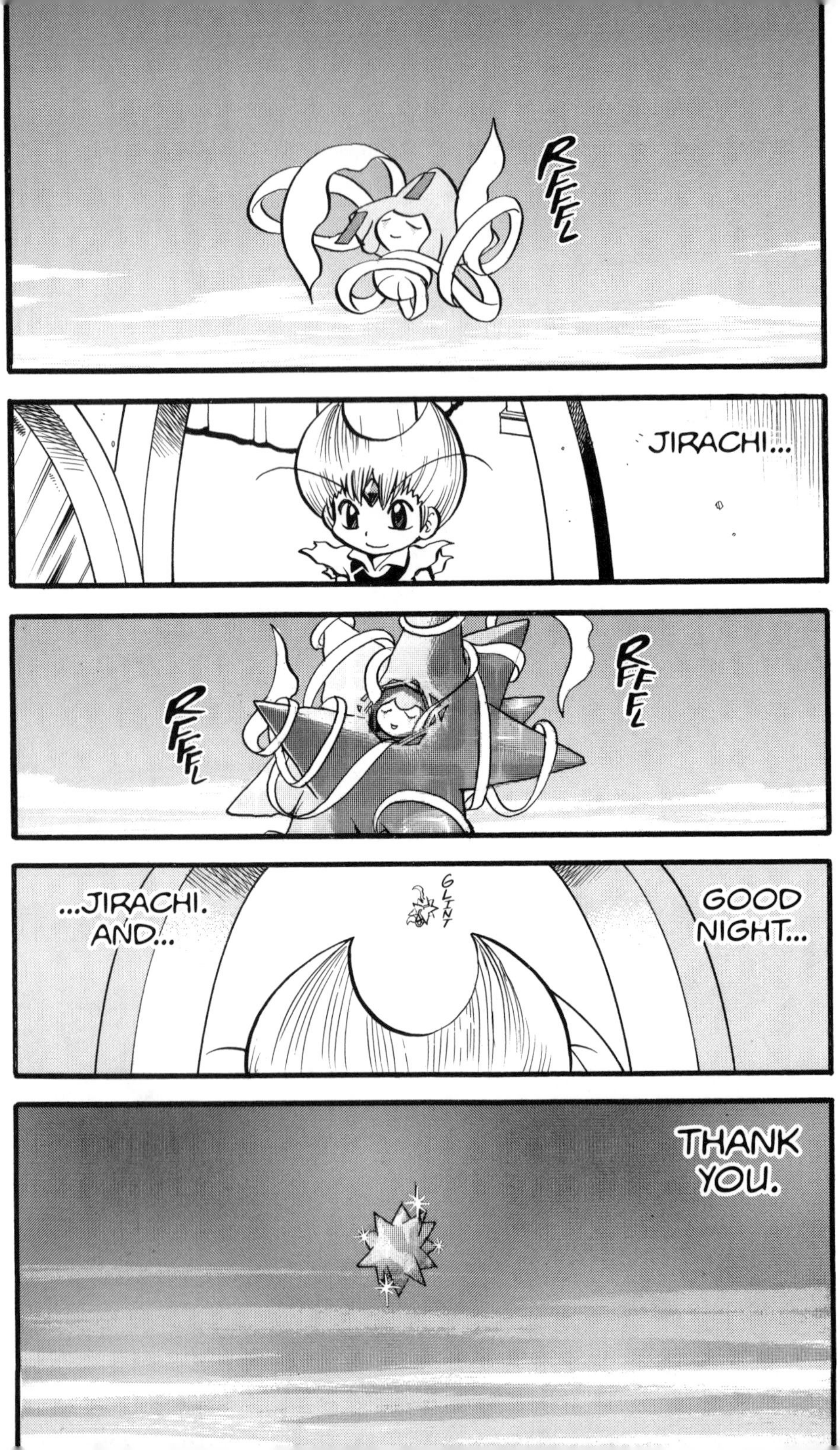
RFFFL
JIRACHI...
RFFFL
RFFFL
GOOD NIGHT...
GLINT
...JIRACHI. AND...
THANK YOU.

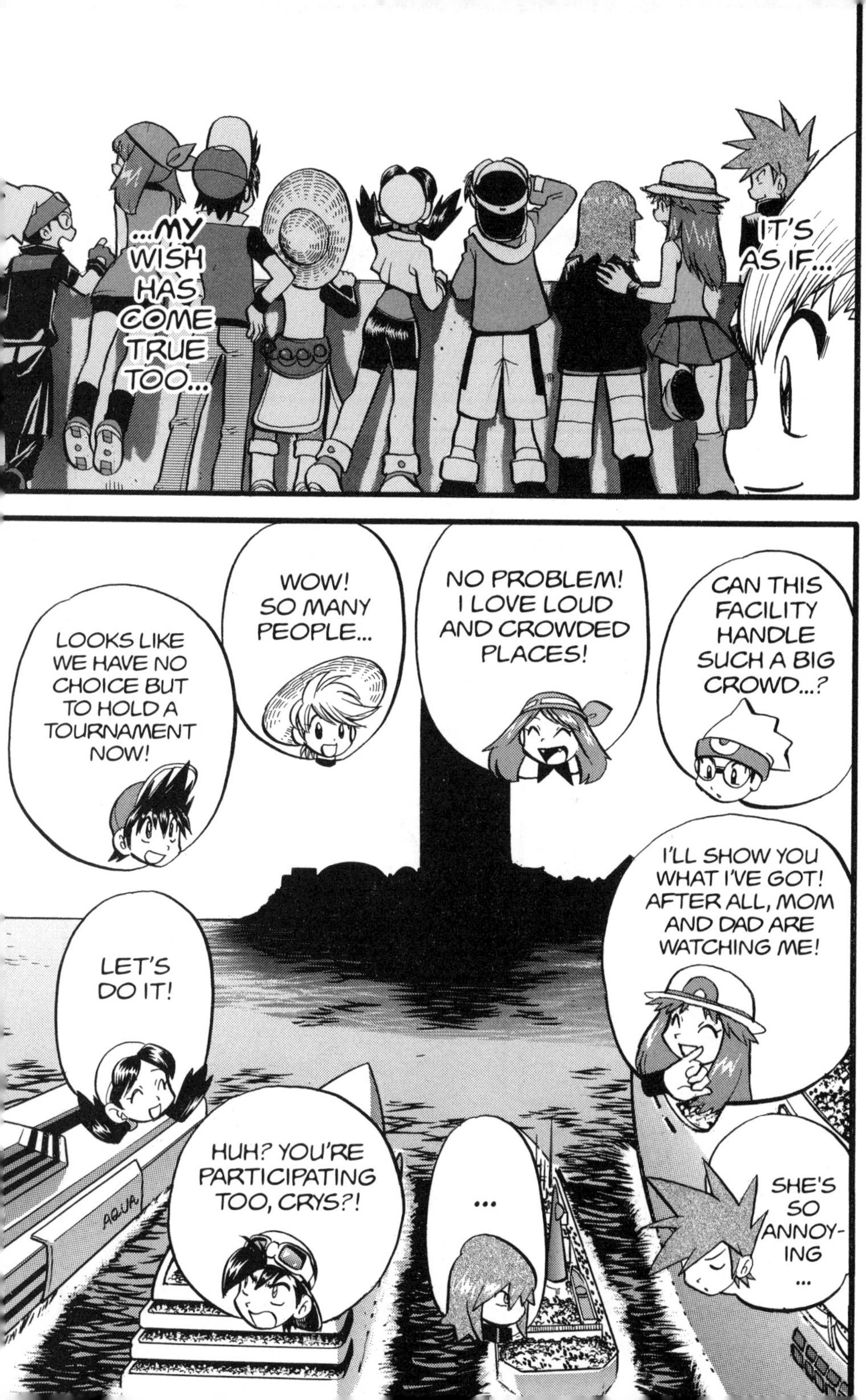
IT'S AS IF...
...MY WISH HAS COME TRUE TOO...
CAN THIS FACILITY HANDLE SUCH A BIG CROWD...?
NO PROBLEM! I LOVE LOUD AND CROWDED PLACES!
WOW! SO MANY PEOPLE...
LOOKS LIKE WE HAVE NO CHOICE BUT TO HOLD A TOURNAMENT NOW!
I'LL SHOW YOU WHAT I'VE GOT! AFTER ALL, MOM AND DAD ARE WATCHING ME!
LET'S DO IT!
SHE'S SO ANNOY-ING...
...
HUH? YOU'RE PARTICIPATING TOO, CRYS?!
AQUA

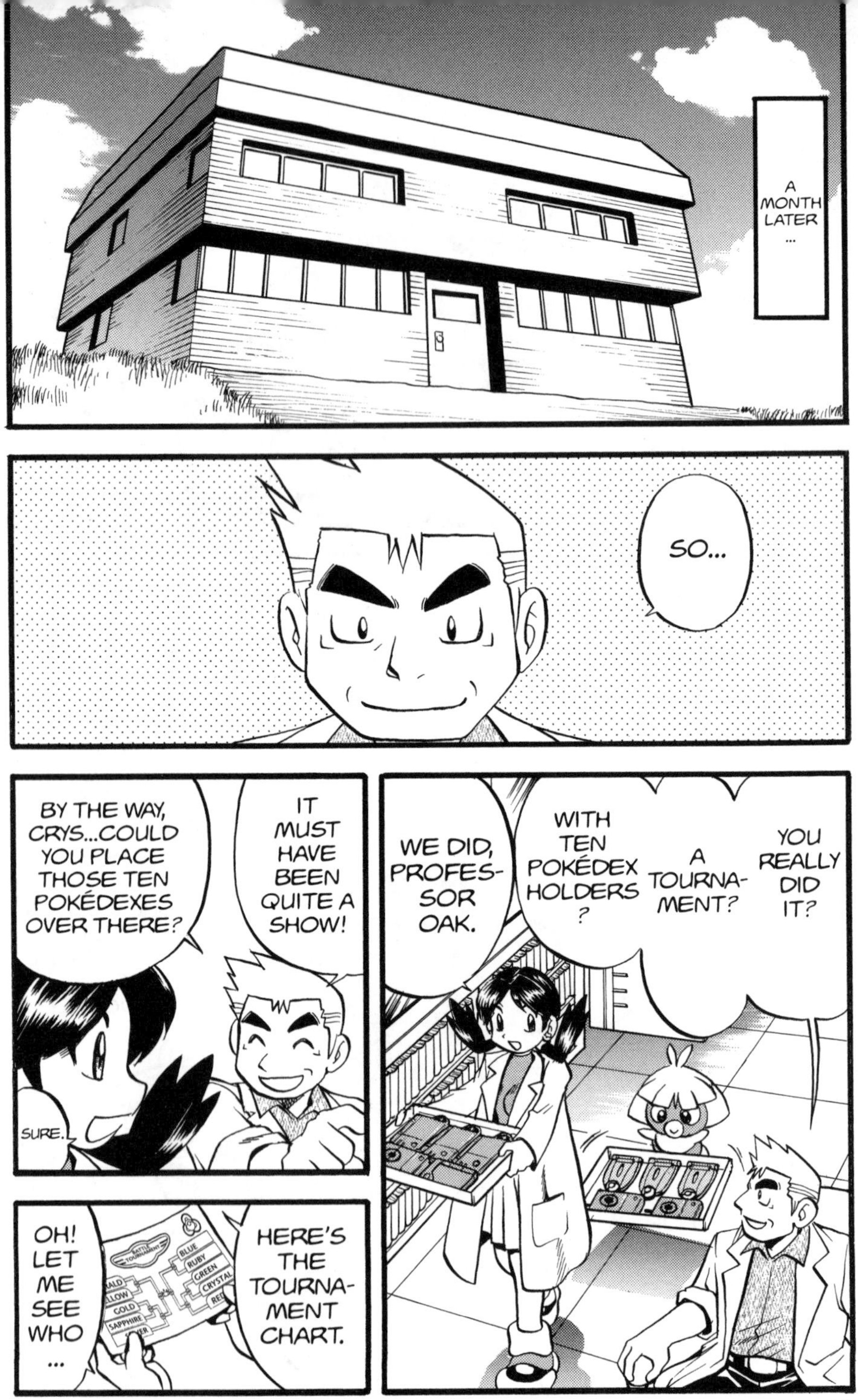
A MONTH LATER ...
SO...
YOU REALLY DID IT?
A TOURNAMENT?
WITH TEN POKÉDEX HOLDERS?
WE DID, PROFESSOR OAK.
IT MUST HAVE BEEN QUITE A SHOW!
BY THE WAY, CRYS...COULD YOU PLACE THOSE TEN POKÉDEXES OVER THERE?
SURE.
HERE'S THE TOURNAMENT CHART.
OH! LET ME SEE WHO ...

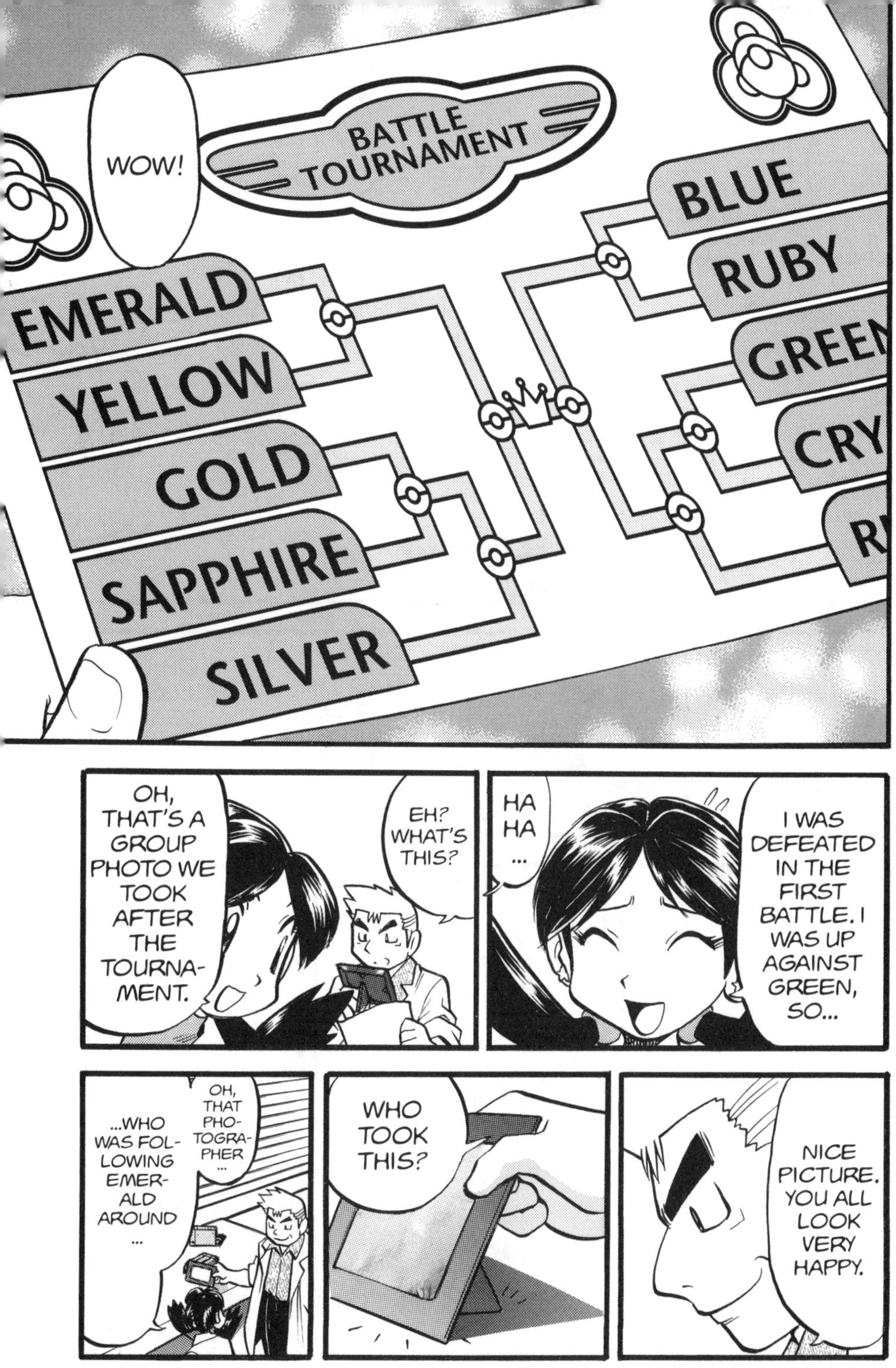
BATTLE TOURNAMENT
WOW!
BLUE
RUBY
EMERALD
YELLOW
GOLD
SAPPHIRE
SILVER
I WAS DEFEATED IN THE FIRST BATTLE. I WAS UP AGAINST GREEN, SO...
HA HA ...
EH? WHAT'S THIS?
OH, THAT'S A GROUP PHOTO WE TOOK AFTER THE TOURNA-MENT.
NICE PICTURE. YOU ALL LOOK VERY HAPPY.
WHO TOOK THIS?
OH, THAT PHO-TOGRA-PHER ...
...WHO WAS FOL-LOWING EMER-ALD AROUND ...

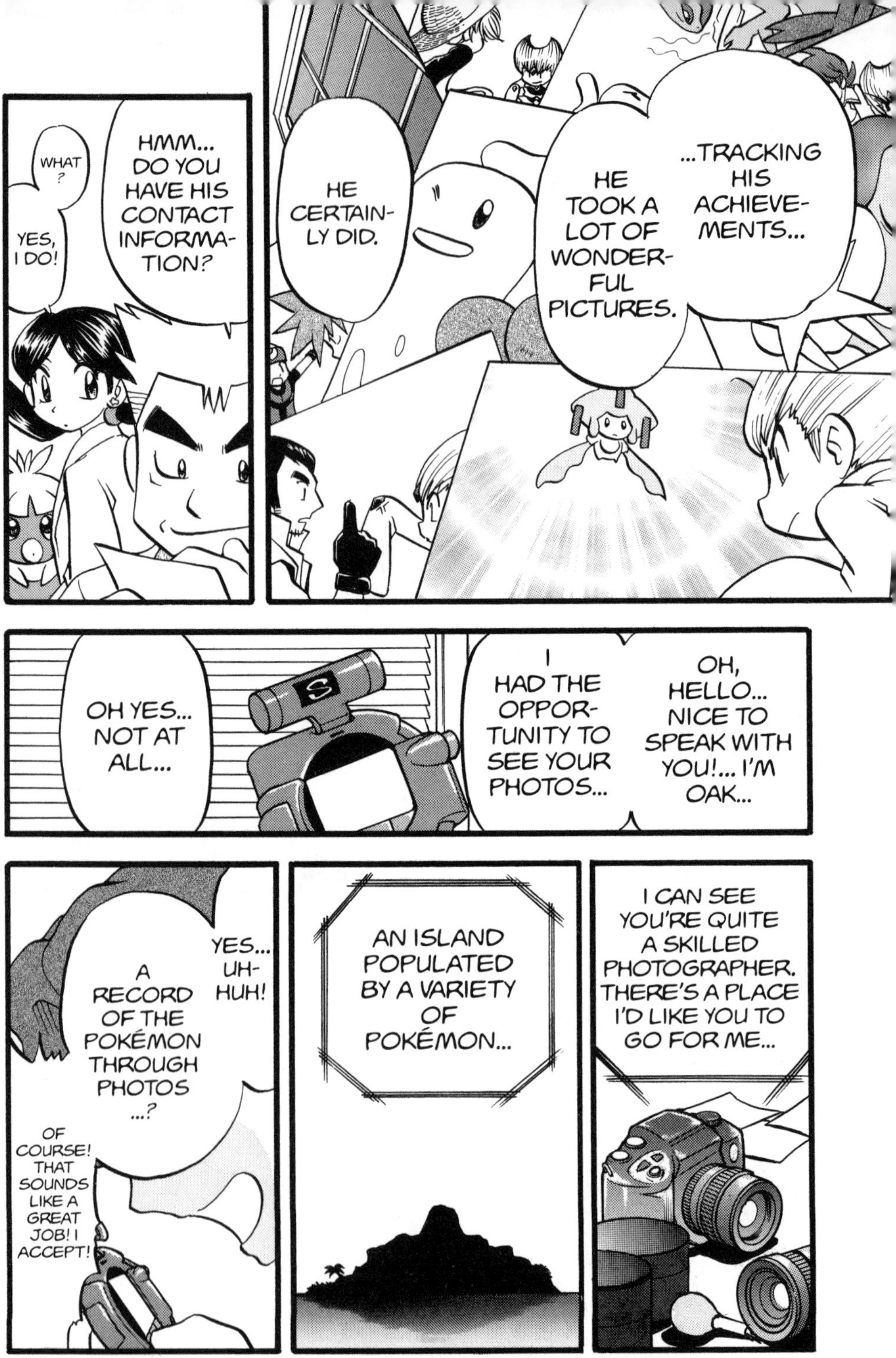
...TRACKING HIS ACHIEVEMENTS...
HE TOOK A LOT OF WONDERFUL PICTURES.
HE CERTAINLY DID.
HMM... DO YOU HAVE HIS CONTACT INFORMATION?
WHAT?
YES, I DO!
OH, HELLO... NICE TO SPEAK WITH YOU!... I'M OAK...
I HAD THE OPPORTUNITY TO SEE YOUR PHOTOS...
OH YES... NOT AT ALL...
I CAN SEE YOU'RE QUITE A SKILLED PHOTOGRAPHER. THERE'S A PLACE I'D LIKE YOU TO GO FOR ME...
AN ISLAND POPULATED BY A VARIETY OF POKÉMON...
YES... UH-HUH!
A RECORD OF THE POKÉMON THROUGH PHOTOS ...?
OF COURSE! THAT SOUNDS LIKE A GREAT JOB! I ACCEPT!

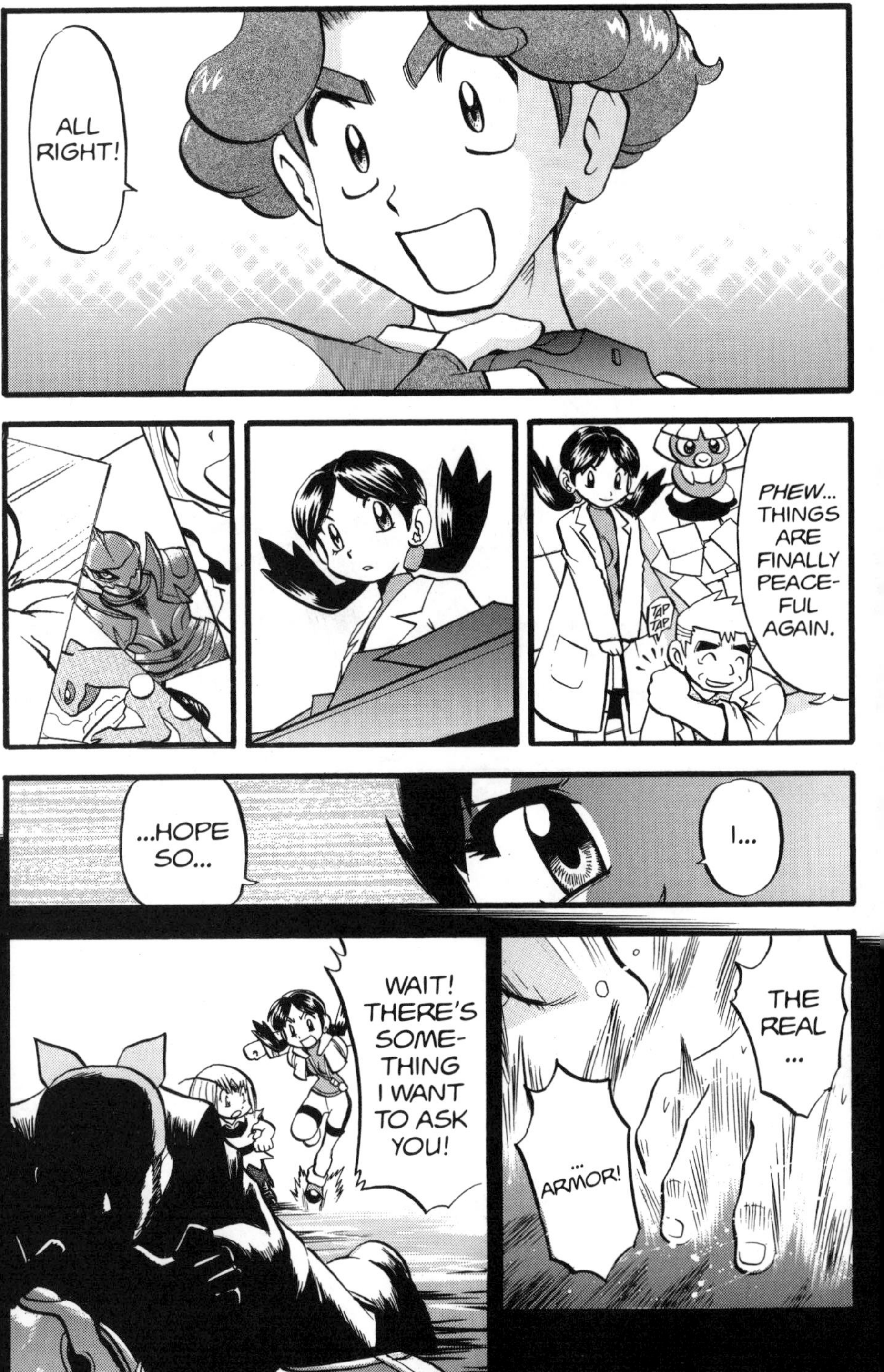
ALL RIGHT!
PHEW... THINGS ARE FINALLY PEACE-FUL AGAIN.
TAP TAP
I...
...HOPE SO...
THE REAL...
...ARMOR!
WAIT! THERE'S SOME-THING I WANT TO ASK YOU!

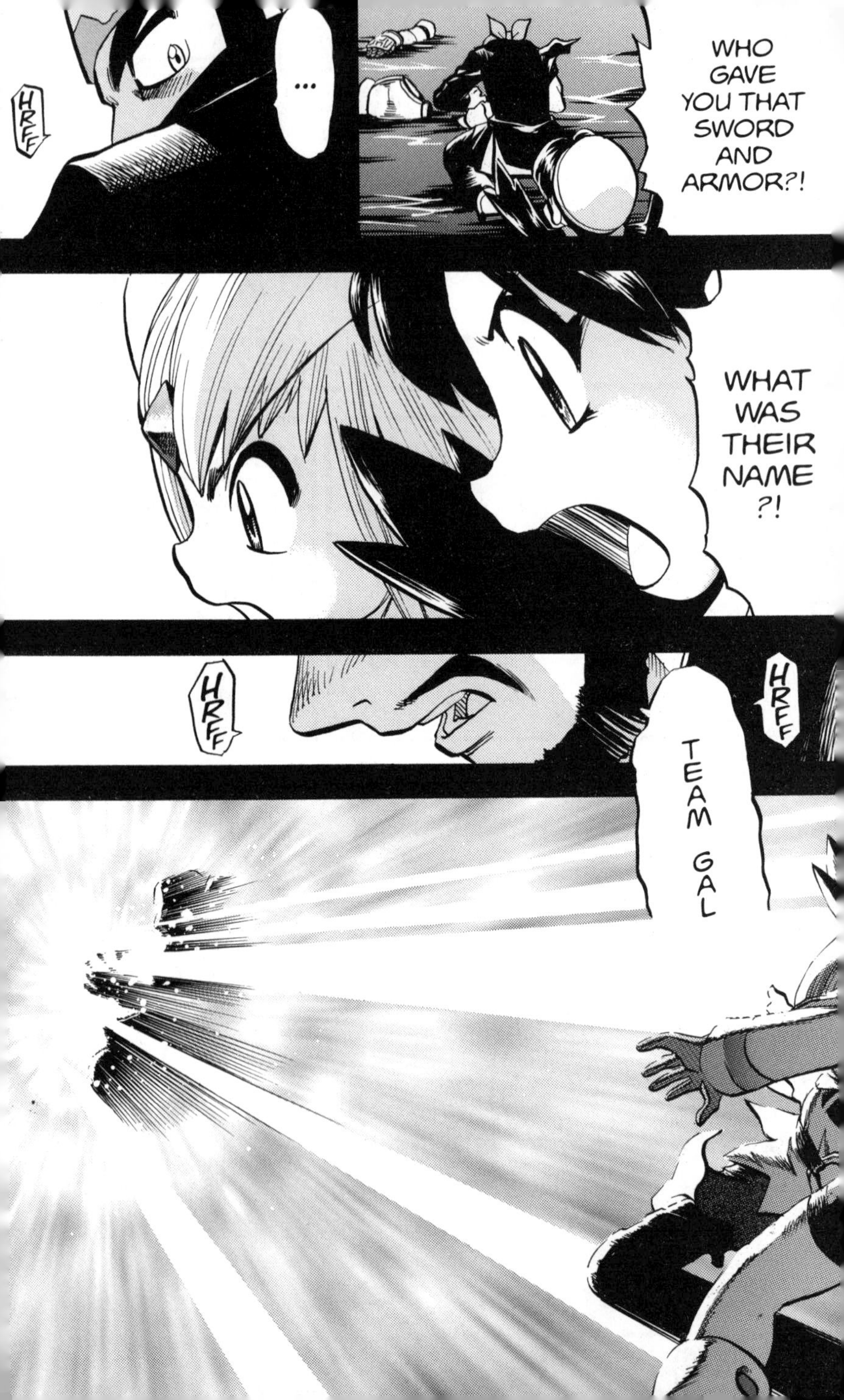
WHO GAVE YOU THAT SWORD AND ARMOR?!
...
HRFF
WHAT WAS THEIR NAME?!
HRFF
TEAM GAL
HRFF

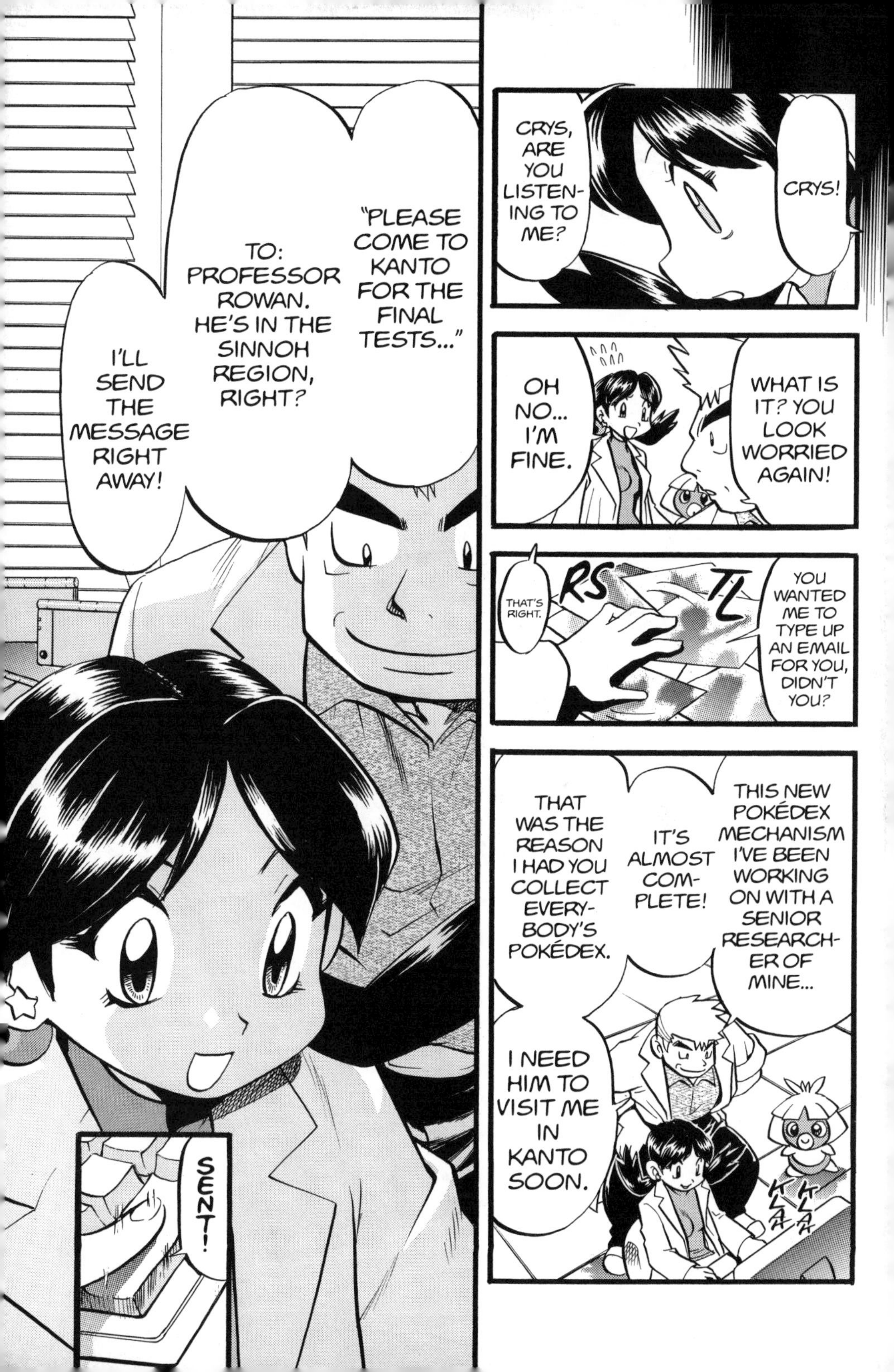
CRYS!
CRYS, ARE YOU LISTENING TO ME?
WHAT IS IT? YOU LOOK WORRIED AGAIN!
OH NO... I'M FINE.
YOU WANTED ME TO TYPE UP AN EMAIL FOR YOU, DIDN'T YOU?
RSTL
THAT'S RIGHT.
THIS NEW POKÉDEX MECHANISM I'VE BEEN WORKING ON WITH A SENIOR RESEARCHER OF MINE...
IT'S ALMOST COMPLETE!
THAT WAS THE REASON I HAD YOU COLLECT EVERYBODY'S POKÉDEX.
I NEED HIM TO VISIT ME IN KANTO SOON.
KLAK KLAK
"PLEASE COME TO KANTO FOR THE FINAL TESTS..."
TO: PROFESSOR ROWAN. HE'S IN THE SINNOH REGION, RIGHT?
I'LL SEND THE MESSAGE RIGHT AWAY!
SENT!

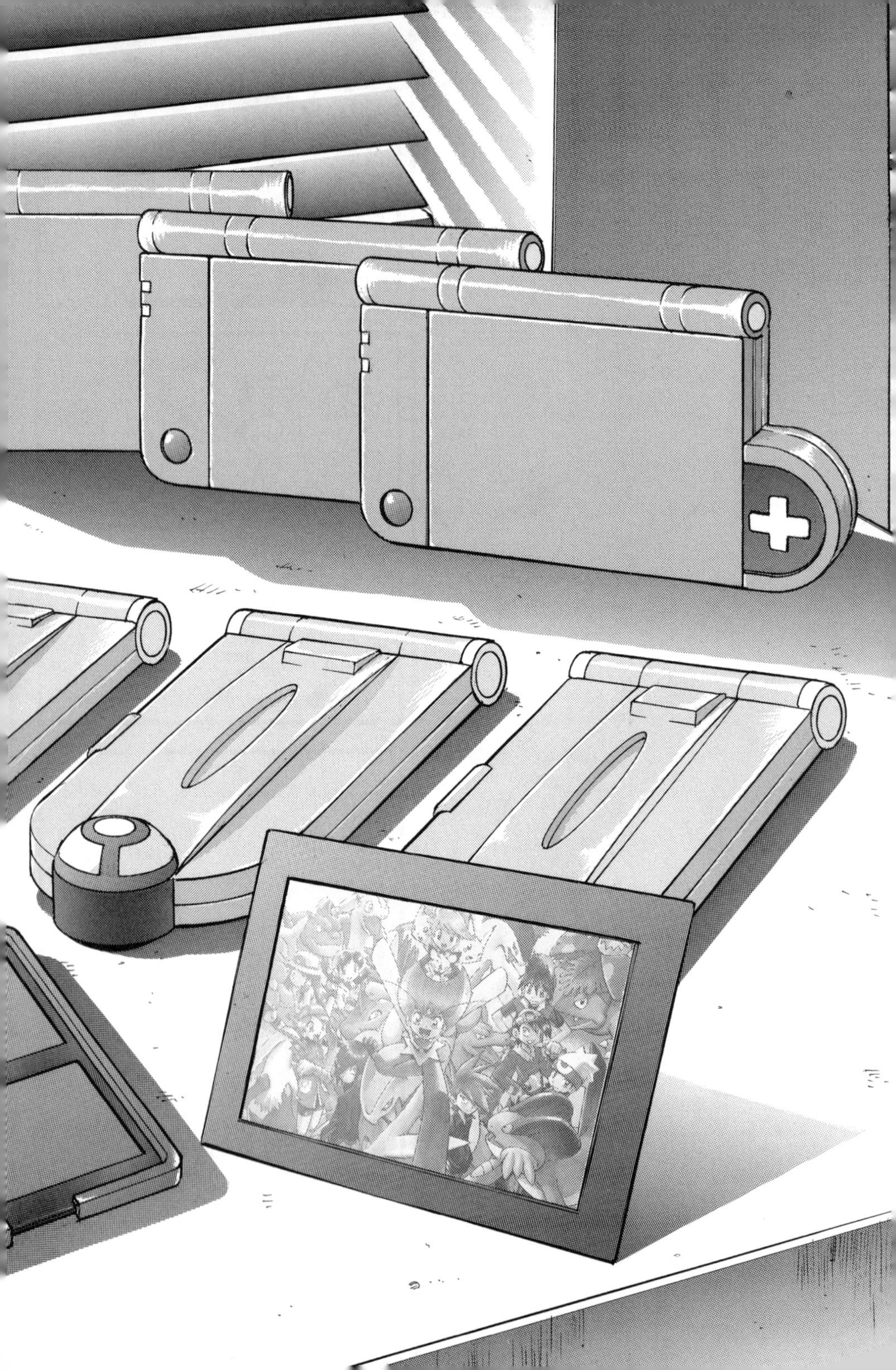

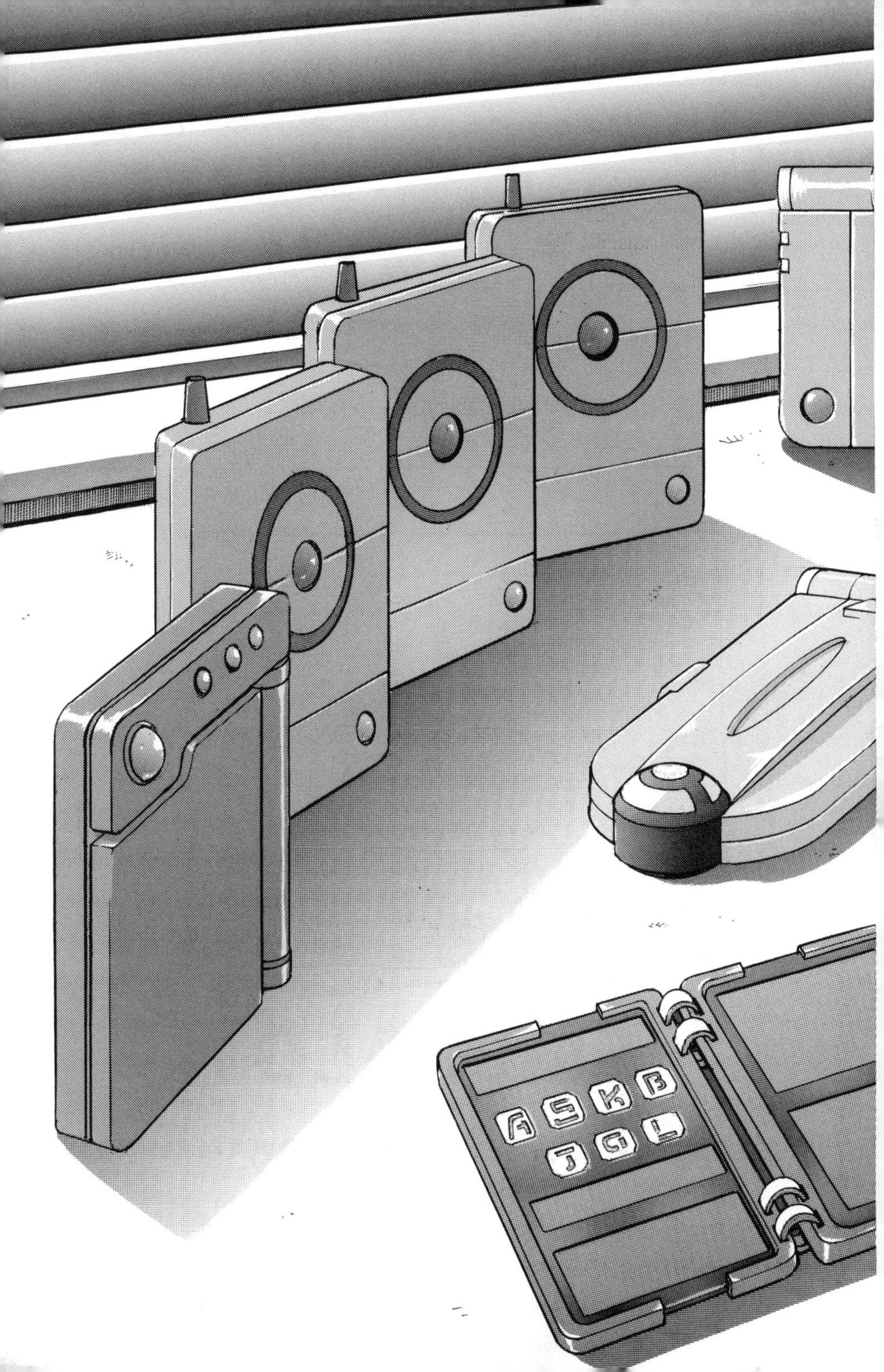
A S K B
J G L

Pokémon Adventures Emerald™

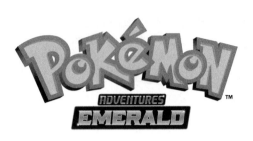

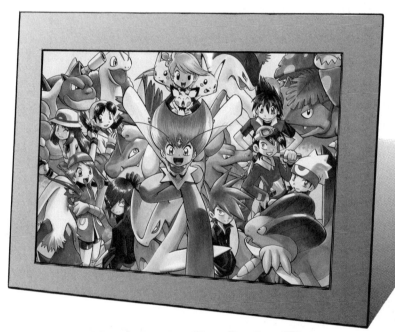

EMERALD

RED • GREEN • BLUE • YELLOW • GOLD • SILVER • CRYSTAL
RUBY • SAPPHIRE

Fin

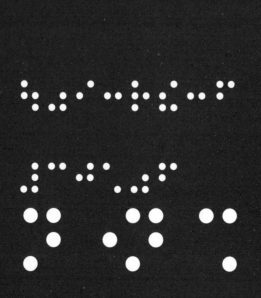

TIMELINE OF EMERALD'S CHALLENGE AT THE BATTLE FRONTIER

SEVEN DAYS OF AWAKENING ▶ ▶ ▶

DAY 4	DAY 3	DAY 2	DAY 1	DAY 0
7/4	7/3	7/2	7/1	6/30

DAY 0 — 6/30

OPENING CEREMONY

(DEMONSTRATION BATTLE AND PRESS CONFERENCE)

DAY 1 — 7/1

BATTLE FACTORY

(CHALLENGE→WIN)

DAY 2 — 7/2

BATTLE PIKE

(CHALLENGE→WIN)

DAY 3 — 7/3

BATTLE PYRAMID

(CHALLENGE→WIN)

DAY 4 — 7/4

BATTLE AT THE ARTISAN CAVE (MORNING)

BATTLE ARENA (AFTERNOON)

(CHALLENGE→WIN)

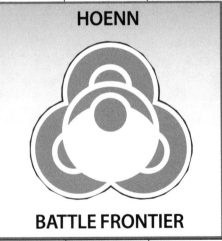

HOENN

BATTLE FRONTIER

DAY 7	DAY 6	DAY 5
7/7	7/6	7/5

BATTLE DOME
(REMATCH–TOURNAMENT DO-OVER)

🇯

BATTLE TOWER
▼
▼
▼
(END OF BATTLE WITH GUILE BEGUN ON DAY 5)

🇦

BATTLE DOME
(CHALLENGE–DEFEAT)

(AFTERNOON/EVENING)
BATTLE PALACE
(CHALLENGE–WIN)

🇸

(NIGHT)
BATTLE TOWER
(FINAL BATTLE AGAINST GUILE BEGINS)
▼
▼
▼

Pokémon Adventures Emerald™

6

The Sixth Chapter

Secret Japanese-Braille Subtitles Decoded!

VOL. 27

Adventure 309: Pike Queen
Adventure 310: If You're Lucky
Adventure 311: Homeland Mud
Adventure 312: Pyramid Adventure
Adventure 313: Flying Star
Adventure 314: Artisan Cave
Adventure 315: The Armor-Clad Man
Adventure 316: Skills of the Salon Maiden
Adventure 317: Scott's Intentions

The Loss of the Wishing Star
Continues in Vol. 28…

VOL. 26

Adventure 303: The Shining Frontier
Adventure 304: The Calming Mud Pellet
Adventure 305: Challenge the Seven Facilities
Adventure 306: The Frontier Brain of Knowledge
Adventure 307: A Suspicious Shadow
Adventure 308: Sending a Request

The Awakening After 1,000 Years
Continues in Vol. 27…

The Sixth Chapter

VOL. 28

The Ten Pokédex Holders
Continues in Vol. 29…

VOL. 29

To the Sinnoh Region...!
Continues in *Diamond and Pearl/Platinum,* Vol. 1

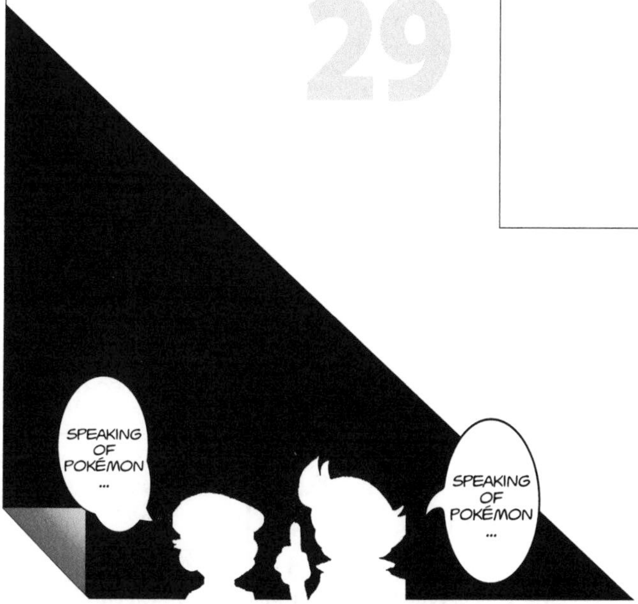
SPEAKING OF POKÉMON ...
SPEAKING OF POKÉMON ...

SPEAKING OF POKÉMON?!

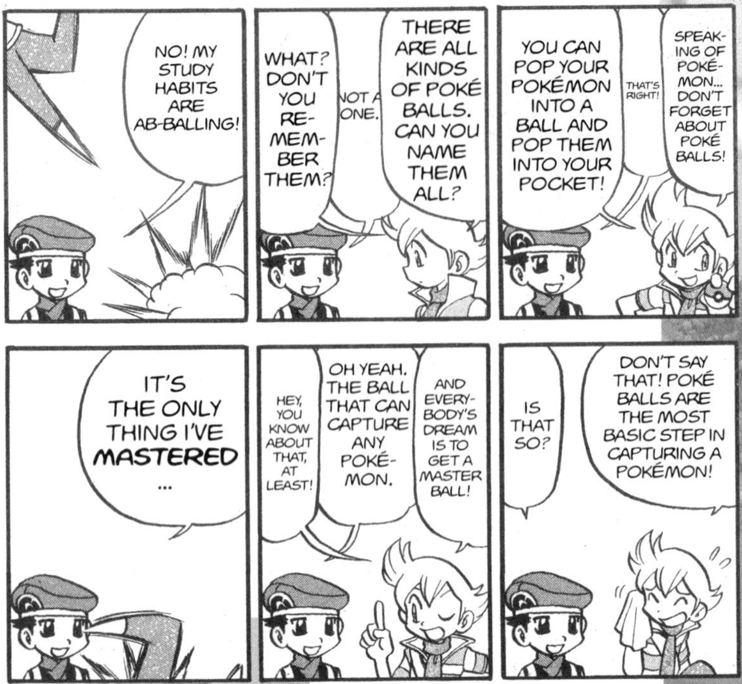
SPEAKING OF POKÉMON... DON'T FORGET ABOUT POKÉ BALLS!
THAT'S RIGHT!
YOU CAN POP YOUR POKÉMON INTO A BALL AND POP THEM INTO YOUR POCKET!
THERE ARE ALL KINDS OF POKÉ BALLS. CAN YOU NAME THEM ALL?
NOT A ONE.
WHAT? DON'T YOU REMEMBER THEM?
NO! MY STUDY HABITS ARE AB-BALLING!
DON'T SAY THAT! POKÉ BALLS ARE THE MOST BASIC STEP IN CAPTURING A POKÉMON!
IS THAT SO?
AND EVERYBODY'S DREAM IS TO GET A MASTER BALL!
OH YEAH. THE BALL THAT CAN CAPTURE ANY POKÉMON.
HEY, YOU KNOW ABOUT THAT, AT LEAST!
IT'S THE ONLY THING I'VE MASTERED ...

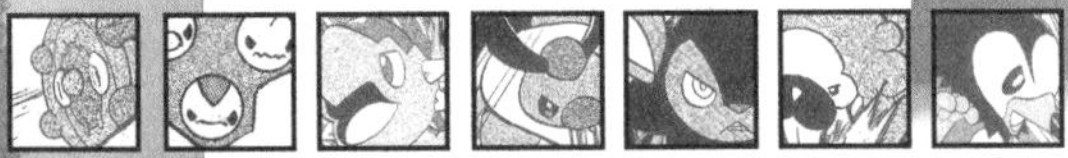

SPEAKING OF POKÉMON?!

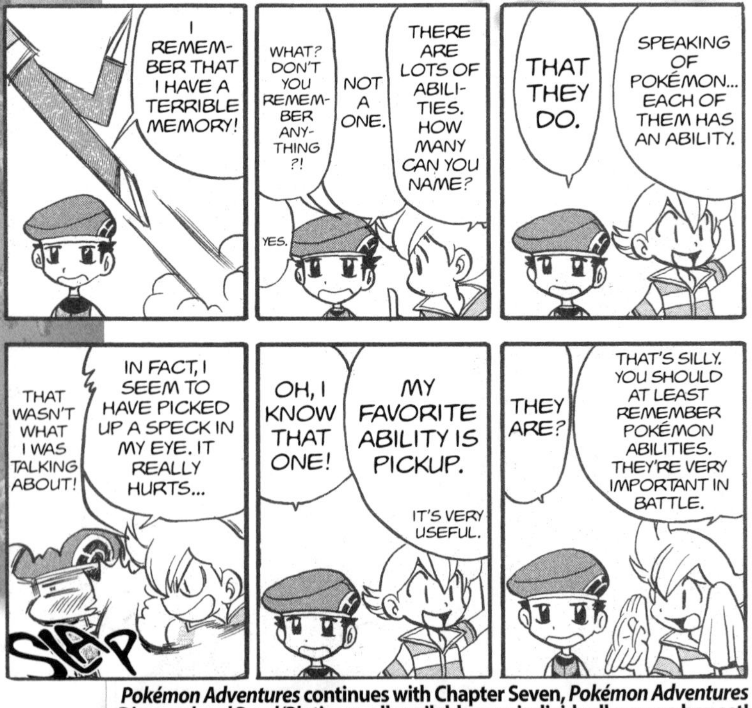
SPEAKING OF POKÉMON... EACH OF THEM HAS AN ABILITY.
THAT THEY DO.
THERE ARE LOTS OF ABILITIES. HOW MANY CAN YOU NAME?
NOT A ONE.
WHAT? DON'T YOU REMEMBER ANYTHING?!
YES.
I REMEMBER THAT I HAVE A TERRIBLE MEMORY!
THAT'S SILLY. YOU SHOULD AT LEAST REMEMBER POKÉMON ABILITIES. THEY'RE VERY IMPORTANT IN BATTLE.
THEY ARE?
MY FAVORITE ABILITY IS PICKUP.
IT'S VERY USEFUL.
OH, I KNOW THAT ONE!
IN FACT, I SEEM TO HAVE PICKED UP A SPECK IN MY EYE. IT REALLY HURTS...
THAT WASN'T WHAT I WAS TALKING ABOUT!
SLAP

Pokémon Adventures **continues with Chapter Seven, *Pokémon Adventures Diamond and Pearl/Platinum*, all available now individually or as a box set!**

COLLECTOR'S EDITION

Volume 10

Story by **HIDENORI KUSAKA**
Art by **SATOSHI YAMAMOTO**

©2021 Pokémon.
©1995–2008 Nintendo / Creatures Inc. / GAME FREAK inc.
TM, ®, and character names are trademarks of Nintendo.
POCKET MONSTERS SPECIAL Vols. 28–29
by Hidenori KUSAKA, Satoshi YAMAMOTO
©1997 Hidenori KUSAKA, Satoshi YAMAMOTO
All rights reserved.
Original Japanese edition published by SHOGAKUKAN.
English translation rights in the United States of America, Canada, the United Kingdom,
Ireland, Australia, New Zealand and India arranged with SHOGAKUKAN.

Translation/Tetsuichiro Miyaki
English Adaptation/Bryant Turnage
Lettering/Annaliese "Ace" Christman
Original Series Design/Shawn Carrico
Original Series Editor/Annette Roman
Collector's Edition Production Artist/Christy Medellin
Collector's Edition Design/Julian [JR] Robinson
Collector's Edition Editor/Joel Enos

Printed in the U.S.A.

Published by VIZ Media, LLC
P.O. Box 77010
San Francisco, CA 94107

10 9 8 7 6 5 4 3 2 1
First printing, October 2021

PARENTAL ADVISORY
POKÉMON ADVENTURES is rated A
and is suitable for readers of all ages.

viz.com

THIS IS THE LAST PAGE.
THIS BOOK READS RIGHT TO LEFT.

FEB 2024